SPECIAL ACCESS

MARK A. HEWITT

To Joe [signature]

Black Rose Writing
www.blackrosewriting.com

The final approval for this literary material is granted by the author.

First printing

ISBN: 978-1-61296-255-9

PUBLISHED BY BLACK ROSE WRITING

www.blackrosewriting.com

Printed in the United States of America

Special Access is printed in Myriad Pro

A salute to the pioneering men of the US Army, US Navy, the Schweizer Aircraft Company, the Lockheed Aircraft Corporation and the Central Intelligence Agency who had the vision to conceive, build, and fly quiet powered aircraft in the defense of the United States of America.

A black program in the intelligence community refers informally to a "closed" or extremely classified program. Black programs are unacknowledged publicly by the government and defense contractors. In the United States intelligence community, the formal terminology for the most-sensitive classified program is ***Special Access Program.***

SPECIAL ACCESS

May 1, 2011. The President announced that the United States conducted an operation that killed Osama bin Laden.

May 5, 2011. The President announced that he would personally thank the Navy SEAL team that killed Osama bin Laden. For four days, the nation was treated to hundreds of stories of SEALs. The public wanted more information about their new heroes.

May 7, 2011. Special Operations Command struggled with issuing a press release that Navy SEALs are grateful for the nation's show of support but are growing angry with the continued focus on their operations, tactics, and tools, claiming it could jeopardize future raids and their safety. "Anything further that comes out could damage their operational security, may reveal tricks of the trade, or even endanger their families."

May 10, 2011. Pablo Reyes, a twenty-two-year retired US Navy commander and former Navy SEAL, was found dead at his home in Denver, Colorado. The Denver Police Department believes Mr. Reyes, a physical fitness instructor at the Johnson and Wales University, was the victim of a random shooting. The case is under investigation.

PROLOGUE

2325L February 12, 1999
Cristóbal Airport, Republic of Panama

As they took turns climbing onto the wing and settling into their cockpits, the two men in black NOMEX and black helmets quickly went through their prestart checks. The man in front lowered the canopy, while the man in back scanned left and right to discern if anyone would notice their late-night departure. It was wasted energy. One of the ground crew had already done that, scanning the area with night-vision goggles.

All clear was a thumbs-up held high for three seconds followed by starter engagement and a slowly spinning propeller. It wasn't just any propeller but one specially designed in the late '60s by an acoustic laboratory in Massachusetts; the prop design was still considered top secret.

Also obviously missing during the engine start sequence was the low growl of engine exhaust. The big Continental 360 should have rattled the windows of nearby buildings during engine start, but it sounded more like a Lionel locomotive. Hot exhaust gases were completely diffused through a pair of large conformal mufflers and long, perforated piping that ran down the starboard side of the fuselage. Lycoming engineers found a way to dissipate the hot gases and muffle the engine exhaust.

The pilot lowered the canopy, flipped ANVIS-9s over his eyes, and silently taxied to the runway.

"Ready?"

"Ready. All clear."

If anyone noticed the little black tail-dragger, he would have doubted what he saw and heard. At 1400 RPM, the pitch-control lever was smoothly programmed to increase the angle of attack of the propeller to the maximum pitch angle. The special reduction gearbox spun the laminated three-prop blade slowly. The three- foot, rectangular blades cut the air in small gulps with no noticeable P-factor.

The last remaining operational YO-3A slowly moved down the runway. A low-noise profile takeoff at night under night-vision goggles is as harrowing as a nighttime catapult launch of an F-4 Phantom off a pitching carrier deck in crappy weather. The pilot had done both multiple times.

At the two board and thirty-five knots, the tail wheel lifted gently off the centerline at the urging of the pilot's forward cyclic inputs. Taking all 5,000 feet of runway, the mains broke the deck before the asphalt ran out. No one in or near the airport heard or saw the airplane take off.

Two minutes later at 2,000 feet AGL, Duncan Hunter pushed the throttle to 3,200 RPM to increase climb rate and speed and leveled off the YO-3A on a heading of 080. In the rear seat, Greg Lynche began checking the FLIR, infrared illuminator, laser target designator, and video recorder.

"Not bad for a thirty-year-old plane," Lynche remarked.

"A thirty-year-old plane with your basic F-16 cockpit. I'm really impressed with the old girl. You also worked some magic with the engine since last time."

"We dropped in a competition Continental. Two spares are in the shop getting the same treatment."

"The last of its kind."

"Like your old F-4?"

Duncan sighed. "That hurt, Greg. Yes, like my old F-4, the last of the man's machines. I hate to say it. They're being converted into drones, and I hate to think they're targets. I love flying this. This is a great airplane in its own way, surprisingly very responsive. You need a good touch to fly this well."

"That's why you're flying, and I'm picture taking."

"Thank you, Sir. Every time I fly this, it's always a little strange having boards for a prop. This is a very cool airplane."

Checking their GPS coordinates, Lynche said, "Let's head 090 and see if we can find the FARC, take some pictures, and head back. If we have time, I want pictures of the port, the oil tankers and storage tanks, and anything else that might be of interest."

The retired CIA Chief of Air Branch was back in his element, hunting drug smugglers and narcoterrorists from the formerly top- secret airplane. Eleven Lockheed YO-3A prototypes were developed for the US Army's use in Vietnam as low-altitude, silent night reconnaissance airplanes.

Derived from several Quiet Thruster designs that would have given Rube Goldberg a stroke, number 007 was the last remaining flyable copy in private hands. Less than twelve people knew of its existence. Only six knew of 007's capabilities.

"I still can't get over how you got this from the FBI. Are you sure you didn't hold a gun to someone's head? Made them an offer they couldn't refuse?"

"Something like that. Someone owed me a favor. You know I was the DCI's personal aide?"

"Greg, you rarely tell me anything about your old place."

"You know after the Judge ran the FBI, he came to CIA as the DCI. I became his aide."

"Yes, Sir. I know that. How'd you get 007?"

"Well, after my tour as the Judge's aide, I became Chief Air Branch. Toward the end of my three years, I had visions of making a CIA aviation museum on some of the land behind headquarters. I had the last remaining A-12 in storage, along with a U-2 and a DC-3 from our old Air America days. I found out this little recce plane was going to be returned to DOD, and there was little doubt it would be scrapped, so I asked the FBI to transfer 007 when they were done with it.

"They told me to get bent. The Judge found out his old place had basically flipped me off. He made a couple calls, and, right before he retired, he somehow had the airplane transferred to me. Actually, the FBI sold it to me for a dollar. Not exactly what I had in mind, but that was the deal."

Duncan shook his helmeted head. "Do you see that? One o'clock, on the horizon."

Old habits die hard. Lynche couldn't see Hunter's visual vector. "What? Where? Ah, looks like a bonfire. It's a little late for a barbecue. Let's go take a look. Take it up to 9,000, and we'll see if that's a good altitude."

Hunter traded air speed for altitude. During the zoom climb the aircraft slowed to seventy-five knots for maximum noise reduction, as it eased into the assigned altitude as if the maneuver were choreographed, then he placed the throttle in the Quiet detent. The reduction gearing was immediately noticeable, as the short-but-wide variable-pitch prop adjusted to maintain altitude and sixty-five knots at just above idle RPM.

The Wraith slipped naturally into glider mode. The only thing the two men heard was the sound of their own breathing in their noise-canceling headsets in their helmets.

"Looks like the FARC having a celebration," Lynche said. "I see about fifteen people. Orbit here while I get this on tape."

"Roger."

After three turns, Lynche said, "This is BS. They're just shooting the shit. Duncan, run the throttle up to 3,500 and quickly back to idle. Point the nose at them. That's good. On my mark...mark."

The sudden power change significantly yawed the aircraft before it returned to trimmed flight. The propeller blades propagated low-frequency noise toward the ground but nothing from the heavily muffled engine.

"Let's see what they do, if anything," Lynche said.

Less than five seconds later, the Forward Looking Infra Red's video recording caught the collective surprise of the group of narcoterrorists. Each ghostly image tried to discern the low- frequency growling sound and from where it could have originated.

As if given an order, all the men grabbed weapons and ran single-file through the jungle. The FLIR caught the white images of their heat signatures and the arcs of cigarettes thrown into the night, as they raced down a jungle path.

"Well, I didn't expect that," Lynche said, nonplussed. "That's an unusual response. Usually, if they think it's an airplane operating without lights, they shoot toward the noise. Now what are they doing?" The FLIR traced ten men running down the path, who slowed as they approached a large structure on the hillside. The men took defensive positions around the makeshift hut.

Lynche lifted his head suddenly, narrowed his eyes, and whispered, "Something doesn't make sense with that response." He switched to the electro-optical sensor, hoping for a better view, then switched back to infrared.

As Duncan kept the aircraft in a tight 30° right turn, the FLIR recorded the terrorists looking into the distance, waiting for another visual or aural cue. It was a game of cat and mouse.

Lynche scanned the mountaintop. The fire was out, though the embers still burned brightly in the FLIR. Three remaining images walked toward the hut.

"That's really odd."

"What is?" Duncan didn't have a sensor repeater among the three multifunction displays and HUD, and had to rely on the old spook's commentary.

"I wasn't sure at first, but I think we know where a batch of hostages is located. Take it up…500 feet. I want to see if we can get better imagery through the roof of that hut."

Hunter gently zoomed to the requested altitude, careful

not to create any whistling of a deflected flight control. The aircraft was specially designed to be noiseless with conformal antennae and retractable landing gear, but, as was demonstrated during low-level flight trials, large deflections of flight controls even at idle speeds could create a medium-range whistle that was audible over a mile at night. Before a YO-3A went on a mission in Vietnam, the aircraft would fly 300 feet over the maintenance shack. If the maintainers heard whistles, rattles, or other noises, the pilot brought the aircraft back, and maintenance placed duct or aluminum speed tape on loose parts of the airframe.

After several flights, the maintenance workers knew where the problems were, and they taped those noisemakers before every flight, so the overhead noise check became an afterthought. 007 sported several strips of black duct tape.

"Right there. I can just make out ten, twelve bodies. Looks like they're against the walls. Probably their hands and feet are tied. That's a great set of heat signatures through that thatched roof. We'll know more when we analyze the tape."

Lynche cross-checked the aircraft's GPS coordinates with the FLIR's symbology and pressed a few commands on the touch screen of the multifunction display panel.

"X marks the spot." The GPS coordinates were imprinted on the video tape.

After orbiting for ten minutes, the two men watched the FARC men laugh and joke with each other, as they relaxed their defensive posture and returned up the hill.

Two minutes later, they lit a smaller fire, while two guards remained at either ends of the hostage hut.

Lynche gave Hunter a vector to depart the location and headed to Cristóbal via the river and port.

Thirty minutes later, Lynche placed his hand on the stick, shook it slightly and said, "My plane."

Duncan responded by releasing the controls and putting both hands up for the man behind him to see. "Your airplane."

"I'll call the chief and tell him we located their targets." Lynche switched from interphone to radio. "Lasko, November X-ray triple seven Lima Sierra."

"November X-ray triple seven Lima Sierra, go ahead."

"Roger, Lasko. I think we're going to need one--two hotel rooms for the night. Can you have a van pick us up?"

"Copy that, November X-ray triple seven Lima Sierra. One- two hotel rooms. I'll pass the message to the Sofitel."

"Roger, Lasko. Thanks for your help, Sir. November X-ray triple seven Lima Sierra, out." He switched back to interphone. "OK, Duncan. We'll do a little low level over the river. I'd like to find a drug lab or two, maybe a find submarine, then we'll head back to the airport. I want some video of oil tankers and oil storage tanks. You can take it home after that."

"Roger."

Once Lynche made out the Saldaña River draining into the Caribbean Sea, he banked hard to the right and pulled the throttle to idle to slowly descend the YO-3A to 2,000 AGL, paralleling the Magdalena River.

After fifteen minutes of near blackness, Lynche shouted, "Your airplane!"

"My airplane."

"I think we have a lab at three o'clock. Spin it, please." He slewed the FLIR to the area that flashed in his NVGs.

"Nice job, Sir. Coming around. Give me a vector."

"Check your nine o'clock, about three fingers above the treeline. I could barely pick it up in my NVGs; I almost missed it. Now it looks like a flare in our FLIR."

"Still no joy. Oh, there it is. Tally ho. Nice catch, Sir. Man, you wouldn't have been able to see that if you were directly overhead. We were at the exact right slant angle."

"Check altitude, and let's orbit here. I want to see if I can discern what's going on."

"Greg, twelve o'clock. I think it's a gunboat coming upriver. Riverine patrol?"

"Let me see." Lynche swung the FLIR to the vessel in the middle of the river and zoomed the image. "I'd say it's a Colombian Navy gunboat. I can make out its ensign waving on the stern. I'm recording this. What do you want to bet they power right by the drug lab?"

"Your next modification should be a repeater for that FLIR. Should be able to dump the video onto one of these screens."

"I'll see about that once we get the old girl home. Yes, Colombian Navy. Looks to be just patrolling."

"Shit. Did you see that? Three IR flashes! Did that drug lab just signal the gunboat? Is that really a gunboat?"

Lynche was completely focused on the FLIR display. "Check your speed. Take her down another 1,000 feet. I want a closer look."

Hunter pulled the throttle to idle and reduced the pitch on the propeller. The glider was reluctant to descend, and Hunter was afraid of using speed brakes or spoilers for fear of creating a whistle.

"That's very strange," Lynche said. "They're going up the little tributary that feeds into the river. Seems like they're expected. Maybe it's the national police at the drug lab, and this is a coordinated op."

"Or maybe the Colombian Navy is corrupt and is in on it."

"Or maybe you're too cynical. Take it down another 500 feet."

"Verify 500 AGL?"

"For the moment. I want to see if I can get some high-granularity video. I want to see if I can tell who's on the boat or who's at the lab. Mark this avenue of approach on GPS. We have time for only a pass or two."

There was no moon, so the area was absolutely dark. Hunter smiled. His pulse quickened. He knew the altitude at which a human could detect the YO-3A was still top secret. He concentrated on maintaining the correct altitude and keeping some level of situational awareness with respect to the terrain. He strayed over the target but away from the gun line. Army YO-3A crews did that every night in Vietnam, sometimes lower if they believed the sound of running water would mask their approach to the target. Purposely flying into small-arms range in an unarmored, unprotected airplane is usually fatal.

Lynche cursed under his breath. "No one's facing the camera." He requested a closer, lower observation altitude for the final run of videotaping. "OK. I believe we can get away with a quick, low-level pass. Shoot the video and get the hell out of here."

"Roger. Seventy-five feet. You're incredible, Lynche. This is exactly why UAVs can't cut it in this environment."

"Just don't hit the spoilers, or you'll flip us into the river. These guys don't like having their picture taken. The FLIR suggests they still have the boat engine running, and they shouldn't be able to hear us. We'll be OK. But if I say, 'Run,' get us the hell out of here. Can you get a little closer?"

"Roger, passing 150 for seventy-five." Hunter dipped the wing and added a little rudder. "And, Sir, you're a little closer. Any closer, and I'm afraid we'll hit something."

"Steady…smile shitheads…. Come on. That's the ticket. Oh, shit…that's Manny! They're loading packages onto the boat. Get us out of here. Let's go to 2,000 feet and watch.

"Roger. 2,000. Uh, Greg, what's that at one o'clock? I see a light source where there shouldn't be one."

"OK. FLIR coming around to one o'clock…searching… searching…."

"Check two o'clock on the waterline, two fingers on the right."

"Tally ho. Shit, Hunter, you found a sub! Dumb fuck is using his flashlight to get aboard the thing. That's incredible."

"Reminds me of the night activity at the Texas border. Everyone couldn't believe how much activity goes on there at night completely undetected."

"I marked it with GPS. Won't be hard to find again. Back to Manny and his band of merry men."

Lynche aimed the FLIR back at the lab and the boat for the maneuver. "So far, it doesn't look like they know we're here. I won't press our luck."

Hunter increased the pitch-control lever and began a gentle climb. Leveling off at 2,000 AGL, he asked, "So who's Manny?"

"Admiral Manuel Vasquez, Colombia's version of Chief of Naval Operations. That looked like he was supervising the loading of bundles of cocaine. I have a hard time thinking he's on the take. Shit. I thought he was a good one. When I was Chief of Station, we gave him a bunch of intel."

Thirty minutes later, the gunboat pulled out of the tributary and headed back the way it came.

"Follow them," Lynche said.

"My pleasure." Hunter flew S turns to keep from overrunning the gunboat. An hour later, the vessel docked at what appeared to be a naval installation at the mouth of the Saldaña. No one took anything off the boat.

"Let's head back to the field. We have to get this tape to the COS."

After taking a circuitous route to the airfield, which allowed Lynche to tape FLIR images of oil tankers and tankers in port, Hunter landed expertly and taxied quickly to an open hangar at the far end of the field. Once the propeller stopped, he opened the clamshell canopy, and the two men stepped out of the cockpits and climbed down to the ground.

The two-main maintenance crew hooked a tow bar to the tail wheel and guided the little aircraft into the hangar, where the wings would be removed and the aircraft readied for shipment in its forty-foot sea container.

Lynche, the first one off the plane, handed a VCR tape to the awaiting Bogota Chief of Station. "John, this is probably what you're looking for. I'd like a copy for my files. Duncan, I'll see you back at the hotel. I'll ring your room after I debrief."

"That's incredible work, Greg," said the COS.

* * *

Bogota newspapers reported the freeing of twelve hostages in an isolated jungle area, where they were thought to have spent the last fifteen weeks. Ten men were killed in a shootout with National Police, and three men were charged with training FARC members in bomb making and kidnapping.

The same day the hostages were rescued, a radio station received a statement from the FARC. The group claimed it was holding nine people for ransom in addition to other hostages for a prisoner exchange. The Colombian authorities reportedly received satellite footage, probably supplied by the CIA, of the hostages' location.

Other articles reported the Armada Nacional de al República de Colombia Commander, Admiral Manuel Eduardo Vasquez, suddenly retired for medical reasons.

The Colombian National Police and the US Drug Enforcement Agency didn't take action against the cocaine submarine, opting to monitor the vessel and the drug smugglers' activities before raiding the area two weeks later. Officials were astounded at the level of technology incorporated into the semisubmersible. After the sub was secured and seven men were taken into custody, an American film crew was brought in to re- enact the takedown of the Volvo-powered, 100-foot-long vessel.

* * *

Two American businessmen flew out of Bogota two days later on American Airlines Flight 2170, first-class. Surveillance video of the travelers going through ticketing and security couldn't positively identify the men, as if the two knew exactly where the surveillance cameras were located. Hunter returned to his job with the US Border Patrol in Texas, and Lynche returned to his office-home near Annapolis. 007's container arrived at the Port of Baltimore at the end of the month and was transported to a storage facility near the airport in Easton, Maryland.

It would be another three months before the Special Access Program, known as Wraith, would again be activated by the Director of Central Intelligence.

BOOK ONE

CHAPTER ONE

0900 December 7, 1984
TRAWING 2 Conference Room Naval Air Station
Kingsville, Texas

First Lieutenant Duncan Hunter, United States Marine Corps, and his fellow about-to-be newly minted Naval Aviators, marched into a classroom for out-processing. The six sailors and one Marine officer sat around the conference table. Before them were file folders and mounds of papers.

Hunter didn't wait to be told to take a seat. The others followed his lead. One minute later, a Navy yeoman wearing a form-fitting dark-blue dress uniform, resplendent with ribbons, badges, and pins, entered the room and began her spiel.

"Gentlemen, I'm Petty Officer Gentry. I'm here to help you process off the air station and help you get on your way to your next duty station. Who needs a pen?"

Six sailors raised their hands.

"The first thing we'll do is fill out a Standard Form 86, a questionnaire for national security positions. You must fill this out in its entirety before you receive your orders. The Defense Security Service will conduct a background investigation on you, since you'll be coming into contact with sensitive information at your new duty station.

"Lieutenant Hunter, it seems you're the special one today. Maybe it's a Marine thing. We need two copies of your fingerprints and some additional paperwork for DSS to complete a single-scope background investigation."

Lieutenant Hunter looked into the blue eyes of the short-haired petty officer, silently questioning the rationale for the additional paperwork. She dropped two blue FBI Standard Form 87s in front of him and handed out white OPM SF-87s to the sailors.

Deep in thought and concern, Hunter tried to understand why some of the Naval officers were going to fly more-sophisticated aircraft than he, like the EP-3 signal intelligence gathering and EA- 6 jamming aircraft, and those pilots only had to fill out one white card. Thirty- year-old Phantoms were a dying breed. They were being replaced by the more-capable and agile F/A-18A, and Hunter was the last F-4 pilot in the training pipeline.

After everyone had his fingerprint cards, Petty Officer Gentry said, "Lieutenant Hunter, please be careful filling out those SF- 87s. They're the only two I have. F...B...I.... Either you've been very naughty, or I'd guess you'll be doing something special."

Six sailors leaned inward to look at the blue fingerprint cards, while Hunter's eyes shot up toward the yeoman, who smiled and gave him a quick wink.

CHAPTER TWO

1300 February 25, 1985

Sub-basement Three
Central Intelligence Agency Washington, DC

The man in the gray suit and dark tie entered the access code into the programmable keypad, pressed down on the door latch, and entered the SCIF. From under his arm he withdrew a jumbo brown Kraft envelope and tossed it on the worktable.

Slicing through the double-wrapped cover with a sharp box cutter, he removed most of the thick package from the FBI, immediately removing the heavy clip from the two-inch-thick stack of documents.

The man scanned a blue fingerprint card that had been process, stamped, and approved by the FBI. Several ten-panel urine screens were stamped NEGATIVE, showing no trace or history of amphetamines, barbiturates, cannabis, cocaine, or opiate use during the last ten years.

A heavily marked-up questionnaire for national security positions provided the backbone for the fifty-five DSS investigator's interviews of the subject's acquaintances, friends, coworkers, and family, as well as copies of military, medical, and school records.

The man reached into the jumbo sleeve and spilled out two dozen photographs clipped together. "Let's see what you look like." He adjusted his necktie before flipping through the black-and-white 8x10 photographs of the subject in his Marine uniform, in a racquetball court, or engaged in other physical activity.

He stopped at the color photograph of the subject in a flight suit, standing on the boarding ladder of a Navy jet, helmet in hand, with a broad smile. He had short, dark hair with no receding hairline and was a handsome, lean, mean, fighting Marine Corps machine.

"Probably the perfect build, weight, and height for a fighter pilot. Not a bad little hero shot," the man said.

After three hours' reading and taking notes in the margins, he reached across the table for a large stamp and ink pad. Flipping open the metal cover, he took the stamp and pounded the pad three times before centering the stamp at the bottom of the cover sheet. APPROVED in red letters remained on the sheet from the ink transfer.

He initialed the page and separated the sections of the package before placing them into an accordion file folder, removed the top from a black ink marker, and wrote HUNTER, DUNCAN USMC across the top of the file flap. He slid back his chair, picked up the file folder, and placed it with similar folders in a four- drawer safe.

Those folders were culled from thousands of subjects who took a battery of simple aptitude tests across America during the '50s, '60s, and '70s. The CIA's Science and Technology Division was interested in the outcome of one single test—how quickly could a subject balance sixteen penny nails on the head of another. Under three minutes was noteworthy. Balancing sixteen nails on the head of one under sixty seconds made the National Clandestine Service want to take a look at the feasibility of recruitment.

Hunter, Duncan, USMC, was the first person in five years to break the code and deliver the solution in fifty-eight seconds. The man charged with identifying unusually capable, talented people for unique and time-sensitive special access programs closed the safe labeled 17 NAILS, spun the dial, and left the tiny SCIF.

CHAPTER THREE

0700 October 10, 1996
Del Rio International Airport, Del Rio, Texas

The overnight thunderstorms blew out just in time. Duncan Hunter sat back in his chair and stared into the distance, as dozens of maquiladoras on the other side of the Rio Grande disappeared over the horizon and into the haze. Aircraft mechanics slogged through the hangar dripping with sweat. In a couple hours, it would be show time.

It was another humid Thursday in Del Rio, and the US Border Patrol's Director of Aircraft Maintenance would soon be on his way to the other end of the airfield either to bring Border Patrol aviation into the 20th century or watch it lapse back into a glorified flying club—or die altogether.

The uncertainty made Hunter nervous. For a former Marine fighter pilot, the feeling was new and a bit unsettling. There was a career resting on how well the presentation went. Depending on who one talked with, it was not a good fit having a former fighter pilot and aircraft maintenance officer with a couple of graduate degrees as the Border Patrol's new Aircraft Maintenance Director. It was an odd choice for a new civil servant with little to no civil aviation experience.

Law-enforcement aviation and FAA regulations were completely different beasts than military flight and maintenance operations, but the GAO report suggested either the Border Patrol get some adult leadership to turn its aviation program around, or it would be shut down.

Not many applied for the job. Hunter was a surprise selection. Within the first hour of his first day, he met the crusty old Chief Pilot for the first time. Charles Rodriguez

24

jabbed a finger into Hunter's chest and spat, "Who the fuck do you know in the Border Patrol?"

Taken completely by surprise by the outburst from the short, heavily wrinkled man in a flight suit, Hunter coolly replied, "You try that again, and I'll break your finger. I don't know anyone in the Border Patrol." He saw a rectangular nametag, a Border Patrol aviation patch, and a shoulder holster containing a 9mm Beretta.

Holstering his finger, Charles snapped, "Bullshit. You couldn't have gotten this job without knowing someone in the Border Patrol. Who the fuck is it?"

Hunter debated his response. "Is that how you got your job, Charles? Who'd you blow to get it? I don't know anyone in the Border Patrol. However, I do know the Attorney General, so don't fuck with me, or I'll make a little call and have your ass investigated."

He turned his back on the pissed-off pilot with a gun and walked out of the pilot's building and into his hangar. Hunter encountered a lot of hostility in the few weeks he was on the job, but, in the short time he was there, he immediately reversed the trend of aircraft crashing every other week due to pilot error or weak maintenance processes. Half the maintenance workers and the junior Border Patrol pilots quietly cheered for Hunter. The senior patrol agents in charge, like the Chief Pilot, avoided him.

Response to the outsider "non-agent" was mixed, but the leadership, including the Chief Patrol Agent and his deputy, was wholly supportive. Half the assistant Chief Patrol Agents kept Hunter at arm's length. The other half became cheerleaders.

It was over a year since they had an aircraft crash attributed to buffoonery, and he'd been on the job only thirteen months. Hunter's encounters with Charles Rodriguez were still strained but professional. Airplanes and helicopters were being fixed as fast as the pilots broke them. For the first time ever, all aircraft went on patrol with all systems working. Every aircraft in the Del Rio fleet was up, ready, and flyable with no deferred discrepancies. The Border Patrol leadership took notice.

The maintenance facility hummed with efficiency and professionalism, and, with the turnaround of the facility and the improved mission capability of the aircraft, the mechanics found themselves with a lot of free time. With ten crashed aircraft carcasses in the Quonset hut out back of the maintenance hangar, Hunter challenged the bored mechanics with a project.

Some of the men began overhauling a crashed Piper Super Cub. When the first overhauled airplane rolled out of the hangar, Hunter turned it into a media event highlighting the mechanics' work—the half that supported him. The aircraft was transformed from a ragged collection of parts, including a bent frame and wings, seized engine, shredded dope and fabric—to a stunning like-new airplane.

His success embarrassed the senior pilots and the other half of the mechanics, who were buddies with Charles. The hangar no longer looked like an Army-Navy surplus store. The mechanics that worked produced like-new airplanes from carcasses that hadn't flown in ten years, and the bright little white airplane in Border Patrol livery stunned the leadership. Other Section Air Operations begged for their aircraft to be overhauled or to be placed on the list for new Super Cubs.

When the Chief Patrol Agent asked Duncan how things were going one day in August, he replied, "I don't understand why your guys don't use quiet airplanes to chase illegal aliens and drug smugglers."

Taken aback, the Chief asked, "What are quiet airplanes? Gliders?"

That conversation set off a chain of events culminating in a flight demonstration and a quiet aircraft presentation. It was a long, bumpy road to reach that point, and it was time to get started.

Hunter checked his Seiko Dive Master. The men giving the presentation should be at their airplane at the FBO.

Driving up to the unique motorized glider, Hunter stepped out of the Border Patrol truck and walked straight toward the thin man with the full head of gray hair, knocked knees, and a smile. He was a distinguished gentleman and wore a white, long-sleeved, button-down-collared shirt with dark-gray slacks. Dull-black dress shoes completed the picture.

"You must be Greg Lynche." Hunter gripped his hand and shook it three times before releasing it to shake the other man's hand, which hung in the air. "You don't know how long I've waited for this day. I appreciate your coming today."

"Glad to finally meet you, Duncan. I feel like I've known you a long time." Lynche and the other man exchanged glances as if sharing a private joke. Lynche immediately recovered and said, "This is Art Yoder."

Once introduced, Hunter shook the hand of the six-foot-four- inch, unsmiling, solidly built companion. It had been years since he saw a flattop on anyone. Yoder sported the same dress code of white shirt with dark slacks.

"Art Yoder?" Hunter asked, looking up at the man. "Army colonel and All-Army racquetball champion? It's been a very long time, Sir. I thought you looked familiar."

"Army Special Forces," he replied, as if that was a separate service. Maybe to him it was. He was obviously a Vietnam vet. His mood eased up a little. "And I did play a little racquetball. Have we played before? I don't recall."

Yoder and Lynche continued to exchange glances. "Sir, we played a couple times while I visited the POAC," Hunter said. "Then I played with Bobby Saunders in Cleveland. He said you and he met several times at the National Singles Championships."

"That was me. That was a long time ago. I haven't played in many years."

"I don't look forward to the day when I can't play anymore." Hunter sensed the colonel didn't want to discuss racquetball. He was there on business and wanted to get on with it.

Hunter tried to get a better look at the quiet aircraft obscured by the two men and finally said, "Greg, I haven't seen any of these except on the Internet."

"Let me show you what we brought for today's demonstration. This is your basic Schweizer SA2-37B two-seat, single-engine, low-noise profile airplane. It's optimized for low-altitude surveillance and reconnaissance. This one has a suite of infrared and electro-optical sensors to monitor activities covertly on land and sea. Endurance about fourteen hours."

"She's beautiful with those sleek, conformal antennae. I expected more a muffler system like the YO-3A. Our pilots will mutiny if they hear fourteen hours. They're old and have to piss every few hours." He grinned broadly at Lynche, hoping for and receiving reciprocation.

"We're early. Have you had breakfast? I know where the best breakfast tacos on the planet are made."

"Sounds like a plan to me."

"Do I need to put security on this?"

"That would be fantastic."

Hunter turned to the driver of the Border Patrol truck. "Alex, can you and Ray make sure no one fingerfucks that airplane? I'll take these gentlemen to Julio's for some tacos and a chat. Want me to bring you back something?"

"Sir, Roy and I will stand guard. We've already had breakfast. Your National Guard Counterdrug Task Force at your service, Sir."

"Thanks, Alex."

First Sergeant Alexandro Duron opened the door, got out, and moved aside so Hunter could sit behind the wheel. Lynche and Yoder entered the four-door vehicle, and Hunter drove off the airport property.

"I forgot how wide open, flat, and dry it is in Texas," Lynche said. "In Maryland, it's wall-to-wall trees."

Hunter nodded. In the rearview mirror, he saw Yoder's eyes following every passing car. His eyes narrowed and brows furrowed.

"Duncan, I have to ask what's the real deal with illegal immigration? I swear every other vehicle we pass has Mexican license plates. Back home, some folks think we should build a fence along the border to stop illegal immigration."

Hunter nodded. "First the tags. Those people have bona fide legal documents. Illegal aliens either have none or have counterfeit papers. That's what makes them illegal. If you have a job and a house in Mexico, you can come over here just like we can go over there to visit and shop."

"Interesting."

"I didn't know any of this until I took this job. It's truly fascinating work. Let me tell you a story. The guy who's watching your plane, First Sergeant Alex Duron, and I went to a little town outside Houston to take delivery of some above-ground storage tanks. I got a G-ride—sorry, an unmarked sedan—out of the motor pool, and we drove six hours to get there.

"Alex had the same shirt on when you met him, Border Patrol green with a USBP patch over his left breast. That's recognized anywhere within 500 miles of the border. In big gold letters on the back are the words AIRCRAFT MAINTENANCE.

"So we drove up to the corporate main office right near the plant. When I stepped out of the car, I looked over to where the huge plant was making six-, eight-, and ten-thousand-gallon above-ground storage tanks, those with the pebbly finish."

"Yeah. I know the kind you're talking about."

"Right. I can tell you that every one of the plant workers watched our unmarked vehicle enter the parking lot. When Alex got out in his green Border Patrol shirt, they threw down their tools and ran for the fence to get as far from the car and that shirt as they could. They were really high-tailing it.

"I told Alex, 'Tell 'em we're not here to bust anyone and to get back to work.'"

Lynche and Yoder smiled, then burst out laughing with a you- have-to-be-kidding-me look. They shook their heads in amazement.

"I can't make that shit up," Hunter said. "It got better. As I turned to the CEO and company leaders who came out to greet us, the CEO had an expression of sheer terror. He tried to find the right words, but what came out was, 'I swear they have good I-9s.'

"I looked at him and said, 'They obviously aren't that good.' The point is there are millions of those guys with completely bogus documents in the country working all kinds of jobs. They have bogus identities. Some are probably stolen. What can you do when the democrats look at each one as a potential voter? It's crazier than you can possibly image. It won't be long before we elect an illegal alien with great bogus papers. Mark my words."

"That's incredible, Duncan. The fence?"

"When you leave here, head north twenty miles past the dam and see how the mighty Rio Grande has carved its way through 500 feet of solid granite. We have this amazing moat two, three, four hundred feet across with walls that are 400 feet high of smooth granite. If someone can cross there, a little fence won't slow him down. Politicians who think a fence is the answer are idiots. They don't come out here to talk to the Border Patrol agents who know what we need to secure the border, and a fence isn't it. You're little airplane might be the trick, though.

"Anyway, go out to the Tucson and Yuma Sectors and look at the desert. That's another natural fence. The Rio Grande is a moat. Strategic fencing from Otay Mesa to the Pacific to separate Tijuana and San Diego is the right answer. Fencing 2,000 miles of open country and private property is pure stupidity."

"That makes sense," Yoder said.

"You can see what's wrong with liberalism here on the border. The liberals go out of their way purposely to prevent law enforcement from enforcing the law, while facilitating other illegal activity. Republicans are in a constant state of war with the Democrats. One side wants to secure the border. The other side undermines the law and the efforts of law enforcement. Pick any topic, and it's the same. Out here, it's the trenches, and you see it all up front and personal.

"If you talk to a Border Patrol agent, you'll find they're all exasperated. To a man they won't say we need fences but surveillance aircraft and more ground agents. It's really simple. When they come over the fence, you need an agent waiting to apprehend them.

"I wish there was a video of Iranian students pouring over the US Embassy fence. Maybe that visual would drive the point home. A fence is only as good as the ladder needed to scale it. It won't even slow people down. You need a law-enforcement officer on the other side to deter or arrest them."

The mention of Iranian students changed Yoder's demeanor for a moment. Hunter wondered if he said something out of line or if the comment resonated with the man with the flattop.

"Duncan, that's the most common sensical…. Is that a word? Thing I have ever heard on the topic."

"Thank you, Sir. The rest of the story is, in 1995 there were only 5,000 people in the Border Patrol. More emphasis is coming our way. What we need are more planes and agents. I think quiet airplanes are the ticket for areas that don't need fences. Ground agents and aviators get it. Strategic fences are needed in metropolitan areas like Laredo, El Paso, and Tijuana. Guess what? That's exactly where they are.

"There's fourteen miles of fence in San Diego from Otay Mesa to the Pacific Ocean. It works, but not because there's a fence. It's because when someone steps over, there's a boot on the ground and an agent right there to apprehend Juan Valdez and his buddy.

"Without an agent to apprehend, a fence barely slows them down, so why bother unless you've got the manpower to apprehend? The real problem is illegal documents in the hands of illegal aliens. There's a whole industry on the other side of the border making counterfeit docs. Fixing that problem is a whole different story. That's the issue no one in politics will talk about."

"What do you mean?"

"Illegal or bogus documents fuel two different parts of the political process. Those on the right produce jobs, like building those fuel tanks. They benefit greatly from low-cost labor, so they make money and grow the business.

"It's a little different on the left. One part is the democrats don't believe in border control and view anyone coming over as a potential voter. The other part's related to bogus documents. The dirty secret in law enforcement, at least here on the border, is when the police or Border Patrol pull over illegal aliens. Let's just call them poor, but they have fistfuls of documents. It's no surprise when one of them gets pulled over and he flashes a Michigan driver's license or a Social Security card issued from Connecticut.

"They get free stuff, whether it's health care or food stamps, under multiple names, then they sell any extra they have. It's another form of welfare. The other thing they do with those bogus documents is vote. What's that Chicago saying? 'Vote early and often?' These folks have it down to an art form. The reason democrats are hostile about voter ID laws is that they wouldn't be able to win an election unless they stole it."

Hunter guided the Border Patrol truck into Julio's parking lot. "If these aren't the best tacos you've ever had, I'll buy you dinner, too."

The men ordered, and Hunter led them to a corner table so they could talk. "Greg, you can expect at least five Chief Patrol Agents and I don't know how many pilots in my hangar. I want you to know the people you'll be dealing with today. The chief's deputies, and assistant chiefs are mostly very conservative patriots. The other chiefs who aren't here are definitely not interested in improving the capabilities of their sector.

"Things are so bad under this democratic administration that some agents siphon gas from seized vehicles so they can get back into the field and catch bad guys. Our budget's really thin, and it's made that way on purpose. So there's no money to buy new aircraft."

"That's not a good sign."

"It might get better soon. I understand Congressman Hernandez or one of his staffers will be there, too. He's the first Republican to win this district, and the BP leadership has high hopes he'll be a magic bullet for the Border Patrol, at least in Del Rio Sector."

Yoder deadpanned, "Sounds like things are looking up."

Hunter smiled. "I also broke the code on how to get money."

Breakfast tacos were delivered to their table with a large bowl of salsa and chips.

"Let me know what you think of the salsa," Hunter said, pausing to take a bite. "There's a wildcard. I don't know the Chief of Air Ops very well. He's hard to read. I think he views me as a competitor, but, by law, I can't take over his job."

"You aren't an agent?"

Hunter shook his head. "No. However, I'm the highest-ranking non-agent on the Border Patrol. I got the job when the GAO almost shut down USBP aviation. It was really just a flying club and might still be in some sectors. Anyway, the Chief of Air Ops Doug Crabb may also come. I think he and a contingent from El Paso Sector will fly in. I can't emphasize enough that this is a very big deal. My chief went over his head to get you here. I'm way out over my skis, too, but Chief Burgher is my sponsor and likes what I provide him."

"You have to have a sponsor," Yoder said.

"10-4. I want you to know there are some friendlies, like Chief Baker from Laredo. He's the first African American Chief Patrol Agent and could be President someday. He's an amazing man. There's Chief De la Montoya from McAllen. He's a close friend of Chief Burgher. Of course, we'll have Chief Burgher here. You can't miss him. He's the tallest guy in the Border Patrol, maybe taller than Art."

Hunter chuckled. "I heard when he was a field agent,

illegals took one look at that giant man and became so docile, Paul just had to say, 'Get in my truck.' After that, my intel isn't so good. The senior pilots have repeatedly claimed the Schweizer doesn't work, and I heard it again yesterday from our chief pilot. I know it's all crap, but they're the senior aviators here. If there's any pushback, that's where it'll come from."

Lynche listened to Hunter talk while biting into a soft, round, filled tortilla. "Duncan, these tacos are fantastic, and the salsa is absolutely the best I ever tasted. You're right. These are amazing. Art?"

"Makes me want another one."

Lynche waved his hands and said, "No mas. No mas!" He returned the remains of his taco to his plate. "The CEO of Schweizer said no one from the Border Patrol has ever expressed interest in his aircraft."

"He told me the same thing when I spoke with him," Hunter said. "I told him I absolutely believe it. It seems reasonable to expect the rank-and-file Border Patrol pilot just wants to do the mission, while older pilots want to fly air-conditioned helicopters during the day, then go home. The older guys will tell any lie to keep from working hard or flying at night. There are several who have ceased being patriots."

"Duncan, these tacos are so good, they must be illegal."

"It's the salsa. It's the best on the planet, and it's one of the best-kept secrets in Texas."

On their way back to the airport, Hunter motioned through the windshield to the clearly visible buildings and expansive maquiladoras on the Mexican side of the border. "There are watchers over there with telescopes. I'll bet heads exploded when you guys landed and I picked you up.

The comment got Yoder's attention. "Watchers?"

"Yes, Sir. I learned long ago we can't do anything without someone knowing or watching us. You can see we're less than a mile from the border. You can see the maquiladoras. We're more effective in apprehensions and seizures when we can mask our operations. I'd move the air operations out to the Air Force base if I could and operate it like, well, like I expect the CIA would conduct air operations."

Lynche beamed broadly. "You're a smart man, Duncan. That's exactly what I'd do."

CHAPTER FOUR

0900 October 10, 1996

US Border Patrol Maintenance Hangar
Del Rio International Airport, Del Rio, Texas

Chief Patrol Agent Paul Burgher, a broad six-foot-six-inch man with hands the size of hubcaps and fingers as thick as screwdriver handles, walked to the seated assembly of Chief Patrol Agents, Deputy Chief Patrol Agents, Assistant Chief Patrol Agents, Patrol Agents in Charge, and a Congressional staffer. Except for the pilots, everyone wore business suits with a tie. The agents in dress suits and flight suits carried their weapons in shoulder holsters.

"I'd like to thank Mr. Lopez from Congressman Hernandez' office for making the trip from San Antonio."

Hunter applauded, establishing the protocol for recognizing each attendee.

"I'd like to also recognize Chief of Air Ops, Douglass Crabb, Chief Louis Baker of the Laredo Sector, Chief Raul De la Montoya of the McAllen Sector, and Chief Ron White of the El Paso Sector. The security folks wanted to make sure I announced this brief is at the TS/SCI level. This requires special access, so everyone's clearance has been verified. Is that correct? I thought so.

"OK. I asked our Aviation Director to see if we could get more information on different aircraft to improve our ability to secure the southwest border. Today, we have Mr. Greg Lynche from the Schweizer Aircraft Company. Mr. Lynche retired from the CIA after a distinguished thirty-five-year career and was a member of the Senior Intelligence Service. He served in leadership positions around the globe as Chief of Station, Chief of Counterterrorism, and Chief Air Branch.

Ladies and Gentlemen, Greg Lynche."

Lynche acknowledged all the dignitaries as Chief Burger did but added Duncan Hunter to the list, which earned Duncan a round of applause. Greg Lynche quickly went over the challenges facing Border Patrol agents and suggested the aircraft he brought could solve most of their problems.

"One of the greatest liabilities to aircraft doing field work was that once an illegal alien or smuggler heard it, everyone scattered." He related an Arab proverb. "The eagle that chases two rabbits catches neither. With a low-noise aircraft, you control the aural environment and are able to identify targets, coordinate an interception, and control the apprehension or drug seizure from an acoustically silent platform. I like it, because you can also look over the border and see what's over there and what might be coming."

Most of the audience nodded and were poised for his next bullet point when the Del Rio Sector Chief Pilot said, "No disrespect, Chief, but we've tried these technologies before, and they don't work in this environment." He seemed proud of his statement, and some of the other agents in flight suits either nodded or rolled their eyes.

Lynche nodded to Hunter and asked, "Art?"

Duncan moved quickly to a cart with a large TV on the top shelf with a VCR player on the lower shelf and rolled the cart in front of the assembly of Chief Patrol Agents. Art Yoder waited for Hunter to turn on the two devices before he inserted a tape and pressed Play.

The Chiefs leaned forward for a better view. The Chief Pilot hadn't anticipated that Lynche would ignore him.

As an image came to the screen, Lynche said, "I don't know who said that, but let me tell you what we did last night on our way to delightful Del Rio, Texas. We took on gas at Corpus Christi and flew along the coast from Brownsville to Del Rio. We flew up the Rio Grande. This is what we recorded of the activity along your border."

For the next hour, Lynche and Yoder relayed where they were and what they saw, highlighting the location and movement of hundreds of illegal aliens, some in columns of 120 or more, and obvious drug smugglers, some in columns of ten to forty human mules carrying huge bales on their backs.

South of Laredo, a dozen horses carried large bales of something across the shallow Rio Grande. In four instances, snakes of seventy to 120 illegal aliens and smugglers passed within twenty feet of Border Patrol vehicles with agents inside.

"We know these are Border Patrol vehicles. We used an infrared night-vision laser spotlight to verify the Border Patrol emblem on the side of the truck as well as the J-tag license plates. We wished we had your radio frequency. We could have helped."

Lynche and Yoder's five-hour flight documented over 1,000 illegal aliens entering the US without being apprehended or detected, as well as over 200 drug smugglers with countless pounds of contraband that evaded detection and apprehension. The FLIR captured an invasion of illegal activity, long suspected but never caught on film before. The shocked audience was in turmoil.

Lynche, beginning his wrap-up, fast forwarded the video. "I think you'll like this. This was extraordinary. We were surprised there had been no activity for a long while when I saw something flash on the FLIR that didn't look like a rabbit or a javelina. You can see from this aspect there's no thermal image, but, when I came around 180 degrees, there's a guy sleeping. If you get on the other side of his lean-to, he disappears. I hadn't seen that before, but I think he's hiding under a thermal blanket.

"Now let me fast forward a bit. Here we go. I think this is a Border Patrol helicopter flying right over the guy. We were at 1,500 AGL at that point, and I think the helo was at 500 feet. And you can see the helicopter had a FLIR ball on the nose.

"The guy on the ground heard the helo coming, threw up the blanket to mask his heat signature, and hunkered down.

We stayed on station for ten minutes, and it looked like, once the helo was out of aural range, well watch what happens. For those in the back, the guy crawls out from under the blanket, stands up, snatches the thermal blanket, and runs east."

The crowd murmured. Some shook their heads in disbelief.

"Mr. Hunter thinks, if you had one of these aircraft flying this corridor, the sensor operator could have talked to ground agents and vectored them into position to capture. I'm sorry. I meant to apprehend those people on the film. Please note the high level of clarity on the video. This quality is possible only with a low-level quiet aircraft and a great FLIR flying above the targets."

"What altitude is that?" A pilot asked.

"That's classified. We were flying between 500 and 2,500 feet, basically north, VFR without lights, to prove our point."

Chief Patrol Agent Crabb looked at Chief Burgher. "We could really use those airplanes."

Crabb turned his head to the Del Rio Sector Chief Pilot and momentarily glared at him. The body language and facial expression were unmistakable. Mr. Lopez from the Congressman's office suddenly stood and walked toward Lynche, Yoder, and Hunter. The five chiefs joined the group in the middle of the hangar, ignoring the other attendees.

Chief Burgher soon left the pack, threw up a big hand, and waved. "That's all, Folks. Thank you for coming. Let's go into the conference room."

Hunter was astounded by the reaction of the senior Border Patrol Agents and whispered to Lynche as he was dragged toward the conference room, "Nice work, Sir."

Art Yoder watched the pilots' reactions. His arms crossed, he walked to Hunter and said, "Duncan, I think you made an enemy for life."

Hunter smiled and nodded. He didn't need to look back to know what happened behind him.

He sat there, staring ahead. The Chief Pilot's rage was

visible. Ronnie Hawley, his assistant, leaned over and said, "Charles, calm down. They'll never be able to buy one of those things."

The Chief Pilot and Patrol Agent in Charge of the Del Rio Sector Air Operations shook his head, stood, and walked out of the hangar to his office. From his desk phone, he made a call. "We have a problem."

He glanced out the window where the Schweizer was parked, shook his head, picked up his old truck keys, and left.

An hour-long meeting with the five Chief Patrol Agents, Mr. Lopez, Lynche, Yoder, and Hunter, resulted in a commitment from the Congressional aide to have the Congressman meet with Lynche and Yoder when they returned to Washington, DC. Hunter sketched out a pilot program with a concept of operations, what Yoder called a CONOP. A handful of quiet aircraft would be used during the night, flown by contract pilots operating from airfields away from the prying eyes of border watchers.

When the issue of funding arose, the aide indicated the Congressman would start work to find funding for three aircraft, but the Border Patrol couldn't count on receiving the earmark, since the funding could and would likely be siphoned off by the Democratic I&NS Commissioner and reprogrammed for something else.

"What about using drug forfeiture funds?" Hunter interjected. The three-second pause was shattered by Chief Burgher.

"That's brilliant, Duncan. I think we could make a case that the aircraft would also be used for detecting drug smugglers."

"Quiet aircraft pilots could contact DEA or Customs just as easily as they could contact Border Patrol agents when they found a drug op going down," Hunter said.

Lynche and Lopez asked simultaneously, "How do you get drug forfeiture funds?"

The men looked at each other and laughed.

"Duncan, you want to answer that?" Chief Burgher asked.

"Sir, I provide an official request to the DEA for what I'd like to do. I've received over two million dollars for several projects, one of which is right around this corner. I think I've broken the code on how to get drug forfeiture funds as well as aircraft and vehicles that have been the property of drug lords."

"What's around the corner?" Mr. Lopez asked.

"Let me show you." Hunter walked around a bulkhead and stopped in a large workspace.

Work benches were outfitted with different pieces of test equipment, including oscilloscopes, multi-meters, radio-frequency generators, power supplies, soldering guns, lighted magnifying glass rings, and rate tables for testing gyroscopes. Special and common hand tools hung from boards and racks of spare parts and consumable items like terminal ends, splices, and light bulbs.

In the middle of the shop was a Piper Super Cub, minus its wings, that was being rebuilt. A mechanic was sticking out from the side, wedged into the cockpit, installing the rudder pedals. All that was visible was the man's jeans and boots and a green polo shirt with BORDER PATROL AIRCRAFT MAINTENANCE on the back.

"Sir, this is the DOJ's first and only FAA-certified Repair Station. I received five hundred thousand dollars to completely establish and outfit a repair station, and we have every piece of test equipment we need to fix law-enforcement aviation electrical and electronic systems. My guys fix Border Patrol, Customs, and DEA aircraft, as well as Department of Public Safety and anyone else who wants to use our repair station. Our clients include aviation units for the San Antonio and Houston Police Departments. We even fixed the governor's plane when it came through here and broke down."

Lynche glanced at Yoder. "What's the advantage of your having a repair station?" He walked up to the fuselage and looked inside the little airplane.

"Sir, take this gyro, for example. Before we had this repair station, if we had a bad gyro, it was sent to a repair station, and they charged us $2,500 to crack open the case and another $3,000 to repair it. Then it took several weeks to turn around. A gyro costs $6,500 new. My guys can overhaul one in a couple hours and give same-day service for less than fifty dollars. We overnight it back to the law-enforcement unit."

Chief Burger beamed.

"What's this airplane doing here?" Lopez asked Duncan. "Are you fixing it?"

"In their spare time, my guys overhaul Super Cubs and return them to the Border Patrol fleet. We have a dozen aircraft that crashed over the years. We get the frames straightened and put in new wiring, an engine, and avionics. After we recover them, we deliver them to the air ops unit that needs them. After the first one was delivered to Laredo Sector, everyone in the Border Patrol wants one of our refurbished Super Cubs."

"And, they're very effective," Chief Burgher said. "You get a young agent up there, and he'll find illegals all day long."

"What are the chances you can get some drug forfeiture funds?" Lopez asked.

"For quiet airplanes? In the past I've asked the DEA to transfer a couple of aircraft that we integrated into our fleet. I haven't asked for specific funds for quiet aircraft, but if that's all it takes, Sir, I'll work it," Hunter said. "I've been very successful in that arena. You need the right justification, and timing is everything."

"I'll brief the DEA chief," Chief Burgher said. "Duncan has some other ideas that would help us tremendously, like the quiet airplanes."

No one noticed Lynche and Yoder quietly exchanging raised eyebrows and imperceptible nods.

As the meeting broke up, the senior Border Patrol agents departed out the hangar's back door, while Chief Burgher escorted the Congressional aide to his vehicle. Lynche and Yoder promised to stay in touch.

After Chief Burgher departed, Hunter turned toward the

large hangar doors toward Mexico. He led Lynche and Yoder back through the hangar and out to the long-wing Schweizer airplane.

"I think that went well." Hunter beamed like a lighthouse on a dark night.

Lynche patted his back. "You're a master of understatement."

He raised a heavy eyebrow at Yoder, who nodded.

Hunter understood it was time to get the old spook and colonel on their way. "I can't thank you enough for coming to our little patch of Texas. You might be able to sell a few airplanes."

Hunter placed his hand on the sun-baked cowling of the quiet airplane, appreciating its lines and beauty and thinking how cool it would be to fly.

"Duncan, would you be interested in a job proposition?" Yoder asked, interrupting the younger man's reverie.

Hunter slowly cocked his head, his brows narrowed. He saw sly smiles etched on the two men's faces. After gently patting the quiet spy plane, he asked, "What did you gentlemen have in mind?"

CHAPTER FIVE

0900 December 15, 1997
Central Intelligence Agency Washington, DC

Training for an operation demanded strategic resources, plans, schedules, and practice. They worked in secret locations in the early days under the watchful eye of a senior intelligence officer in a basement room of the CIA's old headquarters building. Hunter and Lynche, sometimes accompanied by Yoder, nearly drove each other crazy with the level of planning necessary for their CIA handler to approve the operation and receive the official Notice to Proceed. Hunter insisted on full mission planning, consistent with his fighter pilot training. Going from startup to shutdown, he covered every contingency in between.

Wraith ops were one-time flights in and out, in stringent secrecy, and the only surprise Hunter wanted to deal with was a light gripe. "We plan for every situation. We always have a backup plan. We plan for the unexpected. We're dealing with men and machines. Anything that can go wrong will, and whatever happens, it'll come at the worst-possible moment. Greg, your bride will beat my ass if I let anything happen to you. Let's get this show on the road."

The men made mock-ups and models of compounds they would fly over or around. In support of those unique, top-secret Agency operations, overheads, or satellite photographs from the National Reconnaissance Office or the National Geospatial- Intelligence Agency were provided for operations and mission planning. The photographs were extremely detailed, with levels of granularity and resolution not available from commercial sources.

During his first op with Lynche and Yoder, Hunter complained of the lack of training aids to conduct mission planning. The fact that they would fly at night, while their practice sessions took place in a well-illuminated room, didn't sit well with him. He insisted on conducting the tabletop exercises and practice missions with night-vision goggles.

Lynche balked at first, then he saw the value of training until everything on the mission checklist became routine. The DCI's senior intelligence officer monitoring the mission planning asked if there was anything else they could to do improve the success of the mission.

"Yeah," Hunter said. "Get us a full-motion simulator." The three men stared at him, thinking he was joking.

His silence and demeanor conveyed his seriousness. "I know where we can get one. We would just need to upgrade the cockpit and find it a place to call home."

Yoder yawned. Lynche was cranky. He asked, "How do you get a YO-3 simulator?"

"The hard part is acquiring the full-motion platform. Then we need a donor cockpit, but even then, we can make one. Then we need the cockpit updated to resemble the Wraith's, complete with NVG-capable lighting. Ever hear of EDA? Excess Defense Article is like DRMO for airplanes, ships, and anything huge and expensive—like a full-motion simulator."

The CIA handler asked, "Can you give me exactly what you need and a POC? If we get this huge EDA thing, where will it go?"

As Hunter wrote a dozen bullets and handed the list to the man with the blue badge, he said, "I vote for Schweizer's. Saul Ferrier has a building capable, and they could do all the cockpit mods and maintenance on the simulator, and he has a SCIF. We could do mission planning there and practice in the sim."

The second day of mission planning, as the three men entered the new headquarters building, the security crew stopped Hunter for trying to carry in a custom-built resin model of a YO-3A on a long wooden dowel, covered by a Wal-Mart bag to hide its unique features.

Security eventually relented after the DCI got personally involved. Yoder, Lynche, and Hunter passed through the turnstiles with their green contractor badges. "You think maybe one day we can get a large model built and have it hanging up there with its big brother and sisters?"

The three men looked up. Suspended from the ceiling of NHB's glass-enclosed atrium were one-sixth-scale models of the U- 2, A-12, and D-21 reconnaissance aircraft. The CIA developed the U-2 to collect imagery of the former Soviet Union. The supersonic A-12, built by the CIA to replace the U-2, held speed and altitude records that remained unbroken. The D-21 drone extended the A- 12's capabilities into high-threat areas.

"Greg, I think your YO-3A would be in good company."

Hunter's quiet airplane on a stick simulated flying over an overhead of the operational target, just like attack and fighter pilots across most militaries did for briefing and debriefing flights. The little model provided enough three-dimensional frame of reference and different viewing aspects.

"That really is a good idea," Lynche said later. "You really can plan better with a visual aid and study the contingencies. I guess you can teach an old dog new tricks."

"Three cheers for us old farts." Hunter smiled.

CHAPTER SIX

0830 July 13, 1998
Near East Division Offices, CIA Washington, DC

Nicholas Lloyd Dolan scanned a month's worth of weekly reports. The case officer and analyst for Pakistan of Near East Division returned from two weeks' vacation in Zion National Park, Utah, and found his return to work in McLean unfocused at best. Two cups of black coffee weren't enough to kick-start the old gray matter into performing real analysis.

Mondays were always challenging, as reports and dispatches arrived in bundles from the twenty-odd US embassies that submitted them over the weekend. Nick Dolan's indifference to the dispatches from Pakistan almost ended up at the bottom of a manila file or tossed in the burn bag when he gripped the documents and composed himself.

Exhaling, he said loudly, "Focus, Nick!"

A cursory glance of the dispatch from the Chief of Station in Islamabad didn't register anything notable the first time. Upon second glance, though, it was curious. The administrative equivalent of kicking the can down the road, he highlighted the narrative and wrote in the margin in green ink, Check info/send to the FBI & State. Missing from the marginalia was a follow-up by date.

The dispatch was attached under the signature sheet on the message board. Embassy dispatches are at least classified Secret. That one was considered Confidential, the lowest security classification. The dispatch was fuzzy and blurry coming off the printer, but it was clear enough to read.

Verify with DOS validity of citizenship of a candidate running for senator in the state of Michigan. Local asset insists the candidate traveled to Pakistan under British passport in 1980s. Previous confirmation the subject met with suspected terrorists, attended mosque and training camp. Local asset had chance meeting with candidate last month in Washington, DC. Candidate now US citizen?

CHAPTER SEVEN

1100 October 22, 1999

US Border Patrol Maintenance Hangar
Del Rio International Airport, Del Rio, Texas

A jet engaging its reverse thrusters was enough to get Duncan Hunter out of his chair and leave his office to investigate. Stepping into the bright sun, he waited until his eyes adjusted before trying to locate the jet. Del Rio didn't get many jets, as the runway was too short for anything without reverse thrusters.

When jets visited, they were usually filled with exotic big-game hunters heading for ranches with populations of exotic species of horned animals—ibex, oryx, and whitetail bucks with racks that redefined trophy. A quick check of his Rolex Submariner confirmed he needed food soon.

Hunter turned to walk back to the hangar when the Chief Pilot pulled his decrepit Ford pickup in front of the pilot's office and hurried inside.

Patrol Agent in Charge Charles Rodriguez didn't acknowledge Hunter with a wave or a flip of a finger. Hunter didn't expect anything from him but contempt. From the first day, it was contempt. For four years, every day it was contempt. Maybe that day was special contempt.

Hunter, standing in the sun, recalled events leading up to that day. For four years, Hunter observed the internal workings and politics of Border Patrol aviation. Border Patrol Air Operations was a glorified flying club and good-old-boy's network for a very long time. That was the official assessment from the old congressional watchdog General Accountability Office. Hunter's fascination with all things airworthy led him occasionally to steal rides with friendly Border Patrol pilots in helicopters and Super Cubs. On a day when he jumped into the left seat of a helicopter going out on patrol, Hunter was curious when the pilot diverted around what he expected to be prime smuggling areas.

Before Hunter could ask, the pilot said, "Charles doesn't want us flying over this area."

The incongruity of a federal agent being told not to patrol a prime smuggling area made Hunter immediately suspicious.

A curious case of cause and effect occurred when Hunter left on a few weeks of leave or when he was on temporary assignment with the DOJ's Office of Internal Audit. Hunter and Lynche's counterdrug work in Colombia, Peru, and Panama were felt immediately along the major smuggling routes into the US. Hunter would leave and ten days later, the number of drug seizures along the border dropped to nearly zero, because supplies dried up. Intelligence officers or DEA agents in Mexico heard the rumors, "Nothing from Colombia today."

Chief Pilot Charles Rodriguez, seeing the relationship immediately, tried to determine what Hunter was doing for the DOJ's Office of Internal Audit. "Auditing an aviation program" was enough to make the chief pilot and his friends wary of the former Marine pilot with no apparent law-enforcement background.

Several calls to other Border Patrol Air Operations units revealed the hunter sometimes engaged in auditing a USBP program. At other times, Hunter wasn't auditing a USBP Air Operations program anywhere. When those situations occurred, Charles took notes and tried to locate the whereabouts of the Border Patrol's missing Aviation Maintenance Director.

When Hunter worked in Del Rio, his impact on the US Border Patrol wasn't limited to the aviation units but was also felt in the field. He sometimes responded to a field agent's frustration when he said, "Sometimes, we just don't know where to patrol. There are things we can do, like drag roads and cut sign, but oftentimes, we spend a lot of unproductive time chasing getaways."

Hunter suggested folding a geographic information system into the electronic form used to process those who were apprehended for any infraction. The modified form captured and presented geographically referenced data using a point-and-click mouse to pinpoint the location where the illegal alien or drug smuggler was apprehended.

Working with the computer geeks in the IT shop, they developed a pilot system that did just that. After two months of data collection, the results were stunning and exciting. The data was graphically represented as red dots of increasing size to signify the scale of apprehensions. Large red blotches indicated high- intensity smuggling areas, while tiny dots suggested a random or accidental apprehension.

An unintended consequence of the program was that it also pictorially represented dead zones—areas where high-apprehension activity was expected, though the data didn't show much activity. A famous satellite photograph of the world at night indicated civilization, activity, and life, with one exception—North Korea. On a map where areas north and south of the country are fully illuminated, the country is a dead zone without lights.

Just like the North Korea dead zone, the sector map of Del Rio had its own dead zone. The area above Los Reyes Ranch showed hundreds of apprehensions, and the area below it was the same, but the area encompassing the ranch was black, meaning no activity. Hunter knew that was the same piece of property that Charles Rodriguez mandated his pilots avoid.

The penultimate piece of the puzzle fell into place when communications technicians, who serviced the thousands of seismic sensors strategically placed along the border, found the sensors' antennas on the Los Reyes Ranch were clipped, rendering them useless. The technicians reported several heavily traveled routes through the property.

After repairing the seismic sensors and installing several

others while noting their locations, the technicians reported their findings to the sector leadership.

As Hunter sat at his desk one morning, Charles, in full pilot regalia—flight suit, patches, and sidearm—came into the maintenance office. He ignored Hunter's good morning salutation and used the copy machine. A few minutes later, he backed away from the machine with his copies and scurried out of the building like a rat on a mission.

A few more minutes passed and Hunter went to make his own copies and found the Remove Original from Glass light was on.

When he lifted the lid of the copier, the last thing Duncan expected to find was a document stamped SECRET in red letters, at the head and footer, containing the ID number and location of all the new seismic sensors on the Los Reyes Ranch.

Hunter copied the document, flipped it onto his desk, and went to the pilot's office. He greeted several of the pilots, one of whom was standing in front of the pilot's office copy machine making copies.

Hunter walked into Charles' office. "Sir, I believe you left this in the copy machine."

"Oh, yeah. We got new sensor location sheets. I had to update our flight books."

"No factor. Have a great day Charles." He left the building and returned to the maintenance facility and his office. He opened his two-drawer safe, extracted a hefty file, slipped the SECRET document inside, and went out the back door to the vehicle parking area.

Forty-five minutes later, Duncan Hunter left Chief Patrol Agent Burgher's office empty-handed.

* * *

Hunter stood outside for five minutes before a Border Patrol pilot ran out of the pilot's shack. Seeing Hunter, he made a beeline for him.

"Charles just retired," the man said. "If you want to say anything to him, you need to do it now. He said he's had enough and is moving to Seattle."

Hunter crossed his arms as a flurry of activity went through the flight shack. An old white truck was being filled with boxes of pictures and other dust collectors from men in flight suits scurrying back and forth. Some of the mechanics filed out of the hangar and into the flight shack.

First Sergeant Duron joined Hunter on the tarmac. "Did you hear?"

Hunter nodded.

Ten minutes after Duron's arrival, US Border Patrol Chief Pilot Charles Rodriguez led pilots and mechanics from the building as he hurried to his truck. Before opening the door, he gave Hunter a cold, hateful look and shouted, "I know it was you, motherfucker." Rodriguez got in, slammed his door, and drove off.

First Sergeant Duron took a half-step to the side, standing in Hunter's periphery to speak, but Hunter was expressionless and unemotional as the old truck roared away. Hunter turned to stare toward Mexico for a moment, wondering if anyone witnessed the event.

He turned back toward the hangar. "Show's over," Hunter said. "Everyone back to work."

First Sergeant Duron glanced at the pilot's office, then at Hunter's figure as it disappeared into the maintenance facility, and wondered what he just saw.

CHAPTER EIGHT

0900 September 11, 2001
SOCOM Headquarters, McDill AFB Tampa, Florida

"Admiral O'Toole, Sir, your presence is immediately requested at the command post."

"Is this related to the airplane that hit the World Trade Center?"

"Yes, Sir."

"On my way."

Three minutes later, Vice Admiral Mannix "Max" O'Toole scanned his ID card into the card reader, punched in his access code, and entered the SOCOM Command Post. Twelve paces in, he was struck by the quiet and started to speak. On one large TV monitor, members of the Crisis Action Team watched a live feed of a Boeing 767 flying into the South Tower of the World Trade Center.

As a fireball and debris shot from the middle of the South Tower, Admiral O'Toole turned crimson and barked, "We're under attack! Colonel Brown, set Threat Con Delta. Activate the CAT. Let me know when everyone's here."

Telephones rang. Admiral O'Toole moved to his CAT station, inserted and turned the Crypto Ignition Key of the STU-III, and started punching numbers when the device rang. The indicator showed a Washington, DC, area code.

"Captain Jackson, status! Any more aircraft out there? Anything from the Pentagon?"

"Yes, Sir. FAA reports at least four commercial aircraft stopped position reporting. Two jets may be inbound to Washington, DC. Nothing from Command Post."

"Admiral O'Toole," said, answering the STU. "Max, Spook. Do you know what's going on?" Vice Admiral

Ray "Spook" Dunhill, Officer of Naval Intelligence, asked.

"Not much, Sir. We've gone to Delta. We know some commercial aircraft have dropped off the radar, with two probably inbound to you. After that, not much. I think this has to be Al Qaeda or Saddam."

"Max, here's what we think we know. At 0832, American Airlines Flight 11's transponder stopped transmitting. Boston ATC indicated it was hijacked at 0838. At 0841, New York ATC lost communications with a United Airlines Flight 175 and assumed it, too, was hijacked. Those are 767s, and we have no idea how many souls are aboard.

"We think the second jet to hit the WTC was the United. No one has claimed responsibility, and there was no intel this was in the works. We're flying blind. I have a call in to the CTC, but their lines are jammed.

"Here's the bad news. At 0850, American Airlines Flight 77, a 757, also stopped transmitting and may be headed toward DC. FAA is shitting all over itself, and...hold on.... Let me call you back. I don't think there's anything to do right now but take cover and protect your people. Spook, out."

Admiral O'Toole, replacing the handset in its cradle, turned to Colonel Brown. "I need the Delta commander to initiate a recall of his folks and have him get here as soon as he can. Captain Jackson, contact DEVGRU and get Captain McGee on the phone ASAP.

O'Toole and his staff fielded secure phone calls and SIPRNet traffic. It was difficult not to watch the monitors. Fire and smoke poured from two obscene scars in the WTC. A person fell from the building.

Did he jump? M a x O'Toole glanced to the north wall of the CAT at the banks of clocks displaying local times across the globe. In Washington, DC, it was 0937.

Seconds later, American Airlines Flight 77 disappeared from the radar and struck the western side of the Pentagon.

"Admiral O'Toole?" a voice asked louder than the others. "Sir, the Pentagon has just reported the entire building shock."

Everyone in the CAT took a deep breath.

"Sir, the Pentagon's been hit. They're evacuating."

Two minutes later, the CAT's FAA representative announced, "The FAA has ordered all planes in the air to land at the nearest airport."

Smoke and jet fuel permeated the air in the Pentagon. The seventy-year-old Secretary of Defense was one of the last to leave the building and began assisting in rescue operations at the crash site.

At 0959, the South Tower of the World Trade Center began collapsing. A dozen people muttered in unison, "Oh, my God." Members of the CAT and Admiral O'Toole were transfixed, as the building fell into itself.

"Admiral? United 93 is completely off the radar about eighty miles southeast of Pittsburgh. F-16s were en route to intercept, but no new details, Sir."

Less than thirty minutes later, the North Tower collapsed. America was at war.

Several hours later, the President returned to Washington, DC, to meet with his full National Security Council at 2100.

Forty-eight minutes later, Vice Admiral O'Toole joined a STU-III conference call with the SECDEF, the CIA director, and the Chairman of the JCS. Someone spoke without bothering to use salutations or honors.

"Max, we're virtually certain Osama bin Laden and his network were behind the attacks. A check of the passenger manifests of the hijacked flights turned up three known al-Qaeda operatives on the jet that hit the Pentagon. We're learning it's al- Qaeda, not Saddam. More to follow when we know.

"Osama bin Laden is in Afghanistan but exactly where isn't known. We think the killing of Ahmad Massoud two days ago can't be a coincidence."

"Max, the President wants a plan to find and kill bin Laden and destroy al-Qaeda."

Retaliating against Afghanistan, a country decimated by two decades of war, would pose a significant challenge not only to find Osama bin Laden but to find anything worth hitting.

"We'll need to a quick-reaction force in country in very short order to find bin Laden, Sir," Admiral O'Toole said. "I have the commanders of Delta and SEAL Team Six inbound. Getting a large S and D team in country will be a challenge. What are the chances of getting the Pakis to change sides and stop supporting the Taliban and al-Qaeda?"

"The President and the Secretary of State will lean on them, make them an offer they can't refuse," said the DCI.

"When can you brief the President?" the SECDEF asked.

"Sir, we have several plans that are war-gamed and practiced. Twelve hours?"

"We'll do it via VTC. See you tomorrow."

* * *

The War in Afghanistan officially began on October 7, 2001, as the armed forces of the United States, the United Kingdom, and the Afghan United Front (Northern Alliance) launched Operation Enduring Freedom in response to the September 11 attacks on the United States. The President enunciated the goal of dismantling the al-Qaeda terrorist organization and ending its use of Afghanistan as a base. The United States would remove the Taliban regime from power and create a viable democratic state.

* * *

Ten days after the Twin Towers fell, members of the US Army Delta Forces parachuted into Afghanistan and met with CIA agents at the Qala-i-Jangi compound near Mazari Sharif in northern Afghanistan. Based on the most-recent intelligence, Osama bin Laden was holed up in an extensive cave and tunnel system on the Pakistan-Afghanistan border.

Twenty-five SEALs from DEVGRU—the Gold Team—led by thirty-five-year veteran Captain William "Bullfrog" McGee, HAHO parachuted into Afghanistan's Tora Bora area. For three months, snipers of SEAL Team Six killed Taliban and al-Qaeda in great numbers and at great distances but few of the top leaders. The lack of top AQ officials led the SEALs to believe the intelligence was poor and possibly even wrong.

By December 17, the last cave complex had been taken, and all defenders were overrun. No massive bunkers were found, only small outposts and a few minor training camps. A dejected team was extracted to Kandahar by two Blackhawks of the 160th Special Operations Aviation Regiment. McGee debriefed the members of SEAL Team Six Blue and returned to Norfolk. Failing to find and kill Osama bin Laden, Captain Bill McGee was removed as commander of DEVGRU/SEAL Team Six with orders to attend the Naval War College. For all practical purposes, the Navy's most-decorated SEAL commander's operational career was over.

CHAPTER NINE

0805 September 11, 2001
Laughlin Air Force Base Del Rio, Texas

"I know how they did it." Hunter's voice was forceful but hushed. He had called Greg Lynche two minutes after watching the second 767 fly into the South Tower of the World Trade Center.

"Good morning to you, too. What do you mean, you know how they did it? No one knows anything yet. At least, no one's talking to me. This is unbelievable."

He stared at the live TV feed of both Twin Towers burning. "Greg, I don't know anyone at the FBI, but I think you might. You know everybody."

"Hunter, you're scaring me again," Lynche replied half-heartedly.

"Here's the deal Greg. Those two planes had to be hijacked. New York's just one target. Washington is next, then maybe Chicago and LA, but there will be more. I know how they did it, and the guys who helped facilitate the hijackings were Muslim pre-board screeners at the departure airports. There will be significant chaos. I doubt the FBI will be able to move quickly enough. If they don't, they'll lose contact with the accomplices, and the evidence will be erased."

"Whoa, whoa, whoa! Slow down. What are you trying to say?"

"Greg, the only way to get a weapon aboard an airplane, so you can hijack it, is if the pre-board screener, the guy sitting at the X-ray machine on the concourse, either doesn't catch a weapon in someone's carry-on baggage when it comes through it, or he's in on the plan and is told to ignore anything going through his X-ray machine from, say, eight-thirty to nine-thirty. Hell, they can even look up from their screen and see who's in line to come through. It's probably too late, but this is what the investigators will find."

Lynche wrote wildly. When Hunter got into one of his outpourings of consciousness, all Lynche could do was take notes and hang on.

"The FBI will find a group of Muslims were manning the X-ray machines at each of the airport concourses where those hijacked planes took off. If the FBI doesn't tell those airports to lock down all passengers and get airport security to secure every surveillance tape, especially the four-channel video recorders that show what's inside the X- ray machines and who's coming through the magnetometer, they'll lose the data on those tapes.

"You'll see once this has settled down that a fairly large cadre of Muslims, Islamists, got those little minimum-wage jobs and quietly worked their way into being X-ray machine operators and supervisors—someone who could arrange people's schedules."

"…and was told to ignore anything that went through the X- ray machine during a certain window of opportunity."

"Yes, Sir. If we ever find out, I'm afraid those tapes will show maybe one person got a gun through, while the others —this has to be a multi-person mission—have knives or…. What do they call those things with razor blades with a handle?"

"X-acto knives? Linoleum knives? Utility knives? Box cutters?"

"Oh, God. That's it. Box cutters, the perfect terrorist tool you can hide. If one were stopped by accident…anyway, they can be smuggled into a carry-on so easily."

"OK, OK, OK! Let me make some calls. I want to talk to you later on how you know all this."

"Thanks, Greg."

* * *

Later that evening, after four aircraft crashed, Lynche called Hunter and told him he relayed his message to a senior FBI agent and his old boss at the CIA. They thought he was nuts, but, when a retired member of the Senior Intelligence Service begins to relay intelligence, woe be anyone who doesn't act on it.

Immediately after Hunter was off the call, Lynche called someone he was close to who was still on active duty at CIA.

Six hours later, the Deputy Operations Officer quietly told him that over fifty people were being sought in conjunction with activities at the airports in Dallas, Denver, Chicago, Miami, Memphis, and LA. It took FBI field agents several hours to get into the major airports and confiscate the concourse security tapes. Reports soon came into FBI Headquarters that from across the country the concourse security tapes clearly showed several flat box cutters in the luggage of Eastern-looking men going through the magnetometers.

FBI agents at a few airports sat in stony silence, as they picked out the teams of five men with the signature flat metal box cutters going through the X-ray machines. Not once had the operator stopped to check the bag or alert his supervisor of a possible weapon. All four channel surveillance tapes at the other airports showed the same thing.

Camera one showed what was being X-rayed. Camera two showed the passenger setting his baggage on the X-ray machine. Camera Three gave a frontal view of the passenger passing through the magnetometer to see if he carried metal on his body. Camera four showed the X-ray operator at work with the machine.

At eight airports, the four-channel surveillance tapes clearly showed a Muslim man or woman, some women wearing hijabs, operating the X-ray machines. Eight tapes showed the X-ray machine operators all checking their watches repeatedly starting at 0800 local time. They were obviously looking for a face in the magnetometer line. Once the operator identified his marks in the line, he or she focused intently on the X-ray machines. None of them looked up until long after the Eastern-looking men passed through and retrieved their bags from the X-ray machine.

The FBI agents were aghast to learn that within fifteen minutes after the men passed through the magnetometer, every X- ray machine operator asked to be relieved from his or her post and never returned.

Once the FAA ordered all aircraft grounded, another theme was replicated across the eight US airports. Some managers of the contracted airport security firms complained several employees quit, or the employees walked off the job. Some airport security uniforms were found in trashcans in airport restrooms.

When the FBI descended on the airports and demanded employee records, over fifty employees across the country were reported missing. The airport security managers confirmed the missing employees were Muslims, good workers who never gave any trouble. The managers had to make accommodations for them, even helping find a room at the airport, so they could go to prayer.

One manager commented, "They never complained about making a minimum wage plus a nickel. By the way, do you think it's coincidental that over a year ago, I didn't have a single Muslim employee, then, within a month, I had a couple dozen?"

Employee records were taken to FBI offices, and fingerprint cards were processed. Each of the former airport security employees became a person of interest. Police and FBI descended on the employees' home addresses, but the apartments were all vacant. None of the neighbors reported seeing anything unusual. All-points bulletins were issued, but not one of the former X-ray machine operators was found or detained.

When the FAA grounded all aircraft, many passengers on the airplanes left the airport to find ground transportation. At least twenty-four men of Eastern descent were revealed in the surveillance tapes quickly exiting the airport in advance of the X- ray machine operators leaving. FBI agents were able to piece together several plausible situations where five-man teams were to be passengers on six other aircraft flights of Boeing 757s or 737s. Had not the FAA grounded all planes, those aircraft would probably have been hijacked to attack nuclear power-generating stations near major metropolitan areas.

* * *

During the 9/11 Commission hearings, there was no mention of the fifty missing Muslin X-ray machine operators, the six airport concourse surveillance tapes, or the thirty men of apparent Eastern descent who quickly left the six Midwest and Western airports after their flights were grounded.

* * *

FBI agents interviewed Hunter several times concerning his insights into airport operations and how to breech airport security for those of Muslim faith. The FBI report resembled that of the Oklahoma City bombing. Muslins were involved to a greater extent than anyone believed. The US government, specifically the FBI, refused to pursue the case.

Only two FBI agents in Boston were assigned to investigate the hijackers' comings and goings while in Boston. It wasn't until years later, when an al-Qaeda lieutenant being interrogated in Jordan named the imam and mosque from which eight of the ten men who flew the two aircraft into the Twin Towers passed through at one time or another.

Imam Abrahim was instrumental in helping members of his flock secure employment at Boston's Logan International Airport. Two dozen Muslims, who worshipped at the Al-Azzam Islamic Center, worked at the fast-food restaurants or gift shops at the airport for almost two years before moving and attaining pre-board screening positions with the local security contractor, International Screening Services, several months before Osama bin Laden released the cowards from hell and started a war between al-Qaeda and the United States.

CHAPTER TEN

0600 September 12, 2001

Basic Underwater Demolition/SEAL Training Area
Naval Special Warfare Command, Coronado, CA

On the brink of passing out, he emerged from the surf shivering uncontrollably, trying hard to control his breathing and not hyperventilate. After almost five days of exercise, continuous drenching in the super-chilled California surf, with little sleep or food, all twenty candidates struggled in the mild riptide to return to the beach after their rafts capsized and blew away in the wind.

So that's what it's like to see stars, he thought in a flash of coherence before falling face-first into the water.

Eight inches of seawater provided enough cushion to prevent him from breaking his nose, jaw, and neck. He was completely exhausted, with his nose embedded in the sand. Fear of drowning gave him a jolt of adrenalin to his trembling arms as he struggled to push himself up and get his face out of the water. Sandy seawater drained from his mouth and sinuses, choking him.

It wasn't worth it. They would let him die. As the surf withdrew, gently tugging him back into the bay, he momentarily lost consciousness. His quaking arms buckled, and his chest and head fell back to the beach. With the next wave, the cold Pacific shocked him awake again.

Eyes blinking wildly to clear themselves of salt and sand, he exhaled rushes of spit and salty water. He was going to die on that stinking beach. With a loud exhalation, he fell over and stopped moving

Two instructors leaped into the water and screamed at him to get up. Another yelled, "You can make it all go away!"

"You don't want to do this anymore, do you?"

His shivering returned so hard he could barely speak. Finally, his head bobbed up and down.

"He's done. Corpsman, here's another one."

That was the last thing he heard before Petty Officer Sam Miller's eyes rolled up, and his heart stopped.

CHAPTER ELEVEN

0145 June 30, 2002
Hunter Ranch, Del Rio, Texas

After three hours on the road, Duncan Hunter tried to exhale deeply but was overcome by a lengthy yawn that squeezed tears into the corners of his eyes. Physically spent, he couldn't squelch another yawn even if he tried. With the ranch house ahead, he deftly coordinated another yawn with a left-handed press of the garage remote clipped to his sun visor and a right-handed turn of the steering wheel into the driveway.

As the garage door slowly crept up, the truck's headlights progressively illuminated the black-and-white checkerboard floor, blood-red toolboxes, and gray car cover hiding an old, yellow Corvette racecar.

He sighed audibly, waiting for the garage door motor, spawning another yawn and forcing him to stop the truck. He leaked more tears as he stretched his jaw and facial muscles. He guided the Silverado inside, turned off the engine, and closed the garage door.

Hunter, glad to be home, sat in the seat, hands gripping the wheel. He was exhausted from ten days in the oxygen-deprived high altitude of Bogota and by night flying at low altitudes under night-vision goggles. The work, extremely stressful, demanded his utmost attention, many times more than during big deck carrier operations from his fighter-pilot days. Nighttime missions were downright scary and very dangerous. The intense, continuous stress of low-level night flying on the ragged edge of life and death over treetops to spot drug labs or through canyons to find terrorist encampments took its toll in fatigue—not during the flight but afterwards.

A mission was followed by fitful sleep during daylight hours, which always messed up his hypothalamus and biorhythms. He didn't know how Lynche did it at his age.

When he asked, Greg replied, "I never even think about it. You're the pilot. I'm in back playing with the sensors."

Decompression and rest wouldn't occur until Hunter returned home to his bed in Texas. Getting there required a two- stop commercial flight from Miami. He raced the 150-mile gauntlet of Highway 90, where kamikaze whitetail deer stepped into his headlights at inopportune moments, sporadically flooding adrenalin into his system as he swerved to avoid collisions.

Some evenings, the deer stayed on the side of the road, but not that night. After every close encounter, Hunter's skin tingled from the hormonal spike. His body's natural tendency was to compensate with rest.

After completing the exciting midnight run from San Antonio to Del Rio, Hunter's natural inclination was to let his guard down when entering the city limits, because he was tired and knew sleep would come quickly. After five years of flying with Lynche for Art Yoder and "Lynche's old place," Hunter couldn't afford to let his guard down at any point in the kill chain.

Hunter, Lynche, Yoder, and the Director of Central Intelligence were continuously reminded that Hunter was targeted for assassination. Only his wits and situational awareness kept him alive. If it wasn't highway deer trying to take him out, it was other road hazards.

The first unbelievable and bizarre attempt on his life occurred shortly after Lynche and Yoder brought the Schweizer to the Border Patrol in 1996. Two punks in an old truck in broad daylight tried to crowd Hunter off the road toward a deep ditch along a long, clear stretch of Highway 90 between Del Rio and Brackettville.

They'd obviously been waiting for him, as his black Silverado passed through the former home of Buffalo soldiers, John Wayne's Alamo, a German prisoner-of-war camp, and a small Border Patrol Station. Hunter immediately felt the act was intended to be more lethal than lazy or poor driving technique, and he countered the aggressive move with skills learning from a survival-and-defensive driving course.

Braking hard, he modulated the pressure on the pedal while steering into the truck's rear bumper at the right moment and angle. His heavy brush guard's firm bump against the other truck's rear quarter panel unweighted the Ford's truck bed enough to give it a sideways skid. At seventy mph and suddenly going sideways, the driver tried to compensate with a hapless maneuver just when his tires struck an expansion joint in the road bed and stopped.

The truck flipped over and rolled down the center of the highway. Hunter slammed on the brakes and watched the vehicle shed parts and people with each revolution. He sat in his lane, engine idling, tapping his fingers on the steering wheel and wondering, What was that all about?

Reversing direction, he returned to the Border Patrol Station in Brackettville to report the incident to the Chief Patrol Agent and Greg Lynche.

"If I didn't know better," Hunter said, "I'd swear they were trying to kill me."

With the sudden retirement of the unit's chief pilot, three increasingly aggressive attempts on Hunter's life were enough for Yoder and Lynche to encourage the Director of Central Intelligence to intervene. An FBI counterintelligence team was dispatched to the border town and quickly determined that the former chief pilot had ties to a Colombian drug cartel and possibly a militant Islamic group. They even uncovered a potential link to an unsolved homicide.

The FBI and the Border Patrol Chief Agent recommended Hunter be administratively transferred to another duty station or federal agency for better protection.

While some at Border Patrol Air Operations cheered the announcement, the Chief Patrol Agent lamented he didn't want to lose Hunter, because he was the most-dynamic employee he ever had. By the end of the week, the former Marine Corps pilot, who was already teaching graduate school classes for the instructor pilot cadre at the nearby US Air Force base, was transferred to the Air Force under a by-name assignment and became their deputy director of aircraft maintenance.

As Wraith missions continued every other month, Hunter managed the stressors of flying the low-level nighttime ghost over hostile territory. He achieved decompression by returning home to work at his real job, teach courses at night, and play racquetball and relax in his hot tub. With the move from the airport to the air base, Hunter bought a new house closer to the Laughlin Air Force Base complex, although its location was somewhat remote.

The ranch-style home, built by a local orthopedic surgeon, featured a diving pool and in-ground hot tub with a seven-foot satellite dish wedged into a corner. As illegal aliens became more of a problem, trespassing the ranch and even breaking into the house, the surgeon erected a twelve-foot brick wall around the basic living area to encompass the patios, pools, and plants to make it difficult for the average illegal alien to get into the house.

After Hunter moved in, the Border Patrol installed seismic sensors around the property and placed the ranch on their patrol schedule. Intrusion detectors and motion-activated floodlights reminiscent of a warlord's compound found in any third-world country provided a level of security and safety that was acceptable to Yoder, Lynche, and the DCI.

Hunter loved the security, privacy, and lush tropical garden in the backyard. Bougainvillea, Mexican fire bushes, and many different species of palms required a gardener's services to maintain. During summer months, when the sun heated the pool to the high nineties, Duncan stumbled out of his bedroom and wobbled outside to fall into the pool to wake up. At night, after a late evening of work, school, or racquetball, he fired up the Jacuzzi's jets and relaxed in the pulsing, hot, eucalyptus-scented water.

That night, all he wanted was to drag himself into bed with the ceiling fan on high and sleep. He'd brush his teeth in the morning.

He unfolded himself from the truck, extracted his roller board from the truck bed, punched numbers on the keypad near the door to disable the alarm, and entered the kitchen. He glanced at the pile of mail and number of missed calls on his answering machine. They could wait. It was late.

He yawned and started dragging his flight bag to the bedroom when red lights erupted on the security panel. After a double-take, he realized the seismic sensors were showing movement outside the compound walls. Hunter tried to make sense of the flashing lights. He blinked several times, then rubbed his eyes.

Did I miss that? he wondered.

An alarm bell rang in his mind, as he quickly looked through the kitchen and sunroom to see if the motion-activated floodlights were on. After two seconds of scanning the outer wall for signs that the floodlights would illuminate, he jumped when the security system beeped, signaling an intrusion into the compound.

Hunter kicked his bag aside, mashed the Help button on the security panel, and bolted for his bedroom, racing from the kitchen, across the dining room, and down the hall.

As he turned left into the bedroom and directly into his walk- in closet, the first rounds of an AK-47 assault rifle shattered the glass panels in the sunroom. Hunched over in the closet, he pulled up on a folded T handle and lifted a door leading to the storm safe room, taking the stairs two at a time before stopping.

A second burst from an AK-47 sent 7.62 mm bullets raking the house, as he closed the overhead door of the safe room. In the dark, he felt for and located the dead bolts and rammed them home, left and right.

The safe-room door, reinforced with sheets of steel, Kevlar, and bullet-resistant Fiberglas, shut off all light from the bedroom. His skin tingled from adrenalin. In total darkness, his senses became hyperactive. He was breathing so hard, he almost hyperventilated.

Hunter thought a third Kalashnikov joined in ripping apart the house. He reached for the flashlight he always left on the third step and touched the cold metal silently. His heart pounded. In the total darkness, he saw phosphenes with each heartbeat. He almost celebrated his escape, then he realized the basement wasn't designed to repel Kalashnikovs. He might be trapped, but he had to decide whether to stay and fight or go.

When the previous owner decided to install an in-ground pool he was surprised to find the ground was solid rock under six inches of caliche, requiring drills, dynamite, and jackhammers to blast out material for the pool and hot tub. While all the heavy equipment was on site, the surgeon had his architect design a safe room for the occasional tornado that swept across southwest Texas when least expected.

An escape tunnel was cut in the hardened sedimentary rock that opened out into the far corner of the yard in case the safe- room overhead door wouldn't open or the house was on fire. When the house foundation was poured, four inches of concrete covered the tunnel out to where the satellite dish was mounted and the cables returned to the house.

The safe room was the selling point for Hunter and Lynche after the attempts on Duncan's life. Hunter called it the basement in a town that had none. It was the perfect place for his arsenal, telephone, emergency, and survival items, including a gas mask. All those items were across the room in the dark.

The shooting stopped. Hunter's heart pounded in his chest and ears, and he remained frozen in place as if any noise he made might reveal his location. He stayed hunched over the stairs in the darkness when a man's voice reverberated through the reinforced door.

"Not here," he said in Arabic.

Hunter was shocked. *Spanish would make sense, but Arabic?*

He reached to the other wall of the staircase and backed silently down to the bottom step.

"What's that?" someone asked in Arabic.

A second later, Hunter heard the door's T-handle being pulled. The inch-thick deadbolts held. Keeping one hand on the wall, he crept away from the stairway, though he was several feet from his weapons safe.

An AK-47 erupted. The noise was deafening in the rocky chamber, as the man above unloaded his magazine into the door. Hunter closed his eyes and jammed fingers into his ears, as copper and lead slammed into the steel and Kevlar door.

All was quiet again. Hunter opened his eyes, expecting to see beams of light spilling down from perforations in the door, but it held. The men above, conferring in Arabic, were agitated, and Hunter wasn't able to understand their rapid garbled speech.

He leaned against the wall, his eyes closed, while phosphenes danced to the rhythm of his pounding head. *Arabic?* he wondered. He listened for any sound and sniffed for signs of smoke.

He decided to leave. If those men had Kalashnikovs, they might also have fragmentation grenades or dynamite. He pressed the button on his Maglite, and light flooded the room.

He reached for the phone on the computer desk, but the line was dead. He set the light on the weapons safe and punched a combination into the keypad. The LCD read Open.

He slowly depressed the lever, trying to open the safe quietly, but it clicked loudly as the locking mechanism retracted. As he opened the door and reached for his AR-15, someone above shouted in Arabic, "Down there!"

More gunfire came. The sound was deafening in the chamber. Hunter's hands moved from his weapon to a pair of sound suppressors. The relief to his ears was instantaneous. His sense of urgency to leave the safe room and run elsewhere was tempered by other decisions.

He reached for his favorite weapon, the Kimber1911 Custom on the top shelf, stuffing it against the small of his back. Two full clips of .45 ammunition went into his rear pocket, as he grabbed another full clip for the AR-15 and shoved that down the front of his pants. He picked up the AR-15, slid the charging handle aft to chamber a round, and allowed the bolt to slide home.

After a pause, he decided to take the night-vision goggles, slipping the strap over his head.

"Gas mask?" he mumbled. "Gas mask!" He removed it from the pouch at the bottom of the safe and placed the strap over his head.

Bullets pounded the overhead door, as he closed the safe and reset the lock. Snatching his flashlight, he saw the first beams of light suddenly spill down through holes in the door. Three AK-47s roared, sending bullets into the safe room, as he ducked and ran down the escape tunnel. A beam of light illuminated his way, as bullets ricocheted behind him.

The firing stopped. Hunter raced forward as fast as he could, but, with light entering the chamber behind him, he wouldn't reach the end of the tunnel in time. He was trapped. All they had to do was fire one of the AK-47s down the tunnel, and he was dead.

The opening at the end was in sight. Twenty feet to go, and all he heard was the sound of his feet and his labored breathing. Five seconds later, he reached the small vertical concrete pipe and turned around, turned off the flashlight, got on his belly, and aimed the AR-15 down the tunnel. The only sound was his ragged breathing.

He waited for the attack of a fusillade of Kalashnikovs. His eyes and ears strained for any hint of light or movement, as the smell of cordite wafted through his nostrils.

A glance at the luminous markers on his Rolex showed only five minutes had passed since he entered the house.

Three Middle Eastern men stared incredulously at their weapons. In their zeal to hunt down and kill their target, who apparently escaped into a room under the house, they completely depleted their supply of ammunition while trying to chip away at the concrete footer of the safe room entryway.

When they realized they held empty guns, one said in English, "We must go."

They slung their weapons over their shoulders and drew Russian 9mm Makarov Parabellums from their holsters. One man led the other two from the bedroom. They hurried single file from the house to the far side of the compound. In seconds, they were over the high wall, assisting each other to safety.

US Border Patrol agents didn't anticipate a firefight that night. When agents were sent to investigate the seismic sensors that went off near the Hunter property, two USBP Broncos and an airborne Air Operations helicopter were dispatched.

The helicopter was still two miles away, but the crew was able to identify the Border Patrol vehicles moving around the rear of the compound through their FLIR. The sensor operator in the left seat keyed his microphone.

"Three men left the back of the house," he told the men on the ground. "They're coming your way from the southwest corner of the fence. They're carrying pistols and have slung automatics."

The men in the Broncos hit the men with spotlights. An agent demanded over a bullhorn that they stop and put down their weapons.

"Alto! Abandonar sus armas!"

Momentarily blinded, the three men in black fired their Makarovs at the lights and the amplified voice.

The helicopter sensor operator saw hot bullet traces in the FLIR and immediately called over the radio net, "Agents under attack by at least three men. Backup needed at the Hunter ranch!"

Bullets crashed into the windshields, and two random shots took out one of the spotlights, as the drivers responded to their partner's high-pitched entreaties of, "Backup! Backup!"

Soon, twelve USBP four-wheel-drive vehicles, a pair of Texas Department of Public Safety Crown Victorias, and three of Del Rio Police Department's finest officers converged on the Hunter property. The helicopter provided eyes in the sky, radioing to the ever-increasing number of law enforcers the location and direction of the three men as they ran to a Bronco-like vehicle a few hundred yards away from the compound on a nearby access road.

The three entered the truck and tried to drive away. FLIR captured the heat of the men inside and the increasing intensity of the engine compartment. Other vehicles converged. The getaway vehicle wasn't moving very fast. All four sidewalls were punctured by bullets. Soon, the getaway truck was surrounded by headlights and spotlights.

A Texas State trooper used his megaphone and told the men to put down their weapons and get on the ground.

All three men bolted from the truck, rushing toward the loudspeaker as they fired pistols and shouted, "Allahu akbar!"

Hunter remained in the escape tunnel, certain the intruders had given up trying to get at him, but he didn't want to return down the tunnel for fear of booby traps.

He dropped the NVG case and gas mask bag, turned on the flashlight, and looked at the top of the barrel. Steps made of rebar went upward. He stood on the second rung and slid a single restraining bolt free from a manhole cover, which remained in place by a simple counterbalance mechanism. Taking another step up, he placed his shoulder against the cover and pushed. Whatever held the old cover stuck gave way on the third try, and it opened like a one-sided flower in bloom.

As he cautiously raised his head above the edge, he saw the satellite dish and stars overhead. The sound of automatic weapons fire came from the north. Then all was quiet but for the sound of a hovering helicopter.

BOOK TWO

CHAPTER ONE

1400 August 5, 2002
Naval War College, Newport, Rhode Island

Duncan Hunter showed his retired military ID card to the gate guard, who reviewed it suspiciously. After returning the dark- blue card, the guard provided verbal and hand directions to the appropriate parking area.

Hunter drove away from the guard shack, negotiating the black truck and trailer combination through the concrete Jersey barriers. An old, bright-yellow Corvette racecar rested atop the road-weary trailer. After successive right turns and up a short hill, he reached an elevated, nearly empty parking area for about 100 vehicles.

Since it was Sunday, parking was easy, and he took a slot that allowed him to pull straight ahead and depart easily. As he stepped from his truck, a short, round woman wearing heavy spectacles and a long, drab dress walked past the front of Hunter's truck.

"Excuse me, Ma'am. Could you direct me to where I need to check in?"

The woman paused and turned, her eyes going from the car to Hunter. She pointed at the large building near the bay. "Hunter, two oh four." She turned and walked away. She was in a hurry.

Taken aback, Hunter called, "Excuse me, Ma'am!"

The woman paused, slightly exasperated, and asked, "Yes?"

"I'm sorry, but how'd you know my name?"

Confusion showed on her face. "What's your name?"

"Duncan Hunter."

She chuckled. "Duncan, you need to go to Hunter Hall, room two zero four."

He flushed with embarrassment. "Thank you very much." Reaching into the truck, he extracted a black Zero Halliburton briefcase from behind the driver's seat. When he stood, she was gone. "That lady might be big, but she's fast."

At the entrance to Hunter Hall, the guard behind the bulletproof glass rejected Hunter's military ID and demanded he surrender his civil service ID card. He buzzed the double doors, and Duncan walked in.

Immediately inside, he saw a large brass plaque. Admiral Henry Kent Hunter apparently served on the USS Missouri in the Great White Fleet's circumnavigation of the globe from 1907-1909 and distinguished himself during World War Two. "Doubtful he's any relation," murmured Hunter.

After checking in and receiving a room assignment, Duncan walked to his living quarters for the next eleven months. Having stayed at several substandard BOQs during his active service days, he expected the worst. Adjacent to the Navy's Preparatory School, the nondescript, three-story building labeled Number 7 didn't inspire confidence.

He walked up three flights, found room 307 was the corner suite, unlocked the door, stepped in, and was shocked by the spacious, two-room suite's large picture window. After dropping his luggage onto the sofa, he walked to the window and looked at the NWC complex and Narragansett Bay with the Claiborne Pell Bridge in the distance.

He inhaled deeply. "Hunter, you are one lucky dog."

After several trips up and down the stairs to transfer his personal effects from the truck to his new room, he changed into PT clothes and headed out for a run around the base.

Two old aircraft carriers sat in the distance. Hunter ran toward them, noting the scenery along the way.

Twenty minutes later, he stood at the bow of the two unknown carriers. It was almost fifteen years since he flew his Phantom off a carrier. He smiled softly. "I wonder what other surprises this place has in store for an old grunt?"

He turned and jogged into the sunset.

CHAPTER TWO

0700 August 6, 2002
Connelly Hall, Naval War College

The President of the Naval War College, Rear Admiral DiFilippo, was introduced. The lithe man in white with the gold epaulettes walked across the dais to the lectern.

"Good morning and welcome to the Naval War College." "I'm very pleased to see the 527 men and women who represent the finest minds this nation has to offer, as well as those from the fifty-five maritime nations around the globe. You're at one of the US Navy's best locations. The Naval War College is the finest of war colleges. You'll soon see the faculty and staff are the best of the service war colleges.

"The Naval War College is where the United States military does some of its finest thinking. You're here, because you're a proven commodity. I can say without hesitation that your being here means your service thinks enough of you to give you the education you'll need for your next promotion and assignment. While here as a student, you'll help the Navy define its missions. With our international partners, you'll strengthen our maritime security cooperation with other countries. You'll learn to think strategically, and you'll be pushed to think critically.

"This is a very special place for our international students. For as long as the Naval War College has been teaching US officers, it also has a distinguished track record of producing world leaders. Six graduates of the Naval War College have gone on to become heads of state, and seventeen graduates have gone on to become their navy's chief or staff or our CNO equivalent. Over 150 international students have gone on to attain flag rank.

"No other war college in the world has this track record of

excellence. Our international students are some of the brightest, most-distinguished leaders their country has to offer. The friends you make here will last a lifetime. You'll be surprised where your travel takes you. We hear stories all the time that NWC graduates somehow gravitate toward each other in the most-unusual locations at the most-interesting times. Make the most of your time here and get to know your international students in your seminars.

"Your country has invested a great deal in you to get you to this point, and we'll need you more today than you realize. Today we're in a new, unprecedented war against terrorists and extremists. This is an ideological conflict we face against murderers and killers who want to impose their will on free peoples. These are the people who attacked us on September 11. "Some of you have recently returned from the battlefields of Afghanistan, and we'll learn from you. This is a new war. The stakes are high. Once again, we have to change our strategic thinking to fight and defeat these new enemies.

"I'd like to introduce you to your class President, Captain William McGee. We're honored to have Captain McGee, as he recently returned from Afghanistan. Get to know him and the others who recently returned from the fight. The United States Navy is the most-professional, advanced navy the world has ever seen, and the men and women of the Naval War College are determined to keep it that way. Enjoy your time here. Make the best of this opportunity."

"Attention on deck!" was shouted from the rear of the auditorium.

As the assembly of the men and women of the class of 2003 stood and rendered honors, the President of the War College and his entourage departed the dais.

Duncan Hunter glanced at the Navy captain sitting alone in the front row. The heavily muscled SEAL wasn't tall but imposing and distinguished. His white uniform didn't hide the massive black biceps and sculpted physique of a professional bodybuilder. The gray flattop and small, round glasses fit an unlined face that exuded confidence and intelligence. His movements were slow, methodical, and his alert eyes took in everything, missing nothing.

Near the rear of the auditorium, among the fifty-five foreign naval officers, Lieutenant Commander Zaid Jebriel, Royal Saudi Navy, and Commander Nassar Athamneh, Royal Jordanian Navy, paid particular notice to the US naval officer in the front row. Both men wrote down the name Captain William McGee in their notebooks.

CHAPTER THREE

0745 August 6, 2002
Naval War College Newport, Rhode Island

"As officers, we serve the pleasure of the President. What does that mean? Anyone want to define the difference between the Oath of Enlistment and the Oath of Office for Commissioned Officers?" asked the instructor, Dr. Randy Norton, as he abruptly started class.

Half a dozen students still stood, trying to scramble to their seats after the inevitable tentative introductions and first hints of cliques forming. Three international students from Kenya, Colombia, and Rumania were left to themselves. The three Army lieutenant colonels sat together. The three Marine lieutenant colonels sat together at one end of the U-shaped arrangement of tables. Three Air Force lieutenant colonels sat together, and two of the three US Navy commanders sat together. No one talked to the commander with the warfare specialty pin identifying him as a SEAL, and no one talked to the civilian. No one could understand why a civilian was at the Naval War College. Hunter, trying to speak to the SEAL, was leaning over when the instructor asked his question. Folded name cards gave away everyone's identity.

Duncan raised his hand.

"Mr. Hunter?"

"Officers swear they will support and defend the Constitution of the United States against all enemies, foreign and domestic. Enlisted men and women swear they will obey the orders of the President of the United States and the orders of the officers appointed over them."

"Excellent. That's absolutely correct. The President can't fire members of Congress, but can he fire air traffic controllers who go on strike?"

"Congress critters are elected and can't be fired by the President. Nearly everyone else in civil service serves at the pleasure of the President."

Except for the three international students, who had difficulty comprehending the topic and the dynamic, rapid-fire exchange between the instructor and Hunter, the class of fifteen chuckled at Duncan's disparaging comment on Congress.

"Members serve at the pleasure of the President," Dr. Norton said. "What does that mean?"

Hunter was reluctant to answer again. "Anyone?" asked Norton.

Finally, Duncan said, "Political appointees serve at the pleasure of the President. He nominated them, and they remain in those positions unless they resign or until the President asks them to. Not everyone at that level serves at the pleasure of the President. The chairman of the Federal Reserve Board doesn't, and the President can't dismiss him. Neither can he dismiss the director of the FBI, who has a ten-year appointment. There may be others in that category. Vice Presidents can't be fired. I think generally, if the President appointed someone, he can be asked to resign by the President if he isn't doing well or isn't carrying out the President's policies."

"So a President can terminate without cause?"

Hunter sensed a trap. He'd been baited into the exchange, and the instructor was about to pounce on him for showing off. It was graduate school all over again. *I did the same thing to my own students*, he thought.

"I would say," Hunter said, "that despite his unfettered power, there must be a reason for the decision. Of course, at the pleasure of the President implies there doesn't need to be a justifiable reason. The President is the ultimate decision-maker in those things under his purview."

"That's outstanding. That's also an outstanding segue into this course. For the next few weeks, we'll be analyzing and dissecting presidential decisions from George

Washington to the current Commander in Chief. We'll look at the political forces surrounding them at the time of their decision-making process, and we'll look at the men and women who tried to carry out the president's decisions and directives.

"I want you to be especially watchful that at the level of the President, when faced with a real crisis, there's no really right decision. There are military decisions and political decisions. We shall see in almost all cases that presidents are compelled to choose between one or the other. Kennedy either bombs Cuba and starts World War Three, or he does nothing and looks like a weakling.

"Oftentimes, it isn't that the decision is the lesser of two evils. When presidents are compelled to make decisions, as we shall see, many people die. Let's get started."

Three hours later, as Hunter walked from the classroom, someone said, "For a while there, I thought he was looking for a fight."

The SEAL following Hunter out offered his hand before swapping introductions. The SEAL carried himself with poise and confidence, giving his name as Don Jorgenson.

"He wasn't, really," Hunter replied. "He was annoyed I popped up and answered him. It's a classic instructor tactic to get the attention of the new students, because they're the smart ones, and we're the dumb ones. We better pay attention. Otherwise, they'll have no problem embarrassing us in class.

"I just let him know I wasn't easily intimidated. I teach a little grad school myself and thought we'd be a little more advanced than that here."

"That's interesting. Where and what did you teach?"

"Embry Riddle Aeronautical University. I taught just about everything from aircraft and spacecraft development to accident investigation to helicopter operations." He pointed at the badge on the man's chest. "I doubt Embry Riddle has a center on a SEAL base, but I don't know."

"They don't. At air stations, yes. Good to meet you. See

you tomorrow, Duncan."

Hunter glimpsed the Navy Cross at the top of the man's medals, followed by multiple awards for everything else. He was a true war hero. "You, too, Sir."

As Jorgenson walked off, Duncan thought, *Typical SEAL— a man of few words.*

After descending into the bowels of the War College to find the bookstore, Hunter queued with the other students to receive two large shopping bags full of books. The hemp rope handles cut into his hands. There were at least twenty pounds of books in each bag.

Straining under the load he uttered to no one in particular said, "My pleasure reading has just dropped to zero."

The sight of dozens of students laboring to carry the two shopping bags of books across the parking lot to their vehicles was mildly entertaining. The men tried to look masculine and strong, carrying the bags with erect backs, but Duncan passed more than one car with an exhausted male student trying to catch his breath. The female students carried one bag, typically with both hands. As the male students drove away, the female students returned to Hunter Hall for their second load of books. *Hard to be chivalrous when your hands are full of books.*

Hunter dumped the bag of books in his truck and quickly walked to the gym and racquetball courts, hoping to find someone to play against. A former near-world-class athlete, a racquetball champion in the Marine Corps and a National Singles Championship competitor, he didn't anticipate any high-caliber playing at the NWC.

As he approached the courts at the end of the large gymnasium, three men, obviously racquetball players, stopped talking and sized up the newcomer.

"New student?" one asked.

"That's me. Duncan Hunter." He held out his hand. The older man shook it. "Bill Poole."

"Glad to meet you, Bill."

"This is Sanjay. He's the champ around here and our local rocket scientist. This is Bill Hall."

"Sanjay. Bill."

"Duncan."

"Do you have room for a fourth?" Duncan asked.

"Those two are supposed to play," Bill Hall said. "You and me?"

"That'll work. Let me change my shoes and warm up a little, and I'll be ready."

The three men noticed the multiple tags on Hunter's bag, as Bill Poole kept up a running dialogue.

Duncan learned that Bill Poole was Captain Bill Poole, OIC of all international students. Bill Hall was a retired lieutenant commander, USN submariner, and worked at the National Wargaming Center. Dr. Sanjay Prakash was a sonar scientist at the Navy's sonar research lab.

After dispatching Bill Hall in fifteen minutes and Bill Poole in twenty, Duncan moved to the doctor. Twenty minutes later, after many good-natured exchanges of points, Duncan ended the match with a backhanded down-the-line kill shot.

Sanjay said he had to get back to work.

"Thanks for the games," Duncan said. "You have a great touch, Sanjay. Obviously, you play squash."

"Yes, thank you, but there's no one to play with."

"Tell you what. I don't get to play squash very often. I'll get a squash racket, and you can crush me like a bug. My goal before leaving is to beat you at your own game. How's that?"

Dr. Prakash smiled. "That would be great."

The men turned from the center of the court and noticed an observer through the viewing windows. Duncan immediately recognized the SEAL from the front row at class. The miniature, gray-haired Schwarzenegger smiled at him and walked back to the weight room before Duncan and the sonar scientist left the court.

CHAPTER FOUR

1100 August 7, 2002
Marine Corps Recruit Depot San Diego, California

Platoon Sergeant Staff Sergeant Joe Crofton said, "At ease. Recruit Miller, you've done very well. The platoon commander recommended you for meritorious promotion to lance corporal and your choice of military occupational skill. You indicated you want to be a Scout Sniper, 0317. After setting the all-time range record of 250, the battalion commander probably found it difficult not to grant your request.

"I have to tell you, Recruit Miller, that I never heard of anyone leaving the Navy, joining the Marine Corps, and then going straight to Scout Sniper Platoon from boot camp. I expect you to go back to San Onofre and get Recon Marine MOS 0321 before heading to Sniper School. You're one tall motherfucker, Miller, and I'm afraid you'll have your hands full with that course. There'll be tremendous pressure on you to succeed."

"Sir, the recruit will not fail, Sir!"

"Recruit Miller, what's the motto of a Marine Scout Sniper?"

"Sir, one shot, one kill, Sir! Oorah!"

"Recruit Miller, what's the mission of a Marine Scout Sniper?"

"Sir, a Scout Sniper is a Marine highly skilled in field craft and marksmanship who delivers long-range precision fire on selected targets from concealed positions in support of combat operations, Sir!"

"I think the shooting won't be your problem. It's the low crawling that usually gets the best shooters, especially the tall ones. You can hide a dingy, but it's hard to hide a fuckin' battleship. Do you understand me, Recruit?"

"Sir, yes, Sir!"

"Well, good luck, Miller. Work hard, and don't fuckin' embarrass me."

"Sir, the recruit will not embarrass the platoon sergeant, Sir!"

"Dismissed."

"Sir, Dismissed! Aye, aye, Sir!"

As Miller saluted, Staff Sergeant Joe Crofton noticed a tattoo on the back of Miller's hand. The black letters SS were very small. He'd been around several Marine snipers during his career, and they all had that mark in the same place. Scout Snipers adopted the SS banner more commonly known as the World War Two German Waffen-SS insignia.

That tattoo might be premature, he thought, but you have to give the kid credit. He sure shoots like a sniper.

CHAPTER FIVE

0900 August 10, 2002
Auditorium, Naval War College

Directed to proceed to Spruance Hall and the 1,100-seat auditorium for a presentation, Duncan Hunter walked down the port aisle and sat four rows from the front. He looked around to see if anyone from his seminar class would be brave enough to join him. As one of the very few civil servants attending the NWC, he was viewed as an odd bird. Most of the students sat in the rearmost rows, and none came to join him.

As a former college professor, he made it a point to set an example and not be swayed by childish views about sitting at the front of the class. He would not retreat to the rear of the auditorium. Glancing at his Rolex, he wondered when the presentation would begin.

As his eyes lifted from his watch, Class President Captain Bill McGee walked in through a hidden front side entrance. The big, gray-haired man with small, round glasses and a chest covered in ribbons and gold badges strode into view to his place at the front of the assembly. Scanning the class from the back of the hall to the front, he stopped when he saw Duncan.

"Would you join me up front?" he asked. Another glance at Hunter's Brooks Brother's suit, French cuffs, and enameled coin cufflinks told McGee the man wasn't a typical civil servant. He didn't like civil servants, especially those from three-letter agencies. He immediately scolded himself. It might have been a mistake to invite the sharply dressed man to sit with him. He usually disliked men who were younger, taller, and better-looking. He also generally disliked men who were white.

90

While at school, he convinced himself it would be better to sit with a white man than another black man. As the man in the suit moved around the seats to sit beside him, McGee was struck by his grace, fluidity, and composure. He moved like Sean Connery from the old James Bond movies.

Bill McGee momentarily pushed aside his thoughts of disliking the man for another time and place. As a youngster, he'd been infatuated with the James Bond books and persona and was intrigued by the man's amazing cars, gizmos, and unique weapons. However, there were no black James Bonds to emulate, just movie caricatures of cool, hip, soul brothers with afros and guns shooting each other when drug deals went bad.

As a SEAL, McGee was an improbable James Bond. He had his share of beautiful women and exciting adventures at home and abroad, and he got to play with the most-exciting weapons imaginable, classified and unclassified.

After two failed marriages and his last mission, which failed spectacularly, he resigned himself to the fact that his glory days were over, and a new chapter in his life had begun. He viewed the assignment at the War College as a gift, a time to reconnect with his new wife and young daughters, not run off to a far-flung part of the globe to create mayhem under the cover of darkness. Even James Bond had to settle down to become a respectable old fart, but McGee never read that book.

As the man in the suit walked around seats to join him, his movements stirred old memories of the desire to be the guy they called on to save the mission, save the war, and the world. At first glance, the GS guy was at least interesting. He might even be real.

"Yes, Sir," Hunter said, surprised at the request.

Several hundred sets of eyes watched the SEAL enter from the auditorium's lower level and stop in front of the civilian a few rows up. A moment later, the man in the suit stood, walked around a few seats, and joined the SEAL in the front row. They shook hands, and the two sat side-by-side.

The SEAL, resplendent in his white uniform with a foot of ribbons and the SEAL trident, offered his hand. "Bill McGee. I have to sit up front, and everyone's afraid to sit with me."

The former Marine Corps officer kicked in, showing respect for the man with three Navy Crosses, and shook the rock-hard hand. "Duncan Hunter. Glad to meet you, Sir. I'll keep you company."

They sat in the middle of the front row.

Trying to say something that didn't sound stupid, Hunter leaned over and said, "I don't know many SEALs, but I went to flight school with one named Scott Reamer back in '83. I think he was a SEAL during his enlisted days. Somehow, he got a commission, and I distinctly remember he wanted to fly A-6s to provide close air support to Marines and SEALs or something like that. He embarrassed the rest of us when he had to get into uniform with his boatload of ribbons and SEAL badge when all the rest of the student pilots had firewatch ribbons."

McGee broke into a wide smile, showing perfect teeth. Before he could respond, the assembly was called to attention, and the NWC faculty and staff entered the auditorium.

A Marine Corps lieutenant colonel approached the lectern and asked the assembly to take their seats. He made a few comments that ensured no foreign students were present, then said, "This lecture is classified SECRET—NOFORN. I'd like to introduce Dr. Elizabeth McIntosh. She's been with the Central Intelligence Agency since 1975, serving in positions from field agent to chief of station. She's held the George H. W. Brush Chair of International Intelligence at the Naval War College since August 2000. She received a master's in international affairs from Boston College and her PhD in Russian studies from Harvard in 1984. Ladies and Gentlemen, Dr. McIntosh."

The little old lady who gave Hunter directions to Hunter Hall took the stage.

Duncan smiled, shook his head unconsciously, and stifled

a chuckle.

With a nod to the class President, she said, "Captain McGee, Mr. Hunter, and the class of 2003, on behalf of the CIA and the Naval War College, I welcome you to Newport and hope you have a great year."

McGee, noticeably narrowing his eyebrows while continuing to look straight ahead, gave Duncan a nudge at the mention of his name. Like a junior in high school, Duncan nudged back.

"In the weeks after 9/11, the American public knew nothing of a top-secret interagency response. The first clues were news reports out of Afghanistan that a CIA paramilitary officer had been killed, and an American Taliban had been captured. Johnny Michael "Mike" Spann had been a Marine Corps officer before coming to the Central Intelligence Agency's Special Activities Division. Mike Spann was the first American killed in combat during the US invasion of Afghanistan in 2001.

"His partner, Dave, is here today to give you an eyewitness account of what happened at the Qala-i-Jangi compound near Mazari Sharif in northern Afghanistan. I think Dave has some pictures. Dave, it's all yours."

For the next hour, the intelligence officer named "Dave" mesmerized the assembly with how he and Mike Spann entered Afghanistan, met with the Afghan Northern Alliance and Delta Force, and worked their way to Mazari Sharif. They found and interrogated the man the press called the American Taliban. He gave a minute-by-minute account of the subsequent uprising that killed Mike Spann and how Northern Alliance troops, backed by US air strikes, US Army Special Forces, and British Special Forces, crushed the uprising that took Spann's life and almost took Dave's.

He concluded with, "Mike Spann was awarded the Intelligence Star posthumously and is buried in Section 34 at Arlington National Cemetery. Because the Intelligence Star is the equivalent of the Silver Star, Mike was approved for burial in Arlington. Dr. McIntosh, I thank you very much for inviting me. I can take a few questions if that would be OK."

After the assembly, McGee turned to Duncan. "So how does the head spook know you? You CIA?"

Hunter shook his head. "You wouldn't believe me. It's absolutely stupid."

"Try me."

Duncan told the story.

McGee smiled. "That's pretty good. What are you doing for lunch Duncan?"

"I was going to grab something here and then head to the gym."

"That's exactly what I was going to do."

CHAPTER SIX

1115 August 10,2002
Naval War College Café

McGee selected soup and orange juice. Hunter eyeballed the chili and put a diet Coke on the tray. He noticed slight head movement from his companion, as the SEAL's eyes rapidly scanned the café. He tried to veer them toward the open window seats overlooking the bay, but the SEAL suddenly moved toward a corner away from the windows.

That's a little odd, Hunter thought, then forgot about it. "So you went to flight school with Scott Reamer? He was one of my rock stars back in the late '70s. I know he was picked up on an officer commissioning program, then I lost track of him."

"I was a prior enlisted Marine," Hunter said. "I did avionics, comm-nav tech on helicopters. After nine years, I got picked up on the Enlisted Commissioning Program and found out I was selected while on the New Orleans when we were between Honolulu, and the PI. Over the One MC, the ship's captain said, 'Congratulations to Staff Sergeant Duncan Hunter for his selection to the 116th Officer Candidate Course.'

"After spending Christmas in Ologapo, we steamed west, and I was dropped off in Singapore and told to find my way to Washington, DC. I see you're a Mustang, too."

"That was a long time ago. I've been a SEAL thirty of my thirty-five years in the Navy."

"The admiral left me with the impression, if you're here, you'll be promoted. I would have thought you'd have gotten this War College ticket punched long ago. I have a close friend, a Navy captain, who indicated it takes the right sponsor and a well-defined career path. I take it you'll make admiral?"

The man knew how to draw blood early. "Very unlikely. I'm amazed I'm here at this point in my career. I'll probably stay on as staff or faculty after graduation. This will be the first time I actually have two or three years of shore duty and won't have to deploy. I have two little girls who don't really know me, and I'm looking forward to being a dad and watching them grow up. What's the rest of your story?"

"After I got my commission in '82, I went to flight school in Pensacola and went on to fly F-4s."

"That's my favorite jet. Isn't it a little unusual for a Mustang to fly fighters?"

"You have no idea. Scotty went to NECEP and got a degree. The Marines had MECEP but also had ECP. They took guys with some college but no degree and gave them a shot at a commission. My claim to fame was I was the only guy in DOD flying fighters without a degree. Some of my Navy instructors in Pensacola had issues with having a non-college grad in the flight program.

"My skipper in the F-4 RAG, the training squadron, told me I was unique. In the fighter community, that type of unique isn't a badge of honor. 'Get your degree fast and don't advertise you don't have one,' he told me.

"So I got a bachelor's and MBA from Embry-Riddle Aeronautical University. Flying F-4s was a kid's dream come true. Just as I say today, I thought then I was the luckiest guy I knew."

"So how'd you wind up here? You a GS?"

"I'm a 14. The short story is I'm an Air Force civil servant."

"The long story?"

"I jumped out of a jet and survived. I had to deal with an uncommanded roll in my F-4 while on a live bombing hop. It's a big deal to take live ordnance off a base. The jet has to go to the combat arms loading area in case there's an accident. Tell me if this bores you—I won't be offended."

"Not boring—I love the aviation stuff. My dad was a pilot."

"Ok. A few hours before you walk to your jet, the aviation

ordnance shop loads triple ejection racks on the wing stations and then loads the bombs one-by-one. I was going to be dropping six Mark 82s, 500-pounders to get my live bombing qual. I was flying with the skipper leading, and I had an idiot in my back seat. His call sign was Goof, a perfect fit."

"We rode out to the CALA, jumped in, fired her up, and taxied into position. I did my takeoff checks when I discovered a problem with the roll channel of the stability-augmentation system. When I moved the stick side-to-side, it shuddered. I shut off the roll channel, and it was nice and smooth. When it was On, it shuddered."

"Doesn't sound good."

Hunter shook his head. "I've lived by the code that if you aren't happy with a jet, don't take it. There are other training aids and other days to fly. There I was, in a hot jet with six Mk 82s, the skipper leading, sitting on the runway, and my jet isn't working the way I liked.

"I told my backseater, 'I have a problem.' Goof got on the radio and said, 'Cheese, button two.' I told the skipper, 'With Stab Aug on, and I check the flight controls, the stick shudders in roll. I shut off the roll channel, it's nice and smooth. It ain't right.'

"He said, 'It's probably the air system. Happens all the time. You can take off with Stab Aug on and shut it off when airborne.' "I thought long and hard for about one second, not wanting to come across as a weak tit. Finally, I said, 'OK.' We flip back to tower, and tower's screaming at us, because you can't change freqs while on the active runway.

"I thought, 'That was stupid.' It was quickly turning into a shit sandwich. The skipper was raring to go. We got cleared. Ten seconds later, I jam it into blower. I call out what I'm doing for the guy in the back like always.

"Off the peg. 50, 70, 100, 150. We're going flying. 180. Nose is coming up. Gear. Flaps. That was when I stopped talking. I was passing through 300 knots and started to bring the throttles out of afterburner before we hit 350. I thought I encountered some turbulence, as the jet started a slow roll to the right. I added more stick, and it kept rolling.

"In slow motion, I programmed the stick all the way to the stops. I was now deflected all the way to the left. The roll stopped when I was completely inverted. I've come about 180 degrees. I probably looked like a Blue Angel, on my back with six green live bombs pointed skyward. Goof started screaming.

"I took my left hand off the throttles and began to program the cyclic stick forward two-handed. As I was upside down, somehow I had the sense to try to get away from the ground. The jet has several clicks of nose-trim at takeoff, so when you're inverted, that trim wants to pull the nose up, which meant it wanted to move toward the ground.

"Still in AB, I'm fighting the trim, and the forward pressure on the stick puts a few negative Gs on the aircraft. I immediately floated off my seat about six inches, and my head hit the canopy. I remember glancing in the rearview mirror and seeing my RIO completely splattered in his canopy.

"Just as I thought I saved it by arcing away from the ground toward vertical, I realized I was still in burner. I thought it was more important to depress the AFCS disconnect at the base of the stick when the Goof pulled the upper ejection seat handle and shot both of us out of the jet. Because I was fighting to control the jet, I was in an unusual attitude when he panicked and pulled the handle. The dumbass ejected himself into the ground. The 170-degree angle meant he shot across the highway we just flew over, like a flat stone skipping water. He never had a chance.

"When I left the seat a little over a second later, the initiators jammed me into the seat. My torso, seat belt, and leg restraints pulled me in tight, but my head was a little out of position when I took the 20G rocket ride. I shot out parallel to the ground.

"My chute opened parallel to the dirt, and I got one swing when I slammed into some orange trees in an orange grove across the highway. I should have broken my neck and back—at least a leg— but those trees saved my life. It wasn't my day to die.

"I was medically grounded for a spinal compression injury and became an aircraft maintenance officer until I retired. The window between life and death was the 1.5-second delay between when the rear seat leaves and the front seat starts to go. I'm the luckiest guy I know."

"That's incredible."

"Lucky, really. It took a year before I could run a PFT and get back in the racquetball court. I retired in '93 as an aircraft maintenance officer. I looked for a year but couldn't find work until January, '94, and that was in Cleveland, Ohio. I have many interesting stories from my six months of working at Cleveland Hopkins International Airport, including how to scrape ice from inside my car.

"In '95, I went to work for the US Border Patrol, where I got the job as director of their aircraft maintenance program. I taught grad school at night at the local Air Force base for Embry Riddle. My students were shit-hot Air Force instructor pilots. Having a retired Marine fighter pilot for an instructor seemed to work for everyone.

"In 1999, the base commander asked me to consider working for the Air Force. I made the jump in 2000 as their deputy director of maintenance. Two years later, I'm at the Naval War College as an Air Force civil servant. I think it's wild."

"That's fantastic."

"What about you? I know you were a SEAL for thirty years. Anything more and you'd have to kill me."

He smiled and the big black man looked away. "Yeah. Something like that." Hunter smiled at the impressive man. He knew Agency guys were wary of strangers. It takes time to gain their trust and confidence. He could see from McGee's face that the same level of wariness applied to SEALs too.

"My bud was the CIA's Chief of Air Branch. I get the same thing from him," Hunter added. "I know he has some great stories, but he doesn't share much of anything. At least, not often."

Captain McGee blinked three times, then he cocked his head like a dog trying to resolve the sound coming from an ancient music box. "You'll have to tell me that story another time if I'm to get in my workout and get downtown to pick up my wife. Here's one for you, though. My bride used to work in the Air Branch office when I was detailed to Langley."

"When was that?"

"I met her in 1990 while working in the basement."

Pulling a 3x5 card and pen from his suit coat pocket, Duncan wrote quickly. "Here's Greg Lynche's home number. If your bride worked with him, I know Greg would get a kick out of hearing from her. He's a wonderful gentleman."

McGee looked down at the card, then up at Duncan. "You know, that's a little spooky."

"Happens to me all the time Bill." He gave the SEAL an informal salute. "See you later, Good Sir."

As Hunter walked toward the parking lot, McGee reversed direction and went straight to the Security Office.

The petty officer behind the desk asked, "How can I help you, Sir?"

The security officer stepped from his office. "May I speak with you?" McGee asked.

Once the door was closed and pleasantries were exchanged, McGee asked for a full security brief on Duncan Hunter as soon as possible.

CHAPTER SEVEN

1830 August 10, 2002
Quarters #3, Coddington Cove, Middletown, Rhode Island

"Hey, Baby," McGee said. "Does Greg Lynche ring a bell?"

"You mean my old boss at CIA? What about him?"

"I met a fellow stud who says he's Greg's buddy but doesn't have CIA creds. It was a little strange. He gave me Lynche's home number if you were interested in talking to him. I'd like to ask him about this guy."

"That's incredible. I'd love to call Greg." She picked up her flip phone from the table. "He'll be shocked."

She dialed, and someone answered on the second ring. "Greg Lynche."

She recognized the voice instantly. "Greg, it's Angela... Angela Hagerty."

"Angela? What a treat! My God, what's it been? Fifteen years?" He turned away, and his muffled voice said, "Connie, it's Angela!"

For the next seven minutes, the two former intelligence officers caught up on their lives. Angela married "that sailor," as Greg called him. She said Bill was back from the war, and they had two little girls. Greg told her about starting his own business after retiring and added he still had all his man toys —the Porsche, the sailboat, and the airplane.

"Angela, that's fantastic," Greg said. "I can hear you're happy. I'm glad things are going well for you. I'm a little curious how you got my number."

"Bill came home and said he met this guy at the Naval War College who said he knew you well. He gave Bill your number."

"That must be Duncan Hunter. I know he's in Newport."

"Well, there you go. It's a small world, isn't it? Greg, Bill would like to talk to you about…Duncan. Do you have a few minutes?"

"Anything for you, Angela. My pleasure. You have my number. Let's not lose touch."

"Absolutely. Give Connie a hug for me." She handed Bill the phone."

"Mr. Lynche, I've heard a lot about you, but I never thought I'd get a chance to talk to you," Bill said.

"I heard so much about you from Angela and you guys usually kept to yourself," Greg said. "I'm glad you're doing well. She sounds very happy. I know she's glad to have you home."

"I'm glad to be home. Thank you. Greg, what can you tell me about Duncan? He seems really different, but somehow, he's wired into the IC."

"What I can tell you on this line is I met Duncan in late 1996. He could give you the exact date. He was working for the Border Patrol in Del Rio, Texas. After I retired in '95, I started my own company and as the sales rep for an aircraft manufacturer. Duncan called the CEO, who directed him to me.

"He was trying to get Border Patrol aviation out of the Stone Age, and I flew a demo into Del Rio for a bunch of Border Patrol agents and the local congressman. He and I hit it off immediately and have been very close friends ever since. We've worked together on some projects for my old place. He has all the tickets.

"The longer story is much more interesting and would probably take a couple hours to discuss in a SCIF. I think Duncan's a remarkable guy even if he doesn't drink and is the pickiest eater you'll ever meet. He's probably a borderline genius, but he's very down-to-earth. He plays a lot of racquetball and loves teaching for Embry Riddle. Also, he has the fastest reflexes of anyone I ever saw."

"I can tell he's a little different. He carries himself like a SEAL or Delta but in more-subtle ways. You can spot those guys a mile off. When I asked who he was, I was surprised he had no SOF or IC background."

"Let me tell you two quick stories. I have to make this short. Connie and I have a dinner engagement. The first is that he's like Sherlock Holmes and Isaac Newton rolled into one. He sees things other people simply can't see. He uncovered some Border Patrol agents on the take. They were pilots, and what they did along the border didn't make sense to Duncan.

"He started collecting data. It showed something was really askew. It only made sense to him if the chief pilot was somehow on the take. He showed his material to the chief patrol agent, and that pilot and his deputy suddenly retired and moved to Canada.

"The Sector Chief Patrol Agent was amazed that the chief pilot managed to hide his activities for so long. The new guy broke the code on him in short order.

"The other time, Duncan and I were in Miami about two years ago. He came to help me run a display at a trade show. We got in late, and it was dark, and we headed for a restaurant near the hotel. Duncan's always exercising and eating something.

"We didn't get far when a mugger jumped out from between two cars in the parking lot and tried to rob us. Duncan had a bottle of soda he just took a drink from when the guy jumped out and started to say, 'Give me your money.' Duncan threw the soda into his face, and I swear he went on the attack.

"The mugger tried to shield his face from the soda. Duncan grabbed the guy's revolver like Bruce Lee and slammed it into the guy's face. The guy's face was completely crushed. Blood was everywhere.

"In one motion, Duncan kicked one of the guy's knees and bent it completely backward. I heard it snap. That's when the crook started shrieking. Duncan flipped him over and wrenched his arm up, dislocating it. The mugger passed out.

"It took less than ten seconds. Duncan stepped over the body, tucked his shirt in his pants, and was ready to continue walking to the restaurant like nothing happened.

"'Hunter,' I said, 'we have to call the cops.'

"'What for?' he asked. 'I have his gun. OK. We'll stop at the hotel desk.'

"I'll always remember what I said next and Duncan's response. 'I thought you were going to kill him.'

"He said, 'I tried. He had a hard head.'" Bill and Greg laughed.

"Sounds like what one of my guys did down in Panama," Bill said. "Anything else of note?"

"There's actually a lot. I can tell you he's absolutely trustworthy and was instrumental in helping my old place track down Pablo Escobar. Soon after I met Duncan, I ran a check on him, probably like you did. Someone from Langley ID'd him early in his career in the Marines.

"If you see him play racquetball, you'll see he has the right mix of size, athleticism, and instinct that's rare in any sport. My old place wanted to use him to try to put a tracking device on Escobar. Intel indicated Escobar liked to play racquetball in Cartengia. My old place got Hunter to Cartengia and somehow, Pablo met him, and they played. I understand Hunter kicked his ass, but he gave Pablo some lessons and showed him some tricks, too. Pablo was so impressed, he bought all of Hunter's racquetball equipment —racquets, balls, gloves, and bag—for something like $5,000. Hunter didn't have to try to plant anything on Pablo. Escobar got all the tracking devices when he bought the stuff.

"That's another thing. Duncan can make things happen when others can't see how. If you get a chance to watch him play racquetball, tennis, or golf, you'll see right away he's a gifted athlete who doesn't know the meaning of 'quit' or 'give up.'

"Anyway, three days later, my old place gave DEA a tip that led the Colombians to Escobar. I'm sure Hunter got a medal for it."

Bill exhaled deeply. "That's really interesting, Greg. I certainly appreciate your time and consideration. Thank you, Sir."

"My pleasure, Bill. Please tell Angela she made my day. I had a great time talking with you and her. If you want to know more about Duncan, call anytime or just talk to him. Anyway, good night, Bill."

"Good night, Greg."

CHAPTER EIGHT

1400 September 11, 2002
Security Office, Naval War College

Captain McGee received an e-mail announcing the data he requested on Duncan Hunter was at the Security Office. Commander Neal Mihelich, the Security Officer, waited for the SEAL captain. When he saw McGee, he swung open the half-counter door and followed McGee into his office. "Afternoon, Sir."

"What do you have, Commander?"

"Do you want to read it, or can I brief it?"

"Brief."

"Mr. Duncan Hunter, GS-14, Air Force civil service. Born Fort Leavenworth, Kansas. TS/SCI with a polygraph."

"Don't tell me—his mom was a convict."

"She wasn't. His father, Technical Sergeant Lincoln Hunter, US Air Force, held a TS clearance and appears to have been en route to Turkey when the lad was born. Those records confirm the father was assigned to a special access program and a strategic balloon squadron that conducted secret aerial reconnaissance flights into the Soviet Union and satellite states.

"Two brothers. Did well in high school but quit, awarded a GED in 1972 at age seventeen. Enlisted in the Marine Corps. First major note. He has one of the highest recorded GT scores—154. Reportedly refused Naval Academy seat and Intelligence assignment at boot camp. Assigned an avionics technician on an air contract. Awarded Naval Aircrew wings and spent three years with a search-and-rescue unit in Arizona. May be able to pilot small helicopters, like Hueys and Cobras.

"He was always rated the squadron's top sergeant or staff

sergeant, one of many. His enlisted records are filled with interesting notes, such as he found an old F-4 Corsair in the desert north of Yuma, Arizona, and that airplane now hangs in the Marine Corps Museum."

McGee grunted.

"Took college courses at night, eventually receiving a pair of bachelor's degrees, electrical engineering in 1985 and professional aeronautics in 1991, and an MBA in aviation from Embry-Riddle in 1993. In Hawaii, he was squadron duty officer, as a SNCO, of a helicopter squadron when a helicopter had an accident. Appears he took all the necessary steps to secure the accident site and had everyone involved in the accident take a piss test. His actions determined several Marines had THC in their urine, which most likely contributed to the accident.

"A note, 'This event was the galvanizing factor for the Marine Corps' stringent substance-abuse policy,' and SSGT Hunter's actions established the standard response for such an incident. Immediately afterward, he was nominated by the CG and selected for Officer Candidate School.

"Went to OCS in early 1982, commissioned in April, '82, flight school in Pensacola and went on to fly jets in Kingsville, Texas, where he was a distinguished graduate and set several records for airmanship and leadership. Transferred to Yuma, Arizona, to fly F-4s. A note in his flying training record on his very first flight in the F-4 from his instructor, 'He flies the Phantom better than I do, and I have 1,000 hours. Could he be a former USAF pilot? If not, he needs to be dissected.'"

"Does he have a call sign?"

The commander smiled. "Seems like he was the original Maverick,' as he didn't have a degree when he went through flight school. It appears the call sign was awarded early. All his commanders held him in the highest regard. He completed Marine Corps Amphibious Warfare School, and the Command and Staff College while learning to fly the F-4 as a lieutenant. There was a note that, 'no one else in his squadron to include his CO completed those courses.'

"His training was interrupted when he was selected to be a general's aide for the Third Marine Aircraft Wing. Noteworthy, the CG was the former squadron commander of Sergeant Hunter. Noteworthy, he continued his flight training in El Toro flying RF- 4s. Seems like Lieutenant Hunter conducted several investigations while he was the general's aide and was awarded a couple medals for uncovering smuggling operations, but no citations are attached. They could be secret. It seems the general facilitated his TS/SCI clearance, and a polygraph was conducted by the CIA."

"That's highly unusual for an aviator."

"Very. He returned to Arizona to complete his training and served with distinction as a student, but, during a training flight, he ejected from an F-4. He survived, but his R-I-O, whatever that is, was killed."

"I think that's Radar Intercept Officer."

"Yes, Sir. He was severely injured in the ejection and took over a year to recover, was medically grounded and became an aircraft maintenance officer.

"Here's where it starts to get interesting. Seems like Mr. Hunter began receiving unclassified and classified fitness reports beginning as an L-T and ending as a captain. His classified FITREPs are still under seal, signed by the Commandant of the Marine Corps. The CMC also appended a letter to his Officer Qualification Report that tells commanders, quote, 'Captain Hunter can be counted on to perform any mission involving the highest level of special trust and confidence. This letter is to remain attached to this OQR. Any questions, contact CMC, Code 311A.'"

"That's unique, even in DEVGRU."

"Yes, Sir. His unclassified fitness reports highlight he won the Marine Corps Regional and All-Marine Championships for racquetball several years in a row, served on the Interservice team, and attended the National Singles Racquetball Championships ten years in a row. He continued to score the maximum on PFTs—300. Always shot high scores on the range, Expert Pistol and Rifle, and was the 1992 Military Male

Athlete of the Year."

"Say again?"

"He was the 1992 Military Male Athlete of the year. For what it's worth, he won gold medals or trophies in five different sports over a single weekend. Served on the 1993 BRAC commission, was selected for promotion to major, but retired in 1993. Seems he served in O-5 billets as a captain after his accident, as Group Aircraft Maintenance Officer, Squadron XO, Senior Marine Liaison Officer, and Director of Training for all Enlisted Aviation Training. Sir, I really have never seen anything like this before."

"Anything else?"

"Sir, as you requested, he spent five years with the US Border Patrol, and we have some of those records."

"Go." McGee leaned forward and tried to read the report upside-down.

"Seems he was the US Border Patrol's aircraft maintenance facility director. TS/SCI no poly for DOJ. He was the principal aviation advisor to the Chief Patrol Agent and managed aircraft maintenance and logistical support for the second-largest fleet of non-DOD aircraft and sixth-largest aircraft fleet in the US government. He developed and maintained a close working relationship with airborne law enforcement operations and provided technical and direct logistical assistance to the Texas Department of Public Safety, Drug Enforcement Agency, and US Customs Service. I'm not exactly sure what it means that he established and operated the DOJ's and US Border Patrol's only FAA-certificated repair station. He served as aviation subject matter expert for the DOG Office of Internal Audit and DOJ representative for the Interagency Committee for Aviation Policy."

"Grade?"

"GS-13. Transferred to the Air Force, where he's currently the deputy director of maintenance. TS/SCI no poly. I understand his base has over 250 training aircraft, supporting five flying training squadrons. Seems he won several Air Force Productivity Excellence Awards, was the Outstanding Senior Civilian Program Manager, and was selected for the Defense Leadership and Management Program. That's why he's here at the War College. It's their capstone course. He served on the Airport Board at the local international airport, teaches graduate students at Laughlin AFB and Randolph AFB for Embry-Riddle Aeronautical University, and is on the editorial staff of some aviation journal. Sounds like a slacker."

"No poly with the Air Force or Border patrol, but he has a TS/SCI with a poly? How about SAP?"

"Yes, Sir. He's cleared for Special Access Programs."

"TS/SCI with SAP. Anything else in JPAS? Is his poly active? Is that it?"

"That's it for his clearance."

"Anything else?"

"I'm almost there, Sir. There's very little from Embry-Riddle. He started teaching in 1995 in Del Rio. Taught seventy aviation-related graduated-level classes. Is an associate professor. Students primarily Air Force instructor pilots. Instructor of the Year last year."

"Anything from McLean?"

"They refused our request. Seems like there's a war going on, and they don't have time for us. I asked Dr. McIntosh to intervene, but she also got nowhere. I don't know what to make of it, as they always responded to our requests before."

"Anything else?"

"His financial report. It's unremarkable until 1996, and then…."

"Then what?"

"Well, in 1996, he made $80K with his Border Patrol pay and his military retirement and veteran's disability and from the university. In 1997, it jumped to almost $300,000. In 1998, almost a million. For the last four years, he made between $1.2 and $1.5 million dollars each year."

McGee was incredulous. "How has he made millions as a civil service employee and a college professor? Who else is he working for?"

"His W2s indicate a company named GMS, but it's not registered. We can't find anything on a GMS."

The SEAL, staring hard at his security officer, wished he could ask how Hunter was at the Naval War College as a civil servant making millions of dollars, but all he said was, "OK. That'll do. Please shred that. Thanks for your help, Neal."

McGee walked out of the security office and stopped in the middle of the passageway. *Who the hell are you, Duncan Hunter?* he wondered. *It's bullshit that the spook doesn't know you. A TS/SCI with a polygraph? You're CIA. Retired Marine? Air Force civilian? Making a million bucks a year? Who are you?*

CHAPTER NINE

1030 November 10, 2002
Seminar Classroom, Naval War College

"The United States finds itself in Afghanistan, and we're about to go into Iraq if we believe military intelligence." Dr. Randy Norton spoke with a wry grin.

The classes laughed at the implication of the hoary military joke that those two words were the ultimate contradiction in terms.

He continued his lecture on Strategic Thinking. "So is it fair to say we're in a war with Islam or a radical branch of Islam, or is it something else?"

No one seemed willing to answer. Dr. Norton took a breath and asked, "Or is it something else? Mr. Hunter, what do you think?"

"It could be viewed through a lens of good versus evil. It's pure evil for the likes of bin Laden to send almost two dozen men to kill aircrews and turn airliners full of people into weapons of mass destruction."

"So you think this is a case of good versus evil? We're at war with evil?"

"I'm beginning to think so. I find the religious undertones to be striking and polar opposites but not at all incongruent. It's hard to ignore the tangential relationship. Just a few decades ago, we found ourselves in a similar situation with two irreconcilable belief systems— Communism and freedom. We were essentially in a war of ideas and beliefs. Yesterday it was the Russians versus freedom. Today it seems the actors are Islamofascism and freedom. It seems we're fighting evil at a concentrated level."

"That's brilliant, Mr. Hunter. So you're saying Communism was the embodiment of evil? A form of concentrated evil from the Bolshevik Revolution, while Islamofascism is the focus of evil. Does anyone want to challenge Mr. Hunter's analysis that Islamofascism is the new, concentrated evil of our time?"

There were no takers.

"You might be on to something, Mr. Hunter. Can one argue that, as ideologies, both Communism and Islam are or were struggling for dominance? The Bolsheviks called it their struggle against the rich and privileged, and the Muslims have their jihad, their struggle against nonbelievers. Are we fighting these wars to determine if the whole world will become free? Is that your real purpose in uniform?"

"I don't know if we fight for the whole world to be free," Hunter said, "but, the more I look at it, it seems that in a very strategic context that's what our function appears to be. If you take that idea, at least for me, I have a better understanding of why the left is so agitated... aggravated with those who fight for freedom. It's a struggle for dominance. They want to subjugate and control, while the right just wants to protect their freedom and other free men, or to set people free.

"Is it the struggle for dominance? If free people don't fight evil, will civilization, as we know it, be completely destroyed? Khrushchev said, 'We will crush you,' in a not-so-subtle threat that Communism would dominate the world with the backdrop of gulags for those they didn't want to waste bullets on. Joseph McCarthy was painted as a Communist-hating senator who couldn't find them hiding under every bed. Have we learned from that episode, that Joe was right, but the left hid their true ideology very well? Politicians on both sides of the aisle have fought each other as hawks and doves. Are we seeing a kindler, gentler struggle between good and evil?" Many heads nodded.

"What does Islam have to show for itself, besides submit and become part of the caliphate?" Hunter asked. "Isn't Communism, which claims to be a solution for all the world's ills, really just a manufactured crisis? I read somewhere some loon from Hollywood said, regarding Communism, 'It looks so good on paper,' while someone else said something to the effect, 'Don't let a good crisis go to waste.'

"It seems to me that Communism, and now Islam, I should say radical Islam, isn't only a symptom of crisis but a stimulant of one. For the Communists, they manufactured a crisis, the crisis was sold as worker's rights. It galvanized the workers to overthrow their masters, only to become slaves to a different set of masters.

"For the National Socialists, the Nazis, the crisis of the day was presumably the Jews. Hitler galvanized a despondent Germany to eliminate them. I suppose for Islam and Islamofascism, it seems that some foment a crisis surrounding Jews and freedom—submit or die and all that."

Dr. Norton nodded. "Communism was the great alternate faith of man, and still is for many fellow travelers and liberals."

"Only they won't admit they're enamored of Marx," Hunter said.

The remainder of the class watched the two professors go back and forth like watching a ball at a slow-motion tennis match.

Dr. Norton folded his arms and leaned against the lectern. "Bin Laden and his followers see Islam as the only 'true' faith of mankind. Like all great faiths—we're talking a billion followers in China and Russia and a billion Muslims—their strength is derived from a simple vision. The Communist and socialist vision is derived from the concept of Man without God. You see that in the former Soviet Union and Nazi Germany, where churches were demolished, and it was a crime to practice an alternate non-state religion. Communism and Socialism became the state religion."

Hunter offered, "You can say the same thing in many parts of the Muslim world, where Christians are virtually extinct in some places. In others, radical Muslims are extirpating Christians, Jews, and other infidels. Islam is the state religion. Is that why some on the left accuse us of being on another

Crusade?"

"What do you think?"

"I think yes, right now. I better understand the major religions. All had great visions, and they always had different versions of the same vision, which was basically the vision of God and Man's relationship to God. I better understand the First Amendment better and what it means regarding an establishment of religion or prohibiting the free exercise thereof."

Heads snapped back and forth with interest, as the debate reached a heated pitch.

"That's very good," Dr. Norton said. "Conversely, aren't the Communist vision, the National Socialist vision, and the Islamic vision rooted with some organizer, an accomplished agitator and mighty propagandist? Aren't they the vision of Man without God, with the god in their case being the agitator—Lenin, Hitler, and Mohammad?"

"And now that community organizer bin Laden? The time was ripe for someone like him. He has the money to bankroll jihad. I never thought we'd discuss these topics at the War College, but you've opened my eyes."

Those who'd been following the exchange wondered if the ping-pong dialogue was over. Some were glad it was, while others wanted more.

Dr. Norton smiled. "That's a good place to stop. Tomorrow, we'll discuss how does Communism, Socialism, or Islamofascism, whose horrors are on a scale unparalleled in history, where that ideology has killed or subjugated hundreds of millions, recruit some of the best minds to do something like kill hundreds of millions of their fellow human beings. By the end of this class, you'll see why the left looks the other way, just as they're doing in Iraq.

"OK. Your homework for tomorrow. I'd like to see a five-page analysis on, 'If given the opportunity to get their hands on WMD, specifically a nuclear weapon, would Osama or Saddam or the next Ayatollah Khomeini use it? If no, why not? Got it?"

Heads nodded. Hunter gave a thumbs-up.

"Mr. Hunter, can I have a minute with you?" Dr. Norton asked.

"Uh-oh," one wag in an Air Force uniform said sheepishly. "You're in trouble."

After the students left, Dr. Norton said, "You should consider staying here as an instructor to teach. You're really good."

"Thanks, Randy but I'm pretty sure I have to return to my job. I really do have a day job. This is temporary duty for a civilian. If there was a way, I'd consider it in a heartbeat."

"Let me work on it. Bin Laden as a community organizer?" He laughed. "That's perfect. I'll have to add that to my lecture with all the other aforementioned community organizers."

CHAPTER TEN

1855 November 13, 2002
Al-Azzam Islamic Center Boston, Massachusetts

The man in the dark leather coat hurried across the snow-packed street from the train station and entered the mosque just in time for evening prayers. As one of the last to enter the prayer hall for maghrib, he quickly moved to an open prayer rug near the rearmost columns, and removed a small packet from his pocket. No one saw him slip the envelope under the front of the mahogany-colored rug as he knelt and waited for the ceremony to begin.

When the imam stood, the man stood. When the imam ascended the *minbar* raised his hands; he raised his hands. The congregation said, "Allahu Akbar."

Their eyes met, and the man nodded imperceptibly. Folding his hands over his chest and staring straight ahead, he recited the first chapter of the Quran aloud in Arabic. He uncrossed his hands. "Allahu Akbar."

The man went to his knees, bowed, and recited three times, "Subhana rabbiyal adheem," Glory be to my Lord Almighty.

Standing, he recited, "Sam'i Allahu liman hamidah, Rabbana wa lakal hamd." God hears those who call upon Him, Our Lord, praise be to You.

Again he raised his hands. "Allahu Akbar."

The words reverberated in the mosque. He prostrated on the carpet and recited three times, "Subhana Rabbiyal A'ala," Glory be to my Lord, the Most High. Breathing deeply, he rose to a sitting position and said, "Allahu Akbar."

On the first bow, the man slipped an envelope from under the prayer carpet and into his sleeve. After coming to a sitting position after all the rak'as were completed, he recited the second part of the Tashahhud. When he was done, he turned to the right and said, "Assalamu alaikum wa rahmatullah." Peace be upon you and God's blessings.

He inhaled deeply and whispered, "Allahu Akbar."

* * *

The packet contained a detailed dossier in coded Arabic on all twenty-seven Special Operations forces personnel attending or teaching at the NWC. The first name in the half-inch-thick notebook was Captain William McGee. The last was Duncan Hunter. Since the beginning of school, the little notebook reflected the make and model of private vehicles, license plate numbers, and anything of note one could determine by walking past or sitting in class, such as questions asked in class and a person's daily routine.

Zaid Jebriel, Lieutenant Commander in the Royal Saudi Navy, Saudi Intelligence Services and al-Qaeda intelligence lieutenant, retraced his steps from the mosque and headed for the train station for the return trip to Newport.

CHAPTER ELEVEN

1000 December 7, 2002
McCarty Little Hall Naval War College

The informal surveillance on Hunter for the previous two months turned up nothing unusual. McGee gathered the other SEALs, from the junior and senior class, and asked them to keep an eye on Duncan Hunter.

"I want to know what he's doing here, and you don't have a need to know yet," McGee said.

He learned Duncan was a good student, something of a ladies' man, and he went to the gym every day, sometimes three times. Ever few weeks, he invited classmates for an adventure. They left the base, retrieved his car on a trailer, and went to a racetrack in Lime Rock, Connecticut.

One of McGee's SEALs thought Hunter was under surveillance. He noticed a couple of Middle Eastern men watching Hunter intently, as he worked on his car at a storage area where he garaged the race car.

"Bullfrog, it was hard not to stare," the man said. "That's an incredible car on that trailer, and I saw these dudes scoping it out. At first, I thought they were casing the storage units, then I thought they were interested in the bright-yellow Corvette. The longer I watched, I wondered if they weren't watching Hunter like I was.

"He put a car cover over his car, locked the shed with a big padlock, and left. The dudes stayed. I left after ten minutes. Maybe they were watching him, maybe not. They didn't see me."

McGee walked from the library SCIF and found Duncan ahead, browsing a journal. "Hey, you ready?"

"Yes, Sir."

They walked together across the elevated covered

walkway between Hunter Hall and McCarty Little Hall for the weekly intelligence brief. McGee wore his service dress blues with ribbons and badges. Hunter wore a black herringbone suit with bright-red tie. They didn't speak until they approached the auditorium check-in booth and greeted the petty officer checking security badges.

McGee and Hunter took their places in the front row.

"I'm playing in a racquetball tournament this weekend near Boston," Duncan said.

McGee nodded. "I'm taking my family to Boston for shopping and sightseeing. We might stop in to watch if we're in the area."

"I'll flip you the address and name of the facility in an e-mail when we leave here."

"That'll work. Thanks."

There's no finer place to study the art of war than at a war college with a war raging on the other side of the planet. Adding the top-secret facilities of a national war gaming center and the Office of Naval Intelligence solidified the Naval War College's position as the best-equipped war college in the DOD.

The National War College may have held more cachet for politically minded or passive officers and civilians. For the more- active war fighters, the intelligence and information held in the three SCIFs was enough for one visiting democratic US senator. He had a troubled relationship with the Navy and argued strenuously to close the war colleges, especially the NWC. After his visit, he reversed himself and became one of the NWC's more-vocal supporters. The ability to think and war-game through complex situations and contingencies was invaluable to ground and maritime warriors. SEALs war-gamed and practiced whenever they could for every situation.

The doors remained open, and students filed in. McGee leaned over and said quietly, "Less than twenty-four hours after the Twin Towers fell, I was up here with about fifty shooters planning to go into Afghanistan. You can imagine what we were planning."

Hunter lowered his head and cocked it before looking at McGee. Something passed between them. McGee wanted to tell someone what really happened up there in the mountains of Tora Bora.

"I'm pretty sure if you found and killed him, you wouldn't be here," Duncan said. "I can't imagine how that fucker escaped with a bunch of SEALs on his ass. What little I know makes me think it was crappy support and poor intelligence. My bud Greg and I think they should have had quiet airplanes covering the area, but the Air Force wanted to show they were masters of their domain with their high-flying UAVs. Wrong solution."

"You don't know how right you are. You have to tell me more about quiet airplanes when we get out of here."

"Can do easy."

A female Navy commander walked to the lectern. "Good morning. I'm Commander Guilford, Commander of the Naval Intelligence Detachment Newport. I'll be giving your briefing this morning. This brief is classified SECRET NOFORN. Slide!

"On 2 December, fierce clashes between forces of Amanullah Khan and Ismail Khan resumed in western Afghanistan. This fighting is a continuation of a land squabble and isn't related to any operations in the north or east. Slide!

"Three people were killed and five wounded in a gun battle between police and fighters of a military commander in Kandahar. US Special Forces based in Lwara, near Khost, called in AH-64 Apache helicopter support to help chase five people seen moving in the vicinity of the base. A small team of soldiers discovered five rockets in the area where the suspects had been seen, and one person was detained for questioning. The five suspects fled into a building two miles away.

"A US Air Force Predator tracked them into the building. Let's see. Do we have the video?"

She clicked the remote, and a FLIR video replaced the

PowerPoint slides on the front screen. Five ghostly images ran into a one-story building. A moment later, three images emerged onto the roof and looked in the same direction. Fire-control symbology overlaid the FLIR image. The upper-right corner began flashing the word FIRE.

"Wait for it. Wait for it…." urged the commander.

Five seconds later, the picture showed the after-effects of a Hellfire missile launched from the Predator.

McGee muttered, "I hope there weren't any kids in that building."

Hunter sighed and nodded.

At the end of the brief, the commander asked Captain McGee and all other SOF to stay.

"I'll send you that info," Hunter said. "If I don't see you this weekend, have a great time with your family, Bill."

McGee watched the man leave and again wondered what Hunter was really doing at the war college.

CHAPTER TWELVE

0715 December 9, 2002
Wayside Racquet and Swim Club
Marlborough, Massachusetts

What started as a simple way to make a little money without much effort quickly became more interesting. The two men from the mosque were summoned several days earlier by the imam, who said, "I want you to report when this infidel leaves the Navy base in Newport and follow him wherever he goes."

The imam gave them two 8 x 10 glossies of Duncan Hunter, taken at a distance, and his truck. Written on the back of the picture of the Silverado was BIG CAT, the personalized license plate bolted onto the rear of the truck.

"This is a very important mission," the imam said. "You'll be paid well for accurate information. Another team is watching another infidel at the Navy base, and they'll watch you as well. If you fail me, you'll be severely punished. You can't let this man and his vehicle get out of your sight when he's off the base."

He handed them five $100 bills each, and their eyes widened. That was more than they usually made in two weeks.

"We won't fail you, Sahib. Inshallah. Thank you for allowing us this opportunity."

The black truck with the Texas license plates emerged from the NWC's main gate.

Achmed jabbed the napping Muhammad in the ribs. "There he is! Go. Go!"

He fumbled with his handheld radio, which fell to the

floor between Muhammad's legs. As he reached for it, Muhammad popped the Honda's clutch, throwing Achmed rearward, his face jammed into the man's crotch. Achmed tried to yell, but a mouthful of denim stopped him.

Eventually, they composed themselves, looked at each other, and silently agreed not to discuss the episode ever again. They followed the Texas truck in silence.

An hour later, the driver of the truck parked at an athletic club. He slid to the ground, retrieved a long, black bag from the back seat, and walked toward the fitness center.

The little red Honda with faded paint on the hood and top pulled into a driveway across the street from the black Silverado and parked.

"This truck was very easy to keep in sight," Muhammad said. "The infidel is an idiot."

"If the imam wants us to watch this truck and tell him what this infidel does and pays us for it, it's better than working at the airport or those stinky fast-food places. That's women's work." Muhammad nodded. "What if the infidel saw us?"

"What would he say? If he claims we're watching him, I'd deny it. I'd say, 'It's a free country. I can sit here and enjoy the beauty of America, and no one can deny me.'"

"He's from Texas. I've heard that people from Texas are wild. They carry weapons all the time. He has something in the back window of his truck."

"It's called a gun rack," Achmed said. "In Texas, infidels display their weapons in their trucks in the open."

"Americans are all cowards and stupid. This one flaunts his money with a big truck and a race car. Have you seen such a thing?"

"No. It's very unusual here. I haven't seen a race car before. I only hope we're asked to do something else soon. Inshallah."

"Inshallah. What do you want to do?"

"I want to fuck American bitches." He laughed.

"Me, too."

They laughed heartedly and loudly. "I wish the imam would pay us to fuck American whores. Maybe our next job will be to fuck American bitches."

"Inshallah."

CHAPTER THIRTEEN

1045 December 9, 2002
Wayside Racquet and Swim Club

Duncan Hunter was exhausted, having expended more energy than was smart to stay in the game, but he was within one point of sending the match to a tiebreaker.

"Fourteen serves six," the referee on the second-floor observation deck said.

Hunter wiped sweat from his forehead on his sleeve, looked at the receiver, and bounced the worn green ball there times before hitting a lob high off the front wall. The ball arced to the right wall, floating three-quarters of the way back, where it barely touched the wall and dropped four feet from the rear glass panel.

The receiver, not believing his good fortune at the poor serve, immediately assessed his options before driving the ball into the corner. Hunter, anticipating that response, ran toward the right corner, hoping to cut the ball off and quickly return it for a winner.

Traveling almost 150 mph, the racquetball was smashed into a blur as the receiver, made it carom off the right wall inches from the floor and ricocheted to the front wall and left, away from the diving-right Hunter. Duncan positioned himself to reach across his body. At the last possible moment, he reached out and barely touched the ball with his racquet. Like a drop shot in tennis, the inertia of the fast-moving ball dissipated when it touched the racquet, leaving just enough energy for the ball to hit the front wall at the baseboard and roll out along the floor at walking speed. The referee yelled, "Point!"

Hunter's diving contortion resulted in a winning shot he couldn't see. He landed heavily on the floor. His momentum rolled him onto his right shoulder, and, like a tumbling gymnast, he rolled 360 degrees before his legs slammed against the wall to a stop.

He lay there, crumpled on the floor with his feet against the front wall, while his competitor shook his head, turned, and walked off the court.

On his back, looking up at the ceiling, Hunter took a deep breath, rolled onto his knees, and stood. Off to the right of the glass wall, among fifty onlookers, was Captain McGee and his beautiful girls and wife. Hunter stepped through the open glass door and smiled.

"That was Incredible," McGee said.

"It was lucky, and he and I both know it. But I won a game off a professional—a very charitable one. That's all anyone could ask for."

"That guy's a pro?"

"That's Cliff Swain, one of the greatest racquetball players of all time. He's probably already in the Racquetball Hall of Fame. I think he owns this facility. He isn't even working hard, and I'm dying. He's playing for the fans. Trust me. If he wanted to, he could crush me like a bug, and there wouldn't be anything I could do about it. He's been playing with me while he's on cruise control. I'm working way too hard and can't stop. This is how I get my fun. I'll be surprised if I can walk in a couple hours.

"Thank you for coming. Bill, where are my manners? Wow, this is the missus? You must be half-blind. I don't see what anyone could see in Bill. You guys have a beautiful family."

Bill laughed and made introductions. "If you don't mind, we'll watch you finish. This is pretty exciting. I never saw anyone play at this level before."

Duncan Hunter couldn't resist the opening. "I never saw anyone play at this level before, either." All of them laughed.

Hunter changed into a dry shirt with Master Yoda on the back, revealing the cobblestone abdomen definition of a twenty- five-year-old Olympian, not a forty-eight-year-old man. Hunter knew he would lose the next game, but, with

McGee and his family watching, he was inspired to give it a good try and keep the thirty-three-year-old pro honest.

Swain appeared distracted throughout the eleven-point tiebreaker. At 7-7, Hunter and Swain dived for balls left and right, keeping the rally alive. Both sprinted to the front or back walls to return shots.

McGee never saw such a demonstration of blinding speed and never giving up. Any other racquetball player would have long ago quit, as each man with huge quadriceps and calves hammered the ball with all their might, hoping for an incremental edge over the other. Hunter found himself jammed along the right wall, as Swain crushed a passing shot driving the ball behind him. The right-handed Duncan swung his racquet left behind his heels, blindly making contact with the ball.

As happens occasionally in racquetball and lotteries, Lady Luck struck at the right time. The crowd saw Duncan hit what should have been a winning passing shot for Swain, who was totally unprepared for a lucky and unconventional save. Duncan looked composed, as if he designed the behind-the-back-to-the-opposite-corner winning shot.

Swain smiled and raised his hands in applause. "Nice shot...for an old man."

The crowd, stunned at the turn of events, cheered and applauded.

"Point!" the referee shouted.

For the next three minutes, Hunter showed flashes of how well he and Swain were matched. They tied at 9-9, and Swain didn't anticipate Hunter's wicked backhand cross-court shot. Hunter concealed the racquet's position perfectly, unleashing every bit of energy in his torso and legs, concentrated into one small spot at the top of his racquet.

The ball shot off the racquet at nearly 170 mph. Swain tried immediately to change direction only to have his foot touch a drop of sweat on the floor. Even with gum-soled shoes, his foot skidded. The man rolled his ankle and fell hard.

By the time Hunter recovered from his follow-through and waited for the crushing return, he saw Swain on the floor, holding his ankle in both hands, his racquet dangling from his wrist. Play stopped with the winning passing shot. The crowd gasped, as Swain blinked wildly, closed his eyes, relaxed, and rolled onto his knees. He stepped gingerly onto the foot.

Hunter raced to the fallen man, holding out his hand to help him up.

"I'm done, Duncan," Swain said. "Great racquetball. Congrats."

Both men dripped lakes of sweat to pool on the floor. "Are you sure?" Hunter asked.

"You know when you're done, and I'm done. I'll be all right. I just twisted it. Thanks. Great game." Cliff Swain looked over his shoulder and shouted, "Ref, that's it!"

"Thank you, Cliff," Hunter said. "I appreciate your taking it easy on me. You made an old man very happy. I hope someone caught this on video."

The pro, mildly amused, slapped Hunter's back, tossed the referee the ball on his way off the court, and hobbled out the glass door.

Hunter left the court right behind Swain and met a big, smiling Navy captain offered a bottle of water. "Are you guys done?"

Nearly breathless, his chest heaving and shirt drenched, Hunter nodded and removed the racquet's safety cord from his wrist before tossing his racquet and goggles onto a pile of his belongings. "Yes, Sir. He said he twisted his ankle, which should make me the winner. From my old flying days, a kill is a kill. That should also be $500."

Surprise showed on McGee's weather-beaten, heavily lined face. "I guess you're buying the beer."

Hunter drained the water bottle in four long slugs. "Hell, I'll buy dinner as long as I don't have to walk. You guys up for lunch or dinner?"

"I really ought to get them home. Nicole needs to finish

MARK A. HEWITT

some homework, and I have a bunch of honey-dos to take care of."

"I have to study and work on my paper."

"I have to tell you that behind-the-back shot made me think you really are Master Yoda." He almost added that his SEALs considered themselves Jedis but let it pass. There would be another time.

"Even a blind squirrel finds a nut now and then," Hunter said. "It was all luck."

"From my vantage point, it wasn't luck." Moving closer and lowering his voice, he asked, "I wonder if we could talk about your paper."

"Sure. What about?"

"I'd like to better understand what you're working on."

"One idea I'm tinkering with is designed to demonstrate how special-purpose quiet aircraft can be employed in an interagency environment. That's pretty straightforward."

"Can your airplane help my guys?"

"I'd think your guys would be all over this technology."

"Not quite. Talk about weapons and other maritime-related capabilities, and yes. We nearly have an unlimited budget. Go against the Army or Air Force, and we're SOL. I think your little airplane might be a game-changer."

"I think it is, and it has a history of doing so. Want me to call you when I get home, or maybe we can meet in the morning and go down to the SCIF and talk?"

"Let's meet in the morning before class. That was great stuff, Duncan." McGee pointed to the open court.

"Thanks, Bill. Safe travels home." Hunter touched his fingers to his head.

McGee waved in lieu of a salute. "See you tomorrow."

The drive back to Newport was uneventful. Hunter glimpsed the ratty Honda early in the return trip in his rearview mirror but didn't know he was being followed.

130

CHAPTER FOURTEEN

0735 December 8, 2002
Henry E. Eccles Library, Naval War College

Hunter, a little early for his meeting with McGee, was about to stride into the spacious library in Hunter Hall when he noticed a new, shiny brass plaque left of the double doors. The large wooden sign over the doors announced it was the Henry E. Eccles Library. "Let me guess. Another admiral."

Duncan discovered Henry Effingham Eccles was a Rear Admiral and a major figure at the Naval War College from the late 1940s through the 1970s, a man recognized as a thinker and writer about naval logistics and military theory.

"Who knew?" he wondered aloud.

"Who knew what?" a voice asked from behind.

Hunter always found McGee's voice incongruous. It should sound like a hard, demanding drill instructor, but it was more like a radio announcer's voice in tone and timbre.

"Another famous admiral who made a name for himself. It says here Eccles was closely associated with the Naval War College and served as confidante and advisor to successive presidents of the College and got the library named after him."

"Ah. SEALs are difficult to impress. Ready?"

"Yes, Sir."

They entered the building and walked to the SCIF door just to the right inside the library. Ensuring they were free of any electronic devices, they entered.

The clerk behind the counter recognized the civilian but not the captain. "Good morning, Mr. Hunter. You're early this morning. What can I get you?"

"Nothing this time, Tim, but I'll be back later this afternoon. Will you be here?"

"Sir, I'm always here. See you later."

Hunter smiled and waved to the classified-document librarian and led McGee to a desk with two chairs toward the back of the facility among rows of tightly shelved, classified documents. Hunter watched the SEAL rapidly scan the windowless room.

McGee relaxed and sat first. "I still can't believe you beat a racquetball pro. I swear, I rarely saw the ball. It moved that fast. You guys seemed to know exactly where it was or was going. That really was amazing, Duncan."

"Thank you, Sir. What's up?"

"Tell me about your quiet airplane project."

"What do you want to know?"

"What's so special about quiet airplanes?"

Duncan grinned. "I'm not trying to be flippant, but they're inaudible. I think when a SEAL asks, 'What's so special about quiet airplanes,' you're really asking, 'How can a quiet airplane help my guys?'"

"That's it."

"Let me tell you how I thought quiet airplanes could help the Border Patrol, just to establish a frame of reference. Then I'll tell you what my bud Greg and I have done and some of the history I found in this library. How about that?"

"Sounds good."

"First if all, the problem of aircraft doing any kind of surveillance or reconnaissance work is that they're noisy. It's just not sufficient to muffle the engine of a piston-driven plane...."

"...and jets are too noisy."

"Right. The only real solution is a glider, but they have no power, so you need something that can get you from point A to point B and back. The best solution is a prop. The secret is to make it quiet. Props are very efficient, but, like engines, very noisy. If you see a propeller-driven airplane, you hear the propeller and not the engine.

"Back in the late '60s, the Army felt it needed a low-altitude surveillance airplane for reconnaissance over the battlefield, especially at night. The big SR-71s and U-2s had to work during daylight hours for their cameras to function. The problem the Army had in Vietnam was North Vietnam moved hundreds, if not thousands, of VC at night, fixing the bridges we blew up, digging tunnels, and what have you. With thick jungle canopies, the US didn't know how to overcome the advantage the VC had when they hunkered down during the day and went to work at night.

"The state of technology was such that the first-generation FLIRs and night-vision devices required not high-flying airplanes but something that could get low. Hence, the notion of a low- flying, acoustically quiet aircraft to take pictures or relay intelligence real-time was the ticket to success."

"Makes sense."

"The US Army Research Lab pushed several TS contracts to their contractors to make not only a quiet airplane, a motorized glider if you will, but amazing amounts of research went to quiet a propeller so it was virtually undetectable on the ground. A combination of a super quiet prop, a quiet engine, and airframe smoothing, like conformal antennas and such, provided an airplane that could fly low and not be heard at night by a human."

"How low we talking about?"

"Believe it or not, that's still TS. It's in here." Hunter pointed at a shelf of classified documents. I can tell you that, in open sources, guys flying these planes at night were able to get within a few hundred feet above the VC walking along a very noisy river without alerting them to their presence. Those guys also used the first-generation night-vision devices.

"That leads me to the Border Patrol. I viewed the mission of detecting VC movement at night as the same problem as illegal aliens moving at night. Illegal aliens and drug smugglers typically move at that time. Anyone flying a regular plane at night would alert those on the ground to take cover or countermeasures. Some twin-blade helicopters can be heard at night five to seven miles away. Even if the aircraft carry FLIR or low-light cameras, the problem becomes where to aim the sensor. The second problem is when you have a sensor, you have to deal with the soda-straw effect."

"Soda-straw effect?"

"Yeah. Look through a straw, and what do you see? Only what you're aiming at. FLIRs and night-vision devices are great, but if you alert your enemy, the ugly little secret is the bad guys are very adept at thwarting those devices when they hear the aircraft.

"So what does the USAF do? It makes a Predator fly higher and uses better optics for definition. However, high-granularity intelligence goes right down the tubes. How many Afghani kids have been blown up by Predator missiles because of poor granularity of intelligence?"

"Probably too many."

"All I want to do is kill or interdict bad guys. My suggestion to the Border Patrol leadership was, if you didn't alert the bad guys, you increased your chances of locating and apprehending them, because they'd move without feeling they'd been detected. You could even look across the border with a FLIR, a low-light camera, or a moving-target-indicator radar to see what was coming. Couldn't you monitor the actions of the bad guys and radio your ground forces to interdict them? If a bad guy got away at night, a quiet aircraft flying low overhead could easily detect what he was doing and guide an agent to his position."

"Makes sense. Too much sense."

"What little I know of your business, I can see where a quiet airplane would help SEALs when landing on a beach, getting on a ship, doing all kinds of things at night. You guys operate primarily at night, too, and you'd have a pair of eyes watching the battlefield or the ship, talking to you and your guys. I think magical things would happen."

McGee sat quietly, his mind racing over what to say next. "I tell you, Duncan, if I had access to your quiet airplane, we would have gotten bin Laden."

"Probably a long time ago."

"Yes, a long time ago. We went into Afghanistan with the right guys and the wrong equipment, like unarmored HumVees. The Air Force was hell-bent on flying Predators, and they didn't help us find anyone. They blew up a lot of Taliban and al-Qaeda. That's a good thing, but they weren't helpful in our operations after detecting them."

"That's really it. Low-flying aircraft see things in great detail, because bad guys don't think they're being watched, especially at night. High-flying aircraft, with sensors, lose sufficient detail that they're only ten to twenty percent effective. Another area where a Schweizer comes into play is in the jungle arena. By flying at low altitude and checking for heat signatures at an angle, drug-lab heat signatures pop up like flares. Trying to look straight down, the canopy diffuses the heat signature so significantly that you can't detect the lab."

Duncan looked at his companion. "What else, Sir?"

"How do I get one of these airplanes?"

"Such a deal I have for you, but we have to get to class first. Are you serious?"

"As a heart attack."

"We need to talk to my bud Greg. Did your wife ever call him?"

"She did."

"I think you could contact SOCOM and ask why the CIA couldn't reprogram one of its Night Riders for you guys. I can tell you what I did for the Border Patrol. It resulted in Greg Lynche bringing a demo to Texas. That convinced the USBP leadership a quiet airplane was a complete game-changer for the border. I don't think you'll have a problem getting help, but a conversation with Greg or someone from his old place would be very helpful."

Hunter couldn't tell if he saw fatigue or fire in McGee's eyes. "What are you thinking?"

"I'm wondering why I didn't know about these planes."

"I would've been surprised if you did. There are really only a handful out there, and they're very special aircraft. Schweizer sells every one they build, and they don't make many per year. They're usually employed in a counterdrug role. When I was in the Border Patrol, the Democrats in the administration fought the INS at every corner to keep the Border Patrol from getting those planes."

"Say again?"

"The Democratic administration in the mid-to-late 90's wasn't interested in curtailing illegal immigration, and they worked, or their lawyers did, to thwart Border Patrol agents from doing their jobs. The funding for the USBP was horrible. It was so bad, some Border Patrol agents siphoned gas from cars seized from drug smugglers so they could fuel BP trucks and chase illegal aliens.

"You can imagine the conniption they had when the Chief Patrol Agent went to INS for additional funding for quiet airplanes. They laughed him out of the office. If it wasn't for a Republican congressman, who got an earmark for three airplanes, the BP would never have received a dime.

"The ultimate tragedy was that the administration killed the program. There was no way the Democrats wanted the Border Patrol to actually control the border. I found a way to get some money and the airplanes, and the BP leadership didn't tell the shitheads in Washington. The bottom line, Sir, is you'll need a high-power sponsor to reprogram one of these airplanes."

"Let's discuss CONOPS and plan of attack after class."

"I'll call Greg before I go upstairs to see what he thinks. If he can't get you a Schweizer, there may be another solution or two."

"I thought you said these Schweitzers are unique."

"Schwei-zers. They are, but we have to run. It wouldn't look good if the president was late to class. I'll tell you more later."

"I have to tell you, Duncan, I'm going way out on a limb

with this. SEALs have some bad history with the CIA, the FBI, and the NSA. We call them the Three Stooges, because they always failed us when we needed them. When they promised to be somewhere or deliver something, they weren't or couldn't. CIA failed us in Grenada. NSA failed us in Beirut, and 9-11? Hell. Drive by their building on the weekend, and the parking lot's deserted. Don't get me started on the FBI."

"Sounds like a typical bunch of ground guys. Aviation pukes are a little different. Trust me."

McGee looked at the grinning Hunter. "OK. Meet you back here at 1100?"

"Aye, aye, my captain."

CHAPTER FIFTEEN

0755 December 8, 2002
Silent Aero Systems Vienna, Virginia

"What are the chances you can get someone from your old place to demo a Schweizer for a bunch of SEALs?" Hunter asked.

"Well, hello to you, too." Lynche smiled and set down his cup of coffee.

"I'm sorry. I'm late for class, and our class President and thirty-five-year SEAL just discovered what a quiet airplane could do for his guys in Afghanistan."

"I wonder how he found out. OK. I'll make a couple calls. I'm not sure if there's an agency asset in the country. I'll call Nicky to see if there's one in Elmira. Maybe someone can make a visit. Call me back after lunch?"

"You're a gentleman and a scholar."

"You're the scholar."

"Thank you, Sir. Hello to Connie."

CHAPTER SIXTEEN

0730 December 13, 2002
Quonset State Airport Newport, Rhode Island

Hunter arrived at the FBO thirty minutes before Lynche's ETA. At nineteen degrees Fahrenheit, he still wasn't acclimated to the cold, moist New England air and hurried to get out of the cold whenever he was outside. The heater of the 1967 Corvette kept him nice and toasty, as he waited for McGee to arrive and Lynche to land. When an old Green Riviera pulled into the parking lot, Hunter momentarily thought, *Is this the advance party of a car show? What a nice car!*

When McGee pulled up beside Hunter's car, he looked at Duncan and waggled his eyebrows a couple times grinning like an idiot.

Shutting off the idling two-seater, Hunter ignored the cold, as he climbed from his race car. "Holy shit, Batman!" he said, more dramatically than what was called for.

McGee climbed out nonchalantly. "I hope these babies will still be here by the time we get back."

"She's beautiful. Stunning, Bill. '66-'67 Riviera?"

"1965. It was my mom's. I've had it for seven years. One of these days, I'll restore it. Only 37,000 miles—all original. I heard someone brought a race car to school, but I had no idea it was you. My God, that's an incredible car. Is it street legal?"

"Oh, yes. One of my hobbies is this 1967 Corvette coupe. Aluminum block 427. It pumps out 600 ponies." Duncan raised the hood. "There are several racetracks in this part of the country."

"Drag racing?" McGee saw more than a few big-block engines, but the motor under the hood was the most impressive he'd ever seen.

"No, Sir. Grand touring, or GT. Get Ferraris, Jaguars, Porsches, and anything else with a ton of cubic inches and headers and chase each other over a two-mile track. There's a famous track in Connecticut, Lime Rock. I had this out there a few weeks ago. Came in third in a classic challenge race. I was outdriven by a couple of Jags and a Ferrari. I'm still learning. You know behind every great Corvette...is a Ferrari, a Jaguar, and a Porsche."

McGee laughed. He was definitely in a good mood. Hunter said, "It was great fun and wild."

The sound of an approaching airplane interrupted the two men's gushing over their cars. As they walked toward the FBO, McGee glanced back at the two vehicles—Beauty and the Beast.

Three minutes later, a red and gold-trimmed airplane with twin-tail booms with engines fore and aft taxied in front of the fixed-base operator's office. McGee suddenly recognized the aircraft. "Isn't that the BAT-21?"

"Yes, Sir. The civilian Cessna 337 Skymaster or the military's O-2. It's a 1967, one of the very first ones ever produced, and you'll see it's in great shape."

Lynche killed the front engine, set the parking brake, and opened the copilot's seat for the SEAL. Hunter led by shedding his coat and throwing it behind the back seat. McGee took his cue and removed his coat before climbing into the rear of the airplane.

As the two men strapped in, Lynche shouted over the noise of the rear engine, "I love it when a plan comes together!"

After ringing off with Hunter Friday morning, Lynche's first call went to the Schweizer CEO, Saul Ferrier, who confirmed they had a new SA-37B, but it was being prepared for immediate delivery to the US State Department for one of their International Narcotics and Law Enforcement programs. Lynche's next call went to the current head of Air Branch. After he showered and put on a suit, he headed for CIA headquarters for a discussion in a SCIF.

The Chief Air Branch, new in his position and with virtually no aviation experience, agreed to meet Lynche in Elmira to see the aircraft in person and meet the Schweizer CEO and Navy SEALs who were interested in the aircraft. The Air Branch Chief was en route in an Agency Gulfstream G-III.

McGee's calls to the SOCOM and DEVGRU commanders also resulted in an agreement to meet the next day in Elmira, New York. The SOCOM commander's G-III lifted off from Norfolk, Virginia, with the SEAL Team Six commander and XO. The other eight seats were occupied by Special Operations personnel. Everyone wore civvies for the trip, and some had high and tight haircuts. All sported small waists and powerful chests that indicated their true occupation as the world's finest commandos.

Hunter thought he was going along for the ride, but, as soon as he buckled in and put on his headset, Lynche said, "Your airplane." Lynche turned in the seat, shook the SEAL's hand again, and kept up a running dialogue all the way to their destination.

Lynche was amazed at the way McGee's ultra-wide shoulders and thick chest took up the complete rear seat. Hunter fired up the front engine, called the tower, and taxied to the duty runway, ripping quickly through the check list. Early on Saturday morning, there was little traffic.

ATC cleared them direct to Elmira. Hunter ran the throttles to takeoff RPM, checked the manifold air pressure for both engines, and released the brakes. Lynche and McGee continued their discussion on family and cohorts, as the little white and red push-me pull-you bounced down the runway.

The combined tractor and pusher engines produced its unique sound of competing propellers. In the frigid temperatures, November 777SH quickly lifted off.

Ninety minutes later, Hunter dropped the gear and began a straight-in approach to Elmira Regional Airport. Once clear of the active runway, Lynche turned around and said, "My airplane."

Hunter released the controls. "Your airplane." He raised both hands.

McGee was fascinated by the two pilots' back and forth. He hadn't seen or heard of pilots handing over command of an airplane before. He was usually too busy jumping out of one to notice. Every movement and radio call was a coordinated event. Clearly the two men had flown together many times.

"Hunter, you're the luckiest shit on the planet," said Lynche as he taxied the Skymaster toward the Schweizer ramp, where a dozen purposeful men and a portly gentleman were deplaning from two nearly identical white-and-blue Gulfstreams.

Nodding to the nearest aircraft, Lynche said, "I bought that jet. It still looks great."

"Timing is everything good, Sir," Hunter replied. "Let's not park behind one of those jets. If they start up, they'll blow your baby right over."

"Now how the hell would you know that?" Lynche often wondered where Hunter got his ideas. Maybe he just observed things differently than others.

"I've seen what happens when big dummies don't think about such things," Hunter explained. "The guys who fly jets don't think about it. The GA pilots get pissed off when they park behind jets, and the jet flips over their little airplanes when they pull out of the chocks. Happens all the time, really."

Lynche shot Hunter a look, raising his eyebrows twice as he detoured around the jets to the building with the large Schweizer Aircraft Company sign. Thirteen men, some with the best security clearances that could be granted by the US government, stopped walking, their eyes followed the taxiing Skymaster to the closest hangar door.

Before Lynche shut down the engines, a well-bundled, raven-haired woman opened an outside door from the offices beside the hangar. "Gentlemen, please come in out of the weather."

At 10° Fahrenheit and a steady westerly wind, the invite to go inside should have been a galvanizing moment, but no one wanted to break his indifferent stride to the door for fear of being labeled a wuss. The rear prop hadn't fully wound down, as Hunter jumped out and began securing the aircraft, chocking the nose wheel, stuffing intake covers into the open ports on both engines, and covering the pitot tube.

When McGee deplaned the Cessna 337, several men with shaggy hair immediately came over to greet him. In the lee of the airplane, it was obvious the group was oblivious to the cold.

Lynche and Hunter saw love, respect, and admiration ooze from the troops, as they became reacquainted with the legendary SEAL Team Six commander.

Several gave a loud, "Hooyah!" when McGee said something with his frosty breath. After a minute of smiles and short phrases, McGee stepped back and said in a command voice, "Gentlemen, I'd like you to introduce you to SIS Greg Lynche, former Chief of Air Branch, and this is Duncan Hunter. Mr. Hunter is one of us and should have been a SEAL. Call him Apex."

"Hooyah, Apex!" barked several men to a confused Duncan Hunter.

Lynche and Hunter pulled on their coats while standing on the ramp. Hunter, slightly embarrassed by McGee's compliment, was confused at being given a name. He handed McGee his coat.

"Let's get inside," McGee said. "I saw a pretty woman in there who's a lot better looking than any of you."

Lynche walked smartly toward the portly gentleman from the CIA jet. McGee walked toward the slightly open door, leading the troop. He saw Hunter carefully inspecting the Skymaster. Even in bone-chilling weather, habits were hard to break. Duncan performed a post-flight inspection, checking aileron bearings, brakes, tire wear, and the engine for oil leaks. He pushed the Skymaster hard to get to Elmira on time and wanted to make sure he hadn't broken anything on the beautiful red-and-gold Cessna 337.

When he finished, he ran toward the door where the other men disappeared.

CHAPTER SEVENTEEN

1030 December 13, 2002
Schweizer Aircraft Company

Hunter, entering the anteroom of the lounge, was surprised to find no one there. He glanced at the hundreds of pictures of Paul, Bill, and Ernest Schweizer, the three brothers who designed, built, and tested their gliders in the 1930s, then he paused to scan the colored and black-and-white pictures of Schweizer gliders and small helicopters. Having been to the hanger several times, he turned left down the hall toward the offices and conference room, but those were vacant, too.

"Must be in the hangar," he muttered, reversing course down the picture-laden hall to the hangar's double-door entryway.

The sound of the door opening echoed in the large room. Saul Ferrier turned and saw Duncan. "I think we can get started now."

The CEO held court. "This aircraft is the culmination of sixty years of building high-performance sailplanes. In 1966, Schweizer worked with Lockheed to develop a powered motor glider for the US Army in Vietnam. Several prototypes were immediately pressed into service. We received a contract with Lockheed to build another prototype that went into limited production, the YO-3A. Lots of observation airplanes were being built and employed in Vietnam—the O1 Bird Dog and O-2 Skymaster, to name a couple. I think the best-looking Skymaster in America is parked out front."

McGee, arms akimbo, shouted, "Hooyah!"

Twelve men responded, "Hooyah!"

A very proud Greg Lynche smiled and crossed his arms.

"From the R&D done on the YO-3, we developed the SA-

37 motorglider for the Air Force Academy. Greg, you came to us in 86 or so to develop a reconnaissance version of the 2-37?"

Greg said, "Yes. As Chief Air Branch, we worked to develop the airplane you see here. This airplane served as a platform for FLIR and low-light cameras. If you can get a FLIR up close, you can see things in great detail. Nothing I've found does that like a quiet airplane at night. I brought a video that shows the difference between nighttime high-altitude surveillance and low-altitude surveillance."

"How high can this aircraft fly?" asked the thick-necked, small-eared bodybuilder in the group.

"It's fully pressurized to 35,000 feet."

"How low can it fly without being heard?"

"The tested altitude is still classified," Hunter said, "but anecdotal stories from old YO-3 pilots say they could get a couple hundred feet over large numbers of VC, as they worked near or crossed running water. They got close enough with first- generation FLIR to make out who they were viewing. That was the prize for analysts and intelligence officers."

The man wearing four stars said, "That's the problem with the Predators. We can see seven guys going into a building, but you really don't know who they are. If they're seen laying IEDs along the road, the Air Force has no problem taking them out with a half-million-dollar missile. Some of us would like to know who the hell we're blowing up."

"Saul," Hunter asked, "is the conference room set up for showing Greg's video?"

"It is. There's some brunch if you guys are hungry. Shall we? Nicky can show the way."

Lynche and his successor migrated to each other early and spoke quietly, following the brunette. The SEALs and Army SOF almost moved in unison, like a school of fish that changed direction without any noticeable collisions. When the four-star moved left, the solders moved left. If McGee moved right, the SEALs moved right. It was purposeful yet entertaining.

All followed Ms. Nicky.

Hunter sidled up to the head of the company, who stood next to the motorglider's wing. "Saul, anything interesting going on?"

"Want to buy a company?"

"Sir, that's not a good line. I take it, if you sell, these little darlings will go by the wayside?"

"This is probably the last one. They're expensive to produce, and others think they can do the same thing with unmanned systems. You know other motor gliders are being produced."

"Yes, Sir, but they just have an engine. Your airplanes are special purpose, silent, and handmade. I've been afraid something like this might happen. There's a tremendous wave of interest in unmanned systems. The problem is, the decision-makers have no clue what they're getting into when they divert precious funds for unmanned systems and don't question the high cost of reduced capabilities.

"The same systems that reduce the need for pilots require much more manpower to support them. Last year, the US embassy in Peru wanted some unmanned coverage for a counterinsurgency op. Greg's old place couldn't support, so they turned to the Air Force, who sent down two C-130s and a hundred guys to support a pair of Predators. The Chief of Station told them to not get off the airplanes and go home. We did the work. By the way, you guys did a remarkable job with that airplane. I'll build your airplanes if you sell the company. I'm serious."

"Thank you, Duncan." He sighed. "Let's go get a bite before it's all gone."

The Schweizer CEO and Hunter, entering the conference room, found Nicky Tweed, the business director, setting up a sideboard of drinks, cold cuts, soup, and chili for their guests. Each man got a helping plate of meat and cheese and commented favorably on the soup and chili before sitting at the conference table, waiting for the show to begin.

Lynche took center stage, as Nicky handed him a wireless controller. The CIA man, General Jones, and Captains McGee and Goodfellow sat near the front. Saul Ferrier remained standing.

"The real capabilities of the SA 2-37B are amplified when coupled with a high-quality FLIR, such as FLIR's Star Safire and WESCAM MX-20, that offer the greatest-possible detail achievable. There are other aspects of a FLIR that can be helpful. Lights, please."

Hunter turned off the lights and studied the crowd. He saw the same level of interest when he was with the Border Patrol.

A FLIR image was projected on the large front screen, taken during Lynche's and Hunter's run to South America in 1999.

"As you can see by the symbology, this video was shot in Colombia while looking for FARC, drug labs, boat docks, and other campsites. Here's what we thought was a barbecue high up on a mountaintop in the early morning hours when sane people would be in bed.

"We had reports of several US citizens being taken hostage for political and monetary reasons. The Colombians asked the US Embassy if we could locate the hostages. You can see when the airplane revved its engines, the noise from the prop propagated to the ground. Watch what happens."

McGee looked at Hunter, wondering if that was what Duncan did with Lynche.

The video slewed left before returning to its primary focus. Then the camera zoomed to show the men freezing place for three seconds, then they leaped into action, retrieving weapons, running down a jungle path, tossing cigarettes into the bush, and taking defensive positions around a hut in the trees.

Many of the men around the table became animated and cracked quiet jokes. The CIA man furrowed his brow. Saul Ferrier found it fascinating. Hunter took a copy of National Geographic from a stack of magazines and skimmed through the pages. "Definitely not the response one would expect when hearing something strange while partying on the top of a mountain," Lynche said. "Let me fast forward here and show you what we were looking for."

When the video returned to normal speed, white images began walking back up the hill with a couple of bodies remaining in place. The camera zoomed in on the hut.

"The aircrew made a pass directly over the hut at a couple hundred feet. The FLIR clearly shows a dozen heat signatures in the structure. Those were the hostages. With the fire extinguished on the hilltop, the aircrew got as close as they thought prudent.

"When the tape was analyzed, our folks could determine who each of those guys was and could match his mug shot to the FLIR tape. That's what quiet airplanes can do that no other aircraft can. Oh, yes." He let the video continue. "What could you do with this?"

The tape showed a close-up of each terrorist's face with a tiny green dot dancing on his forehead.

"Sniper killshot!" an Army officer barked. "Hooyah!"

The CIA man turned in his chair. "We used a quiet airplane to resolve the Japanese embassy hostage crisis in December, 1996. Isn't that correct, Greg?"

"That's correct, Sir." Lynche momentarily scowled at Hunter, who seemed intently focused on National Geographic.

"For those who may not know, the Tupac Amaru Revolutionary Movement, MRTA, took hundreds of diplomats, government officials, and business executives hostage at the residence of Japan's ambassador to Peru. The media wrongly called it the Japanese embassy hostage crisis. Some of the hostages were released. Others were held hostage for about 125 days.

"The USG choreographed a raid with the Peruvian Armed Forces commandos. We got some SOG snipers in the area, and the overhead illuminated the militant guards along the walls of the compound. Snipers took them out."

Without looking up, Hunter said, "At night."

"That's right," the CIA man said. "All the MRTA militants died."

"Hooyah!" someone said.

"Duncan," McGee said, "your basic CONOP is getting a quiet airplane in position to find targets. Once detected and ID'd, you relay positional information to ground forces for real-time situational awareness. Then the ground forces engage or kill the enemy."

Hunter set the magazine in his lap with his index finger holding a place. "Or any option you want to execute. If you wanted to snatch a high-value target, having a Night Rider as your eyes in the air I think increases your chances of success."

When there were no follow-up comments, his gaze returned to the magazine, then he scanned the room as if deep in thought before gazing at the ceiling.

"Let me tee up another video for a couple more examples," Lynche said. "You guys are smart, but the adversary always has a trick up his sleeve. Here we go. I shot this from less than 1,000 feet over the Rio Grande. This train of people is actually a line of over 120 illegal aliens. Those two vehicles are Border Patrol agents with NVGs trying to find illegal aliens. If we had been able to radio the guys in the truck.... 'Agent Smuckatelli, wake up! Take four paces to the right, and you'll make your quota for the month.'"

Laughs and calls of "Hooyah!" went around the conference table.

"Mr. Lynche, Mr. Ferrier," the four-star general said, "I think your airplanes could be a game-changer, especially for troops in the mountains. What will it take to get a couple for SOCOM?"

"The bird in the hangar is the last one off the line," Ferrier replied. "We have no plans to build any more. It takes about nine months to build one. If we doubled the workforce, we could do it in five months, but with a single jig, that's the best we can do."

"What about the one in the hangar? It's slated for State? I

might be able to borrow it from them."

"It's mine, actually," the CIA man said. "I might be able to let you use it until you get one of your own."

"That would be fantastic, Sir. We need a plan for more quiet aircraft and fast."

Hunter finally looked up. "Sir, Duncan Hunter. There may be a way to get several additional quiet assets in very short order."

Confused, nearly everyone looked at him, but Ferrier and Lynche smiled.

"Sir, there are several YO-3As in museums. Typically, they're on loan from DOD. If you could get them restored, which could take a couple months, you could have half a dozen operating quiet aircraft inside the AOR within three months."

"Tell me more," the four-star general said.

"Sir, of the eleven built, 001 is in the museum in Fort Rucker. I believe 002 is at the Hiller Museum in Washington State. 004 and 006 are in private hands awaiting restoration. They could be persuaded to be loaned to you if they were restored. The same thing with 008. It's with the Confederate Air Force in California awaiting restoration. 010 was used as a parts donor for 011, which is with NASA. Six airplanes."

"What about the other four aircraft?"

"Lost or unavailable," Lynche said quickly.

Hunter didn't flinch or change his expression, but McGee heard something in Lynche's quick, almost-dismissive comment.

The four-star general faced the CIA man. "I think that's a great idea, and it solves a lot of problems. Rob, if we could get your aircraft on loan, we'll work getting the others out of the museums and from NASA." He looked at Lynche. "I take it you'd want them to come here?"

"We don't want to advertise the fact that those aircraft are being restored. This is a secured facility with cleared personnel. Saul, we could expedite the resto-mods?"

"We could put all new wiring with new glass cockpits,"

Saul Ferrier said. "You'd need to select which FLIR you want and any other extra systems, like GPS, encrypted comm, radar hazard and warning. Someone will need to provide a requirements document."

Excitement rose among the men around the table.

"How do we get them to Afghanistan?" the four-star general asked. "They can't fly there."

"These are basic, very special gliders," Ferrier said. "The wings can be removed or installed inside twenty minutes. They travel in a trailer or shipping container."

"Unless someone has other questions," the four-star general said, "I say we have work to do." He stood, as did the others.

The men exchanged good-byes, and the CIA man and the general led the congregation to their jets.

Lynche turned to Hunter. "I can't believe you were reading National Geographic during this. Were there pictures of naked Liberian women in it?"

"You wish. OK, get this. There's an article in here about how the ozone layer has become so big that the tip of South America, the region called Patagonia, is experiencing significant plant damage from the additional UV that isn't being filtered out."

Lynche sighed, closed his eyes, and said, "He's doing it again."

McGee and Ferrier were confused. "What?" they asked simultaneously.

"High levels of UV kill or maim plants, even the hardiest ones in Patagonia," Hunter explained. "Why couldn't we use a UV laser to kill or maim poppies in Afghanistan at night with a Night Rider? We could hit cocoa or marijuana, too."

The three men stared at him, trying to find words to respond.

After ten seconds, McGee said, "That's brilliant. I don't know what else to say. That is positively brilliant."

"I have to agree," Ferrier said. "That's a very interesting concept. Wouldn't take long to determine if someone else thought of it and patented it."

Lynche shook his head. "He does this shit to me all the time, but I have to admit this one sounds incredibly interesting. How'd you come up with that?"

"I had a physics professor who asked, 'How do you make a black hole using the escape velocity equation?'"

The three men stared at him, waiting for the rest of the story.

Hunter walked to the blackboard. "It goes something like this. Escape velocity is...." He wrote the equasion on the board.

"G is the universal gravitational constant, M the mass of the earth, and r is the distance from the center of gravity of the earth."

Ferrier, the engineer, nodded. "That looks right."

All three wondered how that connected with UV lasers and quiet airplanes.

"Something that isn't obvious is that black holes supposedly exist when light can't escape the gravitational pull of whatever you're trying to escape from. In this case, it's the earth. I told my physics professor that if we make V sub e equal to C, the speed of light, then the mass of a photon probably couldn't escape the gravitational pull.

"Since the other values are also constants, you turn the crank and do the math to solve for r, the only variable. So for the radius of the earth, if it were a black hole and weighed what it does today, it calculates to be the size of a medicine ball. Or something bigger than a breadbox.

"Anyway, I was thinking there had to be a similar equation that calculates the probability of kill based on some constants of dosage, dwell, and power. Move some figures around, and I think we could kill bad plants with high levels of UV. It's a function of power and maybe the type of UV. I know UV-C is lethal. Since UV's invisible to the eye, we could zap poppies at night, and no one would know we were there if we used a quiet airplane. The more I think of it, we wouldn't have to kill or torch them. I'll bet we could make them so sick, they couldn't bloom. A kill is a kill."

McGee shook his head and laughed. "Wow. That's amazing, Hunter." He turned to Lynche. "I asked Security to check out Duncan after we met. They pulled his military records and said he had a GT score of 154. No one ever saw that before and thought it was a misprint. It's pure fucking genius. That's what I just saw, and I still can't believe it. That's impressive, Sir."

"Only Duncan could go from ozone holes to black holes to killing poppies," Lynche said. "Hey, I just got it! Ozone holes to black holes. Black holes was an out-of-the-box solution, and so was the ozone hole. I think…"

Hunter looked a bit embarrassed. "Thank you, Sir. I have to say it was the easiest A I ever got in college. Dr. Simmons was so impressed by my answer, he said I just earned an A for the class. I thought he was BSing me, but he wasn't."

"Speaking of which," McGee said, "we have class tomorrow. What do you say you give that big brain of yours a rest, and I sit up front on the way back?"

Hunter gave a thumbs-up. Lynche grinned, and Ferrier smiled, shaking his head.

As the three men bid the Schweizer CEO farewell, they left the warm office building for 10°F sunshine and wind, walking quickly to the Skymaster. Lynche tossed his coat in the back seat and took the left seat to begin the checklists, while Hunter retrieved all the red engines covers and pulled the chocks. McGee waited outside until Hunter finished.

Hunter and McGee got in, tossing their coats into the back seat. Lynche started the engines, called Ground for taxi clearance, taxied to the hold short, set the GPS for Newport return, and received clearance.

"What do you think if we call it Weedbusters?" Hunter asked suddenly.

McGee turned with a big smile. "That has a nice ring to it. Now I'll have, 'Who you gonna call? Weed…busters,' running through my head for the next week."

Lynche took off. "Look for sailplanes. Sometimes they're

thick, but it might be too cold for flying. No heaters in a glider." He pointed out Harris Hill and the National Soaring Museum. "Your airplane."

McGee learned quickly and said, "My airplane," as his hands went to the yoke.

Over the interphone, Lynche said, "That was a lot easier than I expected. I'm not sure what else there is for us to do if Rob and Jones can work out a deal to support Bill's folks in the field. I'll see Rob this week at the yacht club and give you a status report. Bill, you might give it a couple days and ask your guys if everything's going well."

"This is so cool!" McGee said. "I never sat in the pilot's seat before. I appreciate your letting me fly."

As McGee piloted the Skymaster, Lynche showed him the instruments and the communication and navigation systems.

Hunter turned down the volume of the Bose noise-canceling headset and closed his eyes.

After scanning the horizon for traffic, Lynche glanced in the mirror and saw Hunter sleeping. "I guess using all that brainpower at one time is exhausting."

McGee, glancing back, saw Hunter raise his middle finger without opening his eyes. He smiled and said to Lynche, "I never expected to be doing anything like this. It's amazing what happens when you're around Duncan."

"You have no idea."

As Lynche gently bounced them to a landing, he told McGee, "I have to be careful when Duncan lands. He's so used to slamming an aircraft down on the carrier deck, I think he sometimes forgets he's in a Cessna, not a Phantom."

"Oh, yeah. They're so similar." All three men smiled like fools.

Ninety seconds after clearing the runway, Lynche parked in front of the FBO and set the front engine at idle with the prop feathered. Hunter and McGee said good-bye and crawled out of the airplane. Lynche checked the door was closed, waved, and powered away toward the runway.

Hunter and McGee went toward the double doors of the FBO to use the bathroom. They chatted as they walked toward their vehicles. Hunter saluted, as McGee suddenly disappeared out of sight between two cars.

Thinking his friend had fallen, Hunter raced around his car and saw him on his knees, studying the Riviera's underside.

"Old habits die hard," McGee explained. "You can never be sure if some husband or boyfriend would like to see me blown to pieces. I always check when I leave a vehicle parked for an extended period." He moved from the right rear to the right front, searching for anything out of the ordinary.

"That's smart," Hunter said. "I recall discussing doing that during SERE but never thought I needed to."

"Survival strategies, Duncan. In my line of work, they saved several guys here and overseas." After checking the left front wheel well, McGee stood, unlocked the car, and started to slide in. "It's too cold. I had a great time, Duncan. See you tomorrow."

Hunter waited outside his car, as the Riviera drove off. He paused, he looked around the parking lot before he dropped to hands and knees to take a cold, hard look at the race car's underside. "I'd know if I found something."

Seeing nothing out of the ordinary, he got in and started the low-slung beast. The engine rumbled softly, as huge volumes of hot gasses roiled from the dual exhaust in the subfreezing air, nearly enveloping the car in steam.

At the far end of the parking lot, a nasty-looking Honda with bad blue paint started its engine, too.

CHAPTER EIGHTEEN

1000 December 17, 2002 Scout Sniper School
Marine Corps Base
Camp Pendleton, California

"Sir, he's a natural shooter. We've seen a bunch of great shooters over the years come through here, but, as you know, some don't get the conceal-and-maneuver phase and wash out. He's struggling a little with C&M, because it's hard to hide when you're six-eight, but I thought he'd be OK. He's working hard, and you know we work with the ones who come close.

"The lad almost broke the all-time long-range record of seventy-two consecutive bulls' eyes at 1,000 yards at the West Coast meet last week. He was simply incredible. He hit seventy consecutive and won three gold medals, including overall champion.

"I don't know what to make of this report. It seems Miller is being investigated by the FBI for trying to locate and purchase a…." He checked his notes. "…a Unique Alpine TPG-1 with an integrally silenced barrel."

"Is it against the law to look for or purchase a sniper rifle?"

"Sir, that's a yes-and-no answer. It's not against the law to look at sniper rifles, as the basic weapon is considered a standard target rifle, chambered for a .338 or a magnum round where the ammo is commercially purchased."

"But…?"

"Yes, Sir. It's against the law to purchase silenced weapons and especially silencers. Guys go to jail for attempting to buy or make them."

"Ah. Well. Recommendations, Gunny?"

"Sir, he's almost finished with the program. Graduation is

157

next week. He's being investigated and will have to answer some questions. The FBI might not think anything of it, since these guys are being trained as scout snipers. Everyone here loves finely crafted, precision firearms. Half of this group are part-time armorers.

"On the other hand, there may be some imaginary line he crossed that makes him a person of interest. We'll have to work with him a little on concealment and maneuver, but he could be the greatest long-distance Marine scout sniper we ever produced."

"Gunny, I know you'll hate to lose him. Pull him off the program and assign him to the barracks until we get a read from the FBI."

"Wilco, Skipper," he said, feeling exasperated.

"Guns, I'll talk to Legal and see what else we need to do. I'll get back to you by the end of the day."

"Aye-aye, Sir."

CHAPTER NINETEEN

0200L January 15, 2003
White Mountains, Afghanistan

SEAL Team Six-Blue fanned out over the rocky terrain, night-vision goggles suspended in front of their eyes, scanning the mountaintop at 15,000 feet and three feet of snow. Video feed from the Schweizer Night Rider low-noise-profile aircraft, operated by a CIA Air Branch aircrew, provided the team wide-ranging thermal imaging of the battle space.

An Air Force AC-130 Spectre was on station twelve miles away in audio contact with the SEAL radioman and Night Rider. A dozen targets, probably Taliban and al-Qaeda, were on the back side of the mountain, trying to make tea and settle in for sleep. No one was at the top of the mountain, as that would silhouette them for snipers with night-vision scopes.

The sensor operator from the SA2-37B Night Rider broke the silence in the radioman's headset. "Apache, all known seven lookouts are on the north side having tea."

The radioman clicked the microphone twice to indicate acknowledgement.

The Tora Bora cave complex, locally known as Spin Ghar, was heavily protected from above and below by 300 Taliban and al-Qaeda fighters. This mountain had a dozen, while the surrounding hills had ten or more. The closer one flew toward Tora Bora, the more fighters were waiting and watching for US forces.

The group having tea was the first line of defense for protecting Black Cave and the Tora Bora entrance. The fifteen members of SEAL Team Six-Blue, code named Apache, led by twenty-two-year veteran Commander Robert "Roberto" Garcia, flew in from Kandahar to the base of the White Mountains by a single MH-47 Chinook, call sign Cochise, from the 160th SOAR.

Two days of concealed movement in their German military snow-camo gear brought them to the point of surprising the lookout team and trying to snatch the leaders for interrogation. The sensor operator in the Night Rider had a lock on which image was probably the leader. Even through the milky white images, it was clear which man commanded the most respect. The airborne eyeball provided the shooters on the ground a running dialog about where the other men were in proximity to their leader.

Apache's radioman, Dash 5, provided hand and arm signals to the main assault party. A raised index finger indicated priority one, the leader, then he told the others where the rest of the Taliban were. The smell of tea and unwashed Afghanis drifted toward the SEAL team, which was downwind.

Five SEALs crept into position, strung out from the edge of a boulder to the top of the mountain, their Tasers armed. The sensor operator from the Night Rider said, "Perfect placement."

Dash 5 clicked the interphone system in each SEAL's helmet three times, twice, then once.

Backed by five SEALs with silenced M-4s, five men simultaneously stepped from their concealed positions and fired Tasers into five surprised Taliban. The compressed nitrogen propellant ejected two bared darts that tore through the men's kurtas and slammed into their chests, sending 50,000 volts from the pistol grips. The insulated wires from the handgrips delivered a sizzling pulse of electricity, incapacitating the Afghanis' neuromuscular capability in microseconds.

All five Tasers hit the startled men center mass

simultaneously, rendering them momentarily unconscious. The two sleeping Taliban never woke. The two nearest SEALs double-tapped the men's heads with silenced Glocks. Contrary to what many thought, suppressed pistols were still very audible. At night, even a silenced weapon could be heard at great distances.

The SEALs employed a top-secret active noise-canceling system that effectively neutralized any sound coming from their silenced pistols. Flexible sensors weaved into the materials of their uniform forearms and chest protectors analyzed the sound from a noise source and generated another sound exactly out of phase with the incoming sound waves. The result was that a silenced Glock produced a personal sound shadow in which everything but the unwanted noise was audible. The SEALs called it *Pop Stop*.

The SEAL shooters holstered their Tasers and moved quickly to bind the Talibans' hands behind their backs with zip-cuffs and bound their feet with zip-ties. Duct tape strips were roughly placed over their mouths and beards.

Once all the Taliban were fully functional with eyes open, another SEAL injected a sedative into each man's arm. Another SEAL placed a black hood over their captives' heads.

In seconds, the trussed Taliban were sleeping. "Everyone OK?" Night Rider asked.

The radioman replied with a double click.

Commander Garcia ascertained that the op had gone according to plan, with five Taliban bundled for shipment to Kandahar. He flipped up his NVGs and jerked up the hoods of the sleeping prisoners for a closer look.

Twelve minutes after Apache clicked "go," Commander Garcia radioed Cochise they were ready for extraction. Night Rider monitored the other outposts, as Cochise closed on the pickup point.

Aboard the helicopter, Commander Garcia moved to the front of the helicopter and handed the pilot a note to transmit to the command post, which read, One Sierra, four Alphas. They had one Saudi and four al-Qaeda, not Taliban.

Apache radioed Night Rider. "Thanks for the great support, November Romeo. I hope we get to work with you again in the near future. My skipper was very impressed and wanted me to tell you, 'Nice job.'"

"Our pleasure," Night Rider replied. "Know we got you on tape. It'll be at the JSOC tent tomorrow if you want it. Safe travels, Apache, and Godspeed."

"You, too, November Romeo."

CHAPTER TWENTY

0115L January 19, 2003 White Mountains
Nangarhar Province, Afghanistan

Night Rider relayed targeting data to the four SEAL Team Six snipers, first from the FLIR systems' nine-inch ball and TALON IR laser designator, then audio.

"I see three bogeys moving your way. I'm painting the lead dog now. Laser hot!" The Night Rider sensor operator lased the leader with the LD.

Through the 5X60 night-vision scope on the heavily silenced TCI Model 89 Sniper Rifle, the bright-green dot marked the spot. The sniper quickly acquired the target, and his laser rangefinder flashed, 620 yards. The 7.62mm hollow-point left the silenced rifle and hit the lead Taliban right above the heart, passing through his body to strike the number two Taliban below the sternum. Both men went down instantly.

Night Rider lased Taliban number three, as he tried to reverse course and seek shelter, but Sniper Team Two had already acquired the target. In two seconds, he, too, was down. The bullet tore his spine in two, pulverizing vertebrae and spinal cord. He was dead before his head hit the ground.

Before Night Rider could say, "Three down," the sensor operator was surprised to find two new heat sources directly below and to the left of where the Taliban went down.

"Hold your position. Two new bogeys popped out of a hole. They know something happened to their buddies and are afraid to come out and see."

"Can you paint him?"

"Painting now."

Through the NV scope, the target was barely visible, but Night Rider placed the LD dot on the Taliban's forehead. He was zooming in the FLIR for a better view when the Taliban's head exploded in the FLIR's scope display.

"Nice shot. That reminds me of Whack a Mole. I don't see any other activity, but I'm calling in a JDAM to plug that hole."

"OK. We're out of here. Thanks for the help."

Night Rider remained on station, as the sniper teams advanced farther into Tora Bora.

Seventeen minutes later, an Air Force F-16 at 35,000 feet released the first pair of Laser Joint Direct Attack Munitions, L-JDAMS, onto the well-hidden Taliban cave. Riding the beam from the Night Rider, the laser seekers on the converted 500-pound guided ordnance hit their target perfectly just as another Talban cautiously tried to take a peek without getting his head blown off like his brother.

CHAPTER TWENTY-ONE

2100 January 27, 2003
Al-Azzam Islamic Center Boston, Massachusetts

Marwa Kamal was proving to be an interesting Muslima, thought the imam. Educated as a lawyer in the US three years earlier, Marwa Kamal was once active in a youth group at Yale that fought discrimination against Muslims. Born into a wealthy family in Jordan, she attended the best schools in Britain and then law school in the US before being summoned home after 9/11. Her father was furious about her extracurricular activities—joining a pro-Muslim support group that challenged the stereotypes that often associated Muslims with violence and terror. She should be seen and not heard. She brought shame and discredit to her family.

Her father quickly arranged her marriage to a man who promised not to beat her if they married. Of course, he did. She grew discontent, rebelled, and planned her escape. Knowing her husband would sit with his fat friends smoking shisha at the hookah lounge, she left her husband's apartment in a royal-blue cashmere abaya with a button-down front. After applying eye makeup, she ensured the buttons were undone.

She took one look at the room, picked up a small bag, and walked down Shara Street to Prince Faisal bin al-Hussein Square, which US, British, and Australian embassy personnel and tourists frequented, and where the open-air hookah lounge was situated.

Women wearing headscarves were common in the square, but women in abayas were rare. When she approached the hookah and saw her husband chatting with two women without headscarves, she stopped and shouted, "Waleed!"

The stuporous man removed the pipe from his mouth and stared as the woman in the abaya grasped the flaps, ripped opened the fabric, and flashed her large naked breasts for everyone in the lounge.

Two US Embassy Marines and a group of Australian tourists were passing when Marwa told her husband he'd never see those breasts again.

"That's something you don't see every day in Jordan," one Marine told the other.

All who saw Marwa were stunned by the incongruity of the scene. A young woman unable to show her face but exposing her beautiful breasts, curvaceous body, and white ruffled bloomers with coils of chastity knots off her hip... right across the street from a McDonald's.

Several photographers nearly missed the event, but one amazing picture was soon uploaded to the Internet. Marwa covered her body, turned, and walked to the cab stand.

He had hit her and bruised her face, which spurred Marwa to change her life and go where life would be infinitely better. Her student visa was still good for multiple entries, so she took the first jet bound for America out of Amman.

After landing at Boston Logan, she migrated to the other women working at the airport concessions. Soon, she worked in one of the concourses at a grab-and-go restaurant that didn't serve pork. Several men working as screeners, running the X-ray machines at the security gate, began courting her. All heads turned when she walked by.

Mild pandemonium erupted, as word spread quickly, as she approached the checkpoint coming to work or leaving the concourse for home. Many tried to get to know her, but she showed no interest.

Nizar Mohammad was more successful than others to get her to acknowledge him. He was a screener at Boston Logan after 9/11. He eventually passed a background check and was hired by the Transportation Security Administration. He became a supervisor at one of the concourses.

When Nizar Mohammad was away from the airport, he served Allah and provided his imam with information about the comings and goings of the traveling public, as well as how poor airport security remained even after being federalized when ten al-Qaeda terrorists passed through the checkpoint on their way to destiny.

Nizar leaked information to the imam of the stunning woman's beauty and American education, adding he wished to pursue her.

Imam Abdul asked, "What do you know of this woman? Where did she come from? Why does she refuse to wear the hajib?"

"She says she's from Kuwait, but she sounds British and looks more like an Iranian."

"Find out more. Can you get picture? I want picture of her."

CHAPTER TWENTY-TWO

2145L January 29, 2003
JSOC Command Post Khost, Afghanistan

"Killing the enemy is the easy part," the JSOC commander told the Night Rider crew. "Finding them is the hard part. You guys are doing the Lord's work in finding the enemy."

Unspoken was the lack of USAF Predator support. Thequality of Night Rider's intelligence was timely, on target, and actionable, while the high-flying Predator feeds lacked the level of granularity necessary to keep the nation's finest warriors up-to- date with on-scene details, like whether the images were children or men.

During two missions, Night Rider not only found the enemy and positively identified them as bad guys, but they helped kill them with pinpoint, steady, laser-designator accuracy. Forward air controllers wished they could be as effective.

The CIA men, Ben and Jerry, the pilot, and sensor operator did more to help SEALs and JSOC find the enemy, especially at night, than any other available resource. The JSOC commander didn't know how the Schweizer came to be part of his Task Force, but he was damn glad they were there. The next time he saw the DCI, he'd personally thank him and let him know that his little airplane allowed his SEALs to live up to the sniper motto, "One shot, one kill."

When he uttered the motto to himself, the JSOC commander had a flashback. For three seconds, he thought of his mother, a beautiful lady with jet-black hair. Her no-BS personality raised three very competitive boys and kept his dad in line, too.

He recalled the time he and his father went on their first deer-hunting trip in the Colorado Rockies. Their destination was Meeker. Since his father recently retired and returned from tours in Germany and Vietnam, he and his father didn't have any rifles or the other necessary hunting equipment for the trip.

It was a big deal for a family with a limited income to go to the downtown Gart Brothers store in Denver, where Dad bought an elegant Winchester Model 70A 300 Magnum, while he got a generic sporterized 30.06 with four-power scopes, sleeping bags, a tent, and a couple boxes of ammunition for each gun.

After driving up to Meeker on Friday night, the future JSOC commander and his father bagged two huge four-point bucks within thirty minutes of opening day of deer season— one shot, one kill. They raced home to show the family, feeling like hunters, not gatherers.

Mom wasn't impressed. "We spent almost a thousand dollars for rifles and hunting equipment, and both of you took one shot to kill one deer. That's the most-expensive venison in America. We could've bought two Angus heifers." She shook her head and walked away.

The thought faded, and the JSOC commander found himself smiling and unconsciously shaking his head at the thought of his mother poking at her hunting men about one shot, one kill. He now extolled the same virtues of his hunter-killers.

Still smiling, he looked at the SCIF to find everyone looking at him. He took a deep breath and said, "God bless the mothers of warriors."

A couple of "Hooyahs!" reverberated through the room, then he returned to his SEAL and Night Rider missions.

As the Night Rider crew left for their aircraft, the JSOC turned to his Air Operations commander. "If their rate of success keeps up, there may be room for more of those quiet aircraft in theater. So far, those things are a gold mine."

* * *

The Night Rider men took off east to support a significant SEAL surveillance party with two snipers. Intelligence reported a large Taliban meeting would take place in the little village of Pomma. The SEALs wanted to snatch a couple of the leaders, which would mean mission success. If a snatch-and-grab was out of the question, the goal was to ensure the Taliban didn't live to fight another day.

The mountains were curiously free of Taliban and al-Qaeda on the run to the target. Off to the south, an IR strobe flashed twice, twice, and three times.

"Apache, tally on your position." Two clicks sounded.

"Tally-ho on the compound. Several kids marching are around, not looking too happy."

The Taliban leaders woke the hamlet's children and paraded them around the walled compound as insurance. USAF Predators wouldn't knowingly drop a Hellfire when children were visible.

After four full turns in the air, they saw movement in the compound. A head stuck out the door and looked around. The children jumped and walked faster around the building. Seconds later, a steady stream of men of relatively the same height poured from the building and quickly entered five Toyota Hilux pickups and a Landcruiser parked nearby.

"Those are Hiluxes," Jerry said. "Since when do the Taliban drive Hiluxes?"

"Al-Qaeda lieutenants drive them. Osama's main ride is a Landcruiser. Doesn't Omar like a Suburban? Let them know those are Hiluxes and a Landcruiser. Please tell me one of those turds is over six feet."

"Apache, I have six rides coming your way, Hiluxes and a Landcruiser. Certain they're AQ. No tall cowboys in the posse."

Two clicks came in return.

At the sound of the vehicles starting and driving from the compound, Night Rider noticed several heat sources popping up along the valley walls. Two were below the SEALs' outpost, and three popped up above the SEALs. The area must have been a warren of caves that hid security forces from IR eyes.

"Shit! Apache, there are tens of AQ pouring out of caves and moving toward the vehicles' line of departure. I think you need to get out of there. Now!"

"Standby."

"Negative standby. Apache, you have a squad of four twenty- five meters to your south, heading your way. I don't think they know you're there. There's another squad of five above you, about forty meters to your west, also moving your way."

"We need to stop those vehicles. Paint the lead, please. Then targets of opportunity."

"Those fuckers are crazy," Jerry said softly to Ben.

Night Rider quickly refocused the laser designator on the vehicles. "Painting now."

The lead vehicle moved slowly, as Jerry placed the LD dot on the driver's door. Four seconds later, Night Rider confirmed the impact and targeted the second vehicle. Jerry swore momentarily when he saw the bullet slam into the driver's back. In the FLIR, something obviously happened to the lead Hilux, as it began to slow.

Night Rider was unaware of two SEALs moving to intercept the two AQ fire teams moving their way. With the butt plate lodged firmly in their shoulders and eyes focused in NV scopes, they easily found the enemy within fifty feet— point-blank kinetic action range. Each SEAL thumbed the selector level to single on his silenced M-4 and popped off single rounds into the heads of the fighters moving toward them. Most were killed with one shot. Pop Stop squashed the reports.

One AQ with two shots to the head fell backward with his finger trapped in the trigger guard of his AK-47. When he hit the ground, his twisted finger pulled the trigger, sending a burst of rounds into the air and alerting everyone in the valley. Simultaneously, as the second vehicle in the convoy rolled to a stop, the other vehicles dispersed.

"Paint the Landcruiser," Apache ordered.

Night Rider acquired the racing Landcruiser, heading for the valley outlet. As long as the Toyota moved linearly, at that altitude, he easily lased the vehicle's driver door.

"Painting now."

Two SEAL snipers pumped four shots into the Landcruiser. Two seconds passed before the vehicle went ballistic and caromed into a medium-sized boulder and stopped.

"Check my status?" Apache asked coolly.

Night Rider slewed the FLIR turret to the IR strobe to locate the SEAL team. "I have several dozen bogeys heading your way."

Jerry looked up to the RMI to determine their heading and did some quick mental math. "Most moving in from the north. I think it's time to get out of there."

"Can you give Spooky a call and give them a vector? I'm going to be busy."

"Ten-four, Apache. Keep your head down. We'll work on getting the cavalry here ASAP."

Ben immediately called the AC-130H gunship, passing on the request and Apache's frequency, and coordinated their location to be opposite of the angle of fire.

At twelve miles away, the AC-130 crew fire-walled the throttles of the four Allison T56 turboprops and closed the gap in less than two minutes.

The FLIR operator quickly located the SEAL teams. "Tally-ho on your beacons. Take cover. Incoming."

Apache's radio operator and the rest of the SEAL team hunkered down behind the biggest rock they could find and rolled themselves into balls to protect themselves against ricochets from the two 20mm M61 Vulcan cannons that raked the Taliban and al- Qaeda. They heard rounds strike the ground and crack off rocks, then the low growl of the rotary cannon at high altitude.

The four-second burst from the M61s spat 5,000 rounds and decimated the enemy, setting two of the vehicles afire.

"Shit," Jerry muttered in the Night Rider.

The M61s lit the sky, silhouetting the big Hercules momentarily from hot rounds and tracers leaving the barrels.

Ten seconds passed.

"I think our work here is done," Specter transmitted. "We're outta here unless you have something else for us."

"Thanks, Spooky," Apache said. "Nice work. I'll buy the beer when I see you. Out."

JSOC's SEALs and the AC-130 killed so many enemy forces that the dead bodies of the Taliban and al-Qaeda fighters were carted off the field the next day by the truckload.

CHAPTER TWENTY-THREE

0715 February 7, 2003
Henry E. Eccles Library Navy War College

McGee nearly collided with Hunter going into the library. "Good morning, Sir."

"SCIF." It was a command.

"After you, Sir." Hunter followed the SEAL on a mission.

Once inside the SCIF in Eccles, McGee led the way to their table. "I just got some feedback. Lynche's old place has been flying support for my guys, and the results have been fantastic."

"That sounds great."

"JSOC and SOCOM want more quiet airplanes in the AOR."

"OK."

"I thought we could do something from here." "Like what?"

"You're the one with the big brain."

"What are you trying to accomplish with quiet aircraft? Sounds like you have an idea."

"It might be a bad idea."

"Nothing is as toxic as a really bad idea. I doubt you have a bad idea, Sir."

"Maybe we could do something like working on integrating quiet aircraft for DEVGRU. Maybe something unmanned."

Hunter smiled, reached down, and placed his black Zero Halliburton briefcase on the table. Opening it, he handed a folder to McGee. "This is my unclassified research proposal for doing just such a project. I hope the Office of Naval Intelligence will approve it. I have another proposal for developing quiet UAVs. These will be classified research, and we need to get the War College President to approve them.

Want to team on one or the other or both?"

"Hell, yes!" He lifted his eyes from the inch-thick proposals. "You're amazing. Can I read these?"

"Yes, Sir. Take your time."

"Meet you in the café after class?"

"Sir, I think we have an all-hands lecture in Connelly at 1000."

"That's right. See you there."

"Roger."

CHAPTER TWENTY-FOUR

1115 February 7, 2003
Connelly Hall, Naval War College

Hunter and McGee took their usual places in the front of the auditorium. Rear Admiral DiFilippo just finished speaking, and the assembly was dismissed when Duncan's eyes met the admiral's.

"Mr. Hunter, may I have a word with you?" the admiral asked.

"Yes, Sir."

The admiral, stepping down from the stage, offered his hand to Hunter, then McGee.

"I understand you're quite the racquetball aficionado," the admiral said.

"Sir, he beat a pro a couple months ago," McGee said. "I saw it. He's awesome."

"Really? Well, that's helpful. In mid-April, we go to Carlisle, the Army War College, for Jim Thorpe Days. It's a track-and-field meet between the war colleges. Navy rarely wins anything at Jim Thorpe."

"Sir, do they have a racquetball competition?" Hunter asked.

"They do. Would you be able to participate?"

"Sir, I can't promise you a gold medal, but I promise to bring back something. I can't imagine any of the other war colleges having the talent we have here at Newport."

"We have some good players here?" Rear Admiral DiFilippo asked.

"Yes, Sir, we do."

"Hold it," McGee said to Hunter. "Do you think anyone can beat you?"

"That's not the issue. Usually, there are rules in place to

negate a ringer, and I'd likely be considered one. Here's how they do it. They make a team identify their A and B players. Then, most likely, they'll have a couple more people who aren't as good who play doubles. Then a team has a chance of getting three points per school. The best two out of three matches wins.

"So let's say Army and Navy have the same score going in, like six to six. The winning team just has to take two games to win the championship. All the schools bring in a ringer and try to outfit a B player while they hope for a miracle on a doubles team."

"I just want to win something," the rear admiral said. "I don't want a repeat of last year, where we didn't win anything."

"Sir, we'll bring you home something heavy. I'm old and treacherous when it comes to this stuff. I'll organize a team and a winning strategy."

"Sir, we might need your help in another area," McGee said.

"What do you need?"

"Permission to conduct some classified research."

"Topic?"

"Integration of quiet aircraft into DEVGRU. We could give you a brief."

"That sounds interesting. Why do you need my permission?"

"We're told only the President of the War College can authorize classified research. We think we'll have to make a couple of trips to Suitland, Sir."

Rear Admiral DiFillipo smiled. "For you two, permission granted."

"Can I get your John Hancock on this form, Sir?"

He smiled as he signed. "You'll have to let me know when you're done. I'll be interested in your paper." He looked at Hunter. "A gold medal at Jim Thorpe would be nice."

Hunter smiled. "Can do easy, Sir."

As the admiral reached to shake Hunter's hand, he

noticed McGee studying the Royal Saudi and Royal Jordanian Navy commanders sitting together at the rear of the class, chatting among themselves. No other foreign officers remained in the auditorium.

CHAPTER TWENTY-FIVE

2200 February 7, 2003
Al-Azzam Islamic Center

Nizar held a photograph in one hand as he knocked on the door. It opened slowly. Imam Abdul looked at him, then at the offered photo. With the touch of a pickpocket, he drew the photograph from the man's dirty fingers and held the flimsy copy paper to the light. He was impressed.

"Your beauty is striking, worthy of Allah, peace be upon Him," he muttered to the photo. "But you are a whore."

A notion he'd been formulating for days came into focus. Marwa might be useful. First, though, he needed to know more. "She's fair, Nizar. What more have you?"

"Sahib, I was able to see her passport. I stopped her, as she tried to entire the concourse to work. She's Jordanian. Her name is indeed Marwa Kamal."

"Go. I must think."

The 9/11 Commission learned that al-Qaeda relied on a trusted network of a dozen hawala dealers to move money and information around the globe. One of the only two who escaped the dragnet of investigations after the terrorist attacks of September 11 was Abdul Abdullah, or Imam Abdul. The other was his cousin, Imam Atef, in Amman, Jordan. Atef considered it an honor to find more information on the woman.

"Fax the photograph," Atef said. "I work."

CHAPTER TWENTY-SIX

1100 February 14, 2003
Al-Azzam Mosque

The hawaladar in Amman engaged his network of runners and spies. A runner carried money if the amount was small or slips of information announcing the money transfer between the hawala headquarters and the recipient of the transaction. Armed with a photo of Marwa Kamal, a young runner found someone who recognized her.

Imam Atef quickly knew who she was. She fled her husband, a relative of a Saudi family. She shamed him, and the husband would kill her if he saw her again. The disgraced husband blamed the father, who knew his daughter fled to America and continued to send her money, so she didn't have to live in squalor like other Muslim women overseas.

"Nizar, the sacred text says men are in charge," Abdul said. "The Holy Quran says a woman is worth only half as much as a man. It says men can beat their property if the woman gets out of line. That is the way Allah, peace be upon Him, ordained it.

"Men can do no wrong, and everything is to be blamed on the woman. That's why we beat, stone, or hang women for being raped. It's their fault. They caused a man to behave badly, as he sullied another man's property. It's an outrage. That's how Allah, peace be upon Him, ordained it. She has wronged two men indirectly, including all her male relatives. She has sullied her family's honor, and she must pay for her transgressions."

The imam stroked his beard several times. "Nizar, you still desire this woman who has sullied her family?"

"Yes, Sahib. She can make much money, and I'll make sure she pays for her transgressions every day."

"Nizar, Inshallah, I hope you aren't making a big mistake. Bring this Marwa to me. I must be satisfied she won't dishonor you, my son. Bring her, and I will help rehabilitate her."

* * *

Two days later, a proud, beaming Nizar stood beside the head-covered Marwa Kamal. Abdul sent Nizar to sit in the antechamber and commanded Marwa to sit in the chair near the little man's overflowing desk.

"Marwa, I have heard many things about you. Nizar likes you very much. I understand all the men at the airport desire you. What say you, Marwa?"

"I'm not interested in any of them, Sahib. I just want to work and be left alone."

"The airport job is beneath you." He paused for effect; the woman fidgeted and was very uncomfortable. She looked at her feet. "You're a lawyer, Marwa? Do you miss Waleed?"

Hearing her husband's name made her jump. Her head shot up, her heart slammed in her chest, and her eyes shot to the closed door. She couldn't run. Stunned and trapped, she trembled, unable to speak.

Abdul slowly paced in the tiny office; two steps forward, reversed, and two steps back before starting over. He allowed Marwa Kamal to shudder for a long time. He stopped his pacing and asked, "Are you a servant of Allah, Marwa?"

She fought to remain calm. Taking several deep breaths, she finally said, "Yes, Imam Abdul, of course. I'm employed at the airport."

"I'm sure your husband is worried about you, a beautiful woman in a land of heathens and infidels."

Marwa's knees began to knock, thinking the imam would touch her. She didn't want to return to Jordan. She wanted to leave the room.

"I need you to do something for me, Marwa."

"Yes, Sahib." Shaking, she tensed, awaiting his touch.

"I want you to leave your job under good terms. I want you to return to the airport after you're done with a project. You're a good Muslim woman, Marwa. Aren't you?"

"I try, Sahib. Inshallah."

"What I have in mind can't be discussed with anyone outside of this room. This is very important, and I can't let anyone else do what must be done. Can I trust you, Marwa?"

She was curious yet still very afraid. The man's tone suggested he wanted something other than sex. "Yes, Imam Abdul. Of course. What do you wish me to do?" Her voice trembled, and she broke into a sweat, praying she didn't misread the tone in the man's voice and would have to touch him.

"I want you to meet an American man. Find out as much about him as possible. He'll find you very beautiful, Marwa, and I think he'll find it very difficult to ignore you. He'll want to talk to you, take you to dinner. You'll have to go without a head scarf. Can you do that?"

Marwa stopped shaking. She looked up at the imam. "This is very important, yes?" Confused, she was still anxious to leave the room.

"Very important, my child." He touched her cheek and placed his other hand on her trembling shoulder.

"What do you need me to do?"

CHAPTER TWENTY-SEVEN

1715 February 26, 2003
Newport Athletic Club

The imam's watchers did a good job of documenting the infidel's movements. As it had every Wednesday for several months, the black Silverado pickup came into view at approximately 5:15 PM, leaving the Navy base's north gate and headed to the Newport Athletic Club. The watchers reported Hunter visited the fitness center every Wednesday at the same time for two hours. Following orders, they never entered the club to see what the infidel did.

Marwa Kamal moved to Newport. The imam found an immaculate red Mercedes SL380 for her to drive, as Commander Jebriel reported the civilian had an eye for flashy cars and beautiful women. She was given a credit card to buy a membership and a decadent wardrobe that included fitness center clothes. She also had a swimsuit in case the target opted to swim in the club's indoor pool.

Marwa still didn't understand why she was chosen for the assignment. The previous week, she left her aerobics class to sit directly in the center of the stadium seats of the glass-walled court to watch the game of racquetball.

Hunter would have been blind not to notice her. On the first day, when she walked along the elevated seating to find a place, Hunter chased a ball to the back wall and glimpsed the leggy brunette. He tried to remember why he was in the racquetball court, lost focus, swung his racquet, and missed the little blue ball completely. The follow-through upset his balance, and he cartwheeled to the floor.

Laying there, looking up at the lights, he shouted, "Hinder!"

His doubles teammate asked incredulously at Hunter

laying on the floor, "Hinder?"

"I couldn't concentrate with that dark-haired goddess sitting there."

The pause in the game became comical, as other men tried to inconspicuously peek at the stunning brunette in a puffy white leotard with her breasts bubbling from the top. Duncan rolled to his knees and stood.

Folding her arms over the gentle swell of her breasts, she tossed her head innocently. Her long black ponytail floated free until the mane rested on her shoulder, spilling an avalanche of shiny hair across her chest.

As Hunter and the men played, he stole glances at her through the glass wall. Why was she so intently interested in a bunch of old guys playing with a little blue ball? The other women in the club rarely glanced into the court filled with superannuated racquetball champions. She seemed fragile compared to the women he'd known since his active duty days. With her obvious Middle Eastern looks, she was interesting. Nothing like that happened to him before. She was breathtaking, and, while his curiosity was stoked, he didn't want to believe it was mere curiosity on her part that brought her there.

The men played for two hours. She sat there, totally engrossed by the man she was to spy on and befriend. When the men finished, they moved outside the court. They chatted, gathered their racquetball bags and towels, and left the court.

As Duncan gathered his belongings and pulled a towel from his bag, he looked up at the woman who crossed her legs like long tailoring scissors. They made eye contact and smiled.

"Do you play?" he asked casually.

She thought the question could be interpreted two ways, but she merely said, "No. I do not play. You are very good. I would be very bad. I swim and do aerobics."

She was a striking beauty, an intoxicating combination of intrigue and innocence. He detected a slight British accent coming from her full auburn lips, but she didn't look like she was from England. Her olive skin, high cheekbones, and small, round nose made it difficult to place her. She was definitely Middle Eastern but not Egyptian, Saudi, or Paki. Her eyes weren't heavily made up but flashed platinum green with hazel flecks.

Then it struck him—Iranian? One part of her demeanor oozed sensuality while another suggested timidity. Duncan thought she seemed out of place in the club. Her tight white leotard looked new, as it emphasized her full bosom, tiny waist, and shapely legs. Her shoes looked new, but so were his.

Duncan convinced himself the breasts were natural, not bought, and her dark legs were firm and shaved smooth. Long, jet- black hair pulled back over her ears into a ponytail framed her amazing face. He was almost lost in her eyes, and his curiosity was roused, like moving the throttles from his old jet from idle to max.

He remained polite and smiling, as he checked her hand for a ring. Completely at a loss for something bright to say, he said, "I think it's the best sport. It's great exercise, and these guys are a lot of fun." He maintained eye contact as he bent over, untied his court shoes, and placed them in his bag.

"You look like you were having a very good time," she said.

"These guys are great—wonderful players and absolute gentlemen. They're former national champions who invite me to play doubles every Wednesday. I think I give them good competition, and we have a good time."

Slipping his feet into running shoes, he toweled his sweating head and damp arms, then he began to change his drenched shirt for a dry one, then stopped.

"I must be going," he said. "The life of a student is never done." He took a black zippered sweatshirt and sweatpants from his bag and pulled them on.

She responded thoughtfully, as he dressed, "You're a student?" The question almost sounded meek.

He nodded. "I'm at the Naval War College."

She watched his movements, unable to believe he was the man the imam wanted to know more about. He was older and more beautiful than his photograph, gracefully athletic, with eyes and a voice that made her warm all over. She was embarrassed that he stirred a burning between her thighs. His comment that he was leaving caught her off guard. She gathered her coat and jumped up to go with him.

Hunter didn't anticipate that she'd walk out with him. He slung the huge bag over his shoulder and started up the stairs. "See you…. Oh. You're leaving, too?"

"Yes. I should be going home."

He stopped to let her catch up. Holding out his hand, he said, "Duncan Hunter."

She was momentarily conflicted. She was still a married Muslim woman, and it was forbidden for another man to touch her.

Their eyes locked. She reached out and firmly shook his hand. "Marwa Kamal. Very nice to meet you, Duncan Hunter."

CHAPTER TWENTY-EIGHT

2020 February 28, 2003
Al-Azzam Islamic Center

War college surveillance indicated Hunter was frequently the topic of the female students. Issues of fraternization and competing services overwhelmed most desires among the single students, of which there were twenty percent, male and female. Jebriel noticed Hunter warmly engaged female students, while McGee didn't. Hunter often met with female students for breakfast at the school's café. McGee didn't. When Hunter met McGee, they walked quietly to the large library and entered the room he heard someone call a skiff.

Jebriel learned from day one that international students didn't have the authority or clearance to enter the Sensitive Compartmented Information Facility, or SCIF. He tried several times to engage the civilian infidel in conversation without success. Hunter was always polite but refused to talk much with the Muslim students.

When Jebriel overheard one of the female students say, "Hunter makes my panties wet," he acquiesced to the notion that a woman could get close to the infidel, so he dutifully reported the comment and his assessment to his handler, the Imam Abdul.

Allah provided when the beautiful Marwa arrived in Boston. Allah always did. Their al-Qaeda sponsor wanted to know more about the civilian, especially when Abdul received a financial report on Duncan Hunter.

The infidel is a millionaire?" he asked. "How is that possible? He doesn't act like he has much money. There is much more to this man than meets the eye. We must find out more about him. Why is he always with the SEAL McGee?"

The Saudi sponsor wanted that information and more

concerning Hunter and McGee, so he pushed money into the imam's accounts. Once Marwa agreed to befriend the civilian and learn more about him, she was given a nice apartment in Newport. The imam had it bugged for sound and planted cameras in the bedroom, hoping Marwa could get the infidel to talk or at least reveal some useful information in a compromising position. She did well gaining his attention for the last two weeks.

"Ask him to dinner," Abdul told her. "American men can't say no to a beautiful woman."

CHAPTER TWENTY-NINE

1720 March 5, 2003
Newport Athletic Club

Hunter felt it was synchronicity. He walked in, showed his pass at the front desk, and entered the glass court just as Marwa stepped from the aerobics room, drank water from a fountain, and walked toward the courts. They exchanged smiles. He was surprised to see her, and it was obvious she was interested in him. Something about her tickled the back of his mind, though. It seemed safe enough to ask her to dinner.

She was thrilled to see him and planned to ask him to dinner if he didn't ask first. As Hunter prepared to play racquetball, they chatted. Some would have called it flirting.

Before entering the court, he looked at her hard, searching for a word. His mind defaulted to breathtaking. Something about her also screamed, Danger! Danger!

Her heart pounded in her chest. He was an infidel and an enemy of Allah, but he was very good looking. Something about him screamed, Danger! Danger!

CHAPTER THIRTY

1930 March 8, 2003
The Red Parrot Newport, Rhode Island

The weather appeared it would hold off for a few more hours, as the 1938 white Rolls Royce Phantom III pulled up to the apartments overlooking the Atlantic. Duncan Hunter opened the suicide door, stepped from the back seat, and turned to the driver, noticing the words printed on the horn button—Soft/Loud.

Only a Rolls, he thought. "I shouldn't be long." He tapped the driver's door sill and stepped away.

When he turned, he glimpsed a dark-haired woman in the doorway of the upstairs apartment. That could be her. Then again, maybe not.

Before he could start up the cascading stairway, Marwa Kamal stepped from her apartment, shawl in one hand, waving to Duncan with the other. Her little white turtleneck dress hugged every curve. Long, wavy hair spilled across her shoulders like a black wave and obscured part of her face.

Hunter froze. His heart pounded. He couldn't take his eyes off of the woman.

Under his breath, the driver of the Rolls Royce muttered, "Nice job."

He regained some of his lost composure. "I think I'll just stand right here," Duncan breathed.

The driver offered moral support. "Good idea. I think this was the right car for tonight." Hunter, still gaping, nodded.

As she approached, Duncan spread his arms wide. "Marwa, you're absolutely breathtaking."

Her perfume was strong and exotic, almost cinnamon. "Thank you. This is your car?" She offered her hand, and he took it gently, guiding her the rest of the way to the Rolls.

190

She was coyly confused.

"Our car for tonight. My old truck seemed a bit too scruffy for dinner." He opened the door and held her hand as she slid in butt first, knees together, bright red heels lifted over the sill. Her eyes remained on his.

He raced around the back of the large old car and slid in. "The Red Parrot, James."

Marwa brushed hair back from her face. "This is a beautiful car. I've never seen one like this before." The rear seating area featured a small bar with crystal decanter and two wine goblets. She recognized the ancient radio, heater, and clock but couldn't comprehend why a huge speedometer was so prominently displayed. Small cane strips on the doors offset their topaz leather handles.

"James tells me it's a 1938 Rolls Royce Phantom III, or a P3. I saw this car several weeks ago in front of a church, waiting to take a bride and groom from their wedding. I thought it might be a little too much, but now, I think it was the right car for tonight. When you step out in front of the restaurant, everyone will think you're a movie star."

There was a delayed smile and some rapid blinking when Duncan mentioned bride and groom, and he noticed immediately. She tried hard to flush all thoughts of Jordan from her mind and calm herself, relax, and enjoy the night. She couldn't have anticipated such an elegant vehicle and had no experience with such an ostentatious display of wealth. She could hardly believe what was happening to her.

"So, we're going to a red parrot?"

He turned to face her. "The Red Parrot. It's one of the nicer restaurants in Newport. They have great steaks and salads, and the ambiance is wonderful. I hope you like it."

"I'm sure I will." Her accent thrilled him. She slid her hand across soft leather into his.

When she moved, Duncan caught another whiff of perfume. While the driver negotiated the antique limousine through downtown Newport, Duncan provided a running commentary of some of the historical landmarks, including the National Tennis Club, the Naval Academy building during the Civil War, and the summer homes of the rich and famous.

"Marwa, I must tell you that the locals will fall all over themselves when we drive up, and you get out. If you see someone fall or walk into a post, just look at me and try not to laugh."

"You're very funny." Flashing perfect teeth, she lowered her head slightly, which accentuated her cheekbones and stunning sensuality.

"Oh, we'll see." He squeezed her hand gently, and she returned the pressure.

As the Rolls glided to the front of the Red Parrot, several dozen heads moved in unison, following the rare car to a stop, trying to look inside the darkened windows. The driver leaped from the right door and smoothly opened the rear one.

Duncan stepped out and walked around the rear of the car when Marwa swung out her legs wrapped in misty black hose. A little embarrassed, she offered her hand to Duncan, and he allowed her to pull herself to her feet.

Heads craned for a better look, and a local yokel lost his footing and fell off the curb, crashing heavily into a parked car. Marwa retained her grip on Duncan's hand and looked at him with a mischievous smile.

Hunter smiled back and mouthed, "I told you."

The couple turned heads as they walked into the restaurant, and a hundred eyes followed them to their table.

"I have to tell you, Ms. Kamal, you know how to make an entrance," Hunter said.

"I'm glad I had something to wear." She draped the shawl over her shoulders, crossing the ends to conceal her breasts.

He pulled a chair out for her. Marwa wasn't certain what he intended, but she stepped in front of it and sat. He sat beside her, not across the table. A waiter hovered nearby. The air carried the scents of cinnamon and charred beef.

"Water? Wine? Something to drink?" Duncan asked. *Those eyes are incredible.*

"Water with lemon."

"Same for me. Thank you."

The waiter flitted off in a hurry.

"Are you having a good time so far?" He slid his hand across the table and gently took her fingers. She glided her hand into his and squeezed, moving incrementally closer until their knees touched. She didn't look away.

"Yes."

"You make it very difficult for me to concentrate playing racquetball. I almost hurt myself when I saw you sitting there the first time. After that, I tried really hard not to look like an idiot on the court."

"I don't think that is possible. You play very well. I never saw anyone play racquet…ball before. It's very interesting. The ball moves so fast, sometimes I don't see it."

"The guys on the court agreed with me that you have the most striking eyes we ever saw."

"Thank you."

"And, you're incredibly beautiful. I was worried our driver would run into a pole, as he tried to look at you. And when that local crashed and burned, I realized I was the luckiest guy on the planet."

"You're very funny." She giggled, blushed and squeezed his hand again.

He squeezed a little harder. "So tell me Marwa, why have you come into my life? Why are your friends following me, and what do you want from me?"

Shock registered. Color drained from her face. She tensed and tried to pull away, but Hunter held on.

"Marwa, don't say anything yet. I'm a straight-up guy, an honest broker. I won't hurt you. I'll tell you the truth, and I expect the same." He gripped her hand. "I'm pretty good at reading body language, and, from the moment I first saw you, I knew something was up.

"I sense you're in trouble. I know people have been following me and some of my friends, but, for the life of me, I don't know why. I'm a nobody. Well, no one who needs to be followed."

Tension relaxed in her hand. She sat in stunned silence, feeling failure already. She tried to look away from him but couldn't.

"OK?" he continued. "I won't hurt or embarrass you. We're two friends having dinner and a good time. If your friends are watching, they'll see us having a good time."

Her stunning eyes filled with relief. She could tell him. Could he help her? "Duncan, they aren't my friends."

"But someone wants you to get something from me—some information?"

"Yes," she said softly, turning her head aside in embarrassment.

"Are you in trouble? Does someone have something on you? Are you being threatened?"

"Yes," she whispered. "I'm very frightened now. I have failed."

Grasping her hand firmly, he said, "OK. Look at me. I won't let anything happen to you, OK? You have to believe me, but I need to know everything, so I can figure how to get us out of this. Will you trust me, Marwa?"

A tear welled in one eye. "Yes. I'm very frightened, Duncan. I do trust you."

"Can you tell me everything?" He caressed her hand, and she squeezed back and smiled, melting his heart. "Yes, but I do not know where to start."

"First of all, relax. We're close friends who are about to become closer. Tell me about yourself and your family. Tell me how you came to the US and then into my life. I'll tell you about me, which will put you to sleep."

She tried to smile and relax at his attempt at humor. After a minute her tension had almost dissipated, and she held his hand tighter.

"Marwa Kamal is my real name. I'm from Amman, Jordan. My father was head of the royal court in the service of His Royal Highness, the king. My mother...."

"...has to be as beautiful as you. Amazing genes."

She smiled, and her eyes flashed at him. "Yes, she's very beautiful. I always thought my mother was the most beautiful woman in the world." She sipped her drink. "I was an only child. I was schooled in Amman until I was ten-years old. My parents sent me to England and Switzerland to finish my studies. My father graduated from Yale Law School. I also attended Yale and graduated three years ago. I thought I would return to Amman and work at my father's business, but something changed him. He wanted me to marry."

She lowered her eyes at the table, then drained her glass.

Duncan squeezed her hand, and rubbed his thumb over the top of hers in comfort.

After taking a deep breath, she said, "I married Waleed last year. It was the worst thing I could have done."

"That didn't work out?"

"We had significant philosophical differences. In a world where it doesn't matter what a woman thinks, especially an educated woman, such a marriage was doomed to fail. He was not a very compassionate man."

"I'm sorry, Marwa." He had visions of someone trying to hit that dark-haired goddess, and his ire rose.

"Not your fault. I really wished there were a way I could live freely. I came to love and admire America. It's a free society where I could follow any religion without compulsion."

"That puts you and me in the heretic category, I guess."

"So far, I'm not really sure what I am. I know I'm not an atheist, because I believe in God, but God can't be the Allah of Mohammed. My God is kind and merciful. God should not be evil, cruel, mean, and sadistic, as is Allah. Have you ever read the Quran?"

"In English. My Arabic is horrible."

"I never did until I returned to Jordan. All my life, I recited the Quran in Arabic without understanding a single word. About a year ago, I purchased a copy of the English Quran and read the complete translation for the first time. I read some parts in English before, but never the complete book. Last year, I read it cover-to-cover. I also read other references and religious books, including the Bible.

"It validated what I long suspected. The Quran is probably the most evil thing on Earth. Islam teaches nothing but hatred and violence, especially toward women."

"Your assessment is on target. I've worked with the Royal Jordanian Air Force and found them to be what I would call good Muslims—not radical—and they never expressed anything but respect and courtesy with me. The last time I visited, nearly every single one wished me Merry Christmas. I was pleasantly surprised."

"You were fortunate to meet and work with moderate Muslims. I think the line between good and evil is very narrow. If you're busy and working, I believe you're less likely to be influenced by ignorant, vile, corrupt imams. I...I can no longer be part of a cult. I have come to realize cults subjugate their followers. They become blind puppets without minds of their own."

"And, under the control of a crazy person, bad things happen."

"I'm so sorry, Duncan. I didn't want to spy on you. I was so conflicted."

"Your body language at the courts gave it away. Something bothered you a great deal. Let's change the subject. How did you come to the US? What did you do?"

"I ran away from Waleed and came to America. I landed in Boston. I'm familiar with Yale and thought I would find a job in New Haven. I found some women from Jordan, Saudi Arabia, and Kuwait working at the airport who said I could get a job with them, and I'd be safe. I couldn't believe how many Muslim women were working at the airport. Many were afraid of men, and several, like me, had ran away from bad marriages.

"I was working there when Nizar Mohammad from the TSA said I had to see an imam in Boston. The imam knew I had dishonored my family and I had run away from Waleed. He suggested...."

"He suggested if you went to Newport and met me, things would get better?"

"Yes. He wanted me to get close to you and find out more about you."

"Do you know why?"

"I think he's interested in a man called McGayhee or something like that. He wanted to know why you were close to him."

"His name is McGee." Hunter paused for a moment, then he changed the direction of the conversation. "I take it you're fluent in Arabic?"

"Of course, as well as Farsi, French, and a little German." The waiter approached for the tenth time.

Hunter's mind raced. He squeezed Marwa's hand again. "Are you all right? Can you eat?"

She nodded. Green eyes peeked from behind her black hair.

"OK. Let's order. I need to think." The waiter took their order and left.

"So this imam is interested in my friend and wanted you to get information about him from me?"

"No, Duncan. I think he wanted to know why you and he are friends and what you do together all the time. He wants to know who you are. I think someone else wants to know about you. The imam is a...how do you say...?"

"Middleman?"

"Yes. I believe so."

"OK, Marwa. How about this? What were you supposed to do when you had something to tell?"

"I was to drive back to Boston and give my report in person to Imam Abdul. Tonight I am supposed to give my report."

He nodded. "Do you think your life would be in danger if you returned to Boston? Once you reported your findings, what do you think would happen to you?"

She turned her head away, unable to bear such thoughts. "Let me guess. You can just nod."

She looked at him with her incredible eyes, which filled with tears. He took her other hand.

"You think he would send you back to Jordan or turn you over to Waleed. He might even try to touch you himself."

She nodded, her jaw tight. It took her a full minute to compose herself. "There is a concept held by radicals that holds that some Muslims aren't Muslim enough. Therefore, they are apostates. Because they are worse than nonbelievers, they may be killed with impunity."

"Tafkir?"

"Yes. I know in my heart and mind that the imam embraces Tafkir. I would be deemed not Muslim enough if I refused his request. I was so afraid for my life." Her eyes welled with fresh tears.

Hunter's mind was in overdrive. He held her hand in reassurance. "OK. How about this? What if you could start your life over fresh, with a new name, a job, and a place they can't get to you?"

She stared into his brown eyes. "If you're in my life, Duncan, absolutely."

"Thank you, Marwa. We'll have to see what tomorrow brings."

Their eyes locked, and she held his hands tightly. "Do you trust me?" he asked.

"With my life. I was so embarrassed and ashamed. Now, I'm at peace with you."

"I believe you. OK, let's see what we can do to get out of this mess." He reached to his hip and brought his Blackberry to the table, punching a series of buttons. "My plan right now is to get you away from Newport and as far from this place as fast as we can. I'm going to ask a friend of mine to come get you and start you on your way to a new life. Let's see what the Grinch has to say."

He placed the device on the table and took her hands again. "The... Grinch?"

"My best friend and cohort in crime—Greg Lynche." He brought his fingers together to demonstrate two worlds

198

merging into one. "Greg...Lynche...Grinch."

"I'm not going back?"

"Only if you want to. Is there anything you need in your apartment?"

"I have my passport. There are only a few clothes in the apartment."

"Do you know where the mosque is where Abdul preaches?"

"I don't know exactly, but I think I could find it. When Nizar took me to see Abdul, he drove all over Boston. I thought it was funny how he did that and assumed he was lost. Now I realize he didn't want me to know where we were going."

"I get the feeling you knew anyway."

"Yes. My friends and I traveled from New Haven to Boston on the train, the Amtrak. I'm certain the mosque was near one of the stations where we got off. I saw the station and recognized where I was. If I had to run from Nizar, I was going to run to the metro station."

"You're incredible in more than one way. That info is nice to know."

The Blackberry buzzed. Hunter, looking at it, frowned. He punched a few buttons and replaced it in the holster at his hip.

Marwa watched with trepidation.

"The soonest he can get here is Wednesday evening," Hunter said. "There's a storm coming. I knew that, but you're such a distraction, I forgot and can't think straight."

She smiled. "I don't want to return to the apartment."

"I don't want you going back, either. I'll take you home with me. I have enough room for two. Tomorrow, we'll buy you some clothes on the base."

"Duncan, I don't know what to say. I'm so relieved, but I'm still frightened. I'm worried they might do something to you."

He raised his water glass. "It'll be OK. Here's to tomorrow." Still stunned, she copied the gesture.

"Tomorrow," he said, touching glasses. They sipped without blinking, staring at each other.

Two hours after they entered the Red Parrot, Marwa and Duncan stepped outside into a freshening breeze that brought the hint of snow. Marwa's hair and shawl rustled in the wind. Her nipples hardened at the sudden temperature change. Duncan appreciated the sight but also felt embarrassed for her. He hurried her into the Rolls, away from the eyes on the car and the stunning brunette in the white dress.

"To the base, James."

The driver was momentarily confused and then got it. "Your building, Sir?"

"Yes, Sir. Number seven."

The drive to the main gate of the Naval War College was slow and uneventful. Duncan and Marwa held hands. He talked about the school and some of the landmarks. They saw the original war college structure from the 1800s and the huge new education building.

James stopped in front of Building 7. Duncan got out and helped Marwa out, then he handed the driver a folded $50 bill and said, "Thanks again for a great ride."

He offered Marwa his hand, and they walked into the building and then to the elevator. Neither spoke as they rode to the third floor.

The doors opened, and Duncan said, "It's all the way at the other end." He led the way.

He flashed an old brass key to unlock the door and allowed her to step inside first. The door closed behind her, and she turned to Duncan. Marwa looked like a frightened, bewildered, and an amazingly beautiful bird.

"This is home for a couple days," he said. "Let me show you around. Here's the living room, kitchen, and in there is the bedroom. That's the bathroom and closet. I need to get you some clothes. I have some long-sleeved T-shirts and sweatshirts and sweatpants that will work until we buy something for you tomorrow. I even have a new toothbrush.

How's that?"

She clutched her purse, lowered her head, and cried. He took the purse from her hands and wrapped his arms around her. She slowly put her arms around him and sobbed. The faint scent of cinnamon enveloped him as he held her.

When she composed herself, she released her grip, and he reciprocated.

"I have to use the bathroom," she said, removing her wrap and tossing it and the purse on the table in the tiny dining area.

"I'll get you something a little more comfortable," Duncan said. "I'll put the clothes on the bed."

"Thank you."

He watched her walk into his bedroom and disappeared into the bathroom. He had difficult believing the events of the evening.

Several minutes later, she emerged from the bedroom wearing a yellow Corvette Racing jersey that gave her ample bosom plenty of room. Black sweatpants disappeared under the shirt, and elastic cuffs profiled her thin, bare feet. Hunter changed into a similar ensemble and stood looking out the picture window when the bedroom door opened. He turned as Marwa padded into the room.

"That shirt will think it has died and gone to heaven," he said.

"I'm sorry?"

"I'm sorry. I was trying to be funny. Will that work? It isn't too...?"

"No. This is wonderful. You may not get this back. It's very comfortable."

"It's yours. Can I get you something to drink? We have...."

"No, thank you. I'm not thirsty." She paused, looking for the right words, as she sat on the end of the sofa. "I've never been in a room with a man before, like this. It's very strange and yet very liberating. With you, I feel safe. Muslim men would...."

"I think any man would thank his lucky stars to be where I am right now. I've often said I'm the luckiest guy I know. When I first saw you watching us play racquetball, I wondered about you. There was something about you."

"There was something about you, too. When I saw you for the first time in the racquetball court, I refused to believe you were a monster. I couldn't believe you were evil, and someone was very afraid of you."

Hunter walked in from the kitchen carrying a glass of orange juice. He sat across from her in the chair. "I guess I'm just a lovable old fuzzball."

She smiled, which warmed him.

"What have you been doing while I was in class?"

"During the last three weeks, I read constantly. I was very concerned that the apartment was under surveillance, but I was afraid to look for the cameras. I went to the library and spent hours reading. I found an amazing book called Understanding Muhammad by Ali Sina. I also read 23 Years by Ali Dashti. I looked for anyone who wanted to expose Islam for what it is."

"That must've been an eye-opening experience."

"Duncan, this...." She spread her arms and rotated her hands. "...and what you have done for me has been an eye-opening experience. Last Sunday, I went to a church near the library and sat in the back to watch. I was astounded to see a woman leading the service. The paper they gave me said she was a pastor. I thought America was the greatest country in the world if women could lead religious services."

"We can be pretty progressive in some ways. Not all agree, but we seem to get along with each other well enough."

"I sat there and thought, 'I can no longer live like this.' I began to gain courage to convert from Islam. If I had said that a year ago, I would probably be in jail or dead. That imam would've had someone execute me. Women who commit the crime of wanting to make independent decisions concerning their lives are murdered all around the world. My life is in danger and will stay that way if anyone finds out I want to leave Islam."

"I won't let anything happen to you. That's a promise."

"That's what Islam does to you. When you're in it, your life is nothing. You live in fear. I think once you leave it, you're in hell, because you're constantly afraid of losing your life."

"What's keeping you from leaving Islam?"

"I don't know how to go about it. I want to leave, but I want to remain anonymous. I don't want to be killed just because I'm brave enough to tell the truth. I don't want to lose my life, because I don't believe in that evil religion anymore."

"Marwa, I promise I won't let anything happen to you. If you want to leave Islam, I'll do everything I can to make sure you can live your life without fear, the way you want. We're going to start doing that by getting you out of here as soon as this storm passes."

"Do you really think you can do that?"

"I can. I'll need some help, but I have some very special friends who can make it happen. You'll have to trust me."

"I do trust you."

The shift in atmosphere was palpable. Marwa began to look like a little girl who struggled to budge a heavy gate only to find a whole new world hidden behind it.

Duncan felt lost for words. Standing, he said, "Come look at this view. Out there is Narragansett Bay, and that's the Claiborne Pell Bridge in the fog. I'm sorry, actually, that's snow. I'm glad I have this room. The view is spectacular."

"That's beautiful. I think America is filled with wonders."

He nodded. "It is. You have no idea. One of these days, I'll show you many, many wonders. Ah, it's my turn to use the bathroom. I'll be right back."

When Duncan returned, Marwa was still in front of the picture window. He walked up beside her and took her hand. Their fingers slowly intertwined.

She leaned against him. "I'm ready to be free of Islam."

Duncan was taken aback. "I'm not sure what that means."

"It means I don't want to be treated like a slave any longer. I was my father's property, then my husband's. I want to be free, to live without fear. I want to be treated like a woman, a lady, like you treated me tonight. That's what I want. I don't want to return to that life. I want a new life and a new beginning."

Marwa turned toward him. "I want to thank you for saving my life." She buried her head against his chest for a few moments. He held her until she relaxed her grip and slowly looked up at him.

"I want you to make love to me, Duncan Hunter." She placed her head against his chest, her heart pounding.

He took her in his arms. She trembled slightly as she reached up to kiss him, then stopped.

"Duncan, I know nothing about making love. I'm...."

He scooped her into his arms, desperately trying to find romantic words. "Marwa, I think you know how it should be. I'll bet you're a fast learner."

She realized all she knew how to do was bend over and let someone poke her. Her arms went around his neck. "I'm afraid but very excited. I want you very much. Oh, Duncan, you're so good to me."

"Now you know what I've felt since I first saw you. You're the sexiest, most beautiful woman I have ever met. I'll try my best not to disappoint you."

"How could I know disappointment? I know nothing! I don't even know how to kiss." Her flash of exasperation was laced with worry and embarrassment.

He walked into the bedroom and stopped at the side of the bed. Duncan looked at her and gently set her down until her feet touched the floor. Her breasts slid down his chest.

Trying to diffuse her concerns, he asked, "You don't know how to kiss? Why, Ms. Kamal, that may be a little problem."

"I don't. I'm not sure what is to be accomplished with French kissing and the tongue."

"Let's start with a kiss, Ms. Kamal. I'd like you to open

your mouth a little and stick out your tongue a bit. Like that. Now close your eyes."

He looked at the slightly trembling woman as he bent down to kiss her. She anticipated his touching her lips when his tongue barely touched hers and shot electricity through her body. Warmth filled the void between her legs. She felt him growing firm, and her eyes flew open, as she moved against him. "Good, yes?" he asked.

"Very good. Oh, yes." Her breathing deepened, and she pressed her breasts against him, feeling his erection again as their lips touched, and he flicked her tongue. She loosened her mouth, inviting more, and her apprehension melted away.

She pulled back, nearly breathless, their foreheads and upper lips touching. She explored his mouth with her tongue.

His lips locked hers when he inhaled, taking wind from her lungs as air raced through her nose.

She nearly collapsed into his arms when they parted. "I think I'm a very bad learner," she whispered. "Can...can the Grinch come get me next week?"

205

CHAPTER THIRTY-ONE

1800 March 11, 2003
Al-Azzam Islamic Center

Eight inches of snow nearly prevented Nizar Mohammad from meeting Imam Abdul. Snow fell at Boston Logan Airport so fast the snow-removal equipment couldn't keep a single runway cleared enough for the airport to remain open. At 1800, the FAA officially closed the airport until the weather system passed. Traffic was diverted as far west as Chicago and Detroit, which were inexplicably spared most of the storm's wrath. With another two feet expected over the coming forty-eight hours, the Boston Airport Authority sent all nonessential personnel home, while plows and snow throwers removed tons of snow from runways, taxiways, and parking aprons.

What should have been a thirty-minute drive from the airport to the mosque took two hours. Nizar almost ran out of gas. By the time he shuffled into the mosque, he missed prayers and found Imam Abdul nearly apoplectic.

"Where's the whore?" he demanded. "She's supposed to be here. What happened to her?"

"Sahib, the infidel didn't bring her home. He picked her up, but they drove an old white car on the navy base. Mohammad followed the old car to Fall River, but she wasn't in it when it stopped. Also, her car was still at the apartment."

"She must report what she learned!"

"Yes, Sahib. She must still be on the Navy base, getting information from the infidel." Nizar was crushed that Imam Abdul sent Marwa to consort with the infidel. He had never seen another Muslima like her. She had fantastic eyes, and she moved and spoke differently. She stirred feelings in him that were anathema to Islam. He would treat her better than she would ever be treated by her family or former husband. If she gave him a chance, she would see he could provide a good living for her as a TSA agent. He worried the infidel would do something bad to her.

"We will wait another day," the imam said. "I will make some calls to see if she's still on the navy base. You must remove everything from that apartment—all traces, understand?"

"Yes, Sahib."

"Go, and close the door."

Nizar, turning to leave, saw snow falling more heavily than when he arrived. Exhaling loudly, he resigned himself to driving for hours in a snowstorm to remove the audio-visual equipment installed in Marwa's bedroom. His spirits picked up at the thought of seeing a video of her changing clothes. He would be able to see her naked. Thoughts of seeing the nude runaway from Jordan motivated him to hurry, and he flew out the double doors into the blizzard.

Abdul had a bad feeling about Marwa and muttered in Arabic, as he rummaged through the stacks and pamphlets on his desk until he found Jebriel's emergency number. Reaching across the stacks, he picked up the old rotary AT&T Model 500 telephone, set it before him, and looked over the tops of his wire-rimmed glasses to dial the number.

After two rings, he hung up and redialed. Jebriel answered on the eighth ring, as briefed, but he didn't speak.

In English, Abdul said, "I need you." The line went dead two seconds later.

CHAPTER THIRTY-TWO

1930 March 12, 2003
Building 7 Newport Naval Station

Twenty-three inches of snow fell from the slow-moving snowstorm that blanketed the East Coast from Washington, DC, to Bangor, Maine. The President of the War College canceled classes for the first part of the week. A blanket e-mail announced classes would resume on Thursday, the thirteenth.

Boston Logan and Providence Theodore Francis Green Airports were closed, as were Quonset and Newport State Regional Airports. Greg Lynche couldn't take off from Easton, Maryland, and he couldn't land in Newport, until the storm passed and the runways were cleared. The soonest anyone expected to be able to fly was late Thursday. Still, Lynche and Hunter were busy.

Lynche slogged across a heavily plowed and sanded Interstate 495 to meet his old counterpart at his old place, who called the deputy director at the National Counterterrorism Center. He was very intrigued and looked forward to meeting the woman who had been sent to gather information about Hunter and McGee. If someone was watching a SEAL and a civilian, why wouldn't they have all the Special Operations forces attending the War College under surveillance? She could be very valuable.

Lynche relayed the information Marwa provided Duncan. The NCTC deputy expressed his unhappiness with the TSA in Boston and considered Ms. Kamal a "catch" if she provided her bona fides and passed a comprehensive polygraph. If she could run the gauntlet of interviews and polygraphs, the NCTC wanted and needed a sorelymissed resource in the arsenal of counterterrorism weapons—a fully functional, competent, trustworthy Arabic speaker and interpreter. She could also be effective as an interrogator.

If approved, Marwa Kamal would effectively disappear into the black hole of the DOJ's Witness Protection Program. She would receive a new identity with authentic documentation. By the end of the day, the NCTC deputy created a job for her as a senior analyst in Middle East affairs at the CIA's NCTC.

After three days of snow and a war raging and coalition forces staging for an Iraqi invasion slated for the coming week, Agency men wanted their potential new resource in the pipe and processed as quickly as possible. When Lynche told the deputy NCTC he'd bring Marwa from Newport as soon as the weather cleared, the deputy said he'd dispatch a detail to pick her up and immediately jet her to Washington, DC.

The deputy NCTC buzzed his secretary. "I'd like the senior FBI agent to come to my office at her earliest convenience." He picked up the handset of the STU, dialed the Office of Intelligence and Analysis chief at the Department of Homeland Security, and briefed him on the situation regarding Nizar Mohammad, a supervisory TSA agent.

After hanging up with the DHS, he heard a hard knock on the door, and the FBI agent was announced.

"Ms. Storm," the deputy said, "I hope you might be interested in the activity at a Boston mosque. They've been surveilling Special Operations Forces attending the War College in Rhode Island. One of their spies just left the dark side and is more than willing to talk to us."

* * *

Massachusetts State Police reported finding several abandoned vehicles along the stretch of I-195 after snowplows made some headway against the record snowfall that shut down the interstate. Snowplow drivers were careful to plow around areas that appeared to be stranded vehicles.

The state police followed them, stopping at each large hump in the snow to determine if anyone still remained in their vehicle.

After several hours of checking over thirty abandoned vehicles without finding anyone inside, Corporal Mike Knox, Massachusetts State Police, quietly hoped he wouldn't find anyone in the last car. His feet were so cold they cramped, and his arms ached from digging into packed, frozen snow.

When he shouted at the vehicle, no one replied. His shovel struck metal, and he quickly scraped around the area to avoid damaging the car. Five minutes passed before he finally located a door window, cleared it with his glove, and shone his flashlight inside to illuminate a body slumped behind the wheel.

Corporal Knox quickly reversed his flashlight and broke the window with the butt end, knocking shattered glass aside as he reached into the car. The body was frozen solid. The man wore a large TSA patch on his jacket shoulder.

Corporal Knox hung his head at the realization that he just found a law-enforcement officer. He removed his gloves and took a white laminated card from his wallet, which he held up to the beam from the flashlight.

"Saint Michael, heaven's glorious commissioner of police," he began.

"Make us the terror of burglars, the friend of children and law-abiding citizens, kind to strangers, polite to bores, strict with law-breakers, and impervious to temptations. You know, Saint Michael, from your own experience with the devil that the police officer's lot on earth isn't always a happy one, but your sense of duty that so pleased God, your hard knocks that so surprised the devil, and your angelic self-control give us inspiration.

"And when we lay down our nightsticks, enroll us in your heavenly force, where we will be as proud to guard the throne of God as we've been to guard the city of all the people. Amen."

CHAPTER THIRTY-THREE

2030 March 13, 2003
The Bridge Apartments Newport, Rhode Island

Imam Abdul hadn't heard from Nizar for three days. His eyes, ears, and muscle hadn't checked in, and neither had Marwa. He feared the worst. It was entirely possible Nizar had been trapped in the snow when he drove to Newport. Abdul had no way to know if Marwa returned to her apartment. His master in Jeddah would not be pleased with the turn of events.

Snow fell for three days, closing I-195 from Boston to Newport. Nizar's attempt to comply with the graybeard's demands ended when Nizar lost control of the old Maxima at forty-five miles an hour and slammed into the blunt end of a guard rail.

Abdul was forced to cajole Commander Zaid Jebriel to go to the whore's apartment and the infidel's building to see if the traitorous bitch was there. She couldn't have disappeared on the navy base. The weather in and around Newport was every bit as bad as Boston's, and Jebriel's driving skills on snow were so poor, he dared not venture out and had to wait until the roads were sanded and cleared.

As soon as snowplows removed the snow from the roadway, Jebriel swept two feet of snow off his Mercedes and attempted to open the door, only to find all doors frozen shut. He banged and pulled on the door handle repeatedly until the door suddenly broke free, upending the Saudi officer's feet over his head. He remained with his arms and legs spread-eagled, his torso parallel with the ground for a microsecond before he crashed down. His tailbone took the majority of the impact, followed by his head.

One split-second later, Jebriel writhed in pain, one hand on the back of his head and the other cushioning his butt. Momentarily paralyzed by the impact to his coccyx, he tried to move his legs, and they refused to respond. He tried several times until panic at the thought of becoming a cripple and freezing in the hell hole called America seized him.

He was hyperventilating when he finally felt his legs tremble and shake uncontrollably, as the numb nerve in his tailbone slowly responded to the rush of adrenalin and synapses firing garbled commands.

After lying on packed snow for several minutes, his legs responded even more spastically, and he gingerly flexed his toes and tried to lift his legs. Elation filled him, while cold raced through his thin coat and trousers. After four minutes on the ground, his heart rate was almost back to normal.

Trying to sit, he found any movement made his stomach churn, so he laid down and rolled over. He managed to kneel, then, using the Mercedes door handle as a brace, he gathered his feet under himself and stood. The car seat beckoned. He shuffled forward gently and gingerly sat in the car. Unsure his legs would respond, he used his hands to place them into the car. He fished from his pocket the car keys with a trembling hand. When the Mercedes started, he ran the emotional gamut from terror to relief and wept.

Twenty minutes later, the car heater almost roasted him. All bodily functions returned to a bruised state of normal. Taking a large breath, he depressed the brake and moved the transmission to drive to tentatively pull onto the roadbed of the Bridge Apartments, where all Naval War College international officers were housed.

Traffic was light, but driving was treacherous. He drove very cautiously, with the trip to Marwa's apartment taking almost an hour.

As he approached the apartment, he saw three emergency vehicles out front, light bars flashing. He drove straight ahead slowly, unable to contain his emotions, and ignored the pain in his head as he observed what appeared to be police at a woman's door.

One emergency vehicle winched a red Mercedes convertible onto its long, angled flatbed. Jebriel drove gingerly toward the other side of town.

An hour later, he waited to turn toward the War College's main gate. Ignoring spurious muscles spasms, he noticed he was behind two large black Chevy Suburbans with blacked-out windows and multiple antennas sprouting from the roofs. The black vehicles meant to enter the base.

The gate guard waved them to the side, allowing Jebriel to proceed and show his ID to the guard. Jebriel's special ID card for NWC international students allowed unfettered passage onto the base, and the gate guard smartly waved his arm in approval for the old bronzed Mercedes to proceed.

The Suburbans intrigued Jebriel, and he tried to appear inconspicuous as possible while not running over the guard. He glanced at the black vehicles, and, as he moved past the front doors, a woman driver dressed in black glared at him. He stopped at the sign ahead and checked his rearview mirror, as his back cramped from all the torso movements, while the knot on the back of his head throbbed. A white Navy security truck pulled in front of the two Suburbans and approached the rear of Jebriel's car.

Just as he moved forward and prepared to turn right, the Navy truck's blue lights flashed and rotated, and a siren went off. Jebriel hit the brake with both feet and froze, sending spasms down his spine. His head felt ready to burst.

The three vehicles drove past him on the left. Greatly relieved, he crept through the intersection like a snake passing behind a sleeping mongoose. His newfound curiosity told him to follow the intriguing parade of vehicles that turned off their pulsating lights.

When the three trucks appeared headed toward the other side of the small base, their brake lights came on, showing they planned to stop before Building 7. Jebriel drove straight ahead to a plowed parking lot across the street and perpendicular to Building 7, choosing a spot with a good view of the building's front door and lounge. Turning off the engine, he waited. Frost billowed from the vehicles' exhaust up the slight hill, occasionally obscuring his view of the front door.

CHAPTER THIRTY-FOUR

2130 March 13, 2003
Building 7 Newport Naval Station

Two heavily armored black Suburbans idled downstairs. A knock on the door of room 307 announced a contingent of US Federal Marshals had arrived to escort Ms. Kamal to the Newport State Airport. A chartered business jet with a cleared air crew would fly the highly touted passenger to the Warrenton-Fauquier Airport in Virginia, where Agency staff would take Marwa to a safe house for processing.

Inside the room, Marwa held Duncan tightly and was on the verge of tears.

"You can't do that," he said. "Look at me. Marwa, you're an incredibly strong woman. You've come a long way to break free, and now you'll be doubly free. Don't cry or they'll think I was mean to you."

"I don't want to leave you."

"Remember what Bogie said. 'We'll always have Paris.' Marwa, we'll always have Newport. We'll always be close, and we'll be together again soon. I asked you before if you trusted me. You said yes, and now you're ready to begin a great adventure and a new life."

"You'll be fine. These guys will take good care of you. When you have the chance, call me, even if they say you can't. I'll have the Grinch check on you once you're settled. When I'm out of here, I'll visit and see if you forgot any of your lessons."

She buried her head against his chest and clutched him tightly. Finally, she released him and took a deep breath.

"I'm OK and ready," she said. "I don't want to lose you, Duncan Hunter."

"You won't get rid of me anytime soon. I promise. I'll miss

you."

Opening the door, he saw the hallway cluttered with four armed women in black SWAT uniforms. One held a badge and ID in her hand.

"Good evening, Ladies." Duncan opened the door until it struck the door stop.

"Mr. Hunter, I presume?" asked the husky, short-haired US Marshal.

"Yes, Ma'am. This is Ms. Kamal. She's pretty special, so I'd consider it a personal favor if you take care of her."

Two blonde US Marshals stepped into the room, and looked around carefully. One picked up a small rollerboard which appeared to go with the shockingly beautiful woman with damp eyes.

"We will. Ms. Kamal, please follow me."

Marwa looked up at Duncan, reached up one final time, and kissed him hard, flicking her tongue over his lips as they separated. Even with all the women standing around, the electricity and chemistry behind the kiss stiffened him. It was painful to see her go.

She stood back down on her feet, turned, and looked away. Two US Marshals led her down the hall. Marwa walked beside her escort, with the remaining Marshal following. They didn't talk as they marched down the corridor. The only sound was the creak of leather boots on the tiled floor.

Hunter watched them disappear into the elevator at the far end of the hallway. Closing the door, he walked to the window, his heart full of sorrow and optimism. Parting with Marwa was harder than expected. Over the last four days, the couple formed an unbreakable bond. Unburdened from years of training in being submissive, she quickly transitioned into 100 hours of freedom to do anything she wanted, including helping Duncan shower.

Three minutes later, Duncan watched two black Suburbans follow a US Navy security pickup down the outlet road toward the main gate. When their taillights vanished, he plopped on the sofa. The disturbed air reeked of sex.

With his head in his hands, he rubbed his eyes and felt slightly embarrassed. *They must have smelled that, he thought sheepishly. Not much I can do about it now.*

He was acutely aware of *In My World* playing softly in the bedroom. His Blackberry buzzed, startling him from his reverie.

He received an e-mail from Lynche.

Think you kicked over a hornet's nest. My old place says someone, presumably AQ, ordered a hit on her.

Hunter quickly typed a reply. Thought she was low level. Call me when able.

His Blackberry rang immediately with an incoming call. "She's considered low level for now," Lynche said. "I don't think they know she's alive. They're covering their bases."

"She just left. Thanks for all your help."

"I tried to come get her myself, but they vetoed that idea. They want her bad. War with Iraq is coming. I understand they sent a jet for her. She's a hi-pri resource now. It's pathetic that my old place doesn't have many professional native Arabic-speaking analysts on staff."

"Break, break," he said, using military code to change the subject. "Any work on the horizon?"

"Art has a couple things local and down south. Everyone's busy with one war and another on the way. Looks like there'll be lots of overseas work. Africa is completely untapped."

"And completely wild. At some point, we'll need our own jet and C-130. We can't rely on the Air Force all the time."

"Agreed, but we can't afford anything like that. Not yet anyway. What were you thinking?"

"I'm just thinking. Hey, what's the other meaning of Inshallah?"

"Besides God willing or if God provides?"

"That's the one. Inshallah, Mr. Lynche."

Completely confused, Lynche replied, "Good night, Maverick."

217

CHAPTER THIRTY-FIVE

2145 March 13, 2003
Parking Lot Charlie Newport Naval Station

Commander Zaid Jebriel gripped the steering wheel of the creaking, cooling, old Mercedes and gingerly leaned forward, using his sleeve to wipe the advancing frost from the windshield. He expected the people in black to return to their vehicles at any moment.

Minutes earlier, as he turned into a parking space facing Building 7, he observed four women in heavy black uniforms with something partially obscured because of the frost. They stepped from the black vehicles' rear doors. Over the sound of his cooling engine, he heard the doors slam shut a second after he watched them close.

The sole driver in the white pickup remained in the truck, engine running, as the single exhaust pipe leaked a narrow column of steam.

The windshield continued to frost over quickly without the defroster on, requiring Jebriel to move forward and back, inviting spasms from tailbone to his atlas, the topmost vertebra. After a dozen attempts to wipe away the accelerating window frost, he started the engine again, and the defroster quickly cleared the windshield.

He counted five dark uniforms rushing from the building. Confused, he again gripped the steering wheel and pulled himself closer for a better look. The lettering on the back of the nearest figure read US Marshal.

Then he realized they had another woman with long, dark hair. She wasn't in black and wasn't as short as the others. It had to be the Imam's spy. She was a prisoner.

The three vehicles moved away, turning left at the intersections until they were about to pass in front of Jebriel to head back the way they came. Panicked, he tried to get out of their line of sight.

Jebriel twisted, trying to push his head down toward the passenger seat, but his confused spinal cord wouldn't allow him that much latitude or responsiveness in movement. Once his body was in motion, he realized his mistake and tried to protect his face, as he crashed heavily against the dash amid the buttons and levers of the Mercedes' heater controls. His arms, failed to respond adequately to prevent facial trauma.

As the vehicles passed in front of the Mercedes, blood erupted from his broken nose, while broken teeth caromed from the dash toward the passenger seat. Jebriel howled in pain. His back locked in spasms, and his arms went limp. He sobbed in his blood as he lay face down in the passenger seat.

"I hate women!" he screamed, blood spurting across the seat and floorboard.

CHAPTER THIRTY-SIX

2000 April 5, 2003
Annapolis Yacht Club Annapolis, Maryland

"Pick up the phone, Maverick!" an impatient Greg Lynche barked. He and Connie sat on the club porch, enjoying the view of the Chesapeake and the camaraderie of the latest J-105 fleet meet. Three years earlier, Greg and Connie were blessed with a very disciplined race crew and won several races, including the J-105 Sailboat Racing National Championship. They were treated like sailing rock stars and Greg was just re-elected chair of the race committee.

Connie raised a glass of wine to toast the love of her life. Greg, grinning, touched goblets with her. Life was very good in Annapolis and became better when Greg finally concluded that Duncan Hunter was the guy he wanted as a partner in his consulting business. Art Yoder had other ideas. Greg didn't like it at first, but when he and Duncan teamed for one of Yoder's high-priority, high-stakes missions, the money flooded in as Lynche negotiated good terms on the contracts while Hunter planned the operations, ensuring he was at the controls of the quiet airplane.

Connie loved Duncan, because he was always there, taking care of the older, lankier Greg. She loved him even more when he helped push the Lynche family income into a stratospheric tax bracket.

When Duncan drove the completely rotisserie restored Porsche 928 to the club and tossed her the keys, saying, "Happy Birthday, Good Looking," there was nothing she wouldn't do for him.

It broke her heart that all Duncan wanted was meat on the grill and potatoes and beans for dinner when he visited. A visit meant Duncan was taking Greg to some wild place they couldn't talk about.

Greg was exasperated. There was work on the horizon, and he had to reach Hunter.

Patting his hand, Connie said, "Greg, he'll pick up the call in a minute or two. He always does."

After four rings, the Blackberry connected. "Yes, Sir?"

"When are you coming down this way?"

"I'll be in Carlisle the week of the fourteenth through the nineteenth, then I thought I'd stop by."

"Can you stop by Flight Safety on Long Island on the way?"

There was a long pause before Hunter said, "Are you shitting me?"

"I'm not. You're amazing, Hunter. Can you make it?"

"Do you have a time slot? What day?"

"We have the twelfth and thirteenth. The books are on their way. You'll have them Monday."

"I don't know what to say."

"Wait till you see her, then tell me. I just want to confirm that you're the luckiest shit on the planet."

CHAPTER THIRTY-SEVEN

0840 April 9, 2003
A Safe House near Quantico, Virginia

After the end of her seventh polygraph interview, Marwa folded her hands in her lap and waited.

"She's clean," the short, balding, myopic polygrapher said, summing up the week-long marathon of interviews and polygraphs.

Two men and a woman entered the small testing room. "Marwa," the woman in the pantsuit said, "I want to thank you for enduring all the testing and interviews. We have to be assured that someone who comes over is who they say they are. Your SF- 86 was simple, and we've received interim verification of your life and history. Your polygraphs are good —actually, very good. So after we've poked and prodded you for the last couple of weeks, are you still interested in working for us?"

She gave them a tired smile. "I am. I think I can help, and I'm ready to work at whatever you wish for me to do."

"I'm excited to have you on the team, but there are several things we have to do before we can officially bring you aboard for active duty."

"I'm ready to work. What must I do next?"

"We still have a great deal of work to do to bring you into the world, and we haven't been lazy. First, we must give you a new identity. Unless you have objections, we must come up with a new name."

"I won't have any objections unless the name doesn't suit me or is too cute."

The three spooks laughed and struggled to compose themselves.

"Marwa, I'm sorry," the woman said. "We tried to find

something that reflected a professional Islamic woman while acknowledging your natural beauty. We felt the name Nazy was as striking as you are. In Farsi it means...."

"Cute." Marwa took a deep breath and smiled. "It's a beautiful name. My mother was Iranian. I was almost named Nazy. Thank you for your kind words. I think I can be Nazy."

"From this day forward, you'll be known as Nazy. Actually, Nazy Cunningham." The shorter man with a full head of hair and a CIA lanyard filled with ID cards placed a black briefcase on the table, opened it, and extracted a handful of documents and keys. "Miss Cunningham, here's your Social Security card and US tourist passport. We have a Virginia's driver's license, two credit cards in your new name, a bank account, and a long credit history. You have a house near headquarters and a car. I understand it's a nice house and a very nice car. Those came from a different funding source. I believe your recruiter facilitated that.

"Oh, yes. Here's your personal history."

Marwa was intrigued by the narrative and their professionalism. As she tried to adapt to being an employee of the CIA, she was enthralled by the tone and pace of the briefing.

"Nazy Cunningham," the man said, "I'm sorry to hear you lost your husband, Lieutenant Commander Jeff Cunningham, a US Navy jet pilot, several years ago. You graduated from Oxford Law School, where you met Commander Jeff Cunningham in London while he was on an exchange program with the Royal Navy. You fell madly in love, married, and, one month later, he disappeared on a training mission over the Indian Ocean. You were crushed."

Initially confused, Nazy smiled back at him. She eased into a little role play as Duncan taught her. "The poor man. I *was* crushed."

"Exactly. Ms. Cunningham, you have a little royal Persian blood. You emigrated from the United Kingdom twenty-five years ago with your mother and father, a cousin of the shah. You carry yourself well, and, as long as you don't advertise your not-so-humble background, you'll be OK.

"We selected this cover, because we have a few ideas about future operations. Documents, keys, and briefing book are all in the briefcase. The briefing book can't leave this room. John G will wait for you to read it, commit to memory, and then he'll shred it."

"You're very thorough. You've made a good life for me. I greatly appreciate what you've done."

"So when do you think you ready to start work?" the woman asked, leaning over the table.

Nazy Cunningham responded, "After I use the facilities?"

* * *

On the other side of the world, a US Marine tank recovery vehicle cautiously rolled into Firdos "Paradise" Square. A crowd of several hundred Iraqis and reporters from around the world congregated in the square to welcome the Americans. A small group of men struggled to climb the forty-foot statue of President Saddam Hussein and placed a rope around its neck.

A Marine corporal disembarked from the big, tracked, armored vehicle and assessed the situation. He scanned the crowd, looking for trouble, then waved them away. Directing his crew to move the M88 to the base of the statue, he climbed to the top pulley so he could drape an American flag over Saddam's face before adding a chain around the neck of the statue.

At 1548 Baghdad Standard Time, the statue fell. The crowd erupted in unrestrained joy and beat the statue's head with their shoes.

BOOK THREE

CHAPTER ONE

1000 April 19, 2003
Carlisle Barracks Athletic Center Parking Lot
Carlisle Barracks, Pennsylvania

The surveillance was correct. It was easy to locate the distinctive black Silverado with Texas tags. Hunter always parked away from other vehicles, ostensibly to prevent it from receiving dings in the door panels from drivers indifferent to others' property. The infidel went to great lengths to reduce the risk of being hit by other vehicle's doors and to have a bomb placed on his vehicle.

One of the unintended consequences of the infidel's actions was that he made it difficult for anyone to park close to his truck, so someone could drop down between the vehicles and hide something on the truck's frame. Hunter never left his vehicle unattended for long or very often when he was off the Navy War College campus. When he played at the Newport Athletic Club, the parking lot always teemed with people coming and going between their vehicles and the club.

For months, teams of watchers monitored the base gates and determined Hunter's black truck left the base typically only once or twice a week, to drive through a fast-food restaurant, usually fast food Mexican. The other times, he drove to a racquetball club or storage facility near the War College, and either worked on or retrieved his trailered race car for a weekend.

The surveillance on the other men on the list was complete. Their movements were known, and their vehicles were tracked. With graduation looming, the imam insisted on redoubling their efforts to plant a tracking device on the vehicle owned by the last person on their list.

The Royal Saudi Navy commander suggested the arrogant infidel wasted much of his time playing the game called racquetball, and it was widely known that Hunter would go to Pennsylvania for Jim Thorpe Days. The President of the War College opened participation to the foreign officers if they were interested. The one sport where they might possibly participate was *futbol* or soccer. It was nearly an all-international team with naval officers from Australia, New Zealand, Great Britain, Germany, France, Saudi Arabia, and Jordan. The soccer team played well and showed their War College classmates they were masters of the ball and helped the Navy team win a gold medal.

When they weren't playing soccer, the Saudi and Jordanian officers continuously monitored Hunter's movements, his vehicle's location, and windows of opportunity to install a tracking device on the huge black truck. With limited parking spaces on the Army War College compound, Hunter found spots which backed against the tennis courts but his truck was often among other vehicles.

There would be no failure. The men's bronze Mercedes was parked three vehicles away from the truck. It was common for men and women to walk about, going to and from vehicles or in and out of the fitness center.

Jebriel opened the Mercedes' trunk, removed a black Saucony bag, and walked toward the rear of the Texas truck. Athamneh was lookout, his hand resting on the car's horn button. Forty seconds later, Jebriel emerged from under the truck. It took him ten seconds to locate and separate a power wire and strip away insulation, then another ten seconds to insert the exposed wire and transmitter wire into the dual-wire splice connector. As he flipped the clip and squeezed it shut, the wires were connected, crimped, and secured. In another ten seconds, he unwrapped the adhesive strip, activating its chemicals to bond the transmitter permanently to the top of the fuel tank.

He used up the final ten seconds getting out from under the truck and emerging between the two vehicles. Royal

Saudi Navy Commander Jebriel was joined by Royal Jordanian Navy Commander Athamneh at the fitness center entrance. When Jebriel entered the crowded observer area, he saw the infidel Hunter fully engaged playing a racquetball match.

CHAPTER TWO

1000 April 19, 2003
Carlisle Barracks Racquetball Court

Before putting on his safety goggles, Hunter took a quick look around the crowd that gathered at the single court to observe the final racquetball match of Jim Thorpe Days. He watched the Air War College team, led by a dynamic, hard-hitting, left-handed African American with a boxer's build, crush the Army team and the team of National and the Industrial War Colleges. The Navy team also proved to be very tough, winning all its matches.

Air Force and Navy were both 3-0 in their matches, and no one attending Jim Thorpe could have seen the collision of two undefeated teams, especially with Navy in the finals.

Hunter's A-player match with Lieutenant Colonel "Goose" Moncrief drew a standing-room-only crowd. Murmurs of an Air Force blowout came from USAF boosters, while the small Navy contingent waited anxiously. Navy had one gold medal for the games, and had been within an inch of winning another. Navy had split their other matches with the Air Force, and it came down to the finals of the two A-players.

Hunter looked for McGee and Admiral DiFilippo. When he didn't see them, he rocked his head from side-to-side to loosen his neck muscles, tossed his goggles on, and entered the court. As he turned to ensure the door was closed, he saw a pretty redhead jammed uncomfortably in the corner of one of the observation windows. When she smiled, he returned the compliment.

Goose crushed one ball after another during his warm up. He looked at Hunter in disgust, having watched him play a few minutes during an earlier match without getting a good read of his skills and play level.

Hunter lobbed balls to the ceiling on his forehand side, repeatedly not hitting the ball hard but consistently using enough force to have it drop inside the rearmost three feet of the court.

"Change sides?" Hunter asked.

Goose moved to the other side without a word and kept crushing balls with muscular arms that would have made McGee jealous.

Captain Bill McGee and Admiral DiFilippo entered the crowded viewing area, as Hunter entered the court. Some observers recognized the SEAL and the President of the NWC and tried to get out of their way, so they could get a better view of the action on the court. Always one to investigate his surroundings, McGee, his arms crossed, slowly studied the masses trying to squeeze into the limited area to watch the racquetball finals.

Admiral DiFilippo also looked over the crowd. With his hands stuffed into his pockets, he leaned close to McGee's ear and said, "I never knew so many women were interested in racquetball."

McGee momentarily stiffened, smiled, and looked again. Well over half the observers were women. He covered his mouth with one hand and whispered to the admiral's ear, "I don't think you've seen Hunter in his shorts."

The admiral raised his eyebrows and pressed his lips together. "Ah."

It seemed like providence when Duncan changed sides during the warm-up and came into clear view. Several women plastered at the viewing glass leaned forward to see Hunter's huge, medal-winning quadriceps and chiseled calves strutting out from under his little black nylon shorts.

The admiral was duly impressed. With a smile, he replied, "Well, that explains much."

"You're in for a treat, Sir. Duncan can definitely play. He's the best I ever saw."

Hunter, unconsciously trying to turn McGee into a liar, had a poor start and was down 3-11 and about to call time-out. Goose walked over to Hunter and said condescendingly, "You try too many low-percentage shots."

The Goose returned to the service box to serve the next point.

Hunter grinned, turned to the door, and called, "Time out," leaving his opponent standing in the court, smirking.

When Hunter left the court, McGee left his place beside the admiral and moved to the court door. He handed Hunter a towel and bottle of water. "It doesn't look like it's going well."

"Sometimes I take someone for granted or forget I'm playing a southpaw. Today, it's a little bit of that and a distraction. I keep hitting it right back to him, and that redhead is a major distraction. He's a smart player and has lived off guys who forget he's a southpaw. I'll be OK...I think." Giving McGee a wry smile, he wiped sweat from his brow.

Hunter looked up, smiled at the redhead, and made eye contact with the admiral in the back. He also noticed the dark, Middle-Eastern man to the admiral's left. He'd seen him before, thinking he was the Saudi officer who repeatedly tried to talk to him, but Duncan couldn't recall his name.

Admiral DiFillipo gave Duncan a thumbs-up, and he returned the gesture with a wink.

As Hunter returned to the court, it was clear to those watching that a shift in momentum had occurred. Once Hunter gained the serve, he hit drive serves to Goose's forehand, who tried to kill the ball, but every time the ball stayed in play, Hunter deftly scored.

In ten minutes, Hunter rolled off ten straight points and won the first game 15-13. The Navy part of the crowd went wild.

McGee grinned, held out a dry towel and water bottle for Hunter, as he stepped from the court while Goose remained, crushing the little green ball with a vengeance.

"Is that better, Sir?" Hunter asked.

"What did he say to you? It seemed like he said something, and, when you went back in, you were a different person. No more Mr. Nice Guy or what?"

Removing his drenched shirt, Hunter toweled his head and chest. "He said, 'You try too many low-percentage shots.'" He rummaged in his large racquetball bag for another shirt, pulling out a white-collared polo with a large decal on the back with the words, 25th Anniversary National Singles Championships.

As Hunter removed his sweat-drenched shirt, all eyes went to the man in black shorts and white, high-top court shoes. His thirty-inch waist set the demarcation of heavily defined abdomen muscles and obliques, fanning up to solid pectorals the size of soup bowls. As he replaced his shirt, he caught the striking redhead smiling, but he scanned the crowd, oblivious to the women until he saw the admiral, his arms crossed, with a big smile—and the same Middle Eastern man to the admiral's left.

Is he watching McGee or me? Duncan wondered. He glanced at the redhead again. *I think she's a Navy commander.*

She looked at him hard, barely biting her finger, her lips on the edge of a smile.

Duncan smiled to return the gift. McGee talking pushed him into the present.

"He tried to tell you how to play, and you kicked his ass? Oh, that's rich."

"I've played a lot of assholes. Once I played a guy who was so offended by how easily I beat his ass, he wanted to fight me right there on the court. Some guys are nice, but, when they get onto the court, they turn into turds. This guy just thinks he's a better player than he really is. He hasn't hit me or pissed me off—yet."

Twenty minutes later, it was over. Hunter stood in the middle of the court, hugging his sweaty, bald, muscular opponent. It appeared they left the court as good friends. Both were engaging and animated.

The crowd enjoyed seeing great racquetball. When the two men emerged from the court, they heard applause and

"Hooyahs!"

McGee, smiling, offered Hunter a towel and water. "You could have given him a chance in that game."

"Yeah, right. I just exploited his weakness. He really is an awesome player. And, I got lucky with my low-percentage shots." His voice held a tinge of sarcasm.

"I couldn't tell which was a low-percentage shot and which wasn't."

"When he tried them, they were low-percentage shots. He didn't win many points that game."

"Oooo! Be nice, Hunter." Under his breath, he added, "For whatever it's worth, that's the difference between a sniper and a shooter. Snipers practice what would be a low-percentage shot for anyone else."

Hunter nodded at those words of wisdom and shed his sweaty shirt. The admiral pushed his way through the crowd of back-patters and well-wishers. Hunter stood to face the Naval War College President, toweled his head and hands, and accepted the admiral's handshake. The crowd remained around them.

"Well done, Duncan. You made that look easy."

The Middle-Eastern man stood and watched Hunter and McGee, but so did everyone else.

"Mission accomplished, Sir."

The tall, soft-spoken admiral patted Duncan's shoulder with his free hand. "I'm very proud of you. That was a history-making event, and I appreciate your efforts. Again, well done, Duncan."

"Thank you, Sir. Appreciate it."

The crowd thinned. Hunter stood with arms akimbo. The excited admiral looked for something else to say.

"How's the research coming?"

As Hunter pulled on his shirt, McGee said, "Sir, we can brief you when we're back. We're in Suitland this week to wrap it up."

"That'll work. Well, Gentlemen, I have to go rub a little gold medal into the nose of the Air War College President."

"Sir, tell him some old, fifty-year-old, decrepit, blind Air Force civilian got out of his wheelchair and kicked his guy's ass." Hunter made quote marks in the air with his fingers when he said "Air Force."

That brought another smile to the admiral. "You can count on it. Safe travels to Suitland and back to Newport." He shook hands with both men.

As the admiral left, McGee asked, "So, what are you doing after this?"

"I need to find a hot tub or massage before heading back. I'm all checked out. You?"

"We're touring the area before we head back tomorrow. We're going to a place called the Horseshoe Curve to take the girls on a picnic."

"That sounds like fun—planes, trains, and automobiles. Be safe, get earplugs, and I'll see you on Monday, good sir."

McGee was confused. "Planes, trains, and automobiles? Did you say earplugs?"

"You're going to Horseshoe Curve. I think it was the first horseshoe curve for trains in America. It'll be fun. And, it'll be loud."

"I had no idea. Anyway, Duncan, that was great. It's exciting to watch you play."

"Thanks, Bill." He saluted the SEAL as he turned away. Then his eye caught the Middle Eastern man trying to look inconspicuous, as McGee departed. Duncan thought he was imagining things when the man turned away and left the building in another direction.

Suddenly, he caught strong perfume wafting through his nostrils.

"That was exciting!" The busty, redheaded Navy Commander walked up to Hunter's blind side, catching him off guard.

"Thank you. I got lucky today. I'm sorry. Duncan Hunter." He held out his hand.

"Nina Bergman."

"Glad to finally meet you, Nina. I've seen you in uniform

a few times at school." He wanted to add, *That perfume is perfect on you, but it's not as dramatic as Marwa's.*

"I've seen you and Captain McGee in Connelly. It seems you two always sit together."

"I'm told everyone is afraid to sit with him. For a SEAL, he hasn't bit or killed me yet, so I think we're almost friends."

She laughed and smiled. He asked, "Were you playing a sport?" He tried to place her accent and name the scent. Then he got it. New England and Giorgio.

She shook her head. "I helped get all the hotel reservations and logistics worked out. I've been one of the official cheerleaders. Don't you have somewhere you need to be, like getting a medal or something?"

"I think my fellow racquetball guys will pick it up, maybe even Admiral DiFilippo. He was very excited that Navy beat Air Force."

"Seems to me it was you who beat Air Force." She gave a wry grin.

"Shhh." He play-acted and looked around. "It wouldn't be proper to let the Air Force know one of their civilians beat their active-duty ringer."

Nina threw back her head, making her red hair wave in slow motion, and laughed. "Oh, yeah. You can't let that out. That's good. What are you doing now?" Her red hair fell back around her shoulders.

"I was going to clean up and hit the hot tub in the men's locker room to soak my aching body."

She thought for two seconds, then inhaled and smiled. "They have a great hot tub at my hotel in Harrisburg."

He was momentarily nonplussed. "If that's an invite, you're on. Dinner is on me, if you don't have plans." *I hope that wasn't too aggressive or pathetic,* he thought.

Without missing a beat, she smiled and said, "No, that sounds great."

CHAPTER THREE

0800 April 21, 2003
National Maritime Intelligence Center Suitland, Maryland

"Did I see you with Commander Bergman?"

"Will be I waterboarded?" Hunter frowned, thinking, Busted.

"You might get keelhauled."

"Sir, the record will reflect that the good commander offered the hot tub at her hotel to some gold-medal winning Air Force civilian puke. Afterward, they had a quiet little dinner in downtown Harrisburg. She's a great lady, we sat and talked for a good long while and we had a glorious time."

McGee rubbed his eyes and yawned. When he finished, he shot Hunter a look and shook his head. "She is an eyeful."

Hunter changed the subject. "How was Horseshoe Curve?"

McGee nearly shouted, "*Incredible!* We followed the small signs, got there, and didn't know what to expect. We walked up to the viewing area as one train was going up the hill and one was coming down. We were completely surrounded by screaming railroad cars, and the locomotives were nowhere to be seen. It was one of the most-amazing things I've ever seen."

"With two trains on the curve, that had to be loud."

McGee nodded. "I learned when you tell me to do something, I need to do it. I didn't get earplugs for my girls, and it was incredibly loud, almost painful. We complained about our ears ringing afterward."

"What?" Hunter, feigning deafness, leaned forward.

"I said…." McGee realized the joke. "You know, Air Force puke, waterboarding is too good for you."

Hunter was the first person McGee found it easy to be

around. Hunter wasn't impressed or afraid of him, he didn't ask for favors, and he was so levelheaded that McGee could call him a friend. His fellow SEALs were as close as could be, but they trained as a team and had to be. All SEALs had personality quirks, which gave them character. Sometimes, over time, it wasn't good character.

Hunter was one of those rare individuals to whom people naturally gravitated. McGee knew he could ask Hunter anything, and Duncan would do it without thinking anything of it. McGee knew the same worked in reverse.

"Are we ready?" Hunter asked.

"One minute. I have to say this has been fun no matter what happens in there. I learned much about airplanes and especially what quiet airplanes can do for a spec-ops warfighter. I really thought I'd just come up to Newport, be a vegetable, enjoy my wife and kids, and take it easy for once in my life. You opened my eyes and breathed new life into this old guy."

"Thanks, Bill. Teamwork—Hooyah!"

"It's more than teamwork. You didn't have to team with me to do this, and you didn't even blink about who got credit. I just want you to know I appreciate you and want to thank you again."

"Who's your buddy? Who's your pal?" Smiling, Hunter offered his hand, then he led the way into the room and opened the door for the SEAL.

Climbing the stairs to the executive suite, they found the conference room. Uniformed men and women waved the duo inside. Place cards on the conference table directed Captain McGee and Hunter to seats beside the CO. They barely had time to sit down when the room was called to attention.

Hunter wore a black suit as a civilian, but the retired Marine in him was obvious to all. Vice Admiral Jerry Lane, Intelligence Officer and Commanding Officer of ONI, entered and went directly to McGee to shake his hand and exchange a few quiet words.

Admiral Lane turned to Hunter next and shook his head, saying loudly enough for all to hear, "Admiral DiFilippo said you brought Navy a gold medal in racquetball during Jim Thorpe Days. That's fantastic. Well done." He patted Hunter's back and turned to the standing troops before waving them to their seats.

"Captain McGee, Mr. Hunter, I have to say your ideas on quiet aircraft have shaken up some of the old salts here. There's a group that thinks that unmanned vehicles are the wave of the future of Naval Aviation. You argue, quite persuasively, that being unmanned for unmanned's sake shouldn't be the governing factor. Costs and mission should dictate."

Hunter added, "Sir, there's been little research done on quieting aircraft. The most recent is from the sixties."

"And Sir," McGee said, "fielded DEVGRU units supported by a single quiet aircraft have resulted in unprecedented mission success."

"I've heard. The intel from JSOC confirmed, and General Jones was emphatic that we need to get more of those aircraft into theatre. Your research opened our eyes for SOCOM units such as DEVGRU, and now we have work to do. Great work, gentlemen."

"Thank you, Sir," Duncan and McGee said simultaneously. "Do you have any more ideas for us to work on?" the admiral asked half-jokingly.

Hunter took a deep breath. "Sir, I do. It's really a simple concept but not classified. It involves delivering cargo via an unmanned helicopter. It's not sexy stuff, but it would save untold lives and provide the Navy and Marine Corps with a capability they can't appreciate."

Lane, McGee, and the others looked at him quizzically. A slow smile came to McGee's lips. He realized Lynche was right about Hunter's immediate ability to think outside the box.

"Sir, we're having Marines and soldiers getting blown up right now by IEDs while delivering beans, bullets, Band-Aids, and blankets by truck. The roads are horrible. The environment is a saboteur's heaven. The service that gets the right helicopter platform and converts it into a robot will save untold lives and limbs. The best helo for such a demo is the K-Max. If ONI or NAVAIR would take a look and fund a demo, building an unmanned K-Max, I think you'll see that work will set the bar for the next generation of unmanned rotorcraft."

"K-Max?" the admiral asked.

"Sorry, Sir. The manufacturer of the H-2 Sea Sprite, Kaman, builds synchromesh rotor system helicopters, the Husky and the single-seat K-Max. Those designs solve the antitorque problems of trying to convert conventional tail-rotor helicopters into robots. The K-Max could easily be turned into a robot. It's inherently stable, and some smart guy could build a multiple sling delivery system so what my good friend Greg Lynche, the real brains behind this concept, would call an unmanned cargo delivery system.

"The integrated aerosystem could drop off thousands of pounds of supplies at multiple locations autonomously. You can program it. It's optimized for high-altitude work and is built like a tank. You'd get those logistics troops off the roads. The technology could be used for other pinpoint cargo drops, like dumping concrete into the bowels of the Chernobyl reactor instead of sending pilots to a slow, painful death."

Vice Admiral Terry Lane leaned back in his chair. "That's an intriguing concept. How about letting me talk with the NAVAIR commander about what's in the art of the possible? Commander Lance, did you get that?" He looked at the commander with the brilliant gold Naval Aviator wings on her dark uniform, who nodded back.

"Well, Gents, you know we have a war to support. We'd better get back to work." As the admiral stood, so did everyone else. "Again, thank you for your ideas and service. Fair winds."

After the admiral left, McGee and Hunter were detained for several minutes by the others, who wished them well and asked questions. The pretty, short Commander Lance made a beeline to Hunter and asked if he had a business card. They discussed the unmanned cargo-delivery system as he fished a card from his suit pocket.

She was the last member of the admiral's staff to leave when McGee heard her say, "I'll be in touch."

As the two men left the building, McGee shook his head and said in mock scorn, "I can't take you anywhere."

"What?" Hunter asked innocently. "Did I violate some obscure Navy rule?"

"Commander Lance."

"She's a helicopter pilot. She said she and her husband helo pilot have been wrestling with the torque problems for unmanned helos. Hearing about a synchromesh system was an epiphany for her, and she added that my analysis was spot on."

"Oh."

When they reached their vehicles, Hunter removed his overcoat, coat, and tie. He was ready to go and run the I-95 gauntlet back to Newport.

"Well, Sir, see you on the road?"

"Be safe," McGee said.

"Aye, aye." He smiled and saluted.

"You, too Apex."

CHAPTER FOUR

0715 May 5, 2003
Connelly Hall, Naval War College

The lady barber shaved the back of Hunter's neck when McGee entered the shop and stopped in front of Duncan, arms akimbo. Having a pissed off SEAL standing in front of you was not good.

"Have you seen the assignments?" McGee meant the Joint Military Operations War Game, the culminating course at NWC.

"No, Sir. You?"

"I did. I'm JCS, and you're chief of station."

"Chief of station? Don't we have someone from that... office attending? That makes no sense. Are you sure?"

"Oh, I'm sure. It gets better. I checked the script, and there's nothing for the COS to do. I'm busy, and you're vacationing."

"If I'm not doing anything, why bother having the position?"

"Maybe it will all be clear when we get an e-mail about our assignments. I'm off to pick up my books. I also wanted to share something with you, if you have a couple minutes."

"Eccles?"

"Yes, Sir."

"Well, Captain McGee, if you could wait until I pay for this masterpiece of a haircut, I'll walk with you to Eccles."

The barber smiled, as she unclipped the sheet and brushed hair from Hunter's neck.

The two men walked the eighty feet to the library.

"Do you know you're being watched?" Duncan asked quietly.

"Uh-huh. I don't think anything of it. At first, I did. I

241

wondered if they had a reason other than they think I killed one of their brothers or cousins or something. Not many sailors in AQ. Ever hear of the al-Qaeda Navy? There are a couple shitheads watching you, too."

Hunter cocked his head in surprise.

They rounded the corner, dropped their Blackberries into the basket on the table near the door, and went straight to their seats in the SCIF.

"Since we debriefed the admiral," McGee began, "your paper…."

"Our paper."

"Our paper went straight to SECDEF, who, I understand, blew a fuse. Not at us but the Air Force. Usually, it's a bad thing for the Old Man to know your name."

"I hear a but."

"But when someone does something clearly meritorious that impresses the SECDEF, then it's usually OK. Anyway, OSD is conducting another background check on you. I got asked, because we've been seen together a lot. I have no idea what for, but I thought you should know they're interested in you. What kind of tickets do you have?"

"I thought you had all that info. The usual—SSBI, TS/SCI, SI, TK, full scope, yada, yada, yada."

McGee's eyes narrowed. "That's not usual. I mean, for an Air Force civilian in aircraft maintenance."

"Agreed, Sir. I think most folks here were given my range of accesses because of the material we're studying. I could be wrong. In my real job back in Texas, I have no need to know or have access to imagery, but before coming here, I had to have my clearance updated, presumably because of the materials we'd be exposed to."

He didn't tell McGee about his activities with Lynche, which required being read in on several programs as required by Lynche's old place. Hunter started to wonder if SECDEF had been told of Wraith, the name of the highly compartmentalized TS "DCI eyes-only Special-Access Program."

The DCI liked to call them Batman and Robin when they were in Lynche's highly modified YO-3A, with Hunter as Batman, the pilot, and Lynche as Robin, the sensor operator.

McGee watched Hunter, who was clearly thinking fast to resolve a problem. "Nobody needs full scope to come here. Besides, you have one of those fancy TS clearances. That's CIA, Dude." Suddenly, he said loudly, "You're running an Op! Now it all makes sense!"

"What all are you talking about, Sir?" Hunter made quotation marks in the air with his fingers. He'd known the day was coming, and he didn't know how the SEAL would react. They hadn't shared many war stories. Those they discussed were unclassified or came under the heading of need to know. They knew the game but something changed.

"Why are you really here?" McGee had been around a long time and had seen the high and mighty come and go. He recognized Hunter's unusual talent from day one and couldn't rationalize why someone like him was keeping himself under the radar and hiding out at NWC—especially when that person made over a million dollars a year.

"Why are *you* really here?" Hunter asked, deflecting the question.

"You're avoiding the question."

"Bill, before you go off chasing a rabbit down a hole, like you, I'm sworn to secrecy for some things. If SECDEF is interested in me, he may have been briefed on something, but he wasn't supposed to be, and I can't imagine any circumstances where he would be. I'm a little government civil servant. I'm supposed to run in the clear, and, until I get a call, I'm a graduate student here like you. What I really think is this is a coincidence, and maybe you'll get an award or something."

McGee showed newfound respect for Duncan. "So that's how the spook knows you? Why do you think SECDEF is interested in you?"

Duncan shook his head at the first question and shrugged at the latter. "I think it's a ricochet from our joint paper. I can see with some Fruit Loops up the food chain it doesn't make sense having a SEAL on a quiet aircraft paper. It's incongruous and probably suspicious. I really didn't think it would be an issue. It was old research, and ONI wasn't even looking in that direction, nor was NAVAIR. Since we pulled strings to get everyone to Elmira to check out the Schweizer, generals may have talked and that may have raised more than a few eyebrows. I should call the Grinch and let him know there's DOD interest in me. Maybe he can find out."

"If I can help, you can count on me, Duncan. I'm serious."

"Thank you, Sir. Please know the feeling's mutual. It goes, without saying, if I can help you in any way…anytime. Call me."

"Thanks, Apex. I will"

"What's with that Apex thing? I used an apex when trying to pull out a stripped screw head in my old maintenance days."

"Dude, you're an apex predator, top of the food chain—fighter pilot, smart, educated….Have you seen yourself play racquetball? You hit that ball once, and it's a kill shot. You're a killer in pinstripes and nylon shorts."

Duncan smiled and patted McGee's rock-hard shoulder. "I'll take that as a compliment. Thank you, Sir."

"You should've been a SEAL. One of these days, you have to tell me."

"One of these days, I will, but not today. Sir."

CHAPTER FIVE

1100 May 6, 2003
Marriott Hotel Carlsbad, California

"What kind of religion could make people do this?" Sam Miller asked. Like many others shocked by the attacks on the World Trade Center and the Pentagon, Miller continually asked himself that question every time the burning towers flashed on TV, even two years after the national scar.

"What kind of religion could inspire people to do this? The President says Islam is a religion of peace. How is that possible if Muslims killed people on airplanes, then killed thousands more by flying those jets into those buildings?"

For months, many people around him openly mocked and cursed Muslims and Islam. He heard many prison inmates converted to Islam without knowing why. He read about other religions but never took time to read the Quran or understand Islam.

After the 9/11 attacks, he heard many things about Islam but found it hard to believe some of the hateful things. Something nagged at him about the dichotomy, the incongruity between the dialogue and the visual. The President said one thing, but Sam's eyes saw another.

"What kind of religion could make people do this?" It bugged him.

Protracted exposure to abuse, beatings, or other brutality can alter the human psyche. He added protracted combat and brainwashing to the list of personality-altering causal factors. Some survivors transcended the violence and tried to get on with their lives. Some became loners, while others descended into the pits of human hell.

The Marines from Iwo Jima and Guadalcanal experienced the range of depravity their Japanese opponents could throw at them, from combat to brutality. Sam Miller was abused and demeaned in his home as a child and youngster by the men his mother brought home. Her boyfriends beat him when they were high on alcohol or weed. When they tried pharmaceutical cocktails, some of them raped the young Sam Miller.

Recently discharged from the Marine Corps, Sam's life was in a tailspin. He survived physical and sexual abuse from his mother's drunken, dope-head boyfriends until he began to grow and fill out. Seeing what drugs, liquor, and tobacco did to people made him ask himself, Why do people do these things and use bad things?

When he passed the six-foot mark, he turned to schoolwork and fitness as a way to keep men away from him. Eventually, they stopped coming to see his mother. She resented and rejected her son as the sex, booze, and drugs dried up.

When he spurted to six-feet-five-inches tall, Miller became more inquisitive and introspective. He shunned group sports, although basketball coaches begged him to join the team. He began to worry about going to college and finding work. Jobs were rare for any youngster in the poor part of Hamtramck, Michigan.

During a high-school assembly where each military service was represented, the common theme that resonated with Miller from the men on stage was, if you wanted a college education, look to the Reserve Officers' Training Corps. He immediately transferred out of one class into the Junior ROTC. Soon, he distinguished himself as an accomplished marksman with a .22- caliber rifle. His six-foot-seven-inch frame and muscularity helped him maintain an outstanding, consistent shooting position.

He became more interested in the physics and mechanics in a projectile's flight than an arcing basketball. He found more of a challenge in the quiet solitude and accomplishment of taking aim, controlling his breathing and pulse, and sending a bullet to the target. Naturally detail-oriented, Miller's groupings became tighter and tighter. He never missed, often sending a round through the same hole on the target. Then came ROTC shooting matches, which allowed him to practice with match-grade weapons and precision ammunition.

The combination of superior and rock-solid body control and finely tuned weapons catapulted Miller to excel in the sport, crushing the competition from large high schools or in state-wide matches. As he collected rifle trophies and medals, there was talk of Olympic tryouts. The JROTC Master Chief Petty Officer in Charge asked him, "Have you ever thought about becoming a SEAL team sniper?"

For a seventeen-year-old, the thought of using a heavier weapon and more-powerful ammunition to shoot at bad people who hurt others fired his imagination. Finding a sport that capitalized on his natural ability and leave-me-alone personality, he realized any desire to go to college was trumped by thoughts of becoming a secretive commando and lone sniper.

A quick enlistment in the Navy and orders to Basic Underwater Demolition to become a Navy SEAL ended on the beach in Coronado. For the muscular six-foot-eight-inch Miller, a lengthy, difficult swim in the cold Pacific brought on a severe case of hypothermia and cardiac arrest. His dream of becoming a SEAL was washed away.

A Marine Corps recruiter took a chance on the tall, muscular kid with 100 shooting trophies and medals, and sent him back to San Diego for Marine Corps boot camp and a chance to be a Marine Scout Sniper. An unseen gust of wind during the West Coast Regional Shooting Championships prevented Miller from establishing a new all-time long-range record of consecutive bull's eyes at 1,000 yards while garnering three gold medals, including youngest overall champion in history.

He was momentarily filled with glory, as the Marine Corps sniper community prepared to embrace the record-setting hero, when the aftermath of an FBI investigation forced the Corps to release and discharge Miller, humiliating him forever as the "Marine Corps sniper that couldn't."

Mentally and physically crushed, Miller was almost unable to function. He stumbled into a sporting goods store and began selling weapons to people who would engage the salesman with some version of, "What kind of religion could inspire people to fly jets into buildings? I feel I need to better protect myself and my family, and I'm looking for a gun."

Day after day, Miller sold handguns, shotguns, and rifles to men for hunting while some lambasted a religion.

He left his home in Michigan, where one of the largest concentrations of Muslims lived and worked, and went to school. He didn't have a single bad or noteworthy experience with the Muslims in his neighborhood or in school. When he walked past a small mosque, and men poured through its doors, he noted it and kept walking.

Another time when he approached the mosque, he heard a man singing the call to prayers, but it barely registered a thought, other than *That's kind of cool.*

After 9/11, Sam Miller continually asked himself, What kind of religion could make people do that?

After the crushing humiliation of being discharged from the Marine Corps, he decided it was time to find out. He walked across the parking lot from the sporting goods store to the monstrous bookseller to buy a copy of the Quran. With his height, he easily located the religion section and found the English version of the Quran behind a locked case. The cover design intrigued him. The Arabic calligraphy invited questions. He wondered if his notions of Islam as a patriarchal and seemingly violent religion would be confirmed.

A short clerk with thick glasses and unkempt hair unlocked the case and handed the book up to Miller. He tentatively opened the green leather-and-gold embossed cover and page edges. Standing there hunched over, he slowly turned page after page. When he came to the first chapter, with its seven-line message about seeking guidance from a merciful creator, he looked up and wondered how anyone could disagree with that.

He bought the Quran and finished reading it a few weeks later, then he started over. Day after day, he sold guns to people who freely expressed their antipathy to Islam. Halfway through his second reading, he realized he faced a decision.

After confronting a man who came to purchase a pistol and said, "Muslims hate peace. They kill each other for sport," Miller decided to convert. He nearly lost his job, but he studied Islam more intensely. Within a few months, the Michigan-born salesman made his Islamic declaration of faith, or hehadah, at the Islamic Society of Carlsbad.

"I guess it seemed kind of crazy to do at the time," he told the man nearly his own height, "turning to a religion that's so reviled, but I find the Islamic concept of God a beautiful thing. It fits with what I believe."

"You don't have concerns that Muslins flew those jets into those buildings?" said the other tall man.

"I don't. I've come to see America is demonizing Muslims as terrorists and oppressors of women, but now I can't think of anything that's further from the truth. Those who did that horrible act weren't real Muslims. They disrespected Islam. I've always had a good moral compass, and now I have a God I can look up to."

"Thank you for your time. Good luck to you and your beliefs."

"Thank you, Mr. Yoder. I appreciate your time and consideration. I'm sorry you came all this way to talk to me. I know I've found God, and I can continue to shoot and enter competitions. I'm at peace with myself, and that's all I ever wanted."

CHAPTER SIX

0800 May 7, 2003
Classroom 214, Naval War College

Admiral DiFilippo and Captain McGee entered the classroom. The instructors saw the admiral opening the door and barked, "Attention on deck!"

Chairs banged against the walls, as twelve military and three foreign officers rapidly came to attention. The single civilian saw the admiral and was already at attention before the two-star fully entered the class.

Both men pivoted in the center of the room and stopped, award binders in their hands. A photographer filled the doorway and adjusted his flash attachment.

Someone's getting a medal, Hunter thought.

The admiral and McGee paced to the center of the classroom and faced the class.

"Mr. Hunter, front and center."

Hunter jumped at the sound of his name. *Is this what all the noise is about? Thank God I'm in a coat and tie.*

He turned smartly to pass behind his fellow students, pivoted with precision, and presented himself one pace before the admiral. He'd done that a time or two in what felt like a lifetime earlier.

"There's no official ceremony to promote DOD civilians," Admiral DiFilippo began, "but any time a distinguished civilian is selected for promotion, it's a time for celebration and ceremony. Attention to orders!"

McGee opened a navy-blue awards folder and read, "By the direction of the Secretary of Defense, Mr. Hunter is hereby promoted to GS-15."

"Raise your right hand and repeat after me," the admiral said.

"I, Duncan Hunter, having been appointed a GS-15 in the United States Air Force, do solemnly swear that I will support and defend the Constitution of the United States against all enemies, foreign and domestic; that I will bear true faith and allegiance to the same; that I take this obligation freely, without any mental reservation of purpose of evasion; and that I will well and faithfully discharge the office upon when I am about to enter. So help me God."

A flash went off, capturing the two men with their raised hands.

"Congratulations." The admiral shook Hunter's hand, then Captain McGee and the class applauded loudly.

"At ease," the admiral said. "I think this seminar group knows Duncan's contributions at Jim Thorpe, leading his team in beating Air Force and winning the Naval War College's very first gold medal in racquetball. Mr. Hunter unfortunately missed the awards ceremony." The admiral looked seriously at Hunter and asked, "What was more important than getting your medal?"

Before Hunter could find the right words, McGee said, "Sir, I believe he had to get on the road to Suitland."

"Oh. That's right. Well, Mr. Hunter didn't properly receive his gold medal."

McGee held up an engraved Jim Thorpe medal in its small presentation case. The admiral took it from the box, opened the ribbon, and slowly draped it over Hunter's head.

"For superior sportsmanship and for kicking the Air Force's, er, leading Navy over the Air Force Team in racquetball, congratulations." Shaking Hunter's hand again, he patted his shoulder, as the others applauded loudly. A shutter clicked, and a flash discharged loudly, as the admiral and Hunter smiled at the camera. A moment later, Hunter scowled at McGee.

"Attention to orders!" McGee handed the admiral the dark-blue ribbon and bronze medal and read, " To all who shall see these presents, greetings. The Secretary of Defense takes great pleasure in awarding Duncan Hunter the

Department of Defense Distinguished Civilian Service Award for meritorious service and superior performance while serving as student, Naval War College. His contributions in the research and development of special-purpose aircraft concept of operations have significantly enhanced mission effectiveness for the Joint Special Operations Command and the Department.

"Mr. Hunter's conduct reflects exceptional devotion to duty and distinguished service to the United States of America. His actions are in keeping with the highest traditions of the Naval War College and the Department of Defense."

More photographs were taken.

The admiral stepped forward to pin the medal on Hunter's chest, then he stepped back and said, "Congratulations." He shook Hunter's hand again and leaned forward to ask softly, "Come by my office, say 1400?"

Captain McGee and the others applauded. "Yes, Sir," Hunter replied.

A motor drive clicked several pictures with multiple flashes. "Everyone," the admiral said more loudly, "come and congratulate Duncan."

Hunter shot McGee another look, who responded with shrugged shoulders and incredulity. Something about the entire hullabaloo wasn't right.

The admiral and McGee left quietly together. The instructor asked Hunter if he'd mind letting the rest of the class know what he did with special-purpose aircraft.

"I'm sorry, Sir. I'm pretty sure that information isn't ready to be discussed outside a SCIF."

"Well, OK. In that case, let's get back to class. What were we discussing? Oh, yes, interagency operations...."

CHAPTER SEVEN

1400 May 7, 2003
President's Office Naval War College

"You may go in, Mr. Hunter," the secretary announced.

"Duncan, come in, please." The admiral stood and walked around a busy small conference table, intercepted a confused Duncan Hunter, and shook his hand.

Two men and a woman stood and introduced themselves. The tall, thin man was Dr. Stan Lu from the Office of the Secretary of Defense. The balding man was Jim Ebanks, from the Defense Intelligence Agency. The plain woman called herself Dr. Laura Schmidt and was from the Defense Advanced Research Projects Agency.

Admiral DiFilippo waited until all were seated. "Duncan, it seems your research into quiet airplanes caught a few people off guard. As I understand it, it was somewhat timely."

"Yes," Dr. Lu said. "It's very unusual for any of the war colleges to have the records of classified development work. We've been asked to try to find out why the Navy has the classified archives, and hopefully, how and why you came to do your research."

Hunter thought *it was our research* and wondered where McGee was. Since he didn't hear a question in the speaker's preamble, he remained quiet. His expression and body language screamed concern and wariness.

"Duncan, you aren't in any trouble," Ebanks said, frowning slightly. "If anything, you should get a medal for your unilateral contribution to the discipline of aerial acoustics."

"I didn't do anything but dust off some old research and ask why we, DOD, aren't using quiet aircraft technologies. I knew about YO-3As from the men who flew them in Vietnam.

I knew the Schweizers replaced the old prototypes and were very successful in the counterdrug and counterinsurgency roles, and thought they'd be useful along the border when I worked for the Border Patrol. I came here, wondering if the original research was in the archives. Most of it was, so I asked if I could do some related classified research to possibly help Navy SEALs, I'm sorry, DEVGRU in the field. That's really all there is to it."

Dr. Schmidt looked at him over her bifocals. "We were a little taken aback by your recommendation of putting quiet manned aircraft into the inventory instead of unmanned vehicles. The trend is toward unmanned platforms, but your conclusions highlighted that you felt it was a misapplication of scarce resources."

"I tried to find a nice replacement word for stupid," Hunter said. *I probably should not have said that.*

Dr. Lu, a dark, unexpressive Asian, deadpanned, "Why do you think that?"

"Some of it's really simple," Hunter said. "What does it take to put a Predator into a new operating area, say Peru? The answer is about 50 to 100 people, where most are needed just to maintain the aircraft and operate the vans for a group of remote pilots and sensor operators to fly it. The intelligence community can put more capability into the same location with four people, and two are in the airplane—a quiet airplane.

"Then there's the complete vulnerability of your systems. You can work on firewalls and other encryption protection, but what will kill your unmanned systems will be a simple computer virus. It might be five or six years before we hear of any confirmed incidents of classified information being lost or transmitted to an outside source. Then we'll find a virus embedded into the software somehow or somewhere, or a stealthy UAV goes stupid over Iran, where it'll undoubtedly crash into an orphanage or be splashed on CNN.

"Network security specialists will keep wiping viruses from the systems, but they'll find they've been hacked. At some point, DOD will have to face the fact it's under attack. For unmanned systems, that means if they can shut down a single UAV or a fleet of them, they can also hijack them and make them turn on you like a rabid pit bull.

"For a fleet of unmanned aircraft, you're introducing a single point of failure. With a manned aircraft, you aren't. I can still fly it. Unmanned aircraft…." He paused and changed his line of thought. "Imagine the look on a controller's face when he tries to tell an armed Predator to turn left, and it stops talking to him and heads back from whence it came. Instead of human hijackers flying planes into buildings, we'll have some Iranian or Chinese virus hijack not one craft but everything in the fleet. When all your money has been spent on ramping up your unmanned capability, the only thing you'll have left operational will be manned aircraft. By then, you're screwed."

Ebanks smiled. Lu raised his eyebrows.

"The technology is improving daily," Schmidt began. "The cost curve is going down. Unmanned aircraft will soon be less expensive to operate than manned."

"No disrespect, you can choose to believe that but you're flat-out wrong. If you'd done your homework, you'd know there's a growing body of evidence that unmanned systems don't solve problems but simply change their nature. Complex thinkers recognize the paradox. The very systems designed to reduce the number of humans to operate and support them require even more people to support them. Weren't we supposed to be paperless by now and now we go through more paper than ever. It's liberal folly. The current DOD approach to this science project is squandering money that could be used for other things, like building more quiet manned airplanes that cost a third of a Predator, are more effective, and can't be hijacked by a virus."

They waited for him to finish. He got the hint. "So what do you want from me?"

"SECDEF would like you on the Quiet Aircraft Systems Project Office on a team to develop quiet aircraft capabilities,"

Dr. Lu said. "Actually, they want manned and unmanned. After you graduate, you'll be reassigned. The moment we walk out of this office, quiet aircraft development goes full black. It becomes a DOD Special Access Program."

CHAPTER EIGHT

0800 May 9, 2003
Global Mission Solutions Eufaula, Alabama

After the 9/11 attacks, the head of counterterrorism at the CIA investigated the feasibility of hiring cleared private security firms to perform personal security work for Agency and Embassy personnel in Afghanistan and projected Iraq would require even more contractors. The Special Activities Division was stretched to the breaking point putting every available CIA officer into country to collect and develop intelligence. Contractors would help free up Agency personnel for more kinetic activities.

As Marines rolled into Baghdad, the counterterrorism head received approval to hire more contractors to operate overseas. The Agency turned to a few trusted start-up companies for those services, including Blackwater, Triple Canopy, KBR, DynCorp, and others. Several former special operations and SEALs founded defense contracting firms, which provided assessments of terrorist organizations, their techniques, and their abilities.

There was plenty of lucrative personal security detail work for those companies. When the Director of Central Intelligence or the Chief of Counterterrorism needed something more than a terrorist assessment, something special and covert, and they couldn't do it in-house or needed a high level of plausible deniability, they turned to the innocuous-sounding GMS for their expertise in conducting "special activities."

A former intelligence officer and Green Beret, Colonel Arthur Yoder, started Global Mission Solutions as a green-badged consultant for the intelligence community as soon as he retired from the Pentagon. Yoder's claim to fame was being the military intelligence officer of several top-secret operations, including the Green Berets who tracked down and found Che Guevara in Bolivia.

Every week, Lieutenant Yoder left their expeditionary campsite in the jungle, went to the US Embassy, and, from the ambassador's office personally checked in with the President of the United States and gave him a SITREP on a cleared line. After four weeks of tracking Che and his band of terrorists through the jungle, when the President asked Yoder how the men were holding up, Yoder replied lightheartedly, "Sir, they're doing well and are looking forward to getting out of the jungle and getting some ice cream."

Two days later, a single US Air Force cargo plane arrived at El Alto International Airport in La Paz with supplies, including fifty gallons of Baskin Robbins ice cream.

Yoder returned to his troops in the field and said, "Gentlemen, the President of the United States sent us fifty gallons of ice cream with a note. 'Art, get that SOB.'"

Three days later, Che was captured by CIA-assisted Bolivian forces and was executed. The same day, Yoder reported to POTUS their mission was accomplished.

The President responded with, "You tell your men well done, and enjoy the ice cream."

Green Beret Captain Yoder found himself on the lead team of every major special operation, from the infamous Son Tay raid as the intelligence officer to Operation Eagle Claw as a member of the Army's newly formed Special Forces Command Detachment Delta. When a mob rushed the walls of the US embassy in Tehran and held hostages, Delta Force planned for their rescue but failed in the Iranian desert. Eagle Claw ended in disaster when a Marine Corps CH-53, flying off the USS Nimitz, collided with an Air Force C-130 at the Desert One refueling point. The crew chief of the destroyed Marine helicopter, Staff Sergeant Dewey Johnson, USMC, was killed.

Sergeant Duncan Hunter, USMC, Dewey's roommate in Okinawa and on the Nimitz, stood on the flight deck, waiting for his friend to return, when a tall Green Beret walked off the back of the last helicopter and saw the Marine standing alone, waiting. Exhausted and defeated, the tall man changed directions and walked up to the jarhead. With tears rolling down both men's cheeks, Lieutenant Colonel Art Yoder told Hunter, "They aren't coming home, Marine."

Yoder's Cat One Yankee White clearance and one-on-one meetings with future presidents didn't win him any accolades with Pentagon brass. When he retired, he seemed to be on every defense contractor's short list for a presidency for some related line of business. Instead, he opened his one-man shop with a collection of on-call talent for special projects, like the former CIA Chief of Air Branch and a retired Marine F-4 pilot who happened to play racquetball and could land a taildragger at night inside the width of a two-lane road. Yoder collected uncommon or unusual talent that provided a range of capabilities for his customers' needs.

Together, they submitted classified proposals to the intelligence community on known intelligence community shortfalls. Yoder traveled the country interviewing people with special talents. Human resources and civilian personnel offices for three-letter agencies or billionaires weren't equipped or capable of finding unusual, specialized, one-of-a-kind talent. There are thousands of Cessna pilots but only a handful of astronauts who can fly supersonic aircraft. There are a couple hundred fighter pilots but only a handful who could pass a piss test and a full scope polygraph. Of that group, maybe one or two could land a glider at night inside a baseball stadium or steal an F-14 from an Iranian air base.

Finding people who could do that kind of thing was Yoder's specialty. When he was contacted and negotiated a contract, government or commercial, they were very lucrative and made him and his cohorts increasingly wealthy for performing nearly impossible missions. When a workforce held improbable skills and talents, executing improbable missions with plausible deniability, he generated a great deal of interest and more incentives for success.

Greg Lynche planned to let the phone ring. He was

preoccupied with sliding the kitchen door just enough and shoot the damn deer licking seed from his large bird feeder.

Sighing, he shouted at the deer, set down the BB gun, and ran for the phone. "OK, I'm coming. Greg Lynche."

"Good morning, Mr. Lynche. You busy?"

"Art! Good morning. I hoped you got my e-mail. Where are you?"

"I was at Camp Pendleton. I interviewed a gent who won a major rifle championship and could shoot seventy consecutive bull's eyes at 1,000 yards. I thought he would be a good fit for that project with your old place."

"Sounds like you were disappointed. You didn't give him a job?"

"It was a waste of my time. I should have said he was a world-class shooter who suddenly found Islam."

"Uh, that sounds like a bad combination."

"If I'd known, I wouldn't have stopped. He seems at peace with himself. Anyway, I'm sitting in the Admiral's Club at LAX waiting to get out of here. What have you heard?"

"The neighbors down south are shitting in their own mess kit." Lynche sat at his computer and double-clicked Internet Explorer.

"I'll be in the area tonight if you think we'd be interested."

"I'll throw some steaks on the grill."

"Thank you, Sir. See you soon."

Lynche quickly typed an e-mail to Hunter. Call me.

CHAPTER NINE

2000 May 9, 2003
Annapolis Golf Club Apartments

Greg Lynche, hearing a car door shut in the driveway, hurried across the Persian rugs and opened the door to find Art Yoder with an overnight bag. The tall man thrust a bottle of wine into his face.

"Louis Roederer Cristal Rose, 1998." Yoder pushed through the portal, leaving Lynche on the stoop scrutinizing the salmon-pink label.

"I think this will go well with the filet." It wasn't every day he sipped $500 wine.

"I gotta piss." Yoder set his bag in the bedroom doorway, used the head, and wandered back into the kitchen.

"Must be something ugly if you're bringing a '98 Roederer. The beef's almost ready," Lynche said.

"First of all, we have to celebrate our new acquisition. Second, your old place wants to see if we can intercept some hot materials and maybe find some tunneling activity on the other side of the border—Nogales. As you said, they're going nuts. Easy weeklong surveillance out of Tucson. We also have to install some radiation detectors on 007."

"Hot materials? You mean...?"

"Radioactive."

"In Mexico?"

"The intel suggests a drug lord was paid a couple million to get it from Monterey into the US. Supposedly, he's going to use his tunnel. The FBI and Border Patrol think it's in Nogales. Ever been there?"

Lynche shook his head. "Dirty bomb materials or something else?"

"No need to know."

"Hmmm. When do we need to be in Nogales?"

"Your old place and the NRO and NSA tracked it from Iran. The Navy's shadowing the ship. Intercept window begins in two weeks. The detectors will be here tomorrow. Saul has a sheet-metal mechanic and an avionics tech en route to do the install. The Bobsey twins have 007 out of the can and in the hangar and are doing some upgrades to the container."

"Have you seen these detectors?"

"I have not. When we get to Arizona, we might have a chance to check them for airworthiness or see if they'll whistle. Like last time, you'll do some low-level flights and duct tape anything that looks like it'll tweet. Saul assures me they'll be fine."

He let Lynche ponder what would be necessary for the next mission.

"When does Duncan graduate? When do we pick her up?"

"I'm heading down to Miami tomorrow and get checked out. Do you want to go?"

"Can't. Have to head to Jordan for a meeting with the Prince—His Royal Highness, not that little fuck who likes purple crushed velvet."

Lynche was momentarily confused, but for someone who didn't know what a Chic-fil-A was, Yoder wasn't surprised.

"Duncan's scheduled for the first week of June, but we should be able to get him to graduate early, or he might be able to take leave. It shouldn't be a problem. If there's a problem, he'll find a way, or I'll make a couple calls.

"Also, he was notified that SECDEF wants him to help with developing new quiet aircraft technologies. Seems like his paper struck a chord with someone at NAVAIR and OSD. All Quiet Thruster research and his paper went full black."

Yoder's brows furrowed. "That could be good and bad. Do they know anything about Wraith?"

"I talked to Rob. He assures me our cover's solid, but I'm really worried about our operation getting exposed. SOCOM got five of the six available YO-3As. The NASA administrator told SECDEF to fuck off."

Yoder almost choked at the joke. He wiped his eyes with a smile. "That didn't help."

"Nope, but the little lady Duncan met certainly has."

"Do say! Have you seen her?"

"I haven't, but Rob assures me she's incredibly beautiful, and her Iranian mother has that Sofia Loren thing going on. The real news is she was fully debriefed, polygraphed, made a citizen, and is now a GS-13 in the NE Division. What's she's producing is turning heads."

"I sense a but...."

"Not with her. She has a thing for cryptology. I hear she took apart a couple coded messages from AQ and busted the code. We picked two high-value individuals off the street. She has a nose for this kind of work."

"Glad she's on our side."

"Along with the good comes some bad. I think 007 is at risk. I don't trust SECDEF, and it won't take him long to find out I have 007. Then all hell will break loose."

"Maybe I should brief him."

"If you ask me, I think he already knows and maybe doesn't care we're just working for my old place and doing great work. On the other hand, he could demand I return it. On the other hand, maybe DCI briefed him."

"Let's think about this. Ready to eat?"

"I'm ready to get the cork out of this bottle."

"Amen to that!"

CHAPTER TEN

1230 May 19, 2003
President's Office Naval War College

Admiral DiFillipo and Captain McGee shook Hunter's hand for the last time. "Sir, truly this was probably the best experience of my life," Hunter said. "I absolutely loved every bit of the school, and I could see coming back here as an instructor if there was ever a need for someone like me."

"Let me work on that," the admiral said. "We might be able to make you a professor emeritus, and you'll always have standing here. When you're done playing with OSD, you could come back and teach. You'd have to get a PhD at some point, but that's down the road."

"Admiral DiFilippo confirmed I'm staying on as a faculty member until I retire," McGee said. "Maybe I could work a deal to stay on full-time after I retire."

"Could you see us together again?" Hunter asked. "That would be asking for trouble."

"I think it would be fantastic," the admiral said, then he paused. "This isn't for release, at least, not yet. I think I told you I was going to retire next month?"

"Yes, Sir."

"Well, CNO called this morning and said he was sending me down to be the superintendent of the Naval Academy." Hunter, showing genuine surprise, offered his hand. "Congratulations, Sir. I know that means a promotion. Did that come out of nowhere?"

"It did. There are some problems in Annapolis, and the staff thought I'd be the right guy to settle things down."

"Sir, that has to be a first. I've never heard of the President moving to become the academy superintendent. Amazing things happen to good guys when their college wins a gold medal at Jim Thorpe."

The men laughed heartily. It had to be true.

"Good luck, Sir," Duncan said. "You know I have some friends in Annapolis…."

"Duncan, if you're in Annapolis, I expect you to call me, so we can get together. Do we have a good e-mail address for you?"

"Sir, your secretary and half a dozen others have it, as does Captain McGee. I guess I'd better get going on my next great adventure. If you're in the area or need me for anything, please don't hesitate to call."

The admiral gave him a thumbs-up, which signaled their good-byes were officially over. McGee walked out of the office with Duncan.

"Well, good Sir, I never thought this day would come," McGee said. "You did a lot for me, and I want you to know you're…." It seemed like the big SEAL was searching for words and fighting back tears. "…really special. You should have been a SEAL. You would've been a great one. I want you to have this."

He opened his hand to reveal a gold SEAL trident. Hunter was taken aback, and clenched his jaw, fighting back his own tears. "This is the only warfare specialty pin that's the same for officers and enlisted," McGee said. "It symbolizes that Navy SEALs are brothers in arms. They train and fight together. You and me—Mustangs. You'll always be my brother in arms, Sir. Thank you for everything."

"Thanks, Bill. I don't know what to say. You're amazing, good Sir."

"Stay in touch, Apex. That's an order. Fair winds and following seas, Sir." McGee saluted. Hunter thought McGee looked like a Roman God in that uniform.

Hunter returned the salute. "WILCO, Bullfrog. Take care."

He watched as McGee executed an about face and marched off without looking back. He looked at the Trident in his hand before closing his fingers tightly around it while fighting back tears. He wiped his sleeve across his eyes.

Duncan Hunter bounded from Hunter Hall, jogged across Cushing Road, and took the steps up to his truck. Checking his watch, he shed his suit coat and drove from the Naval War College compound pulling his trailered Corvette. He headed up Luce, negotiated the obstacles adjacent the guard shack, and drove toward the roundabout.

As he approached 3rd Street, he noticed the woman in the headscarf quizzically looking at his truck. Checking his side mirror, he frowned when she followed the trajectory of the Silverado.

"I wonder how long it'll be before they realize I won't be coming back," he muttered.

Speeding through the roundabout, he drove across the bridge at Narragansett Bay on his way to the old Naval Air Station Quonset Point, renamed Quonset State Airport.

He stopped at the FBO, crossing five parking spaces, and left the engine running. As he got out, he reached over the truck bed rail and retrieved a black ballistic nylon B-4 bag.

By the time he turned around, Bob from the YO-3A support crew crossed the parking lot and said, "I'll take good care of her, Duncan. See you in a few days."

Duncan shook his hand, looked both ways, and hurried across the parking lot to the FBO. Four minutes later, he closed the door and crawled into the copilot's seat of the waiting Gulfstream G-IVSP. "Thanks for the lift, Greg."

Lynche flicked Hunter's red tie, as he bent over to get seated.

"My pleasure. OK. ATIS info. Winds calm, your altimeter is set, and the tower freq is set. GPS is set via direct to Sierra Vista— 2500 miles. She's full of gas. Questions?"

After buckling into his seat, Hunter slid dark aviator sunglasses through his hair and onto the bridge of his nose. He arched his eyebrows several times before shaking his head in wonder and glancing at Lynche.

Lynche's lips moved behind his microphone, as he looked over and said, "Your airplane." Hunter smiled, looked forward over the yoke, and replied, "*Our* airplane, Sir."

The stunning, red-and-white Gulfstream shot across America. What had once been the $40 million private coach of a Colombian drug lord was seized in Ft. Lauderdale by the DEA. It should have been sold at fair-market value. The funds would have been deposited into the Drug Forfeiture Fund to help pay for counterdrug efforts and similar programs. Seized assets were also provided to other government agencies that needed special equipment if something became available.

Operated by a contractor out of Vienna, Virginia, a little-known US Quiet Unmanned Aircraft Research Laboratory had a long-standing request with the DEA for a Gulfstream G-IV or G- IVSP to be used in quiet-aircraft studies. It would be heavily modified with instruments and sensors to conduct classified and unclassified quiet aircraft research. When the informal network was activated with the news that the head of one of the biggest cartels in Colombia had his jet seized and confiscated, the head of the DEA had to get personally involved in the transfer of the jet, as every federal agency head wanted the plane for his organization.

The paperwork the DEA held clearly demonstrated the document was awarded a very high priority to conduct research "up to top secret" and the lab had been on the "hi-pri" list for years. The DEA administrator called one of the points of contact listed on the Request for Forfeiture Funds form.

When Greg Lynche answered the phone, the DEA administrator asked, after some formal introductions, "So, Greg, how is it you got a jet? Don't tell me, but you owe me big time."

CHAPTER ELEVEN

0430 May 26, 2003
Sierra Vista Municipal Airport, Sierra Vista, Arizona

On the third night of flying the Wraith along the border, monitoring activity in and around Nogales, the radiation detector startled both pilots. They studied the caution light on the multifunction display, as a mild, "woop, woop, woop," warbled in their headset. Then it stopped.

"OK. We got a hit, but I can't tell where it came from."

"What if I descend? Maybe we can pick it up again. I marked our position."

"Let's. While you're doing that, I'll rewind the tape and see what we missed while we were shooting the shit."

"I'll call Art." Hunter depressed buttons on the display.

"Roger."

Duncan selected the Fox Mike frequency, pulled the trigger switch past the interphone detent to transmit. "Redbull, Jaguar."

"Talk to me, Jaguar."

"Roger, Redbull. Got a single hit at 31-20-25 point 08 November and 110-56-21 point 07 Whiskey. Dash Two is looking at the tape to see if we missed any activity when the sniffer started barking."

"10-4. Confirm a single hit at 20-25 decimal 08 and 56-21 decimal 07."

"Read back correct. I'm orbiting the mark, but no more joy." From the back seat, Lynche flipped a selector switch and said, "Bingo. Redbull, we got a truck and the house on the dark side. We had a hit. A hot box was moved from a bread truck to a one-story ranch. There are several houses in the area with thick, probably concrete, walls. If you have your friends ready to move, I can paint the location."

"10-4. Monitor the house and surrounding area. I'll be right back after I contact the friendlies. Also, check for activity on the other side. They may move it immediately. We think it might take them awhile to get it to the other side."

"Roger, Redbull. Standing by."

Art Yoder turned to the Tucson Sector Chief Patrol Agent, the FBI regional director, and the worried little man from the Nuclear Regulatory Commission. "It's show time, Gentlemen."

The information from Ali Akmanni was right on target. He was ten for ten. Ali was picked up in Pakistan when he opened his cell phone on the outskirts of Peshawar. Thirty seconds later, a Predator launched a Hellfire into the building of men, women, and children.

A slight miss enabled al-Qaeda's chief of intelligence to crawl from the rubble and the body parts of his friends into the arms of two SEALs augmenting the CIA's Special Activities Division. The man's shattered left arm and compound-fractured leg required immediate attention.

The SEALs positively identified Ali Akmanni, removed their individual "blow-out" medical kits, and tended the man's injuries while the CIA officer called for a medevac helicopter.

One hour later, Ali was pronounced dead for the press pool in Kabul, but he was very much alive in the Army field hospital in Bagram. His condition stabilized after three days. Under cover of darkness, he was transferred to Jordan in a CIA cargo aircraft, where he was to be subjected to enhanced interrogation techniques.

After having his life saved and given the promise that no harm would come to his family, all the fight went out of Ali. He became a fountain of information and provided actionable intelligence. He gave them the location of Khalid Sheikh Mohammed in Rawalpindi, Pakistan. He knew the last-known location where the Taliban leader Mullah Mohammed Omar was hiding, as well as Osama bin Laden and Ayman al-Zawahiri safe houses in Pakistan and Iran.

He also provided information about a large quantity of radioactive Cesium-137 that al-Zawahiri wanted to smuggle into the US and release into the air in major cities or deposit into drinking water supplies. Iran had an overabundance of Cesium-137, one of the more well-known fission products after splitting uranium and plutonium atoms from their secret nuclear power projects.

Ali knew enough of the Iranian operation to move Cesium-137 into America that Ayman al-Zawahiri stayed along the border and continued to conduct al-Qaeda operations from Iran. Two shipments of Cesium-137 would be moved by ship from Bandar Abbas, the main base of the Iranian Navy and home to several shipping companies on the narrow Straits of Hormuz.

The first attempt to move twenty-five pounds of Cesium-137 was mysteriously lost when the small freighter began taking on water near Djibouti. The crew abandoned ship and were rescued by a French Navy frigate. Very few people knew that SEAL Delivery Team 1, from a US attack sub, boarded the Liberian-based freighter at night in semi-rough seas, located the radioactive slug, and scuttled the ship with several magnesium thermite strips which quickly ate holes in the hull. Still undetected, the six men of SEAL Delivery Team 1 slipped back over the freighter's side as it sank.

The next shipment was scheduled to be smuggled across the US border. In collaboration with a high-ranking member of Iranian Intelligence and a Mexican drug cartel warlord infatuated with pretty young Iranian girls, he offered to move whatever his friend wanted "one at a time" if they would keep a supply of fourteen-year-old Iranian girls coming to his casa. The load would be delivered to a parking lot outside a tiny mosque in Tucson.

The operation was briefed by the Director of Central Intelligence and approved for interdiction on US soil by the National Security Council. Confidence in Ali's information was high, and the interdiction strategy required an almost immediate response and oversight capabilities of a special group of patriots with Special Access operating a quiet aircraft with special sensors optimized for low-altitude operations. Derived from sensors developed for space applications, the YO-3A's wings were modified to integrate several cascading strips of an ultrasensitive, delicate, aerogel-backed, optically stimulated luminescence detectors.

Department of Energy specialists postulated that the radioactive material to be smuggled across the border would be easily read by overhead sensors at all US ports of entry. A small package of lead-lined radioactive material couldn't be totally shielded, so a minute level of radiation could be detected under the right circumstances.

The Wraith detected something hot at the proposed transfer location, as described by the recovering and increasingly well- cared-for Ali Akmanni. US Border Patrol intelligence officers, frequently operating on either side of the US border, were alerted by cell phone from their chief.

Encrypted text messages were exchanged via BlackBerry. The six-man interdiction crew donned personal-protective gear and bullet-resistant vests and moved to their vehicles. Interdiction forces in Nogales were on high alert.

Two hours later, the Wraith picked up the load to US Nogales. The FBI wanted to interdict the receivers of the materials in the US, and several agents were vectored to the right house and vehicle by the Wraith's IR laser designator.

Thirty agents from FBI, DEA, and Department of Energy took down the houses on both sides of the border and caught the vehicle with the radioactive load. The US transfer point was over 1,000 feet from the Mexican border, a distance unheard of in law- enforcement circles.

Lynche recorded the takedown of the house.

When it was clear that the job was complete, Yoder spoke into his radio. "Mission complete. RTB."

* * *

Mexican newspapers reported the takedown of a tunnel by the Mexican Army under the byline, Drug Cartel High-Tech Tunnel Falls to Ejercito Mexicano.

BOOK FOUR

CHAPTER ONE

0630 July 29, 2004
Deputy Chief Near East Division Office
CIA Headquarters

The previous night, Nick Dolan sat in his recliner. Newspapers and magazines were piled high on either side of the worn-out corduroy Easy Boy. A bottle of Heineken rested on a coaster, while a half-eaten bag of popcorn lay in his lap. Had his ex-wife seen him like that, she would've been furious.

A lifelong Republican who practiced his politics in the voting booth and living room, his curiosity got the better of him, and he turned to the Democratic National Convention on his big screen.

"Are they really going to nominate that guy? He was a misfit when he was in uniform. He's been a complete fuck-up as a senator, and he's running as a war hero? Reporting for duty? You're totally unfit for duty! Give me a break!" he yelled at the TV.

He drank beer and popped a few fluffy kernels into his mouth, as the keynote speaker was introduced. Taking a deep breath, he sighed.

"Why are Democratic women so homely?" Shaking his head and looking into his lap, so he didn't have to look at the Hollywood woman behind the lectern, he listened to her speak in her halting, breathless voice.

Dolan heard the keynote speaker was a Michigan state senator and a US Senate candidate. Music and applause in the background increased in volume and intensity, drowning out the keynote speaker's name. He looked up, expecting to see another homely woman take the podium. When he read the title bar at the bottom of the screen, introducing the keynote speaker, he was shocked.

His jaw fell open, and his brain tried to reconcile what he saw and what was in one of several hundred files in a safe at work. After his beer-tinged synapses resolved the problem, fitting all the pieces of the puzzle in his brain in a dozen milliseconds, he shot from his chair, sending popcorn and beer flying.

"Whiskey Tango Foxtrot, over!" he shouted at the big screen television, poised like a sumo wrestler ready to attack.

Dolan slept fitfully after listening to the neatly dressed senator and the sycophantic interviews that followed. His thoughts were on the unusual name on the file in his old office safe and his reaction to that information. In the morning, all the way to the office, Dolan debated what to do and who to talk to. Who else knew of that file? Probably not a high crime or a misdemeanor, most of the material in that file was interesting at best. Some of it could be detrimental to an up-and-coming US senator. Most people would simply ignore the comment in the context of the euphoria surrounding the convention spirit.

After the rousing keynote speech and the questions posed by the lickspittle press regarding his presidential ambitions, one of the senator's remarks perturbed Dolan enough to keep him awake all night. One of the secret code phrases of al-Qaeda was uttered on national television by a charismatic politician, who spent time in Pakistan in a terrorist training camp under a British passport.

Without disrupting his daily routine, Nick Dolan greeted his secretary, read the dispatch board, and settled behind his desk with hands surrounded the large mug filled to the brim with black coffee. He drained the mug, which advertised his Marine Corps roots, and headed out of the office for the offices and cubicles that made up the Near East Division.

He decided to ask the new employee to get the file from the archives, to have someone else's name on the chain-of-custody document to deflect any scrutiny as to why the deputy was interested in the file of a US citizen that should have been turned over to the FBI or NCTC a long time ago.

He found the cubicle at the end of the aisle. Unlike the work spaces of his other direct reports, this one was neat, sterile, and gray. Stopping at the doorway, he was greeted with bright platinum-green eyes, offering a script with several names.

"Good morning, Ms. Cunningham," Dolan said. "Could you please retrieve these files from the archives and bring them to my office?"

He wanted to watch her and her skirt walk to the vault of archived paper files at the end of the office, but he knew he would soon be treated with her presence and slow departure from his room. He almost ran back in anticipation of the shapely Ms. Cunningham and the file.

When she knocked on the door, he barked, "Enter!" one of his favorite holdovers from his days in the Marine Corps. A Navy SEAL entered, offered a stack of files, and began discussing the findings and analysis of their newest analyst.

"Have a seat, Danny. I was expecting Ms. Cunningham to bring these."

"Sorry to disappoint you, Nick. I know I'm not as good-looking as Nazy, but I ran into her in the vault and offered to bring these to you."

Everyone on the floor, including the women, stopped and stared whenever Ms. Cunningham left her cube or returned to it. The deputy was especially smitten, even though she rebuffed his suggestions of going out for drinks after his recent divorce.

"No factor. Thanks for the files. What do you have?"

"I know you're new to this position. I didn't know how much you knew of what we were doing, or what we've been doing."

"Only what I get from the weekly report. After that, not much."

"OK. For starters, Ms. Cunningham's been working with us for the last year. She's provided analysis and perspective on three of our projects. Suddenly, all have yielded amazing results."

"I know her first job was to help interrogate some high-value al-Qaeda. I understand she'd walk into the room, and the little goatfuckers never saw anything like her. She ripped them a new asshole in Arabic, and they spilled their guts. Then she discovered what happened to the Iraqi general who did all Saddam's purchasing."

"That's when I was assigned upstairs. I remember during our first meeting, she said Saddam had to have had a trusted agent to purchase materials and equipment for the production of WMD—biological, chemical, and nuclear. She targeted his ID from thousands of documents and hundreds of files brought back from the initial push into Baghdad. Nazy ascertained a certain Iraqi major general traveled frequently to Moscow and Paris, and his travel preceded significant weapons and equipment deliveries to Baghdad.

"But we still didn't have a name. Then she had the idea to monitor the Iranian Revolutionary Guard to see if they'd help identify the general, thinking they'd actively seek him out for his crimes against the Iranian people. All of Saddam's general officers were targeted, but we didn't know all their names. Anyway, those two pieces were a stroke of genius. She was able to ID him and was able to triangulate his location in Kuwait. The little shit ran to Kuwait City, right to a compound where his family lived for years."

"That's outstanding. Clearly top-block analysis."

"She said he'd probably be amenable to helping us and would want something for his work. Somehow, she knew that the man kept documents on everything he bought for Saddam— receipts, contracts, shipping and receiving papers—copies going back over twenty years. They were insurance of some sort. And, she was right. We sent a team to talk to him and convinced him to give us copies of the contracts, equipment and materials lists, delivery orders, and receipts of payments—usually in millions of gallons of oil."

"Food for oil, my eye." Dolan felt a little jealous when Cox spoke of how closely he worked with Nazy.

"We knew that was a sham. What I'm here to tell you is that the intel on WMD in Iraq was actually greater than previous estimates. Nazy pored over those documents but couldn't find where the materials and equipment was moved. Everything—what, when, and how—was there, but not the location. She asked if the analysis team asked where it was, but no one did.

"Two weeks ago, we went back and convinced the general to disclose where the materials and equipment went before US forces rolled into Baghdad. Last week, Team Six verified where the WMD went and where the equipment to manufacture biological, chemical, and nuclear weapons were stored until Saddam could retrieve them.

"What I want to tell you before you hear it from anyone else is that an hour ago, a flight of six Navy F/A-18s crossed the Syrian border and deposited twenty-four canisters of napalm on top of twenty-four GBU-18 bombs that were placed atop two warehouses twenty miles outside Aleppo. It's now true that there are no large caches of WMD in Iraq or anywhere else."

Dolan isolated the file he wanted, flipped it open, and scanned it while listening to the SEAL. "Oohrah! That's amazing."

"She's amazing in more than one way."

"She was working on something else for you?"

"She did, for us and the CTC. She asked if we were tracking the family members of OBL and Zawahiri. Devout Muslim men will go out of their way to have their families nearby, and we should be able to track them to where OBL and Zawahiri are holed up. The question provided insight into how she thinks and how obvious a strategy that would be. She sees things we don't. Professionally, she's a rock star in this business. I think she's a welcome addition to the NE."

"She's more than a welcome addition to the NE. She has energized her division. Her insight and analyses are on target. She's amazing."

"It's hard to believe she's Muslim. We certainly think she's amazing, and we appreciate her—all of her," Lieutenant Commander Danny Cox added with a sly smile.

The two men grinned in silence, lost in their thoughts, knowing any shared or articulated salacious thought would get one of them in trouble with the HR Nazis. Cox was about to leave when Dolan, wearing an expression that showed he had something else on his mind, asked, "Danny, can you keep a secret?"

The SEAL assumed the topic was Ms. Cunningham and held out his hands. "Of course."

Dolan closed the file and slid it to Cox. "Last night on TV, this guy said, 'We have a righteous wind at our backs.' It's hard to believe it wasn't a coincidence when you look at his file."

Cox's brows narrowed. He cocked his head in surprise at the quote. When he opened the file, he sifted through two inches of loose paper. "Who is this guy? He looks a little familiar."

"He delivered the keynote speech for the Democratic National Convention last night. He's the junior state senator from Michigan running for the US Senate."

The dark-haired SEAL raised his head and met the spook's eyes. "Fuck me." He started over from the beginning, scrutinizing the documents carefully. The dispatches from Islamabad outlined how the tall, skinny man and his traveling partners tried to be inconspicuous, as they moved through hotels and markets before dashing into a mosque known for its fiery imam who railed against the Great Satan and Israel.

Cox flipped through dispatches and case officer notes until he came to the Xeroxed copies of British passports and visas under an alias, as well as a more-recent copy of the man's US passport. Closing the file, he handed it back. "This shit could get someone into a lot of trouble."

"I agree. I'm not sure I can share this with upstairs or the CTC, not even the FBI. There's part of me that screams, 'I need to wait and see what develops.' The dude went to Pakistan and did the tourist terrorism bit, then he utters one of al-

Qaeda's secret greetings on national TV. In essence, he said, 'I'm in.' What do you think?"

"I'd say you have a problem, Marine. I'd take a page out of that Iraqi general's playbook and copy this, then put it in a safe place." He held up the file. "You never know when this shit might come in handy."

"That's what I was thinking. In this business, we've seen what happens when you start a file on some weak tit, and, before you know it, you have a real problem on your hands. I guarantee you the first time bin Laden's name was mentioned and a file started on him, no one ever thought he'd become the most-wanted man on the planet."

"You have a point."

"Danny, I've got a bad feeling about this guy. The history on him is blank since he last traveled to Africa and Pakistan. He obviously used an alias when he traveled. You can see he went by another name with an Indonesian passport. He got into school as a foreign student under that name. Regardless of how he did it, if he's a US citizen, I can't have an official file on him. FBI would kill me. The DCI would drag me out the front door with my head on a pike."

The SEAL shifted uneasily in his seat. The history between CIA and SEALs seesawed over time from good relations to poor to bad, then back to tolerable. The CIA was supposed to capture, develop, analyze, and act on the intel it collected and synthesized. The law changed over the years, stripping the intelligence community of effective methods and procedures necessary to develop intelligence on a range of bad people who were OCONUS.

The relationship was better in the NE on the strength of two personalities. The former Marine and deputy chief and the SEAL got along well. Military liaison officers, cast in supporting roles, augmented appropriate distribution of specific information.

"I'll tell you what," Cox said. "My guys will do a little research into this dude. If we find anything that's open source, we'll share. It might take awhile. You have funds for a little travel expenses?"

"Send the travel requests to me, as well as the expense reports. No renting Cadillacs! We aren't the GSA," he admonished half-heartedly.

The SEAL gave him a wounded look.

"Thanks, Danny. I've been thinking about this all night. It's over-the-top strange. I can see if he gets elected to the Senate, one of these political dickhead appointees upstairs or at FBI will start poking around to see if we have a file on him. Then it will disappear into a hole. It might happen a lot faster than I'd give them credit for."

"That would be the time when your ass disappeared into a hole, too. It's never dull here in NE. That's exactly why I hate politics. Thanks for sharing that with me."

Dolan narrowed his eyes slightly. "Danny, there's one more thing. We're chasing a couple hundred Iraqis and Taliban. This thing is a distraction, but it has all the hallmarks of a fraudulent entry with bogus documents."

"At the very least."

"Just like Atta and the others on 9/11. I have to find someone at CTC to run with this. I don't have many contacts there."

"I may be wrong, Dolan, but there's no urgency to do something. Maybe the smart thing is to let us research this guy and get back to you when we find something. If you think this is huge, you'll have to tell someone at the CTC or the FBI."

"I think it'll stay in my safe for now."

"That might be the smart thing." Cox paused, debating what he was thinking. After a couple seconds' silence, he lost. "Have you ever read The Art of Worldly Wisdom? Somewhere around chapter 149, it reads, 'Let someone else take the hit.' Maybe someone else should work it."

Dolan leaned back, crossed his arms, and smiled. "SEALs can read? Who knew?" As soon as he finished, though, he saw the wisdom in the nugget Danny tossed him.

Cox stood and rubbed his middle finger across his

temple. "I'll let you get back to work."

"Thanks for letting me bend your ear. That's actually pretty good advice."

"Thanks, Dolan. Actually, it's a great little book."

"The irreverent side of me is thinking that if I can't find someone to take the hit soon, you have to promise you'll tell someone if anything weird happens to me."

"What do you mean weird? A fatal paper cut, rats gnaw off your toes, or you fall into a wood chipper? Something like that?" He gave a toothy smile.

"Exactly." Dolan stood and grinned, one finger fully outstretched and pointing at the SEAL.

Danny Cox left the office, closing the door respectfully. Dolan returned to his seat and crossed his arms in thought.

After several minutes, he leaned forward and thumbed through the file. "Danny Boy, I think you're right. I need to buy a couple books ASAP."

CHAPTER TWO

1845 December 22, 2008
Lansanya, Guinea

A cold wind prickled his skin, annoying him further. It wasn't supposed to be cold ten degrees north of the equator. It wasn't the rainy season, but intermittent storms racing west across central Africa made it cold since he was soaking wet and exposed to the elements.

Lansana Conte, President of Guinea, hobbled from the Mercedes to the porch of his house. By the end of the week, he would be buried twenty yards from where he died on that porch, but, for the moment, the man 1,500 yards away dripping wet in a ghillie suit was in a hide. He couldn't shoot the old man.

The shot would be technically difficult. The wind was inconsistent, with approaching and departing thunderstorms. The house sat in a large clearing, with the only avenue of approach for a shot from the front. The only place to blend into the surroundings was a copse of mahogany trees split by the access road one mile away from the ranch house.

The man concealed himself well. His suit moved in the wind the same way as the surrounding foliage. His outline gave a three- dimensional breakup rather than a linear one. Over twelve vehicles passed within five feet of his location during the last three days. A black mamba raced over the heavy barrel of his sniper's rifle in pursuit of drier trees.

Following a brief coup d'etat, Conte became President after Ahmed Sekou Toure, and, like most African self-proclaimed presidents, suspended the constitution and avoided assassination from within his ranks of supporters. After the sixth failed assassination attempt, when his favorite bodyguard was wounded, Conte went on state radio to goad adversaries while vowing he wouldn't be manipulated by those from abroad. A Muslim, he quietly ordered his soldiers to attack people who gathered to protest his ascension as President. Instead, the soldiers went on a rampage of rape, mutilation, and murder.

One week after a seventh failed assassination attempt, a frustrated opposition party leader complained to the inner circle of bankers, lawyers, and other Guinean power brokers that Conte was destroying the country and needed to be eliminated from the political scene. The Guinean Director General of Civil Aviation volunteered to reach out to one of their many benefactors, first in Doha, then Abu Dhabi. The wealthy Saudi promised a very special solution soon. By the time the director general returned from his travels to conferences and his family in Atlanta, a professional assassin was awaiting him at the new hotel in Monrovia, Liberia.

It was a strange, tortuous road from world-class marksman in the US to soldier for hire in Africa. Tall, soft-spoken, Sam Miller, now known as Zaafir, sensed he would soon get the old man to stop for two seconds, so the heavy 300 Winchester Magnum soft point could travel the 1,500 yards and penetrate his chest.

The rain stopped, and Conte's bodyguards moved in and out of the house, preparing the black Mercedes 500 SEL for travel and signaling a departure into town for dinner and meetings. Zaafir calmed his heart and slowed his breathing.

The stock jammed into the pit of his shoulder, the muzzle resting firmly on a large, downed branch. Zaafir recognized the signs that the President was on the move. A door holder opened the entry door, barking out commands to those by the car, which was idling with the air-conditioning on high.

He increased trigger pressure, the sights rock solid, when Conte stepped into the doorframe and checked to see if it stopped raining. He raised his arm and began speaking when a bullet tore through his chest. His last words were never recorded. He was dead before he hit the wooden porch floor.

The following day, the President of the National Assembly

announced that Conte had succumbed in his bed "after a long illness" without specifying the cause of death. Six hours later, a statement was read on TV announcing a coup d'état.

"On behalf of the National Council for Democracy and Development, the government and institutions of the Republic have been dissolved."

CHAPTER THREE

1530 August 29, 2008
Full Spectrum Training Center Hondo, Texas

"Shooters! Assume the position! This stage of fire will be twenty-five-yard rapid fire. This stage of fire involves two phases of six rounds each. Load and lock one magazine. Revolver shooter, load six rounds."

The words reverberated from the public-address system, across the ten-foot dirt berms and down into the shooting butts. The speaker spoke in three or four-word staccato bursts to ensure being heard on the firing range. Movement at each firing station was smooth, fluid, and crisp. Each shooter felt imbued with an unstated sense of urgency. In seconds, dozens of bullets would be precisely fired into human silhouettes. For the life of a paper target, it was a good day to die.

Duncan Hunter stepped into his combat firing position, feet shoulder-width apart, and loaded six .357 Magnum rounds individually into the cylinder of his match-grade, six-inch, blue Colt Python. The cylinder locked, the ventilated barrel pointed up and downrange.

Greg Lynche, standing to Hunter's right and perpendicular to the target, slammed the magazine home on the Beretta .38 caliber pistol. He pulled the slide back to chamber a round. Satisfied it was loaded and locked, he held up the muzzle at a forty-five-degree angle while pointing downrange.

Art Yoder looked over the ten shooters in the firing line, left then right. He brought the microphone to his lips. "Ready on the right? Ready on the left? All ready on the firing line? Shooters, you may commence firing when your targets appear!"

In unison, the ten shooters flicked off their safeties with their thumbs, aimed, and waited for their targets to face them.

With an unconscious nod that all shooters on the firing line were ready, Yoder pressed the big red thumb button in the control booth to activate the target-positioning mechanism. He reached for binoculars, as ten targets turned ninety degrees to face the shooters.

Immediately, the big percussion of the Magnum load from Hunter's Colt overpowered the sound of the lighter loads of the .38 calibers on the line. His target received six shots in a tight, circular group the size of a silver dollar, confined to the head, dead center above the imaginary bridge of the nose.

Yoder glassed Hunter's target. Holes appeared every second and a half as he watched.

After the sixth round, Hunter quickly opened the cylinder and ejected the long casings. A speed loader filled the cylinder with fresh ammunition. With his left thumb, he pushed the cylinder closed. Hunter's shoulders and feet didn't move while he unloaded and reloaded his revolver. The weapon barely moved.

Once loaded, he made a coordinated movement of aiming and squeezing the trigger. His next six shots formed an elongated heart in the middle of the black target, right where Hunter imagined a heart should be.

Yoder, smiling, returned his binoculars to the table.

When the firing line grew quiet, Yoder picked up the microphone. "Cease fire! Cease fire! Clear and table all weapons. Do we have any saved rounds? Any saved rounds? No saved rounds. Shooters, safety your weapons! Assistants, check all weapons for safety before releasing them to holster.

"Thank you, Ladies and Gentlemen. That's a wrap. After you pick up your brass, I'll meet you in the conference center."

He removed his sound suppressors, placed the microphone in its cradle, shut off the power to the PA system, and left the control box.

* * *

Ten shooters walked down the center walkway to review and patch their targets. Hunger and Lynche stood side-by-side to admire their handiwork. Lynche, frowning at Hunter, handed him a length of black stickers.

"I'm surprised I even hit the target," Lynche said. "When I wasn't jumping as that cannon of yours went off, I kept trying to sneak a peek at what you were hitting. Nice groups, Mr. Jones."

"Why, thank you, Mr. Smith. It looks like you got all yours on the target this time. Does that make you the most-improved shooter?" He tried to look away with a wry grin, as he peeled black stickers to cover the holes on both their targets.

Lynche waited until Hunter looked at him, then he rubbed both his eyes with his middle fingers. "One of these days, I'll find something I can do better than you, Asshole." He kicked gravel at his friend.

Both men laughed while walking back to the firing line. As Lynche and Hunter approached Yoder, arms akimbo, Yoder made eye contact with Lynche and nodded toward the conference center.

They walked off together, talking animatedly.

Hunter, still not part of the inner circle, knew how to keep his distance and thoughts to himself. He removed the Colt Python from his holster and secured it in a small, black, hard plastic case before he followed the two. From his perspective behind them, a couple thoughts came to his mind. Yoder lost some weight, and his color wasn't good.

Hunter filed away those thoughts.

* * *

The week at Yoder's training center at the old auxiliary airfield near Hondo, Texas, was an annual affair designed to get all of what Yoder called "his protégés" together for a variety of refresher training, tailored to their special operating environment. With the exception of Yoder's new capture, LeMarcus Leonard, a smart young airport manager with other fascinating skills that appealed to Yoder, all the protégés were busy with a defensive-driving refresher that would reacquaint them with the techniques of driving backward at seventy miles per hour, then spinning the car 180° to continue the same direction at high speed.

Before the defensive-driving phase, nine students conducted weapons familiarization, where every protégé identified, learned, disassembled, and fired weapons from around the world. That training was a holdover from Yoder's Delta Force days. If there was a reasonable chance that one of his charges might come into contact with those weapons in a prisoner or hostage situation, that person needed to know how to use it.

After that came three hours in the fine art of bomb making using common household chemicals. Duncan and Greg had become master bomb makers and quickly assembled a smoke bomb from potassium nitrate, sugar, baking soda, and a urinal cake. They "tested out" when their amalgamation was smashed together and burst into thick smoke.

Lynche and Hunter left others in the bomb-making bunker to experiment with some of the new compounds in the latest iteration of det cord to see what was possible with high-speed, rope-thin explosives. After everyone completed the refresher courses, they were subjected to SERE for professionals, where Survival, Evasion, Resistance, and Escape techniques were reviewed and practiced for business executives. All the protégés tried to evade being found and captured in a scenario where a hotel was overrun by terrorists.

They experienced the helpless feeling of being captured, bound, gagged, and subjected to harsh interrogation techniques expected in a hostile Middle East country. All but LeMarcus Leonard participated. He already completed that portion of the training.

Yoder had been looking for a computer-savvy single black male who could pass a drug test and polygraph, and could do covert work in Africa. After a three-year search,

Duncan Hunter met the hardworking assistant manager at the Jacksonville International Airport and felt he was a possible fit. He informed Yoder.

Twelve hours later, Yoder flew into the airport and interviewed the quiet, composed man with no military experience but who could leverage a laptop computer to destroy Yoder's credit rating or empty his bank account in five minutes, if he wished. Yoder, always a high-and-tight Special Operations soldier, didn't like LeMarcus' sweeping cornrows, but he didn't articulate his displeasure with the ethical hacker's hairstyle.

After the drug test and polygraph came back negative, Yoder became a fan of cornrows, and LeMarcus became a fan of the man who quintupled his pay. By the end of the week, LeMarcus was in training with a small group of former US Army Delta Forces. In a highly compressed six-month schedule, LeMarcus Leonard conquered his fear of scuba diving and heights by jumping out of airplanes while training as a tier-one counterterrorism and special mission specialist. At the end of his immersion training, he could have reported for duty as a weapons specialist replacement in the vaunted 1st Special Forces Operational Detachment Delta, cornrows notwithstanding.

* * *

Duncan Hunter entered the conference center to find Yoder and Lynche standing at the far end of the bar, each sipping a draft beer. The men lamented that the new DCI was a prick and how difficult he was to work with.

"We wouldn't have been able to create Wraith with this dickhead in charge," Lynche said.

Yoder looked at Hunter and neatly poked a finger into Duncan's chest. "We hand-delivered the DCI a one-page white paper to kick off that program. This idiot requires a full, government-approved proposal. That's what you get when you install an Air Force weenie as DCI," Yoder said in disgust.

He removed the offending finger and waggled it at Lynche.

"I'm at my wit's end. I can't get in to see him, and he won't take my calls. Greg, you have to talk with him, spook to spook."

"I'll see what I can do, but I don't think he'll listen to me, either."

They seemed to agree they had a plan and looked at Hunter for concurrence. There was an awkward pause, because Hunter had something else on his mind.

"Art, please don't take this wrong, but you look like shit. How are you feeling?"

Yoder was about to drink more beer when he froze, put down the glass, and rubbed his eyes. Lynche thought Yoder might deck Hunter for such an insolent, direct question. Anyone who talked to Colonel Art Yoder like that never remained standing for long.

"I do feel like crap. Thank you very much, Duncan. Not much I can do about it." He drank beer and stared at his feet.

Lynche's curiosity rose. He'd never before seen Yoder so disarmed.

"Art, your color's all wrong for you," Hunter said. "I had a friend who swam in the waters of Kenya, and he picked up a parasite. He dropped weight, and his coloring looked like yours. Not meaning to pry, good Sir, but have you seen a doc?"

Yoder gave Hunter an impassioned look, finished his beer, and said, "Let's go into the office."

Stunned, Lynche followed the two men to the top floor of the conference center and into the director's office. Lynche closed the door behind him.

Yoder plopped into a big black judge's chair and spun it to look out over the training center through the huge picture window. It was unusually quiet in the room. The only sound came from a Texas-sized, Texas-shaped wall clock.

Without bothering to look at the two men, Yoder said, "I

need a pancreas transplant on top of the damage done by two parasites that wrecked my kidneys and liver. Like your buddy, it looks like I picked them up while in Africa chasing some dumb-ass Muslim warlord. It's amazing it took them twenty years to kill me."

After a moment, he swiveled to face Lynche and Hunter. "This was my last training session with the group. They tell me I'll be dead in a month. Soon, all this will be yours."

CHAPTER FOUR

1230 December 30, 2009
Roberts International Airport Monrovia, Liberia

Airport manager LeMarcus Leonard stepped into the muggy sunshine and onto the parking ramp for a final walkabout. The jet reported its position to the control tower. They were forty-five minutes out. The tower supervisor reported an updated ETA to the airport manager every five minutes. Leonard wasn't nervous. It was just another recovery and launch of a small jumbo jet on an international flight. He was aware, however, that everyone in Africa was watching or would hear of the flight.

The US Transportation Security Administration's small staff of observers was in place to monitor the processing of passengers and their baggage off the big jet as well as those booked on the returning flight. Her Excellency, the President of Liberia, would be the first one off the inaugural nonstop flight of a US air carrier. LeMarcus envisioned a string of Liberians and Americans would follow at a discrete distance and descend the stairs to the ramp. Then would come supporters who helped make the event happen.

The US ambassador would follow shortly thereafter, then probably the tall, white banker who'd been with the President when they worked at World Bank. Probably after the banker would come the ultra-corrupt Director General of Civil Aviation who did everything he could think of to prevent that day from occurring, short of kidnapping LeMarcus Leonard and feeding him to the fish in the Farmington River. Probably the last one out of business class would be his boss. That was his way.

LeMarcus scanned north, not expecting to see the inbound jet but to double-check the ramp for cleanliness.

293

New red baggage loaders, new white tugs, and new blue baggage carts were neatly aligned and had words stenciled on their sides, Gifts from the People of the United States.

Twenty baggage handlers in crisp tan coveralls awaited the signal to offload the jet.

The only eyesore to the north was a decrepit YAK-40, a relic of the latter days of the civil war that ripped the country apart for almost fifteen years. Once the private airplane of Victor Bout, better known in the international press as the Merchant of Death, the three-engine Russian business jet sucked a white-headed crow into the upper engine during landing flare and was never repaired. It sat in the weeds a half-mile from the terminal. Sometimes, it was the only airplane on the field.

LeMarcus nodded at the freshly whitewashed control tower. The six bullet holes that pockmarked the facade had been expertly patched. With new glass, radio antennas, and light gun, the Robertsfield tower looked like any tower at a small American airport. He glanced south at the flight's approach end of the runway and smiled, knowing the jet would fly right over the little hamlet of Smell-No Taste. Few travelers on the jet were aware of the airport's significance during World War Two, where Robertsfield was originally built by the US government as a staging area for aircraft to check the expansion of Axis powers in North Africa.

When hundreds of American aircrews prepared for their flights north, Army cooks prepared hundreds of meals for the pilots, mechanics, and support personnel. The Liberians living in grass huts near the field and along the Farmington River smelled the food being prepared but couldn't get the soldiers to surrender samples and let them taste the strange, odiferous concoctions the airmen ate.

He sighed at the sight of the old main terminal building, embalmed in shrink wrap to hide the damage from the Liberian Civil War. "Still work to be done there," he muttered.

He noted the president's limousine was ready at the VIP terminal just as a cacophony of yelling and applauding erupted. The jet turned over the Atlantic for its approach to the runway. LeMarcus crossed his arms and smiled, hearing a reporter behind him shout into his microphone.

"The return of an American carrier and direct flights to the United States for the first time since Pan Am's withdrawal is a major step in the recovery of not just the airport, but Liberia itself."

LeMarcus, chuckling softly, walked toward the baggage carts, marshaled and ready. The handlers stiffened as if preparing for inspection. He knew he wouldn't be mentioned on the radio or in the print media as the ROB airport manager or the man who reversed the downward slide of Roberts International Airport, formerly Pan American's hub and alternative landing site for the Space Shuttle. He did it despite the director general's shenanigans. After one year, he and his boss kept their promise to the newly elected President, the first woman President on the continent, to return the airport to its former glory and usefulness.

The hard part would be to get it approved for direct flights to and from the US. Her Excellency knew, for Liberia to grow and heal, a direct link to American was necessary. She articulated her view and strategic plan for Liberia to the US ambassador, who, of course, offered help. The newly appointed ambassador fired up the men and women of the Economics Section, including USAID and USTDA, to help reconstruct the country's airports and aviation infrastructure.

Finding someone who could transform a war-torn, decrepit airport into something usable and functional, capable of safely handling jumbo jets with hundreds of passengers and tons of cargo, seemed an impossible mission. The ambassador thought long and hard about the challenge thrown to her from Her Excellency when a faint, pleasant memory of airplanes and airports crept into her consciousness. She reached for the huge Rolodex on her desk, spun it, and stopped at the business card of a former colleague from the Naval War College who knew a few things about airports, airplanes, restaurants, and hot tubs.

One month later, Duncan Hunter landed with an A&E team to assess the condition of the country's airports. In a month, they developed an airport master plan, presented it to the President and ambassador, and won a modest contract to reconstitute the Roberts International Airport.

While Hunter worked and entertained, Lynche and Yoder aggressively searched America for the right airport manager. Hunter found the young rock star manager languishing at the Jacksonville International Airport. LeMarcus Leonard was shocked that some unknown white dude would seek him out and offer him a unique, challenging project in Africa.

His arms crossed, LeMarcus waited and worried at the thought something would go poorly on the president's big day, when she brought America's biggest airline to Liberia.

He stopped when he was underneath a professionally made banner that read Welcome to Liberia Delta Airlines. The crowd watched the big jet move toward and turn above the Firestone Plantation, leveling its wings over Smell-No Taste, and land halfway down the runway. Several minutes after touchdown and back-taxi, the Boeing 767, with The City of Monrovia stenciled on the nose, taxied to a stop at the terminal.

The two monstrous engines drowned out any celebrations on the air side of the airport. When the engines stopped, fifty airport workers leaped into action, while dignitaries positioned themselves to receive their President. A mobile staircase was expertly positioned at the aircraft door. An airline employee ran up to check the gap between airplane and stair.

The door folded into the fuselage, and out stepped the dignified Liberian President to a loud, worshipping crowd. Everyone else in the jet waited until she stepped onto her native soil.

LeMarcus marveled at the pomp of the office while wanting to fuss with his employees over how they serviced and unloaded the plane, wondering when his boss would finally come out the door.

When Duncan Hunter reached the bottom step, LeMarcus waited with open arms.

"Look what you've done!" Hunter shouted, smiling and offering his hand.

LeMarcus grabbed his hand enthusiastically, pumped it once, then the men hugged and stood back to admire each other.

"Nice job, good Sir," Hunter said. "Looks a lot better than last time. Did you put a giant condom over the old terminal building? That cover's artwork is beautiful."

LeMarcus was so emotional he couldn't speak for a moment. Hunter, seeing the man's predicament, placed an arm over his shoulder to walk through the terminal toward customs.

LeMarcus stopped. "Did you see what's going on at the other end? The construction?"

"Yeah."

"Looks impressive. It's far enough from the runway that we could add a parallel runway, and they'd still have plenty of ramp space."

"Just like how you drew it up."

Their conversation was decidedly vague regarding the hangars and office spaces being built for US Special Operations Command.

"I had help, but it's incredible you've been able to get this far along. How's the house?"

"I'm still living in the compound, while the houses are refurbished."

"I'm sorry, but we had to refurbish them. The A&E team wanted to tear them down and add a hotel. I'm pretty sure those are the original Pan Am station manager's house and his staff's houses. They had too much historical significance to be destroyed. You'll have to show me how they're coming along. If we have time, show me the project, too."

"Can do easy."

"So how's it going? Ready to come home?" Hunter tried an impish grin, but it came off as goofy.

"No!" He shook his head. "This is an amazing job, Boss. Not a day goes by when I'm not totally exhausted. You asked if I wanted a challenge. This is definitely a challenge, but it's unbelievably rewarding. I have 400 people counting on me every day. I meet Her Excellency every month. She treats me like I'm someone special. There's nothing I wouldn't do for her."

"She is an amazing woman. The last time I talked to her, she was thinking about adopting you."

LeMarcus knew there was a modicum of truth in that compliment. They stood quietly for a moment before LeMarcus Leonard spoke again.

"Anyway, we've been doing really well since TSA approved the airport. Now we have a dozen air carriers landing throughout the week. Royal Air Muroc lands every other day. Brussels, Ethiopian Air, and Virgin Nigeria all have offices with weekly flights. We're the only real moneymaking enterprise in the country, and we're making a boatload. This year, we'll make one million. Last year there was nothing."

Hunter, grinning, nodded at the director general of civil aviation waddling through the receiving line. "He can't steal from the airport anymore. USAID sees you as a trusted agent and good steward of the US taxpayer's money. They can see you making a difference. TSA is overwhelmed by what you accomplished. Without you and your leadership, there would be no Delta. You've done really well. You'll get a nice bonus, too, though I don't know what you'll spend it on."

"Thanks, Duncan. I appreciate it."

"You're welcome. You deserve every bit of it. Did I see three new fire trucks in the firehouse?"

"Four. And we received a bus and three mowers in the last delivery. The assholes wanted me to sign for the bus when it had missing engine parts and broken windows. I told them, well, basically...."

"Fuck off and die? Get the damn thing fixed, and then maybe I'll sign for it."

"Just about." It was LeMarcus' time to offer an impish grin.

"You're a national hero," Hunter said.

"Thanks to you."

"Nice try. By the way, your clearance came through—TS/SCI at Lynche's old place."

"That took awhile."

"Ten-four. Just keep doing what you're doing."

"There's something new every month. My first day, when you busted those Filipino smugglers, I never saw it coming. I was so naïve. I thought you were joking about customs clerks sitting at a desk but not at the one with the sign No Bribes Taken at this Desk. I thought you were screwing with me."

"Real life is much more interesting."

"You see it here. The Nigerians are always trying something, but the Chinese are the real masters. If there's a Chinese in line, he's got something. We check his bags, and sure enough, he's smuggling diamonds. If I were back home, and the liberals knew what I was doing, their heads would explode."

"That would be a sight. There's something refreshing when a liberal's head goes pop. You can hear it like a melon dropped onto concrete."

"You're bad."

"I know."

Hunter was the last person to clear customs, and his bag was the last one on and off the baggage carousel. LeMarcus told a security detail, "Take Mr. Smith's bags to the car."

Hunter gave each man a dollar. It was time to monitor the outbound passengers for the return flight to Atlanta. LeMarcus and Duncan stood along the wall of the passenger lounge and observed Liberian security scrutinizing passports, tickets, and personal belongings going through the X-ray machine. Hunter watched six passengers pass through the magnetometer when a very tall black man with dark sunglasses queued for the inaugural return flight followed by a big-boobed woman in local dress.

Hunter nudged LeMarcus' shoe to get his attention. They watched the black man and others go through a double screening.

"Hear anything about the Guinean President dying?" Hunter asked.

"He was old," LeMarcus said nonchalantly.

"He was shot."

"Where'd you hear that?"

"Greg still has contacts. Someone wanted him to hurry up and die. That's the price you pay to be a politician or a warlord in Africa. Someone's always trying to knock you off. I appreciate your being careful and living in the compound. I have visions of the director general trying to knock you off or feed you to the fish."

"You and me both."

"What do you think about the tall one?"

"Just what I was thinking." LeMarcus raised his hand, and the chief of security ran up.

Hunter didn't hear whatever they said, but, after a minute of animated conversation, LeMarcus said, "The chief pulled him out earlier and double-checked him and his checked bags. He's clean. He's flying an Arabic name with an American passport. I flagged him for an intrusive search when he arrives in Atlanta."

"That'll work."

Over years of being asked outdated security questions, international passengers stopped listening or giving any credence to airborne threats when someone at the ticket counter or in airport security asked, "Has anyone unknown to you asked you to carry an item on this flight?" or, "Have any of the items you're traveling with been out of your immediate control since the time you packed them?"

The bosomy lady in the wild, orange, African-print dress largely ignored the questions and answered, "No," although the man ahead of her paid her handsomely for the privilege of checking an additional bag of his through to their destination.

Zaafir Miller was being scrutinized by the TSA for Secondary Security Screening Selection, not because his name was on the No-Fly list, but Miller was one of two passengers with a one-way reservation who paid cash for his ticket. Both booked reservations on the day of the flight.

Miller assumed the additional security originated from a similar name, Zaafir Muller, a German Muslim who was tracked on the Terrorist Watch List and hadn't left Germany in weeks. Zaafir Miller was highly aware that his size commanded second looks in airport security queues. The one white and two black men were obviously airport employees who wanted to ensure everyone saw the big man being hassled.

CHAPTER FIVE

0735 April 19, 2010
Helmand Province, Afghanistan

For the past seven days, poppy farmers and their Taliban masters were in a state of high dither. The messages from Allah were clear—stop growing poppies. Every night, farmers raced into their fields to find the stench of hundreds of dead or dying poppies. Some plants were lifeless and discolored, others shrunken and curled with drooping stalks, and everywhere was the faint smell of burned dung. Even watching or sleeping in the field, the workers saw and heard nothing. Thousands of healthy plants surrounded thousands of sick ones.

The Taliban initially thought the Americans were crop dusting, spraying their fields with poison like the Russians did thirty years earlier, but the farmers didn't see or hear any aircraft. They couldn't find residue on any of the poppies. Some leaves were marred with discolored streaks, while others appeared perforated with tiny holes, but there were no mites or other infestations.

The farmers planted sharp, straight rows of poppies stretching over 100 feet. Deflated, defeated plants defined one side, while a row of healthy green plants stood straight and unaffected on the other. The rows of flattened dead or dying plants curved with sharp points and definition.

"Why is it curved here and straight there?" Mansoor asked, remembering something he saw in a Kandahar bazaar. "Father, I've seen something like this before the Taliban. A music cover, called a crop circle. These are no circles, but they might make a design. It may be a message from God. Inshallah."

The farmers looked at each other, unable to see the

design from ground level. After consulting together in great trepidation, Mansoor was elected to climb the valley walls for a better look.

Three distinct shapes carved into the poppy fields became clearer the higher he climbed. Having seen Allah's writing before, Mansoor trembled. His bladder released, and he fell to the ground, wailing.

* * *

Lynche and Hunter walked to the rear of the dark AFSOC C-130. The aircrew waited for their Code 2s to board. The YO-3A with the Weedbusters multiple laser system was secured in the cargo hold in a conformal container specifically made for C-130 transportation. When they arrived in Jordan, outside of Amman, the quiet airplane was transferred to its seagoing 10x10x40 foot shipping container and loaded on an intermodal container chassis for its short ride to Aqaba.

The next day, the container was transferred to a ship bound for Baltimore. The support crew of Bob and Bob had first-class accommodations aboard the ship for the two-week return to America.

Opium production continued to increase, since the Americans arrived in Afghanistan in 2001. The State Department had projected opium production would increase in 2010 and in 2011.

However, opium production dropped significantly in 2010 due to an unknown plant disease that killed off much of the crop.

CHAPTER SIX

1100 April 21, 2010
Near East Division CIA Headquarters

Nazy Cunningham patted herself from breast to waist to ensure she shed all her electronics. She put her right hand in the HandTrac biometric scanner while a camera verified her iris print. Green lights flashed when she inserted her ID card into the reader. Locks released loudly, and she entered the SCIF. She crossed the dirty carpeted floor. Her high heels crushed hundreds of tiny chads into the thick pile, while thousands held fast on the floor and along the walls of the cubicles from static electricity generated from the monster shredders in the room.

Nazy went straight to the classified terminals that linked the US embassies to a secure network. She eased herself into the decrepit conference chair. Delicate fingers raced across the keyboard, entering login and password. Interlacing her fingers in her lap, she waited.

One minute later, the system came alive, and a few mouse clicks took her to the page she wanted. Ignoring the classification headers and footers, she stared at the middle of the black-and- white monitor in disbelief.

Confirmed requested subjects arrived Islamabad Intl Airport 24 Oct 2006. ISI monitored their departure from airport to a compound in Hazara region. No record of any departure. Photo attached. Compound under protection of local military base.

She clicked the attachment icon, waiting for the file to open. After twenty seconds, a very detailed color photograph popped into view and highlighted a three-story structure inside very high walls and protected by a heavily fortified metal door.

She placed her hands flat on the desk, leaning closer for a better look, as she contemplated her next move. What to say, and to whom? Inhaling deeply, she closed her eyes for a moment.

When she returned to the present, she scrolled and clicked the mouse buttons to close the window and attachment before logging off. As she quickly left the room, she ground more chads into the carpet with each step.

Nazy's heels clicked on the tile in the hallway leading to the office of the Director of Operations. Her mind raced, as she rehearsed what to say. She walked past two secretaries without a greeting or acknowledgment that they were alive, knocked on the director's door, and entered. Five graying men in gray suits and dull ties stopped talking and looked up as the NE director entered and closed the door behind her. They admired the fleeting callipygian view and were nearly caught as their eyes ran the length of her legs when she quickly spun around.

Steeling herself, she took a deep breath. "I found him."

First annoyed, then confused, the Director of Operations blinked twice before locking eyes with her. "Who did you find?"

Her green eyes flashed from the sunlight pouring through the window, as they darted to each man's face. Save for the DCI, the CIA's uppermost leadership waited for her response.

"Bin Laden."

The Director of Operations smiled and spread his hands, asking for clarification.

The Director of the National Clandestine Service asked, "Pakistan?"

"Are you sure?" another asked.

"I predicted when he finally quit running, he'd send for his family," she said. "We just received confirmation that three of his wives traveled to Islamabad in late 2006. The ISI ensured they made it to a compound outside a military installation thirty miles from the capital. The compound is a fortress unlike anything else in the area. We should put it under surveillance for a positive ID. They've been there three-and-a-half years. He's there."

"Stake your reputation on it?" asked the man with little hands from the NCTC.

"Sir, he's there. I guarantee it. I just can't prove it at the moment."

The Director of Operations lifted his eyes from Nazy's shoes to her nose. "OK, Nazy. Be ready to brief the director in ten minutes. Show him what you've got. You were right on all the others. I hope you're right on this one. I think this meeting's over."

CHAPTER SEVEN

0700 June 9, 2010
Roberts International Airport Monrovia, Liberia

LeMarcus Leonard drove while the two men slept. Hunter snored lightly, while Lynche sounded like an oncoming freight train. LeMarcus reached over the seat every few minutes and jostled Lynche gently, quieting the noise. The road from the airport to the cutoff for the Kendeja Resort Hotel remained surprisingly smooth after years of wear and tear, as United Nations armored personnel carriers routinely scarred the asphalt running into town or out to the airport. Fatigue, the steady drive, and the decent suspension in the Toyota 4Runner quickly put the two pilots to sleep after another all-night mission monitoring al-Qaeda and drug smugglers coming from South America.

West Africa, from Casablanca to Lagos, had long been a cesspool of terrorist and narcoterrorists activity, but with nations not very friendly to the US, it was unlikely any head of state would allow any ISR missions to be flown from their countries. There was little Americans could do to interdict or disrupt the flow of drugs or terrorists coming to or leaving Africa. Unmanned aircraft, with their ridiculously high accident rate, couldn't be spared for missions in West Africa with its even-more-volatile flying environment and remained in the Iraqi, Afghani, and Pakistani theaters. Even if there were available assets with which to conduct ISR missions, there were no airfields from which to operate—until recently.

What looked like a string of business jet hangars and commercial office spaces on the other side of the runway at Roberts International were the newly constructed hangars and office spaces of US Special Operations Command. For the past week, low-noise-profile ISR flights went up and down the coast, highlighting pirate strongholds, drug-running berths for surface and submersibles, and unmarked airfields from which a cornucopia of drugs and blood diamonds flowed.

LeMarcus was mildly frustrated with Hunter for not bringing him into the fold with whatever operations he and Lynche conducted.

"LeMarcus," Duncan explained, "first, you aren't cleared for this, and you haven't been read in on this SAP. It's better this way. When there's a need for you to know, I'll let you know. You can help by keeping everyone away from the hangars and ignoring what we're doing."

Early that morning, as LeMarcus drove out to the hangar, he saw something, or thought he did, make the turn to the runway threshold at the far end of the field. He never heard an engine, and, by the time he drove up to the hangar, the large fold-up doors were in their fully down position. Hunter and Lynche walked toward him.

"Hotel please, good Sir," yawned an exhausted Hunter, as he slid into the front seat.

"I'm getting too old for this shit," Lynche grumbled, gliding into the rear.

LeMarcus began asking about the airplane when Hunter interrupted him and waved his hand before the man's face. "These aren't the droids you're looking for."

"Boss, I'm worried."

"These aren't the droids you're looking for," Hunter repeated. "One of these days, we might have to let you in on what we're doing, but not today, and maybe not ever. It just depends."

"Depends on what? I think it might be some cool shit." "LeMarcus, you aren't cleared for this. The less you know, the better. How about for now, we get us old farts to the hotel, so we can sleep. We should be done in a day or two."

"OK. One of these days, I want to do some fun stuff."

"Maverick, one of these days I want to do some fun stuff, too," Lynche said sleepily from the back seat.

"Maverick?" asked LeMarcus.

"It's a long story. One of these days, I'll tell you. How about the next time we're here?"

LeMarcus gave up. Hunter yawned. By the time LeMarcus left the air side of the airport, his passengers were sound asleep.

"These aren't the droids you're looking for?" LeMarcus mumbled. "While I'm looking for smugglers and terrorists and such, I'll bet you're looking for flying saucers or some shit."

"If I told you, I'd have to kill you," Hunter said. "Let's not go there, Obi-Won LeMarcus. We have plans for you, and we can't do them if you're dead."

CHAPTER EIGHT

1930 July 2, 2010
Presidential Suite JW Marriott Washington, DC

Duncan Hunter, entering the suite, tossed his keys on the table in front of the couch, put his briefcase on the credenza, and hung up his suit coat. As he pulled off his tie, the in-room phone rang.

"Yes?" he asked.

"I'm sorry to bother you, Sir," the concierge said, "but you have a visitor, a young woman named Ms. Nazy Cunningham."

Hunter's internal alarm went off. They planned to meet Friday and take an extended drive to the Tidewater Virginia area. "Thank you. Send her up."

When he let Nazy in, instead of unbridled sexual chemistry boiling over in the doorway, she walked right past him. Hunter never saw her like that before. She was agitated, worried, perhaps livid.

Nazy tossed her purse onto the couch and sat down. "Duncan, the man's an idiot."

"Which one?" He knew she'd been hounded for a date by several men at headquarters and the NCTC, and she was being promoted to the senior intelligence service. He also knew she'd been summoned to the office of the Director of Central Intelligence for a project.

"All of them, really. All of them but you. Why are you so different, Duncan Hunter?" She kissed him and squeezed his hand.

"Baby, that's been asked many times, and I don't know what it means. I'm just me, an average guy trying to do an above- average job. So who's the idiot? I might know him." He thought he was being funny.

"The DCI."

Suddenly, it wasn't funny. Mind racing, he squeezed her hand. "What has that idiot done to get you fired up? I'd be shocked if he asked you out."

It was obvious she was upset, or she would have waited to tell him the following day.

Nazy took a deep breath. "He said, 'I understand you're our highest-ranking Muslim. I was wondering how you were able to get into the CIA and other Muslims can't?' I was so shocked, I didn't know what to say or do. Then he said, 'The President wants me to do some Muslim outreach. It's my top priority, and I need help.' He wants me to help him."

"The man is definitely an idiot. Then again, all of the president's appointments are imbeciles. They look like the clientele in the bar scene of Star Wars. What did you say?"

She looked concerned and confused. "Duncan, I sensed real danger in that man's office. I had no idea what to expect, and I didn't want to be there."

"You mean other rumors besides his being gay?"

"That's neither a secret nor the issue. Well before I was assigned to lead the Near East Division, there were rumors about him, only I knew they weren't rumors, and I sensed a trap. I wanted to run from that office as fast as I could. Then I thought, 'What would Duncan do in this situation.' I swear, thoughts of you calmed me instantly. I've learned so much from you. You're always helping me, mentoring." Duncan Hunter broke out in a broad grin.

"I composed myself and asked, 'What did you have in mind, Sir?'

"He said, 'Human Resources hasn't been able to recruit a single Muslim. They can't pass background checks or polys. I'm at my wit's end. We need to hire more Muslims.'"

Duncan shook his head. "If you see blood shooting from my eyes, you'll know my head's exploding. Muslim outreach is this man's priority? What am I missing? Is the rumor he's lost his mind?"

"You aren't missing anything. Ever since I came to the

Agency and nearly every job I've had since my first day has been either developing intelligence to fight Islamists or work to keep Islamists and radical Muslims from infiltrating the Agency and other government agencies. There are plenty of Islamic apologists and defenders. I used to be one, you know."

"Yes, I know. That was a long time ago in another life."

"I thought it was obvious. He's the DCI and should've known I renounced Islam years ago. Obviously, that bit of information isn't in my file." She took a deep breath. "When we went to dinner at the Red Parrot—I'll never forget that night, Duncan—I realized that even what the West considers good Islam is terrible. I long felt it was the wrong way to live when I was in school at Yale, but I was conditioned to think Islam was the ultimate way of life. I was Jordanian. Life was good. I didn't have to wear a veil or head scarf, but even then, women were still considered less than a whole person. We were simply property."

"If you submit to Islam, it means you're a slave, man or woman. It doesn't matter. Someone controls you. At dinner, you said you wanted to help me. I ran away once from my husband, and I wanted to run away from that disgusting imam, but no one ever said anything like that to me. You treated me with kindness and respect."

"Somehow, you knew I was in deep trouble, and you jumped in to help me escape. As I sat there, looking at this beautiful, wonderful man, someone I was sent to spy on, you just wanted me to be free. At that moment, that was all I wanted, to enjoy the freedoms Americans take for granted."

"When we were in your room, and I changed into your workout clothes—I still sleep in that shirt every night—I knew right there my life would be a thousand times better if I walked away."

He tried to lighten the tone. "And, I helped."

"Yes, you helped, in ways you may never know." She brought his hand to her lips and kissed it, tears welling in her platinum-green eyes. "I was afraid I was walking into a trap. The rumor is, when the director was a senator and met with his Saudi business partners sometimes in Riyadh or Dubai…. I don't know how to say it, but the senator liked to have young men and little boys."

"Really?" He paused, waiting for her to continue.

"And a Saudi prince facilitated everything. I know it's true."

"Say again?"

"I know it's all true. I know the senator and the prince raped those boys. That's why I was very uncomfortable in his office. Somehow, he knew I knew."

"That's a terrible secret to carry around."

"Duncan, it gets worse. I haven't been able to share this with anyone, and I'm afraid someone will find out the rest of the story about our director."

"That's bad enough. I take it you received intel from the women you ran when you were stationed in Riyadh and Abu Dhabi?"

She nodded. "One of the prince's fourteen wives, no longer his favorite, was a nurse and had the dubious duty of cleaning up those boys after the men finished with them. I need water."

Nazy got up and fetched a bottle from the in-room refrigerator and returned to the couch, where she drained the bottle before starting again.

"She met me in one of those male-run lingerie shops. It was the only place to get nice things from Paris. I didn't wear nail polish and always wore an abaya when I left the embassy, and I thought I was fully incognito, but somehow, she knew where I worked and passed me a note."

"She found you? Your cover was blown? You never told me that."

"I didn't tell anyone. Apparently, she found out from her husband, the prince, who found out I worked at the embassy from Senator Frank Carey, ranking member on the intelligence committee."

"What? Holy shit." Hunter ran his hand through his hair. "I

was pretty sure he knows me or at least knew of me when he visited the embassy. Somehow, he passed that information on to his buddy, the prince. I couldn't figure out how or why. Three months later, I came home. I wanted to tell you, but I just couldn't. I was so embarrassed.

"He can go to jail for blowing your cover."

"That's not all Duncan."

"There's more?"

"Yes, Duncan, maybe much more. Only to you and no further, not even Mr. Lynche."

Duncan always tried to be fully supportive to Nazy. There wasn't much he couldn't share with Greg. "For the moment, OK." Nazy took a deep breath, gripped both of Hunter's hands, and locked gazes with him. "Ten of those boys, who'd been raped by the new Director of Central Intelligence, flew jets into the World Trade Center and the Pentagon. I think the President knows Director Carey's secret."

Duncan looked thoughtful, internalizing what Nazy said. He released her hands and rubbed his eyes. Nazy squished her lips together on the verge of tears. She waited for Duncan to support and comfort her. When he changed the subject, as if he dismissed her concerns and problems as insignificant, she was taken aback.

"Well, Ms. Cunningham, I suggest we get something to eat. You can stay here tonight. We can pick up your things on the way to Tidewater."

Nazy was incredulous. "You still want to go to Tidewater?"

"Why not? We made plans, and there's nothing in what you told me that warrants canceling the trip."

Her anger rose, and she snapped, "How can you take what I've just told you with so little emotion?"

"Baby, it's because I can't do anything about any of it right now. I need time to assimilate what it means that the DCI probably impregnated ten of the 9/11 hijackers. The bit about your cover being blown is worrisome, but there's not much I can do other than listen, support, and love you."

Nazy gave him a blank stare. Where was the thoughtful loving Duncan? Staring at her shoes, she slowly shook her head. She planned to tell him everything, but he was dismissive and uncaring. Fury started building in her. She was hurt and looked for the words to tell him how much he hurt her when he spoke again.

"Before we go down for dinner, I have something for you. I was going to give this to you tomorrow evening."

She watched indifferently, as he went to the credenza and unlocked his shiny black Zero Halliburton. Taking out a package of legal documents, he handed them to Nazy.

"What are these?" she asked.

"Your divorce papers."

"My divorce papers? I don't understand."

"You're now legally divorced from that nut job of a husband of yours in accordance with Sharia and Jordanian law."

"I don't understand. Why…? How'd you manage this?" The lawyer in her thumbed through the legal documents. Raised seals, stamps, and dozens of signatures attested to their veracity. It was true. She was a free, single woman.

"I have a good friend who's a lawyer and a specialist in Sharia with close connections to the Jordanian royal family. Your former husband was caught in a compromising position with an underage male cousin who was being groomed as gift to a high-ranking US official from Prince Bashir.

"Your husband was given a choice—either agree to your request for a divorce or face his uncle's wrath for despoiling the gift. He was also told that he would receive the originals of the still photos and video evidence once the divorce was final."

"Why didn't you just tell his uncle? Then I would've been a widow."

"We couldn't guarantee the outcome. As a widow, you would've been subject to Sharia as it applied to a woman in a widowed state. You know that."

"Of course. You're right. I should've thought of that, but I'm so overwhelmed by your ability to finally free me completely. What of Waleed? Will he not try to appeal when things quiet down? After all, he has the evidence."

Duncan's gaze went to the floor. His tone was cold and matter-of-fact. "His funeral is tomorrow."

Nazy, stunned by the turn of events and Hunter's lack of emotion, slowly shook her head in disbelief. Suddenly, she realized how little she knew about the man who loved and protected her for years. "You had no intention of letting him live. You let him believe that by granting the divorce, he'd be able to continue his life as before. You lied to him."

"I wouldn't call it a lie. Let's say he assumed one thing when I meant something else. It's what liberals do. Waleed was evil. I won't lose any sleep over his death."

Nazy's hands balled into fists. She was furious. "He wasn't evil. He was stupid, lazy, and venal. He was self-absorbed, but he didn't deserve to be lied to and set up by you to be killed."

Hunter was slow to anger, but once roused, it was strong. "Let me remind you that you were the one who ran from that abusive husband. You agreed to the imam's plan to spy on me. I seriously doubt you've thought much of Waleed in the last six or seven years."

Nazy's eyes fell to the documents before raising them to Duncan's again.

"I fell in love with you and have spent the last seven years protecting you, caring for you, and loving you. You wanted freedom. Baby, you have it."

Nazy, overwhelmed by events, was still hurt and angry. "Then I'll take it. I think it's better that I go home rather than stay here tonight."

Duncan couldn't believe she wasn't overjoyed, so he retreated from his position, feeling hurt and angry. *What was her problem?* "OK. Your choice. I'll walk you out."

Nazy picked up her purse and turned to go. "No. I need to be alone. I can find my way out."

Hunter was crushed as she left the room, and struggled with himself, wondering if he should run after her or let her go. He stood there, feeling confused and rejected. Finally, he stared out the large picture window, trying to let her go as his heart broke.

CHAPTER NINE

1935 October 19, 2010
Kandahar Air Field Afghanistan

After a week of maintenance problems with their US Air Force transportation, Lynche and Hunter walked off the rear of the C-17 and headed for the Air Operations Center.

"You can always tell you're in Afghanistan," Lynche said. "It always smells like shit."

"Weren't we just here? Where else on the planet can you breathe this level of fecal matter in such a glorious setting?"

Lynche wasn't amused. The team was a full week behind schedule, primarily because Hunter insisted on installing a radar- detection system in the YO-3A. Installation and checkout of the system proved more challenging than envisioned. Four modified "fuzz buster" automotive police radar units had been velcroed into each corner of the canopy, two in front and two in back. If the system didn't prove its effectiveness in detecting a radar signal, the time-sensitive targeting mission would probably be scrubbed for the first time. The Wraith crew wouldn't fly near the edge of Iran without an early detection warning system.

The mission was to observe poppy farmers harvesting poppy seed, and, more importantly, locate where the Taliban kept its seed stock. Before 9/11, the Taliban prohibited the growing of opium poppy. Once the US invaded the country, the only avenue for hard currency for the Taliban came through the drug cartels via the harvest of 300,000 hectares of opium poppies. The Taliban subsumed and controlled poppy production, threatening farmers and their families with death or worse.

The Taliban warlords were furious that opium production had been severely curtailed earlier in the year from an unknown disease that reduced the harvest by almost 40% from the previous year. Several Taliban masters coordinated the effort to determine the root cause of the blight, taking samples of sick plants and trying to discern what killed them.

The drug lords in Teheran and Islamabad were at a loss to explain why the poppy plants died overnight. Under a microscope, no one found traces of chemicals or insects. The dead plants were found in areas where some farmers claimed it was the work of Allah and that they had displeased Allah by cultivating opium poppies. The Taliban beheaded those who refused to return to the fields and harvest the remaining opium sap. Once the drug lords had the attention of the families' remaining members and forced them to return to work, two trusted agents transported several of the affected plants to be analyzed at the Universities of Teheran and Islamabad.

Botanists there suggested the plants exhibited the traits of being in the sun too long or being subject to high levels of UV. That still didn't explain how the plants shriveled up and died at night. Although they saw the warning, the Taliban were cautious and didn't believe the symbols in the fields were written by Allah.

With the poppy bulbs completely scored and empty, and all opium-producing poppies harvested, it was time to harvest the seeds for next year's crop by drying the remaining brownish bulbs. The farmers would soon collect the seeds in small sacks under the watchful eyes of Taliban members carrying AK-47s. As they did since the beginning of the war with the US, the Taliban would smuggle the seeds across the border into Iran and store them for safekeeping until the winter snows spilled from the mountaintops and it was time to sow the next crop.

The mission for Hunter and Lynche was to operate as close to eastern Iran as they could and locate where the poppy seed stock was held until the Taliban returned for the next planting season. Flying the single-engine airplane over three provinces in southern Afghanistan, operating over Iran, and returning to Kandahar was the most-dangerous mission the old spook and his sidekick had been asked to perform or could imagine.

The DEA suggested the estimated two hundred pounds of seed represented several billion dollars in opium and heroin. 200 pounds of gold would net only half a million dollars. Several US intelligence sources that were studying the problem suggested a small group of couriers would make the border crossing at Zaranj in Nimruz Province, and the seeds would be held at a private compound in Zabol, Iran.

Due to its proximity to American and coalition forces in Afghanistan, Iran put into position early warning systems and Russian S-400 surface-to-air antiaircraft missiles. For the mission, the Wraith had been painted with a special radar-absorption material that cost $35,000 a gallon. JSOC would have two AFSOC MH-60H Pave Hawks Combat Search-and-Rescue helicopters with USAF para-rescue jumpers positioned within a ten- minute response to a downed Wraith in Iran.

The container holding the YO-3A was being transferred from the Air Force's newest cargo jet to the large, white, portable hangar at the far end of the Kandahar airfield. The team's stellar mechanics, Bob and Bob, were again on hand to get the aircraft from its shipping container, install the wings and batteries, fuel the aircraft, check for leaks, and prepare it for a night launch. They weren't young, virile mechanics but spry gentlemen over sixty, former US Army YO-3A mechanics who relished their time with the very special prototype aircraft in Vietnam. When offered an opportunity to keep 007 in the air, they were very interested.

When Yoder indicated their pay would approach six figures for every month-long mission, Bob and Bob, always adventurers, were completely sold, dedicated, and motivated that the aircraft would be able to execute every flight. For eleven years, the four-man team never missed a contract, and 007 never experienced so much as a burned-out light bulb.

007's shipping container was a self- sufficient maintenance shop and supply warehouse. With custom carbon fiber foldout workbenches, spare engines and parts, tools, fuel, spare sensors, multimode FLIR, and low-light cameras, Bob and Bob could work on or test any system, including conducting an oil analysis of the engine oil after each flight.

The completely unarmed 007 slowly grew heavier over the years, with the addition of night-vision compatible cockpits, cockpit and seat ballistics protection, dual radios and batteries, special multispectral black camouflage paint, and, more recently, the Weedbusters multiple-head UV drug eradication laser system and the alternate secret, six-bladed quiet propeller for high- altitude work in Afghanistan.

The JSOC commander and Greg and Duncan were briefed by Jill, a short, stocky blonde agent and their CIA liaison. She wore body armor with tan cargo pants and had a Beretta holstered to her hip. Taking one look at Lynche, she knew she'd seen him before at the original headquarters building.

"I remember you from the OHB," she said. "I was just getting started. Nearly every day, I saw you walk through security in a suit heading for the top floors."

Lynche, who'd been retired almost fifteen years, was more than a little embarrassed that she remembered him, but she hadn't made an impression on him.

Hunter sensed something between them. "Can we show Jill the jet?" He called anything he flew, save a helicopter, a jet; something he learned from his days with the Air Force. Jill told them she was one of the very few agents who had a private pilot's license. She was cleared to brief the two contractors, but because Wraith was a Special Access Program, she didn't have the access or the need to know.

"I'm sorry I don't remember you, Jill," Greg said. "You should see this airplane."

"I'll give you a ride."

The general, a ground officer, offered his Level 7 up-armored Suburban. All vehicles at Kandahar had various levels of ballistic protection to meet client needs. US

321

government contractor vehicles were typically armor levels 3 or 4, providing low-level handgun protection, while government vehicles were typically armor levels 5, 6, or 7, providing high- to ultra-level armor-piercing rifle protection. There were a few level-9 vehicles that had extra armor-piercing rifle protection for visiting dignitaries who would've had a level-7 stroke had they been placed in a lesser-protected vehicle.

On the ride down the flight line, the two spooks chatted about the old days. Hunter thought the two-inch-thick windows were a bit much until Jill indicated the heavily fortified guard shack was the most-dangerous location in the area.

"Even after ten years, we usually have someone blow themselves up every other day," Jill added.

Hunter felt he was being rushed, and his warning sense tingled like crazy. He and Lynche left the C-17 without body armor, and he felt exposed like on their last trip. Next time, he'd make sure he had body armor on the airplane.

* * *

Three hours after landing in Kandahar, 007 had her wings, propeller, and batteries installed. The flight-control cables were attached and checked, and engine was fueled and oil checked, the FLIR vacuumed, and the windshield cleaned. With no need for a quiet takeoff, Hunter had the aircraft airborne with gear and flaps up inside 500 feet.

"Things are going well," Hunter said sarcastically. Almost a little too well, he thought.

Fifty minutes later, things in the airplane began to not go so well. They were heading for their first observation point, a small village in west Helmand Province, which had been under constant surveillance by MARSOC Marines for two weeks.

"Unusual activity with several black-turbaned men, most likely Taliban, have arrived. The village is in terror."

The scout sniper begged to take out the Taliban.

Hunter pushed the Wraith to its limit, and the big prop enabled them to hit 225 knots. At that speed, the little airplane bounced around, hitting air pockets that shook the airframe.

After six tries, Lynche contacted the overlook Marines.

"It appears two Landcruisers were loaded with multiple sacks of what appeared to be grain," the Marine said. "They left the valley thirty minutes ago. No villagers appear to be harmed."

"We're late," Lynche told Hunter. "Shit, shit, shit." He consulted his maps and the available roadways that headed toward Iran, but their airspeed and all the bouncing around made map reading a challenge. "Ouch," he said several times. "Mav, you're killing me."

Hunter throttled back to 180 knots, and the aircraft quit yo-yoing up and down. "How many Landcruisers do you think will be on the road? Not fifty. Two should be easy to spot. No wonder we were getting banged around. There's almost sixty knots on the nose."

"Not good, Hunter. We're still about sixty miles out."

"It's not I-95 down there. I think the best they can do is thirty miles an hour. They're still a couple hours away. Friggin' headwinds aren't helping our cause. We were in such a hurry to get out of there, I didn't ask if there would be any assets in the area. It would be nice if JSOC had a Predator to pick up our bogeys. Even an AWACS would help."

"Good idea. Can't hurt to ask." Lynche spun radio knobs until the assigned encrypted frequency appeared in his night-vision goggle capable-LED window. "Mary Kay, Holeshot."

"Holeshot, Mary Kay. Go." The encryption made Jill's voice sound like she was underwater.

"We were wondering if there are any big eyeballs in our area. Looks like our chickens have flown the coop and have about an hour's head start. I'm afraid we may not be able to overtake them. The headwinds aren't cooperating. Over."

"Let me check. Hold one, Holeshot."

They waited for four minutes. "Holeshot, Mary Kay."

"Mary Kay, Holeshot. Go."

"Regret no buzzards or other Predators in the area. I'm sorry. Anything else I can do for you?"

"We thought as much, but it was worth a try. How about a weather update? We've hit much higher winds than forecast. Over."

"Standby, Holeshot."

That time, she took ten minutes to come back. "Holeshot, Mary Kay."

"Mary Kay, Holeshot. Go."

"First base is reporting thirty knots at 180 gusting to forty- five with blowing dust. At one-zero-zero, sixty knots gusting to seventy. Over."

It was Hunter's turn to say, "Shit."

"Thanks, Mary Kay," Lynche replied. "See you on the flip flop. Out."

Hunter lowered the nose and descended to 7,000 feet AGL. Twenty minutes passed. "Reminds me of my time with the Border Patrol," Hunter said, "when our pilots went out on what they called fire watch. You can see all the little campfires of the goat herders in the NVGs. During the winter, our pilots would launch after midnight in a Super Cub with NVGs, look for campfires made by illegal aliens, then guide agents to the fires. I never would've guessed there would be dozens and dozens of campfires out there."

Thirty minutes later, on the horizon, they saw the lights of the city of Zaranj.

"Greg, eleven o'clock, two vehicles. What are the chances?"

Lynche slewed the big FLIR and zoomed the image to maximum. "Two vehicles that are probably Landcruisers. Your Marines are wonderful."

"All Marines are wonderful."

"Yeah, right. What happened to you?"

Hunter wanted to roll the Wraith on its back and shake

the rudders to get Lynche's attention, but they were late and heading toward Iran. A gust of wind nearly flipped the airplane over.

Hunter fought to keep the YO-3A tracking toward the two Landcruisers headed to Iran.

Then the modified fuzz-buster automotive police radar detectors mounted on either side of the glare shield lit up with a row of red lights and squealed into their headsets. Hunter flipped the plane on its back and pulled the cyclic to four Gs, pointing the nose to the ground before rolling the little airplane back upright at 5,000 feet AGL.

"What the fuck is that?" Lynche asked, shouting to be heard over the squealing radar detectors.

"They're painting us with their radar. I'm trying to break lock and get low and lost in the clutter. I'm looking for a missile launched our way."

"I'll try to keep tabs on the trucks," said Lynche.

"Bird in the air! Shit!" The surface-to-air missile came off the rail from Iran. In Hunter's NVGs, the SAM's engine heat started as a flare in the distance that grew with each second. He reverted to his twenty-five-year-old training to avoid incoming missiles, but this time in a prop plane.

A pilot in a combat situation must be aware that under certain circumstances he may place himself and his plane in a dangerous situation. A pilot didn't want to turn away and lose sight of the bogey, because that meant he would be dead soon. Hunter wasn't a man to retreat, but of all the options he had available, masking the airplane in ground clutter was the only viable alternative. They needed to get down on the deck to defeat the missile, which was rocket-powered and had a head start. IBM's Blue Gene would still be trying to find the best solution. He had to turn his back on the missile.

"Hold on!" Hunter shouted.

The aircraft was in one-G flight as Hunter slammed the throttle to idle, rolled the plane aggressively on its back, and pulled. He fixated on the G meter and programmed the stick to his belly until the needle stood on the tick mark between six and seven. His NVGs slipped over his eyes under the high Gs. Taking his hand off the throttle, he held the goggles in place.

In his old F-4 days, he would've used the throttle hand to grab the oxygen hose connected to his face mask to guide his head and eyes to keep in sight of the bogey, because his head and helmet weighed six times normal, and no one's neck muscles could keep himself upright and focused on the bad guy under that load. Lynche's helmet slipped over his eyes, as he strained to hold up his head.

Halfway through the reverse Immelmann, the front radar detectors stopped flashing and squawking, and the aft pair took over. Halfway through the turn, Hunter checked his instruments. Lynche, completely unaccustomed to even short bursts of six Gs, tried to breathe and stay conscious. His vision narrowed and blackened to an unfocused spot the size of a softball. He hyperventilated through his nose, his teeth gritted and tightened, while straining his stomach muscles as hard as he could. He knew they would die in a few seconds, blasted from the sky.

Looking straight down with a missile inbound, the radar altimeter was off, and the barometric altimeter unwound like a spinning top. Without a horizon or depth perception, Hunter kept the G on the aircraft, deployed the speed brakes, and unfeathered the prop.

As he acquired ground and leveled off barely ten feet above the dirt, a flash behind the airplane rocked both aviators.

Lynche's tunnel vision quickly disappeared. Black returned to color, as the G forces relaxed. He was still hyperventilating and finally managed to control his breathing.

"Fuck it. Let's get the hell out of here." He didn't want to admit the adrenalin rush loosened his bladder a bit.

Ten minutes passed, then Lynche said, "Shit. I think I wet myself."

"We'll both need clean flight suits and new seat pads after this op."

Lynche wanted to laugh, but nothing came out. He barely responded to anything Hunter said. Hunter, recognizing shock symptoms, allowed Lynche time to recover.

Halfway back to Kandahar, Lynche finally spoke on the intercom. "That was some fancy flying, Sir. That's why I thought I'd need a fighter pilot for this kind of work, but I never really thought we'd have to avoid missiles. I couldn't have done what you did. I'm grateful you saved my life."

"I was worried you'd beat my ass for bending 007. There was a period when I thought the wings would snap off. We may've lost the speed brake. It doesn't seem to work anymore."

"Did that...? How...how'd you get that missile to hit the ground?" Lynche spoke quietly, because he had a splitting headache due to the post-adrenalin rush.

"From my old Top Gun notes," Hunter said nonchalantly, "nearly all missiles have a rate bias built in that leads an aircraft. It's the same thing you do when you lead a duck with a shotgun, and you let the duck fly to where the shot will be. Same principle. Missiles have a proximity fuse, so when it gets close to something hard, it blows up.

"I just hoped it would track us...I'm sorry...lead us as we were heading toward the ground. It guessed where we'd be. That dumb Russian missile guessed wrong, or it flew into the ground. Either way, we're still alive and flying."

"That was too fucking close. I'm starting to think you need a new sidekick."

"I thought I was the sidekick." Hunter inventoried his systems and scanned his instruments. "Greg, it wasn't that close."

"It wasn't that close? Are you shitting me?"

"We probably had another half-second, maybe a full second. Good thing this baby handles like a little fighter. Otherwise, we would've been toast. Besides, I couldn't do this without you. We're a team, and you're the man. Don't you forget it."

"You're incorrigible, Maverick."

"Incorrigible would be my middle name if I could spell it."

After Hunter took evasive action and recovered, the aircraft didn't handle the same. It was more challenging to fly and was a little squirrelly on landing. Bringing it down safely, he taxied to the white shelter at the end of the field.

When he and Lynche got out, they were shocked to see how the frame had oil-canned. It was twisted, and several metal panels were warped and rippled. Strips of speed tape and several rivets were missing, while others were loose. Shrapnel shredded part of the speed brake, which hung by one attachment bolt.

Bob and Bob shook their heads in amazement, as they inspected the airframe and engine. YO-3As were prototypes and not production, fully-tested aircraft; they were designed for stable flight in cool night air, not for acrobatics or violent evasive maneuvers. From their days in Vietnam, no YO-3A had ever taken as much as a bullet during nighttime missions. 007 looked as if it had been on the losing end of an inadvertent Lumshevak.

After a quiet debrief and dinner with Jill, Hunter and Lynche entered the hangar, as Bob and Bob disassembled 007 and secured the wounded wings and parts in the container for its trip home.

Hunter, arms crossed, talked to himself. "We were set up. Someone leaked the mission."

Lynche's head jerked toward his friend. "What?"

"We were set up. They knew we were coming and targeted us before we were close to the border." He stared at the work being done in the container.

Lynche didn't like it when Hunter knew something and wouldn't share. It was serious, and Lynche never considered the obvious answer. He steeled himself to ask, "Do you know who?"

"I have a pretty good idea."

"Who?"

Duncan's tone was neutral. "It might be Nazy."

Lynche placed his hand on Hunter's shoulder and gave him a shove. "What? Are you nuts? She's as loyal as you or me. Besides, she doesn't know about Wraith unless you told her. Then there's the fact that she loves you and would die for you. She'd never betray you. None of that makes sense. Nice try, but find another answer."

"Someone knew we were coming. It has to be someone at your old place. I thought the DCI, but that's impossible. That leaves a very thin thread back to Nazy. She doesn't know about Wraith, but maybe she does. I'm having a hard time coming to grips...."

"You aren't making sense, Mav. Take it from the top."

"Greg, Nazy isn't happy with me. She didn't like what I did to get her divorce. She has more sympathy for that bastard deceased husband of hers. She seems to have more feelings for him than any of us. I don't understand Nazy Cunningham anymore."

"Whoa and stop! I don't know where that came from, and it's hard to believe anything other than she loves you. She'd die for you. She would never betray either of us."

"Something isn't right. The timing is too coincidental." Not wanting to talk about it anymore, he shook his head before turning away.

Listening to his friend and reading his body language, Lynche finally understood what had been driving Hunter for the past several months. As Duncan Hunter walked away and disappeared into the night, Lynche gritted his teeth and clenched his fists—the only way he could vent his frustration with Hunter without losing his composure.

As Bob and Bob lashed 007's bent, buckled wings in their padded cradles, Lynche went up to and extracted the satellite phone from its yellow case. In a minute, the connection went through.

"Connie, we have a problem."

CHAPTER TEN

1000 October 22, 2010
NE Division SCIF, CIA Headquarters

Nazy Cunningham sat at the head of the small oval conference table, tapping the end of a pencil against the hardwood. She was deep in thought. It was six months since she claimed to have located bin Laden's hiding place. The directors of the National Clandestine Service and the National Counterterrorism Center just left with their horse-holders in tow, caustically letting her know their surveillance of the alleged bin Laden compound in Pakistan had not yet yielded a single photograph of the world's most-wanted terrorist.

It was true three of bin Laden's wives and several of his children were in the compound. It was also true there was no obvious clue that Osama bin Laden was there or had ever been there. Their collective frustration boiled over, as every Agency asset was leveraged to determine the probability that Osama bin Laden was hiding in that compound.

After six months, the probability still remained at 90%, which was better than anything the intelligence community had come up with in nine years of looking in every haystack for the needle that was Osama bin Laden. Nazy didn't know, but she assumed several groups of special operations people were practicing assaults for that compound. She knew the President had been briefed and directed the DCI to keep developing the intelligence. The CIA had to provide better odds. It had to give a definite, positive ID that Osama bin Laden was in that compound before the President would authorize a raid into a foreign country and invade an ally.

Convinced there was nothing else they could do other than continue surveillance on the unique compound,

Nazy Cunningham pushed back her chair and stood. She collected her files and CIA- emblem-embossed notebook and left the SCIF. As she reached for her pager, it startled her, vibrating and chirping in her hand.

Looking down, she recognized Connie Lynche's private cell phone. A sense of dread swept over her. She sluggishly walked toward her office, fear of the unknown and the creeping feeling that Duncan was in great pain spurred her to hurry.

She flicked the door behind her, as she rushed to her chair. The door slammed shut, an unusual occurrence for the NE Division office. Dialing an outside line, she punched in the Annapolis number.

Connie answered on the first ring. The four-digit caller ID meant the call came from Langley. She immediately pressed the Talk button and said, "Meet me at the Ritz Carlton, Tysons at 1230. It's urgent."

"Just a minute, Connie. I have a mission debrief this afternoon. I can't just leave here."

"Nazy, this isn't a request. If you have any residual feelings for Duncan Hunter, you'll be there."

Before Nazy could reply, Connie hung up. Nazy redialed, but the call was immediately sent to voice mail. Nazy slowly shook her head in disbelief. What was it about? Was Connie now interfering in Nazy's love life?

Convinced that Connie's instructions indicated that Duncan was probably physically all right, Nazy shook off any thoughts he might be injured or dead and reevaluated her schedule. Fingers flew on her keyboard, followed by a rapid mouse, urging her calendar in Lotus Notes to load. She noted the debrief scheduled for 1300 with the DCI had been canceled.

Stunned, she stared at the screen. "What are the chances of that happening?" she asked softly.

While the cancellation left her free to meet Connie, she shunted aside thoughts of missing a rescheduled meeting with the DCI while she was at the Ritz Carlton. The DCI was too mercurial to call, cancel, and reschedule staff meetings all in one day unless he was traveling.

She checked the time and comforted herself with the thought that she could accomplish other time-sensitive work before leaving Langley for the hotel. It would also take her mind off Connie Lynche and what she might have to say about Nazy and Duncan. She habitually scanned her office. The safes were locked, the desk clear, and she quickly logged off her computer.

She stood and went out the door, taking the stairs to the fifth-floor SCIF, heels clicking on the old tiles, her blue badge swaying with each step. Once at the entrance, she saw the warning in huge red letters—Electronics Prohibited. She removed her pager, placing it in the wooded cubby outside, then patted her pockets to check for other electronic devices.

Her hand went into the biometric hand-reading device, and she turned toward the camera with her ID card up so the software could read her iris. A flashing green light accompanied the opening of the electronically actuated door locks. She pushed down the door lever and stepped into the special- purpose SCIF.

As the door closed behind her, she called, "Anyone here?" When no one answered, she stepped between two massive shredders and tan cubicle dividers to her work station in the corner, her high heels crushing thousands of tiny chads that layered the carpet near two massive shredders.

She recently returned from Guantanamo Bay, Cuba, and hadn't fully completed transcribing her interrogation of two al- Qaeda terrorists brought in from Pakistan and Yemen. Ever since the new administration reversed the protocols for interrogating the most-hardened terrorists with what the press and DOD defined as "enhanced interrogation techniques," the Executive Order restricted CIA personnel to use the rules contained in the US Army Field Manual—Human Intelligence Collector Operations.

With the new rules in place, as anticipated by intelligence executives, al-Qaeda and Taliban prisoners completely stopped talking and refused to cooperate with military and Agency personnel. Nazy suggested to the Deputy Director of the National Counterterrorism Center she might get them to open up better if an Arabic woman with an Arabic accent asked the questions. After a few hours, even the hardiest men were so infuriated; they lost control or whimpered in her presence.

Arriving at night in a black abaya, Ms. C entered the interrogation rooms like a ghost and left like a conqueror, soon gaining a reputation as a secret weapon in the interrogation wars.

Nazy shook the mouse to wake the computer and logged onto the system. In moments, she accessed the database from which hours of audio between the two men and her had been loaded into the system. Placing headphones over her ears, she listened to herself talking with the terrorists.

On one screen, she typed each word in Arabic. On the dual monitor, she transcribed the conversation in English. She started and stopped, taking one sentence at a time, clicking the mouse to advance the recording before pausing, typing, and approving the translation.

After thirty minutes of concentrated transcribing, she was startled when she felt the SCIF door slam closed. She lifted an earpiece and was ready to shout, "Nazy here!" to let the person know he wasn't alone when she heard the DCI's voice. She froze, afraid to breathe.

"...they're alive, but their airplane was completely wrecked."

Another man's voice, deeper and more direct than the effeminate DCI, responded, "The two will be grounded for an extended period of time. By the time the aircraft is repaired, their contract will expire, and we can bring this work back in-house and start using our unmanned systems."

At first, she didn't recognize the voice, but she felt it was the Chief of Counterintelligence. That man kept his mouth closed, rarely saying a word in meetings for fear of flashing his incredibly bad teeth. He also smelled bad, and Nazy inhaled quietly to determine the invisible man's identity.

The SCIF door handle unlocked, and the DCI said, "I approve of shutting down Rath. Put a closed tab on the file and lock it away."

"Will do, Sir."

Three seconds later, the SCIF door slammed shut. Nazy blinked several times and slowly exhaled, trying to make sense of the conversation. She knew Duncan and Greg were contract pilots for Langley and were out of the country, but she didn't know which program they were on. In the very highly compartmentalized world of Special Access Programs, she had no need to know.

As she pondered what the men said, she suddenly understood why Connie called. Nazy checked the gold Rolex Duncan gave her, performed a few mental calculations, and settled on terminating the transcription session, as her focus was gone. She closed her work and hurried to her office, sending more shredder detritus into the depths of the old carpet.

Operating on autopilot, too stunned to think clearly, she entered her office. After closing and locking the door behind her, she shut down her computer. She stowed the key in her office safe, collected her handbag, briefcase, and coat, then unlocked the door.

Once in the corridor, she checked for traffic before locking her door and setting the cipher lock. Nazy walked down two flights of stairs before catching the elevator to the main-floor lobby. She left the old headquarters building and walked toward the parking lot.

When she reached her Mercedes, she looked around, expecting to be stopped. Very few people were about, and they were more interested in getting out of the weather that had turned overcast and blustery than noticing someone leaving in the middle of the day.

She placed her gear into the trunk, got into the driver's

seat, and left the parking lot. As she approached the main gate, the guard gave her a half-salute and waved her through.

Once on Highway 123 heading toward Tysons Corner, she felt mildly aggravated with the unusually heavy lunchtime traffic. Taking a deep breath, she looked carefully both ways and concentrated on driving.

* * *

When Nazy arrived at the Ritz Carlton, she pulled into the underground garage, found a parking space near the stairwell leading to the hotel, got out, grabbed her handbag, and walked toward the elevators. She pushed through the hotel lobby toward the restaurant, her heels announcing to all that the woman in the black power suit was in a hurry.

Connie Lynche nursed a half-full goblet of red wine at a table for two near the fireplace when she looked up at her visitor. Under furled brows, Nazy's green eyes flashed.

"Well, I see you made it," Connie said. "I didn't think you'd show up."

Nazy hesitated, tempted to snap back. "I know why you called me."

"I doubt you know anything after you walked out on Duncan."

Before Nazy could respond, the waiter came up and asked if they were ready to order.

Connie returned the two menus and said, "Two cob salads and two iced teas."

The waiter half-bowed and walked away.

Nazy took time to compose herself. "I didn't walk out on him. I told him I needed time to think. I was shocked that he arranged for my divorce and Waleed's death. Duncan knew the outcome."

"Let me get this straight. You told the man who rescued you from a life of bondage, saw to it that you were able to make a whole new life for yourself, who loved you from the moment he set eyes on you and arranged to make sure you were free from any threat of retaliation, that you needed time? To do what? Mourn the cruel, evil man your family married you to?"

"It wasn't like that," Nazy said defensively. "I've never seen Duncan as cold and matter-of-fact as he was when he told me what happened. It was like he stepped on a bug."

Connie worked very hard not to raise her voice. "You silly fool! He stepped on a bug for you. Duncan is either black or white in his views. There are no shades of gray. When he cares for someone, he'll go to hell and back for that person. If someone walks away from him, he turns his back. Unfortunately, he can't let you go, so he's been taking chances he never would have before you came into his life. The latest episode almost killed him and my husband. Thanks to your betrayal, they almost died."

"What are you talking about?"

"You blew their cover."

"What? I don't know anything about any program involving Duncan or Greg, other that what I heard in the hallway earlier today."

"Of course, you do."

"No, I don't. I have a good idea what Duncan and Greg do, but Duncan never told me anything. We're in the business of keeping secrets. He said it was for my own safety."

Connie's confusion showed on her face. She sat back so hard she almost dropped her wine.

"Is Duncan OK?" Nazy asked. "Are Duncan and Greg OK?"

"Yes, they're fine, but they almost died. Duncan saved Greg and their airplane."

"It seems that man's always saving someone."

"You have no idea."

"You love him, don't you?" She said it matter-of-factly, almost accusatory. Nazy's eyes were wide open.

Connie smiled, trying to suppress a laugh, but she knew Nazy knew the truth. "Yes, I love him. I'd do anything for him. He loves me like the sister he never had. You don't know how lucky you are, Nazy Cunningham. Duncan's one of a kind, and he's nuts about you."

The admission completely disarmed Nazy. She breathed deeply without taking her eyes off Connie. Marshaling her thoughts, Nazy whispered, "Connie, when I was getting ready to come over here, I overheard the DCI and another SIS talking about what had to be a special access program called "Rath," and the pilots were almost killed, and the aircraft almost destroyed. It had to be Duncan and Greg. They were almost hostile in their discussion. Why?"

The waiter appeared with two salads and teas. As he walked away, Connie felt the tension leave her back. "Are you sure he said Rath?"

Nazy noticed the change in Connie's tone without registering the change in her stress level. "That's what he said. "I'm almost positive it was Rath, but it sounded like it rhymed with bathe. I didn't catch it perfectly. I don't know any English word that sounds like bathe but starts with an R. As I drove down here, I thought that was why you called me."

Connie went from confrontational to friendly. "You're right, only I thought you were involved in the program, and you blew their cover."

Nazy, confused by Connie's sudden 180° turn, bit into her salad. "First, I don't know what program he's on. Second, I'd never do that. I love Duncan. I'd never do anything to hurt him.'

"I know you do, but he thinks you were somehow involved in the mission being blown. Why would he think that?"

"I don't know."

After a few seconds' silence, Nazy asked, "What am I supposed to do now?"

Connie paused, then opened her handbag and extracted an airline ticket envelope. "You're flying to Texas this afternoon. Duncan's headed back, and you need to be there when he arrives. You need to tell him what you overheard and convince him you didn't, that you wouldn't ever betray him."

Nazy was bewildered by the sudden change of direction

in the conversation. Dozens of thoughts crowded her mind, as she slowly accepted the envelope. She almost said she couldn't go, that she had work to do, as she opened the envelope and saw a first-class round-trip ticket from Washington Reagan to San Antonio. The flight departed at 3:30 PM.

She checked her Rolex and realized she had plenty of time, even with DC traffic, to get to the airport. When she looked up, she asked, "How am I supposed to get to Duncan's?"

"Carlos will pick you up. I called, and he's expecting you. I'll call again when I leave and know you're on your way. He'll make sure you get to the house. I know you have a key, but you don't have the current security code, and neither do I. Carlos has it."

Nazy's eyes fell on the ticket, then she looked up. "Thank you, Connie."

Connie forced a smile. "My pleasure. Eat your salad. I need to think."

44444444

CHAPTER ELEVEN

1800 October 28, 2011
The Yellow Corvette Ranch, Fredericksburg, Texas

Flying first-class, Nazy was one of the first passengers off the American Airlines flight. Although it was late October, southwest Texas was still subject to triple-digit temperatures, and San Antonio was experiencing some of its warmest weather in many years. The temperature on the jet bridge was stifling, so she hurried up the long, tiled passenger walkway toward the air-conditioned relief inside the terminal. By the time she reached the end of the jetway, her brow was damp, and she shed her suit coat. She went to the women's restroom. The trip to Duncan's ranch was another couple of hours away with few opportunities for a bathroom break.

Connie emailed Nazy that Carlos, Duncan's ranch manager, would pick her up at baggage claim. He would drive the Hummer Duncan used for runs into town and to irritate environmentally sensitive liberals, but mostly because the oversized, black monster was a tank, modified to protect the occupants from mayhem. The Hummer carried an additional 1,000 pounds of the latest armor-piercing, and rifle-protection technologies, while the supercharged Corvette motor under the hood was specifically tuned to allow the heavy truck to run away from trouble with ease, on the road or off.

The fuel tank was bullet-resistant, reinforced with quarter-inch AR500 ballistic steel, and blast-proof. The self-sealing tank used bladder technologies to prevent the tank from leaking fuel if punctured by hostile rounds. The huge tires were run flats composed of an outer shell and a strong internal rubber shell that would continue functioning at high speeds even when shot multiple times. The glass surrounding the cabin was replaced with 40mm bullet-resistant multilayer polycarbonate glass.

Nazy, riding the escalator downstairs, walked through baggage claim with her briefcase. When she stepped through the automatic glass doors, the San Antonio heat assaulted her. Carlos Yazzie stood beside the immaculate black Hummer and jumped into action when the striking woman appeared in the doorway. He raced to take her bags.

Men and women along the curb jerked their heads to stare at the beautiful, raven-haired woman who inspired such a dramatic response from the driver. No one would have guessed that the woman in white silk and the black skirt was a senior intelligence officer in the service of her adopted country.

"Welcome back to Texas, Miss Nazy. It's been too long since we last saw you."

Nazy smiled at the fit, ruddy Apache with the high-and-tight haircut. Like all proud jarheads, Yazzie still wore his hair short after he retired from the Marine Corps. "It's good to see you, too, Gunny. How is Theresa?"

Nazy resisted a little, then let Carlos take her briefcase and hovered at her side until they reached the Hummer. As Yazzie opened the passenger door and stepped aside, he said, "Feisty as ever, Ms. Nazy."

He turned his body and head toward the curb to prevent anyone from seeing the skirted woman indelicately enter the truck. When Yazzie felt his charge was safely inside and composed, he checked to make sure all of her body parts were safely inside and composed before closing the immensely heavy door. He moved quickly around the rear of the idling truck, placing Nazy's briefcase on the back seat. Once behind the wheel and buckled in, he continued talking as he drove from the terminal.

"Yes, Ma'am, she's feisty as ever. She has aired out the house and provisioned the kitchen. Captain Hunter is due home later tonight."

Leaving the airport complex, he drove north on Interstate 10 toward Fredericksburg. The seventy-mile trip passed in companionable silence.

When they arrived at the compound surrounding the main house, garages, and outbuildings, including the Yazzie quarters, Carlos parked at the front door and helped Nazy out. A rotund, sprightly Theresa emerged from the house and met them on the porch. The two women embraced and exchanged greetings.

Carlos opened the door and waited for the women to enter. He carried Nazy's bags in one hand and motioned the ladies to get out of the heat with the other. Once inside, he took Nazy's briefcase to the guest room beyond the main living area.

Once Carlos was out of earshot, Theresa looked hard at Nazy. "Are you here to try to make it up to Captain Hunter or tell him good-bye?"

"I'm here to make it up to him."

"Bueno. He hasn't been the same since you went out of his life."

"How did you know?"

"I've known him a long time, ever since he saved my Carlos from becoming a washed-up drunk and kept him in the Marines. Captain Hunter hasn't been the same man since he returned from Washington."

"I'll make it up to him if it's the last thing I do."

Theresa hugged Nazy again. "I know you will. You're a good woman."

As Carlos entered the foyer, he lowered his head. "Theresa, we need to go."

The two walked out, and Nazy closed the door behind them before walking into the main living area that made up the main part of the house. She noted the LeRoy Neiman over the fireplace. The painting was of Duncan and his old Corvette after Duncan won the Vintage Grand Touring Championship at Monterey, California, the previous year. The room, decorated in the warm tones of the southwest, included Navaho rugs and pottery, leather furniture, and southwest watercolors by local artists.

Opposite the Neiman, suspended in the corner, was a six- foot Apache war bonnet with double rows of foot-long eagle feathers descending in long tails to the carpet, worn only by chiefs and warriors. Carlos Yazzie presented the family ceremonial bonnet to Hunter, the greatest chief he knew, for saving him from a life of despair and misery. Nothing similar to the war bonnet existed in the Middle East, and Nazy always found the golden eagle feathers, ermine trim, and fancy beadwork unique, striking, and elegant.

After admiring the painting and headdress, she went down the hall to the kitchen, brewed a cup of tea, and returned to the living room to wait.

* * *

The Fredericksburg FBO was shut down for the night when the stillness was broken by the sound of a jet crossing the threshold, inbound from the east. Ninety seconds later, the pilot keyed the microphone to the special frequency to turn on the runway and taxi lights. After landing and clearing the taxiways, the pilot keyed the microphone to extinguish the lights, as the Gulfstream taxied to a large hangar at the far end of the airport.

The engines were shut down and the stairs lowered. One man exited the aircraft and walked into the hangar through a side door.

A bell sounded, as the hangar door slowly folded up toward the ceiling, while interior mercury vapor lights gradually increased in brightness.

Once the hangar door was retracted to the ceiling, the man stepped away from the door switch and toward an aircraft tug in the middle of the hangar. The white tug's engine started easily. In less than five minutes, a tow bar was pinned to the nose wheel, the jet was towed into the hangar, and the landing gear chocked.

Duncan Hunter loaded his bag and old leather flight jacket into the black Aston Martin parked inside and drove the sleek Vantage out of the hangar, set the brake, and returned to the hangar to lower the door and turn off the lights.

Ten minutes after landing the big jet, Hunter drove into the hot Texas night.

* * *

When he arrived home, he was surprised to see lights on in the house. He noticed lights on in the Yazzie house, too. He paused, then realized Connie must have called Carlos to tell him he was on the way back.

Duncan used the remote to raise the garage door and pulled the Aston Martin into its assigned slot. After he shut off the engine, he clicked the remote a second time to lower the door, removed his bag from the trunk, and entered the house via the kitchen door, noting Carlos hadn't reset the alarm.

As he reached for the light switch in the kitchen, he tensed, feeling the air in the kitchen had been disturbed. He caught the faint scent of cinnamon. Duncan quietly set down his bag and flight jacket on the granite countertop, removed his Sig Sauer P290 from the holster on his back, stepped out of his shoes, and quietly walked toward the front of the house.

As he approached the living room through the kitchen hall, he barely caught the slight rustle of fabric against the leather couch. Crouching in the dark hall, he said, "Stand up. Put your hands were I can see them, and step away from the furniture." Without thinking, he raised the tiny gun to firing position and clicked off the safety.

Nazy, dozing, was startled by Duncan's voice. She turned toward the sound in panic, tripped, and fell.

Duncan, shocked when he saw Nazy fall down, moved quickly toward her, gun still in his hand. When he reached her, she was beginning to rise. He offered his hand, but she pushed it away.

"I'm glad you're a good shot. You could have killed me," she said.

"Nice to see you, too, Ms. Kamal. What the hell are you doing in my house in the middle of the night?"

"Connie told me you were almost killed on your last assignment and blamed me for blowing your cover. I came to tell you I had nothing to do with that, nor do I know anything about Rath."

"Remind me to take her off my Christmas card list. Wait a minute. Rath? What are you talking about?"

"The Special Access Program you're on. Something to do with flying airplanes."

Duncan paused, his mind suddenly clicking into high gear. Clicking the safety on the gun, he holstered it, removed the holster and gun, and set them on the coffee table. "How'd you hear about this Rath program?"

"When I was leaving the office earlier today on my way to meet Connie for lunch, I overheard the DCI and another man. I think it was the Chief of Counterintelligence. They were almost laughing about the near-death of two pilots and destruction of their aircraft. The DCI said he'd approve shutting down Rath. He wanted the file closed and locked away."

"Are you telling me you aren't read into this Rath program?"

"Yes. That's correct. That's what I'm trying to tell you."

Duncan saw for the first time that she was cool and collected, not her usual weeping self when their relationship crossed the line regarding her insecurities. He suddenly realized that the woman he loved from the moment he first saw her had grown from a weak, compliant Muslima who'd been dominated by her father and then her husband into a confident, independent woman who knew her own mind and wasn't afraid of a challenge.

He took her in his arms. "Well, Ms. Marwa Kamal, you've

come a long way...."

Nazy angrily pushed him away. "Never call me that again. My name is Nazy Cunningham. I left Marwa Kamal and her baggage behind when I realized that you freed me—completely—from Waleed, his family, and Islam."

"Then you forgive me for getting your divorce from Waleed?"

"There's nothing to forgive. You did what was right and had to be done. I was stupid to realize it at the time."

Duncan took her in his arms. "So, Ms. Cunningham, shall we make up for lost time?"

Nazy kissed him. "Absolutely, Mr. Hunter. I suggest we turn off the lights and lock the house."

Hunter gazed into her sparkling emerald-green eyes. "I need you to wait one moment. I'll be right back."

As he raced toward the kitchen, she felt confused. They had magically reconciled, and he was running off?

Seconds later, he returned, his flying jacket bunched in one hand. Stopping before her, he smiled, and she returned it if for no other reason than they had cut the Gordian knot and were moving on to securing the house and walking down the hall to the master suite.

Hunter became serious. His lips pressed into a thin line, and his breathing rate went up. She worried, as he reached into the pocket of his battered leather flight jacket.

Taking a deep breath, he said, "I agree, but before we do so, I have something for you."

She looked at the battered Tiffany blue box Duncan took from a jacket pocket. He opened it and took out the ring box nestled inside, then he opened the ring box to reveal a blue-white, two-carat diamond solitaire set in platinum. "Ms. Cunningham, would you do me the honor of allowing me to change your name, yet again, from Cunningham to Hunter?"

Nazy's eyes widened. Taken aback, she began crying. "I take that as a 'yes?'"

Laughing through her tears, she said, "It's most emphatically a 'yes.'"

Duncan, taking the ring from its nest, placed it on Nazy's left hand. She jumped into his arms and kissed him passionately.

When she let him go, he whispered, "*Now,* we should lock up and turn out the lights."

Nazy nodded and said breathlessly, "I'll stay right here." She admired the ring on her hand and gently shook her head.

* * *

Theresa and Carlos watched from the caretaker's house as the lights in the ranch house went out, and the outside alarm signal turned red.

Theresa turned toward her husband. "I think she made it up to him."

CHAPTER TWELVE

1045 November 1, 2010
Schweizer Aircraft Company

Saul Ferrier supervised the offloading of the blue-and-white shipping container with a stylized Thunderbird crudely painted in the middle of the box. He couldn't believe the condition of the 007.

Hunter bent the frame and wings of the forty-year-old quiet airplane, and Schweizer engineers calculated the aircraft had probably been taken to its never-to-exceed limit. The G-meter indicated it experienced G forces equal to a one-quarter G away from both wings failing catastrophically, snapping off during the dive to safety.

There days later, the CEO reviewed the data and repair costs and called Lynche. "With all the parts we have to manufacture, it might be cheaper to buy a new airplane."

"Uh, Saul, are you making any new YO-3s?"

"Oh. Yeah, I see your point." The tacit acknowledgment was that the 007 was several orders of magnitude better than the aircraft Schweizer produced for the CIA when Lynche was the Agency's Chief of Air Branch.

"What we really need to do is start saying, 'No,' to amazingly crazy shit. Trying to operate in Iran was probably in the felony stupid category. Duncan thought we could do it, but he insisted on the fuzz busters. They did exactly what he said, and he did the right thing to save our lives and the plane. We'll fix it and call it a business expense."

"She can't be replaced unless you were to find another one."

"DOD returned all the YO-3As they borrowed. Their owners were happy to have them back, and I doubt we'll ever get another one from them. I don't see them leasing one to us or even letting us buy one outright. Their owners know they make interesting air show aircraft, and those guys love reliving their low-level nighttime exploits during the war."

"You have to face facts. She'll be out of action for months. Duncan broke her good. It's unbelievable you two defeated a missile."

"I know, and I know we really need a spare. The only good news is the new director doesn't have a lot of work for us. He has a different agenda. The last mission was overly dangerous, so I wonder sometimes how they knew we were coming."

Lynche had been thinking about how close he and Duncan came to being shot down. The JSOC commander was astounded that Iran fired on an aircraft over Afghanistan. He said, "That's a first."

Lynche let the thought go. "I know Duncan's working on it. He knows those guys better than I do."

"Let me know. We need the work. I'm afraid our days of building quiet airplanes are over."

"Say it isn't so!"

"Greg, we haven't had a new order since 2006. It's probably time to scrap the jigs and tools. I'll see after we repair 007."

The two men nodded, stepping toward the white and red Skymaster on the ramp.

"Let me know, Saul. I'll talk with you later."

"Tell Duncan I said, 'Howdy.' How is the lad?"

"Who knows? All I know is, he's driving across America in a bus. He likes taking in the mountains and valleys during daylight hours and at ground level."

"Is he driving alone?"

"I don't think so. Connie assures me he has a companion."

"Ah. All's well now?"

"I certainly hope so."

BOOK FIVE

CHAPTER ONE

0900 March 31, 2011
CIA Headquarters Washington, DC

The armored limousine passed through the main gate without stopping. Security guards in black SWAT uniforms, their H&K machine pistols at the ready and ear buds jammed into one ear, were alerted to the approaching vehicle carrying the Director of Central Intelligence. As the limo passed the checkpoint, high- definition cameras scanned the vehicle's underside, instantly comparing the picture to previous images to detect any change.

By the time the rear bumper passed the first of the pop-up barriers, green lights embedded in several posts and on the computer in Radio Control flashed steadily, signaling the all-clear.

Two minutes later, the DCI exited the limo in the underground garage, walking through double glass doors to the open private elevator for the nonstop ride to the seventh floor executive suite.

He turned to the control panel, held up a blue card with his photo to the camera lens, and waited until a green light illuminated. The doors closed silently, signaling approval for the occupant to proceed to the selected floor and to hold on.

Six seconds later, one of the fastest elevators at CIA stopped on the seventh floor. Another second later, the doors fully opened.

Stepping into the hallway, the DCI approached his office door, which opened automatically. Hank, his long-time secretary and a former male model, held the door, and greeted him with an appropriate, "Good morning, Sir," and followed the DCI into his inner sanctum. As Frank Carey removed his suit coat, Hank placed a steaming mug of coffee —sugar, cream, spoon, not stirred—on a leather coaster, took one look around the office, and departed, closing the door behind him.

Carey slid his tall, corpulent frame into the dark-brown leather chair, gripped the spoon, and stirred while he read the left side of the dispatch board. It showed copies of all the dispatches from every embassy and office around the world received within the last twenty-four hours. No immediate actions were on top. Routine actions followed.

After half an hour, he closed the cover of the dispatch board and lifted the right metal divider to find April's calendar of events. He scanned through the proposed calendar for anything he didn't want to commit to when he stopped at April 15. Hank indicated that was Tax Day in highlighted pink, as well as a Broken Lance Exercise in blue. Nothing seemed out of the ordinary, and he was about to close the folder when his eyes returned to the Broken Lance Exercise entry.

Even in deep thought, Carey was a shallow man. He wanted a trip to Dubai. It had been too long since his last adventure. The prince had two new toys for him to enjoy, but he needed to be in his office in Washington, DC. The president nagged him about his failed Muslim outreach initiative. The president didn't want to discuss the whereabouts of Osama bin Laden unless the CIA had an "airtight case" with photographic evidence at a minimum. A positive DNA match was preferable.

As a former ranking member of the Senate Intelligence Committee, Carey knew the American people wanted their pound of flesh with the capture of bin Laden, while the intelligence community wanted him for all the secrets in his head. KSM had spilled everything he knew under repeated sessions of simulated drowning procedures, called "waterboarding."

During the previous administration, American and European liberals screamed and railed against the enhanced interrogation techniques. They engaged in a collaborative effort to define waterboarding as torture, arguing that civilized countries didn't torture prisoners. The controversial change in definition gave the political left more ammunition to manufacture crimes against the former Republican administration. Former DCIs were repeatedly excoriated by congressional Democrats and some moderate Republicans on the Agency's use of the newly defined "torture."

One of the previous DCIs, a former Air Force intelligence officer, was often puzzled when liberals and their socialist, Marxist, communist, and fascist friends around the world sang the same song about waterboarding's being torture.

"What is it that has their little panties in a wad this time?" he asked.

When a dispatch from the US embassy in Pakistan appearing on the morning message board referred to a previous dispatch of a certain "former British subject now attending a major US university," but was "now a US citizen running for office," it was considered either wrong or disinformation at best. The timing was infinitely curious. Someone in the Near East Division must have started a file of the "subject named individual."

When the former DCI took a rare trip downstairs to NE, he was stunned to learn there had been a file, and the referenced dispatch as the topmost document. At a glance, the author of the dispatch outlined the SNI "had met with a string of known imams, terrorists or facilitators." The DCI tucked the file under his arm and never returned to the NE Division.

The outgoing DCI surrendered several dozen "DCI Eyes-Only" files upon his departure. The new DCI was astounded that there had been a "DCI Eyes-Only" file on the new president in the DCI's personal safe, but it was enormously, almost suspiciously, thin. What he found, however, was explosive. The new DCI saw the file as a ticket to greater success.

The 0600 call from the President awoke the DCI's young lover, who reached over to the other nightstand to silence the BlackBerry. A crotch in the DCI's face and the unique ring tone startled him awake. Carey screamed, "Don't touch that!"

Carey answered the secure electronic device with, "Good morning, Mr. President." A minute later, he terminated the call with, "Yes, Mr. President."

The President was shaking him down again. That time, it was for a million dollars to be sent to a bogus solar-energy company. For the last two years, the President ordered his cabinet members to do crazy, even zany, things. DOJ was to look the other way on voter intimidation or voter fraud issues. The Democratic President's voting rights laws existed only to protect a special class of voters. The Department of Homeland Security was to look the other way on illegal immigration and to sue states trying to protect their borders. He sent a message to the Muslim world that the US was pro-Islamic by prosecuting CIA agents and military members who apparently violated a terrorist's right to kill Americans.

The Department of Energy was ordered to spend hundreds of billions of taxpayer dollars on bogus solar or wind energy projects as investments in the green energy industry, which would require constant, massive government subsidies in order to operate.

Carey didn't like the view when he was forced into a box. He saw the President, like all closet socialists, couldn't help himself when it came to abusing executive power.

"He's going to destroy this wonderful party, my friends, and me," Carey muttered. "He won't listen to reason, and he can't quit the trajectory he's on. Someone has to step up and do something."

Right before he tossed a metal binder into his out box, a thought occurred to him. He opened the dispatch board on his calendar and focused on the Broken Lance Exercise entry again. Then he caught himself staring blankly at his bookcase. He leaned back his head, moving the huge leather chair back, too, and raised his arms over his head with fingers intertwined.

For ten minutes, his brain churned over the Broken Lance Exercise. Suddenly, he brought down his hands and sat upright, a devious expression on his face. "I think that just might work."

CHAPTER TWO

1400 April 1, 2011
Dulles International Airport Dulles, Virginia

The millionaire, unmarried, liberal senator from New England was a surprise nomination from the President. Frank Carey spent a good part of his five-term career in the company of politicians and businessmen in the Middle East. His company provided a range of foodstuffs, primarily fruits and vegetables, for markets from Morocco to Pakistan. He made several fortunes with his partners in Saudi Arabia and Dubai. Prince Bashir inherited his oil fortune from his father and got into the business of providing goods and services for thousands of oil-field workers who clamored for fresh fruit, vegetables, and beef. Camels, goats, and chickens were plentiful in the kingdom, but beef was scarce until Senator Carey suggested the prince visit the King Ranch in Texas and check out the Santa Gertrudis brand, known the world over for their ability to adapt to harsh climates.

Prince Bashir bought a starter herd of 2,500 of the cherry-red cattle and had them shipped to his 20,000-acre ranch in Saudi Arabia. A processing plant was built, and the Zebu brand of beef dominated the finer restaurants from Istanbul to Djibouti and everywhere in between, especially at canteens supporting the extraction of oil from 10,000 wells. The tip from Carey made Prince Bashir an international star on the cattle market. Attending cattle auctions around the world, he secured the finest Santa Gertrudis bulls from Texas, paying record prices every year. He reciprocated by facilitating exclusive contracts for Carey inside and outside the kingdom to feed the tens of thousands of oil-field workers in Africa and on the Saudi Peninsula. They shared a passion for making money supporting the gold that came from the ground, as well as a passion for sharing pretty young men and tight little boys. Bashir sent spies everywhere to find the best boys and men to satisfy the craving he and Carey shared for the pretty and undefiled.

The former senator also used his position on several committees to make massive stock trades ahead of legislation, a practice that drew yawns in Congress but was considered insider trading with significant jail time if anyone else tried it. Carey shared those blockbuster changes in legislation with Bashir, enabling him to get ahead of the markets in Europe, Asia, and the Middle East.

It was a marvelous relationship. The senator provided Bashir with information, and Bashir provided him with young men and boys. An ethics investigation into his relationship with his live-in lover, who was caught running male prostitutes out of the senator's house in Washington, nearly derailed the setup. Worth nearly a billion dollars, Carey was able to buy his way out of trouble and escape scrutiny the same way a previous president escaped removal from office. Being impeached wasn't removal, and the findings resulted in less than a slap on the wrist.

The recent presidential nomination spelled trouble for the intelligence community, as the partisan liberal Democrat was approved by a single vote in the Senate. The new president began demanding outcomes at the CIA. More minorities needed to be hired, as well as more attorneys brought in to oversee the out-of-control Agency that provided poor intelligence for the run up to the invasion of Iraq.

There were no weapons of mass destruction. "The president lied, and people died," was the refrain from the left. The new president's solution was that the intelligence community needed more professionalism and oversight, so another war wouldn't be started based on bad intelligence. Those who provided that professionalism and oversight were almost 100 attorneys, the majority of whom had radical legal backgrounds from US nonprofit organizations across the country. A significant number of those organizations defended terrorists brought to trial when they weren't actively working behind the scenes to overthrow the US government. Soon came demands from inside the Agency to lessen the number of direct actions by CIA and the IC, "based on shoddy intelligence."

Terrorism became a bad word at the White House. Islamic extremist were even worse words. The senior intelligence service officers at the NCTC were systematically discouraged from more-aggressive action on al-Qaeda and others under the auspices that the intel didn't support the action—per the judgment of the new attorney corps.

Ten months after his confirmation, sitting before the House Intelligence Subcommittee, Frank Carey let it slip that he was executing the president's wishes to hire more minorities and conduct Muslim outreach. The response from Republicans was disbelief and outrage. The White House immediately disavowed any such plan to have the CIA, FBI, or even NASA conduct outreach to Muslim countries.

When a congressman from Texas asked the NASA administrator about the Muslim-outreach plan, a NASA spokesman said, "The initiative was very real until somebody slammed the brakes on it."

The only problem at the CIA was that every career executive, analyst, and case officer saw the DCI's efforts for what they were—to interject by fiat unqualified, unsecured people into the one agency entrusted to keep the nation's secrets. Frank Carey tried, but every Muslim brought before human resources failed the background investigation and polygraph.

The DCI was incensed that not a single Muslim could pass the BI or polygraph. Every month, the president asked, "How are you coming on Muslim outreach?"

Every month, the DCI replied, "Not well, Mr. President, but we're working hard to make your vision come true."

The president suggested background investigators and polygraphers were deliberately rejecting candidates and undermining the DCI's authority. He added that perhaps the inspector general should investigate. When the IG began questioning the CIA's rank and file, every CIA employee clearly understood they were being targeted by a hostile president. The DCI felt the same way but for different reasons.

The president disrespected him often. He saw it many times before. Someone who claimed to be tolerant of bisexuals conducted himself in a way that made it clear he was disgusted by the idea. The president avoided being alone in the Oval Office with the DCI. When he was, the president was rude, crude, and demanded better results from his priority projects, including greater minority hiring to include openly gay individuals. More Muslims needed to be in the ranks, too. He warned Carey to investigate his out-of-control agents.

Previous presidents were briefed daily by a senior CIA official or the DCI in private. The new president was initially briefed every day by the DCI and a senior intelligence officer. After three months in office, the president received his daily brief weekly. After ten months, it became biweekly. The vice president or the Chief of Staff received the PDB in hardcopy. A CIA agent dropped it off with one of them, as directed by the DCI, and returned to McLean.

Ten months after the president's inauguration, the DCI's daily operations meeting included a significant change of status from red to yellow-green. NCTC agents believed they finally found Osama bin Laden's location with ninety percent probability. He was in Pakistan in a town near a large Pakistani base that was the Paki equivalent of the US Military Academy. The DCI requested a personal audience with the president to discuss the granularity of the intelligence.

Once granted, they met. The president was obviously uncomfortable, as the DCI gave him the details. The president looked shocked, and it took him several moments to compose himself for a reply.

"When you're 100% sure, we'll take action. I don't trust

those clowns at your place. They've proven they don't know what they're doing, and I won't risk my presidency on a ninety-percent solution from a bunch of losers who failed to find WMDs. Now get out."

Successive meetings with the president resulted in similar aggression toward the DCI and a similar assessment that the odds were still ninety percent. SIS officers of the NCTC were stunned, then resigned, when the DCI announced, "Until we have photographic evidence, we're to continue developing our intelligence."

They secured a safe house, high-powered telescopes, and as much eavesdropping equipment they could muster without drawing attention to themselves. Months of surveillance resulted in not one single photograph or voice print. The compound was too unique even for the wealthy side of Islamabad, Pakistan. With Howard Hughes gone, no one else on the planet was that much of a recluse.

The president unveiled his reelection strategy to his staff, announcing he would have a blockbuster announcement soon. The DCI was furious and dejected. The POTUS was going to go after Osama bin Laden when there was 100% confirmation, which could be any day. He wasn't about to let such an opportunity slip by.

"It was given to me, and it's golden," he nearly shouted at the DCI.

He walked from behind the Resolute Desk and put an index finger in the middle of the DCI's chest. "Don't fuck this up, or your ass will be out on the street in a minute. Then you can go butt fuck all the little boys to your heart's content."

That was the final straw. Carey was ready to quit, then thought better of it. He was smart enough to know that he didn't think straight when he was angry. It wasn't time to have some lickspittle cocksucker or political lackey agree with him, console him, and make him feel better. The confrontation had just moved to another plane. He had two opposing thoughts, each fighting for clarity. One was to seek advice from a very trusted source, so, as he did for thirty years, he called Bashir.

"Will you be in Washington anytime soon?" Carey asked.

"I can be there by the end of the week, my friend. Will that be OK? I haven't had my little airplane out in a very long time."

* * *

The white, green, and gold Boeing 747 landed at Dulles and parked near the executive terminal across the ramp from where the lesser princes parked their Gulfstreams and smaller Boeings.

Carey's second thought dominated his waking hours. It was becoming painfully clear to him, his friends, and even his enemies that the president was bad for the country and horrible for the Democratic Party. Carey saw himself as a victim, like Claus Schenk Graf von Stauffenberg, who was maimed while serving the Fuhrer only to discover that Hitler was unadulterated evil, a man hell-bent on destroying Germans and Germany. Von Stauffenberg slowly came to the conclusion that he was the best person to organize a movement to save Germany by stopping Hitler. He was under no illusion that the mission would be suicide if it failed, but for him, a shattered war hero, living under such tyranny was worse than death. Von Stauffenberg got close enough to plant a bomb near where Hitler stood and barely escaped the blast.

Carey was being consistently and emotionally maimed by the president.

During Cabinet meetings, after the press withdrew, the defeated faces of the Cabinet members were similar to the faces of Hitler's generals before von Stauffenberg tried to kill him. The man became a churlish tyrant, and the DCI became the frequent butt of cutting remarks around the table. Carey left the White House livid, like a lover scorned. He was so supportive of the president during the campaign and after the election and often fantasized about being with him, but those fantasies were replaced by lethal ideas and thoughts of revenge.

When the president couldn't appoint his communist radical supporters to key positions, he was forced to appoint those he could control, not lead. The DCI was the most outrageous appointment. His history in gay rights and scandalous associations were slightly offset by his longstanding position on the Senate Intelligence Committee. When the president hinted that he knew of Carey's overseas pastimes, Carey knew anything he did or didn't do would be subject to blackmail.

Then the president finally crossed the line by shoving his finger against Carey's chest.

"You pushed me too far, Mr. President," Carey muttered when he was alone. "You grossly underestimate my ability to fight back. You're nothing but a Detroit thug, and I won't take your shit any longer."

The DCI and the Saudi prince met on the prince's jet. Carey reverted to his obsequious persona. "Bashir, you definitely know how to travel. I'm always in awe of your little airplane."

After a handsome young man in makeup brought tea and pastries, Carey discussed his concerns and ideas. Prince Bashir was enamored of the tall, arrogant senator and expressed his sympathy.

"At some point, he needs to go away," Carey said, "but I'm afraid the only option is to kill him. He's the most protected man in the world, but I think I know of a way."

"Very interesting. Tell me more."

"I have information that there's a group of military commandos, Navy SEALs, who've been trained for this mission, which is to kill the president. They could do it, but they have to be properly motivated. They're only compelled to shoot him if he were held hostage or kidnapped."

"Americans plan for the most bizarre contingencies. Very interesting. What's your plan?"

"I will compel the SEALs to kill him. Otherwise, they'll

watch their comrades die. I think it's a good plan, but there must be something dramatic to incite these professional killers into action. They're very protective of each other and are willing to die for a fellow SEAL."

"It sounds like a good plan. It might take awhile before these SEALs are properly motivated to take…. How do you say…?"

"Appropriate action?"

"Yes. I think I can help. I'm aware of a man in Africa who may have the long-distance shooting skills. It might take several weeks before I can arrange a meeting."

"I can't ask you, dear Bashir, to become personally involved."

"My dear Carey, you can't do it. I'll develop a plan. How much do you think this business is worth to this man? He must be…."

"…appropriately motivated?"

"Yes. Appropriately motivated. That's very good. I believe I can also locate some of those SEALs."

"I believe you're anticipating some of the challenges I face. I don't think I can provide much information without raising awareness. I must maintain distance from this."

"I can handle this. I'm very good at arranging things, yes?"

"Bashir, you're wonderful. I'll owe you greatly, my friend."

"I just thought of something Carey. I wonder if there's a file on the president. I'd be very interested to know if there is such a thing."

The request caught Carey momentarily off guard. "I'll find out. You're correct. It would be very interesting to know if there is a file."

"Please let me know."

"I shall, Bashir." Carey bowed in respect. "You're the best, a great friend."

"It's the least I can do for one of my very best friends."

"I'll pay whatever's necessary."

"We can worry about that later. Let's talk about it when you visit Riyadh. I have two very nice toys for us to play with."

"Maybe aboard the Sa'ad?" He envisioned his private cabin on the prince's yacht. "Inshallah. Thank you, Bashir. I must go.

"Shukran."

"Please soon, my friend. It has been so long. Ma'assalama."

CHAPTER THREE

2315 April 15, 2011
Near East Division, CIA Headquarters Washington, DC

For nearly six straight hours, Nazy Cunningham and her analysts in the NE Division pored over the latest on-line release of nearly 10,000 secret documents. Most had been classified at one time as confidential or even secret. The administration hailed the release of the documents as "a great thing" and done in the name of "free speech," while Republicans called the act "unmitigated treason."

Those at the CIA and the National Counterterrorism Center hoped the release of the documents from the State Department wouldn't compromise any ongoing operation. Early analysis after three hours of scrutinizing thousands of documents had most of the agents confident that the data dump would have little or no impact on current operations.

At the five-hour mark, nearly every analyst in the division agreed that everything released on that go-round was trash or OBE, overcome by events.

One little line in a two-part dispatch from Pakistan that Nazy almost overlooked because of its Confidential classification was not only intriguing but potentially explosive. On the second page was a casual remark from a low-level Pakistani intelligence administrative clerk: "There is great interest within ISI of a huge compound near the military academy. CIA is watching the house."

Nazy spun in her chair, logged onto the classified intranet, and typed a memo to the deputy directors of the CIA and the NCTC.

* * *

FLASH. Potential location of OBL identified in latest online release doc #5467. Could be enough to put officers at risk or alarm occupants of compound. Expect immediate media discovery and release. Plz advise/respond. End.

CHAPTER FOUR

0500 April 30, 2011
The White House

The call to the DEVGRU commander went through in less than two minutes to the secret base in east Afghanistan. The President got right to the point.

"Captain Cox, I don't have to tell you this is a history-making event. I want you to know I appreciate you and your men's service to our country."

"Yes, Sir." The old SEAL wondered if the guy wanted a trophy.

"I have trust and confidence in you and your men to carry out this mission successfully."

"Yes, Sir. Thank you, Sir."

"Captain Cox, I know you know what commander's wishes are. Am I right, Captain?"

"Yes, Sir. What are you looking for, Sir?"

"Captain Cox, I'm looking for assurance that he doesn't leave that compound alive. Am I clear enough?"

Captain Cox heard warning bells in his head. "Yes, Sir. Understood, Sir."

"Thank you, Captain Cox. Good luck. We never had this call, did we?"

"I don't know what call you're talking about, Sir."

"Thank you. Make me proud. Good luck and good night."

"Good night, Sir."

The line to the STE disconnected. Cox looked at the receiver in disgust, replaced it in its cradle, and turned to his assault team. Members sat on any available flat spot in the small, modular SCIF.

He said matter-of-factly, "He wants the fucker dead."

A moment passed, then Chief Petty Officer Lampard spat,

"Is that another way of saying he doesn't want him interrogated?"

"Or waterboarded?" someone in back asked. "Don't we want to know where Zawahiri is?"

"How about Abu Sayyef?"

"You're shitting me!"

Captain Cox raised his hand, and the men fell silent. "Dunk, Chase, Spike, Spock stay. Everyone else take a walk."

When the last SEAL departed the SCIF, Cox asked, "The president said he wanted assurances that OBL doesn't leave the compound alive. He invoked commander's wishes and we-never-had-this-conversation bullshit."

Four confused, long-haired, bearded men looked at each other.

"I've rarely been this mad, and I'm disinclined to honor his wishes. If we find that murderous bastard, he needs to be interrogated until his seventy-two virgins waiting in heaven won't want to have anything to do with him. If I'm out of line, speak now, and I'll relieve myself of command. Am I clear?"

Commander Mike "Dunk" Jordan spoke quickly. "Skipper, I vote we take the bastard alive if at all possible, just as planned. He needs to squirm and talk."

"I second the motion," Chase Mosely said.

"Count me in," Spike Klug said. "The bastard has to pay."

"I agree," an incredulous Matt "Spock" Mott said, "but how the fuck will we pull it off?"

"You're the brains of this outfit, Spock," Cox said. "I know you can come up with a plan that'll make your mother proud. Americans will sing your praises one of these days."

"All right, Skipper. How much time do I have?"

"What can you do in two minutes? We take off in ten, and I have to piss."

Spock thought fast. "I'm done. Want to hear it?"

"I'll hold it. What's the plan?"

Spock recommended an immediate burial at sea according to Muslim tradition. That was a touch none of them could have imagined.

"That's perfect," Cox said. "Gentlemen, I think we have a plan. What do you say?" He placed his fist in the center of the men. The others bumped fists with him.

"Hooyah!"

"Now I'll go piss. It'll be a long flight."

CHAPTER FIVE

2200 May 1, 2011
The White House

"Who the fuck told them to bury him at sea?" the President squealed.

The Vice President, the Chairman of the Joint Chiefs, the SECDEF, the DCI, and the Secretary of State didn't have an answer.

Though he didn't realize it, the Secretary of State came to the rescue. "Mr. President, none of the Islamic nations would take the body. It sounds like the commander made a great snap decision in hindsight. Pictures of the body are being processed at the CTC."

The president was livid. His vitriol was incongruent against the success of the mission to kill Osama bin Laden. That bin Laden fought back, and a SEAL was forced to kill him, was one of the many contingency scenarios practiced. The world's most-wanted terrorist was killed. Around the world, people celebrated or lamented bin Laden's death.

DCI Carey tuned out the harangue, rehearsing his lines mentally. The president wrapped up the meeting, telling everyone to leave the office.

"Mr. President, sixty seconds?" Carey asked.

The president plopped in his chair and spun around, turning his back on the room, as three people filed out. "You have one minute, Carey."

The DCI walked to the front of the Resolute Desk and waited for the room to clear. "Mr. President, here's a partial file of your activities when you were traveling as a British citizen on your British passport and visiting the man you just killed."

The President turned slowly to face the DCI and stared at

the file in his hands.

"I have the only full copy of your file. Your secret's safe unless... you fuck with me."

"That's bogus shit, Carey. I can't believe...."

"Mr. President, you'll announce the vice president has health issues, and you'll make me his replacement in one month. Before the election, you'll resign due to health reasons. If you don't heed my advice, the whole file will be released. You'll be exposed as a fraud and a traitor, and you'll be frog-marched out of this office and thrown in jail."

Carey tossed the file dismissively onto the desk, turned, and said, "Good night, Mr. President." He walked out, leaving the President of the United States in utter shock.

CHAPTER SIX

2230 May 1, 2011
The Yellow Corvette Ranch Fredericksburg, Texas

The BlackBerry vibrated, and Secret Agent Man announced it was Duncan's favorite spook calling. "You're awake at this hour?"

"Turn on your TV," Greg whispered.

"What channel?"

"It won't matter. I think we got him. Talk with you later."

Hunter jogged from the garage into the living room, snatched the remote, and hit the All On button. Five seconds later, the President materialized at a lectern.

"Good evening. Tonight, I can report to the American people and the world that the United States has conducted an operation that killed Osama bin Laden, the leader of al-Qaeda and a terrorist who's responsible for the murder of thousands of innocent men, women, and children."

Duncan was transfixed. The one mission he and Lynche were never part of had been executed. He thought of his old friend from the Naval War College. "Well, Bill, wherever you are, I hope that ghost has finally been put to rest."

CHAPTER SEVEN

1000 May 4, 2010
Dallas Motor Speedway Dallas, Texas

Dozens of national and local reporters filled the White House Briefing Room. The spokesman, still basking in the afterglow of the Navy SEAL team's operation, announced, "The president announced he would personally thank the Navy SEAL team who killed Osama bin Laden."

For four days, the nation was treated to hundreds of presidential vignettes regarding his leadership and political courage during that part of American history. The message from the White House was controlled. The media and press weren't allowed to ask about the former senator's previously stated virulent antiwar political views when he opposed the wars in Afghanistan and Iraq or when he introduced legislation to end them.

While the president's polling numbers were expected to rise meteorically, the favorability bounce quickly died, as Americans were more interested in hearing about the assault on Osama bin Laden's compound and to hear more stories about SEALs, past and present. Nearly everyone in America was more interested in their new heroes than the man who authorized the operation.

Hunter emerged from the toilet carrying a twelve-inch cardboard box and paused to watch the lapdog media on TV. Lynche, engrossed, saw Hunter frowning and turned off the set. Hunter continued his vector to the door and stepped down from the motor coach. Lynche followed with a bag and two sodas.

"I wonder how many victory laps he'll take before the media realizes he didn't do a damn thing?" Hunter asked. "He acts like he pulled the trigger. For someone who hates the military and is a pretend commander-in-chief, that's disgusting. It's like the CEO of General Motors rushing to Paris to congratulate the Corvette racing team after they won Le Mans. When he gets there, he kicks the driver out of the car and takes victory laps while he waves to the crowd, saying, 'Look how great and brave I was.' The man's a total fricking incompetent and an embarrassment."

Lynche shook his head. "Wow. Where'd that come from? I have to say I like the analogy, especially in this venue."

Duncan hadn't been overtly political for as long as Lynche knew him, but, with the recent election of the junior senator from Michigan, Hunter showed a distinct shift in outlook and displeasure with the new president. There was something about the erudite politician that impressed Lynche while arousing Hunter's suspicions.

Lynche and his wife were swept up in the high emotion of the election of a historic figure. Some called him a transformational politician. Hunter thought Lynche lost his ability to rationalize. What little was known about the man from Michigan was carefully squelched and obviously choreographed.

Hunter found it difficult to get excited about a red-diaper baby raised by committed Marxists, mentored by committed Marxists, baptized by a committed Marxist, schooled by committed Marxists, and being given kudos and policy advice by committed Marxists. Why those topics weren't the subject of the media was one of the greatest mysteries of the election.

The media's cultural code of silence and disinterest in the senator's past didn't resemble how the old Communist-run Prada was controlled by the Kremlin, but it resembled the Mafia- influenced *omertá*. Within Mafia culture, breaking *omertá* was punishable by death. For all its vaunted tolerance, the political left consistently demonstrated a militant intolerance for dissent. As any Republican soon discovered, any questioning of the Democratic candidate or the new president's background and character was punished by a thousand cuts from the media.

Hunter, like millions of other Republican sore losers, sniped and fumed, resigned there was nothing to do until the next election.

Hunter just returned from several high-speed laps on the banked track, testing the car's integrity before handing it over to his mentor and friend. The yellow race car easily sustained 150 mph with a string of other high-performance Corvettes. The weather was perfect for racing. He and Lynche had long planned to get away from the mission grind and do something fun.

When Connie Lynche wanted to give her husband lessons at a racing school for an anniversary gift, Duncan offered to provide the car, track, and the lessons. At first intrigued, Lynche became intimidated when he saw the huge oval raceway with high-banked track. His confidence was shaken as the line of cars roared around the speedway's NASCAR track. A banked track was an unnatural driving environment for him, and when he wasn't worrying about killing himself, he worried he would damage Hunter's favorite antique racecar.

During the break-in racing sessions, Hunter and Lynche sat under an awning attached to the motor coach. Lynche opened the bag, and he and Hunter ate Texas brisket sandwiches before the next session began.

"The guy's disgusting," Hunter said. "What he's doing is disgusting. I'll be glad when I can turn on the TV and not see his face."

"Mav, I'm embarrassed that I voted for him."

Hunter wiped barbecue sauce from the corners of his mouth. "That's why I quit watching. Break, break. New subject. It's your turn, good Sir. You saw how easy it is. I guarantee you'll have a blast. You'll have fun, Mr. Lynche."

"So how was it?"

"It's very spooky the higher you go. The car seems to want to climb right up the bank—a minor steering correction. It's intuitive, so you'll feel it. Then keep up with whoever's in front of you. It's your turn." He opened the box he carried from the coach and handed Lynche a new black helmet wrapped with thick plastic with the word Grinch painted on the back in yellow letters.

"Wow. Thanks, Mav. I still can't believe you'll trust me with the Beast." He wondered if learning to race was a bad idea, but it looked like he would really have to do it.

"You always trusted me with your Skymaster. No factor. Ready to hit the track?"

"I'm not driving that fast."

As Lynche walked to the bright yellow-and-black 1967 Corvette, Hunter shouted, "If you piss on my seat, you'll buy me a new car! Go have some fun. I have a feeling our days in the sun are coming to a close."

CHAPTER EIGHT

1200 May 7, 2011
The Presidential Suite JW Marriott Washington, DC

The pretty blonde reporter with the word FOX on the microphone spoke to the camera. "We're getting reports from JSOC headquarters that Navy SEALs are grateful for the nation's show of support but are growing angry with the continued focus on their operations, tactics, and tools, claiming it could jeopardize future raids and their safety. A JSOC spokesman issued the following statement.

"'Anything further that comes out could damage their operational security, may reveal tricks of the trade, or even endanger their families.' It was a subtle hint that the men of SEAL Team Six would rather this episode in their glorious history pass— the sooner, the better. Back to you in New York."

Nazy Cunningham pulled the sheet up to her neck, sat up, and leaned against the headboard. "Everyone in the building is in a jubilant mood. The SEALs brought back boxes of laptops, hard drives, and cell phones. The director has been in a horrible mood since bin Laden was taken down. Rumor is that the President almost fired him, because he was looking for someone to blame for all the secret documents posted online. Then a couple days ago, he was bouncing around like he won the lottery. If you're already almost a billionaire, why would you do that?"

"Maybe he's had enough," Hunter said. "You found Osama bin Laden, and it was your finding of the dispatch that forced the White House to approve the raid. As for the DCI, he should be a hero. What does he have to prove? Maybe he has a new boyfriend."

"I don't know. I think it's something else. Women's

intuition."

"What does that tell you?" He raised bedroom eyes at her.

She smiled and almost giggled. In a sexy voice, she said, "My women's intuition tells me you missed me very much."

"That's true. I came as fast as I could, but I figured you'd be busy for several months with the haul they brought back."

"The CTC and the FBI are doing all the analyses. I'll actually have a few days off."

"Hmmm. So what does your women's intuition tell you I'm thinking?" He gently tugged the sheet covering her breasts.

"Why, Mr. Hunter, I think you're very glad to see me." The pressure on the sheet gently released.

"Why, Ms. Cunningham, I think your women's intuition is on target again."

CHAPTER NINE

2100 May 9, 2011
Naval Support Activity Millington, Tennessee

The former fighter pilot Commander-in-Chief left the political stage after eight years with American forces fully engaged, hunting down and killing terrorists in several locations on several continents. The troops loved him when he showed up in Afghanistan in the middle of the night on Thanksgiving to serve them turkey dinner and pumpkin pie. They loved him when he jumped in a jet and landed on a super-carrier coming back from the war. He wanted to fly onto the big deck in a Navy F-18, but the Secret Service vetoed that idea. They didn't want an uncleared, non-Yankee White pilot taking the President for a joy ride in a jet.

The President relented by flying onto the USS Abraham Lincoln as the copilot of an S-3A Viking with an airsick Secret Service agent in the back. They loved him when he left office, often to meet returning warriors from the war when they landed in Dallas, Texas.

The election of the junior senator from Michigan was viewed as cautiously optimistic. For most of the uniformed services, they reserved judgment. The new president's proposed social engineering policies were anathema to the rank and file, while his dubious past associations with domestic terrorists, radicals, and communists stretched the limits of credibility. No president could be that far to the left. Honesty, integrity, and leadership were what mattered to the military, both the officer corps and the enlisted ranks.

The new president's reported associations were incredible and so radical as to be unbelievable, almost un-American. His pastor of twenty years was a venom-spewing racist and anti- Semite, as were his college professors. His neighbors were aggressive radicals and communists actively working to overthrow the government.

There was the head of a large, Black Muslim terrorist group and a husband-and-wife team that made national news as part of a group of unrepentant domestic terrorists who bombed police stations and military installations, killing dozens in uniform. It strained the limits of credulity to believe any American citizen could have been elected being the most-liberal senator in the Senate, or being close friends with avowed communists and Marxist radicals, or were cozy with unrepentant domestic terrorists.

For the mainstream press, the new president got a 'Get Out of Jail Free' card. His past associations were viewed as immaterial. After all, he only lived in the neighborhood, and it wasn't possible to choose one's neighbors, professors, or pastor.

For a large segment of the intelligence community and professional military, warning bells rang when the conservative, informal media began to accumulate information on the new president. Several military members refused their deployment orders until he could prove he was a natural-born citizen, per the Constitution. When the president's autobiographies clearly stated he was the son of a British subject and therefore should have been one, too, the press and the left went into hyper-drive to protect their newly elected liberal standard bearer and dismissed anyone who brought up the issue as a nut or an extremist. The national mood reflected the national employment rate—very bad and getting worse.

The country seemed to be bumping around the edges of civil war, with the president openly pitting class warfare and fomenting what some suggested was the beginning of a race war. For the intelligence community and the military, a shift in policies and priorities meant military heroes were removed from commands and replaced by liberal-minded, docile officers, while the intelligence community leadership embarked on fulfilling the president's priorities of Muslim outreach and hiring more minorities, including those who were openly homosexual.

Morale within the two communities entrusted with national security was at an all-time low, but that was never reported in the press, nor were the reasons for the decrease. It became clearer every day to some that there was an active plan to emasculate the IC and the military. To some, the president crossed the line, and a growing number of his former supporters began working against him and his radical policies.

After three years, despite what the press portrayed, the president was a polarizing national embarrassment. For a military man or woman, there was an expectation of confidence and leadership from the Commander-in-Chief whoever it was. It was very difficult for senior and junior military members to respect their Commander-in-Chief when the president didn't know the words to the Pledge of Allegiance, refused to put his hand over his heart while the nation anthem played, avoided being photographed with the American flag or a cross, bowed before Muslim leaders when traveling abroad, and spoke well only when he had a teleprompter. Without the device, he sounded like a buffoon.

For someone marketed as the smartest Harvard lawyer ever to hold the office, he completely lost the respect of the majority of the military when, during an awards ceremony at the White House, he called a heroic Navy Corpsman a "corpse man" several times. To the military, it was obvious that the president was a reader, not a leader.

No one was fooled when he began to take the stage with dozens of Stars and Stripes, neatly folded, prominently displayed. He even started wearing an American flag pin, eliciting comparisons from the political Right to Dracula being able to overcome garlic.

With campaign promises leading to legislation that specifically targeted the good order and discipline of the military, morale continued falling. Polling trended toward a steady decline in American confidence in the president.

Pollsters stopped polling troops. Those who returned from firefights in Afghanistan uttered sentiments to family members like, "Feel sorry for those Air Force and Marine aircrews having to transport the POS. We were the lucky ones."

Some joked privately, "An illegal alien, a Muslim, and a communist walk into a bar. The bartender asks, 'What can I get you, Mr. President?'"

When the CIA told the president in August, 2010, that they knew with very high probability Osama bin Laden was located in Pakistan, the president forced the military and intelligence community to continue developing intelligence and waited months before ordering an attack. A massive intelligence leak that strongly suggested Osama bin Laden's location in Pakistan compelled the president to order a nighttime assault. He told the Chairman of the Joint Chiefs he still had to "sleep on it" before giving the execution order.

On the first of May, the president announced that the United States conducted an operation that killed Osama bin Laden. Osama bin Laden was taken down by a large contingent of US Naval Special Warfare Development Group, formally DEVGRU, informally as SEAL Team Six. Afterward, politicians had to applaud the president's leadership in killing the world's most wanted terrorist.

The political left and the media stepped up their slobbering over the president, marketing how brave he was and over-extolling the organization that did the deed.

Five days later, the president announced he would personally thank the Navy SEAL team who killed Osama bin Laden when they reached the United States. For the next four days, the politician and his fire team of media lapdogs ran around the country, basking in the afterglow of the heroics of the men who did the work. Each audience received more details of the mission from the president, as well as DEVGRU's internal workings. The media interviewed and profiled SEALs past and present.

Immediately after returning from Afghanistan and

meeting the president, the commander of DEVGRU called the SOCOM commander and complained bitterly that the president's comments and unauthorized portrayals of DEVGRU by the White House press corps brought significant, unwanted limelight on the operation and the men of SEAL Team Six and their families.

The JSOC and SOCOM commanders were both livid, and the politically correct message to SECDEF and the Joint Chiefs was that "Navy SEALs are grateful for the nation's show of support but are growing angry with the continued focus on their operations, tactics, and tools, claiming it could jeopardize future raids and their safety."

SECDEF issued a press release without clearing it with the White House, which said, in essence, "Shut up, Mr. President." It appeared that the White House heard the message.

Perhaps it was coincidence that the day after POTUS was briefed they knew where Osama bin Laden was located, and the intelligence community and DOD were told "continue to develop your intelligence," the SECDEF ordered the SOCOM commander to draft plans for a search-and-destroy raid. He also announced his retirement would be soon. He had it with that worm.

Then a SEAL was found dead.

CHAPTER TEN

0700 May 10, 2011
The Denver Post
Denver, Colorado

Pablo Reyes, a 22-year retired US Navy Commander and a former Navy SEAL, was found dead at his home in Denver, CO. The Denver Police Department believe Mr. Reyes, a physical fitness instructor at the Johnson & Wales University, was the victim of a random shooting. The case is under investigation.

CHAPTER ELEVEN

1400 May 14, 2011
Arlington National Cemetery Arlington, Virginia

Thirty-six SEALs in dress blues marched in a column of twos behind the horse-drawn carriage transporting one of their own, Commander Pablo Reyes, to his final resting place. Another one-hundred friends and mourners from across SOCOM and the Navy quietly gathered around the burial site awaiting the hearse and escorts to arrive.

SEAL pallbearers marched into position, as the hearse arrived. They gently lifted the wooden casket from the carriage and lowered it to the telpher crane deck. The Commander Chaplain delivered the rites. A bugler played Taps. A bagpiper played Amazing Grace, as every SEAL approached the casket in single file.

In a movement reminiscent of a football being spiked to the ground, each SEAL stuck a gold SEAL trident onto the casket, saluted, and moved on.

Soon, 66 of the US Navy's most famous warfare specialty pins adorned the casket lid. SEALs past and present, merged into a single line and assembled at the top of the hill for a few words together.

The crowd mostly dispersed when Captain William McGee, US Navy (Retired) and still an imposing figure in a black suit, turned to Commander Frank Ford and said, "Disco, we have to stop meeting like this."

"Aye, aye, Sir. Hey, I guess I'll see you this fall at the war college—if you're still there."

"I'll be there. Call me when you get in."

"Wilco. I'm heading to Memphis for a promotion board. You take care, Bullfrog." The men shook hands as they departed.

"You, too, Disco."

CHAPTER TWELVE

0600 May 17, 2011
The Commercial Appeal
Memphis, Tennessee

Commander Frank Ford, Executive Officer of SEAL Team 2, was found dead along a stretch of road at the Naval Support Activity in Millington, TN. Millington PD reported that the case was under investigation and was ruled suspicious.

Commander Ford was a precision parachute jumper and an avid sharpshooter. With a striking ability to control his emotions in the most- dangerous situations, he was known for leading men with calm resolve and confidence. Over a 25-year career, Ford rose to become a Commander in the Navy, leading SEALs and joint and combined units that helped capture key Taliban and al-Qaeda leaders. Mr. Ford's remains are scheduled to be returned to his home of record, Beaufort, South Carolina, arriving Monday evening at the Savannah International Airport. A Mass will be offered at 9:30 AM Thursday at Our Lady of the Sacred Heart Catholic Church. Funeral arrangements are being handled by the Helton-Hilburn Funeral Home. In addition to his mother and father, he is survived by two brothers, Robby and Richard.

CHAPTER THIRTEEN

2100 May 22, 2011
The Virginia Pilot
Norfolk, Virginia

David "Mako" Petersen, of Virginia Beach, died on Saturday, May 21, 2011 at the Norfolk County Health Care Center. David was born on August 11, 1956 to the late Raymond and Mary Petersen in Orange, CA. He married Anita Zingaro in September, 1999 in Bay St. Louis, MS. David was a world-class swimmer when he joined the US Navy. He and his wife lived most of their lives in Virginia Beach. David was a proud Naval Officer, spending over 30 years in the service of his country. He was preceded in death by his wife, Anita, and son, James. A memorial Mass will be held at a later date at Sacred Heart Catholic Church in Honolulu, HI. Interment will be in the National Memorial Cemetery of the Pacific.

CHAPTER FOURTEEN

2100 May 28, 2011
The Washington Post, Washington, DC

Stephen "Speedy" McCreedy, a longtime Boy Scout leader and US Navy officer, died Friday, May 25, at the Bethesda National Naval Medical Center. Commander McCreedy was a decorated US Navy veteran whose combat experience reads like a list of the biggest battles to have taken place in the Afghanistan and Iraqi Theater of Operations. Arrangements pending.

CHAPTER FIFTEEN

2100 June 7, 2011
Green Parrot Bar Key West, Florida

Todd Walters, The Key West Citizen reporter, approached the Key West PD detective. "We'll report tomorrow that Commander Donald Jorgenson, USN, was found dead in the parking lot of the Green Parrot Bar in Key West, Florida. No further details are known, and the KWPD is investigating."

"That'll work, Todd. Thanks. Call me in the afternoon to see if I have any news." The thin, balding reporter, dressed in jeans and a flowery green Tommy Bahama shirt, ambled away from the crime scene to file his report or find another place to get a beer.

Unaccustomed to murder and mayhem in the tourist town, the Key West Police Department quickly notified the NAS Key West duty officer that one of their officers had been shot and killed, and the body was en route to the morgue. Senior Petty Officer Mario "Curious" Curiel, SEAL Team Four, called the DEVGRU duty officer to report that his commander had been killed. The team had been partying in their favorite Key West bar, and, when the commander hadn't returned from the parking lot, true to his call sign, Curious went to investigate and ensure the gentle giant of a commanding officer wasn't being harassed by punks in the parking lot, like the previous evening. Curiel stumbled around outside for a minute before dropping to his knees to scan the underside of the vehicles. He quickly saw someone on the ground.

He ran around the truck to find Jorgenson, face up, parallel between two trucks, not breathing. Curiel first thought some SOB ambushed Jorgie and shot him at point-blank range. He immediately assumed a defensive-aggressive posture and flattened to the ground, scanning the underside of every vehicle while placing his fingers on Jorgenson's neck in the hope of finding a pulse.

When he was assured he wasn't in danger from armed hippies, he turned the commander over. The sight crushed Curiel, and he sank down on his butt. As he assimilated the information that his commander and friend were dead with an exit wound the size of a grapefruit, he paused to reflect. Having thirty-four sniper kills to his credit, Curiel recognized the trademark destruction of a long-range, soft-nosed, hollow-point rifle bullet. Trying to make sense of it, he slowly concluded that Jorgenson was taken out by a sniper who might still be targeting the area.

His senses were immediately heightened, and he took another peek at the underside of the vehicles when he saw an odd piece of paper rocking in the breeze under the other truck's front axle. He grabbed an edge and brought it closer. An inner voice warned him to move, so he crawled low as fast as he could, scattering gravel with every step and keeping as close to the other vehicles as possible.

With the entrance in sight, he paused, scanned the area, pushed off, and sprinted through the doorway. Running to the barkeep, he said, "Dial 911 and get an ambulance and the cops here. Someone's been killed in the parking lot."

When Curiel flew into the room and shouted at the pretty bartender, Petty Officer Russell Johnson watched, knew they needed quiet, and unplugged the jukebox. The SEALs stood when Curiel rushed toward them.

While Curiel scrolled through numbers on his cell phone to call the DEVGRU duty officer, he said, "Jorgie was taken out by a terminator round. He's down in the parking lot. I found this. Don't anyone touch it."

The DEVGRU duty officer was shocked by Curious' call and directed the TEAM to return to base as soon as possible.

* * *

Lieutenant Jim Bourne, call sign "Still," turned to the duty chief and took a deep breath. "Commander Jorgenson is down in Key West."

"How?"

Still recovering from the shock of Jorgenson's demise, Bourne ignored the question and said softly, "That makes four SEALs from Little Creek who've been shot in the last two or three weeks. That can't be a coincidence."

Reaching for a black binder, he flipped it open to a list of personnel recall numbers. He started at the top with Captain J. O. Biggers.

A young woman answered and shouted, "Dad! Phone." A few seconds later, a voice said, "Captain Biggers."

"Sir, Lieutenant Bourne, Command Duty Officer."

"What can I do for you Still?"

"Sir, I just got word Commander Jorgenson was killed in Key West. Chief Curiel said it looked like a sniper took him out. I told him to have the team return to base."

"I'll be there in five minutes. Out."

Captain Biggers rushed through the door in four minutes and barked, "SITREP!"

The Command Duty Officer followed him into his office. Biggers inserted his crypto card into the STE and turned to Lieutenant Bourne.

"Sir, no new info. Team Four is still being questioned by the locals at the Green Parrot. SOCOM has not been notified. I've drafted a FLASH message for your release. Sir, I think that makes four SEALs KIA'd in the last two weeks—three active duty and one retired in Colorado."

"No shit, Sherlock," Buggers mumbled. "That'll be all, Still. Thanks. Pull the door behind you."

The information panel on the STE indicated it was ready. Biggers pushed the #1 button to speed dial the SOCOM commander's private line.

After three rings, Admiral Don Shaw answered. "Secure, Sir?" Biggers asked.

Shaw waited for the STE card to work through all the

cryptological algorithms in two seconds, hearing the tone in the headset change to signify the call was secure. "Good morning, Juice. To what do I owe this pleasure?"

"Sir, Team Four Commander Jorgenson was killed in Key West at 2205, reportedly by a sniper. Key West PD and NAS Key West PMO are on the scene."

"Shit." The admiral inhaled sharply. "That's four in what, three weeks?"

"Yes, Sir. There's more. The chief who found Jorgie also found a piece of paper near the body. I'm told it was a message cobbled together from scraps of newspaper. The message read, Kill the one who ordered the hit on Osama bin Laden and I'll stop killing SEALs."

The admiral stepped to his desk, lowered his head, and closed his eyes. "Say again?"

Biggers repeated the message.

"Shit. That's all we need now. Where's the message?"

"Our boys still have it. One of our petty officers has it and thought it shouldn't be further contaminated. I think we have to turn it over to the FBI and let them work it."

"Agreed. Do you have a FLASH drafted?"

"Yes, Sir. I didn't think it was prudent to mention the message at this juncture."

"Agreed. OK, Juice, release the FLASH. Tell your guy to hold onto that message, and I'll contact the FBI. They'll get hold of him. We need to brief all SEALs that someone's on a SEAL hunt and to take precautions. Everyone needs to remain on base to the greatest extent possible. You know the drill."

"Aye, aye, Sir. Wilco."

"Juice, we thought something like this would happen after Osama bin Laden was killed, but I didn't think it would be quite like this. Talk to you tomorrow."

"Yes, Sir. Juice, out."

Admiral Shaw, SOCOM commander, received the call from Captain Biggers and repeated the process with the vice chairman of the Joint Chiefs, Marine General John "Horse"

Wright. Wright briefed the Chairman, who contacted the FBI director, who contacted the Attorney General, who mentioned it at the morning National Security Council meeting.

Sitting around the table chatting were the DCI; the Secretaries of Defense, State, and Homeland Security; the National Security Advisor; the Attorney General; and Secret Service Director Marty O'Sullivan.

Before the president and vice president arrived, O'Sullivan raised one eyebrow and asked the Attorney General, "Did you say, 'Kill the one who ordered the hit on Osama bin Laden, and I'll stop killing SEALs?'"

The others stopped talking and looked at the former Navy SEAL and fifteen-year Secret Service veteran, and newly installed Secret Service Director.

The AG spoke quietly, briefing the others about the four SEAL team commanders who'd been killed and added, "The FBI is investigating." It was "obviously the work of a right-wing extremist." The Secretary of Homeland Security tightened her jaw and ground her teeth. Her temples bulged, while she nodded in assent. O'Sullivan asked to meet with the Chairman, the Secretary of Defense, and the director of the CIA after the meeting. The AG asked to be included.

The President and Vice President entered the room. O'Sullivan nodded and left, as he wasn't a member of the council.

The president and vice president weren't briefed. No one at the White House or in the Situation Room had any doubt who "the one" was mentioned in the killer's note. The political right ridiculed the left and the president for being so arrogant when, during the Democratic convention, he galvanized the screaming crowd by saying, "We're the ones we've been waiting for." That sent 60,000 supporters in the football stadium into a frenzy.

The two-way implicit threat on the president was clear.

When the Attorney General was notified, the FBI dispatched agents in Florida, Colorado, Virginia, and Tennessee to investigate the four SEALs' deaths. Agents began searching airline, train, and credit card records for anyone who'd been at all four locations.

CHAPTER SIXTEEN

1400 June 8, 2011
Secret Service Duty Office, White House Washington, DC

The Secret Service Director closed his office door. "I'm taking this one seriously. From what I've heard so far, I think we have a major problem."

The Chairman of the Joint Chiefs, the Secretary of Defense, the Director of Central Intelligence, and the Attorney General were all on tight schedules, and the president's meeting always ran long.

The DCI muttered, "What's got your panties in a wad, Marty?"

The other three men grinned.

"I think this is serious shit. While you were in the Situation Room, I got a brief from our liaison at the FBI. The initial analysis is some fruit loop wants a SEAL to take out the president, and there's enough...." He waved his hands in the air. "...atmospherics to suggest that a SEAL would be encouraged to take unilateral action."

"Like that's going to happen," the Chairman said. "After taking out Osama bin Laden, this is ridiculous."

"I don't think we should overreact," the SECDEF said. "This sounds like overreaction and a poor analysis."

"No disrespect, Sir. I have to take this one seriously—and personally. You don't know these guys. I can see someone looking to be a hero. There's someone who wants to be like Mike Murphy. A real hero. In June, 2005, Lieutenant Mike Murphy exposed himself to enemy fire and left his covered position to get a clear signal with his cell phone. He provided his unit's location and requested immediate support for his team. He was shot several times and died from his wounds, earning the Medal of Honor."

"Some of the guys will view this attack on their fellow SEALs as an extension of the war, and he will try to save his teammates. He'll look to be a hero. All it takes is one try."

"What are you suggesting?" the Attorney General asked. "A SEAL will try to kill the president?"

"I think it's a possibility," O'Sullivan said. "I can't dismiss the probability, however small. If another SEAL is killed, there'll be more pressure on one of the less-stellar SEALs to do something. I think there's a good chance that a minor player would do anything to protect his fellow SEALs. I was a SEAL for fifteen years. If someone gets it into his head that his only way out of the situation is to protect his teammates...." He shook his head.

"The one thing you don't want is a pissed-off SEAL on your ass," SECDEF said. "We know no one can stop someone with a SEAL's skill set."

"You're saying the president will be targeted by a SEAL?" the Attorney General asked. "Are you serious?"

"What do you want me to say?" O'Sullivan asked. "Everything is hunky-dory? It isn't. It sounds like we have someone who doesn't want to go into the history books as the guy who tried to kill this president, so he found a way to get a surrogate to do his dirty work."

"A rogue SEAL?" the Attorney General asked. "That's blackmail on a horrific scale."

"If he's capable enough to take out four of our finest warriors," the SECDEF replied, "we could all be in the crosshairs before this is over."

"Any intel on the wire?" O'Sullivan asked.

"Not that I'm aware of," the DCI replied. "I'll talk to the deputy CTC and see if they've heard anything. We need to find this shooter. Marty, you need to lock down the president as much as you can, and limit his public exposure and public appearances. Since he's campaigning, that's going to be a challenge."

"We'll see if there have been any snipers booted from the services in the last ten years or so," the SECDEF added. "I don't want to, but we should probably brief all SEALs, and they'll need to submit to a poly. I can't just confine the SEALs to base. They have work to do. If they refuse a poly, they're done." His BlackBerry buzzed on his hip.

"You mean give them all a polygraph?" O'Sullivan asked. "Sir, that will piss them off. What if they all fail, because you insulted them? You can't fire them all!"

"I'll have the FBI working overtime on this," the Attorney General said. "Highest priority. I'll brief the president and the vice."

The SECDEF sighed, thinking the AG was a lightweight. "We'll engage the full resources of the IC to see if we can find some leads," the Director of Central Intelligence said. "I propose we have our deputies ramrod these investigations and brief daily. Anything substantive, we can brief at my place."

"Full court press," O'Sullivan said. "Thank you. I appreciate the help, Gentlemen."

"Who do we know with the skill set to knock off SEALs?" the DCI asked.

"There aren't many," the SECDEF said. "An effort like that will take a lot of money, too."

"With the killing of bin Laden, there must be a Middle East connection," O'Sullivan said.

The SECDEF nodded, while he read something off his handheld device. The DCI seemed startled for a moment, while the AG remained clueless.

"Do we need to investigate the backgrounds of the SEALs who were killed?" O'Sullivan asked. "Are there any common threads that link all four of the guys?"

As he placed his BlackBerry back in its holster, the SECDEF asked, "Besides the fact they all were in the initial wave that went into Afghanistan to find Osama bin Laden and all attended the Naval War College at the same time? That, and there's been another SEAL killed we didn't know about."

CHAPTER SEVENTEEN

1800 June 8, 2011
Secretary of Defense Office Pentagon, Washington, DC

The SECDEF, glancing at the file, waved the admiral away. As the door closed, his breathing rattled in his ears. The conversation with the Office of Naval Intelligence commander still ran through his head.

"Of all the men killed this month, they were SEALs during Jawbreaker from October to December, 2001, and they were ordered to the Naval War College during 2002-2003. One Saudi naval officer also attended the international class at NWC in 2002 and was later identified as an al-Qaeda lieutenant from a detainee in Gitmo in 2008."

"Go on," said the SECDEF.

"Commander Zaid Jebriel, Royal Saudi Navy, is the son of Prince Bashir Mohammad Jebriel, a Saudi oil billionaire who's believed to have bankrolled several AQ operations. Also noteworthy, Team Six took one of the prince's sons captive in 2003, and that lad's still in Gitmo. Sir."

"It's a little thin, and it isn't perfect, but it's the best story I've heard to date," the SECDEF said. "We still don't have any idea who the trigger puller is."

"There's one more pretty obscure link. When Ops processed the dead SEALs to close out their clearances, it seems all were read in on a Special Access Program called Broken Lance. Other SEALs in the building claim they never heard of it. ONI has no visibility into that program. Do we know who else has been read in on Broken Lance?"

When the door closed behind the admiral, the SECDEF whispered to himself, "Only a dozen SEALs, the DCI, the AG, and…me."

CHAPTER EIGHTEEN

1800 June 8, 2011
Secret Service Office Western Campus of St. Elizabeth's
Washington, DC

The Secret Service director pushed away from his desk and walked to the window overlooking the DC skyline. He stood there for several minutes, arms akimbo, before finally asking aloud and to no one, "What are the chances they were all part of Broken Lance?"

CHAPTER NINETEEN

1045 June 9, 2011
Paul's Pure Gas Station, Fredericksburg, Texas

The former 1950s-era Chevrolet dealership across the street from the even-older Pure gas station had both been quietly rehabilitated. The twenty-foot white-and-blue Pure sign on the corner was reminiscent of a small water tower. Fresh paint sparkled in the Texas sun. Old-time gas pumps with glass tops and racks of oil cans and other antique signage were reminders of days long past.

The gas pumps were fully functional, but the station didn't sell gas at the advertised price of nineteen cents per gallon. The two-bay garage was usually fully active. Mechanics worked on antique cars held aloft by old-time hydraulic lifts with single pistons, just like they were in the good old days. Paul's Pure Gas Station was part of the city's long, expansive Americana Main Street that was home to the greatest string of old- time specialty and antique shops in Texas. At the other end of the street in the tourist-trap town of Fredericksburg was the National Museum of the Pacific War, where thousands of sightseers visited every day, rain or shine.

Across from the Pure Gas Station was an old bank building on one corner, holding the corporate offices of Quiet Aircraft Technologies. After the passing of the old warhorse, Art Yoder, Lynche and Hunter consolidated and continued their contracting work under newly established front companies—Lynche in Maryland and Hunter in Texas.

At the other corner sat the old car dealership with fresh glass, restored neon signs, and new plaster and tiles. In the showroom were six collectable Corvettes from the '50s, '60s, and '70s, along with an immaculate 1974 Jaguar XKE. The old sales lot, which once held 100 cars for sale when the Stempel dealership was running, was reserved for car clubs or organizers of car shows. Sometimes it was used by old-car aficionados when they visited the Main Street shops.

In the back of the dealership, in the former repair shop, a thriving phalanx of automotive artisans, craftsmen, and mechanics were quietly busy restoring two dozen rare motorcars. Also in the rear of the dealership sat a long, tall, air-conditioned single-bay garage that held a forty-foot maroon motor coach Duncan and Nazy took out to see America when they weren't working. Nazy Cunningham loved traveling to see America's beauty.

The BlackBerry vibrated on the red toolbox, signaling an incoming e-mail. Duncan sighed and stopped draining fluids from his race car, which sat atop a single-piston lift at Paul's Pure Gas.

Catchment pans were strategically placed to capture oils from the engine, transmission, and differential.

By the third buzz, Hunter snatched the device and looked at the display. He didn't recognize the address. Two presses of the Track button brought up a message that read, "Apex, Bullfrog."

Hunter, stunned to see those two words, immediately typed rapidly. "I was just thinking about you, with your guys finally getting OBL. I hope, good Sir, you've been able to put that ghost to rest."

As so often happened with military people, they meet and got to know each other only to lose touch over time. That happened with Hunter and McGee, too.

"OK, now," McGee replied.

"Good Sir. Haven't heard from you in a long while. Hope you and the family are well."

"Would like to talk with you. Better to see you in person. Would like to take a plane ride. Best from Newport if able."

"Verify you'd like to see me in Newport, RI?"

"ASAP. Very important."

"Roger, Sir. Can do. Be there tonight. Can you talk? Call

my number?"

"That's very fast. Thx. Voice comm. not good. Plz text. Text is best."

"Wilco. Out."

Three additional punches of buttons, and Hunter heard Lynche's phone ring in the handset. He answered on the third one. "Mr. Hunter."

"Mr. Lynche. What's going on with you?"

"Connie and I are on the boat in the middle of a race."

"Remember my buddy from the Naval War College, the SEAL?"

"I do. Huge fucker. Snap your head off like it was a twig."

"He wants to see me at Newport ASAP. I got the impression he's in some kind of trouble. Just sent text messages. He didn't want to talk. I thought I'd take the jet and see Whiskey Tango Foxtrot is going on. I also thought 007 has to be about ready."

There was a long pause. "Greg? You still there?"

"Yes. Listen, I got wind of something's up at my old place but nothing more. My bud from there had to leave a race meeting in a hurry. He gave me a look that said something was up. I don't know how they could be related, but…."

"Nazy's out of pocket. Want me to pick you up? I can be there in three hours."

"Easton? Call when you're an hour out?"

"Wilco. See you in a bit."

Hunter disconnected. Scrolling down his phone list, he punched a button. Bob answered on the first ring.

"Yes, Sir?"

"Are you in a place to ready the jet for an immediate takeoff?"

"No, Sir. Bob's at his place hunting. Nothing was on the schedule."

"No problemo. I'll take her solo. Don't know when I'll be back. Any issues with her?"

"Sir, you wound me."

"Sorry, Bob. I knew but still had to ask. Will call when I'm heading back, OK?"

"I'll call Wolfman at the FBO. He'll have her out of the barn and ready for you. Safe travels, Sir."

"Thanks, Bob. Out." He scrolled through more contacts and punched another button.

Rudy Cervantes, his sometime race mechanic and pit crew, answered on the first ring. "*Señor* Hunter. What's up?"

"Rudy, I have to go out of town, and I have the beast up on a lift with all her fluids running out. Can you come over and replace the drain plugs, then service the little darling?"

"Sure. Anything else?"

"Make her ready. I'd like to run the Nevada Open Road Race next week before we head to Lime Rock."

"For you, *el jefe*, can do easy. I'll see you when you return."

"Thanks, Rudy. I'll set the alarm. Take care."

Duncan looked around the restored two-bay '50s gas station, as he wiggled out of his threadbare coveralls with the Frontier Airlines patch on the back. Hanging the faded beige coveralls on the office coat rack, he stroked them for a second. They belonged to his father when he was a line mechanic for the airline, and they were the only thing Duncan had left of his father's life.

Lincoln Hunter died seventy-seven days after being told he had inoperable cancer, and he suffered greatly through the early days of chemotherapy and radiation treatments. Duncan was twenty, a sergeant in the Marine Corps, and he was assigned as a helicopter crew chief for the local Search and Rescue unit at the Marine Corps Air Station. Where other SAR units flew the medium-lift CH-46s, Yuma, Arizona, had the smaller UH-1 Hueys. Crew chiefs flew the left seat, effectively being copilots and admittedly the luckiest assignment for an enlisted man in the Corps.

There was no other place in the Marine where a snuffy could fly in the copilot's seat of a helicopter every day, sometimes twice a day. When his mother suddenly called to ask him to come home, Duncan raced back to Denver and felt his world collapse as he watched his father die. Dad died on the Marine Corps' birthday, November tenth, forever stigmatizing that date as a time of sorrow for Duncan.

Duncan turned off the CD player in the middle of the Moody Blues' *I Know You're Out There Somewhere*, looked around to see if he forgot anything, then turned off the lights, set the alarm, and locked the door behind him.

Bob called the FBO and had the owner, Josef "Wolfman" Wulfkuhle, prepare the jet for departure. When Duncan arrived, he stopped at the terminal to file a flight plan and get a quick weather brief. Flimsy in hand, he stopped at the men's room. Even with autopilot, he didn't dare leave the cockpit to relieve himself at the rear of the jet.

He jumped into the Hummer2 and sped toward the entry gate, where rows of executive and T hangars stood. He swiped his card to open the access gate. Once inside airport property, he checked his rearview mirror to ensure the gate closed before speeding toward the hangar. To his right, he saw the hangar door was open, while to the left, the G-IVSP was being towed into position in front of the terminal. Duncan drove the truck into the hangar, got out, and walked to the corner to press the Close button before leaving the hangar and walked to the parking apron where the Gulfstream sat.

As he approached the jet, he looked back at the hangar to ensure the door closed, then went into pilot mode. He scanned the plane's exterior for any defects, making sure tire condition and pressures were OK. He walked under and around, looking for anything that was loose, missing, or damaged. The gear pins had been removed, as had the pitot, intake, and exhaust covers, which should have been stowed by the Wolfman.

Duncan opened the baggage compartment and saw all the covers were in place, as were a spare nose and main wheel assembly, toolbox, and jack. The gear pins, with their long, red- and-white Remove Before Flight tags, lay on the top step, as he climbed the stairs, grabbed and counted the three pins, and entered the jet.

The Wolfman stroked his long beard, as he watched Hunter move quickly around the jet and up the stairs. When the door closed, Wolfman removed the chocks from the nose wheel, walked to the large red fire extinguisher abeam of the jet, placed sound suppressors over his ears, and waited.

Hunter sat in the left seat. In a sweeping, fluid motion, he turned the battery switch on, engaged the APU, buckled his shoulder and lap belts, and positioned a headset over his ears to listen for ATIS information on the VHF. As the little jet turbine at the rear of the airplane spooled up and engaged the combining gearbox, Duncan's hands flew over switches, knobs, and buttons.

With a flick of the generator switch, the cockpit was awash in lights. Display panels came alive, radios hummed in the background, and hydraulic system indicator needles jumped to fully pressurized. A quick scan of the instrument panel indicated everything was working, as he engaged the #1 engine starter switch.

Speaking to himself, he double-checked the pocket checklist on his knee. "Off the peg, thirty percent, lever to idle. Good pressure, and we have light off. Looks good. OK, number two. Off the peg, thirty percent, lever to idle. Good pressure, and light off. Two engines in the green, brake pressure good, GPS set."

He pressed the microphone switch. "Tower, November nine, nine, nine Sierra Hotel, taxi one with Delta, clearance on file."

He moved the throttles to eighty percent to start the jet rolling, then returned them to idle.

"November triple nine Sierra Hotel, you're cleared taxi to runway eighteen. Hold short for release."

Wolfman spat a load of chaw in an arching splat and muttered to himself as the jet's engines spooled up beyond idle RPM, "Damn, that man's fast."

CHAPTER TWENTY

1715 June 9, 2011
Easton Municipal Airport, Maryland

"Hola!" Greg semi-shouted, doing his best kabuki dance to fit his six-two frame into the Gulfstream's cockpit.

Hunter monitored the lanky man's legs and elbows to ensure they didn't bump any switches or buttons. He didn't shut down the starboard engine, and, once he heard the cabin door close behind Lynche, he started the port engine and called the tower for taxi.

When he was in the cockpit, the former fighter pilot displayed the sense of urgency and economy of motion to get an airplane airborne and ready to fly as quickly as possible. At least with the Gulfstream, he let Lynche take his seat before throwing the throttles to eighty percent to pull out of the chocks and take a hard right turn.

Once Lynche had his headphones on, he said, "I swear you do that just to see me bounce around."

Hunter gave him a "Who me?" look.

"November triple nine Sierra Hotel, Tower. Cleared to taxi, runway 04. Hold short."

On the interphone, Hunter said, "Good evening, good Sir. Hope I didn't ruin your evening. I hope Connie's still talking to me."

"You send her flowers. She loves you. You can do anything, and she'll still love you. I think she loves you getting me out of the house. I never send her flowers. She tolerates me."

"You obviously never read The Art of Worldly Wisdom. Chapter 1348 clearly tells you to send a woman flowers often to keep your ass out of trouble."

"You're full of shit."

"It could happen. And it can't hurt."

Lynche smiled. The two amigos were back in their element, bantering in an airplane on an adventure.

Once they were airborne, Lynche asked, "So what the hell's going on with your SEAL friend?"

"I thought I lost track of him, but he popped up on my BlackBerry. I'm not sure how he got that particular address. I suspect maybe Ferrier gave it to him. I don't know what the issue is, but he was very circumspect. The atmospherics of Bill emailing me on our emergency address is bad karma. Traffic, eleven o'clock, low. Forty-five minutes ETA."

"Tally-ho. How's Marwa? I'm sorry. Ms. Nazy Cunningham."

"As beautiful and sexy as ever. I told you she visited a couple weeks ago. I laughed when she said all she's doing anymore is reading dispatches from Middle East embassies, morning, noon, and night, and running a few spies. I hear your old place loves her enough to promote her again."

"That's an understatement. The Agency has always had trouble recruiting Middle Easterners and Muslims, even for administrative work like transcribing documents or being an interpreter. When Nazy passed a full poly on her first try, which was unheard of for Muslims, current or former, she was set. She's been a gold mine for the Near East Division. She'll be SIS. That'll be a first. You know how to find 'em."

"Wasn't that hard. She chased me. She renounced Islam and is no longer a Muslim in my eyes or hers. Once that bond was broken, like you said, she was off. God, that woman's beautiful."

"Like I said, I don't know how you do it, but you know how to find 'em."

"I guess I'm a chick magnet."

"What you really are is full of shit. You're just lucky."

"I was thinking we could swing by Elmira and check on 007 on the way back."

"That'll work. Saul's been going through the airplane and updating it with better threat-detection systems."

"You mean our modified fuzz busters weren't good enough? They saved our bacon."

"You saved our bacon. I still dream about that night, thinking we were going to die. I wake up sweating and nearly out of breath. If that's what PTSD is about, then I'm a believer. I was fucking terrified and couldn't do anything about it but watch."

"Are you serious?"

"I swear I don't know how you did it and why it doesn't affect you."

Concerned, Hunter looked at his friend to see if he was being serious or making banter, then he returned to scanning the instruments and sky. The color weather radar showed no systems up the coast or ahead to Rhode Island. It was one of those rare, clear days when, at 35,000 feet, he could see the lights of Washington, DC, Baltimore, Philadelphia, and New York City all the way to Boston.

"You know I taught a course on human factors in aviation, and I'd say if it didn't affect me it's because of training. It's hard to provide a level of realistic training for kids going into combat, because all the training in the world can't prepare you for the horror of seeing a buddy blown up beside you."

"I can understand that," said Lynche.

"In the fighter community, we train for combat as best we can. The realism is very good to the point that when you're actually in a situation, such as hurtling jets at one another at 1,000 mph or having SAMs come at you; a pilot has seen it before. He has practiced defensive maneuvers and can react properly.

"You're still scared shitless, but, after a few hours in a simulator, it becomes a 'no-brainer, I can do that' issue. The reality is, there are guys who can do it and guys who can't. They stop and move on to something else. For the young ground troops, watching body parts flying through the air isn't part of the training and can't be. I hate to say it, but that fucks up even the most- hardened trooper, at least for a while.

"The kids who returned from Iwo Jima weren't the same and wouldn't talk about the war. We're a lot smarter now and can better train our troops and even treat some of the shock. Greg, they've got guys returning from multiple deployments who are locked up. They can't talk to their wives or kids, but you put a trained golden retriever in the room, and the dude acts normal. He talks to the dog and reacts with his family like he's OK again. He just unlocks. You can't believe it unless you see it."

"I won't get a dog."

"Come on, Greg. He'll keep you warm when he isn't humping your leg."

"OK. That's enough. Break, break. New subject. What will we do when we land?"

"When I landed at Easton, I sent Bill a text message giving our ETA. He wrote back and said he'd meet us at the airport. I sent him the tail number."

"He's running it like an op. Maybe we should just meet in the jet with the APU running. No one can eavesdrop with that on. If this is really important, I wouldn't feel safe talking inside the FBO."

"I'm curious what could get the most-decorated SEAL to call and want to see me. If I didn't know better, I'd say he was afraid of something."

The two men looked at each other with a sense of dread. They flew the remaining leg of the flight in near silence.

SPECIAL ACCESS

CHAPTER TWENTY-ONE

2030 June 9, 2011
Newport State Airport Newport, Rhode Island

Lynche piloted the whole way, landed, and taxied to the FBO. A marshaler with flashlight wands directed them to a parking spot in front of the executive terminal. Hunter unstrapped, started the APU, and headed for the door.

Lynche shut down the engines, navigation, and communication gear but left the external lights on. Hunter unlocked and opened the door, then lowered it. When it touched down, Hunter was surprised to see McGee racing up the stairs carrying a backpack. Once at the top step, he filled the doorway momentarily before stepping into the cabin away from the entrance. He shook Hunter's hand.

"You brought a jet?" he asked.

"It's good to see you, too." Hunter smiled; McGee was very serious.

"Can we go somewhere?"

"In this, or in town?"

"Away from here. When you said the airport, I hoped we could fly someplace where I'd feel a lot safer."

"OK." Hunter turned to look over his shoulder. "Greg, let's fly direct to Saul's. Now." He pulled up the stairs, closed and locked the door, while Lynche started the starboard engine.

Hunter pointed to the captain's chairs in the cabin. McGee filled up the closest one and leaned back, while Hunter sat on the edge of the second seat to face the old SEAL. Hunter continued to smile, but McGee continued to be stoic.

"You probably haven't heard, but some SEALs have been killed—by a sniper."

"I'm sorry, Bill. I haven't heard anything about that.

Where?"

"Memphis, Denver, Key West, and I think Norfolk and Washington, DC."

"Holy shit!"

"Remember the SEAL in your seminar group? Jorgenson? He was killed a few days ago in Key West. I don't know if you knew Reyes, "Disco" Ford, Petersen, and McCreedy."

"Those don't ring a bell. You and Jorgenson were the only SEALs I really knew at the War College. This is so incredible, I don't know what to say. In the States? A sniper? How's that possible?"

"All those guys were in our war college class."

Hunter asked the obvious. "Are you saying you're on someone's hit list?"

"That's part of it. Here's the other part." He reached into his backpack and brought out a black metal case the size and shape of a paperback novel with wires hanging loose. "This is an old tracking device. It was on my Riviera. I started to restore the car a couple months ago and found this sitting on my gas tank with the wires spliced into the hot wire of the sending unit. At first, I thought it was a bomb, but I had it checked out. It's a first-generation GPS tracking device made in Germany, circa 2002."

"The time we were at school?" McGee nodded.

"The other part is there was a note left near Jorgie's body. We think he went out to his rental in the parking lot and found the note on the windshield. It read, Kill the one who ordered the hit on Osama bin Laden, and I'll stop killing SEALs."

"How many other SEALs were in our class? I vaguely recall somewhere between eight and twelve."

"Ten."

Lynche started the other engine.

"You're in danger," Hunter said. "OK. We can get you somewhere safe. What about your family?"

"Angela and the girls are in Europe with her parents. I

410

think they're OK. They're after us, some of the SEALs from Team Six."

"Why? Payback for killing Osama bin Laden?"

"Maybe. I think there's more, but I don't know if there's a connection."

"OK. Let me help Greg get this beast airborne. You can have the jump seat."

As Hunter stepped into the cockpit, Lynche said, "I called Saul. He'll meet us at the airport."

"Ten-four. Good thinking, Grinch."

Lynche and McGee traded salutations and handshakes, as McGee unfolded the jump seat and wedged himself in the remaining cockpit space. Hunter handed him a set of headphones. "I really appreciate your coming," McGee said. "I'm at my wit's end, and there's no one I could turn to or trust. The more I thought about what was going on, I felt you might not think I lost my mind and would hear me out."

He paused for the men to run their takeoff checks and radio calls. McGee watched Hunter's legs moving, as the jet turned. Looking out over the nose, he saw they were tracking perfectly down the taxiway's centerline.

Ten minutes later, Hunter said to Lynche, "Your jet," and turned in his seat.

"My jet." Lynche promptly switched on the autopilot and turned in his seat to face McGee, eliciting a smirk and frown from Hunter. Lynche didn't intend to miss any of the conversation.

"What do you think's going on, Bill?"

"In my thirty-plus years in the Navy, I never shared classified information with anyone unless he had the clearances and accesses and need to know—until now. I know you were cleared, and this can't leave the airplane or be traced back to me."

"That's fair. You show me yours, and I'll show you mine. Deal, good Sir."

"I was part of a discrete group of SEALs read in on a program called Broken Lance. It was an op to rescue or take out the president if he was taken hostage by unfriendlies."

"Holy shit!" Lynche exclaimed.

"You're probably heard of the term Broken Arrow for the loss of a nuclear weapon," McGee added.

The two men nodded.

"Bent Spear, Dull Sword, and Empty Quiver were other reporting terms that resulted from the accidental launching, firing, detonating, theft, or loss of a nuke. When we weren't chasing terrorists around the world, we did a lot of exercises in various places practicing scenarios, such as if we lost a nuclear weapon. All those programs came from a strategic plan to deal with the loss of a nuke. In the case of Broken Lance, though, it was the loss of the president."

"I never heard of Broken Lance, but that doesn't mean a lot," Lynche said. "By the time I was senior enough to be trusted with strategic information, I was knee-deep into counterterrorism."

"I doubt you would've heard of it," McGee said. "It was a Special Access Program; only fifteen bodies read onto it at one time. Anyway, I was under the impression that no more than ten SEALs from Team Six had been active and read-on the program at any one time, all officers. We ran scenarios and practiced the op two or three times a year."

"What do you mean?" Hunter asked.

"We'd get an op order, and two-man sniper teams would jump on an AC-130 or C-17 and jump into an area to make our way toward the target and shoot a facsimile—at a range of over one mile in the dark."

"Hold it. You were part of a team that planned to assassinate a sitting president, even held hostage? What kind of program is that?"

"One that only about fifteen people in the US government know about. There are ten SEALs, POTUS, the SECDEF, the DCI, the Attorney General, and the Secret Service Director. When I retired I was read-off, and someone else should have taken my place."

"That's incredible. How would you initiate something like

that?"

"SEALs always accompanied the president overseas. They were totally undercover, usually part of the advance party that did pre-security checks for Air Force One. Once it was confirmed that POTUS was kidnapped and held hostage, the SECDEF, the DCI, and the Attorney General had to agree to the provisions of a secret executive order signed by JFK in 1962. He was the original Lance or Lancer, living in Lancelot or some such shit. If the three of them agreed, Operation Broken Lance would be authorized. If we were in-country with POTUS, we'd be notified and try to rescue him. If that wasn't possible, we'd execute our orders."

"Were there times you didn't travel with him?"

"If we weren't traveling with POTUS, well, we were on twenty- four-seven recall. Anything we did was priority one. Only half of us could be out of the country at one time. What was briefed when we were read-on was that Kennedy determined the American people didn't want to see their president subject to torture or paraded around after being captured. A president would likely be tortured for information. The country would be at risk, and the government would become completely dysfunctional.

"The vision I have is when the Iranian hostages were taken in 1980 for 444 days, imagine if POTUS had been visiting the embassy. Or when Saddam was abused by his people after they found him in a hole in the ground and was turned over to the Iraqis. It was also considered a suicide mission, as once in-country, we didn't expect to get out alive. It was a volunteer assignment."

Hunter shook his head. "I don't know what to say. That's incredible, Bill."

"Now five of the more senior former Lancers have been taken out by what we think is a sniper, ironically using the method and weapon we trained on to take out the president."

"You mentioned the Secret Service director also knew. I guess he didn't get a vote?"

"Several of the Secret Service directors were former SEALs and a former Lancer. Like O'Sullivan is, or was. I'm not sure what JFK was thinking when he put the onus on the Navy for that work, other than he was once a naval officer. In '62, he created special operations commands and the Green Berets and SEALs. I guess if someone had to take him down, he wanted a fellow naval officer to put him out of his misery."

"So what do you think is happening with your guys?"

"I don't know. Five of my friends are dead, and most likely I'm targeted as a former Lance member and leader, or because I was at the war college the same time you were. Remember, we were under surveillance the whole time we were at school and never knew why or who was responsible. Then I find a tracking device on my car."

"All Nazy knew was to get info on why I was hanging out with you. She never mentioned anything about tracking devices."

"Duncan…who's Nazy?"

"Sorry. She was the woman sent to spy on me. She's now a…."

"She's SIS, Chief of Near East Division," Lynche said quickly. "She's also Duncan's fiancée."

The information confused McGee more than it helped, but the retired Senior Intelligence Service agent in the left seat knew how to condense information.

"Bill, you were the focus of everything back then," Hunter said. "I assumed it was something to do with your role in chasing Osama bin Laden or killing al-Qaeda shitheads. I was collateral."

"So did I."

"But once Nazy came over to the dark side, that operation soon ceased, as I understand it. Greg, didn't the FBI take it down?"

Greg nodded. "I don't get any of the connections. It seems pretty weak."

"I agree it's weak, but it's a better connection than what the National Security Council thinks it might be—someone from the Middle East with an ax to grind against Team Six after they took down Osama bin Laden."

Hunter frowned as he thought. Then he said, "OBL and OBL."

"What?" the other two men asked simultaneously.

"Osama bin Laden and Operation Broken Lance. That's weird. Is that weird? What do you think's going on? Who's behind this?"

"Duncan, I don't know," McGee said. "You're the smartest guy I know, and you see things us Billy Ray Joe Bob Average types don't. That's why I called the CEO at Schweizer. I didn't know where you were, but he did. I'm glad you came. You have to tell me how you've got a jet. Part of me wants to hear you stole it from a scumbag when he wasn't looking."

"That's pretty close. Try drug-forfeiture program. It's a former drug lord's private coach. We got it from the DEA several years ago."

"Why does that not surprise me? That's a great story."

"You really have no idea who might be involved?"

"My knee-jerk reaction is al-Qaeda or the Pakis or Saudis, but the Broken Lance connection is screaming, 'Look at me!' and I can't see anything obvious. Those who are read-in on the program are patriots."

"I'd argue that the previous group was patriots. I'm not convinced this crop is anything but closet communists. The current AG isn't friendly, and the DCI's a flaming queer. Both have a different agenda by direction of the president. As much as I dislike them, I can't conceive of how they'd organize anything that would put you and the other SEALs in the crosshairs, unless he put a contract on you guys; but why would he do that?"

"You know the AG wanted to try a couple SFALs for Interrogating an AQ terrorist. The idiot isn't on our Christmas card list. For that matter, neither is the DCI or the President. The whole SEAL community is infuriated with them, specially the president, who's running around the country high-fiving every swinging dick he sees. We feel his politics have put the whole SOF community in the crosshairs. Now we've got five dead SEALs."

Hunter and Lynche let that simmer for a moment before Hunter tried to vector the discussion into more informative directions. Lynche said, "I haven't considered the Attorney General, but you're right about him. Why him, or why not him?"

"He's too stupid and too wrapped up in trying to establish social justice bullshit at the DOJ," Hunter said. "He's not smart enough for something like this."

"OK, not the AG. Too stupid. The SECDEF? That makes no sense at all," said McGee.

"Agreed."

"What about the DCI?" asked Hunter.

"That bothers me more than a little," Lynche admitted. "I know he is not one of your favorites and I still have a problem with motive."

Hunter thought over what Nazy told him about the man, but he didn't want to explore that avenue yet. "What if it's a diversion?"

"What do you mean?" Lynche asked.

"Politics. What if you're targeting SEALs to draw attention away from another op? Or what if you target SEALs to take them out of action, to neutralize them. How about this? What would happen if SEAL Team Six was completely taken out? What is it that you guys do, that, if you stopped, it would create a vacuum in capability that someone could exploit? I really don't know what-all you guys do."

"Well," McGee said, "DEVGRU's mission includes pre-emptive, proactive, counterterrorist operations, counterproliferation—especially WMDs—as well as assassination or recovery of HVTs. I'm sorry. That's high-value targets from unfriendly nations. Also, DEVGRU is authorized to use preemptive actions against terrorists and their facilities. We kill the enemies of the United States."

"Hooyah!" Hunter smiled. "How'd Jorgie die again? There was a note? How did the shooter know he was in Key West and would step outside? Did you know where he was?"

"Last question first. Green Parrot Bar."

"How do you know that?" Hunter unconsciously scratched the side of his face, remembering how he took Nazy to the Red Parrot in Newport.

"It's our...a SEAL hangout in Key West. I was briefed about Jorgie, how he was shot and what the note said. I'm totally bewildered how anyone knew he would step outside to make a call."

"It's unlikely he was tracked there by one of those little black boxes," Hunter said.

"Agreed."

"What if he had an appointment to make or receive a call?" Lynche suggested. "I expect the FBI will scour his cell phone records. How'd the other guys die? Were they similar, at other SEAL hangouts?"

"What I know is that all were shot outside except for Pablo. He was found inside, but the cops thought he was the victim of a random shooting. There was a bullet hole in his living room window."

"Could have been our guy."

"Yes, Sir. That's what I believe now. No doubt in my former military mind."

"Do you know if they're planning another op?" Hunter asked. "I mean, after taking out Osama bin Laden, what does a SEAL do?"

"Blow up Iranian nuclear facilities, create mischief in Korea, sink Libyan ships, shoot pirates—fun shit."

"I didn't hear that," Lynche said.

"Anything else rattling around there?"

"It's all so weird," McGee said. "It doesn't make sense. Most SEALs so dislike POTUS that some have been doing their own research into who he is. Some have had to be counseled to follow orders or resign. I hear of active-duty guys thinking he's a commie plant. His associations scream communist. Do you know a communist? I don't, but he's surrounded by them.

"For thirty-five years, all my efforts have been dedicated to bringing down the Soviet Union and to kill communists, and now our president's one. I hate to say it, but I'll go to my grave thinking the man's a puppet for the communist party."

Hunter realized that was the most he'd ever heard McGee say. "You mean like the Manchurian candidate?"

"Exactly."

"Anyone find anything?"

"This is technically hearsay, but I consider the source as reliable as if you or Greg told me. Back in 2003 or 2004, well before the election, a very senior SEAL, a good friend of mine and the guy who probably led the raid on Osama bin Laden's place, had been working at the NE Division and said he saw a two-inch-thick dossier on the man. A long-retired case officer started a file on him when he went to Pakistan in the '80s on a British passport while attending college in the US. That sent red star clusters all over NE Division.

"The list of suspected terrorists he saw, complete with photos, was supposedly a who's who of really bad guys and probably included Osama bin Laden. We killed most of them since 2002. The rest are probably in Pakistan or sitting in Gitmo.

"When the senator from Michigan started making national news, I think right after we got out of the War College, the deputy chief pulled the file and made a duplicate. In today's context, my buddy said the information's so explosive it would rattle the foundations of the democracy."

"If he was attending school in the US on a British passport," Lynche said, "and went to Pakistan, that would be enough for a field agent to trigger a case file or mention in a dispatch."

"Somehow, he secured a US passport," McGee said. "Copies of both were in the file. The deputy hid the duplicate in plain sight and contributed to it when he could. Here's the kicker. The deputy chief was astounded when the DCI personally came down to NE Division and demanded to see what, if anything, they had on the man. I understand the deputy opened his safe and handed the file to the DCI, who didn't even sign for it. It was never returned."

"When was that?"

"2008. Before the election. The previous DCI."

"Hold it," Lynche said. "If the previous DCI came down and asked for the file, then he somehow knew the senator was the subject of an inquiry. Probably it came up in a weekly report or on the dispatch board. If he really traveled on a British passport, how'd he become a state and a US senator?" Hunter and Lynche looked at each other.

"I would've expected the case officer or the deputy to do something," Lynche said slowly. "There's paperwork...chain-of-custody regulations...."

"That deputy did," McGee said. "The guy was a former Marine. Duncan, I thought you'd appreciate that. He's dead, too. Happened a couple months ago, about the time this all started."

"There sure are a lot of dead guys in this discussion," Lynche said. "Sounds like more than a coincidence. How'd that happen? Don't tell me. Similar to the others?"

McGee lowered his head and nodded, trying to make sense of the seeming coincidence.

"Nazy's boss was found with a bullet wound to the chest a couple months ago," Hunter said. "He was the chief, not the deputy, but he used to be Deputy NE. She moved up to chief."

The two men stared in shock.

"What would you do if someone has been killing your friends, and you thought you'd be next?" Hunter asked.

"I called you," McGee said. "We're getting the hell out of Dodge, flying...it looks like west."

"I was thinking the president has friends in Pakistan, but that doesn't make a lot of sense, either, does it?" Hunter asked.

McGee pondered that.

"Bill, how close were you to getting bin Laden?" Lynche

asked. "I read several accounts from the commander of US forces in Afghanistan at the time, as well as the senior CIA agent on the ground chasing him. One says we don't know whether bin Laden was at Tora Bora. Some sources said he was. Others said he was in Pakistan."

"I learned at school, reporters get it about fifty percent right. The guys with clearances and Special Access won't say anything unless they're disgruntled or ready to retire. Tora Bora and the Zhawar Kili cave complex were teeming with hundreds of Taliban and al-Qaeda. My snipers engaged every target we saw. One of my sniper teams killed over fifty of the bastards. The Air Force bombed the shit out of the surrounding area. What they didn't bomb, Predators hit targets of opportunity. Multiple assets, including strategic assets, were so thoroughly looking at that area, we'd see a mouse crap. We could've taken Osama bin Laden out to 2,000 yards or put an LD on his forehead or let the Air Force bomb him back to the Stone Age.

"Try as we might, we never positively acquired him. We were the closest group to where we thought he was, but we never saw him. The truth is we chased a radio. He was already in Pakistan. He had one of his trusted agents carrying a radio. He was smart enough to know we'd triangulate his position, so he had someone carrying a radio with a recording of him giving directions.

"Like a dumb hound dog, that was the only place we looked. We were so close that when others, like Delta and CIA SOG, called for air strikes, they were denied, because it would have meant killing me and a dozen of my SEALs, Team Six. CIA and Delta were pissed, but few knew Team Six was that close. We were on top of them, and we came in from the Paki side. Everyone else came from the west.

"Osama bin Laden wasn't there. Even if he really was at Tora Bora, the commander of US forces in Afghanistan wasn't going to let anyone blow us up, too. The SOCOM commander and I were relieved of command for not finding bin Laden. I don't think I ever told you that. Shit rolls downhill.

"We took a chance at finding him at Tora Bora. We expected the Taliban and al-Qaeda to protect their west flank, as they had the Pakis in their pocket and didn't need to protect the east one. There are a ton of theories about how Osama bin Laden escaped. They're probably all true. Having him taken down in Pakistan only proves the Pakis had him and knew where he was all the time. If you think about it, would he really thumb his nose at the US after 9/11 and just hide out in the Afghani mountains? His history was always hit and run. He whacked the head of the Northern Alliance, started the ball rolling for 9/11, and ran to friendlies in Pakistan."

"I always found it incredible he would have stayed in Afghanistan after the Towers fell," Hunter said. "The last democratic president sent a dozen Tomahawks after him for just.... Oh, that's right. That idiot was another Islamic sympathizer and bombed an aspirin factory."

"I can attest that was wag the dog and all that," Lynche said.

"We knew he was in Pakistan, but we didn't know where. The ISI wanted us to look in their so-called tribal regions, but those people were mainly enemies of the ruling party. If Americans were killing them, then that would be a good thing."

Hunter focused on the big black man's dark eyes. "I don't want to see another of you guys taken out. We have to be able to do something to lock them down. Can we war-game this a little? Say it's the Broken Lance or Lancer connection. Is it really a sniper who's taken out your guys? Are we sure, or is it we don't know?"

"It's absolutely a sniper," McGee said.

"How'd the first guy die? Do you know?"

"We heard Pablo was found dead in his home. We thought he was the victim of a random gunshot."

"Bullet wound?" Hunter fired questions at McGee.

"Heart. Single shot."

"The next guy?"

"Disco Ford was found dead along the perimeter road on the Navy base in Memphis at night."

"Bullet wound?"

"The same—heart, single shot. Regarding Petersen and McCreedy, I'm not sure how. I only heard about Petersen from a friend, and that's when I texted you. I heard McCreedy was pronounced dead at Bethesda. Jorgie was shot in the parking lot of the Green Parrot."

"Where and how?"

"Heart, single shot. All of them. With terminator rounds."

"Terminator rounds? What's that?" asked a shocked Lynche.

"It has a special jacket that slows it immediately after penetration and spreads out until it's two inches wide. It blows a hole out the other side, sometimes grapefruit-sized, sometimes volleyball. It's one-shot, one-kill ammo. They're illegal for anyone but the SOF and are super-controlled. The UN banned terminators for combat."

"Fuck me." Lynche shook his head.

"What about the CIA case officer, the Marine?"

"He was found dead in his backyard. The dog was howling, which alerted the neighbors. They thought it was a heart attack, but, when they turned him over and saw the exit wound, it was clear he'd been shot."

"In the heart, single shot?"

"Yes, Sir."

"Big fucking hole in his back?"

"Yes, Sir. Terminated."

"Five or six guys; six kill shots? I'd go out on a limb and say all six single shots were terminator rounds to the heart. Isn't that a signature shot? I'll go out on another limb. I'm sorry, but isn't it obvious that somehow the DCI is behind this, because the case officer's dead? That can't be a coincidence."

Lynche and Hunter looked at each other, then at McGee.

"It can't be a coincidence," Hunter repeated.

CHAPTER TWENTY-TWO

2050 June 9, 2011
24,000 Feet above New York State

"I have to admit, it's pretty damning," Lynche said. "All vectors point to him, but I can't fathom why. All those SEALs and the case officer can't be a coincidence."

"I think this is important," Hunter said. "Suddenly, this has reached the level of spooky. Full disclosure, Bill. Greg and I have been working indirectly for the DCI, past and present, on a number of activities. I told you long ago someday I'd tell you what I was doing. Here it is."

Lynche pursed his lips and nodded.

"Greg and I fly an old top-secret spy plane for the CIA doing work no one else can do."

"Like what?" McGee asked.

"We've located hostages held by the FARC and in Somalia. We've located a dozen submarines used to smuggle drugs from Colombia and Peru. We've killed poppies in Afghanistan with a laser. That's for starters. All at night with a quiet airplane."

"I knew it had to be something like that. That's very cool."

Hunter paused for a moment. "This could be bad for all of us."

"You think?"

"If the DCI's behind this, we all have to be careful."

"Agreed. I knew there were few people I could trust, and I kept coming back to the DCI. He has crazy assets at his disposal. That's why I used disposable cell phones."

"That was smart," Lynche said. "We need to make sure it's him. Will someone please tell me what his motive is?"

Hunter suddenly closed his eyes and shook his head. "I think...I might know."

They looked at Hunter, disbelief spread across their faces.

He opened his eyes again. "We have to land."

CHAPTER TWENTY-THREE

2130 June 9, 2011
Schweizer Aircraft Company, Elmira, NY

The Schweizer CEO greeted them by saying, "Captain McGee, you haven't aged a day since the last time you were here. These two are older and uglier, of course. What an unexpected surprise."

The men decided not to discuss with Saul Ferrier the goings-on with McGee and the mess with the SEALs.

"Saul, we need to work in the SCIF, at least the Green Room, for a few hours," Hunter said.

The Schweizer Green Room was a secure facility for people with clearances to have secure meetings, develop classified proposals for government, as well as hold and store sensitive government or company proprietary documents. Every six months, a security team from the CIA inspected the facility and reviewed procedures to ensure all government documents were properly handled, stored, and disposed of per strict classified regulations.

The three-and-a-half-foot-high shredder in the middle of the room looked like it could disintegrate a New York City phone book into a billion chads in seconds, and it could. Also part of the semiannual check of the SCIF and Green Room was a sweep of the rooms for listening or eavesdropping devices. Additional external checks of the facility included testing with a laser-monitoring system to determine if communications could be intercepted when other access to the room was impossible.

Green rooms and SCIFs with windows were often outfitted with countermeasures to negate the effectiveness of a laser- surveillance system. The company, famous for making high-end waveguide speakers and noise-canceling headsets, also quietly developed the best noise-canceling systems for the Agency SCIFs and corporate SCIFs involved with the intelligence community.

Russian laser transmitters directed at the window of a room used to pick up the reflected laser and convert it into electric signals, which, after filtering, were amplified and fed into recording devices. For the SCIF at Schweizer, whatever was said in the room stayed there. The three men felt they weren't under surveillance at the moment, but they didn't want to take any chances while on the ground.

Ferrier asked if they wanted to see the progress on 007 before going into the SCIF. Lynche and Hunter, so preoccupied with the crisis facing McGee, completely forgot why they flew to Elmira.

Hunter looked at Lynche for approval, because McGee wasn't read in on the YO-3A program. When Lynche gave an imperceptible nod, Hunter said, "Absolutely, Saul. I hope she's getting close."

The CEO, smiling, walked toward the hangars. After McGee shared the details of Broken Lance, there should be a measure of reciprocity between them. Still a government employee, Hunter wondered if he would pass the next poly test from Lynche's old place when the interviewer asked, "Have you ever shared classified information with someone not authorized to receive it?"

I'll cross that bridge when I come to it, Hunter thought.

They passed through the adjoining delivery hangar, where three dark-blue helicopters, bearing San Antonio Police Department livery, sat in the middle of the light-gray floor, their tail rotors almost touching. Ferrier slipped into his role of host and tour guide to visiting VIPs. No special-purpose airplanes were being built, but several dozen small training helicopters were in various states of assembly.

Several minutes later, they completed their circuitous trip at the far side exit door, hit the push bar, and stepped outside into darkness punctuated by floodlights. Ferrier waited for Hunter to bring up the rear and close the door.

They stood on an elevated concrete walkway that connected the factory to a stand-alone hangar. A door with heavy cipher lock and electronic sensor barred their advance. Ferrier took a small, tear-drop-shaped button on the end of a lanyard from his pocket and held it beside the sensor. Immediately, an unseen powerful mechanism slammed ten locking lugs open, startling everyone but Saul, who punched buttons, flipped the handle, and stepped inside. He walked to another keypad, turning on light switches, as he quickly disengaged the alarm. The hangar was one giant safe.

As the mercury-vapor sodium bulbs slowly illuminated the area, the men saw the dark shape of the YO-3A sitting in the middle of the floor. McGee instantly realized it wasn't the same aircraft he saw years ago in the delivery hangar. Hunter and Lynche admired the view of the airplane that saved their lives. The paint appeared to suck all light from the quickening bulbs, because the matte finish didn't reflect any of the light from the overhead lights.

As the view improved, Lynche was reminded of a Broadway play and how the lights transitioned from dark to partial illumination in minutes, with an ever-growing spotlight on the stage.

Saul Ferrier loved the unintended consequences of the slow lighting system. Some suggested he had a flair for theatrics and installed the system just for that purpose. The real reason was more for safety and expense. Mercury-vapor sodium bulbs were standard for hangars with fueled aircraft, and they were cheap. Ferrier built the hangar when he and Greg signed the deal to produce the SA2-37B for the CIA and State Department. The successor to the prototype YO-3A was a rugged, handmade, handsome feat of engineering excellence, hence the term, "special-purpose low-noise-profile airplane."

The hangar not only protected the special-purpose aircraft from weather but served as an enclosed space in which to assemble the disparate unclassified pieces from the factory into a functional classified aircraft. A handful of mechanics with top- secret clearances installed wings, horizontal stabilizers, and the special propellers. Deemed the Vault, it was used to store, repair, or disassemble the unique spy places. The hangar also held one of the few CIA-approved SCIFs outside the Washington, DC area. Entry was limited to those who had Special Access and need to know. Helping to restrict the viewing public from observing the factory's internal workings and its aircraft testing and deliveries, Lynche in his former assignment staffed some overhead restrictions of Elmira's airport with the three-letter agencies. The NRO and NGA approved the security measures and ensured commercial activities couldn't get better than one-meter resolution satellite photographs of the little factory that produced the quietest airplanes in the free world.

When briefing key government personnel, Ferrier or Lynche said, "Area 51 and this airport are protected out to 100-meter resolution." Anyone trying to view the Elmira Airport from satellite photographs would be confused and disappointed when they saw nothing but vague shades. The US government hadn't enabled that area for some reason.

The government went to extraordinary lengths to ensure overhead resources were unable to take usable pictures of the SA2-37B when the aircraft was finally moved outside for testing. It wasn't until late 2009, when production of that airplane ended, that the moratorium on satellite coverage was lifted.

Saul Ferrier's love for all the things related to the development of powered gliders led to one of the most creative work spaces aviators ever saw. As lighting completely flooded the hangar floor, McGee saw, suspended from the ceiling, the original "Quiet Thruster" QT-2 Prize Crew and the Q-Star, the first- generation of quiet aircraft developed with Lockheed in the late 1960s. A four-foot-wide mosaic band of classified photographs of the QT programs and all the testing created a line of demarcation across the hangar's three walls.

Lynche and Hunter walked toward the repaired, remanufactured YO-3A with appreciation and whistles. Lynche's deck shoes squeaked with every step.

"Yes, she's ready," Ferrier said. "We think the laser-cut carbon-fiber panels will add at least fifteen knots to the top end. We finished putting in the armored panels and seats today."

Ferrier turned to McGee. "Bill, this is our shrine to these amazing aircraft. The Green Room's over there. Opposite that is the SCIF. The shitter's down the hall. I'll be right back."

Saul Ferrier went through an unmarked door with a cipher lock and returned two minutes later. "I disabled the alarm in the Green Room. It's all yours. I'll leave you to your business. Have you had any food?"

"Food?" Hunter asked.

"I vote Italian," Lynche said.

"Paisano's," Hunter begged.

"What else is there?" Ferrier chuckled at their expressions. "Bill?"

McGee stopped walking, arms akimbo, mesmerized by the two aircraft suspended from the ceiling. "Those are the weirdest goddamn airplanes I ever saw. People actually flew those?"

CHAPTER TWENTY-FOUR

2225 June 9, 2011
Schweizer Aircraft Company

Three men filed into the room carrying bags, boxes, and drinks, setting them on the small conference table.

"So you think you know?"

"It's more a point of interest that may explain a possible motive. The DCI has a long history of abusing little boys."

"That might do it if it mattered," Lynche said. "Isn't the fuck openly gay?"

"What if some of those boys grew up and flew jets into the World Trade Center...."

"Holy shit."

"...and the Pentagon?"

"Are you serious?" McGee asked.

"I am. The president might know, too."

McGee waved his arms to invite more. "From the top?"

"Nazy had been assigned deputy chief of station in Dubai," Hunter began, "able to come and go to and from the US embassy for almost two years, developing incredible intel on the highly secret groups supporting al-Qaeda as well as other terrorist and radical groups. She was mentioned in dispatch weekly.

"Her network of women in Dubai, Abu Dhabi, Riyadh, and Jeddah provided bits of information that, taken together, gave pieces of the puzzle of the secret lives of princes, kings, sheiks, and their friends. Most of Prince Bashir's friends were obviously Arabs who, whenever they could get together, were offered the customary tea and parties.

"For Bashir's American friends, they were offered pretty young men and even boys. Senator Carey had a long business relationship with Bashir. Some of the men were willing, but the boys generally didn't know what would happen to them. Some of the prince's wives were sent to clean them up after Carey and the others had their way with them.

"Some of the boys were returned to their families with a significant payment from the prince, Carey, or both. There were even parties on the prince's 200-300-foot yacht. I understand some of the men and boys never returned from those trips. One of the wives fell out of favor with the prince and sought to escape from the trajectory of her life and her wretched husband. By chance or design, she met a woman working at the US embassy...."

"Nazy?" asked Lynche.

Hunter nodded. "...and became a significant resource. After a while, she began telling Nazy things that were going on, who was coming to see the prince, and, most curiously, the important Americans. When the Americans came, there were special provisions made—special food and drink and nighttime entertainment. Nazy started a file on them."

"After a late meal and the prince's favorite blend of shishi from a hookah, it was time to turn in. Just like a scene from that ranch in Nevada, instead of half-dressed, heavily made-up women to satisfy the needs of cowboys and businessmen, the Americans chose young men and boys. Sometimes, the prince made the boys turn around and drop their pantaloons, so their little asses could be inspected. Sometimes, the Americans wanted to see the men's cocks and fondled them to see how big they were. Reportedly."

"The senator from Massachusetts always selected one of each, a young man to do him, followed by a boy for desert. He probably squealed with delight. The wife, a nurse by training, was sent to take care of the boys after the men finished with them. Most of the prince's wives were professional women, just like Osama bin Laden's little harem —PhDs, doctors, and lawyers."

"At first, the boys had no idea what happened to them or

why. Poor families offered pretty sons with promises of money, and they'd be taken care of with education expenses or cars or better apartments. One of the uglier secrets was that some of the boys defiled by Americans grew up hating Americans. We saw them on tape walking through the airport, as someone thought they made perfect suicide bombers or pilots of hijacked jets."

"This is all documented?" Lynche asked, incredulously.

"Yes. Prince Bashir's actions are well-documented. The Americans who visited him are well detailed. I understand it's a comprehensive, noteworthy file. Nazy didn't collect all the intel."

"It's like a twenty-five or thirty-year file on the DCI. The information Nazy developed over her two years between embassies enabled the leadership at NCTC to gain a better understanding of why some suicide bombers blew up Muslims, while others focused on Americans. They had the names of the young men and boys. Case officers opened files and tracked the lives of young Muslim men, especially those who were part of the sex-slave trade."

"That was the information Nazy developed. The intel on the Americans was explosive, especially the openly gay senator from Massachusetts and a frequent visitor to the prince's compounds. So, when the senator's name was announced as the new president's nominee to lead the CIA...."

"I don't like the sound of this," McGee said.

"...well, you can imagine how Nazy was shaken to the core. She'd been running several women when one she didn't know approached her in a store and slipped her a note. It was obvious someone had blown her cover, because the disgruntled wife walked right up to Nazy, who was undercover in an abaya, and gave her a note that read, Know you work at the embassy. I have information. I need help."

"She wanted to escape from Saudi Arabia. Nazy thought it had been Carey who blew her cover, because he was visiting the embassy when it happened. It was the only link she had. Nazy's afraid something bad will happen to her since that senator is now the DCI."

Lynche mashed his lips. "Why didn't you tell me this?"

"Greg, you know I don't like Carey, and I don't like the President. I rarely talk politics with you, because you voted for the guy. I didn't want to come across as piling on."

There was a long pause. Lynche and Hunter rarely had cross words, and there were almost no secrets between them. Lynche sighed, "Connie and I kinda got wrapped up in the hope-and-changey thing. It was a mistake I have regretted every day since. It was the dumbest thing I ever did. For whatever it's worth, you were—are—right about him, from the beginning."

Hunter gave a pensive nod. "Thanks, Greg."

"This could be bad," McGee said.

"Nazy said the day the President nominated Senator Frank Carey, all files on the gentleman were turned over to the deputy director, the acting DCI. Carey may or may not have them. Her name has to be on some of those reports and dispatches."

"Which name?" Lynche asked. "Her cover name?"

"Yes, Sir. But I think her real name's in her personnel file, and we have to assume the DCI knows that Nazy was at the embassy when he was abroad."

"The deputy had to be...," Lynche began, "had to get that file. Where it went is anyone's guess."

"Duncan, you have to get her out of there," McGee said. "She could be next."

"I think it's either you or her," Lynche added.

"Bill, I appreciate your using the disposables. Do you have any more? We probably need to have Saul get us some more in town."

"That's a good idea."

"I have a couple others."

"I want to call her to see if she's OK. The love of my life and someone I admire and stand in awe of are probably both being targeted by the director of the CIA and/or a world-class sniper. Oh, by the way, for some reason, he also wants the President dead. Mr. Lynche, have you done anything lately to get on the DCI's shit list?"

"I hope not. It would ruin my retirement."

"I was just thinking. I'm having thoughts that there's a sense of urgency to warn Nazy, but she also might be the only one who can find the file on the president. It must be hiding in plain sight."

"You have a point."

"Do we know any more, Bill?"

"No. Danny's in Afghanistan. I'm certain he led the raid in Pakistan. Maybe he even shot the bastard for me."

"We need a plan," Lynche said, stating the obvious.

Hunter stepped to a large white board on the wall and began writing.

Plan to thwart shooter from Nazy and Bill
Plan to profile shooter
Plan to discover source of DCI's actions
Plan to discover who sent the shooter
Plan to get files on the president and DCI

"How's that? Did I miss anything?"

"Do you plan to eat?" Lynche asked.

Hunter cocked his head and grinned, glad to see he and Greg were close friends again.

"I don't think so," McGee said.

"First, I want to see if Nazy's OK. If she is, we need to see if she's a player. If we assume the shooter's after Bill first, she won't be targeted until Bill's killed."

"Thank you for your concern," McGee said with a wry smile.

"These are our priorities—protect you and Nazy. I think we might have some time with Nazy. If we can interdict the shooter from getting at you, she's clear."

"Unless the DCI takes direct action."

"Let's not go there for a moment. How about we get

word to her to see if she's OK? Maybe she can sense any change in the atmosphere at your old place. If she feels safe and is game, what are the chances she could find those files?"

"I like it. Send her an e-mail. Text her. Then we can eat."

"I'll step outside and use the unclass system. I can send text messages there, and I can receive them on my BlackBerry. If she's home."

"That'll work," said Lynche.

"Save me some pizza," demanded Hunter.

CHAPTER TWENTY-FIVE

2300 June 9, 2001
Schweizer Aircraft Company

HEY, 91321 CAN'T TALK SEND 2 BB
JUST GOT HOME U OK?
CAN U GO BACK 2 WORK MAY BE SAFER
YOU CANNOT CALL ME?
WISH I COULD TALK CANT CHANCE AUDIO OR E-MAIL
UR SCARING ME
KNOW ILY ANYTHING WEIRD W/UR BOSS? BIG D
NO NOTHING NEW IF THAT IS HELPFUL
WANT 2 GIVE U FULL DETAILS 2 DANGEROUS NEED U
    SAFE THINK BEST N UR OFFICE 4 SEVERAL DAYS
I COULD GO BACK, TAKE CLOTHES
GOOD PLZ WEAR UR BA NEED FAVORS
U WILL PAY WHEN ICU 91321
WHAT DO U NEED
NEED U2 FIND FILE ON OTHER FORMER SENATOR. 10-4?
UR PREDECESSOR BUILT 20 YR FILE, MADE COPY N HID IT
    N PLAIN SIGHT
UNDERSTAND BIG D'S BOSS FILE
10-4 ALWAYS AN AVENTURE WITH ME. PROMISE IF
    ANYTHING LOOKS STRANGE GET 2 SAFE PLACE FAST
    PLZ
WILL TRY MY BEST
STAY AWAY FROM WINDOWS N HOUSE. MOVE FAST BTWN
    CAR N HOUSE TEXT WHEN SAFE N PARKING LOT
OK
WILL COME 4U IN COUPLE DAYS CAN U DO THAT
ANYTHING 4U 91225
91225 22 22 13 CU SOON

CHAPTER TWENTY-SIX

2315 June 9, 2011
The Green Room, Schweizer Aircraft Company

Hunter closed the business development director's office and ran through the quiet manufacturing plant back to the vault. Stepping inside, he was again stunned by the clean slick lines and elegance of the design of the newly carbon-fiber-skinned YO-3A. Schweizer's engineers and Hunter met every year to discuss airframe and system improvements. Over the past ten years, the little airplane traded many metal airframe components for precision-fitted carbon fiber panels.

007 and her sisters were prototypes. A production special-purpose quiet aircraft would have been over-engineered in several areas to improve its flying characteristics and its low-level performance from flight tests and simulations, all designed to increase its quietness. Ten years of such improvements and new, longer wings would likely have garnered a thumbs-up from the master of Lockheed's design and engineering, Kelly Johnson.

Hunter told his graduate school students, during his Aircraft and Spacecraft Development classes, "A beautiful aircraft is a great flying aircraft. There's always a certain elegance in form and performance in the great aircraft. Consider this. What would you do to make the SR-71 or the Concorde better? That's how you recognize greatness, when you can't improve it."

None of his students, from the F-15 and F-16 pilots to the guys flying heavies, had ever heard of the little, obscure YO-3A, but they would certainly recognize that 007 would be a great flying airplane and would be very effective.

Hunter stood there for a moment, smiling. "Think you can find a sniper in a haystack?" His voice echoed in the special hangar before he re-entered the Green Room.

"Where we at?"

"What about Nazy?"

"She's OK. Doesn't think anything weird's going on and is going back to her office to look for the POTUS file. I asked her to wear her body armor and stay at Langley until we come for her."

"That sounds like a plan."

"She's a little scared. I'm worried about all of us. Where are we at, or did you just eat it all while I was gone?"

"There's more than enough, even for you."

Duncan loaded Italian onto his paper plate, sat at the table facing the whiteboard, and looked at the list of items. He started talking. "I'm thinking, if we're lucky, one and five are at work. I think the middle three are related. DCI has to be the key."

"It might be helpful to profile the shooter the best we can, then war game the options," McGee said.

"I'm all ears," Lynche said.

McGee, standing, walked to the board. "The guy's an American, not from any of our coalition partners or the Soviet bloc. He's able to move too freely and hit multiple places across the country."

"So he isn't a Muslim itching for some kind of payback that you and your buddies deserve?"

"That's perfect. You have to challenge my assumptions and assertions. No attribution, right?"

"Correct."

"Why not a Muslim shooter?" Lynche asked.

Hunter was in his usual mode of observing and thinking. "First of all, they aren't that good. I think our shooter's a world-class marksman, and he's been to sniper school. He's a trained US military sniper."

"Why wouldn't they be that good?" Lynche asked. "Don't they go to sniper school?"

"They do, but it's the quality of the course. Then there's the whole mobility issue. I just can't fathom how a Muslim could kill five SEALs at long range. I'm trying to say it isn't that they aren't capable, but they haven't had the specialized training and practice. You have to maintain your proficiency to shoot ultra-long distances."

"What I'm hearing is sniper school is like Top Gun or Fighter Weapons School," Hunter said. "Only the best of the best can kick it up a notch, like my racquetball. It's a huge leap from being an A player to an Open player. I see where first-tier allies could go to Top Gun, but I'm unaware if we allow all foreign pilots access to that information and training."

"I'm sure all the yellow and red books I read had Not Releasable to Foreign Nations—NOFORN all over them, or Release to the UK, Canada, and Australia only. So I think any of the questionable Islamic countries would be excluded from first-tier training. The same case could be made for the sniper."

"Agreed," McGee said. "He's US. I'm starting to think a spec-ops guy gone bad."

"What about a convert?" Hunter stared into McGee's eyes.

"What?" Lynche asked.

"A convert. How about someone who was a sniper, went to jail, found Islam, and got out with a chip on his shoulder or was properly motivated with money?"

"Unlikely," Lynche said. "You can't buy weapons if you have a felony."

It was getting late. Duncan rubbed his eyes. "Did you really say that, Greg? News flash. I could probably go into town and within a couple hours buy a half dozen beautiful documents that could be used to get me ammo and weapons. All I need is money and the balls to do it. Your old place is a master of bogus documents. Behind Langley, there are a dozen places south of the border."

"So we think former sniper or SOF, possible convert."

"You still think there's an Islamic component?" Lynche asked almost sheepishly, his liberalism trying not to ooze out.

"I do. SEALs killed Osama bin Laden, and now SEALs are

being killed. That isn't random. Occam's Razor. This has to be something simple, and the DCI is obviously involved—somehow, some way. Nazy indicated the DCI had a close relationship with a Saudi prince who facilitated his habit with kids."

"Former sniper or convert?" McGee asked. "Sounds like both are the best solution."

"OK. Let's assume we know how they did it. The DCI has to be running a sniper."

"Or a sniper team via a surrogate," McGee said. "Too hard to do directly."

"I'd think it would be hard to run a team, although the Washington, DC, snipers worked as a team, but I'm no expert," Lynche said.

"If they were Marines or a SEAL sniper team," McGee said, "they could run all over the country or downtown Washington, DC, and you'd never know it."

"I first thought a team could be a player," Hunter said, "but I'm more inclined to think this becomes infinitely more complicated if there's a team. I can wrap my head around a middleman talking with a single shooter. Who could do this besides a single sniper?"

"There are several things to consider," McGee said. "One is range. Up to 1,000 yards, and you have a lot of players. Beyond that, it's rarefied air—the difference between you and me playing racquetball."

"So a pro, a superstar with a rifle? How many of those guys are out there?"

"Actually, maybe one hundred worldwide," said McGee.

"Greg, are there any snipers at the CIA?" Hunter asked. "There might be, but that wasn't something we did. We left the long-range stuff to Bill's guys and Marine Scout Snipers and such. We'd try a surrogate to do the dirty deed or be much closer, like trying to poison Castro. I'm not sure we have ever taken anyone down via an internal sniper. Maybe we have. I've been away a long time and don't know."

"No doubt some at the NCS have those skills. I can't

imagine CIA taking out a SEAL stateside, though. Someone rogue, maybe, but not an active-duty guy. He would've popped up on a polygraph."

"I think we've got two possible scenarios," Hunter said, "Broken Lance and that mosque. Because of what you and your guys did in Afghanistan, the mosque is tantalizingly simple. My radar homed in on them, but if they've been raided and shut down, and you haven't been molested until now, that screams why and who? Technically, how could anyone locate your friends who were shot? Credit card transactions? Military orders? Cell phones? Bill, that timeline of when the killings started, it was like a forced march starting from…."

"Denver. That was first, with Pablo Reyes."

"Right, Denver. Then Memphis, Norfolk, Key West, and Washington…."

"Who could move from middle America, find and locate a SEAL, one of the most highly trained killers on the planet, determine his daily routine…?"

"All in the span of a few days," McGee added.

"…find a weakness and avenue of approach, then take a shot all without being seen or heard," Hunter finished. "Who can do that?"

"I could do some of it," McGee said, "the trigger-pulling part. Someone has to provide the intel on who, what, when, and where. We just don't do that. We take action on actionable intel developed by intel geeks. Where are you going with this line of reasoning?"

"Is that something a smart one at a mosque could do or have done?" Hunter asked cautiously.

Lynche looked at him curiously. "My knee-jerk response is no. There's no connection."

Hunter thought hard for a couple seconds. "No one thought on the day of 9/11 that there was a nationwide conspiracy at airports. What was it, Greg? Over sixty Muslims working for contracted security firms that disappeared from half a dozen airports when the FAA shut down the airspace?

441

That was a pretty good network."

"Really?" McGee asked. "I didn't know that. Were Denver and Memphis on that list of airports?"

"Denver was," Hunter said. "It's been so long ago, I think so, but I'm not 100% sure of Memphis." Hunter searched the deep recesses of his memory. Was Memphis part of the original group of airports unreported in 9/11? There was Dallas, Denver, Miami, LA and…Memphis.

"CIA could do it if they had the names and SS numbers," Lynche said. "They could send out teams. So could the FBI, which would be more likely, and they investigated the Muslim-airport connection."

"Memphis was one of the 9/11 airports," Hunter blurted. "I remember now. Don't you find it odd that the former DCI took the president's file and the case officer is now dead? Five SEALs are dead in cities near where some 9/11 players were, and there's this little tiny thread that connects DCI with Broken Lance?"

"I still can't get my head around why the DCI would want to kill off a bunch of SEALs," McGee said.

"I think the better question is why would the DCI want to off the president," Hunter added. "'Kill the one who ordered the hit on Osama bin Laden, and I'll stop killing SEALs.' He wants the president killed by SEALs, and he's putting great pressure on the SEALs, especially the Lancers, to do the dirty deed. Isn't that the question? Why?"

"Maybe he's tired of the president's shit?" Lynche was embarrassed when he said that and couldn't believe he let it out. "Maybe the president wants him to do something he doesn't want to do. I don't know what that could be, but the DCI's a powerful Democrat, and the president's a radical…."

"He's a communist," McGee said quickly. "Community organizer is code for communist sympathizer. He and his band of commies have brought up charges against several SEALs who supposedly abused some fucking terrorist. Democrats don't want to admit their party has been hijacked by communists and radicals."

"There's a difference?" Hunter asked, amused. "What's the difference between a democrat and a communist? A communist actually practices border control and respects the military. This coke-sniffing dude despises guys in uniform, and the nicest thing I can say about him is he's a rabid socialist and a closet Muslim, in my humble opinion. Anyway, is there something there?"

"What do you mean?" Lynche asked.

"To me, it's obvious the president is the real target, and Bill's SEALs are expected to pull the trigger. What could POTUS do to make the DCI want to kill him?"

"You mean, like blackmail? You think the president is blackmailing the DCI?"

"That's one thought. Any others?"

"What could he be blackmailed for? He's openly gay. It used to be that was the biggest taboo—catch someone in a compromising position and manipulate him. That's Spycraft 101."

"What if he had AIDS?" McGee asked.

"I wouldn't think that would do it," Hunter replied. "You want to kill the president for fear he'd tell the world you have AIDS? I don't think so."

"I'd agree," Lynche said. "It would have to be something really horrendous. I don't think liking boys is enough. The rich bastard would just quit and have all the sex he wanted. I have a hard time thinking it's blackmail."

The three men were quiet, looking at each other, waiting for someone to speak.

Hunter, who was never bashful at floating trial balloons, asked, "What if he had an epiphany?"

"Who?"

"DCI."

Lynche rolled his eyes. "What are you thinking, Duncan?"

"He had an epiphany, an awakening. He suddenly realized a great truth."

"And, that is to kill the president?" Lynche, feeling tired, was exasperated.

"To make it stop."

"What are you talking about?" McGee sensed Hunter was about to right their foundering ship.

"When someone can't take it anymore, what does he do? If they hurt from cancer and realize it won't get better, sometimes they kill themselves. Postmen go postal. A husband has enough of his wife running around on him and kills her. A wife has enough of her husband's beating on her, so she runs away. German generals think Hitler is off his rocker and try to blow him up. Sam Doe had enough of Liberian President...Tolbert, so he marched him to the beach and slowly turned him into fish food."

"It was a colonel," McGee said. "Von Stauffenberg. Hitler had him shot."

"The price of failure," Lynche said.

"I only got fired," quipped McGee.

"When this is all over, I think it'll be something like this," Hunter said. "Motive starts to make sense with this scenario. I'm at a loss to explain it with anything else."

"OK," McGee said. "What next?"

Hunter walked to the whiteboard and drew a line through the words Plan to discover source of DCI's actions and said, "We need to add to this list, Interdict shooter. We need to stop him."

"He can't get Bill if he's here," Lynche said.

"At some point, Bill doesn't show up. What would you do? Roll to your next assignment. DCI finds out we helped Bill, he'll have us shot." Hunter lowered his chin to his chest.

"What are you thinking?" McGee asked.

"I think the shooter's in Newport waiting for you to return home or work—maybe even the gym—to take a shot at you right in the heart, one shot, one kill. Then he'll go after Nazy, Greg, or me. I still don't know how he knows where the SEALs are, but the DCI has his fingerprints all over this. I think we take 007 to Newport and try to find him and take him out before he takes you out."

"Are you thinking of using me as bait?" McGee was

444

curious and incredulous.

"I think we need to find this guy. Based on what we know, you think you're next. I think you're right. This guy is on his way or is already in Newport to target you. I think we can find and stop him. How do we stop a sniper?"

"A better question might be is how would you target yourself?" Lynche asked.

"You mean, how would I turn this into an op? Go offense?"

"How would you do it? I know we can find someone with the FLIR if they're outside. If they're in a building...."

"Or a vehicle," Lynche added.

"I'm not sure I like this idea," McGee said slowly.

"You have a better one, good Sir? I'm all ears," Hunter said. "Who can we call for help? I think we're on our own."

McGee didn't like the finality of Hunter's conclusion, but he knew he was right. As he tried to think of an alternative, his mind raced through thirty years of lessons learned in combat, trying to find a way out of his predicament. Subconsciously, McGee flexed his muscles and balled his fists. He realized he was out of ideas.

Lynche and Hunter watched McGee wrestle with himself.

Then the big man relaxed and rubbed his callused palms together. "OK," McGee said. "Here's how a SEAL would do it."

CHAPTER TWENTY-SEVEN

0100 June 10, 2011
Millerton and Elmira, New York

It was so simple. He began with the address, which he typed into the Find Location block. In seconds, through the magic of satellite photography and software, designed to mesh an extensive collection of high-resolution satellite imagery into a coherent, seamless picture, the image processor and analysis algorithms enabled the Northern Hemisphere to rotate from over the Atlantic toward New England.

A forward scroll of the mouse, and the image resolution increased exponentially and zoomed to the maximum government- allowable resolution for civilian imaging. Additional zoom increments triggered embedded software to overwhelm program software limitations and distort the images.

EarthZoom and StreetZoom options provided enough resolution to establish the lay of the land, potential avenues of approach, the footprint of the target structure, and latitude and longitude coordinates down to the second of latitude. The EarthZoom feature with precision coordinate was especially helpful, as it enabled planning without having to shoot a back azimuth from the point of impact.

Clicking the Tools menu, he selected Compass. A single click pinned a From location, and he noted the coordinate. He dragged the mouse to the next location and double-clicked to receive the calculated azimuth to the house from the treeline.

StreetZoom facilitated sufficient granularity of the surroundings that potential cover locations were easily noted. He was looking at a God's-eye view of the house, roof, and systematically examined the outlying copse of trees that appeared best suited for a hide. Clicking the Tools menu again, he pulled down the Ruler and measured the gap between the house and treeline fifteen degrees to the left of the stoop. It was 1,250 yards.

Miller saved the images and details of the next hunt and shut down his computer. He expected to receive more information in the morning. It was time to rest before the next e-mail arrived.

* * *

One hundred fifty miles away, McGee finished with, "That's how I'd do it. It's the only solution. It provides the right cover and an escape route from the area. That's where we'll find him. I might even be able to shoot him, but I think I want to talk to him first."

Hunter and Lynche exchanged solemn glances; McGee just nodded his head.

CHAPTER TWENTY-EIGHT

2000 June 10, 2011
Chief Near East Division Office CIA Headquarters

Nazy Cunningham awoke in her office, not an uncommon occurrence for some of the senior intelligence service executives in the CIA. Since receiving messages from Duncan, she scrambled through her house in Vienna, racing through every room to ensure the windows and doors were locked, packed a roller board, and grabbed her "go bag."

Five years earlier, when she received an assignment to Saudi Arabia as Deputy Chief of Station, Duncan helped her pack a "go bag" of essential items to take in an emergency, such as the evacuation of an embassy. Never once thinking she'd have to evacuate her house, she was well prepared for it but was emotionally drained. She had hundreds of questions for Duncan, primarily, "What's going on?" and "Why do you need a file about the president?"

As she oscillated between concern for Duncan and bursts of energy to select a week's worth of clothes, several conflicting thoughts crowded through her mind. She thought the file about the president was just a rumor. They'd been told it was long in the past, and there wasn't anything in it, anyway.

She also realized the DCI had been curiously absent from most of the executive meetings recently. The deputy ran the show. Was that related to whatever Duncan was doing?

The Chief of the Near East Division wandered the sixth floor, visiting everyone and telling them how much she appreciated their working crazy hours in support of the document release and analysis of some of the documents taken from Osama bin Laden's compound.

After walking through all the NE offices and talking with

everyone, she was pleased to find they complied with the "clean-desk" requirements. CIA employees and contractors were responsible for clearing their desks when they left the office at the end of the day. Extraneous papers were either shredded or locked in a storage space. Over the last few weeks, it was very difficult for supervisors and the chief to check all the offices at the end of the day. There was so much material from the Osama bin Laden raid and not enough storage or four-drawer safes, the intelligence professionals of NE feared they would miss something important, so supervisors didn't confiscate or destroy any folders or papers employees may have left on desks.

Six weeks after the raid, the NE had just begun to return to normal, and clean desks were everywhere. People went home to their families or took well-deserved vacations. If something like a file was left out in plain sight, there would be consequences for policy noncompliance. Duncan would have said Nazy was "going 1,000 miles an hour."

Worn out, she returned to her corner office at the end of the hall, plopped into her seat, kicked off her heels, and spun to look outside. Floodlights illuminated the predecessor to the Air Force SR-71, the last remaining A-12 "up on a stick and not in a museum" as Duncan lamented every time he saw it.

Unhappy with herself for not finding anything, she tried to console herself that there was no such missing file on the president. She didn't like disappointing Duncan, and his request to locate a mythical file hurt. Duncan had done so much for her, but the file simply didn't exist. He would understand.

She'd been going nonstop once she was confirmed as the Chief of the NE Division, and she felt exhausted and defeated. She didn't want to go to the garage where her smartphone was to send Duncan a message that she failed. Even SIS couldn't bring cell phones into the building, and she was in no hurry to make the half-mile trek to her car and send him the bad news.

She spun around to face her desk and saw the three-cushion sofa that was her bed the previous night. Not comfortable, but it'll do, she thought.

She had little appetite. The cafeteria, with its 100 tiny ponytail palms in the windows, was closed for the evening. I'd go for Mexican, but I promised Duncan I'd stay on campus, she thought with a sigh.

Nazy reflected how far she came since leaving Jordan and meeting Duncan. Everything about him thrilled her. For seven years, she worked with other high-powered executives and agents in the intelligence community, but none had what Duncan did— her heart. He was the most exciting man she ever met. Everything around her reminded her of him.

The sofa brought back sweet memories of Duncan and her in that room naked, curled together under a blanket, listening to Moody Blues. Nazy scanned the opposite wall and its bookcase of reference materials. It resembled the racks of books when Duncan was in school at Newport. Nazy hadn't thought much about the five shelves filled with a variety of history books left from her predecessor, some related to the art of intelligence-gathering or fighting terrorists.

In stockinged feet, she walked to the racks of books. "Maybe there's a sleeping aid here," she said.

Titles on top, such as The Art of War Gaming; Data Mining and Predictive Analysis: Intelligence Gathering and Crime Analysis; The Strategy of Conflict; Psychology of Intelligence Analysis; International Terrorism: Challenge and Response; A Place Among the Nations; Fighting Terrorism: How Democracies Can Defeat Domestic and International Terrorism; A Durable Peace: Israel and Its Place among the Nations; stirred her curiosity.

"A big Netanyahu fan," she said, taking down Terrorism: How the West Can Win and thumbing through the pages. She would have to read that someday, if her schedule ever slowed down.

Nazy returned the book and scanned the second, third,

and fourth shelves' titles, noting The Art of the Long View: Planning for the Future in an Uncertain World.

On the next shelf, she saw The Campaigns of Napoleon; Nimitz; The Peloponnesian War; From Beirut to Jerusalem; Peacekeeper; Crisis of Islam: Holy War and Unholy Terror.

"Similar and overflow from the top," she murmured.

She crouched down, unladylike in a dress, balancing on the balls of her feet with her bosom crushed against her knees. "Biographies?" She fingered the titles. "I won't be reading MacArthur, Napoleon, Gandhi, Lenin, or Mandela anytime soon. Jefferson, Washington, Truman. Maybe Teddy Roosevelt, Churchill, and Kennedy."

Her eyes suddenly locked on several narrows books in the corner. One spine was so dark, she couldn't read the title or author, but the other two caught her off guard. The author's name seemed out of sync with the others. She smiled.

"OK. With all these great books, why would you have two autobiographies from the current president in the darkest corner of the bookshelf? In plain sight."

With a delicate finger, she rocked the two books toward her, grasped them, and stood. Though she knew she was alone, she subconsciously looked around her office. The outer door was closed, and the secretary was long gone. All the safes were closed, with red magnetic signs reading Closed and Locked.

This has to be it, she thought, slipping into the heavy leather chair behind her desk. She flipped open the first book and thumbed through the pages, expecting paper to fall out or to find a hollowed area with a key or thumb drive inside.

Nothing occurred. She set that book aside and flipped through the pages of the next one with the same result. Something was different, though. The pages were slicker and whiter than other mass-market books, and the print was different.

She looked closer, and one corner of her mouth rose in a wry grin. She began reading. When she turned to the center of the book, she saw a copy of a British passport issued to the president with his name and picture inside—evidence of the bearer's nationality and immigration status from one of the territories of the United Kingdom.

Nazy was shocked. Her heart raced, and she found it difficult to blink. She couldn't resolve the conflict of the documents she held and the person she saw on TV, who'd been crafted by the media into a smooth, erudite Harvard attorney constantly, viciously attacked by right-wing elements.

With a large breath, she recovered and blinked her eyes several times. After a moment, she flipped through the pages and saw copies of embassy dispatches, college applications, matriculation-exemption documents, Social Security number applications, close-up and long-distance photographs. Other pages showed copies of attendance rosters at socialist and communist gatherings, church sign-in sheets, and license applications. There were visa applications and over forty dispatches from Islamabad.

She read fragments of the tiny print. It was clear, but some documents warranted a magnifying glass. She had 300 pages of material on bond paper held between the hardbound covers of two books.

"Something the S&T could have assembled," she said softly. Then it struck her. She drew her hand to her mouth.

"It's true. Oh, my word, it's all true."

Pausing for a moment, she said, "These might be the only documents that can prove the president's detractors were right."

She glanced around the room, as another worm of an idea crept into her consciousness. There were many questions about how the old NE Division chief died. Rumors that an ex-wife killed him had circulated for a few days, but the crushing workload and the high tempo at the Agency meant that rumors died quickly.

However, some wondered not only how he died but why.

Nazy knew the material in those books were the reason

the former chief's life ended so abruptly. When she heard a knock at her door, she jumped.

"Ms. Cunningham?" asked a familiar voice, galvanizing her thoughts and actions.

She quickly closed the book and smoothed her suit front. "Come in, Sir."

When Director of Central Intelligence Carey strolled in, Nazy was stunned, and she felt a jolt of adrenalin race through her. "Director Carey, I thought you were out of the country. What can I do for you at this late hour, Sir?" She remained the consummate professional although her knees were banging together.

The DCI rarely wandered down to the sixth floor, and he was never in the building at night. She wondered if he intercepted Duncan's messages.

"I noticed you were still here. You and your people have been burning the midnight oil lately." He laughed internally and smiled before composing himself and closing the door behind him.

"Yes, Sir. Someone said the information coming out of the CTC is like trying to take a sip from a fire hose. It was too much to analyze all at once. We got through the last of it today. My report went to the deputy and should be on your desk soon."

"That's very good." He waved his hands downward. "Have a seat, Nazy."

He always mispronounced her name as NAY-zee, while everyone else called her NAH-zee. Someone once told her he was from a certain part of Massachusetts where people had trouble with A's and R's.

He wedged himself into one of the two leather-bound office chairs facing the desk. "I see you're reading our president's book."

She hid her concern when she thought he might reach for it. To avoid temptation, she smiled and put the books in the bottom desk drawer. "Yes, Sir. Part of my professional reading. He's had an interesting life." As she waited, her knees were knocking together so loudly she thought they sounded like cymbals. She struggled not to shake.

He studied her for a few seconds. Finally, he took a deep breath. "Nazy, from what I've heard, you and your team have done very well over the last couple of months. Your selection as Chief NE has been validated several times over. You found the gem in that illegal documents release that forced DOD to move up the raid schedule. You also found—what was it?— ten others that showed there were WMD in Iraq that were moved to Syria. That State didn't share those dispatches with us was treasonous, and I've talked to the Secretary about it. I'm not sure anything will come of it, I'm afraid."

"Yes, Sir." She tried not to smile. The room felt colder after he walked in, as if evil emanated from him like perfume.

"I'm sorry the president's Muslim-outreach initiative didn't catch on. I thought you'd benefit greatly from that. I thought the Agency would benefit, too."

"Director Carey, Sir, I'm not sure you're aware that I renounced Islam eight years ago. I thought I could provide some guidance to possibly locate some good Muslims suitable for recruitment. I believe unless you have someone like me, who renounced Islam, the Agency will always have trouble hiring and integrating Muslims into the IC. They won't be able to pass a polygraph, and, if they haven't renounced Islam and Sharia, I don't believe you can trust them with national secrets." She couldn't believe she just said that.

The DCI had an agenda. Lowering his eyes and voice, he said, "Your assessment was on target on that. It looks like over the last couple of years, just about everything you touched has been golden. The deputies agree you have the Midas touch."

"Thank you, Sir. That's most kind. In all fairness, my team made it happen. It has always been a team effort. It wasn't just the Nazy Cunningham show."

Retaining his submissive posture, he picked at his cuticles. "Well, the president thinks you were instrumental in Osama bin Laden's takedown. Your analysis with his wives identified the compound, and NE and CTC surveilled it. You found the dispatches that mentioned that town in Pakistan as a special- interest location before the CTC. He was very interested in the analyst who forced him to authorize a raid before we were sure. He didn't want to do it unless we were 100% sure. We were never going to be that certain. He wasn't happy when I told him. I probably shouldn't tell you, but just between us girls, he was furious at me, and, by extension, you."

"I'm very sorry, Director Carey."

He raised his head to look Into her eyes, then flipped his hand dismissively. "It worked out, and now he's a hero. He came to recognize that you were a key part of the team that made him look like a hero."

"Thank you, Sir."

"He wanted to know if it was a fluke on your part or if you were a superstar. I said you were in the Beatles category of superstar, that you also found Iraq's WMD in Syria when everyone else was looking at Iran, and your other successes in Saudi are what catapulted you into the chief's position and SIS."

"Thank you, Sir. Those successes were team events. I appreciate the kind words." She kept it short, sweet, and team- oriented as Duncan always advised her.

"Nazy, the network you developed was, and still is, producing actionable intelligence. That's very hard to sustain. It takes a rare officer who can go in and survive scrutiny for a long time and leave a functioning network after the case O leaves."

Nazy's sensitivities were in full-suspicion mode. He wanted something, and she knew it wasn't a date. "Thank you, Director Carey." It seemed he was taking a lot of time to arrange his thoughts and what to say next.

"Nazy, I need a couple of favors."

Here it comes, she thought. "What do you need, Sir?"

The DCI sucked a lungful of air. "First, the president wants to give you a medal—the Intelligence Medal of Merit."

Her knees stopped shaking for a moment, as if warm air suddenly blew up her skirt and stopped her shivering. "Sir, thank you for your trust and confidence in me. I appreciate the accolades, but I really don't think I deserve something like that."

"Well, Nazy, I nominated you for the medal, and it's been approved. The president wants to give it to you in person, at the White House at noon this coming Tuesday. I know you had a speaking engagement at the Marine Corps War College during that time, but I would greatly appreciate it if you'd change your plans and attend the ceremony at the White House."

"Director Carey, thank you again for your trust and confidence in me. I suppose putting it in the mail or having you present it to me privately isn't an option?" Her mind raced. Is this a trap? Does he somehow know I have the file? Why this, and why now? It's too much too fast.

"Sir, I'm not comfortable breaking my cover for a political ceremony. It's not that important to me. If there was some way I didn't have to go...." She realized he asked for more than one favor. "Sir, you had another favor?"

He looked as if he appreciated the change in subject. He wasn't accustomed to a Muslim woman who was so direct and strong. He hadn't believed a Muslima could walk away from Islam, but she didn't act like any other Muslima he ever met. She wasn't easily intimidated by him or any man.

The rumor about her was that she might be gay, but the men and women who asked her out always struck out. She was different but always professional. He needed her help. He assumed offering the medal would make her ready to do anything for him, but he was wrong. He needed to ask his question in a different way. All he could do was toss the dice and see if she would play.

"Nazy, I'm sure you've heard some of the rumors surrounding our president."

She wasn't sure what that meant. "Clarification, Director Carey? I'm not sure what we're talking about. I know of no presidential rumors."

"He asked me to see if there was a file on him. Republicans erroneously repeat the charge that he went to Pakistan."

"Director Carey, he stated he went to Pakistan in his book."

"Would there be a file on him?"

Her mind raced. "Sir, we don't track intel on US citizens. That's the purview of the FBI. If we have anything in dispatch, it gets pushed to them via our FBI liaison. If there was anything, there would be a record of when, where it went, and who received it. I've never seen or heard anything. This might be the CIA, but it would be hard to keep a secret like that in this place."

"Could you get into the database and see if there was anything on him, any information transferred to the FBI? I'm unfamiliar with the actual process."

"Sir, I'll ask the deputy if he could give me some direction. I'm...."

"I'd rather we kept this between you and me for right now. If there was anything, I'd think it would be in the NE. Would there be anything on his father, for example?"

"I understand his father was a British subject. I could see if his name is in the database. I could e-mail you my findings."

"Nazy, this is unofficial. If you find anything, just stick your head in the office and tell me. I think it should be a quick check of the file database. If there is a file, where is it, and where did it go?" He thought it would be perfect to have the bitch who screwed up the president's plan to wait and kill Osama bin Laden later to be the same one who exposed the file on the president. There had to be some record of the file transferred to the personal file of the DCI.

Though he thought she was good-looking, she was a bitch to make him work so hard for his requests. She was much stronger than she seemed and wasn't as easy to manipulate as he thought.

"Sir, that shouldn't be difficult to ascertain," she said. "I'll get on your calendar and report what, if anything, I find."

He smiled and stood. "Thank you, Nazy. Go home, have a good weekend, and practice what you'll say to him." He reached over the desk to shake her hand. "Congratulations." Her firm, confident grip surprised him.

As he turned to leave, he kept his back toward her as he said, "I'll tell him I caught you reading his book when I told you about the medal. He'll get a thrill out of that." He walked to the door.

Nazy, still standing, wondered if that was all he was after.

Suddenly Carey stopped and turned. "Can you keep a secret?"

"Absolutely, Sir."

"There'll be a big announcement on Monday and a ceremony on Tuesday. I really hope you're there. I would consider it a personal favor. Thanks again, and good night."

Then DCI Carey turned and was gone.

Was that it? she wondered. He wanted to ask me something else.

Kicking off her heels, she ran to the door and locked it.

Back behind her desk, she withdrew the two books from the bottom drawer and took a magnifying glass from the center drawer. As she read, she could barely focus on the copies of the documents before her.

* * *

Nazy could not sleep. She sat up from the sofa, her head in her hands. "I have to get out of here. I have to get these to Duncan."

CHAPTER TWENTY-NINE

2300 June 10, 2011
USS Stockdale, DDG-106
Carl Vinson Carrier Strike Group Indian Ocean

The gray HH-60 lifted off from Spot 3 of USS Carl Vinson, heading for the fantail of USS Stockdale, three miles south. The Landing Signal Enlisted guided the aircraft onto the flight deck. His lighted coveralls and illuminated wands marked the X on the darkened ship. The pilot flew a slow, coordinated angled approach to the landing spot.

The LSE signaled Stop Forward Motion by crossing the wands overhead, and then, in a single motion, brought the crossed wands to his knees to signal Land Here. The pilot deftly obeyed and landed easily, the tail wheel touching down first, then the mains.

With the parking brake set, and the aircraft just barely touching the deck, the pilot programmed the collective stick full down to set neutral pitch of the main rotor. As the crew chief stepped off the aircraft, two blue-shirted aircraft handlers raced out and attached chains between the aircraft and ship. A moment later, the two rocked and pitched with the waves as one.

The LSE motioned with one wand for the awaiting passengers to approach the aircraft. Three heavily armed men escorted litter bearers and an injured warrior to the helicopter. In two minutes, all passengers were aboard and the stretcher secured. The crew chief, reentering the aircraft, closed the sliding door.

On the LSE's signal, the blue shirts broke down the chains, ran back to their stations, and hunkered down against the impending 100 mph rotor wash. The LSE looked right and left, twirled one wand to signal Ready for Flight, then brought both wands together over his head three times, as the pilot incrementally pulled up on his collective and centered the cyclic and the rudder pedals to keep the ball centered in the Turn-and- Slip Indicator. He raised the aircraft straight and level.

As it broke contact with the flight deck, the LSE pointed his wands to his right for the helicopter to Depart that Direction. The aircrew put the TACAN needle on the nose, destination Navy Support Facility Diego Garcia.

American liberals screamed that the remote island was more than a little-known launching pad for the wars in Iraq and Afghanistan, and Diego Garcia housed a top-secret CIA prison where terror suspects were interrogated and tortured. Rather than some version of Alcatraz or Devil's Island, the facility supported flight and maritime operations in support of Operations Enduring Freedom, Iraqi Freedom, and other coalition missions in the Indian Ocean.

An extension of their lease agreement with Great Britain, terrorists captured on the battlefield of Iraq and Afghanistan weren't to be processed or transported to Diego Garcia. Detainees weren't jailed or subjected to enhanced interrogation techniques but rather given nonstop rides to Guantanamo Bay, Cuba, or other places. SOCOM and DEVGRU quietly maintained a SEAL team presence on the island for contingency operations. Some submarines operating from Diego Garcia were outfitted with SEAL delivery vehicles.

CHAPTER THIRTY

0630 June 11, 2011
New Haven, Connecticut

A white work van idled at the far end of the parking lot of the big blue box home-improvement store. Long metal ladders were lashed to the roof rack. The rear windows were obscured with cartons. Windscreens and side windows were covered with sun shades.

In the center of the cargo floor rested an Islamic green-and- silver mat fringed along top and bottom. The design was based on the village where it was woven, the Kaabah artistically woven at the top. A qubla finding compass, to indicate the direction of Mecca, specifically toward the Kaabah, was affixed above the center of the prayer mat to ensure proper facing for ritual prayers. The man waited for the Call the Prayer to play from his Azan alarm clock.

As the muezzin began his song, a tingle ran down the man's leg. "This is indeed one of the prettiest sounds on Earth," he whispered to himself.

Once the call ended, the man said quietly "Allahu Akbar," dropped to his knees, bowed, and recited three times, "Subhana rabbiyal adheem." Once the ritual was complete, the man prepared himself and the vehicle for departure.

The rising sun was low on the horizon. He lowered his visor, pulled onto the interstate, and drove east. Traffic was light for that time of the morning. The van slid behind an 18-wheeler, and the two trucks cruised one mile under the posted speed limit. The windshield-mounted GPS display indicated fifty-four miles to Newport. ETA was fifty-eight minutes.

CHAPTER THIRTY-ONE

0700 June 11, 2011
Newport State Regional Airport Newport, Rhode Island

Hunter turned to line up on Runway 22, gear down, landing checklist complete. He reached over to touch the landing gear indicators. "Double-check 1-2-3 gear down. I do that, because Greg landed gear-up with his airplane a few years ago." He concentrated on the landing area, windsock, and engine instruments.

"No shit?" McGee asked.

"I understand it was a good landing. It chewed up the centerline paint, and the airport billed him for that, too. One of these days, remind me to tell you the time I was doing carrier quals and had an unsafe nose wheel."

Seconds later, Hunter flared the aircraft until it gently touched the runway. When he lowered the nose, he deployed thrust reversers and stepped on the brakes.

McGee was impressed. As they taxied from the runway onto the taxiway, he said, "I thought you carrier guys slammed down on the runway. I didn't know we were on the ground until I watched the nose drop. I'd never be able to do that."

"A lot of it is pilot technique, but the aircraft has great struts. Business execs don't want to have their martinis dumped into their laps on touchdown, so they build in a lot of travel in those struts. It works well when there's a little wind down the runway."

Hunter shut down the port engine on the taxiway and taxied to the small general aviation terminal, where he stopped and set the brake.

"Showtime," Hunter said, as he and McGee crawled out of the cockpit into the cabin.

McGee removed his shirt, and Hunter helped hang the OD- green plate to the man's chest, then helped him get the shirt over his head and the plate. Hunter nodded and gave a thumbs-up, swung the big silver handle behind him, and unlocked the door.

Before lowering the door and stairs, he turned to McGee.

"Text me when you get home."

"Yes, Dear."

"Good luck, Bullfrog. We'll be overhead in a couple hours."

"It's a good plan. We'll get him."

Hunter lowered the door, and the stairs folded out. He offered his hand, and the big SEAL took it and squeezed.

"Be safe." He rapped the big man's chest and heard a muffled thunk.

"I will. Again, thank you, Duncan."

The aircraft rocked slightly, as McGee hurried down the stairs. Hunter monitored his progress to the small terminal building before raising and locking the door. He climbed back into the cockpit, started the number-one engine, and taxied to the runway for takeoff. As he waited for clearance, he felt they had a good plan, and he wondered how Nazy was doing.

* * *

Hunter and Lynche sat in rapt attention, listening how SEALs set up and practiced for Broken Lance and how a determined enemy could defeat a SEAL sniper team.

McGee stepped to the white board and barked at Hunter, "Do you remember your five-paragraph order, Marine?"

"You mean SMEAC—Situation, Mission, Execution, Admin and Logistics, and Command and Signal?"

"Correct. I'm impressed." McGee quickly wrote on the board.

Situation
Enemy: Unknown Sniper Team: DCI and friends

Activity: SEALs KIA—CIA CO KIA Location: Den, Mem, Norfolk, KW, DC

Time Observed: Night Equipment: Terminators/300 Mag/NOGs

Capability/LimFacs: Easy travel/ long-range targeting

COA: Attack Bullfrog/Girlfriend/ H&L in order

Mission

Who: A Team; 3 Amigos

What: Stop shooter/ID enemy, stop DCI 7 friends

Where: Newport/DC When: ASAP

Why: Live long and prosper How: 007 & help

Execution

Exploitation Plan: Bait & Switch

Desired Endstate: Kill shooter, stop DCI & friends

CONOPS: Harden target/find shooter with 007/neutralize weapon/ shooter

Maneuver: Bait with Bullfrog Fire Support Plan: Bullfrog TBD

Admin/Log: Body armor Comms

Command: On my signal

"Do we want to kill him? Don't we want to know who sent him?" Hunter's question hung in the air like a blood-filled tick on a baby's nose. The shooter had already killed six men who were patriots and friends. It was apparent that the DCI facilitated those deaths. During the Revolutionary War, thirteen-year-old Andrew Jackson saw patriots and friends killed by the enemy. Refusing to kowtow to a British officer brandishing a saber, he was slashed across the cheek. He carried that scar for the rest of his life and knew what to do with an enemy—you kill them. When you kill them was an option.

McGee saw patriots and friends killed by the enemy and had a pretty clear-cut idea what to do with the enemy, but he was professional enough to kill them only after they no longer served any purpose. The current enemy had some explaining to do first.

"Do you mean, can we make him talk?" Lynche asked.

McGee, lost in thought, erased the word kill after Desired Endstate and replaced it with interrogate. "I can make anyone talk," he said emphatically. "SEALs put the special in special operations."

That outburst affected Hunter and Lynche differently. Hunter was definitely in the government's corner when it came to using "enhanced interrogation techniques," as the press called them, which encouraged a terrorist or other related scumball to give up his secrets. How effective those techniques were was the subject of significant debate in political circles.

Lynche was on the other side, feeling that such techniques didn't work, and it was immoral to use them. His thirty-five-year career with the Agency and access to Special Access programs gave him unusual insight into the process, particularly concerning what worked and what didn't.

Hunter spoke with former prisoners of war and read their books about the effectiveness of a wide range of interrogation techniques. Alistair MacLean broke when his nails and teeth were removed by Japanese sadists. Ayman al-Zawahiri broke when his Egyptian captors used car batteries and battery cables on his testicles. Getting someone to talk was a matter of leverage. Slapping prisoners around or keeping them awake or exposed to hours of the Chipmunks singing was D league. Having someone's nuts bolted to a DieHard or watching a friend's head be lopped off, as the swordsman shouted, "Allahu Akbar!" was big league. SEALs were consummate professionals playing in the pro league. Hunter spoke to avoid a potential conflict or unauthorized disclosure. "I think we nab him first. Maybe he'll flip and tell us what he knows and who sent him. I know you want this shithead dead, and so do I. I also want to know who sent him. I doubt it was the DCI directly."

Lynche visibly relaxed.

McGee's gaze softened and returned to the board. "Did I miss anything? Fire-support plan—to be determined. I'll work on that when I get to the house."

"We talked earlier about luring him into a firing position. How do we do that, Bill?" Hunter asked.

"He has to determine how he wants to set up the kill shot based on the available avenue of approach and set up a hide. It might be outside, which is very difficult to do in a metropolitan area for any length of time. Ideally, you fire from a building. I should say a team does better from a building in a combat zone. The team needs protection. They could use a vehicle. A van is most likely if he's a less-sophisticated shooter. The DC sniper used a car and fired from a hole in the trunk while the lookout drove. If you have to be exposed, you have to be able to hide in plain sight."

"I'd think it has to be big enough to hide a rifle and a shooter."

"Correct. Most likely a pickup or a van. Anything would have to be modified, so the shooter can take one shot and disappear. Here's the advantage we have. You have only a limited number of available hides when you determine the avenues of approach. If you're able to shoot a back azimuth from the impact point location, then it's really easy."

"Back azimuth?" Lynche asked.

McGee drew a basic sight picture on the board. "If I wanted to kill you on your doorstep, I'd ideally go to your porch, turn around, and look for openings in trees and the terrain, any open avenue of approach to identify possible firing positions along that vector. If there are a lot of trees, there may be only one avenue of approach, maybe none. Then you have to monitor the target's routine and determine where he goes and what he does to find a window or opportunity, shoot a back azimuth, find points of interest, and resolve a firing solution."

"How does your house compute as a target?" Hunter asked.

"Front yard, I'm toast. Back yard, I'm OK."

"How was it done? How will he do it? Do they all suggest the possibility of night-vision scopes and silencer?" Lynche appeared to be thinking of one thing for those questions. He seemed distracted.

"It's possible. I'm thinking, what if the guy had access to Pop Stop?" McGee asked.

"What's that?"

"A noise-canceling system you wear. It knocks down the sound of a silenced weapon to that of a fart. You can just about shoot a high-powered rifle from anywhere, and the double-silencing systems make it nearly impossible to hear unless you're standing beside the shooter. If he had Pop Stop, he could operate anywhere, even in a neighborhood, and you'd never know your neighbor was shooting a .300 Winchester Magnum."

"That sounds like amazing shit." Lynche was impressed.

"His MO has been to use terminators. Maybe he has a new-fangled silencer that allows him to operate in urban areas. Regardless, I expect he'll anticipate I'll be in some kind of danger, and I'll probably wear body armor. I expect him to use an armor- piercing round. The challenge is regular body armor and ceramics won't stop a 7.62 AP."

"That's what worries me," Lynche said. "It used to be the case an AP would cut right through Kevlar and barely slow down." McGee sounded like a man walking down death row.

"Armor-piercing bullets are strengthened with special copper or nickel-alloy jackets that shred on impact to allow the hardened, penetrating slug to continue through to the targeted substance. It isn't enough to just have an armor-piercing bullet. You need a modified barrel to take advantage of the bullet's ability. This guy aims for the heart."

Hunter looked at the two men, who seemed dejected and defeated. "What if I said we have some lightweight material that provides 7.62mm AP protection?"

"It doesn't exist," McGee said. "There's nothing like that we can use."

"Sir, no disrespect. The seats in 007 were upgraded to provide 7.62 mm AP protection as well as the floors and side panels. Special Access Program from the IED labs. It's some kind of titanium-tantalum hybrid matrix weave using nanotechnology. Amazing shit. Bullets splatter like a snowball hitting concrete, and the stuff doesn't deform under a 7.62 barrage. If it's a .50 caliber AP, we might be in trouble, but if we can double the material, it would stop an elephant. We have enough left over that we can make a small vest."

McGee brightened immediately. "Like Eastwood's 'Man with No Name' in A Fistful of Dollars?"

Hunter nodded.

"Will it work?" Lynche asked.

"As long as he hits Bill in the chest." He pointed at McGee. "You might get some broken ribs and be knocked down if we don't get to him first. He's a good shot. One shot, one kill. Doesn't miss."

"Show me this magic stuff," said Bill McGee.

"Can do easy. There's enough left over to cut a decent-sized piece to make a wearable vest. Saul wanted to put a couple pieces in the wings for the fuel cells, but there was only enough material for one tank. He couldn't make it work and keep the wings balanced."

"How come I'm always the last to know about this?" Lynche complained.

"You're always sailing and keeping Connie happy. You leave the details to me."

"What if we don't get there in time, and he has a slight, uh, mis- hit?" Lynche asked seriously.

"I'll never know," McGee deadpanned. "My guts or brains will be blown out, just like Osama's, when Team Six blew his brains out."

Lynche didn't like the finality of failure.

"Bill, we can do this. We can find and beat this fucker. I think we can protect you from above, but the airplane isn't armed. I'm afraid we need someone else to respond once we locate the asshole."

Hunter opened his mouth to reply, but McGee held up a finger. "I left off Fire Support Plan from mission planning. I had an idea what we could do. Now I know what we're going to do."

Hunter gave a thumbs-up.

Lynche brightened and waited for the big man to explain.

"Here's the plan," McGee said.

CHAPTER THIRTY-TWO

0705 June 11, 2011
Newport State Regional Airport

The white, empty Toyota Tacoma's engine kicked over, accelerated, and returned to idle. McGee stood inside the FBO terminal, starting his truck remotely while surveying the parking lot for anyone hiding or observing. When the car didn't blow up on ignition, he knew the assassin preferred rifles over explosives.

He had to run the gauntlet from building to truck. When he felt there was no discernable threat, McGee bounded from the FBO terminal. It was nearly impossible to lead a quickly moving target at great distances to resolve a firing solution. As he ran, his head swiveled back and forth, looking for threats from any quadrant. He knew he looked frightened, as he pushed the unlock command on his fob.

The truck's lights flashed the electrical equivalent of command received and doors unlocked. The metal plate on McGee's chest swayed asynchronously to his thundering steps. His Nikes pounded the pavement, and a jet turbine spooled up in the distance, making him feel alone but not abandoned.

He knew Hunter would be back. All McGee had to do was stay alive and wait for reinforcements. First, the killer had to find him.

He dropped to the ground, checking the underside of the small pickup, including the wheel wells, truck bed, and hood. It was awkward being on the ground with forty pounds of bulletproof material strapped to his chest. Getting up with a sense of urgency was more difficult than anticipated. Normally, he could handle a forty-pound plate on his chest when doing sit ups. McGee felt exposed and so he hurried.

Rolling to his hands and knees, he pushed up from a tire. Wedging himself into the cabin, he slid the key into the ignition, threw the gearshift into Drive, and sped off before the door closed.

Two men at the far end of the parking lot yawned and stretched at the increasing sound of the approaching business jet. They followed the man and the white truck to the airport two days earlier. The only lit building along the main road appeared to be the executive terminal, where a small jet sat on the far side of the building with its engines running and lights off.

"I can't read the tail number," the driver told the passenger, as he went down the access road, turned into the employee parking lot, and positioned the car so it had a full view of the building's front door and tail of the jet on the other side.

When the jet came alive with activity, some external lights flashed, but the driver still complained, "They still no show the number."

The jet slowly disappeared from view, its lights flashing. Minutes later, the driver pointed toward the departing aircraft. The passenger nodded, withdrew a black smartphone from his shirt pocket, and quickly tapped the screen. During the next thirty-five hours, several jets and propeller airplanes came and went from the other side of the building, but the man from the white truck didn't show.

When the jet awoke Omar, he jostled Hamid awake. Unlike the other aircraft, the white-and-red jet kept making noise soon after it stopped on the other side of the building. Omar nearly missed the big man as he ran from the building and disappeared behind the white truck. He was shocked when the pickup suddenly sped off.

"Follow him!" Hamid shouted.

The old Honda Civic started and lurched from the parking lot. In seconds, the driver was able to see the fast-moving truck ahead. Hamid watched the Toyota, as Omar weaved in and out of traffic. The truck headed toward the owner's small ranch home north of Newport.

The passenger lightly touched the screen of his smartphone and typed, Man return airprt. Drive 2 hous. Pleased with himself, Hamid sent the message.

CHAPTER THIRTY-THREE

0715 June 11, 2011
Newport State Regional Airport

Hunter sat at the hold short waiting for the Piper Cherokee to land. He listened to ATIS, adjusted both altimeters, checked the windsock, and rescanned his instruments. Just as he was about to check the progress of the Cherokee, his peripheral vision caught the red flashing light from the BlackBerry clipped to his flight bag. An e-mail or text message had been received.

"Takeoff checklist complete," he said playfully. "Same day rules apply, Mr. Cherokee." Hunter was anxious to get started but wasn't going to be rushed. The aircraft was slow to land, and knowing he had some time, he grabbed the BlackBerry and punched in the access code.

Found it, was all Nazy had sent on the subject line.

Hunter stared so long the device went into its power-saving mode, and the image faded. He pushed the Select button again, then jumped when the device vibrated and rang.

On way home with books. All there, plus more. I need 2cu.

He used both thumbs to type a quick reply. 10-4. Plz go2 grinches will come 4u soon txt when there plz.

The control tower called, clearing Hunter for takeoff. Again, his BlackBerry rang and buzzed.

There is more very scared need ttty asap.

When I land will call grinches be safe ttys.

K.

CHAPTER THIRTY-FOUR

0730 June 11, 2011
Claiborne Pell Bridge Newport, Rhode Island

Eastbound traffic was stopped at the toll booths. Car parts lay scattered across four lanes. A dozen eighteen-wheelers, panel trucks, and light vehicles awaited the emergency to be cleared from the longest suspension bridge in New England. A young woman trying to send a text message while driving was hit head-on by a young man who'd been fired from his job, snorted some cocaine, and got into his car to see how fast he could go up the bridge. Airbags saved the lives of the distracted youngsters, now being attended by emergency medical technicians.

The dull white van disappeared among the dull whites of cargo trailers and their idling tractors. Resting in the passenger seat, the tablet computer emitted a ringtone rap from new hip hop that flooded the airwaves in California, signaling, you have mail, Dude.

The driver reached across the engine cover to retrieve the device. One hand, with a thick crosshairs tattoo, flitted across the touch screen, providing security codes and commands to open e-mail. He had so much to do. He expected updated information on the target in Rhode Island. Two taps of the screen finally opened a window.

Address: 7445 Polo Court Drive
Vehicles: White 4dr Tacoma 23-KYSI
Black 4dr Land Cruiser 24-RREW
Family is away
The target is in house
No unusual activities.
Returned from airplane trip 7:00 AM June 11

No further information at this time. Bettawfeeq Inshallah

Two more taps opened the attachments that gave pictures of the target, dated 2003 and 2004, in uniform and civvies, and pictures of the house and a driveway leading up toward the house.

Traffic finally began to break up, as two ambulances raced counterflow to those waiting to cross the bridge into the historic town of Newport. The man smiled. It was time to get to work. He reached for the GPS and input the address. He had 14.7 miles to go.

"You can run, SEAL, but you'll just die tired. Allahu Akbar."

CHAPTER THIRTY-FIVE

0830 June 11, 2011
Sikorsky Memorial Airport Stratford, Connecticut

Greg Lynche lined up the YO-3A on the short grass strip. The two-story farmhouse and barn held plenty of vehicles, mostly trucks and tractors. He looked for a windsock, found a small red one indicating a slight, steady crosswind. Double-checking the wind direction on his GPS, he was satisfied. He had the throttle on idle, flaps full, and gear down, with the aircraft's nose pointed toward the end of the strip. No aircraft were in the area or on the ground.

"Double-check one, two, three gear down," he said, momentarily recalling the lapse that led to his new routine of double-checking, placing his fingers on the three landing gear position indicators to show they were indeed down and locked.

It was several months since he had flown 007. Duncan was the designated pilot for the operation. Although Greg flew when they were airborne, it was rare that he took off or landed the aircraft. There were no pleasure flights with 007. It was a top secret workhorse under a Special Access Program contract with the CIA.

007 had been flown in daylight only once in the last ten years—and that was today. He worried he'd do something stupid with the tail dragger and ground loop the aircraft after touchdown or smash the brakes and flip it tail over nose, with no wind, in the daylight.

"OK, Lynche. Just like all the other landings. Don't fuck this up. Gear down triple-check." He was distinctly nervous.

The owners of the private landing strip never heard the aircraft circle overhead, land, or taxi to the far end of the treeline. Lynche powered up the engine and spun the tail around for an expeditious departure, keenly aware of the Wraith's extended wings. He shut down the engine, selected Battery *OFF*, raised the canopy, and unbuckled his shoulder and lap belt and his helmet chin strap. The farmhouse and vehicles were at his two o'clock. No one came running out with a shotgun, pitchfork, or camera.

He already decided he'd wait until someone from the house came to investigate. The benefit of having a noiseless aircraft was that one could operate unobtrusively. Still, it was hard to hide a matte black, one-of-a-kind, spy plane in plain sight.

While he waited, he typed into his BlackBerry his GPScoordinates, and that he was safe on deck twelve miles north of the old Bridgeport airport, now called Sikorsky Memorial in tribute to Igor Sikorsky of flying boat and helicopter fame.

Hunter responded with a text message. He, too, was on the ground and on his way. He called Lynche's house from the FBO. No one answered, and Nazy didn't reply to his text messages. Text messaging became the communication mode of choice. When encrypted, texts enabled complete privacy to exchange messages with each other without fear of compromising or intercepting the message.

The BlackBerries carried by Nazy, Lynche, Hunter, and the two Bobs used data network authentication using an unbreakable encryption key. The software successfully passed highly advanced security tests conducted by the Israeli Ministry of Defense, and the CIA's Science and Technology Directorate. What the team didn't want to do was come under the scrutiny of the NSA's ECHELON computers, which could break any encrypted voice or data transmission. They felt they were flying under the DCI's radar, but Nazy's last text message and the lack of an answer at Lynche's house phone gave Hunter increasing cause for concern.

Before the three men implemented their plan to find and

interdict the sniper that may or may not be on his way to Newport, text messages were sent to Bob and Bob: Come to the factory ASAP. Need the support gear/trailer plus fuel. Plz hurry and be safe.

CHAPTER THIRTY-SIX

1730L June 11, 2011
USS Texas, SSN-775 Diego Garcia, Indian Ocean

In a ceremony that traced its origin to Navy Lieutenant John Paul Jones, Captain Danny Cox presented himself to the Officer of the Day, saluted, and, in command voice, said, "Request permission to leave the ship, Sir."

The ODD responded, "Permission granted, Sir," returned the salute, and piped the captain off the Texas. Over the 1MC, the OOD announced, "DEVGRU, departing."

Captain Cox took two steps down the gangway, turned toward the stern, saluted the national ensign, about-faced, and continued down the gangway onto the pier. A sedan and driver awaited the SEAL Team Six commander to take him to the Bachelor Officer Quarters.

Two hours earlier, Captain Cox had returned from SOCOM for the second time in a month. A week after the highly publicized takedown of Osama bin Laden, several SEALs from the mission were conspicuously missing, with other members of DEVGRU filling in for their friends still in the war zone. After a weeklong goat rope encompassing a couple of dog-and-pony shows and a grip-and-grin photo op between SEALs and POTUS, Cox became increasingly more furious and concerned. The president suddenly seemed to have discovered the military and how wonderful it was. SEALs and especially Team Six were national heroes for taking out Osama bin Laden, and the Pentagon and SOCOM looked to milk the operation and the SEALs' success for everything they could.

Cox debriefed SECDEF and SOCOM and strenuously

voiced his concern that the continued focus on DEVGRU operations and tactics would likely jeopardize future operations and the men's personal safety.

"There will be retaliation," he said sharply. "It's just a matter of when. This shit needs to stop. Anything further that comes out could damage our operational security, might reveal tricks of the trade, and could endanger our families. *This shit must stop and now!*"

The SOCOM commander agreed and SECDEF came around to their thinking. A public affairs statement was issued, and the SECDEF briefed the president to cool it. After the brouhaha died down, as Captain Cox headed back to Baghram, the OOD informed him a retired SEAL died in Colorado under suspicious circumstances. Under normal conditions, he would have gotten more information and attended the funeral. Over the years, SEALs developed a somber ritual for a downed comrade, and a funeral wasn't to be missed unless a SEAL was otherwise engaged, like at war.

Cox significantly underestimated the challenges ahead. Over the previous month, he and his little band of co-conspirators were frustrated and grumbling about what they should have done and what needed to be done. Whatever struck the SEAL commander as the right and proper thing to do with the world's most wanted terrorist later came to strike him as folly.

"We should've just killed him," he told the USS Texas commander, a Naval Academy and Naval War College classmate.

Danny Cox and Dallas Smith were roommates at Annapolis and remained close. Dallas knew Danny would do great things in the SEALs, and Danny knew Dallas would do great things in the submarine corps. At the USS Texas change of command, Captain Cox was invited to say a few words.

"Who else would be better to command this amazing boat than someone named Dallas, who was born in Amarillo and has brothers named Houston and Austin?"

Cox knew he probably overstepped the bounds of friendship by involving Dallas and the Texas, but Dallas Smith disagreed strenuously.

"Ox, I know you'd do the same for me if the roles were reversed. I think you did an incredibly brave thing. In hindsight, with everything you told me, there wasn't any other choice. My assessment is this will take a little longer than you'd like. We have to get him to the right place in the hands of the right guys. That's our job. The Texas is the right boat at the right time to help."

Cox grabbed the man's outstretched hand and squeezed.

Danny Cox was a very hard man, and the strain on him was incredible.

Dallas Smith watched the eyes of the big man called Ox. He thought they would well up, but they did not. Ox quickly composed himself and took a deep breath. "Yes, but where and who?"

"I think we need outside help, someone with connections."

"That leaves only one dude—Bullfrog."

"Bullfrog?"

"Captain Bill McGee. He was the Team Six commander who led the first S&D into Afghanistan after 9/11. Shit for brains was already in Pakistan. The man's a legend in SEAL circles and he has connections out the wazoo. He and I spent time at the CIA, Team Six at different times, but even there, he was a rock star."

"Sounds like a real patriot."

"He is and he can keep a secret. I'll see if he can help. If anyone can at our level, it's him. Either that, or he can give us a vector. We need something more than just holding the bastard in the brig."

Cox unlocked his BOQ room and dropped his kit on the sofa. He sat at the desk, pulled a laptop from his briefcase, turned it on, and accessed the Internet. He'd been thinking what Dallas said and thought for a moment that he and Dallas could be shot for perpetrating one of the greatest bait-and-switch routines in history. When the President wanted Osama bin Laden killed instead of captured and interrogated for everything in his head, Cox couldn't execute the order or complete the mission. Killing Osama bin Laden was the right thing, but with the president changing the op order just as Team Six was about to embark aboard the helicopters, Cox knew something was very wrong. The plan had always been to snatch him, take him alive, and pump him for info.

Following the president's bidding would clearly have been a high crime, if not outright treason. Months of practice to ensure the team could take Osama bin Laden alive came down to a phone call to change the plan.

As the clock ticked down to their time to mount up and depart, Cox told his team, "We want to know what's in that fucker's head. Too many innocent people died because of that fuckstick. The American people want to know what's in his head, so we can find out who his buddies are, hunt them down, and kill them. I want to know what's in that fucker's head. I want to empty it and then fill it with something more than lead. He won't get off easy with a bullet in the brain. He needs to talk. He's going to talk, and he's going to pay."

When the assault team lifted off from its base in Afghanistan and headed to Pakistan, the recurring question of why the president wanted Osama bin Laden dead remained unanswered. The situation created a conflict within Cox. For twenty-five years, his job was to follow orders, kill America's enemies, protect his country, and complete the mission.

The president gave him an illegal order. He wanted SEALs to cheat thousands of families who lost loved ones and wanted vengeance. The president wanted Cox to cheat millions of Americans out of what was rightfully theirs.

Vengeance didn't come from a quick shot to the head.

In the helicopter, drowned out by engine and transmission noise, Captain Danny Cox vowed, "I'll kill his ass, but not before I've extracted every bit of intel from him, then I'll cheat that fucker out of his seventy-two virgins."

Five weeks later, no one would have believed that a handful of SEALs could have orchestrated the death of Osama bin Laden in his bedroom, only to have him sitting quietly in the brig of one of America's newest attack subs, awaiting interrogation.

CHAPTER THIRTY-SEVEN

0800 June 11, 2011
7445 Polo Court Drive Newport, Rhode Island

McGee made it very difficult for any long-range sniper to reasonably target him around his property. He moved robotically. He walked, stopped, and faked a step in one place, and then went in another. He ran until he was inside the house.

Once inside, he raced to the basement, where he kept excess gear and weapons accumulated over thirty-five years of naval service. He rummaged through several parachute bags, stuffed with different uniforms, and selected two dark-green ghillie suits, two sets of dark camouflage tops and bottoms, and half a dozen armored vests of different weights and materials, Kevlar and ceramic.

He carried them upstairs and dumped them on the sofa. Returning to the basement to one of three 2.5-foot-by-5-foot gun safes, he keyed in the electronic code, unlocked, and opened the door. Taking a deep breath and mentally inventorying what he felt he needed, he first withdrew a heavily customized M-4 with laser sights. From the top shelf, he grabbed a single fully-loaded, extended-length clip; he slammed it home and pulled the charging handle. He was locked and loaded with the selector set to SAFE.

His next selection was a Weatherby .300 Magnum with 12x scope, laser sighted to 1,000 yards. He rocked a box of ammo toward him and extracted six rounds, pushed two into the magazine, and racked another in the chamber. Checking the safety was on and scope covers removed, he set it aside.

He removed a pair of Kimber Tactical Custom 1911 pistols. From the top shelf, he selected a pair of magazines, checked they were hollow-points and fully loaded, rammed the clips into the handles, and pulled the slides, chambering a round before flipping the safety selector to On. He slid one into a holster, and the other went into the space between the small of his back and his cargo pants.

From the bottom of the safe, he took out four medium-sized plastic cases containing binoculars, spotting scopes, and NVGs. He closed the safe, gathered his weapons and optics, and climbed the stairs.

Over the next thirty minutes, he established a sniper hide in his living room. He closed all blinds except for the ones covering the large picture window facing the driveway. He arranged some of the furniture in the center of the room, then removed lamps to the dining room, overturned the sofa, brought two coffee tables close and draped camouflage uniforms over everything. One spotting scope was set up on a table to look out over the driveway and out past the road.

As he placed the spotting scope on the table, he didn't see a white van trundle down the road or the driver who looked carefully at the house up the long driveway. McGee was determined if a sniper was able to target and kill his fellow warriors, then a sniper was needed to neutralize another sniper. He told Hunter and Lynche that the other SEALs never knew they were targeted for assassination. If they knew, they would have taken aggressive action to protect themselves and their fellow SEALs. They would have gone on the offense and hunted the would-be hunter.

Like most professional warriors—SEALs, Green Berets, Rangers, and Marine Recon—they weren't only users of weapons, they were masters. Over time, professional warriors experimented with different types of combat arms, from those that were merely useful to those that were purely lethal. They collected those that impressed them.

McGee's collection of weapons reflected raw lethality and elegance, and he selected the cream from thirty years of firearms testing to become his crop. His only hope was that his counterattack effort wasn't misdirected. He shifted the armor plate on his chest, as he hunkered behind the slightly armored hide and dragged a laptop toward him to send text messages to Hunter and Lynche that he was safe at home. Phase one was in place.

While he ate a banana, McGee relaxed for a moment and checked his e-mail. There wasn't any other SEAL or trusted agent in the Newport area for him to be friendly with. He was comfortable teaching graduate school for coming generations of warriors at the Naval War College, but, when he finished class, he looked forward to coming home and seeing his family.

Workouts at the gym dropped off to three times a week, not three times a day. He felt the time spent with his growing family was more important. His girls were nearing driving age, and he looked forward to intimidating any young stud who cast an eye toward one of them. The love of his life, his kindred spirit, Angela, drove him wild with pride and passion. Three former wives couldn't compete with the service to his country and his young SEAL pups. He wanted to live long with Angela at his side. He didn't want it to end.

Not surprisingly, the e-mail in his in box was filled with hysteria, anger, grief, or bravado from other SEALs who became aware of the string of friends who died of terminator bullets to the chest. He shifted his position, moved his chest protector slightly, becoming more attuned to his predicament. As he scrolled through the list of e-mails, one stuck out. It was from Ox, Danny Cox, SEAL Team Six Commander and hero of the free world.

"What does Ox have to say? I hope he isn't gloating."

The e-mail was two short lines: Got your buddy. Any ideas what to do with him?

McGee was confused. "Got my buddy? What the hell does that mean?" He checked the date and time and saw the e-mail was sent only twenty minutes earlier.

That made no sense. Was the message hung up in cyberspace for a month and was finally being delivered? His heart racing, he put his head in his hands as he rubbed his eyes.

"I would've thought my buddy would mean OBL, but OX and the Team delivered his ass to Allah. What's he trying to...?"

McGee's head jerked up, his eyes wild. He moused and clicked Reply, then typed, There are times when cheating is the most sacred of duties. What can I do to help?

Two minutes passed, then he received a reply. Need a better place to play 20 questions. Plan to leave Texas soon.

McGee burst out in loud, raucous laughter. He hadn't laughed so hard in a very long time. "Holy shit. That's incredible, Ox. You're fucking incredible." He was struck by the incongruity of the situation and was ready to type a reply when a new message appeared in his In Box

Hope to catch the 775 Thursday. May be OOA/C for a month. He typed quickly. Let me work a pickup. Check back in 24? McGee, setting his laptop aside, sat upright, the M-4 and Weatherby at his side. He stole a peek over the camouflaged sofa, as his mind raced. Ox had gone rogue. It wasn't like him to wander off the reservation—not Ox. After almost ten years of chasing Osama bin Laden and the highly publicized victory tour by the president, the IC and SOF communities were livid that the terrorist mastermind hadn't been captured and interrogated as planned.

"Something pretty dramatic must have happened for Ox to snatch and hide him," he mused, unable to think of a reason for it.

Why hadn't the team captured Osama bin Laden and interrogated him? They'd still be heroes, and America would still love them.

The only weird thing had been the president's recent actions. Suddenly, he acted like the military was a great thing. His newfound concern and admiration for the men and women in uniform was completely bogus. There was nothing in there that would make Ox snatch Osama bin Laden and hide him.

Then McGee realized someone changed the orders.

SECDEF couldn't do it unilaterally. Only POTUS had that power.

"Holy shit. Ox, you're a true patriot." McGee became excited when he thought about what his friend did and the ramifications of being able to ask Osama bin Laden twenty questions, as Ox put it. He needed to talk to Lynche and Hunter. That was more their area of expertise—when you're inside the other side of Special Access. McGee reflected he would still need help and thought, *Maybe the old spook still knew how to conduct a rendition or a place to interrogate someone.*

"And, maybe I can be part of it," he said. "If I survive this."

He sent a quick text message to Hunter and Lynche. Have to make sure I live. Need you more than ever. Have new info.

He set the laptop aside five minutes later without getting a reply. A little dejected, he reflected for a moment and said, "I wonder who the hell they dumped in the IO?"

CHAPTER THIRTY-EIGHT

0800 June 11, 2011
Office of Security
CIA Headquarters Washington, DC

Nazy Cunningham looked like the impeccably dressed senior intelligence service executive in a gray suit skirt, white silk blouse, black pumps, and free-flowing hair spilling across her shoulders.

A black backpack over her shoulder provided a little incongruity, as the security guards overtly admired the view. Her heels clicked across the stainless and granite headquarters entrance.

After four hours of fitful sleep on the sofa, she dragged herself down to the HQ gym for a workout and shower. She was alone in the aerobics and cardio room, lifting a few weights. After nearly an hour of intense exercise, she went to the women's locker room, where she undressed, wrapped a towel under her arms, and entered the sauna.

Nazy sat down, pulled her legs to her chest, and broke down. She was on the edge of confusion and drifting toward helplessness. Duncan was always there to listen to the trials and tribulations of the new immigrant and high performing intelligence officer. He was there to catch her when she "got too far over my skis," as she learned to say. He was demonstrably proud of her and highly supportive of and confident in her abilities. Between sobs, she just wanted him to look at her, talk to her, hold her, tell her she'd be OK, and they'd take a vacation soon.

The material in the two books was comprehensive, with information and dispatches from MI6 and Mossad detailing the activities of the skinny, chain-smoking kid with big ears and a penchant for making friends with some of the world's most lethal terrorists. Suddenly, he was the President of the United States.

Drenched in sweat, with tears rolling down her face, she slowly calmed herself, left the sauna, and walked naked to the shower. Composed and invigorated, she dressed quickly as if going to a meeting, tossed her backpack over her shoulder, and headed toward the parking garage.

She entered her red Mercedes SL380 and immediately checked her BlackBerry for messages from Duncan and exchanged short notes that she'd been successful, was frightened, and needed to see him soon. She didn't understand why he wanted her to go to Greg Lynche's, but it seemed important to him, and he was being protective of her. Duncan was guiding her and it made her smile.

She glanced at her backpack, then out the front window. The old Mercedes started easily and the air-conditioning hummed in the background as she drove. Soon, she turned toward the main gate.

As she approached security, she slowed and braked for the black-clad, M-4-toting security guards. She rolled down her window, and the guard's eyes rocketed from her legs and eyes to her décolletage.

She presented her blue badge.

"Ms. Cunningham, the Chief of Security has authorized a random search of your vehicle. Please turn off the engine, exit, and open the doors, hood, and trunk. Please provide your badge, license, registration, and proof of insurance."

Nazy momentarily froze, then lowered her head and complied, removing documents from her console and purse. "I've never had to do this before. Is this normal procedure?"

One armed guard positioned himself to watch her slide from the sports car. "Yes, Ma'am. This is normal, just a random spot check. Your badge and license?"

The three guards attempted to maintain their professionalism, but Nazy saw their eyes following the movement of her legs in the car. She pulled the hood and trunk levers, mashed her knees together, opened her door, and swung her legs over the sill and stood. She walked around the car to lift the trunk and open the passenger door. Bending over to unlatch the hood, she lifted it before walking back to the gate.

The three men watched her closely. Thinking the bored guards had the show they wanted and the stop was part of the harassment package for leaving the compound on Saturday morning, she was momentarily distracted when the guard on the other side of the car removed her backpack from the front seat and emptied it onto the car's convertible top.

She hesitated, unable to shout, "No!" Frozen in place, she nearly fainted when the guard extracted the stack of books, looked at them, and thumbed through each. When he closed the books and continued rummaging through her gym bag, she turned to the other two and watched indifferently as one guard scrutinized her documents and copied information onto his clipboard.

From her peripheral vision, she saw the other guard replace the books in the backpack and replace it on the seat. After her papers and badge were returned, she walked around the car to close the trunk, passenger door, and hood before getting in the driver's side. She brought her knees together and slid into the seat, moving her legs under the steering wheel, as she gently closed the door. It wasn't the time for her to lose her composure. She wanted to slam the door, but her fury and fear were contained for the moment.

"Thank you for your participation, Ms. Cunningham. Have a great day."

The guard in the shack picked up the telephone, as the little red car drove off. He was answered before the second ring.

"Security, Jamerson," a voice said.

"You're right, Jim. She does have the best legs in Virginia."

CHAPTER THIRTY-NINE

1700 June 11, 2011
7445 Polo Court Drive Newport, Rhode Island

McGee studied the activity along the treeline. For several hours, squirrels intermittently played chase while birds flitted about. He panned the spotting scope left and right, looking for disturbances in the background, his mind taking pictures and comparing them to his mental archive. Nothing changed.

Hunting for a professional sniper trying to get into a firing position undetected is very challenging but not impossible. At scout sniper school, the final exam for newbies was the culmination of a land-navigation course to get into the general area, evaluate the surroundings and environment to improve a ghillie suit that would mesh with that environment, and transition to conceal and maneuver.

Graduates learned their lessons and tricks to move so slowly that multiple spotters couldn't detect them reaching a firing position even in daylight. When the sun started falling in the west, detecting subtle changes in the background was nearly impossible unless the sniper made a mistake and telegraphed his location and intentions. Treelines were especially useful to hide in if the shot could be made from deep within the foliage, not from the edge. Animals would flee from humans tromping around in the brush and cover, and avoided them as quickly as they could.

Evidence of someone moving in the bush was usually the sudden appearance of birds leaving the area. After birds left, usually four-legged critters scattered to make room for the intruder.

Once the sun set, the rules changed. McGee recalled his participation and successes and failures during Broken Lance exercises, parachuting into an area at night and quickly navigating across unknown territory to get into position with GPS and night-vision goggles to illuminate the way. Animals rarely refused to get out of the way and would highlight an intruder's presence.

Several small animals at the wood's edge maintained their search for food and weren't alarmed. A pair of rabbits munched grass at the edge of the trees, and a pair of squirrels raced around another. McGee maintained his vigilance at the spotting scope when his mobile device vibrated. Lynche was on his way and Hunter was nearing Newport.

It might not occur that day or the next, but the three men were positive a sniper would come for McGee and had to be in the area. The pattern of the killings, the modus operandi, the logistics and timing virtually assured them that the killer of the SEALs was either bearing down on Newport or was in town preparing for the hit. They felt the momentum shift in their favor. Unlike the SEALs and their friends, who were killed one-by-one, McGee maintained a close network of friends and other SEALs, first through e-mail and then through social media. What began as a forum for students at the War College to stay abreast of class assignments, world events, and school programs grew into a hydra of chat rooms, blogs, and resumé banks.

McGee was connected, and, as events occurred and were reported daily, information, pictures, articles, and trends funneled into his mailbox. Through the noise of hundreds of email or social network postings, a picture emerged with a few SEALs passing away at different locations. That the three dead SEALs were related by three separate events might not have been noticed, except they were McGee's men in battle in Afghanistan, his classmates at the War College, and his teammates on Broken Lance.

Too many unique coincidences would have otherwise been missed. McGee analyzed the pattern of killings and the direction of travel of the killer. He and his friends were fully aware of the threat.

They went into full protection mode and had prepared to go on the offensive. All they needed was an op order from the Bullfrog. McGee called Hunter.

Lynche caught a break with the owners of the grass strip. A former Green Beret, who served in Vietnam, lived in the farmhouse with his son and daughter-in-law. The son was a former Army helicopter pilot who flew a crop duster and sprayed nearly every field in a seventy-mile radius of Bridgeport, Connecticut.

The father and son initially had difficulty believing Lynche's assertion that he was on his way to an air show and had to set the interesting black plane down for a precautionary emergency landing. When the two were invited to look at 007, Lynche was proud to show off his rare plane.

It looked fairly innocuous if not hideous with its huge canopy, long glider wings, and massive, six-blade propeller. The crop-duster pilot looked at it carefully, noticing it didn't have the required registration identifier on the side. He almost asked, "Where are your N numbers?" but thought better of it.

When a black airplane without identification lands in your back yard, it probably didn't pay to ask too many questions. Hidden from view was the equipment that made the YO-3A a bloodhound of the sky—the forward looking infrared thermal- imaging gyroscopically stabilized ball was folded into the fuselage when not in use or stowed for takeoffs and landings.

The former Green Beret looked over the aircraft, from nose to tail and tried to remember when he'd seen something like it. His son studied the aircraft with a skeptical eye. The black paint, huge six-bladed propeller, and twenty-foot muffler screamed it was a spy plane.

"That's a Yo-Yo!" his father suddenly shouted. "I remember now. I knew they were called something strange, and I remember they were...hugely successful."

"What do you mean, Dad?"

"There was a small number of these aircraft. They weren't painted like this, but they were the original stealth airplanes. They were so quiet, the Cong couldn't hear them. They flew only at night over Vietnam and Cambodia. Those pilots never came back from a mission without contacting the enemy. What else? Oh, yeah, those Yo-Yo pilots couldn't do enough for us. I don't know of anyone who took a round. That's one special airplane, Mr. Jones."

As the son listened to the old man, he walked around the aircraft for a better view of the instrument stacks in the cockpits. With the canopy raised, the crop duster noticed the flat glass panels, few analog gauges, and the data plate in the cockpit.

Manufactured by the Lockheed Corporation Type: Y03A
Serial Number: 007
Date of Manufacture: 02-14-1969

"Lockheed," the crop duster said. "Maker of the most famous spy planes. Forty years old. Never seen anything like it. Damn…."

"Damned if it doesn't look like one of them spy planes James Bond would've flown," the young man said, obviously picking up on an unstated theme.

The Green Beret and Lynche looked at each other, as if sharing a telepathic secret.

"Maybe your kinda air show and mine are different," the father suggested.

Lynche raised his eyebrows with a grin that garnered the old man's approval.

"You need anything, Mr. Jones, you just ask."

The son wanted to retreat into the house and let the thin old guy alone with his strange airplane.

"Thank you, Sir," Lynche said. "My partner will be here soon with some parts, then we'll be on our way."

"No bother, Mr. Jones. If you need to come back here for any reason, please feel free to drop in. You made an old man's day. Thank you, Sir."

"Much obliged, Sir."

* * *

Nazy Cunningham checked in near the time that Duncan arrived at the grass strip. She was safe at Greg Lynche's house. Taking a circuitous route to Annapolis, she wasn't followed.

Connie and Nazy had a long girl talk about their men, their work, and what was in the black backpack. Connie was highly skeptical of Nazy's analysis of the documents bound under the hardcover and dust jackets until she reviewed them herself.

Nazy was enthralled at the dozens of cardinals and sparrows on several hanging bird feeders suspended from trees in the Lynche's back yard. Connie sat in stony silence at the kitchen table, reviewing page after page of the scanned material. She and Greg voted for Republicans and Conservatives for the past thirty-odd years, but they voted for the Democratic candidate during the recent election, believing he might do an OK job. Connie hoped change was finally in the air. It was more a vote against the weak Republican candidate and his squeaky-voiced vice presidential nominee.

Connie was the more-vocal supporter of the president when Duncan visited. He knew how to get her politics cranked up by throwing barbs at the man and his administration. Over time, Duncan was convinced he was a flaming communist and a charlatan.

Suddenly, Connie found herself reading classified documents that exquisitely demonstrated that the man in the White House was someone other than whom he and the media portrayed. One item of interest came through several documents. Dispatches from the UK and Israeli intelligence services, some dated fifteen years earlier, proved that the man holding the highest office in the land had been a British national for almost thirty years; not American. The rumors from the political right wing, that the president and his friends were spending millions of dollars to keep the range of scholastic, passport, and birth records from public view, were laid bare before her eyes in the CIA files.

Provided by both MI5 and MI6, the files contained copies of college applications, transcripts highlighting non-residency and poor academic performance, bank records, and a British passport that demonstrated several dozen visas and significant foreign travel, primarily to the Middle East. The British Secret Intelligence Service Foreign Section provided several transcripts of conversations with reputed or known terrorists in Pakistan and Afghanistan involving the young man while attending US colleges, including two meetings with Osama bin Laden and several members of the al-Qaeda hierarchy in the late 1980s and early 1990s.

Forty pages into one book, Connie couldn't contain her embarrassment and pain any longer and collapsed, sobbing. Thirty minutes later, she and Nazy deposited the two books in Lynche's safe in the basement, knowing the information could be life-threatening to whomever carried them.

They put Nazy's Mercedes into the garage, out of sight, and Connie drove them to the Annapolis Yacht Club for dinner. They hoped men in black helicopters and black uniforms with black guns wouldn't come for them.

Hunter transferred weapons and body armor from 007 to his rental car. He and Lynche playfully synchronized watches before starting out for Rhode Island.

In a couple hours, the Wraith would be airborne again with Lynche at the controls and using FLIR to spot the shooter.

* * *

When three deer bolted from the copse, McGee was shocked but not surprised. He knew a killer would come to the woods, and he finally arrived. He brought his laptop close and typed a brief message.

He's here. Right on time.

CHAPTER FORTY

2030 June 11, 2011
7445 Polo Court Drive Newport, Rhode Island

Hunter felt a touch of nostalgia while crossing the apex of the bridge leading into Newport. The Naval War College brought a smile to his face, and warm memories flooded his thoughts. He wondered if the two mothballed aircraft carriers that had been his turnaround point when he jogged were still tied up to the north. He barely saw them between bridge parts flashing by. He tried unsuccessfully to locate Building 7 in the distance, his home away from home for a year and the place where he taught Nazy how to make love to the Moody Blue's *The Other Side of Life.*

Hunter relived certain salacious events when he realized the vehicle ahead was braking, and he almost rear-ended the pickup. He still had a young man's reflexes and crushed the brake. Though he over-steered, he mercifully avoided a collision.

The spike of adrenalin made his skin tingle and shot his heart rate up, making his face flush. Everything from the passenger seat shot out of it and now lay on the floor.

"That would have been bad," he muttered. "That woman will be the death of me, but I'll die with a smile."

He powered around the truck that trundled ahead of him, the driver not realizing he almost had a Camaro impaled on his bumper hitch.

The GPS gave directions to where McGee felt Hunter should make his approach to the wooded area. Traffic was light once Duncan got through town and headed north and east of Newport. Winding his way through the Rhode Island countryside, one minute after turning from the smooth roadbed onto a poorly maintained road, the husky GPS female voice announced, "Destination on the left."

Hunter saw a long strip of tall trees in the distance to his right. As the bumpy road swept left, his headlights illuminated a line of evergreens and a small, low-level sign that read, Wet Socks Curve.

A minute later, his headlights marked the rear of a van with old, black California tags and a pair of extension ladders on the roof.

"And no external markings," he said softly, creeping along until he parked in a cutout 100 yards from the other vehicle. The dusty white van looked out of place on a deserted lover's lane near the ocean frontage.

Hunter sat for a second, then slid down in the bucket seat, anxiously reached behind him and retrieved helmet bags, one after the other, and his body armor vest. He wiggled out of his sweatshirt, flipped the vest over his head, and snugly fastened the Velcro strips.

From one bag, he extracted earphones and an AN/PRQ-7 handheld radio; stuffing the ear buds into his ears and the jack into the radio, and turning on the volume. As the radio hissed in his ears, running through its algorithms, Hunter replaced his arms and head in the sweatshirt.

He keyed the microphone. "Ramrod, Maverick."

"Go, Mav," Lynche replied.

"Where you at?"

"I should be there in three or four mikes. Give me a vector?"

Hunter rolled down the window and fished out an IR beacon from the helmet bag. He turned it on and placed it on the car roof. Only someone with NVGs would be able to see the pulsed IR focused upward in a cone.

"Tally ho, Sir. Be there soon."

"Ramrod, there's a van parked just south of me. Can you see if anyone is in it or in the area?"

"Ten-four, Mav. Anything for you."

Hunter rummaged through the bags and extracted a Taser and spare clip, a handful of thick plastic restraining strips, his helmet and NVGs, and a medium-sized zipper pouch containing a six-inch .357 Magnum Colt Python.

"I have you, Mav. No one's in the van. It's fairly cool. I don't see anyone in the immediate area, just some deer. Shut that beacon off."

Hunter retrieved and extinguished the beacon before rolling up his window.

"Are you ready?"

"As ready as I can be. Bullfrog says he's right where he should be, and you just said there's no one in the area. The shithead has to be hidden pretty good in the woods if he isn't popping up on the FLIR. I'll let Bill know we're on the scene."

Hunter stepped from the car, clipped the radio to his hip, and placed the Colt in the holster at the small of his back. He energized his BlackBerry and sent a message to McGee.

2 here n on offense. Cover me.

* * *

The brush in New England was unlike anything he ever encountered. Thick brambles made crawling in a ghillie suit impossible. Every bit of loose material became snagged on thorns or fallen branches. He walked, hunched over to clear a way, slicing through vines and branches with garden clippers. Every twelve feet, he extracted, crushed, and dropped a chemlite to mark the path.

Ingress was more difficult than anticipated. He should have gotten into position sooner. He might have to spend the night if the current opportunity was missed.

The underbrush was damp and quiet underfoot. Annoyed and aggravated, he slowly stood, Russian NVGs strapped to his head. His height helped him look over the brush and fallen branches. The man cleared the area 180° to the right and 180° to the left. All was clear in the spit of woods and in the distance. Off to the west, he saw both farmhouses identified by overhead satellite photographs.

He was anxious to finish, because big money lay ahead.

He felt he could be a little reckless and plow through the brush without alerting any humans. There was no one within 700 yards, and the target was completely exposed at 1200 meters and would receive visitors in a few hours.

No one knew he was there—the ultimate ambush predator. The Brotherhood provided the necessary intel, but they probably just walked out there with binoculars to watch the man and his family to note what he did and when.

It was the last of the SEALs. Then he faced the long drive to Texas. First, he had another fifty feet to go before reaching the forward edge of the battlefield.

He bent, snapped, shook, and dropped another six-inch IR chemlite to mark his trail.

* * *

Duncan, wearing his helmet with the ANVIS-9s suspended in front of his eyes and battery pack on his back as a counterweight, found that walking with NVGs was a bigger challenge than flying with them. His AN/PRQ-7 radio was connected to the helmet pigtail, adding to the over-balancing problem.

As he walked toward the copse on the distance, the image in front of his eyes wobbled back and forth, and his brain immediately tried to overcompensate for the movement, making him dizzy.

He stopped, flipped up the NVGs, and the disorientation ceased immediately. "You can't walk and wear NVGs simultaneously, dummy," he muttered to himself.

Lynche provided a running commentary in Duncan's headset. With no other human activity between the vehicles and the woods, Duncan moved quickly to the edge of the wood, the expected point of intercept.

"Nobody?" he whispered. "Is the guy from the van over the side shrimp fishing?"

"Nobody," Lynche replied. "I have horses, cows, deer, and rabbits but no people. Well, you're people, but I don't see anyone else."

"Bullfrog texted he has him. He should be visible on the other side of this wood."

"I didn't see anything on that side. I've been focused on your approach to the back side of the wood. I think you're OK to the edge and move to the south. I'll work the opposite side to see if he's dug in or something."

"Good plan. Out." Light from the last-quarter moon came from a waning crescent above broken skies. Hunter put one hand on the helmet for stability and jogged the remaining distance to the copse. It was momentarily amusing to think he ran like Forrest Gump, but, as he decelerated, he became suddenly serious.

The trees seemed to suck all light from the area, and it was very dark. The moon was no help. He began to think it wasn't a good idea after all. He surveyed the area and flipped the NVGs over his eyes, then he almost jumped out of his skin when he saw an IR chemlite in the wood, illuminating a path into the copse of trees.

He froze, his mind racing. Of course he has NVGs! And standing here makes you a target! Do something, *big* dummy!

He scanned the area slowly for a human, gun barrel—anything. Finding nothing, he stepped away from the animal trail with the chemlite, reached to his side, unclipped the PRQ-7, and hit the transmit button twice to get Lynche's attention.

"Yes, Mav?"

He typed a message on the keyboard and read on the LCD. IR chemlites at entry. Where is he?

Lynche responded, "No joy as of yet. Bullfrog's mail says he is in position. Copy?"

Hunter pressed the transmit button twice in reply. "Copy chemlites. Mav, the wood's 100 feet across. I say continue south and come up the face slowly. I'll drop down and see if he's dug in or is under a thermal blanket."

Hunter, pressed the button twice again, and moved

slowly to his left. With his left hand on the helmet, he patted the Taser in his pocket.

* * *

The McGee house was well illuminated. Porch lights flooded the landing with a yellow bulb to chase away bugs. The picture window was curtained with enough backlight to discern movement from outside if someone passed in front of a lamp. Miller, in position, studied his surroundings. He had a clear path to the front of the house.

Checking his digital watch, he said softly, "Thirty-five minutes to go, give or take."

* * *

McGee double-checked his NV scope through the crack in the door. He couldn't see the shooter or the barrel of his rifle, but he was convinced he was staring straight down the barrel of death with an eight-inch-wide silencer.

He turned and typed a message.

* * *

Lynche's BlackBerry flashed red in the cockpit, but he didn't notice the message: Check rifle barrel with silencer the size of a two-liter soda bottle.

* * *

Lynche had the YO-3A on autopilot with altitude hold in a 15° angle of bank. He scanned the instrument panel for trouble and found none, so he resumed looking at the FLIR screen for large variations in thermal signature. There weren't any. The edge of the wood was filled with fallen trees and bushes and trash from years of farming and plowing. Some people tossed their refuse into the woods after climbing the cliffs and rocks near the ocean. The thermal signatures showed a hodgepodge of hots, colds, and irregular shapes, but nothing that looked like a human in a firing position—or any humans at all. Lynche felt increasingly frustrated, as he couldn't differentiate any semblance of a man hiding in the trees and trash. He saw Hunter clearly stalking the killer, but he couldn't find the shooter.

Greg Lynche's frustration spilled over into his radio. "Mav, hold your position. I can't find anything. You're coming up on an area that's hot with detritus, but I can't see anything that might be human. I've got trash, downed trees, and metal poles that might be fence posts. If I were trying to hide, that's where I'd be."

* * *

Hunter keyed the transmit button twice. He saw the area ahead. In the green shades of the NVGs, he vaguely saw what was bothering Lynche, but he couldn't make out anything human, either.

* * *

Lynche disengaged the autopilot and rolled the aircraft away from the wood, scanning his instruments and finally noticing the slow red flash of his BlackBerry reflecting off the standby attitude indicator.

The Wraith's wings wobbled, as he tried to fly with his left hand and manipulate the BlackBerry with his right. He pressed the track button to open the application and read, Check rifle barrel with silencer the size of a two-liter soda bottle.

Awareness hit him. "I saw that!" Lynche shouted angrily. "Fuck!"

Tossing the device into his shirt pocket, he rolled the aircraft over, back to parallel the treeline.

505

* * *

A small dirty pickup truck, with an illuminated Pizza Hut Delivery sign on top, slowed as it approached the entrance of the access road, turned off Polo Court, and headed toward the farmhouse, kicking up a rooster tail of dust. It was right on time.

Miller jammed the sniper rifle deep into his shoulder socket and calmed his breathing. Pressing the Russian NV scope to his eye, he watched the reticule stabilize on the door with a minor rise and fall of the crosshairs in syncopation with his soft breathing and heartbeat. He panned to the truck, bright triangle of light atop, then placed the crosshairs back on the front door.

* * *

The headlights filled the night-vision scope, saturating the electronics, and the internal safety software shut down the image in the scope. McGee instantly understood what his adversary had planned. He created an innocuous diversion to bring him to the door. He cursed at himself as he should've anticipated that.

The sniper counted on the resident confronting the driver at the door. McGee would walk into the telescope's crosshairs, fully exposed for the critical seconds of the bullet's flight, as the sniper squeezed off his shot.

When the truck stopped in front of the house, McGee had a decision to make.

* * *

Lynche engaged the autopilot, took his hands off the controller, and was back on the FLIR. He rolled the thumbwheel on the joystick controller to zoom in on Hunter with the bottle- looking device, also in view. In shades of

506

white and black, Lynche was immediately aware of the significance of the thing at the end of the long rod, and it took on a hideous, lethal quality.

He shouted into the microphone, "Mav, stop! You're almost on top of him. One o'clock, inside the treeline. He's under something, maybe a big tree. The big round thing is a silencer."

* * *

Hunter was in midstep when he heard Lynche's shouted warning and froze. He slowly turned his head toward one o'clock and saw the huge, round thing on the stick, but he didn't see what was attached to it. The silencers he was accustomed to seeing and what was in his eyepieces didn't register. He thought it was an old soda bottle and waffled in incredulity and disbelief.

"You're too close!" Lynche shouted. "Back up, back up, back up! Get out of there!"

Lynche helplessly watched Duncan slowly reverse course. Fear filled him, as he screamed into the microphone, "Get out of there! Move!"

* * *

The pizza delivery man braked to a stop, shut off his lights, and put the transmission into Park. He jammed to the music coming from the subwoofers and checked his cell phone for the time, making sure he would receive the $100 tip for delivery of three pizzas at exactly 9:30. He had one minute to go.

* * *

McGee knew he and the driver would be shot unless he acted fast. He shifted the plate on his chest, stood, and ran to all of the lamps, knocking them over and plunging the house into darkness.

He jumped back over the sofa and checked the NV spotting scope. It recovered, and, in the viewfinder, he saw Hunter stepping back very slowly. Hunter was in mortal danger and needed to run.

* * *

Miller heard something to his left. He slowly pulled his face away from the scope and faced the noise. He blinked at the silhouette of a man wearing a helmet and NVGs slowly stepping backward.

Adrenalin led shock. His heart jumped, as his mind realized someone knew where he was. His finger slipped from the trigger guard. His hand slid off the stock grip and into the cargo pocket of his pants. His hand went around the metal handle, and his finger went through the trigger guard while his thumb slid the safety to Off.

In one continuous motion, Miller pulled a silenced 9mm Sig Sauer from his pocket, aimed the laser pointer center mass, and shot the silhouette three times.

* * *

Hunter thought he was making great progress retreating quietly when he was suddenly blinded by light, pressure, and pain. The impact of the first bullet in his sternum threw him straight back. The second also found his sternum, and the third bullet slammed him hard and continued his rearward trajectory.

The soft-point bullets over-centered his body mass and overwhelmed his brain to respond to the fall. He went down flat on his back. The double jolt to his system knocked all the air from his lungs, replacing it with fire. His head hit the plowed earth hard enough to dazzle his eyes. Astonished at being shot, he struggled to breathe and fought to remain conscious.

*   *   *

McGee watched Hunter suddenly jerk backward and fall on his back. He moved to the Weatherby and fumbled with the stock and sight picture in a coordinated effort, forcing himself to remain calm. Through the NV scope, he acquired the huge silencer.

*   *   *

In the FLIR, Lynche watched the thermal energy of the hot bullets trace their impact into Hunter's chest. The energy expended in the body armor flared slightly in the FLIR, as Hunter fell.

"Nooo!" Lynche wailed. Hunter didn't move.

*   *   *

Miller slipped the NVGs over his eyes, looked, but didn't see anyone else. The interloper wasn't moving much. His body shook with shock. He raised his head toward McGee's house, where all the lights were out. The timing seemed odd.

He realized he'd been made and followed. He needed to abort the mission and leave. His mind racing, he realized going back through the woods would take too long. He needed to get out of there. First, he had clean-up work to do.

*   *   *

McGee jammed the stock into his shoulder, trying to steady the reticule bouncing in syncopation with his pounding heartbeat. The scope settled down in a few seconds, and he watched a dark mass emerge from the wood, the grotesque silencer on the rifle in one hand, a machine pistol in the other. He took up the slack in the trigger and was surprised when the firing pin slammed, sending the soft-point bullet downrange. He extracted the spent case, reacquired the dark mass, and fired twice more.

* * *

The Weatherby .300 Magnum belching fire from the doorway was enough to make the pizza driver freeze, turn down the music, and try to understand what just happened. When the second round cracked overhead four seconds later, a primal urge to flee took over.

He slammed the transmission into Reverse, stomped on the accelerator, put his head down, and backed up as fast as he could.

* * *

The dark mass of burlap, cloth, and twine moved purposely from the hide toward the downed man, a pistol visible in his hand. McGee knew the sniper would quickly close the distance and fire two shots into the body on the ground; he'd double-tap Hunter.

McGee's first round cracked over Miller's shoulder, making him duck and start for the body on the ground when a second shot cracked and tore through the heavy material at his waist, and jerked him around.

Miller stopped, reassessed the folly of going after the body, and fled. The third round cracked over his head, encouraging him to run hunched over along the treeline.

* * *

Lynche watched in rapt fascination as three white-hot laser beams traced a long path from the farmhouse to the wood, getting close to but missing the shooter. The minimal thermal signature of the shooter turned and ran along the edge of the trees toward the parking area. Lynche wondered what materials the man was wearing.

But he had to stop him. Lynche hadn't given much thought how he'd do that when he saw the shade of white thermal image of Hunter roll to his hands and knees, stand, stagger, and move after the shooter, in an arc like Hunter had just gone three rounds with Dizzy Izzy.

Lynche yelled and bounced around the cockpit like a frenzied cheerleader at a ball game.

* * *

"Yeah!" McGee shouted, seeing Hunter stand up.

In his excitement, he lost sight of the sniper and took several seconds trying to reacquire him in the scope. He saw Hunter chase the man down the treeline. McGee leaped to his feet, shed his body armor plate as if removing his shirt for a fight, grabbed his M-4, and raced out the front door.

* * *

The pizza driver had tried to drive in reverse, lost control, and found the only tree stump in the front yard with which to collide. His rear axle was suspended on the stump, wheels spinning.

When a huge black man came flying out of the house with an assault rifle, the driver squealed, "Shit!" stood on the brake, selected Drive, and mashed the gas.

When nothing happened, he fumbled for his phone and tried to call 911 on the touch screen, but his hands shook too hard and he couldn't manage it. When his fingers didn't work, he became petrified.

A truck approached from the house. The pizza driver knew he was going to be killed when the truck stopped next to his and the driver shouted, "Get into this truck. *Now!*"

After a one-second delay, the pizza driver did what he was told.

* * *

Hunter stumbled, wobbled, before finding his footing. He saw the different shades of the shape disappearing into the night, paralleling the treeline. His chest was on fire. Incendiary air filled his lungs with each step.

Hunter pressed his arms to his sides to keep his obliques still and moderate the pain that ran through his chest. As he closed the distance, he removed the helmet from his head and swung it at the top of the dark mass.

* * *

Lynche scanned his instruments and saw he was still in a level turn. He returned to the FLIR scope and shouted, "You're a fucking animal, Maverick! Get him! Get him! Get him!"

He watched Hunter collect himself and run toward the sniper, closing the gap with each stride. In a few seconds, which seemed to take forever from 1,000 feet, Lynche watched Hunter collide with the man, knocking both of them down in a heap.

"Tase him! Tase him!" he shouted.

The dark mass was down but recovered quickly. In seconds, it looked as if he was getting the best of Hunter. Lynche raised his head from the scope and looked around the cockpit for something—anything—to help Hunter. He paused, lurching forward as his brain tried to formulate a plan. In a flash, without looking, he reached left and down to the Laser Designator and Weedbusters control panels like he'd practiced in the simulator and flipped two switches on. The left multifunction display panel came alive.

Glancing at the FLIR scope, he saw the big man kicking Hunter's ass. Hunter fought back in slow motion, trying to kick the man's knees, only to miss like a drunken flailing fighter. Lynche returned to the instrument panel and punched a few letters on the multifunction display, keyboard, and selected FLIR under Control Options. Advisory system status illuminated on the MFD: LD Ready. WB Ready.

Lynche returned to the FLIR to watch the dark mass uncoil his shoulders faster than the rest of his body, and hit Hunter with a roundhouse with the back of his arm. Hunter took the blow hard and fell on his face. The white image of Hunter didn't move.

The hulking mass of shades of white rocked back and forth slightly. Lynche realized he would watch Hunter be killed a second time when the man started looking around for his rifle and pistol.

* * *

McGee shouted at the shocked, skinny youngster as he closed the door, "What's your name?"

He raced out of the driveway, spinning back wheels tried to find purchase after bouncing across the asphalt on the road, as they headed for the distant copse of trees.

"S...Steve. Steve Krasic."

"Steve, Bill McGee. We're heading across this field, hopefully to catch the motherfucker who almost killed you."

"What?"

"I shot at him first. Let's hope I tagged him before he gets away. Hold on."

* * *

Lynche programmed the dot on the FLIR viewing scope with the joystick, placed it a few feet in front of the slowly moving dark mass, and mashed the thumb button on the joystick.

BANG appeared before the mass of white. The laser designator carved out two-foot bright-red letters in front of the thermal mass. The software used for laser light shows at basketball arenas and carving Arabic letters in Afghani poppy fields produced the desired effect.

513

The man stopped, his arms hung out and forward as if catching a medicine ball.

"Come on, Asshole. Look up and smile for the camera," Lynche oozed ominously.

* * *

Miller was slightly dazed but furious that he'd been attacked. He had to get away, but he had to get his guns first and kill the infidel. He saw his rifle in the moonlight ahead and walked toward it when BANG appeared before him in big red letters.

He froze; he tried to understand where the laser came from. It had to be from above. He looked up and scanned the sky.

* * *

The FLIR captured every small movement in the varying shades of black and white of the mass. Adrenalin pounded at Lynche's temples, as he waited for the moment to attack. The man clearly saw the letters appear before him and was shocked still.

He stopped, trying to make sense of where the letters came from. The hulking glob of white energy decided it should investigate, not run, and slowly looked up.

* * *

Lynche read the man's body language perfectly. He pushed the coolie hat switch on the top of the control stick to select IR.

WB Armed appeared on the multi-function display and in the FLIR's symbology.

He zoomed the FLIR to max and placed the laser

designator low on the man's forehead. His thumb pressed the button on the control stick to Laser.

* * *

Miller's eyeballs exploded as the invisible laser beam shredded his corneas, irises, sclera, and eyelids, as if a hundred razor blades raced across his face at the speed of light. Vitreous media burst with the release of pressure and gushed down his cheeks.

Lynche released the switch after one full second. Miller's hands went to his eyes, but he was too late. Screaming in agony, he fell to his knees.

"You don't fuck with my partner, Asshole," Lynche screamed.

* * *

The primal scream of a man in agony jolted Hunter back to the present. He pushed his face out of the dirt and spat to clear his bloody dirty mouth. In the moonlight, Hunter saw the large mass writhing and screaming in agony a few paces away. Unsure what happened to him, Hunter struggled with a sense of urgency to make his arms and legs move and pushed himself up. He staggered for a moment, his damaged ribs screamed against any sudden or radical movement.

Nearly exhausted, Hunter slapped a pocket to check for the Taser. He struggled to draw the stun gun from the pocket and wobbled over to the screaming man who lay on his back, jammed the Taser against his side, and pulled the trigger. The man's body went rigid as 50,000 volts burned into his body.

Hunter collapsed and fell over. The Tasered man's body snapped taut, like instantaneous rigor mortis, and he stopped screaming. Points of light danced in Hunter's vision. He was in extreme pain but adrenalin flooded his body, as he anticipated the man recovering and fighting back once again as the Taser's shock wore off.

Forcing himself to reload the Taser, he rolled on his side and zapped the man again, this time in the neck. Feeling more energized, Hunter knew he didn't have much time. He pushed the pain of cracked ribs to a far corner of his mind and rolled the tall sniper onto his face.

Laboring with every breath, Hunter extracted the locking plastic handcuffs from his pocket. His ribs fought him with every exertion. Lights exploded before Hunter's eyes, as he pushed the man's hands through the openings and pulled the remaining strip of plastic tight. Hunter heard the zip of the strip across the tiny metal stop.

Sitting on the ground, Hunter looped plastic restraints over the man's legs, drew the straps tight, and fell over with exhaustion and pain, and curled up to protect his ribs. He rolled onto his back for sweet bliss and the release of pressure and pain.

* * *

One minute later, McGee and the pizza driver drove up to two humps on the field. They got out of the Toyota and McGee drew his pistol, running toward the mess of cloth and burlap. He didn't expect to find the man in the ghillie suit sobbing like a girl, hogtied, face down, ready for transport.

He saw Hunter on his back, breathing hard. Hunter rested, trying to catch his breath and look for Lynche and Wraith in the night sky. He didn't see anything, but he felt a disturbance in the air as the long-winged black bird flew low, right over his head.

The air shook as if an eighteen-wheeler doing 100 mph passed them standing on the roadside. The pizza driver, trying to make sense of what happened to him, was almost knocked down by the invisible pressure wave.

"What was that?" he asked. "Shit!"

Hunter looked at the kid and McGee, then asked, "Who are you?"

"The pizza guy," McGee deadpanned.

"You ordered pizza?" Hunter asked incredulously, his ribs killing him with the effort to speak.

"Steve, there's a flashlight in the glove box," McGee said. "Get it and see if you can locate any weapons out there. Duncan, are they in this area?"

Hunter labored to answer. "Yes, Sir. Thanks for coming to the rescue. There has to be a rifle…and a pistol. My helmet's out there. The asshole also had NVGs."

"Man, I thought you were dead. I saw you go down."

"Owww! I must've broken some ribs when that asshole shot me. I didn't search… him. Check him. The bastard's huge."

"I'll get him. What did you do to him?"

"I didn't do anything. He hit me hard and rang my bell. When I looked up, he was screaming, holding his face."

Miller, recovering from the debilitating stuns from back-to- back Tasers, whimpered from his shredded eyeballs. Steve returned, wide-eyed after collecting a rifle, a pistol, a fighter pilot's helmet, and a pair of night vision goggles with a head harness.

Duncan stood gingerly, relieving Steve of the helmet. "I have to get my NVGs. They must've fallen off when he shot me. I can get another battery pack. I hit that dude in the head, battery first. He has a hard head."

"Let's get him in the truck," McGee said, his tone menacing. "I want to talk with him." Duncan Hunter was too tired and hurt too much to reply.

The pizza driver and McGee dragged the trussed man to the back of the pickup and lifted him onto the tailgate, rolling him unceremoniously onto his side. Blood covered his face.

Hunter staggered toward where he thought his NVGs fell off.

Minutes later, aided by McGee's headlights, he found them, leaned over, and held them up for the others to see. He slowly walked to the truck and gingerly crawled into the rear seat, then he moaned with every bump as they drove out of the field. The pizza driver watched Hunter with fascination.

"Could someone please tell me what happened in the last five minutes?" Steve asked.

"Sure," McGee said. "The guy in the back seat stopped a terrorist trying to kill me after he killed five of my friends. Your terrorist buddy tricked you to get me to the door, so he could shoot both of us with that crazy rifle you picked up."

"Oh." Steve thought for a few moments, realizing the big man beside him probably saved his life. "What will happen to me?"

McGee parked behind his house and turned off the engine. "Steve, I really appreciate your help tonight. I know there'll be a lot of pressure on you to share what you saw. We can't afford to let that happen. If you talk about it tonight, somehow it will get back to some very bad people, and I can assure you they'll find you and hurt you and your family, in ways you can't imagine. Did I miss anything, Du...Maverick?"

"No Sir. I think that summed it up pretty well."

"You guys CIA or something?" Steve asked.

"Mr. Pizza Man," Hunter strained to say, "if we tell you, we'd have to kill you. The gentleman saved your life. You can repay the favor by keeping your mouth shut about all of this. You seem to be a nice guy. I don't want to kill you."

Steve Krasic took several breaths before looking at McGee. "I won't say anything. I promise. Thank you for saving my life."

"Forget about it," the former SEAL said. "I'm serious. You just need to forget about it. It's our little secret, OK?" He offered his hand.

"OK." Steve shook hands and realized the man's muscular hand could have snapped his like a twig. It was quiet for a moment, as if something passed between them, then he stepped outside.

Hunter's loud exhalation from the back seat broke the quiet. "Hey! Did you bring any pepperoni?"

CHAPTER FORTY-ONE

2200 June 11, 2011
7445 Polo Court Drive Newport, Rhode Island

Hunter was astonished when McGee pushed the kid's small pickup off the stump and got him on his way. Unable to help, Hunter supervised. Bill dragged the shooter from his truck without any care for the man's health or injury. A killer of SEALs wasn't going to be coddled.

"Stay here," McGee told Hunter. "I'll be right back."

"10-4. I have pizza." Duncan remained on the porch.

The retired SEAL quickly lowered the tailgate and rolled the man off the truck. He fell heavily to the ground, groaning and moaning, as he was moved. Completely defeated, he didn't try to fight back.

McGee dragged the overly tall man into the house by his feet, through the kitchen, and down the stairs to the basement, not caring that the man's head banged roughly on the stairs. He checked the man's plastic cuffs and lifted his head to study him. Blood covered his face and still oozed fresh streaks. He roughly wiped off his face. He'd never seen such a wound on a human being.

The word BANG was burned into his face across his eyes, or what was left of his eyeballs. All that remained were bloody sockets and what looked like thousands of minute, razor-thin cuts. Dropping the man's head on the floor, he walked upstairs.

"You'll keep," he said over his shoulder.

He went outside and touched Hunter's shoulder. "How are you doing? I think you earned that Trident tonight. Dude, you were awesome."

"Thanks, Bill. Just an average guy trying to do an above-average job."

They laughed. Hunter tried not to hurt himself. They looked at each other for a few seconds, then started talking simultaneously.

"There's something else...."

"I need to tell you...."

Hunter threw up a hand. "You first, Bill."

"Bin Laden's alive."

Hunter stared at him for a second, then slowly set down his pizza. Two could play that game. "Nazy found the file. The president's a documented fraud."

"That could be a problem."

"Constitutional crises are above my pay grade. What do you mean Osama bin Laden's alive? You mean it was a bait-and-switch? The public isn't supposed to know?"

"No. I'm fairly certain Ox called an audible at the line. The press played it up as a search and destroy, but, for whatever reason, they took him alive and didn't kill him. They're holding him. I expect Ox would like someone to relieve him of the turd, so someone could interrogate him. That's my interpretation."

Hunter was at a loss. Like a racecar with a broken transmission, he sat in place, trying to make his brain go. The past month had been one national photo-op orgy after another, one article of phony presidential courage and leadership after another. The slovenly press rolled over on its belly for the White House every way it could, while SEALs and special operations were touted as the new heroes of America against their will. Meanwhile, the president basked in the glory of media worship.

All the showboating was for naught. Osama bin Laden wasn't really dead. Why not? Suddenly, Hunter's brain started working and eliminated all possible motivations why a senior SEAL commander wouldn't execute his orders.

"It must've been an illegal or improper order," Hunter said, "or an order whose strategic implications were deliberately being ignored."

He knew that the on-scene SEAL commander must have

determined that killing Osama bin Laden wasn't a strategic imperative, while having him alive to tell his story was. That story would include the inner workings of al-Qaeda and where his supporters were the intelligence community didn't know about, along with other gems of information the National Counterterrorism Center would like to know. Dumping the body into the Indian Ocean was a red herring. The SEAL commander was a patriot for all the right reasons, while following some illegal order would have been wrong for all the wrong reasons.

The matrix logic picture came into focus, and Hunter grinned. "Now that's a patriot." He laughed, and it hurt, but he couldn't help himself.

McGee wasn't laughing.

Hunter stopped. "What are you thinking?"

"Danny Cox reached out to me to see if I could help. I don't know how, but I have friends with a jet and some senior contacts in the CIA."

"You're so lucky. Where is he?"

"The Indian Ocean, Diego Garcia. He's on a sub or will be soon."

"Diego Garcia? No shit. I killed a man there once, in my enlisted days."

"OK. How, pray tell?" McGee gave him an incredulous look, YGTBSM. He waved his fingers to indicate, Give me more.

"We were on a cruise. We pulled into port for fresh fruit, milk, and stuff. I weaseled my way off the boat and went to the racquetball courts for a game or two. I was totally screwing with this supply officer, running him back and forth, when he fell over and died. I thought he slipped and hit his head on the concrete floor. When I checked his pulse, I freaked and yelled for help. I did CPR, but nothing worked. His heart exploded. The Navy wasn't very happy with me and said I killed their supply officer."

"I can see the episode left you crushed."

"There was a moment when I thought I'd be thrown in

the brig—Marine enlisted turd killed one of the Navy's finest. It's not like I stabbed him. Anyway, Sierra Hotel. Do you and...?"

"Cox—Ox."

"Do you and Ox have a plan?"

"I was hoping you might come up with something. What about the president?"

"I'll have to come up with a plan for that." He pulled the pizza box close, picked up a slice, and bit into it.

"Can you come up with a plan for Osama bin Laden?"

"I can come up with one. How much time do we have?"

"They set sail Thursday, Diego Garcia time. I'm not exactly sure, but I think they have him squirreled away on a sub, the USS Texas. If I had him on a boat, I'd want him off before we pulled out of port. This is an incredible secret, and I can see if it gets too far from comfortable, Osama bin Laden really will be tossed over the side and we won't learn anything from him. Hell, it might already be too late."

Hunter's mind power-shifted through several gears, trying to keep up. "Ahhh. So there's a significant sense of urgency to make this happen. If we don't get there in time, do you know where they're heading? How would we get him off a sub?"

"I don't know where they're heading. Once underway, it could be months before they pull into port. If the sub has a SDV, a SEAL Delivery Vehicle, getting someone on or off is relatively easy. I expect they have one if Ox is highlighting the Dallas. It just depends."

"Where and when?"

"Right."

"Best to pick him up at Diego Garcia, I'd think."

"Probably."

"I think we can get there, but we may need help. Then we have to find a place to take him."

"I think that's the hard part." McGee looked away for a moment, then looked Hunter in the eye. "You have a better idea?"

"Not at this time. I'm still trying to assimilate all that happened since you called." He yawned, exhausted from being shot, fighting the sniper, and trying to use his brainpower to understand the latest revelations. Exertion and lack of sleep, plus intense pain, were getting to him. He fought back the idea that he was getting too old for crazy stuff.

Who else could do it? No one they knew could be trusted with the information on Osama bin Laden and the president, and do something about one or both of them. Greg might have a contact or two, but he was retired, and contacts for a couple of retired men were especially perishable and growing deader by the hour.

Maybe fatigue clouded his mind. More likely it was the realization that if something had to get done, it had to be by himself and Lynche.

The thought frightened him. "Bill, I don't know anyone else who can do this but Greg and me. It's too time-sensitive for something this important. The jet has the legs to get us to Africa and probably Doha or Abu Dhabi. I may have to three- or four-hop it. We need to start soon. I think we can do it. What do they call it in the press? Extraordinary rendition? This definitely falls into the category of extraordinary."

"Agreed."

"First, we need to find out who sent that asshole." Hunter gently jerked his thumb over his shoulder.

"That's my job." The man with the gray flattop and round spectacles could have smiled, but he was dead serious.

"We need to find out who sent that asshole."

"I will take care of him. I will find out, and I will take copious notes. A p e x, w e need you to get the other asshole."

Hunter understood. McGee didn't need help or a witness. The words we need you sounded suspiciously like Hunter was jumping into the category of reluctant patriot. He wasn't doing it for himself, Lynche, or McGee, but for something much larger—the American people. He had to find the answers to the questions thousands of innocent people had been asking since that fateful day in September.

McGee saw that Hunter finally understood. Hunter would have given his friend one of his informal salutes, but his ribs hurt too much.

"Welcome to the war, Apex," McGee said softly, then he corrected himself. "I think I'll start calling you 'Maverick.' It's a better fit for you."

"Aye, aye, Sir. Do you have any painkillers for these ribs? Can you give me a ride back to my car?"

"Are you a pussy or what?" McGee joked, hopped to his feet with the reflexes of a cat, and jogged into the house. Returning a few moments later, he handed Duncan a bottle of water and a handful of pills. He watched Duncan take six of the little white capsules and wash them down.

"Will you be OK?" McGee asked.

Hunter nodded and stood. "Let's giddy-up, Kemosabe. We patriots have work to do."

CHAPTER FORTY-TWO

1300 June 12, 2011
Easton Municipal Airport, Maryland

Hunter and Lynche received their departure clearances to Lajes Field in the Azores from Baltimore Air Traffic Control. GPS and departure frequencies were set. Hunter jutted his thumb in the middle of the cockpit to indicate his part of the takeoff checklist was complete, and he was ready to fly.

Lynche taxied the jet from the hold short to the centerline, braked, and ran up the throttles. Satisfied the jet's systems were operating as advertised, he released the brakes. Lynche immediately noticed the jet didn't accelerate as quickly as usual.

With a full load of fuel for the first leg, a 2,600-mile six-hour trip to the island paradise of the Azores, the jet took more time to rumble down the runway and achieve flight speed.

Once the gear was checked up and locked, it took over thirty minutes to reach their cruising altitude of flight level 450. Hunter's flight plan ensured they'd land under cover of darkness, making the job of professional and hobby tail-watchers difficult. If a tail watcher identified the aircraft's owners and operations through an Internet search of the aircraft's N number in the FAA registry, he would have found that the registration number belonged to a jet from an oil-drilling rig company in Roswell, New Mexico.

From Lajes, their next stop was Monrovia, Liberia, then on to Dubai. From Dubai, they would fly to Diego Garcia. With the autopilot engaged, Hunter left the cockpit and wandered to the cabin for the first sleep shift.

They'd been incredibly busy for the last thirteen hours. Greg flew the Wraith back to Elmira, and Ferrier put the ghostly aircraft back in the Vault until Bob and Bob arrived to take her to their Maryland hangar.

Duncan left Newport and headed directly back to the old Bridgeport Airport to retrieve their jet; then went to Elmira to pick up Lynche. The worst part of the flight was opening and closing the cabin door. The strain on Duncan's back and abdominal muscles nearly made him queasy and he squealed like a girl. He responded by taking the rest of McGee's medications.

Lynche hadn't been waiting too long for Duncan to arrive and raced onto the jet, flying it to Maryland. Duncan slept fitfully in a recliner in the rear of the Gulfstream.

* * *

The sun was just peeking over the horizon when they pulled into Lynche's driveway. Between houses, Hunter commented there were already golfers on the course. Though he and Lynche were also technically retired, they were too busy to take time off to beat little white balls around the links. Duncan couldn't even think about golf. His ribs were killing him. It was a struggle to breathe or take a full breath.

Connie and Nazy were shocked to see the unshaven, bent- over man, obviously in great pain. Connie wanted to give him painkillers and let him sleep. Nazy wanted to hold him, but Duncan's front and back were both heavily damaged from the impact and shockwave of the bullets striking his armor, crushing muscle and hammering his internal organs.

Nazy responded with a long, passionate kiss that brought Duncan out of his reverie. He wanted something to drink, more painkillers, and to see what Nazy smuggled from CIA headquarters.

What she had could be solid gold if one were a Republican lawmaker with cojones. The impeachment train would leave the station and plow through the White House despite a firestorm of Democratic supporters screaming, "This is a high-tech lynching of a president with a funny name who doesn't look like other presidents."

As Duncan lay on Lynche's sofa, thumbing through the books, Nazy and Connie taped his back with white medical tape, while Greg told them how Duncan fought a tall dude who had killed Navy SEALs.

Several dozen pages into the first book, anger welled in Hunter at the thought that the man in the White House was a fake, a master of deceit and deception. He was overcome by a strange numbness, as if all power and energy were sapped from his aching body. His arms tingled as if asleep, while his legs were shells of their former muscular selves. He couldn't move them. As prickly heat flushed his face and chest, he couldn't feel anything.

As he read through even more pages, he became aware that what he read was too incredible. He was unable to admit to himself that the reason for his disorientation was that the material was true. Before blood spurted from his eyes, he gently closed the book and felt the sensation melt away. He was himself again, and he was angry.

Lynche left out some of the details of the previous evening, like Duncan's being shot and how Lynche used the Wraith's laser to disable the bad guy. The women obsessed over the wounded warrior lying on his stomach.

When Duncan turned over, he revealed three hideous black-and-blue welts, each the size of a grapefruit, with a one-inch raised circular white dot showing the impact point of the 9mm slug. Nazy said it resembled some of the bruises Duncan acquired during racquetball matches.

Connie was more abrupt. "You were shot. When were you going to tell us you had been shot!?"

"Please tape the area while I'm still conscious. I'm pretty sure I have a couple broken ribs. Body armor works. I'm lucky to be here."

Their realization was palpable.

"You were shot?" Nazy looked at Connie, then at Duncan. "Really?"

Duncan nodded. She saw he was all right and certainly better than functional.

"Are you trying to make me a rich woman?"

"Don't make me laugh." He opened, scanned, and closed the second book. "Well, that will create a constitutional crisis. It's not my problem; way above my paygrade. Greg, the GOP will have a field day. They'll want to undo every piece of legislation that closet commie ever signed. They'll demand the FBI yank him and his family from the White House and have them shot."

"They won't be shot. What do you think this is, Russia?" Lynche attempted a little ridicule.

"Maybe not yet. He's a fake and ran roughshod over the Constitution, though. These documents prove he's not a natural-born citizen. He was a British subject who ran around the globe using an alias for years. The media and the Democrats have protected his ass with every excuse in the book, including calling anyone who disagrees with his radical takeover of the government 'hood-wearing racists.'

"He's also been consorting with Islamo-fascists and bin Laden. These documents will stop him and his buddies. Maybe they can make a special wing for fellow traitors and this guy at Gitmo." He held up on the president's newly discovered apocryphal biographies without wincing in pain. The tape on his back was very helpful keeping his muscles free of strain. "We can't sit on this. I have an idea to get the ball moving, but first, we need to tell you that Greg and I are leaving for a few days."

"You can't go like that," Nazy said.

"I can, and I must."

"And you, Greg?" Connie asked.

Greg, looking at the floor, nodded. "Duncan needs help flying the jet."

"Where are you going?"

"I'd rather not say. Let's just say it's of national and strategic importance." He didn't look up.

"And, time sensitive," Duncan added, thinking about the

material in his hands, as Connie interrupted his thoughts.

"Greg, you're supposed to be retired from that stuff," she pleaded.

"We're going to pick up Osama bin Laden."

Lynche raised his head, surprised at Hunter's calm demeanor and outburst. The women were shocked.

"You mean his body?" Connie asked.

"If something happens to us, you need to know the whole story," Hunter said.

Nazy helped him pull on a long-sleeved T-shirt, first the left arm, then she pulled it over his head and double-checked the tape on his chest and back before threading his right arm through the remaining sleeve.

Hunter stood and told them the whole story, starting with McGee's e-mail, the SEALs being killed, interdicting the sniper, worrying about Nazy, Greg's flying solo at night, Hunter's being shot, and the revelation that the world's most-wanted terrorist wasn't sitting at the bottom of the Indian Ocean with a hole in his head but was on a US Navy warship, very much alive and apparently unharmed.

Someone needed to take him from the Navy and transfer him to the appropriate hands for interrogation to find out what was in his hate-filled head.

"I've thought about it," he said, "and there really isn't anyone else I know—we know—who we can trust with a secret like this. There's more to the story, and I'm interested in that, but it isn't important how and why Osama bin Laden wasn't killed in that raid. What's important is extracting what he knows. It's very disconcerting to read old embassy dispatches that our president had a couple meetings with him when he was young. When the president had the chance to take Osama bin Laden out, he dallied for months and put off the whole IC and SOF, ostensibly for political reasons, like the election. When I read those dispatches, I really want to know if we have an al-Qaeda branch in the White House."

"Once you pick him up, then what?" Nazy asked. "Where will you take him? Who do you have in mind to interrogate him?"

"I don't know anyone that close at my old place who can stick his neck out that far past a Presidential Directive, even if he isn't who he says he is," Greg said. "Do you know anyone we can trust with this information? First, no one would believe you. Second, it would take too long to get someone to move on official business. The unintended consequences of telling a civil servant might be to sign your death warrant. No, this has to be closely held. The DCI is complicit in some way, and he would never authorize an op. That leaves us with ourselves. I see this like breaking fine china. You broke it, it's yours. Whatever you do with it is your business."

For a moment they were silent, then Duncan's BlackBerry vibrated with an incoming e-mail.

Hunter punched the center button, quickly moved past the security screens, and read. "You've love this. It's from Bill. Quote, you were next and last on his hit list. He was going to Texas after Newport. Not the girlfriend. Why target SEALs? Why were you on his list? He doesn't know. He just pulls triggers. Is given a name and address and real-time info via e-mail at every location. He doesn't know but believes local mosque provides watchers and info on his targets. Emails end with good luck and God willing in Arabic.

"Replies to e-mail he received that mission is completed. Paid well. History: Failed SEAL training and USMC sniper school. Former world-class shooter. Born in US as Sam Miller. Converted to Islam. Hired as sniper in Africa, killed opposition leaders. Worked out of Sudan, Mali, Nigeria, Liberia, Congo. Paid by Saudi middleman. Tracked him down as the ops chief of one Prince Bashir out of Dubai.

"Break. Break. He RX info from local mosque at every location. Believes mosque in Boston watched my house and me. Have his laptop but can't get in. No other questions possible. PS. Ox excited cavalry coming. Needs list of what you need. Send to me and I'll forward. Out."

"What does it mean 'no other questions possible?'" both women asked.

"I think the guy who shot me is meeting seventy-two Virginians right about now." Hunter distorted the prize of Islamic martyrdom with heavy sarcasm. He suppressed a desire to poke at Greg about the effectiveness of enhanced interrogation techniques, but they were short on time, and he was distracted by knowing he was next on the hit list. Why him and how was that possible?

As the two men and two women came to grips with their parallel situations, Hunter asked for help thinking through the problem. They had a lot to do before their date with destiny.

The discussion around Connie Lynche's kitchen table began with Hunter outlining his proposed concept of operations. Nazy and Connie would disassemble the two books, scan the documents into a file, and have several hundred copies made. A photocopy business would do the work, but they had to avoid anyone scrutinizing the documents.

Nazy and Connie vetoed that idea. They offered a counterstrategy that the easiest and safest way was to scan each document, redact certain entries, and place them on an innocuous web site for all to see—just like the most-recent download of hundreds of classified documents onto the Web. They would provide the web site to the media and Congress. Hunter kyboshed the whole plan until they returned, but the ladies could scan all the documents from the books.

While they did that, Greg and Hunter would fly around the world, retrieve the terrorist, and find a place to hold him and someone to interrogate him. Hunter acknowledged that part of the plan hadn't been completely thought through, and he was open to ideas.

McGee's assessment that his friends had a jet and contacts within the CIA, along with the idea of spiriting someone away who was officially declared dead, was only one of several tips of submerged icebergs of logistical challenges. Getting to Diego Garcia was easy, though not for civilian aircraft. One needed prior permission before embarking on a flight to the middle of the Indian Ocean.

Then there was the security. It wasn't possible to sneak a gnat onto an aircraft on a military base under the watchful eye of security forces south of two major ground conflicts. There would be records of the trip—fuel receipts, tower logs, aircraft registration numbers—and a host of other unexpected speed bumps to negotiate and obviate before any measure of success could be celebrated. The unintended consequences of bending any one of the logistics links would mean the operation could end in a disaster like the mess at Desert One, Operation Eagle Claw. Hunter was familiar with the total process, from soup to nuts as logisticians were fond of saying. There was no back-up plan, much like the Apollo mission to the moon. There was no time to practice either. They either planned and executed the operation perfectly, or people would die, or worse.

First, there was the minor issue of releasing the documents, long suspected in some quarters by one of the political parties while ridiculed by the other, that proved the commander in chief was really the communist in chief or charlatan in chief. Either way, he was disqualified from legitimately holding the highest office in the land.

Hunter wanted to expedite their release and handle it himself, to avoid endangering those around him from unintended consequences. He knew he had to be very careful. The political left viewed the media as an extension of leftist and socialist policy. The former administration couldn't fart without the media screaming about a manufactured crime against humanity.

The current occupant of the White House was markedly worse in several areas. When he did something stupid or illegal, the media just yawned. The political right expected the media to report unbiased news and couldn't believe they wouldn't or couldn't. The power grab of radical forces trampling over the Constitution, coupled with the dishonesty of the Democratic left, their communist friends, and the de facto state-controlled media provided enough incentive for any patriot to expose the president, their party, and the fifth column as totally corrupt and complicit in more than just simple impeachable offenses.

Hunter hoped the release of documents would also release the Hounds of Hell from the halls of Congress. He was unconcerned that armed vigilante and veterans' groups across the country would crawl over broken glass to help overthrow the dictatorial, illegal, and illegitimate government.

As McGee drove Hunter back to his rental, Hunter released a steady stream of thoughts, concerns, and challenges they had to overcome. "We need to make this as inconspicuous as possible, in and out with as little fuss and visibility as we can get. And, we'll need help—not crazy help, just help. Can you see if your guy in Diego Garcia holds enough sway to ensure our jet isn't on their landing history? I want to land there under cover of darkness. We'll need a full bag of gas when we leave.

"For us to be successful, I have a vision of one of your guys borrowing a full fuel truck of Jet A or JP-8. Since it's Diego Garcia, with all those Air Force jets going through there, they have JP-8. Ideally, they need to meet us on the ramp in some remote location. Parking in front of base ops with all those floodlights won't be helpful.

"If I have to, I think I can remember how to operate an R-11, a 6,000-gallon refueling truck. We might have to take almost half of it to allow a 4,500-mile leg. I think we'll need a guy in the tower to make sure no one accounts for our landing and takeoff. That'll be the hard part. There was a famous scene in A Few Good Men where the duty controllers and the tower logbook were brought in as evidence. We don't need something like that."

McGee nodded. "We need to run it like a Special Access Program. Dudes with clearances are going to have to put their jobs and clearances on the line."

Hunter agreed. "Do you think we can get a couple of SEALs for support? I envision a continuation of effort of what they're doing right now. There has to be a rotating guard to make sure Osama bin Laden doesn't wander off or hurt himself. We'll need them for a few days. I know, at some point, they have to be replaced or returned to duty. Maybe we can drop them off in the Azores. I'll figure something out. Maybe they have a Cadillac chit they can use. Maybe Ox will have an answer."

"I don't think that'll be an issue. We couldn't even begin to think about doing this without Ox's help. Since he reached out to me, I sent him a message saying I have two trusted agents to help him." McGee's focus was on the prize. "Have you given any thought who we can reach out to for the interrogation?"

"I'm working on it. There are a thousand things that can go wrong just getting there and then getting off the island. Our chances increase exponentially if the right guys are in place to help. I'll be counting on them to be there."

McGee, stopping behind Hunter's car, turned toward him. "I think I need to go with you, but I don't know how long it'll take to play twenty questions with our boy."

"I'm not sure what I can do about that. We need that info from him."

"Maverick, I agree, but I don't see how I can go with you unless that shithead we left at my house is dead when I get back."

"If that happens, call me. I'll pick you up. Otherwise, we probably need you here as command post."

"Roger. Be safe, Sir."

"Aye, aye, my captain."

Connie Lynche's questions brought Hunter's mind back from its reverie.

"How long will you be gone? Will you be incommunicado? Where will you go and for how long? Who'll interrogate him? That's the purpose of this whole adventure, right?" Her stress showed in the way she launched bullet questions while trying to understand the enormity of the problems her husband and Duncan faced.

Nazy remained quiet and composed.

"I don't know how long we'll be," Lynche said. "This is way outside my lane, and you know how I feel about torture."

Hunter ignored the verbal slap from his friend. "I'll figure out something. I'm certain if I tried to waterboard him, I'd drown him. You know how clumsy I can be."

He tried to spin and pick up the books filled with their impeachable evidence only to inflame his obliques and ribs. Grimacing for a moment, he caught his breath and composed himself.

He handed the books to Connie. "Please put these in the safe until we're back. I need to figure out how and to whom to send this data."

Greg and Nazy watched in rapt attention, engrossed by the way Connie approached Duncan and slowly took the books, as if they were the only ones in the room, and she was going to drag him off to the bedroom.

"It'll cost you," she cooed.

Greg and Nazy stared at her flirtatious audacity. If she wanted to relieve some of the tension in the room, she failed miserably.

Duncan didn't play. "It always does, Connie." He hugged her and kissed her cheek as if she were his sister.

Connie feigned hurt, turned, and disappeared into the basement.

With all the imagined sexual tension released in the room, Hunter said, "We need to get going. We'll need to pick up a few things before we take off."

"Are you sure you'll be OK?" Nazy asked.

"I'll be fine."

"He'll be fine," Greg said. "Look at him. After he'd been shot three times, that shithead looked like he was kicking his ass. Look at him now, hardly a scratch. He's an animal." Playful sarcasm dripped from every word.

"What do you need to do?" Connie asked, returning to the room.

"I need someone I trust and who can speak Arabic," Hunter said. It was either the fatigue or the pain that affected his normally sharp mind. The moment he finished speaking, he slammed his eyes shut and cringed.

"I speak Arabic," Nazy said coolly in Arabic, before switching back to English, "and I'm a trained interrogator. You can't trust me?"

Duncan Hunter opened his mouth to speak, but nothing came out.

CHAPTER FORTY-THREE

0500 June 13, 2011
The Washington Post

Associated Press. CIA Director to Become VP

In a surprise announcement yesterday, Vice President Jack Bowen submitted his resignation to the President, citing health concerns. The President accepted the VP's resignation with sorrow and said, "Jack has been a thoroughly fantastic vice president and confidant. I will always miss his wise counsel." The President nominated the Director of Central Intelligence, Frank Carey, to fill the vacant seat, only the second time the vice presidential vacancy provision of the 25th Amendment has been implemented. It is expected there will be widespread approval to confirm in both the Senate and the House today. The White House announced a noon ceremony in the Rose Garden tomorrow, 14 June, for Frank Carey to take the oath of office as Vice President of the United States.

CHAPTER FORTY-FOUR

0500 June 13, 2011
The Newport Daily News

Newport—Firefighters were dispatched to Wet Socks Curve off Polo Court in Newport County Sunday night for a vehicle fire. According to Jeff Wright, chief of the Volunteer Fire Company of Newport County, the vehicle was an older Chevy van with California license plates. Human remains were found in the vehicle, but the body was burned beyond recognition. Wright said residents of the area heard possible gunfire or fireworks the night prior but did not see anything unusual. Firefighters were on the scene about two hours, and there were no injuries. A Newport Community Ambulance was also on scene.

CHAPTER FORTY-FIVE

1200 June 13, 2011
CIA Headquarters Langley, Virginia

The Old Office Building was in complete disarray with the vice presidential nomination of the DCI. Agency liberals quietly applauded the nomination. Agency conservatives quietly celebrated by softly humming Ding-Dong! The Witch Is Dead, which was heard throughout the cafeteria and into the atrium. Agency liberals were not amused.

The announcement that the DCI was departing the premises, hopefully never to return, came to some employees and contractors like an answer to their nonstop prayers. Others viewed the ascension of the DCI to the vice presidency as a plus, a way to maintain liberal grip on the government. Had there ever been a worse director? Even the Agency historian couldn't remember.

Liberals excused the DCI's radical behavior to job pressure and his efforts to clean up the mess "left over from the previous administration." Conservatives were more pragmatic, seeing that the DCI was interested in only advancing himself, his friends, and his agenda from the start, not what was in the best interests of the Agency, the Intelligence Community or the United States.

Conservative Senior Intelligence Service executives pegged Frank Carey as an opportunistic predator who promoted himself and administration friends while demoting others who were viewed as challengers or who appeared to be unwilling to accept his leadership style. Carey acquired lackeys and obsequious lampreys eager to do his bidding, killing missions or gutting Special Access Programs inimical to the administration. Rarely seen off the top floor unless he wanted something, there was no love lost between the politically appointed DCI and his personal staff and the career civil servants who worked their way up the ladder and the Agency floors.

Carey wanted to get out of the building as soon as possible. The position served its purpose. He had the president's file in a safe location, and he tried to race from the building and settle into his new office when he ran into the deputy director of operations seeking an official pass down and debrief. Even an outgoing DCI becoming vice president had to be debriefed when leaving oversight of Special Access Programs.

Carey tried to dismiss his official responsibilities as the head intelligence official, telling Deputy Wayne Okine, "You got it. I nominated you to be my replacement. I'm trying to get out of here. The VP left at a most awkward time." Carey grinned unabashedly.

"Director Carey," the thirty-year career intelligence officer replied, "as long as you're alive and breathing, you have to be debriefed about ongoing missions and SAPs. I need about thirty minutes for a debrief and pass down, then we can help you leave."

Carey was too distracted to catch the man's slight expression of distrust and subtle words of sarcasm. Hank, the DCI's personal secretary, had been madly packing the director's personal effects and asked, "Director, Sir, what about this gun and naily thing?"

"Absolutely not. I don't like guns, and I don't know what that thing is. Leave them."

The deputy director took a deep breath and said, "Hank, I need thirty minutes of the director's time. You can resume packing when I leave. Thank you."

The secretary was taken aback. Rarely had anyone been so rude to him. When Carey nodded, the effeminate Hank left the office.

Deputy Okine handed papers to the DCI, one by one, summarizing each. "Sir, I need your signature on these documents. The red X marks the spot. On these, you agree not to divulge any information, including hints, of ongoing SAPs. Thank you. This one is to respond to a State request for some help to discern the whereabouts of a handful of hostages held by Somali pirates. This one's for a mission in Peru to locate the remaining Shining Path leadership...."

"Can't you do those?"

"No, Sir. DCI only, and you're still the director. I'll have to go to the president to get authorization for the SAP, and that might take weeks or months. It may take months for your replacement to be confirmed by the Senate. These are very time-sensitive, as others have been."

"OK." The DCI signed two dozen documents, including ten-year funding authorization for the front company Quiet Unmanned Aircraft Research Laboratory. Carey avoided any snide comments. He just wanted the deputy out of his office and out of his hair.

When all the documents were signed, Deputy Okine offered his hand. "Thank you, Sir. Congratulations, and good luck."

"Thank you, Wayne. Good luck to you."

Deputy Director Okine sped from the office, almost knocking over one of his colleagues.

"Hank, get back in here!"

Instead of Hank's voice, he heard three knocks on his door. "What!?" shouted Frank Carey.

Nazy Cunningham stuck her head through the doorway.

"Excuse me, Director Carey. I have the information you requested."

Carey stopped packing and tried to remember what he needed from that woman.

When his confusion became obvious, Nazy said, "You asked me to do a quick check of the file database."

"Yes! Yes! Come in. Close the door. Thank you. What do you have, Nazy?"

"I know you're busy, Sir, so I'll be brief. There was a file, and it appears your predecessor took possession of it. It hasn't been returned to active files, nor is it in the archives. It wasn't sent to the FBI. That's all I have."

Frank Carey tried to make sense of Nazy's report, quickly running scenarios through his mind. Did he have the only file on the president? It sounded like it. In that case, it was time to get Nazy out of there. "Thank you for your service, Nazy. That'll be all."

"Director Carey, the White House informed the deputy my medal ceremony has been postponed indefinitely. Thank you for your help, and congratulations, Sir." She turned, unlocked the door, and left.

Carey plopped his bulk into his chair wrinkling his brow as he tried to recall what medal ceremony she meant. Finally, he remembered.

He raced to his door and stopped when he saw no one at Hank's desk. He needed Hank to open his safes, so he could check the contents. "Where'd that little cocksucker go?"

Nazy hurried down the stairs, swiped her access card to leave the stairwell, and walked into her office. She glanced at her Rolex for the time and saw she had plenty of time to reach Reagan National Airport. Extracting her diplomatic and tourist passports from her top desk drawer, she thrust them into her suit pocket, ensured all her safes were locked and spun the dials one last time before checking the handles. Grabbing her purse, she went out the door to leave the building.

CHAPTER FORTY-SIX

0100L June 15, 2011
Navy Support Facility, Diego Garcia

"Neptune one zero zero, you're number one, clear to land, runway one three."

"Roger. Neptune one zero zero, clear to land, one three."

Forty seconds later, the jet crossed the algae-covered beach and the instrument landing system. The jet's white underside was momentarily bathed in the floodlights designed to illuminate the landing gear without blinding the aircrew. No wheels watch was on duty at the end of the runway at that late hour, as the airfield was officially closed.

After six hours of overwater flying, the white-and-red jet was feet dry. Two puffs of vaporized rubber signaled the landing, followed by the lowering of the nose onto the centerline. Hunter controlled the trajectory down the runway with his toes on the rudder pedals. No thrust reversers were needed for the two-mile- long concrete strip.

As the jet passed midfield, the tower controller said, "Neptune one zero zero, maintain this freq. Turn off far end and report clear of runway one three."

The man standing beside the tower controller unclasped his hands, giving two thumbs-up. "OK. Can you activate his clearance to Djibouti using this call sign?"

The controller took the script and read it. "Easy."

As the jet decelerated toward seventy knots, Hunter lightly touched the brakes to slow the Gulfstream to a crawl, as he approached the red lights marking the end of the runway. He and Lynche were hyper-alert, as they didn't want to do anything stupid after getting that far, like overrunning the runway or missing a taxiway, or dropping a landing gear off into the sand or dirt. Hunter controlled the left turn with differential braking and thrust, depressing the left brake pedal while advancing the right throttle a little. He didn't take any chances with nose wheel steering, which could have sent the jet one way or the other.

"Neptune one zero zero, clear one three," he said. "Neptune one zero zero, proceed to marshal with wands."

"Tally on wands."

"Roger, Neptune one zero zero. Maintain this freq. Services on scene."

"Roger, Tower. Hope to be off in fifteen mikes." Hunter unbuckled his lap and shoulder belts. Lynche started the auxiliary power unit, as Hunter guided the jet to a stop and placed both throttles to cutoff and turned off the external lights when the taxi marshal crossed his wands.

"Your jet," Hunter said, climbing from his seat into the cabin, wincing with pain from any quick movement. "I hope we don't get arrested," he muttered. "That would piss me off."

With the cabin depressurized, Hunter turned off the cabin lights, unlocked the door, and lowered the air stairs, again grimacing from muscles pulling across bruised ribs. He stepped out into the darkness and down the stairs one at a time and came face-to-face with a shadowed man with a flashlight covered by a red lens.

"Bullfrog sends his regards," Hunter said.

"Ox. The pleasure's all mine, Maverick. Thank you for coming. I have a fuel truck if you can just show us where it needs to go. When we're done, we'll load the cargo."

"This way, Sir."

A shadow emerged from abeam the aircraft, where an R-11 refueling truck unwound a refueling hose. A man dragged the nozzle toward the refueling panel, as if he had refueled many Gulfstreams in his day, though not one in the middle of the night without its lights. Then again, maybe he had.

He attached the single-point refueling nozzle to the aircraft, ran to the truck, and engaged the power takeoff and fuel pump.

Thirteen minutes later, the R-11 offloaded 2,500 gallons

of JP-8 and filled the Gulfstream's fuel tanks. The man uncoupled and

retracted the hose, stowing the nozzle in the truck. He drove off quickly without saying a word or even looking at Hunter.

Ox flashed his red-lensed light into the night. Seconds later, two men carrying a stretcher with a body passed Hunter and Ox. As the men wrestled the stretcher up the airstairs, Ox spoke to the ground.

"You want to ask me a question, Maverick?"

"I do. Why'd you do it? Bullfrog wasn't sure."

"The president called me in Afghanistan and strongly suggested he die in Pakistan. We trained for months to take him alive, so we could interrogate him. At the last possible moment, POTUS said, 'Kill him.' With all the intrigue surrounding our commander in chief, and the fact that I saw a file on him at Langley, killing our man was probably an illegal order or, at the least, a high crime."

"I was convinced there was something inside that asshole's head that our very liberal POTUS wants squashed. My SEALs were the instruments to make that so. Americans deserve to know the truth about their president, especially this one. What about you? How'd you get pulled into this?"

Hunter was surprised. "Me? Bullfrog and I were at the Naval War College. I'll let him fill you in on the rest of the story. Let's just say it's been a long, strange journey to get here. My view is that I see what our enemies are doing to good people. Fighting them is a full-time job. Whatever flavor of enemy—liberal, Marxist, socialist, commie, radical, Islamo-fascist—I'm beginning to see them for what they really are and what this is; a battle between good and evil."

"The democrats have the devil as the head of their party."

"You're right, Ox. Something's definitely wrong with that guy. You did the right thing, Sir."

"Welcome to the fight, Maverick."

"You're a great American, Sir."

"Thank you. Now let's get you out of here."

"I hope we can finish what you started and gave us."

He offered his hand. Hunter tried not to have his crushed as SEALs were wont to do, giving the hand a good shake before saluting the patriot.

"I have all the trust and confidence you can," Ox said. "Fair winds and following seas, Maverick."

"Semper *Fi*, Ox." Hunter turned and ran up the airstairs, pulling them up behind him while trying not to look like a wimp, as his damaged ribs screamed at him. At the sound of the door closing, Lynche started an engine.

Hunter saw two men in black discarding their gear to get comfortable in the huge chairs. In the aisle rested a stretcher with a man on it.

Hunter gave the two SEALs thumbs-up, and they responded quietly.

Four minutes later, Hunter raised the landing gear as they passed 200 knots and said into the microphone, "Feet wet."

Lynche, nodding, scanned the instruments bathed in red light.

When they passed through 10,000 feet, Lynche chortled, "That wasn't so bad. Now what do we do?"

"I hope you set a course for Djibouti."

"Of course. I understand they have a nice hotel now."

"Maybe we'll check that out next trip. Your turn to sleep. I'll wake you in four hours."

"Do we really have Osama back there?"

"It was dark. I didn't see a beard. I have to take their word for it."

"Could be a rumor."

"I hope he doesn't piss on the carpet."

"Ugh. Don't fall asleep."

"Good night, Dear."

CHAPTER FORTY-SEVEN

0200 June 15, 2011
The Bedford Park Islamic Center Boston, Massachusetts

Assad Tammam and his brother walked out of the mosque and across the parking lot to his car. He was exhausted and frustrated. For the last two days, he and his brother tried to determine the whereabouts of fellow mujahidin last heard from near Newport, Rhode Island. Cell phones went unanswered. Apartments hadn't been visited. Two brothers disappeared.

Assad, the trusted one, was the one to contact as a last resort. It took ten years to reach the pinnacle of airport security at Boston International Airport as TSA shift supervisor. As a key law enforcement and supervisory official, Assad had unfettered access to several databases, as well as the instant messaging system for law enforcement and intelligence community officials. The No-Fly List, the Terrorist Watch List, All-Points Bulletins, and other information generated from local law-enforcement activities and the Terrorist Screening Center were very useful for the Brotherhood to monitor the success of their operation and for his standing as a mujahidin behind enemy lines. American infidels were so stupid.

* * *

"No, Sahib, I have no new information. No BOLO. Forgive me. There have been no be-on-the-lookout announcements for anyone unusual. The wires have been very quiet, Sahib."

The imam glared at the man, sighed, and slowly shook his head. "No information at all?"

"No, Sahib. Our brothers have not checked in, and there

has been no announcement of an untimely death. Your brother may have been caught, but I have no information. Normally, I have access to all information. I'm very good at my job. Imam, there was, however a report of a shooting and a vehicle fire in the area our brothers were watching," Assad said.

"Thank you, my son. Please leave me. Contact me if there's any change in the information."

Imam Abdul shuffled behind his desk, as a disappointed Assad wheeled from the little office and closed the door behind him. Thick cigarette smoke whorled the air as he left.

The little man crushed the smoldering butt, fished out a pack of cigarettes from the center drawer, lit the Camel, took a long drag, and placed the cigarette in an overfull tray. He swiveled ninety degrees to face a computer monitor, keyboard, and mouse.

After several keystrokes and mouse clicks, he was in the private chat room in the United Arab Emirates. Lack of sleep and worry contributed to his inability to focus. He struggled to find the right phrasing to report their failure.

Abdul noticed one other online, probably one of the prince's many sons. He began typing. Our brother did not arrive today. I'm most concerned we haven't heard from him. I hope he's safe. Inshallah.

He sent the message without hope of a quick response. The message was on its way with an overexaggerated pointed index finger pressing the Enter key. He crossed his arms on his chest, reached for the smoldering cigarette, and was about to leave the room when a window popped up to announce, A is typing.

Moments later, Abdul was horrified to read, Leave McGee. He sat transfixed. The response wasn't in passive code designed to thwart American intelligence-gathering methods. Confusion was replaced by more anger.

As his leathery hands balled into fists to pound the sides of the computer stand, he became aware of noise outside his office. Something ululated, growing in intensity.

"What's that?" he muttered in Arabic.

Reaching for the stubby cigarette, he tried to ignore the wailing siren and deal with the problem facing him on the screen. His benefactor and sponsor had just broken a twenty-year protocol. Two mujahidin from his flock and a brother-in-arms were missing. The local target was apparently not neutralized.

"What's going on?" he wailed, clasping his hands in prayer. His cell phone vibrated in his shirt pocket. It was Aasim, one of his lost sheep.

"Why have you not called?" he shouted. "Hello? Aasim?"

There was no side tone. Staring at the phone, he realized he just received a text message. He pressed buttons, making several mistakes, until he opened the correct screen and read, Fire.

"Fire? What does that idiot mean by fire? What's that noise?"

He took one more drag from the cigarette dangling from his mouth before jamming it into the ashtray. Smoke billowed around him, as he rushed around the desk to the door.

When he threw open the heavy wooden door, white smoke eddies raced into his office, and the fire alarm claxon increased in intensity by thirty decibels. He looked at the cell phone again and read, Fire.

His eyes bulged, and his lips puckered as he tried to move his frozen legs. The first molecules of burned wood entered his nicotine-saturated sinuses, as the smoke in the hall increased in intensity.

Abdul tried to move, torn between self-preservation and immolation. The coward in him galvanized his legs to function. He raced down the hall, robes flowed with each step, away from where the smoke billowed until he reached the exit and was about to press the crash bar and step outside when he realized he couldn't leave things in his office.

"Passport, books, money.... Computer!" His thoughts raced, taking inventory of what he needed and where the items were. He had to retrieve them if possible.

Spinning around, he saw the smoke thickening. "I can make it," he muttered.

Taking a deep breath, he coughed and raced back into the cloud.

CHAPTER FORTY-EIGHT

1300L June 16, 2011
Roberts International Airport Monrovia, Liberia

LeMarcus Leonard and his airport employees had the arrivals and departures of airline aircraft down to an art form. Unlike American or European airport managers, LeMarcus met every arrival aircraft that landed and offloaded, and he monitored the departure operation as the airlines worked to herd their passengers from the lounges onto the aircraft to meet departure schedules. The arrival of the United Airlines Boeing 777 was routine, except that one passenger required special handling by the airport manager. Duncan told LeMarcus that the woman would find him.

In a sea of blue, tan, and white shirts and coveralls, she saw him first. After watching thousands of passengers embark and disembark, few piqued Leonard's interest. Those who did were subject to enhanced screening. Most who were pulled off to the side were hauled off to jail for various infractions—carrying concealed weapons, exotic animals, diamonds—or for submitting a bogus or stolen passport at Customs. Trained in the observation of people and their behavior, LeMarcus Leonard was one of a handful of specially trained profilers able to discern the microexpressions and microbehaviors of criminals, and he was nearly as effective as a polygraph interviewer.

When the striking woman with long, black hair gingerly stepped down the stairs onto the tarmac and looked straight at him, she rang all his bells. He tried to concentrate on the other passengers, but his gaze kept returning to the woman until she walked right up to him. "You must be LeMarcus," she said. "I'm Nazy Cunningham."

* * *

LeMarcus tried to keep his eyes on the road, not on the woman sitting beside him. It wouldn't do if anything happened to that special lady. Duncan Hunter made it perfectly clear that LeMarcus needed to ensure she arrived safely at the hotel. Getting to Africa by air was the easy part. Once anyone landed on the continent, though, and had to go somewhere, nearly every road in Africa was fraught with intrigue and danger.

As LeMarcus approached the only real limited visibility corner in a semi-jungle area, he flashbacked to an event a month earlier where he routinely braked heavily to negotiate the tight corner only to come to a complete stop when he encountered two dozen men with machetes in the middle of the two-lane.

He leaned on the Toyota's horn to encourage the harvesters of date palms to leave the roadway. He was ready to put the truck in reverse if the men made any aggressive moves, but they simply resumed their slow trajectory across the road, ignoring the horn.

LeMarcus was glad no one was on the road, as he turned without having to use any of Greg Lynche's special defensive driving techniques with Ms. Cunningham aboard. He ran the gauntlet of Airport Road every day from Robertsfield to his high-walled compound near the US embassy. The destination of his special cargo was the beachside Kendaja Resort, open to the Atlantic Ocean.

He approached trucks and buses looking as if they had just escaped a metal crusher, as they wobbled down the road, belching thick, black smoke, overloaded with cargo or people. Most of the taxis he passed on the side of the road had broken windscreens and crushed body panels. They resembled yellow carcasses pressed into service after months in a car-crash derby. Since taking the job as airport manager, LeMarcus was involved in three accidents along Airport Road, including one fairly serious rollover when he swerved to avoid a child who fell into the roadway.

His passenger wasn't prone to small talk. She seemed

more fascinated by the scenery—families living in makeshift mud or grass huts, children dressed in bright clothing walking along the highway, unperturbed by the cars and trucks racing a few feet away. LeMarcus gave up trying to find out about the woman Duncan asked him to pick up when she got off the airplane and take her to the hotel. That's what he was going to do.

He tried acting as tour guide. "We're passing through the village of Smell-No Taste. They're on airport property, but they've been here so long, the government wouldn't think of evicting them. Many of them work at the airport."

She turned, her emerald-green eyes flashing wide. "They look like they're doing OK. I expected more obvious famine, starvation, or emaciation. They seem well-fed. It's a shock to leave civilization like Washington, land in Africa, and the first thing I see is jungle and this level of poverty."

He was about to reply when something surprised her. "Oh, my!"

"It's not unusual to see men and women relieving themselves on the side of the road," he explained, "or, like that older woman, without a top. She's the exception. I think they have dementia. There are a lot of people with horrific injuries sustained from the civil war, including mental injuries. The closer we get to town, the more people are nicely dressed or fully clothed. They wear suits and beautiful African dresses. Kids have school uniforms just like back home."

"It's incredible. I had no idea. I appreciate the information, Mr. Leonard. I've never been to Africa." She continued looking out the Toyota's windows.

LeMarcus resumed his dialogue. "As we get closer to the river, we might see someone selling fish or deer on the side of the road. Those baskets we passed are filled with charcoal they take off the roadbed. You'll see a quarry at the top of the hill. A dozen men turn big rocks into small rocks or gravel, all with hammers. On the horizon is where the Liberian army lives and trains. US military are in there all the time as instructors and advisors."

"Is that an antenna in the distance?"

"That's an old Omega navigation transmitter. I think it's the tallest structure in Africa, at least for a few more days until it's demolished. Too many base jumpers get hurt, and they're supposed to turn that property into a market or something."

As he pulled into the driveway of Liberia's newest ocean resort, the woman turned and handed him a folded piece of paper. LeMarcus' heart skipped a beat, then it calmed immediately.

"Duncan said you can pick up these things before he lands," she said. "Here's some cash. The top five items are must-haves. After that, they're nice-to-have. Thank you for showing me the sights. See you later tonight, LeMarcus."

Two men in flowered print shirts raced to the truck as LeMarcus and Nazy exited their doors. After the woman walked through the sliding doors, followed by the baggage handler and doorman, LeMarcus jumped into the truck.

Before putting the vehicle into gear, he removed the paper from his pocket and read the words in beautiful cursive.

Fully charged car battery
Battery cables
Ten rolls duct tape
2 large 9 volt batteries
2 buckets
Scissors

LeMarcus looked through the glass doors at the woman, no longer a sexual object, standing at the reservation desk. His expression showed a man who'd been filled with joy and suddenly found himself caught in a tragedy.

"What the hell are you guys up to?" he muttered.

CHAPTER FORTY-NINE

1200 June 16, 2011
The Bedford Park Town Crier

Islamic Center Firebombed

Police closed Park Lane Road through Bedford Park following a fire in the early hours of June 15. Firefighters were called to the Islamic Center in Bedford Park just after midnight to a blaze at the rear of the building. Police are treating the fire and the circumstances as arson. Although no one was reportedly hurt, several people remain missing. The fire completely engulfed the main structure, causing considerable damage to the heavily fortified property. Police envisage the road will remain shut for some hours as forensic inquiries continue. Officers, who believe the incident may be linked to a series of burned-out vehicles along Park Lane Road, are keen to speak to anyone who saw someone acting suspiciously near the building or recall seeing a car speeding away. Police investigating said, "It appears an accelerant was used, and our immediate priorities include establishing who started this fire and why, and making motorists aware."

CHAPTER FIFTY

2300L June 15, 2011
Roberts International Airport Monrovia, Liberia

The outcome depended on a thousand things going right and nothing going wrong. Hunter stretched his luck past the breaking point, casually assuming they'd get a bag of gas in Djibouti- Ambouli International and continue on their way. If not Djibouti then Mombasa or Lagos. He didn't anticipate their jet becoming the subject of an international search.

When the Djibouti-Ambouli International Airport denied their landing clearance, Hunter and Lynche called the airport via their satellite phone to inquire why. The authorities mildly suggested they stole the aircraft and were flying it under a bogus tail number, a typical MO for drug smugglers coming in from South America. They suggested they were tracked across Africa and avoided position calls to avoid paying overflight fees sent via the Flight Information Region network.

Lynche and Hunter looked at each other.

"Set course for ROB," Hunter said, reaching for his flight computer.

"ROB? We don't have enough gas. Distance to ROB is 3,250. We have enough gas for only 2,600 miles."

"Maybe." Reading out the fuel flow for both engines, he started tapping numbers into his device. He pulled one engine to idle and trimmed the aircraft, as it slowed and slewed, then he checked the fuel flow again and rate of descent.

Lynche watched intently.

"Let's see if we can get to 450 nice and gentle," Hunter said. "I think we can do it single engine. We have good tail winds this close to the equator."

"You're shitting me."

"Single engine will add 110 miles over dual. We have a healthy equatorial tailwind. I predict we'll run out of gas 100 miles out of ROB."

"Why are you so happy? You just said we'd run out of gas 100 miles out!"

"I think I can squeeze another 100 miles out of her. We'll see how well I can really fly this beast."

"You're crazy."

"It's been said before. Be glad there are no real armed forces that can shoot us down. I'm not going to be able to sleep. Want to go back and get more shuteye?"

"Really? I want to watch this."

"It'll be eight hours."

"OK. See you in four."

Six hours after Lynche left the cockpit, he returned, expecting to find Hunter asleep, but the man was full of surprises.

"How'd you do that?" He pointed at the fuel quantity gauges. "We've been flying single engine at maximum range, maximum endurance. If the fuel gauges are calibrated on our side, we'll run out of gas only twenty miles short of the field. That's Accra at your three o'clock. Abidjan is on the nose. How are they doing?"

"I'm certain Osama thinks he's going to Gitmo. The SEALs said you're flying a roller coaster."

"That's because I have been. I shut down number one. Number two doesn't burn as much as one. I try to maintain altitude, but it naturally descends. I get to 350 and fire up the engine, then I climb back to 450 and do it over again. I'm taking a nap. Don't let me sleep more than fifteen minutes past Abidjan."

"Roger. My jet."

Hunter, lowering his chin to his chest, was asleep instantly.

* * *

An hour passed, but Hunter felt he had been asleep only a minute when Lynche woke him.

"Mav, I think we need to start descending. We're 100 miles out with 1,000 pounds of fuel. We're toast."

"Not yet. We'll run out of gas." He yawned and stretched, making his ribs ache anew.

Lynche felt perturbed and anxious. They'd come so far, only to crash in the Liberian jungle short of the field. He watched the GPS count off seven miles per minute.

Hunter checked fuel quantity and flow, then wrote figures on his knee board. At ten miles from ROB, he cinched the shoulder harness straps tight and did the same with his lap belts. "I have the jet."

"Your jet." Lynche was intrigued by his partner's calm demeanor, though seeing him tighten his harness was confusing. And scary.

Hunter reached for the engine-control lever and shut down number-one engine. Lynche somehow got the message and quickly tightened his shoulder and lap belts, as the jet slowed and descended. Hunter trimmed the nose and held the jet on altitude until airspeed bled off rapidly to 200 knots. At 190 knots he lowered the landing gear and set the flaps to full.

The additional drag nearly departed or destabilized the aircraft, Hunter corrected with the rudder pedals until the jet settled down. Lynche was as nervous as one of his paranoid cats.

They were falling from the sky at 10,000 feet per minute, wings level, at 170 knots.

"Call LeMarcus," Hunter said. "Make sure no one's on the runway. I can do this only once." He stared at the instruments, flying the nose of the aircraft to maintain 170 knots.

The altimeters unwound faster than Lynche had ever seen.

They were eight miles from the field and 35,000 feet above ground. "This is like riding a frigging runaway elevator,"

Lynche said.

"What do you call this maneuver?"

The jet passed through 30,000 feet at six miles from the field. Fuel flow increased on the operating engine, as the air became denser.

Hunter kept control of the nose, not letting them fall too fast. Lynche finally understood what he intended. Then they were five miles out at 25,000 feet.

"Dirty penetration," Hunter said. "Call out the airspeed if we go below 170." He was fully engaged with coordinating the approach with the runway, looking outside to acquire the airport.

Passing through 20,000 feet, Hunter turned the yoke to increase bank angle slightly. He acquired the runway lights, but there were no strobes off one side, and he returned the wings to level.

Three and a half miles from the field, Lynche wanted to ask, "Is this how you do it on a carrier?" but was afraid of interrupting Hunter's focus.

The needle bounced between 200 and 300 pounds of fuel, the engine at idle, and fuel flow increased rapidly in the dense air. Lynche feared a flame-out. Crashing in the jungle was a real possibility.

"November one zero zero," LeMarcus said over the radio. "Cleared to land runway two two. Altimeter two niner niner two."

They were two miles from the field. As the jet roared through 15,000 feet above the runway, Hunter maintained 170 knots on the indicator and said calmly, "One two three, landing checklist complete."

Lynche spoke to the tower. "November one zero zero, cleared to land runway two two, two niner niner zero." He subconsciously leaned back in his seat as the jet screamed perpendicular to the runway lights, flying directly over Roberts Field at 10,000 feet.

Two seconds later, Hunter fully deflected the yoke to the left to achieve a 45° angle of bank in his attitude indicator. He kept pressure on the stick for 270° of turn, and continually looked down at the runway lights and mentally calculating the proper sight picture.

The two-mile runway was fully lit. They were very high and coming down very fast.

"We're high," Lynche said.

"High is OK. We have lots of runway. Give me the landing lights, Sir." He maintained his sight picture of the runway in the inky blackness through 5,000 feet in the left turn and ignored the instruments. It was all sight picture now.

As the runway lights started to converge and level out, Hunter slammed the yoke and rudder to the right, snap-rolled the jet wings-level, and arrested the descent with a hefty pull of the yoke. He jammed the engine to the firewall for two seconds, then back to idle.

The rate of descent slowed to 2,000 feet per minute. With five seconds of wings-level groove time to line up the aircraft on the runway's centerline, Hunter input a "right for line up" correction and returned to wings-level. Landing lights illuminated the runway's landing threshold.

He flared the nose, keeping a nose-high attitude to let the Gulfstream decelerate on its own to the ground. The main landing gear gently touched down right over the displaced threshold. Four seconds later, Hunter allowed the nose to touch on the centerline.

Lynche pumped both fists and shouted toward the front windscreen, "Yea!"

Hunter lifted his feet from the floor to apply even pressure to the toe brakes, as the jet cleanly decelerated under 100 knots. At fifty knots, Hunter guided the jet onto the first taxiway.

Once they were clear of the runway, the runway lights went out. While they were still rolling, Hunter indicated he knew where he would park and fired up the APU and shut down number two. Lynche shook his head in disbelief as the fuel tanks read less than forty pounds. They had less than six gallons in the airplane, assuming the indicators read correctly.

Hunter brought the rolling jet to the edge of the tarmac, depressed the right brake, and swung the jet ninety degrees before stopping. Exhaling loudly, he said, "Welcome to Monrovia, Mr. Lynche." Unbuckling his harness, he took a deep breath.

Greg shook his head in disbelief. His partner simply smiled like the cat that ate the canary.

"That was a first," Greg said, helping Hunter shut down everything in the cockpit.

"That probably was. Definitely not in the operator's manual." Hunter was very somber, as he shut off the APU and all other systems. Had the long and lanky Lynche not been flailing in the cockpit trying to leave his seat, he would've noticed Hunter's hands trembling slightly. As pumps and motors shut down, the aircraft gradually became quiet.

From the dark cabin behind them, someone said, "Sometime soon, I need to change my shorts."

Hunter, Lynche, and the SEALs laughed.

Osama bin Laden didn't get the joke.

CHAPTER FIFTY-ONE

0700 June 17, 2011
United States Naval Observatory, Washington, DC

Vice President Frank Carey stepped out of the black limousine, admiring the quaint, three-story house at Number One Observatory Circle, the official home and residence of the Vice President of the United States. The previous day, he didn't care about moving into the house, preferring to remain in his Bethesda mansion. He assumed the Secret Service would have to provide security at his home and compound. He could make a little money.

However, when the Secret Service director asked if the new vice president would move into the official residence with all its underground bunkers and communications systems or remain at his house in Bethesda, Carey reconsidered. He wanted to see the house and all its furnishings. Even if he moved in, he wouldn't be there long.

With the potential of an exciting, new underground playground for him and his partner, Carey said, "Let's go see it."

Secret Service Director Marty O'Sullivan rode in the number- three armored Suburban of the eight-vehicle caravan. He met the vice president as the portly man struggled to leave the limousine. Once he was out and composed, ready to receive the SS director, O'Sullivan motioned for him to take the lead and instructed, "We will provide security for the VP and his family either here at the official residence or at your home, Sir."

The SS director acted as tour guide of the house and underground facility. Carey wasn't interested in the upstairs but wanted to see the basement. The entourage remained outside the study and private office.

562

Carey maintained a disinterested look about the rooms. "I suppose the help is off. The place isn't that well-maintained. I expected much higher-quality furnishings."

"Sir, all the furniture and pictures in the house were donated from past vice presidents. The Smithsonian can provide you with something more to your liking if these aren't sufficient for your needs."

Carey nodded, waggling his jowls, as O'Sullivan showed him where the secret switch to open the passageway to the elevator was located. The elevator dropped quickly 70 feet to the bottom, where an underground bunker and modern communications center lay before Carey's eyes.

"This is more like it," he said, running his fingers along the walnut conference table and high-backed leather captain's chairs. Wandering in and out of the naturally cooled spaces, he looked in the gym, bedroom, and kitchen. "This has a high coolness factor."

O'Sullivan nodded.

"What's the latest on the threat on the president?" Carey asked casually. "I haven't heard of any new dead SEALs."

"Mr. Vice President, the remaining SEAL from the Naval War College list is Captain Bill McGee. As of this morning, he was alive and well in Newport, Rhode Island. I spoke with him myself. He hasn't seen anything out of the ordinary. It appears that the targeting of SEALs stopped with the Norfolk killing."

The vice president turned cold. "Are you sure?"

"We remain on high alert. The Navy and DEVGRU know they're being targeted. Once they think someone's out there targeting them, they'll do whatever is necessary to protect their own. If they find the shooter, they'll move heaven and earth to find out who's responsible. If they can discern the responsible party, they'll hold them accountable. There will be hell to pay, and SEALs will extract revenge."

Color drained from the portly man's face.

O'Sullivan, trained in a myriad of behavior recognition techniques, read the vice president's curious response. He decided not to show the man the remaining tunnels, safe rooms, and storage at the opposite end of the control room of the underground bunker.

"Maybe the reason they haven't heard anything is that the SEALs took care of the shooter," Carey offered, "so the threat to POTUS has been eliminated."

"Time will tell, Mr. Vice President. Will this be sufficient?"

He nodded. "I'll take one for the team and move in." Carey walked toward the elevator. The tour was over.

O'Sullivan couldn't begin to comprehend what was going on in the new VP's mind. His response to a SEAL's retribution for the killing of SEALs was more than odd. It signaled he knew more than he let on, but so had the discussion with Captain Bill McGee.

CHAPTER FIFTY-TWO

1400 June 17, 2011
Roberts International Airport Monrovia, Liberia

Liberia's main airport always played a key role in aviation and geopolitical history. Liberia's air role during World War Two began when President Franklin D. Roosevelt directed the legendary head of Pan American World Airways, Juan Trippe, to expand and modernize the airline's facilities in Africa, the Caribbean, and Latin America in preparation for war. He also required a Pan Am Clipper flying boat be dispatched to the Port of Monrovia to retrieve a world-altering cargo—sandbags of uranium ore from the Belgian Congo, from which Enrico Fermi would carry out the first successful nuclear chain reaction.

The president funded several improvement efforts for the upcoming war, which included expanding runways and tarmac and built officer housing for the Ferry Command of the US Army Air Corps. The airfield adjacent to the Firestone Plantation was assigned the code name "Thomas Jefferson" and later changed to Roberts Field in honor of Liberia's first president.

Hamlets of grass huts sprang up near the airport, where locals made themselves available for whatever work they could find. Some harvested sap at Firestone just across the river. Cured natural rubber from Firestone was loaded onto planes at Roberts Field and flown to a dirt strip, offloaded, and trucked two miles to awaiting Pan Am Clippers for the flight to the United States.

In January, 1943, on his return from Casablanca, President Roosevelt visited the bustling Roberts Field and rested for several hours at the airfield's commanding officer's bungalow along the Farmington River. Liberia wasn't subject to the various coups and wars its colonial neighbors were constantly engaged in. It was viewed as an American colony, the home of free slaves living in peace since the early 1820s. As Liberia grew, so did its place in aviation history.

In the 1970s, Roberts Field became a Pan Am Africa hub for 747s transiting from South America for the Middle East or South Africa. World-class catering from French chefs filled the cabins of the new transiting jumbo jets. In the early 1980s, the main runway was doubled in length after Roberts Field was designated a Space Shuttle emergency landing site.

The Roberts Field airport was run by senior Pan Am employees for over twenty years. The manager and his staff lived on the airport in houses along the river.

The airport closed during the civil war under Charles Taylor but was still active as a smuggling hub for Viktor Bout's private fleet of Russian cargo aircraft, moving huge arms shipments into various civil wars in Africa in the 1990s and later.

Osama bin Laden, under the watchful eye of a heavily armed US Navy SEAL, sat quietly at a table, eating chicken and rice, in the same building that was once a staging point for uranium ore destined for America, which once accommodated a war-weary US president, several Pan Am station managers, and the Merchant of Death.

When he heard an approaching vehicle stop outside the house, he knew it was his last day on earth. "I've been waiting for this moment. I'm at peace."

He tried to convince himself he was at peace, but his fingers shook slightly. He didn't want them to see he was afraid. He overestimated the Americans' ability to find him, as well as America's resolve to interrogate him. How could he have been so blind?

"al-Zawahiri; you betrayed me.

"al-Zawahiri; I trusted you, and you betrayed me.

"al-Zawahiri; how could I have been so blind not to have seen the signs? You betrayed me.

"al-Zawahiri; why did you wait so long to betray me?

"al-Zawahiri; I will be strong." He would try to be strong. "Ayman was strong as a young man, and he broke. I won't break. I won't. I will not break. al-Zawahiri; I trusted you, and you betrayed me. I've given Allah everything, and the Americans took everything from me."

After several minutes, he turned his head left and stared at the two grocery bags and automotive battery. He wondered what the Americans were waiting for.

Lifting his head, he turned to look at the big man with the big gun. "Kill me!" he shouted in Arabic. "Kill me!"

* * *

Twenty-five miles away, a rested Duncan Hunter walked under huge palms, scaring away dozens of large, green lizards with orange tails that ran ahead or over the sides of the elevated wooden walkway. Two white-headed crows hopped away before taking flight and landing a few feet away, scolding him for making them move.

Hunter's footfalls loudly continued along the apparently Picasso-inspired bizarre walkway, where wood, elevation, and confusing directions conspired to keep one on his toes and on the path.

After checking in, an exhausted Lynche took a misstep off the walkway and tumbled eighteen inches below into a thorn-free succulent. The seventy-year-old former spookmeister hurt something, but, since it wasn't fatal or oozing blood, he was too tired to worry about it. Dragging his tired ass back onto the elevated walkway, he shuffled to his room and to bed.

Thick, puffy clouds continued to race west to do mayhem as the seedlings of a hurricane. Hunter confidently strolled toward the table under the thatched roof gazebo. He counted noses in the distance, seeing Nazy, Lynche, and the SEAL who introduced himself as "Spock."

Spock wore civvies, his olive T-shirt showcasing sculpted biceps. LeMarcus wasn't there, because he had an airport to run. The three people at the table engaged in small talk, as Hunter approached.

They stopped talking as he took an open seat and tossed a pharmaceutical package on the table. Blue tablets sealed with metalized foil caught their attention.

"Remember to take your anti-malarials," Hunter said. "I nearly forgot, but a tiny bastard kept buzzing in my ear and reminded me."

Lynche took the card with plastic blisters, pushed a pill through the foil backing, and handed the card to Nazy. She took it without comment or expression. Lynche realized his mistake.

"What an idiot," he said. "I'm sorry, Nazy. I should've offered it to you first."

Cunningham took one and offered the package to the SEAL, who politely declined.

"No thank you, Ma'am. I'm already on the regimen."

Greg tried to stifle a yawn but couldn't. The SEAL yawned, followed by Hunter, then Nazy. She gently punched Lynche's shoulder.

"See what you started?" she scolded.

Hunter raised his hand toward the waiter at his stand near the main building. "Anyone order food yet?"

"Waiting for you, Sunshine," quipped Lynche.

The foursome quietly ordered from the menu and accepted bottled water and juice for drinks. Two of the three men were exhausted from flying and traveling for days. Spock looked ready to run a marathon backward. Lynche falling off the walkway, despite his assurances he was all right, concerned Hunter. He was in great shape for his age, but they'd been through four days of physically nonstop, emotionally draining effort.

"How are you feeling, good Sir?" Hunter asked.

"Shoulder a little sore. Could've been a lot worse."

Hunter patted his friend's opposite shoulder, and Lynche feigned a new wound. There was plenty of fatigue but there wasn't much sympathy around the table.

"Everyone OK?" They nodded.

"Then we should eat and head to the airport to get started. Any idea how long it will take?" He looked into Nazy's eyes, but Spock answered.

"He's terrified," Spock said. "I think he'll talk freely. We stripped him of every ounce of protection. He saw one of his wives try to take a bullet for him. His sons were killed. We shaved and loused him. He begged me to shoot him several times." Spock's demeanor changed, as if he suddenly wanted to talk and get his information out.

"You speak Arabic?" Nazy asked.

"I understand some, enough to order a beer or a Coke. He's a typical rich Saudi who's had it easy all his life. He's not very bright and is definitely a coward. He's scared shitless. Excuse my language, Ma'am."

Nazy nodded.

"I could've popped him ten times. He just stood there when we burst in like it didn't compute that men in black were there to take him away. He just froze and pissed himself. Two wives rushed to protect him without weapons. I stepped through them and hit him with my Taser. My backups tased the women; his wives.

"I zip-tied him while he was still flipping and jerking around, then carried him upstairs to the helicopter. The rest of the team took care of the women and gathered evidence. We made the room look like he'd been shot. No one on the chopper knew he was just knocked out with a sedative.

"I cut off his clothes, inspected him, and wiped him down before putting him into a uniform. Even with the helicopter blades swirling around, he smelled really bad. We expected that, too."

"You cut his hair and shaved his beard?"

"I did. Yes, Ma'am. Right there on the chopper. I wasn't gentle."

The men smiled. Nazy remained fascinated.

"I'll bet that was tough. You were the point guy, Spock." Hunter beamed with pride, his arms crossed.

"Yes, Sir. I was the belly button. I wanted to kill him for America, but it wasn't his time to die. The team was very surprised when we got the go order. We'd been waiting for months."

"That order was given because of Ms. Cunningham." Hunter nodded to the ponytailed brunette.

"Thank you, Ma'am. I don't know what you did to get the president off his skinny little ass. We could've done it months earlier. The team wasn't a happy group, like stallions tied up in a burning barn. You guys Agency?"

"She is," Lynche said. "I was, and he's something—he pretends to be a pilot or an intellectual or an athlete. Or something."

"Sir, I really don't like flying. I don't mind jumping out of airplanes or falling asleep to get somewhere. I don't know what you did last night, but you scared the hell out of me."

"Sorry, Spock. I guess I should've made one of those flight attendant courtesy calls." Hunter looked at Lynche. "Is there even a way to make an announcement from the cockpit?"

The SEAL was confused when Hunter added, "I really haven't been flying that long. I had no idea what I was doing up there. He wakes me up, and the next thing I know, we're falling out of the sky."

Color drained from Spock's face, and his jaw dropped. "Don't believe a word of it," Lynche said, coming to the man's rescue. "He's an old Marine F-4 pilot, and he isn't very funny. The asshole scared me, too."

Nazy was confused.

The SEAL straightened and offered Hunter his hand. "Ooh- rah, Sir. My dad was a Marine."

"Semper *Fi*, Spock."

Lynche almost spoke but thought better of it.

"The real brains behind al-Qaeda was Zawahiri," Nazy said. "Osama was the money man. He got a lot of praise for it. In the Middle East, if you dole out money to poor people, they'll do just about anything you want."

"Yes, Ma'am," Spock said. "Personal observation—the dude's been forcibly extracted from his life and comfort zone. For the last six or seven weeks, he's been completely terrified. He isn't a soldier or warrior. He's a coward who's in way over his head. I think he'll tell you everything without much prodding."

Food was served. The conversation turned to banalities while the wait staff hovered nearby. Hunter pinched off pieces of toast, trying to lure birds close to the table. Gray-headed sparrows and European starlings flitted close by, fighting over the pieces, when a brown bird with bright-red eyes flew into Lynche's hair.

Everyone stopped eating and watched the bird try to gain purchase on his head. Its red-and-yellow bill raced around Lynche's full head of grey hair, chasing an invisible bug before giving up and flying away.

"Did he crap on me?" Lynche asked, exasperated.

"It doesn't look like it," Nazy said.

"What kind of bird was that?" the SEAL asked.

"That was a yellow-billed oxpecker," Hunter said deadpan. They broke up immediately and laughed aloud. Spock covered his eyes with one hand, turned his head, and fought to compose himself as tears filled his eyes. He dabbed them away with a napkin. The shift from serious work to levity was instantaneous.

"Ox...pecker," Spock said with a mischievous grin, starting another round of infectious laughter.

Lynche and Nazy were confused by the laughter and coughing coming from the big, strong, powerful SEAL. Hunter grinned with amusement and understanding.

"I think his boss goes by Ox," Hunter explained. "And I'm serious. I know my birds, and that really was a yellow-billed oxpecker. That's funny."

Another fit of laughter swept through the table.

Once the waiters and waitresses moved away, Lynche said, "I hope you're right, Spock. Duncan knows I have issues with torture. I don't want to be around, and I don't want to know, but after watching Duncan handle that jet and get us here in one piece, I realized I'm not the smartest guy on the planet. Maybe I ought to be a little more open-minded on certain things. That's my way of admitting that, because of the situation, I haven't fully thought this out."

Before anyone could respond, Hunter stretched and yawned. "The situation is this. These guys have been telling us day in and day out they're going to kill us. One day you open your eyes and find some version of Dr. Evil holding a .44 Magnum to your forehead, with the barrel and front sight jammed against your skin.

"What do you do? If you're a liberal, Marxist, socialist, communist, Islamo-fascist, environmental whack job, radical, or any of the other dumb-ass panty-waisted bed-wetters out there, I suppose you let the asshole shoot you. If you're a conservative, a capitalist, a patriot, an American, an Israeli, or British Special Forces, or even if you have just half a brain, you snatch the gun from Dr. Evil and beat the shit out of him before shooting him six times. You put the film of what's left of Dr. Evil on the Internet."

"If you have to piss up his nose to get him to tell you where they're hiding the keys to the Mark Ten thermonuclear device, you keep water coming until he calls uncle. You title the film, Negotiating with Dr. Evil."

"So when this turd has not only been threatening me, my family, my friends, my fellow Americans, and my country's friends, and I now find myself having that gun pressed against my head, I intend to do something about it. I won't worry or second guess what the idiots on the other side of the aisle think of me. 9/11 was the day that opened my eyes."

The outburst surprised them all. "Amen, Brother," Spock said softly.

"I think the marvelous Ms. Cunningham can get our distinguished guest to spill his guts, and all talk of torture or enhanced interrogation techniques will be moot. But if we can't get him to sing, we don't have much time to dick with him. In this case, I want what's in his head that'll hurt our families, my fellow Americans, and my country's friends. If he doesn't respond to negotiation, then nothing ventured, nothing gained."

Hunter took a deep breath and continued. "As far as the world's concerned, he's already dead. There are places on this continent where it's common to see human road kill. Life is cheap, and no one cares. There are no laws in this country or on this entire continent where flogging a dead man is a crime. I'll bet Osama bin Laden will take one look at Ms. Cunningham, then at the car battery with jumper cables, and he'll decide to say anything to keep talking to the mellifluous voice coming from her beautiful face."

"You may be right," Lynche said.

"I was the secret weapon at Gitmo," Nazy said. "When all else failed, I could get them to talk." She looked at Hunter with hurt and disdain. "And, I never used battery cables."

The men smirked.

"Amen," Spock said. "Let's get this show on the road. I'd like to get home sometime."

"Meet in the lobby in fifteen minutes?" Hunter asked.

They all nodded.

As Hunter walked to the main building, he called over his shoulder, "I need to get food for Spike."

Before the other three left the table, Lynche said, "Always a Marine officer. I have to tell you that someone close to Duncan died in the World Trade Center attack—an off-duty flight attendant on the American Airlines flight. He doesn't talk about it much. I understand she was an old neighbor who lived across the street. They even dated in high school. So it's kinda personal."

"I didn't know that." Nazy appreciated the information.

"My kind of guy," Spock said.

"Mine, too," Nazy and Lynche said simultaneously.

CHAPTER FIFTY-THREE

1900 June 17, 2011
Roberts International Airport Monrovia, Liberia

Nazy, Spock, Lynche, and Hunter left the brilliant sunshine and high humidity outside, as they entered the back door and passed through the kitchen of the old airport manager's house on the Farmington River. Upon seeing the woman and three men, the most people bin Laden had seen in weeks, he knew they were the CIA interrogation crew he expected and feared.

"You don't intimidate me!" he shrieked. "I have rights."

Nazy, translating without looking at him, sat behind the Saudi. Osama bin Laden glared at her, as she left his field of vision.

Nazy and Greg immediately got over the shock of seeing the terrorist struggling against his restraints. Hunter ignored the man and removed his backpack from his shoulder in front of bin Laden, then he walked to the plastic grocery bags LeMarcus brought from town to extract a roll of duct tape. He tore off a piece, walked up to the prisoner, and backhanded him hard. While bin Laden recovered from the surprising blow, Hunter slapped duct tape across his mouth and stubble.

Lynche turned his head, thinking he had to leave the room. But he stayed.

On the drive from the hotel to the airport, Hunter and Nazy chatted quietly in the back seat. Lynche occasionally heard what they planned to do and how they hoped to get the terrorist to break.

As Lynche drove, Spock snoozed beside him, and the lovebirds in back discussed how Hunter would encourage Osama bin Laden to talk. Though Lynche might have heard the words "getting his attention," he knew Hunter would torture the man.

Lynche convinced himself that when Hunter reached the point where he couldn't watch anymore, he'd go outside, take a long walk, and ignore the whole thing. However, when Hunter slapped bin Laden, Lynche was instantly mesmerized.

Hunter was first and foremost a pilot and college professor of aviation. He had no training or history in interrogation, and neither did Lynche. Feeling anxious, Lynche saw that the situation could get out of hand, and they'd soon have a dead terrorist to dispose of; their mission for naught.

Nazy was a trained interrogator for the Agency. Lynche had difficulty comprehending that she'd have sanctioned such activity, and his gaze went from bin Laden to Hunter to Nazy, seeking answers to the questions ricocheting in his mind.

Her expression was mild shock and stunned horror when Hunter unleashed his hideous backhand. Lynche saw his friend play racquetball enough to recognize the powerful choreographed uncoiling of his torso with his feet instinctively placed to capture the full energy transfer to the point of impact. Spittle flew from Osama bin Laden's mouth. Lynche expected his jaw to be broken or to see teeth tumble from his mouth, but it didn't happen. He felt Hunter's interrogation was spinning out of control and steeled himself for a confrontation. Lynche crossed his arms, sending the unmistakable and powerful body language that he disapproved, but stayed rooted to the floor.

Osama bin Laden glared at Hunter, then he looked toward where the woman in the headscarf disappeared. For some reason, she wanted to hide her face. He bounced in his seat, hoping to overturn the chair, but Spock stepped up and held it steady. Spike, disinterested and hungry, left the building, thinking the show was about to start. He had food to eat.

"Tell him, 'You don't have any rights.'" Hunter took several newspapers from his backpack. All came from May 2, 2011, and the headlines read Osama Dead! He tossed them onto the table in front of the man. "Tell him, 'As far as anyone is concerned, you're already dead.' Translate, please."

Nazy spoke rapidly in Arabic.

Osama bin Laden was stunned. His eyes turned upward to see Duncan withdraw a roll of white plastic cord and a small electronic device with a switch, setting them on the table.

"Whatever I do to you," Hunter said, "I'm doing to a dead man who's sitting at the bottom of the Indian Ocean. Translate, please."

Nazy brought a chair to the far end of the table and sat. She didn't look at bin Laden as she shook her head, but she translated as asked.

Osama bin Laden was confused. He blinked his eyes wildly. Everyone watched Hunter walk to the far side of the room, armed with a two-foot, five-inch-thick piece of mahogany in one hand. In the other he held dull white loops of cord that resembled clothesline.

"Count one, two three, in Arabic, please," Hunter said. He swung the wood against the concrete floor. The low-frequency thudding was unmistakable, showing the wood was solid and dense. In one movement, he placed the log against the opposite wall from Osama bin Laden and looped the white cord around the middle of the log in a series of half-hitches, until there were three tight, white loops against the dark-brown wood.

Hunter took pliers from his pocket and cut the end to separate the roll with the clove hitch on the wood. He walked to the table and placed the cord directly in front of Osama bin Laden.

Evil eyes bored into Hunter's back, as he retrieved the little black box and pulled wires from it as he walked toward the piece of wood. Hunter bent over and carefully inserted a wire into each end of the white cord. Suddenly, the device with wires contrasting the white cord took on an ominous quality. Osama bin Laden unconsciously leaned to see what Duncan was doing.

When Hunter stood, he raised the little black box to his waist. "Fingers in your ears. Please count to three in Arabic."

Nazy did as instructed. On "three," Hunter pressed the red button, and a muffled explosion filled the room with concussive power. The white cord instantly vaporized on the mahogany and severed the log into two equal parts.

Bin Laden, shocked by the power of the detonating cord, remained stunned as Hunter moved quickly to bin Laden and wrapped three loops of the innocuous-looking cord around the terrorist's right wrist. In abject terror, bin Laden fought the duct tape, shaking his head vigorously. Spock kept the chair firmly planted on the floor.

Hunter clipped the end of the cord, inserted the wires into the detonation cord, and set the little black box on the end of the table. Hate filled the terrorist's eyes, and Hunter looked at him from under his brows.

Hunter turned and walked to the other side of the room. All eyes followed him, as he picked up the jumper cables and strolled back to the front of the table. With a black-covered clamp in one hand and a red-covered clamp in the other, he walked to the front of the table and squeezed both clamps, bracketing the deadly black box and revealing sharp, copper-colored teeth that would have made a prehistoric raptor envious. Duncan Hunter held them in front of his face, admiring the workmanship and functionality before thrusting the clamps into the edge of the table and releasing the tension. Sharp copper teeth dug into the old wood, emitting a grunt from the friction as the wood was punctured and crushed.

Osama bin Laden's eyes never left the black-and-red insulated clamps, following their path to the table. Fear replaced hate. The table's wood wasn't rotten, but the clamps had strong springs and sharp teeth. Wondering just how bad the sadist in front of him would hurt him, he began to hyperventilate.

"Translate please. Here's the deal. You know how Ayman al-Zawahiri was tortured by the Muslim Brotherhood. Just so there is no ambiguity, Muslim brothers used jumper cables like these and clamped them on his testicles like this. He talked."

Hunter opened the black clamp and removed it from the table, walking to where bin Laden sat. He jammed the meaty part of bin Laden's right hand into the V of the clamp and released the tension.

Half-inch copper teeth tore into his soft flesh, muscle, and bone. Thick blood oozed from the clamp. Osama bin Laden shrieked and howled against the tape on his face. Spock held the heavy wooden chair firm, as the man tried to pull his hand and arm away from the duct tape but failed. Blood dripped to the floor.

Lynche's pulse quickened, but he didn't move. Nazy closed her eyes and momentarily looked away.

Osama bin Laden thrashed against his restraints and screamed into the duct tape but tired quickly. The chair rocked back and forth as he broke down; the fight was leaving him.

After a moment, bin Laden's energy was spent, and he wept. Hunter squeezed the jumper cable and removed it from the weeping man. The relief on his face was instantaneous. He hated the American.

Nazy asked if he needed medical attention. He nodded. "A little."

Spock moved in with a first-aid kit from a cargo pocket and quickly dressed the flesh wound. Admiring his handiwork and applying two Band-Aids, Spock retired to his position against the wall.

"We can do this the hard way or the easy way," Nazy translated. "You tell me what I want to know, and no battery cables. You lie to me, or spit at her.... Translate please."

Osama bin Laden raised his shaven head to look at his tormentor. Hate was gone, replaced by fear.

"...and I push the red button before I bolt your balls to

the battery. Do I need to demonstrate the power of my battery?" His inflection was chilling.

Nazy translated.

Osama bin Laden shivered; his breathing increased. He was terrified. He shook his head.

Hunter's expression didn't change, but he knew he had him.

"You cooperate, and I won't hurt you. I'll remove the tape. We can have a friendly talk on a variety of subjects I want to know, things I think you want people to know. When we're done, I'll put you on a jet and point you toward Mecca, and we're out of your life forever. I promise."

Nazy struggled to keep up with Hunter's machine gun words.

Lynche was shocked by Hunter's promise. He was lying, and he thought Osama bin Laden knew it.

"You lie, or I think you're lying, and you lose your hand," Hunter continued. "Then I'll clamp your balls with these clamps. As they crush and shred your testicles, I'll hook you up to that battery."

Hunter took three steps to the battery on the floor, attached one end of the cables to the terminals, then he quickly banged the two uninsulated ends together, creating a spectacular shower of sparks. Brilliant white light flashed in the darkened room. Tiny balls of molten metal fell to the floor from the blackened ends. The smell of ozone filled the room.

"You'll hear your testicles shatter before you feel them explode. You'll know why Zawahiri was a broken man, why he talked. I don't want to hurt you. I only want to know what really happened. Am I clear?"

Nazy translated in rapid-fire Arabic. The last group of words, apparently translated more easily.

Osama bin Laden, inhaling the scent of vaporized metal, gazed at the blackened ends of the clamps, then he nodded toward Hunter. He stopped hyperventilating, and his breathing relaxed.

Hunter still anticipated bin Laden would try to fool him.

When he withdrew a large pocketknife and opened the blade to reveal a wickedly serrated edge, bin Laden's eyes bulged, and he tried to back up in the chair, anticipating pain and terror from the madman.

Hunter slowly peeled the tape from bin Laden's face and cut the duct tape from his left hand and arm, allowing him to use one hand.

Bin Laden wiped his mouth. Hunter went into the kitchen and returned with a bottle of water. Bin Laden took small sips. As he quenched his thirst, Hunter removed the clamps from the table. The additional freedom of motion and movement seemed to energize the terrorist. He ran scenarios and rationalized his responses to expected questions. He wouldn't make it easy for the American.

His microexpressions gave him away. The SEAL snapped his fingers to get Hunter's attention.

"He's still thinking about how he will lie," the SEAL said.

Nazy, resplendent in dark-blue headscarf and abaya, didn't look at the terrorist as she said, "Your family is well. They weren't harmed. The men came for you to ask you questions. Please cooperate, and no harm will come to you. We can tell you're thinking about not cooperating. Please banish such thoughts. You're a great leader sheikh. You're a true knight for Islam. You fought Zionists and infidels. Please answer my questions fully and with dignity, and no harm will come to you."

The terrorist turned to Spock, as the SEAL revealed his wireless Taser. Osama bin Laden learned to fear the black stick with the red bulb on its end. When a SEAL flicked the switch to *On*, and the stick crackled with tens of thousands of volts, bin Laden learned to do what was asked. Four hits from the bang stick was enough. By turning on the device, the SEAL reminded bin Laden there was at least one other way to die while screaming.

Osama bin Laden took a thoughtful, deep breath and asked, "What do you wish to ask me, my child?"

Nazy nodded, and the SEAL de-energized the Taser. Nazy

didn't look at Osama bin Laden directly. She conducted and recorded the discussion as if it were an interview.

"Why did al-Zawahiri betray you?"

"I knew it." Osama bin Laden shook his head and told her what he thought about their last fight and the accusations—and where he thought the Americans would find him.

Nazy asked question after question from her list. She took notes in the margins, as the high-tech recorder rolled on. Lynche completely recovered from his earlier stage fright and brought chicken and rice and water for the terrorist.

OBL slowly ate between questions. Several times, he challenged Nazy's assertion of where he kept account numbers, accounts, and computer access codes. "I hid them were no one would find them. In two Bibles!"

Hunter and Lynche recognized the Arabic word for Bible.

"The Americans expected to find radios and the Internet but did not. No Internet. Radios were built into the walls of my studios. Very difficult to find."

For several hours, the terrorist and the intelligence officer in the headscarf discussed the inner workings and funding of al-Qaeda, the treachery of Zawahiri, planning for 9/11, Osama bin Laden's escape from Afghanistan, and the move to his house in Pakistan.

They discussed his family, his health, and his future with a bounty on his head. Did he ever think America would come for him? How did Pakistan fail to protect him?

They established a dialogue that was non-adversarial but spirited at times. When Nazy felt he was equivocating, she looked at Duncan with a tinge of incredulity Osama immediately recognized. He never apologized to her but offered to restate what he meant, hoping the sadist across the room wouldn't question his answers.

Nazy asked, "How did Bashir become involved? We know he provided some of the martyrs for 9/11."

"You know about Bashir?" Osama bin Laden blurted. "Your intelligence is very good. Ah, he had the resources."

Nazy nodded. Bin Laden unconsciously shook his head in disbelief.

"He provided all martyrs. He liked young men. I disapproved, but al-Zawahiri was insistent. We needed quality, educated, English-speaking martyrs to go to America. We didn't have quality mujahidin in Afghanistan for such martyr operations. Bashir had many men willing to please Allah. Peace be upon Him."

"Newspapers reported twenty martyrs for 9/11, but we know there were many more."

Osama bin Laden glanced at Hunter and nodded. "Yes. We planned ten aircraft, with five muj per aircraft. Martyrs from Britain."

"And, they passed through airport security where Muslims worked. Many airports," Nazy stated.

Osama bin Laden, showing a little surprise, nodded again. "Bashir's concept was a very good plan. Mujahidin and shaheed were excited to serve Allah. We didn't expect they would stop the aircraft from flying."

"Always Muslim boys?"

"Of course. Shaheed, volunteers, a martyr over many years. He cultivated many for his business and al-Qaeda. His favorites were well provided for."

"Like funds for college? He gave money to poor families for their boys." She was exhausted, and the information came from the terrorist's mouth faster than she could write.

"Exactly. You know this, too? Remarkable. Yes, he provided money to families. Boys would go to Europe. Money for colleges."

"Is it fair to say all you had to do was entertain Bashir and his friends, and he'd provide them and their family's money?"

"Yes."

"The American president visited you when he was a young man. Several times."

Osama bin Laden blinked several times. "Yes. I don't remember him very well. We saw many interested in jihad."

Nazy looked at him, clearly not believing his words.

Osama bin Laden saw she didn't believe him. "He visited Pakistan and Afghanistan two times. I saw him two times. I remember the large ears. I could not use him. He was very weak, bookish and boring. Only wanted to talk. I sent him back to Bashir. Bashir said he had a project for big ears. Sent him to America schools. Bashir suggested politics. Becoming president was a surprise."

"Was that your idea or Bashir's? That sounds like your idea, Sheikh." She felt she was at the threshold of learning something significant. She glanced at Hunter for relief only to find him yawning.

"Thank you, but no. Bashir." An epiphany struck bin Laden, and his eyes brightened.

"And, then he tried to kill you. He sent soldiers to kill you. Why?"

Bin Laden's hand throbbed, but he smiled and chuckled. Suddenly, he smiled at Hunter, then he turned to Nazy, nodding with understanding.

She translated, "This is why you let me live."

Everyone in the room jumped when Spock energized the bang stick. Static electricity sizzled in the room.

Nazy's expression implored him to turn it off and put it away.

Osama bin Laden sat quietly, thinking. He looked at Hunter, at the det cord, the battery cables, the SEAL, and the black wireless cattle prod.

Hunter checked his Rolex Submariner. It was 3:35 AM. "Now or never."

Nazy didn't translate.

"You promise to put me on airplane?" She translated for Hunter.

"I promise to put you on an airplane. A jet." He was deadly serious, no emotion. Time's up, he thought.

"I don't know the answer to your question," bin Laden told Nazy. "I know only his father is Muslim. He's Muslim. He speaks perfect Arabic, as well as you. He affirmed his Muslim faith. Al- Zawahiri got him Pakistan passports. Al-Zawahiri may know more. He was Bashir's lover long ago. He worked for or has helped Bashir grow his fortune. Bashir is very proud of his president. That's all I know. Not sufficient to send soldiers to kill me."

"But you planned to kill him?"

"Yes. The vice president is an idiot. Al-Zawahiri and I thought to have the president killed, and that idiot would follow. As president, the idiot would bring America to its knees. Bashir had a special man who could do it, but he refused. He would do anything to protect his president."

The enormity of what he just said was masked by the quiet that followed Nazy's translation. The group, on the verge of exhaustion, was stunned.

Osama bin Laden's eyes pleaded for understanding. "Did I provide the correct answers you were looking for?"

Hunter listened to Nazy's translation and nodded. "Tell him, 'Thank you.' He did well. Now he has a plane to catch." He nodded imperceptibly to the SEAL.

As Nazy translated, relief spread across Osama bin Laden's face. Spock silently stepped behind the terrorist and covered his nose and mouth with a cloth saturated with chloroform. The old terrorist was unconscious in moments.

Nazy, exhausted from the marathon interrogation, instantly perked up as OBL thrashed in the chair. "You lied to him."

"I wouldn't call it a lie. Let's say he assumed one thing, and I meant another."

"Like Waleed?"

"Yes, Ma'am. Like Waleed."

* * *

LeMarcus Leonard walked up to the observation deck of the control tower and waited for the jet's taxi lights to illuminate. "Leave it to an old fighter pilot to say he'd be ready to leave at 0430, and at exactly 0430, he turns on his taxi lights," he told the dozen geckos near the ceiling of the slanted glass container.

LeMarcus flipped the runway master switch to *On* and pushed the big Runway and Taxiway switches forward. Out of the starless night, white edge lights appeared instantaneously. When he looked up from the airfield lighting control panel, he saw the position and anticollision lights of the aircraft he knew to be a white-and-red Gulfstream IVSP already on the taxiway, heading toward the runway. The jet didn't wait for control tower instructions.

The pilot taxied to the midfield intersection of the runway, made a gentle left turn to line up on the centerline, and departed Roberts International.

When the aircraft was obviously airborne, LeMarcus toggled all the lighting switches to Off, took one look around the observation deck, and descended the stairs.

* * *

Osama bin Laden awoke with a massive headache. He tried to lift his head from his chest. His eyes hurt, and his sinuses were on fire. He tried to take inventory of his surroundings but couldn't identify where he was. It was nearly pitch black.

He tried to focus on his hands, but it was too dark. Though relieved he could move his hands, he couldn't see them. The effort made him very tired, and he had difficulty breathing.

Wherever he was, the air was stale, dusty, and thick. The high humidity smelled of old rubber and mold. Sensing significant pressure on his arms, he tried to move them, but they were restrained. He gave up trying to gain his bearings. It was still dark. He laid his head back on his chest and slept.

* * *

He awoke with a start two hours later, unable to breathe freely, and thought something touched his leg. The sun bore down on him from his left—from an airplane window? Opening his eyes to the bright sunshine was very painful. Recoiling, he slammed them shut.

He turned his head, squinted, and opened his eyes. He was a little groggy from the chloroform but realized he was in an airplane cockpit. He looked away from the sun streaming in from his left. He was in the pilot seat of a medium-sized airplane. Becoming more aware of his surroundings, he saw he wore a heavy leather seat belt with shoulder straps, and his lap was full of chicken and rice.

"Did I vomit?" he muttered, swaying from side-to-side. His arms and legs were heavily taped to the armrests in the captain's chair, while his feet and legs were taped to the seat mounts. There was no white cord on his wrist, but he couldn't move.

He started to panic. He couldn't move, and breathing was difficult. He couldn't fill his lungs with air. Perspiration rippled across his brow and dripped from his nose.

The early morning sun beat down on him directly through the cockpit windows, magnifying the sun's thermal energy onto the side of his face, making him hot on one side and cool on the other. Dust particles were suspended in the thick air. Dust rode eddies with every forced breath.

He squinted, trying to focus on his surroundings while testing the security of his restraints. He saw the instrument panel—three banks of instruments in a column in the middle of the panel suggested he was in a three-engine aircraft. He shielded his eyes from the sun by moving his head away, craning his neck as far to the right as he could.

His chin touched the socket of his right shoulder. At least his sensitive eyes were away from the sun's focus.

"Why am I in this airplane?"

He noticed the cockpit door was open over his right shoulder. The other seat and instruments were intact, the cushions dark and gray. Everything was covered in dust, as if the cockpit was a time capsule. He looked at the instrument panel to the small placard between the large and small instruments—RA 87573.

Though he knew he was in an aircraft cockpit, he was unfamiliar with the controls, instruments, or gauges. The numbers and letters were in Cyrillic. Looking for something to free himself from the tape restraints, he inventoried potentially useful items. There was glass in the instruments. His gaze went to the glare shield, where, in his periphery, a wet magnetic compass was mounted.

He tried to continue his inspection of the cockpit, but the sun was too bright, severe, and painful for his unprotected eyes.

Between blinks, he tried to focus on another item resting atop and centered from where he sat, partially obscured from the coruscating sunshine coming through the cracked, bubbled cockpit window. Through squinted, watery eyes, he saw the device was vaguely familiar. It had a dark outline, but the direct sunlight prohibited even a momentary glance.

He leaned forward to get away from the glare of the full sun as best he could, trying a minutely different angle to see what was on the glare shield, but his limited movement didn't yield the desire results.

"What is that?" he mumbled.

It was still completely obscured by the blinding sunlight. He was aggravated that he couldn't see it. Every attempt to reposition himself to look at it was met by full sunlight in his eyes.

He looked down at his lap. "Why is chicken and rice in my lap?"

Then he saw and felt it. The cockpit grew progressively darker, and the thermal pressure of the sun on the side of his face ceased, as a cloud passed between the sun and the aircraft's window, gradually extinguishing the sun's fire on his retinas, releasing him from his contorted, bowed position, though still restrained by the pilot seat's shoulder straps.

His eyes went to the dark figure centered on the glare shield. He stared in confusion, as his jaw dropped. If he knew

English he would have been able to read the words on the base of the figure—World Trade Center Twin Towers Statue 9/11 Commemorative Model.

Fury replaced confusion. Arabic invective and spittle flew around the cockpit, as the cloud passed, bathing the man in bright sunlight again, just as a huge rodent climbed his leg.

OBL tried to scream and kick it off. The shoulder and lap belts, as well as the tape on the armrests, held him tight. The rat, ignoring the movement and the stifled screams, nibbled at the chicken and rice in the man's lap.

Soon, the cockpit was filled with rats.

CHAPTER FIFTY-FOUR

0915 June 20, 2011
National Counterterrorism Center

The deputy director of the NCTC walked around his desk and offered his hand. "Nazy, it's so good to see you. It's been so long. To what do I owe this visit? We've missed you around here." He offered her one of the two chairs before the desk and took the other one to face her.

"Dr. Rothwell, I plan to post a package for you. It will probably arrive in the mail room tomorrow, maybe Wednesday."

"Nazy, why would you have to send me a package?"

"Because the contents of the package contain several thumb drives of an interview with Osama bin Laden before he died. There are two others that have Agency documents that demonstrate the president isn't who he says he is and may be an al-Qaeda sympathizer, at best."

While the shocked, balding man attempted to assimilate the information, Nazy stood. He made several attempts to speak before finally managing a coherent sentence.

"How were you able to get that information?"

"How isn't the issue. The issue is, I love working here, and I want to continue to do so. I have this information. Some would say it's 'golden' and contains much actionable intel. I need someone I can trust to take it, analyze it, and, as we say, work it."

"So you trust me? Well, well, Nazy Cunningham. Maybe this is the beginning of a beautiful relationship. You know I'm very fond of you. I've said several times we'd make a dynamite couple."

"Yes, you have, Dr. Rothwell, many times. Here's my offer. You take the intel you receive in the mail and you protect me if my job at the CIA is threatened in any way. I don't want the question of how I acquired these to be an issue. The NCTC will learn where al-Zawahiri is and how AQ really conscripts martyrs. Our friend Prince Bashir has a network in Europe and the US. This information will be a...how do you say? A big feather in your hat? I want to be left out of this. No exposure."

"Of course I'll protect you. Whatever it takes." The man was almost slobbering and his eyes raced from Nazy's eyes to her bosom.

"For your assistance," Nazy said, "I won't file charges against you for your continual sexual harassment. Our relationship is and always will be a professional one. Thank you for your time and consideration, Dr. Rothwell. Good day."

Her heels clicked, as she stepped toward the door and left the sitting man agape and crestfallen.

CHAPTER FIFTY-FIVE

1230 June 20, 2011
County Sheriff Department Phoenix, Arizona

Greg Lynche sat patiently in the waiting area of the hustling office building of the County Sheriff Department. The sheriff was a national figure for his no-nonsense stance on illegal immigration and compliance with the law. Routinely vilified by the political left and the national media, the entire department was always alert for reporters and journalists seeking an audience with the sheriff in order to embarrass him or destroy his career.

Lynche requested the audience, telling the secretary that he wasn't a reporter but a citizen with information. "I'm former CIA and in JPAS. I can give you my numbers, and you can check my bona fides."

"That won't be necessary, Mr. Jones. I can squeeze you in at noon on the twentieth."

Greg, after flying almost forty hours in the past week, flew commercial to the meeting. It was mundane and boring being in first class from Ronald Regan National to Phoenix Sky Harbor, hiding under a sleep mask and sleeping all the way.

Like all senior law enforcement, the sheriff was a busy man and ran late. Twenty-five minutes later, he rushed past his secretary with a posse of deputy sheriffs trying to keep up. A bigger man in real life than on TV, he consistently barked directions to his staff.

Lynche felt Hunter should have come. He was more at home with loud, earthy types.

"Next!" the sheriff hollered from his office at 120 decibels.

The secretary waved Lynche to the door with a sense of urgency.

"I don't have all day!" the sheriff added.

Lynche scurried in, offered his hand, and showed his ID. "Aren't you a little out of your jurisdiction, Spook?"

Greg offered him a black portfolio with a gold PanAm logo in one corner. "Sheriff, here's a batch of documents from a patriot who was shot down in the performance of his duties. He hoped one day someone would be able to make sense of these."

The sheriff gave him a look that meant, I'm not impressed.

"What are they?"

"There's an illegal alien in the White House. These are the documents to prove it."

The sheriff's motions became more measured. Mr. Lynche had his full attention. The big man wearing the big badge leaned back in his chair and stared at Lynche for a moment, sizing up Mr. Jones. "What do you need from me?"

"My assessment of these is that a crime has been committed. What the nature of that crime may be is out of my purview. I'm an old intel guy, not enforcement. You have the tools to prove if these documents are fake or real. I know they're real, but the man who collected them so someone could do something about it paid for it with his life. An armor-piercing bullet tore through his heart from over 1,000 yards. He was killed by a Muslim sniper."

In his "good-ol'-boy" voice, the sheriff said, "You know I'm under federal investigation for potential civil rights violations, and there's another separate federal probe accusing me of abuse of power."

"Yes, Sir, I'm aware."

"Well, I'll have a look. I love the sound of liberals' heads exploding. These will surely give them a fucking stroke. Thank you, Mr. Jones, if that's your real name."

"Thank you, Sheriff. You know the drill. We never had this conversation. Good day, Sir."

* * *

The man leaving the sheriff's office was never adequately identified. All records of his visit to the sheriff were expunged. No photographic evidence was retained. Any video of the interior of the department with Lynche's presence was subject to a major computer glitch, and the video recorders in the server room all had to be restarted with fresh DVDs. The sheriff snapped the old discs in half over his office trashcan.

* * *

At the end of the day, after a careful review of the newly discovered documents, the sheriff called a press conference to announce he was conducting an investigation into a batch of documents that significantly questioned the immigration status of key individuals in the current administration. His team would use all the forensic tools available at their disposal to determine the authenticity of the documents. An announcement of the department's findings would be forthcoming.

A snarky young reporter, with fussy hair that ended in a rat tail, raised his hand at the conference. "Are you suggesting the president is an illegal alien?"

Other members of the press pool giggled.

"No. I'm not saying the president is anyone but who we know him to be. It's just that some of the documents, used in an official capacity, such as the president's birth certificate, appear to be forgeries. Uttering forged or forging documents is a criminal offense. Someone presented these as official government documents on a government web site affirming their validity."

"If someone used these documents to secure government services or employment, and the documents are demonstrably false, then a crime may have been committed. It's my job to find out if a crime has been committed. Next question."

CHAPTER FIFTY-SIX

1530 June 20, 2011
Secret Service Office
Western Campus of St. Elizabeth's, Washington, DC

Bill McGee approached the security checkpoint and said to Duncan, "How many men in black does it take to protect this little gate? At least six, apparently."

A massive hydraulic ram barrier was raised in full defensive mode. It looked as if its maw could crush dump trucks when it wasn't repelling tanks. Red paint, traffic lights, and gate arms completed the Checkpoint Charlie scene.

One of the men in black motioned Bill to stop and lower his driver's window. As the window slid into the door, a menacing fisheye camera lens the size of a softball telescoped to the edge of the vehicle and stopped. All that was missing was eerie music and sound effects in the background, as the device could have doubled as the snake-like probe from The War of the Worlds. The thick Lucite eyeball flashed little red lights around its circumference.

McGee turned to face the camera, giving the operator a clear shot of his eyes for the iris-recognition system. Flashing red lights turned to steady green, then withdrew like an eel slipping back into its cave. He gave his and Hunter's driver's licenses to the man in black shades and black assault regalia —black hat, black Glock, black M-4, black earpiece, and black Secret Service Protection Division patch.

With a nod from a similarly attired man in black at the computer station in the heavily fortified, sandbagged control van, the face and ID matched the entry clearance personally approved by the director.

In one synchronized motion, warning bells sounded. The traffic lights turned green. The tank barrier folded into the ground, and the gate arms raised. The man in black returned the licenses and signaled McGee to proceed with a simple snap of his wrist.

McGee, driving through the gate, approached several black Suburbans and Tahoes with blacked-out windows and every known black antenna available to man, mounted on their roofs. At the office building at the end of the drive, McGee was surprised to see a custom placard atop a stanchion signifying he was Captain Bill McGee VIP at the Secret Service headquarters, as he slipped the non-black rental car into the designated parking space.

"I always loved being an O-Six," McGee told Hunter.

Several black clones from the main gate appeared from nowhere to hover in the periphery. Apparently, they were scanning their sectors from behind their black shades, their lips moving continuously.

As the two men emerged from the bright-red rental car, Director O'Sullivan bounded from the building wearing a black suit and tie. McGee and Hunter looked at each other and chuckled, glad they wore gray and red.

On the drive in from the BWI airport, Hunter debriefed McGee on the events of the past week and vice versa.

"I'm not sure what more we could've done," Hunter said. "The girlfriend, as you like to call her, did a great job asking questions and getting him to speak."

"I heard he was induced."

"I would say he responded well to electricity. Spock said he was a coward who was already very tame. I guess they used a bang stick or some wireless Taser system on him. When Spock turned that thing on, Osama bin Laden sat up straight and looked directly ahead, a true Pavlovian response.

"I brought blue-collar tools. I had a big Die Hard and cables. When I banged them together, and the sound, flash, and burnt metal filled the air, your boy talked. I didn't have to waterboard him. I did threaten to bolt his balls to the Die Hard."

"Dude! I also heard you put him on a plane."

595

"I told him I would. And I did. I'm a man of my word."

"More, Marine. I know there's more."

Hunter sighed. "There was a YAK-40 that had been on the field since the late '90s. Spock and I taped him to the seat while he was still sleeping off the chloroform. There was already a big hole in the underbelly, someone poked a hole in the fuselage with a forklift and rats and mice were able to get inside and make nests there. I always expected to see a black mamba creeping along the seats.

"I dumped the remaining food we had, chicken and rice, into his lap. I figured if he didn't wake up, the rats would chow down on him for weeks. If he did wake up, and the rats didn't get him, then the heat of being in that cockpit would slowly cook his ass.

"I think treachery is one of the circles of hell. Until that time, he would see I left him a little memento. He'd be able to see it and think about it until his last conscious moment, or Allah took him home. Or the rats ate him and turned him into little rat turds."

"A memento?"

"If I remember correctly, it had the words, World Trade Center Twin Towers Statue 9/11 Commemorative Model on it. It was nine inches tall. I set it in front of him on the glare shield."

Bill McGee drove down the I-495 beltway for ten minutes without speaking. "That was absolutely brilliant, Maverick. I said you'd make a great SEAL."

"I wouldn't want to give SEALs a bad name. I am already an honorary SEAL, if I recall." He smiled for a moment before his thoughts returned to the present. He felt he aged five years in the last week. His ribs were still sore to the touch, and any attempt to turn over in his sleep resulted in stabbing pain and shortness of breath. His chest sported bruises that covered him in pastels of dried blood and dead skin. His injuries weren't helping his love life.

"So we're going to see the Secret Service Director? Whiskey tango foxtrot, over?"

"Marty O'Sullivan, a former SEAL Team Six and Lancer. Rooster to his friends. Red hair, or it used to be. Smart, lucky bastard, in the right place at the right time. He left the SEALs after fourteen or fifteen years and got a job at the Secret Service.

Worked his way up the food chain and made director. He called me while you were entertaining in Africa."

"He called you? You're close? Was it a friendly chat?"

"He wanted to know how I was doing. I think he knew I was next on the hit list, and when nothing happened to me, he wondered why. I can't believe he's clueless."

"How would he have known? That makes no sense."

"While you were having fun in the sun in Liberia, I was able to investigate on my own. I went through the asshole's van and found all kinds of crap. There were a couple guns, 400 fifty-dollar gold pieces, a prayer rug, and a computer. Somehow, when he got back to his van, he got careless and started a fire. Wasn't much left by the time the fire department got there.

"The amazing thing was, I spotted someone watching my house, then a team of two. I took out one and followed the other to a mosque near Boston. I hear that place burned down, too."

Hunter looked at McGee. "A burned-out car's one thing. The mosque had to hit the blotters nationwide."

"I couldn't help myself. Then with that idiot Carey becoming VP...." He let the thought evaporate as he turned into the St. Elizabeth's campus, the former home to presidential assassins and the insane, and the new home of the Secret Service.

* * *

After salutations, the Secret Service Director said, "Thank you for coming, Bill. Good to meet you Mr. Hunter."

Three Secret Service agents on black Segways raced past the men.

"What's with all the heavy metal?" McGee asked.

A dozen more agents on the silent, two-wheeled devices crisscrossed in front and to the rear of the three men, as they walked toward the old building.

"Training class. You were coming. I thought our newest class could use some beginning VIP escort and counter-surveillance training while you were on campus."

"Ah." The two old SEALs smiled at each other.

O'Sullivan gestured for McGee to lead the way through the double doors, with a stop at the ubiquitous security desk to exchange licenses for badges. Hunter followed McGee, who trailed O'Sullivan into his office.

McGee and Hunter were immediately stunned by the director's workspace. A stand-up desk of black chrome and black granite was flanked by racks of electronics and communications equipment. A large brass chandelier competed with half a dozen monitors suspended from the fourteen-foot cathedral ceiling.

A small conference table rested atop highly polished cypress floors. Walls and windows were famed with large plaster neoclassic antebellum moldings. O'Sullivan offered seats and drinks from the turn-of-the-century bar topped with the only piece of granite in the room that wasn't black.

Immediately, the dynamics between the two old combat warriors was palpable and fascinating to Hunter. It was like two professional fighters who met several times in the ring and found themselves at a social event, trying to be professional and pleasant, working hard not to let past long-fought wars rekindle into flames. Hunter saw the same kind of latent testosterone between pilots flying fighters and racquetball players in near-professional-level tournaments. Someone had been the king of the hill once, only to be slapped down by a younger bull. Old resentments were rarely, if ever, mended or mentioned.

Hunter didn't think the two men would allow the situation to degenerate into barbs or fisticuffs, but clearly, someone needed to be an adult and run the meeting.

"The asshole who tried to kill Bill shot me three times," Hunter said. "My partner neutralized his ass."

O'Sullivan broke eye contact with the other SEAL. "Your partner?"

"Sorry, Sir. Special Access Program. You aren't cleared and don't need to know. Something's on your mind, though, or you wouldn't have called Bill."

The two former SEALs looked at each other, and McGee smiled.

"Marty, I briefed Duncan on Broken Lance. If I hadn't brought him into the fold, I wouldn't be here. I have the feeling you know something about the shooter. You know a whole lot more."

"I think we all need to lay our cards on the table," Hunter said.

"I have the feeling you know more than you're letting on about why the shooter suddenly dropped off the grid," O'Sullivan said. "I was keeping track of all the Lancers in CONUS. Bill, you're right, after a while we expected you were next. I know you know it's true. There were reports from your neck of the woods that a van caught fire, and there was gunfire in the area. I called you, and supposedly, you're none the wiser, just like last time."

McGee sighed and looked away. "Marty, that was a long time ago and isn't relevant to this discussion. The last time, you were doing an investigation. Are you doing an investigation this time, or are you offering to help?"

"I can help where I can. Something's going on."

"I'm fairly certain that, if we were three very close friends," Hunter said, "we could solve this together. I was shot three times. I'm ready for some help."

"Marty, I don't need help, especially your kind."

Hunter saw the conversation approaching critical mass. He wasn't sure what McGee's irritation was with O'Sullivan. McGee hadn't discussed the fact that he had issues with the Secret Service Director. He came willingly. Something was missing.

As if he were rushing into a burning house to save the family cat, Hunter threw himself into the fray, protocol and rank structure be damned. "Marty, you asked us to come down. Something triggered... something in you inspired you to call Bill. What was it?"

The two SEALs stared at each other. Marty broke the lock to answer the question.

"The new VP knows more about the subject than he should. I said something to the effect that SEALs will do whatever is necessary to protect their fellow SEALs. If they find the shooter, they'll find out who was responsible, and hold them accountable. The SEALs will extract revenge. When the color drained from the VP's fat little face, I thought it was a curious response."

"I've been around politicians a long time. They don't give a shit about anything but themselves. The color drained from his lips—a sure sign he was about to pass out and that he knew more about this issue than he should."

"We think the DCI—the former DCI—was behind it," McGee said. "There's a lot of circumstantial evidence to support it. He had an intermediary do the dirty work. A sniper. A Muslim sniper."

O'Sullivan sat up slightly, his interest diffusing the tension in the room. "His response to a SEAL's retribution for the killing of SEALs was more than odd."

"Would that be because now he's part of the Broken Lance calculus?" Hunter asked. "Instead of being the approval authority, now he could be...."

"...the target," the SEALs said simultaneously.

"One of his buddies, Prince Bashir," McGee said, "did the dirty work. He hired the shooter, a world-class marksman, failed BUDS and Marine Scout Sniper school. One of Bashir's sons was at the Naval War College. One's sitting in Gitmo, and one was killed in Afghanistan.

"The interesting piece is Duncan was also on the shooter's list. He was targeted after me."

O'Sullivan ran the lines through his head. "I won't ask

how you know that. You're positive it isn't the Broken Lance connection?"

"Absolutely. The intersection of our relationship was the Naval War College. If the yardstick to get on Bashir's shit list is to kill or jail one of his kids, I don't know how I could ever have gotten on the list," Hunter said.

He turned to McGee and pointed at him. "Bashir's the key. He provided all the 9/11 terrorists to bin Laden. Bashir took care of his little boy toys and funded their education while caring for their families. Osama bin Laden suggested he knew Bashir was very close to the president when he was a young man in the '80s. We took it that Bashir is probably running the president. If you look at his actions and policies in the Middle East, they don't make sense. Now look through the prism of being run by a Saudi prince who fosters worldwide terrorism, and things suddenly start making sense."

"Whoa, whoa, whoa! What are you talking about?" O'Sullivan barked.

"Duncan, ahem, 'interviewed' bin Laden before he died," McGee said. "He learned a few things."

Hunter, withdrew a thumb drive from his suit pocket and handed it to O'Sullivan.

The director was confused.

"The documents on that thumb drive prove the president isn't who he claims," Hunter said. "Bin Laden and Bashir provided all the terrorists for the 9/11 martyr operation, which was in play for ten aircraft across the country. Bashir provided the shooter to kill SEALs. Bin Laden wanted that shooter to kill the president but was vetoed by Bashir.

"We made the leap in logic that Carey ordered the hit for the SEALs to kill the president. We haven't figure out why he did that, but if you look at what happened in the last week, suddenly, if a SEAL killed the president, Carey would be the next president."

O'Sullivan gave Hunter a hard look, trying to digest the

staccato of information.

"It's safe to say at this moment that Bashir's completely wired into the White House and CIA and Saudi intelligence, probably MI6, too," McGee said.

"Bashir and Carey are very close," Hunter added. "They had sex parties with boys and young men. Billionaires can buy anything and anyone. I don't know what you'll do when you review those documents."

Stunned, O'Sullivan tried to assimilate what he just heard.

McGee, who finally relaxed and became animated in the discussion, turned to Hunter. "I still don't know how you got on Bashir's hit list.

The pause in the conversation allowed O'Sullivan time to assimilate all the information. He sat, listened, and tried to assimilate his guests' rapid-fire discussion.

"I couldn't have been on Carey's list, because, when I'm working, I work directly for the DCI," Hunter said. "If I was a problem, he could've pulled my clearance and I would return to a normal life or he could've taken me out so easily, my body would never show up. I had to have done something well before Carey's tenure to be on Bashir's list. I think I finally figured out why."

"Occam's Razor?" McGee asked.

"Yes, Sir. Simple. Strip out all the distractions. There had to be a Naval War College list. You said Broken Lance exercises were planned. Carey had to be read on, and then he used the OBL exercises as the cover to target SEALs. CIA had to have had the OBL names on file—CIA polygraphs and all their little SAPs—but no one but the NWC players were on Bashir's list.

"Somehow, I got on that list, and it might have been an innocent addition when I starting sitting with you during assemblies. I think my name was also known somehow by Bashir for all the counterdrug and counterterrorism work I'd been doing. If Bashir's boy was in the audience as an international officer, you have to be the prime target after returning from the fight. I was just collateral."

McGee nodded. "That makes sense."

O'Sullivan tried to make a point but retracted his finger. "The rest of the story I haven't shared with you was that I'd been targeted for assassination before I was assigned to the war college," Hunter added.

The two men were taken aback, partly because the assertion was given without passion.

"Yeah. That's one thing that wasn't highlighted on your security brief."

"That's basically why I went to the Naval War College. The Agency felt I needed to leave Texas for a while. We never fully understood why a handful of Arabs tried to take me out. I barely escaped. I had a couple of international officers try to make nice to me while we were at school, then I had my little favorite Muslim woman try to spy on me. There had to be a counterdrug connection before the war college. I had no idea then, but I think Bashir had to be involved. That, and we were both trailed for a while at the Naval War College."

"One of these days, we might find out," McGee said.

"I doubt it. If it wasn't an accident, then somehow Bashir knows I've been working on some very special counterterrorism and counterdrug programs. Hunter placed his fingers over his eyes, trying to tie together all the threads. "If I was targeted by accident at the Naval War College…."

"But you were targeted before," McGee said.

"What are we talking about?" O'Sullivan asked.

Hunter took a deep breath. "Yes, at least three times I know about." His mind was in overdrive, recalling the odd events of the '90s and his days at the US Border Patrol. "All our work was counterdrug in South America. A Saudi prince in South America is incongruous. It doesn't make sense."

McGee held up his hand. "Marty, I think we need someone inside to request a full investigation on Bashir. Maybe there's a connection here."

"I agree."

The big SEAL nodded. To his surprise, the Director of

the Secret Service did, too.

"Bill, Duncan, I'll contact you directly when I get the info," O'Sullivan said.

"That's fantastic, Marty," Hunter said. "Sir, I really could use the head. Every time I travel to Africa, I bring back a bug that attacks my insides for a few days. I'm sorry."

When the director stood, Hunter thought he would offer him the use of his private bathroom. Instead, he said, "I'll get you an escort."

"As long as he doesn't watch, that's OK." The men grinned at the obvious retort.

After ten minutes in a tiny hall bathroom, Hunter emerged to face another heavily armed man in black. The escort silently walked Hunter to the director's office.

He found the two former SEALs standing at the antique bar, sipping drinks and laughing like long-lost friends. After returning their badges, Hunter and McGee exchanged good-byes and promises before getting into their rental and driving away to run the outbound security gauntlet.

Once clear of St. Elizabeth's, Hunter asked, "What changed while I was away?"

"The long story was Marty ran an investigation of me and my guys when we were lieutenants. Some weapons were lost at sea. It was an accident. I told him there wasn't anything to investigate. He was like me—a young buck full of piss, leading SEALs into all kinds of mischief and mayhem. We were teammates but not close.

"You and I are light years closer by comparison. He had his conclusion, that one of my guys lied about the loss of a sniper rifle and something else, but it was all bullshit. The equipment went right over the side of a LPD, the Denver, when the helo we were going to ride in was in its landing phase. The rotor wash caught the rifle case, and it and a few other things were blown over the side.

"My guys and I were anxious to get on our helo and be on our way, but the wash nearly shoved us and all our equipment over the side, too. We reported it, and Marty wrote his findings to support his conclusion. He didn't give me the courtesy of telling me he would accuse me or one of my guys of stealing the rifle.

"I got the tape of the landing from the ship, and the video showed the case going over the side. It was a major breach. He was removed from the SEALs. He never apologized that he was wrong. When you went to the head, though, he did. He said he grew up a great deal and did a very stupid thing. He left the Navy and got into the Secret Service. I said he did pretty well for himself."

"Hmph."

"He said he was young and dumb from a liberal school, but he grew up during that episode. He wanted to tell me he was wrong but couldn't do it. He was too embarrassed. He said he's now very conservative. Protecting the president's the hardest thing he and his guys have ever done, and the VP is a frigging degenerate."

"That's an understatement."

"Then he surprised me. He said it was obvious that Operation Broken Lance needed to be activated, if he knew anything about such a program."

They rode in silence, as McGee took the off ramp to the airport terminal road.

Suddenly, Hunter looked at McGee. "POTUS?"

"No. The VP."

"That's unexpected. If anyone deserves it, he definitely does. Let me get this straight. Are you saying Lancers are going to take direct action on the VP?"

McGee stared straight ahead. "You know better than that. That subject requires Special Access. Sir, no disrespect, but you aren't cleared for the program. I know you haven't been read in on this."

"But I'm an honorary SEAL." Hunter was half-joking.

"That may be true, Grasshopper, but you aren't a Lancer. You did your part. You were wildly successful. We SEALs have to do this. The less you know, the better. You need to track down Bashir."

"Maybe we can do that. Lynche and I have another mission. We're off to Djibouti to look for hostages and hostage takers."

"I'll make a couple calls on Bashir. See what I can find out." As the rental pulled up to the American Airline terminal at Reagan National, McGee offered his hand. "Have a nice day, Mr. Hunter. Safe travels, good Sir. Please stay in touch."

For the very first time that Hunter could remember, McGee saluted Hunter first, as he drove off.

CHAPTER FIFTY-SEVEN

0900 June 29, 2011
The White House Washington, DC

Three six-foot, red metal disks were rolled into place by the groundskeepers. A fire truck and ambulance and their crew stood at the ready. Sniper teams emerged from the roofs of federal buildings outlining the flight corridor. Specially approved visitors and friends lined up on the lawn for arrival. Eyes strained against the sun, trying to see the immaculate and famous flying machine.

The flight of three green-and-white VH-3Ds from Marine Helicopter Squadron One turned toward the greatest landmark in the District of Columbia. At six miles, the Washington Monument split the center windscreen, as the lead helicopter made a final correction to arrive on target, on time.

"Countermeasures ready," the copilot said, a US Naval Academy graduate from the class of 2002. "Three minutes to jink."

The pilot, class of 2000, pointed at the Radar and Homing and Warning indicators, as they flashed green in the indicator mounted above the pilot's glare shield. The crew chief double- clicked his interphone key, signaling he was in his seat and buckled.

"Two minutes," the copilot said after sliding doors hiding chaff and flare dispensers opened at the rear of the helicopter.

"Decoy checklist complete." Green lights illuminated on the instrument panel; they were Armed. The IR Beacon flashed Hot.

"One minute."

The crew looked forward, left, and right for any telltale

smoke trail of a shoulder-fired weapon. They were in the critical window. The crew's pulse rates jumped an additional forty beats per minute, as they scanned for any visual recognition of an incoming missile. The mission of the decoy wasn't to avoid an incoming missile but to intercept it. If countermeasures failed, the decoy helicopter would be placed between a heat-seeking or radar missile and the president's helicopter. Every day was a potential suicide mission for the Marine One aircrews.

"Thirty seconds. Twenty. Ten. Break."

The two helicopters' infrared generators flooded the National Mall with enough IR energy to attract 500 Sidewinders. From the ground, before the lead Marine helicopter reached the Washington Monument, the helicopter pitched hard right toward the Capitol. The number-two helicopter pitched hard left. The third continued its steady approach between tall trees to the White House lawn. The pilot expertly arrested the aircraft's forward momentum and hovered the big Sikorsky over the red discs, then he added a little differential pressure to the rudder pedals to turn and align the landing gear over the big red discs. He centered the pedals and programmed the collective down to set the landing-gear tires directly in the middle of the red metal plates. The rotor disc quickly decelerated with the application of the rotor brake.

A moment later, the forward cockpit door was lowered and a Marine Corps Sergeant in full dress blues stepped out, awaiting the Commander in Chief to emerge. As the leader of the free world stepped out, the Marine on the ground rendered a razor-sharp perfect salute.

For the first time since he was inaugurated, the president didn't return the honors rendered. He didn't wave to the small crowd but proceeded to the Oval Office, finding the Vice President standing in the middle of the beige rug, running his finger across the famous Resolute Desk.

"Measuring the drapes?" snapped the President.

"No, Sir, Mr. President. I'm just delivering the papers from the Attorney General—your resignation and a full pardon for any crimes you may have committed while in office. I've already signed and dated it July first, as agreed."

The Vice President was torn between glee and concern. Carey's plan to leverage the president out of office on his timeline was thwarted by an unknown force. He couldn't shake the thought that Nazy Cunningham forced the President to move up his timetable to kill bin Laden and she knew about the file on the President. He couldn't fathom how she could have obtained the whole file when only a fraction of it resided in his safe.

His train of thought snapped when the President shouted, "I thought we had a deal!" Moving to his chair, he stared at the documents.

Over the previous ninety-six hours, a Constitutional crisis erupted in America. Hundreds of classified and confidential documents spanning the five decades of the President's life were given to several law-enforcement agencies across the United States. One hundred members of Congress and 100 newspapers and TV stations across the country received softbound copies of the same documents from an overnight delivery service. 100 copies of the same documents also appeared resting atop a long banquet table in a conference room at the Washington Ritz Carlton. An easel announced the topic of the conference. In large gold lettering it read, *Corrupt Lapdog Media and Their Inability to Vet a Communist or Radical Candidate. Conference materials inside.*

Media outlets across Virginia and Maryland received e-mail invitations. Curiously, the New York Times and the Washington Post didn't receive one. Hyperlinks to copies of the same documents were posted on the Internet on several liberal and conservative blog sites. No one claimed responsibility for the outpouring of the documents, but the FBI determined the billing address for the printing work was from a recently burned-down mosque. The credit card used to print, publish, and dispatch the 300 copies was traced to a bogus address in California. The owner was a suspected illegal alien. The FBI and the NSA were apoplectic.

Though ridiculed by the Democrats and the media as forgeries of a vast right-wing conspiracy, the documents were quickly subjected to forensic analysis and validated as genuine.

The information they contained painted a picture of a young Muslim radical traveling domestically to attend socialist or communist conferences. He also attended a terrorist training camp in Pakistan while enrolled in America's finest Ivy League schools. Intelligence documents showed that he consorted with a Who's Who of Islamo-fascist and radical Muslim leaders. The news that he obtained counterfeit documents and established a new identity in the United States, just like some illegal aliens crossing the Rio Grande, prompted some members of Congress and the press to call for immediate investigations and impeachment.

When the British and Israeli prime ministers met at a joint meeting in the Azores and affirmed the immigration and surveillance documents from their respective intelligence services were legitimate, Congress moved to meet in emergency session. Bipartisan articles of impeachment were drafted for the president.

The president signed the letter of resignation and handed it to the vice president.

"Mr. President, you know I didn't do this. I thought I had the only copy. It's obvious there was more to the file than I had." Carey was ill knowing there was another copy of the DCI's file, but was at a loss of understanding of who could have made it? *Who had it?*

"That's bullshit. If you didn't do this, then you'd better watch your back. You're next, and you don't even know it. Now get out of my office. This is still my house."

CHAPTER FIFTY-EIGHT

2330 June 30, 2011
United States Naval Observatory Washington, DC

The Secret Service Director dismounted from his black Suburban and was joined by his Deputy, who silently padded from the residence's side entrance to the director's side. A column of two Secret Service agents in black battle dress on matte-black Segways approached the Suburban slowly. Once past the men, they leaned forward slightly, silently racing off into the night.

The two men monitored the Vice President, as he stepped from the limousine and entered the official residence. They stood there for a moment before O'Sullivan commented, "Well, he's on his way."

The Deputy knew who "he" was. A humiliated, vanquished President boarded Air Force One for the last time at Andrews Air Force Base, on a westerly heading. With the recent revelations of the President's Muslim roots and bogus documents, rumors abounded regarding his destination, most assuming it was the Big Island of Hawaii or somewhere in the Middle East.

The following day, Vice President Frank Carey would be sworn in as the next President of the United States and would spend his first night in the White House as President. The Secret Service Deputy Director left the White House Secret Service detail monitoring several work crews, some packing the President's belongings and repainting the Master Suite, Sitting Room, and the Lincoln Bedroom before the new leader of the free world moved into the world's most famous residence.

The Vice President didn't see the President off, choosing instead to attend an official function at the British embassy.

At the end of the night, the ambassador of the United Kingdom presented the Vice President a bust of Sir Winston Churchill to be prominently displayed in the Oval Office. The bust sat in the front seat of the Director's Suburban, strapped in with a seat belt.

"The Founders would turn over in their graves if they knew a rabidly gay man and his lover were going to occupy the White House," the Deputy Director quietly lamented to O'Sullivan. Staring at the antebellum building, he shook his head as if witnessing the unbelievable.

"Our job is to protect them, not judge them," O'Sullivan replied noncommittally.

Both men were breathing hard after facing several trying days and nights for the Secret Service leadership. Since the document dump, threats on the President's life jumped a hundredfold. The common theme was, If Congress and the Justice Department *doesn't* do something to remove the un-American president, patriots will.

The complete Secret Service was on twelve-hour shifts, working on and off. Stress rippled through the organization, and the two leaders of the organization hadn't slept in days.

Since both men stopped moving, they yawned as if on cue. If they didn't start moving again soon, they'd fall asleep standing up.

After another yawn, the Deputy said, "A friend of mine on the Hill the other day said, 'May you live in interesting times,' was a Chinese curse. It's been an interesting week, Marty. I hope it's over soon."

"You got a friend?"

They shared a chuckle at the old joke.

"We have a big day tomorrow," O'Sullivan said. "I say we get out of here and let the A Team take it."

"Roger."

Director O'Sullivan punched the transmit button on his wrist microphone. "Chuck Wagon; Eagle and Falcon departing Star Base to quarters."

In the black earpiece, a voice replied, "Ten-four, Eagle.

Good night, Sir."

As if they'd been waiting for permission to move, the two men didn't walk in opposite directions toward their vehicles until the command post operator replied, "Good night, Sir."

As the Director approached the black Suburban and rolling command post, he glanced at the small observatory in the distance before entering the vehicle and driving off.

* * *

A single Secret Service agent in black battle dress, mounted atop a Segway, approached the outermost observatory of the five on the property, stopped, and dismounted. The electronic device stood perfectly still, balanced on its two wheels, as the agent approached the observatory's antique metal door with its partially frosted reinforced glass.

A low-watt light bulb, suspended from a fixture with a rain shield, barely illuminated the concrete landing and handrail. With one black-gloved hand, the agent unscrewed the bulb until it broke contact with the power grid and went out. With the other, he extracted a mechanical lock pick from a cargo pocket and thrust it into the old Yale lock, manipulating levers and pins until all the tumblers fell into place.

He twisted the oblong brass handle. Three seconds later, he was inside, peering out of a window of the old National Observatory. He watched 110 yards away as several Secret Service vehicles departed from the front of the Vice President's official residence.

The agent turned and removed his helmet. Cool air flowed over damp hair momentarily, as he retrieved night-vision goggles from a cargo pocket and pulled them over his head, adjusting the harness for a snug fit and turning on the power. In seconds, the interior of the observatory was visible in shades of green.

A thirty-inch telescope filled the binocular. Filigreed

mirror arms with curls, whorls, and ionic volute connectors and mounts supported and accentuated the unique ancient instrument. The agent swept the room on the balls of his boots, then returned his gaze to the stairwell leading down into the telescope pit.

Stepping high over the small chain that discouraged the public's access, his soft soles cushioned each step, as he stepped gingerly down a slightly winding staircase and around the arced walkway, glancing at the turntable, gears, and old motors of the antiquated telescope's mechanical base.

Halfway around the circular pit, the agent stopped at the lone glass-and-metal door with a metal plate that read, Power Room. Trying the old-fashioned knob, he found the door unlocked, so he returned the mechanical lock pick into his cargo pocket.

Stepping inside, he surveyed his surroundings. The room was as deep as a one-car garage but only half as wide. Three large filigreed power junction boxes were mounted along one wall. One featured a long, thick ornate arm nearly parallel to the floor. "Pull the arm" was the direction given, but it didn't move.

He stepped back and reassessed the situation and his instructions. He pulled it horizontally, and it immediately extended half a foot. He heard metal slide against metal in the small room, then there was the hint of rushing air from the small wall. A downward push of the arm made the wall pivot on its center. Cool air filled the room with dust and debris, mostly the remnants of dead roaches and moths.

He stepped inside to face the wind and total darkness. NVGs capture and amplify electromagnetic radiation outside the natural range of vision. Without any photons to be captured or amplified, the device was useless. The agent braced himself against the wind and slipped his hand into a cargo pocket to pull out an IR penlight.

Depressing the button flooded the area with photons and reactivated the NVG's photo cathode and multiplier. In a second, the phosphor screens were green again.

A green staircase stood before him, with a tunnel leading to the control center under Number One Observatory Circle.

* * *

"Mr. Vice President? We have an emergency!" a voice shouted from the hall.

"Wait! Don't come in! I'll be out in a minute!"

The Secret Service agent rounded the corner of the bedroom, a Sig Sauer P229 with a heavy silencer drawn and pointed skyward. "Intruder alert!" he whispered.

The corpulent, naked vice president, standing at the edge of the large bed, withdrew from his bent-over partner's ass and turned to the agent.

The agent lowered the 9mm and shot the man face-down in the bedcovers in the back of the head, twice. With a heavy hand, he grabbed the startled vice president by the throat and pushed him four steps backward into a nearby chair, then he jammed the silencer under the rolls of fat under the man's chin and pulled the trigger.

The wall behind the chair erupted in a spray of blood, brains, and hair. Placing the silenced Sig on the floor, the agent checked the exit wound at the back of Carey's head and whispered, "That's for killing my friends."

* * *

Twenty minutes later, a lone Secret Service agent on a Segway motored along the inside perimeter of the Naval Observatory compound and out onto Observatory Lane. He didn't stop or wave to the Park Police at the gate. Secret Services agents don't wave.

After several switchbacks and turns onto Tunlaw, a dead-end street, the Segway stopped behind a white Toyota Tacoma at the end of the drive. The agent lowered the tailgate and deadlifted the 125-pound Segway into the back of the pickup, rolling it onto its side.

Two minutes later, the Toyota pulled onto Wisconsin Avenue and followed the directions from the GPS toward Rhode Island.

CHAPTER FIFTY-NINE

0430L July 4, 2011
Djibouti-Ambouli International Airport

The Joint Special Operations Command liaison officer, the CIA's Deputy Director of Operations, and a dozen senior agents from the NCTC sat in rapt attention. The only woman in the pit of the NCTC's small auditorium was Nazy Cunningham, the Chief of Near East Division. She announced they had a significant lead on the newest, most-wanted terrorist on the planet, Ayman al- Zawahiri. Information received from recent sources confirmed there was a heavily fortified, isolated compound in Sana'a, Yemen, only a stone's throw away from the country's military hospital and military academy.

"The coincidence of the location near a major military facility and the basic construction of the compound are striking. There's nothing else like in anywhere in Sana'a. It's remarkably similar to the OBL compound in Pakistan. One noteworthy item—over a dozen of al-Zawahiri's family members have transited the Aden International Airport over the last five years, and most of them haven't left the country.

"Four hours ago, surveillance confirmed two of al-Zawahiri's wives entering the compound." She indicated a point on the screen with her laser pointer.

"It doesn't look like it lends itself to a raid," the JSOC colonel said to no one in particular.

"Or bombing," the DDO replied.

"I'm surprised he'd still be there after Osama bin Laden's much publicized death," the NCTC deputy said, undressing Nazy with his eyes. She refused to make eye contact.

"We have some MQ-9s, some Reapers, in Djibouti," the JSOC colonel said.

"And we have some capability in that area that might be able to provide nighttime close-ups from the air," Nazy Cunningham added. "The request went out to POTUS for interagency coordination and SOCOM approval. We'll have eyes on the target this evening."

"What kind of capability would that be?" the JSOC colonel asked.

"I'm sorry, Sir. Special Access. Next question?" Nazy asked.

* * *

Bob and Bob sat in lawn chairs in the cool breeze outside the inflatable hangar, waiting for their pilots and bosses. Two days into the mission of locating Somali pirates and hostages taken from several ocean-going vessels, the Wraith was retasked by the Acting DCI to recon a compound of a possible terrorist leader in Yemen.

Hunter and Lynche, acknowledging the mission change, made the three-hour trip from Djibouti to Yemen to orbit the target compound in a calm, cloudless sky. Low-light video and FLIR images of the compound and surrounding area were streamed live to a satellite and returned to SOCOM command centers on three continents.

Two armed Reapers with a pair of Hellfire missiles orbited six miles high, their remote pilots sitting anxiously in their "cockpits" halfway around the world in a bunker in Nevada. After three hours on station, there had been no movement on the ground or within the compound.

Hunter maintained his left-handed turn at 2,000 feet of slant range, and Lynche radioed they'd be "bingo" fuel in fifteen minutes—their fuel reserves would be too low to continue the mission.

Just as Hunter was about to break off their shallow turn over the large town of Sana'a and return to Djibouti, the engine chip detector lit up, its bright-yellow light shattering the dull mood in the cockpit.

"Knock it off, Greg. We got a chip light. We're out of here."

Lynche barked into the microphone, "Hey, I've got movement." He zoomed the FLIR to maximum resolution.

"Belay my last," Hunter said. "We aren't going anywhere." He studied the bright-yellow light, then scanned his instruments for secondary engine indications. For the moment, all was well. Hunter shook his head and hoped the decision to stay wouldn't kill them.

The image of an older man in a turban stepped out of the shadows of the house and into the doorway of the topmost room. The fourth-generation FLIR showed, in shades of white, the different temperatures of the man's face, torso, and background. A pudgy face framed with glasses with a distinct cold spot in the middle of his forehead appeared in the FLIR scope. The momentary profile and head-on view of Ayman al-Zawahiri, al-Qaeda's new leader, from his waist to the top of his head, stunned the SOCOM commanders. The low-flying aircraft delivered crisp FLIR video via a couple of satellites.

Hunter tried to reset the press-to-test switch of the chip detector. The bright yellow light remained on. Something metallic had likely completed the electrical circuit across the center post to the case of one of the three magnetic chip detectors, one of two on the engine. Something metal must have made the connection, something as tiny as an insignificant sliver of chrome off a bearing sleeve to a ball bearing from a failed main bearing. If the engine rotating and friction components were shredding pieces of metal, the engine could die within seconds. Crashing anywhere over a downtown city in Yemen would be fatal.

Looking at the image in the FLIR, Hunter tersely directed, "Paint the target."

Lynche, selected the laser designator and mashed the button; he keyed his microphone over the encrypted carrier. "Laser hot!" He struggled to keep the dot on the cold spot in the middle of the man's forehead.

* * *

"Fire!" shouted a dozen people in Tampa, Abu Dhabi, and Las Vegas. Two military and a CIA attorney conferred over the shoulders of the two remote pilots at Nellis Air Force Base, seemingly awaiting concurrence from the other two that the target was legitimate, and firing Hellfires was an ethical use of lethal force.

"Approved," the attorneys said one after the other.

The two remote pilots launched two missiles, followed by two more, three seconds later.

"Fox four," said the air-to-surface missile shooters. "Four birds in the air."

Lynche rolled the thumb wheel to zoom out, as the terrorist stepped back from the doorway to highlight the building and make note of the large, overhanging roof that prevented any viable overhead imagery from satellites.

"I think that's the shot they were looking for," Lynche said. "We're too close. We could get fragged."

Hunter said, "Keep the heat on that room." This could get real ugly, Hunter thought.

"Missiles inbound!" a voice erupted in their headphones.

Hunter kept his orbit with a potentially sick motor. The first flash completely blinded and washed out the FLIR. Three successive detonations and white-hot pulses immediately followed in the FLIR scope.

Hunter cheered, pumping his fist. He composed himself and focused on the yellow light of the engine chip detector. "Now we're done! We're getting out of here! Let base know we might need a pickup."

They flew south-southwest toward the Red Sea, running through all emergency procedures and recovery scenarios.

Scanning his instrument panel, Hunter said, "No secondary indications that something is failing or failed. Oil pressure and quantity indicators are steady. The motor isn't torquing or misfiring. I'm going to trim the prop to lower the torque on the gearbox and engine. We'll fly it and watch it."

Reducing the pitch on the propeller meant they would

decelerate, spending more time over the Red Sea on the trip back to Djibouti.

"We won't land at any airport," Hunter said. "There's nowhere to put down in Yemen without killing both of us."

"You're crazy, you know?"

"What would you have done...differently?" Hunter offered.

Lynche stared silently at the brightly illuminated chip light. "So far, so good."

Hunter tried to reassure Lynche that the light was either an electrical short or fuzz on the detector. "Still no secondary indications."

He headed toward the island of Jazirat in the middle of the Red Sea.

An hour later, their aircraft was "feet wet."

"We've got 250 miles to go at eighty knots," Hunter said.

"This will be fun. ETA 0400 local. At least it will still be dark."

Lynche stared at the yellow light, wondering if that was how their lives would end.

Hunter was concerned by the way his friend was obsessing over the chip light and not the great work they had done over Yemen. After their mission to track Afghanistan's poppy seed stock ended with the Iranian missile force shooting a missile at them, the seventy-two-year-old Lynche became noticeably more cautious and worried about their missions. And the interrogation of Osama bin Laden completely changed him. Once vivacious and outgoing, Lynche became markedly introspective. Hunter tried to engage his friend in discussions to kill time and take their minds off the yellow light that dominated everything else in the cockpit. "I think you're a hero, Mr. Lynche. Nice work."

Hunter checked his mirrors and saw Lynche hanging his head in the rear seat. He waited for a minute without hearing a response. He wasn't going to give up on Greg Lynche, at least not yet.

"I finally received some e-mail," Hunter offered. "That BlackBerry vibrated nonstop for five minutes. I should've stuck it in my pants and enjoyed myself."

Lynche didn't lift his chin from his chest, as he keyed the microphone and gave a forced laugh. "You got e-mail?"

"Yes, Sir. It's Africa. I'm still amazed we can get e-mail here. After four days of no e-mail or service, I guess someone finally paid their frickin' phone bill, and wa-la, we have service again." He waited for Lynche to reply. When he didn't, Hunter said, "Happy Fourth of July, Mr. Lynche. You look pretty good for being 235 years old."

"Thanks."

"Connie said not to let you get into any trouble."

"My bride still sending you e-mail?"

"All the time. She wants me to take care of you. How come nobody ever takes care of me?"

"I took care of you. I zapped that fucker right between the eyes."

"Yes, Sir, you did. I probably didn't say thank you enough."

"We're even now. You saved my life, and I saved yours."

Hunter allowed that to sink in. He didn't think Lynche had been keeping score. They'd been through a lot together over a very long period of time.

"I get the sense from her note that you created a ruckus when you went to Africa. Something else you haven't shared with me? I always took you for a gun runner or arms smuggler, for the good side, of course."

"No need to know. No SA for you. Anything else interesting?"

"Nazy might be promoted out of the NE and into the NCTC as deputy director."

Lynche sat up and raised his helmeted head in the spacious canopy. "Whoa! When were you going to tell me that? I didn't see that coming. Maybe I should have. I guess it depends on who did what with her interview material."

"Bullfrog gave me that sniper's laptop, and I turned it over to Nazy. I'm not sure if anything was in there. We'll never know unless she tells me. She's getting more like you, starting to leave out some of the finer details or not say anything at all."

"You know I promised to carry that stuff to my grave."

"Me too, but how will the world know you were some CIA rock star? Dude, if you were in the military, they would've named a planet after you for all the stuff you did."

"Now how would you know that?"

"I have my ways."

"Thank you for the vote of confidence. That was a long time ago."

"Are you counting all the ships down there? It's like a friggin' parking lot at Wal-Mart on Saturday night, with all the Wal-Martians waddling up and down the aisles."

"Did you say Wal-Martians?"

"That's right. Do you even know what Wal-Mart is, Mr. Ivy League? If you did, you'd know that's where all the democrats and liberals shop on Saturday night. It's a show from outer space, minus all the freaky science sounds."

"You're yanking my leg."

"When we get home, I'll send you the link. Break, break. New subject. Did you hear anyone at JSOC say we have a new president?"

"That's probably not news. What you did with those documents was a stroke of genius. Your little trick of sending them out the way you did probably sent him packing."

"I'm not sure if you got the rest of the story. Connie sent us an e-mail. Basically, it read that a constitutional crisis was averted with the swearing in of the Speaker of the House. The president resigned and was last seen in Hilo, disembarking from Air Force One...."

"Speaker of the House? What are you talking about?"

"What I was going to say was, the new Republican President told the American people that a full investigation was underway on the former President. Congress agrees to fix the citizenship ambiguities in current law, secure the northern and southern borders, and establish a national identity card and harsh penalties for those who abuse the law. No one ever saw the murder-suicide coming."

"Murder-suicide?"

"I'm reading between the lines. I think the Vice President was either the murderer or the suicide. We probably won't know until we get home."

"Holy crap! I didn't know."

"Sixty minutes out. Still looking good. For whatever it's worth, I never had to fly over open water with a chip light before. Frickin' spooky. I have newfound appreciation for helo guys flying over water. You never know when the beast will quit."

"Tell me about it." Lynche finally looked out over the Red Sea.

"Connie also said immediately after the new President's speech, the ports of entry swelled with outbound traffic. Thousands of poorly or undocumented workers left their homes, businesses, and vehicles to get out of the country. Just think of all the new jobs available."

"Anything else from my bride?"

"I think I covered it all. But I think we lost LeMarcus."

"What do you mean?"

"It's election time in Liberia. I'll bet the President throws the current director general of civil aviation into jail and offers the job to LeMarcus. He'll be a Liberian national hero and will become the head of the ICAO or something. Maybe he'll find a babe of his own, and we'll never get him out of there."

"He was fantastic. Our loss if it happens."

"I also have bad news. Remember Chief Burgher?"

"I do. Good man. Big, tall fucker."

"I got an e-mail from a retired Assistant Chief Patrol Agent that Chief Burgher's funeral is tomorrow. He had cancer and didn't want the chemo. He was a great guy. He was like you in a lot of ways, Greg. I'd do anything for him or you. I would've gone to his funeral."

"I know you would've. While you were at the Air Force, Connie and I had dinner with him several times. I was very impressed."

"The other piece of information from Jerry concerns my old buddy, Charles, the Chief Pilot." He emphasized the man's name. "I remember."

"Jerry said Charles Rodriguez was found floating in a river in Canada. Since he was a fisherman and a drunk, they figured he had a heart attack or had too much to drink and fell in. What law enforcement didn't tell the media was that he had a bullet hole in his head. His skull was so thick, the bullet bounced around in his cranium until it got tired of turning his brain into gray pudding."

"Did he say gray pudding? I think you're ad-libbing."

"It could've happened. What he did say was that during the funeral, my name and Charles' came up. Seems like everyone in the Border Patrol knew I had something to do with Charles' quitting and running off to Canada. Jerry said one of the old Del Rio pilots was there, and he said, 'Charles took a great interest in Hunter and started a file.' He added when I was off auditing an aviation program. That was enough to make the chief pilot and some of his friends a little wary of the former Marine pilot with no apparent law enforcement background. Isn't that wild?"

"Something didn't make sense with that shithead. He probably figured out that somewhere down the road, whenever you left town for an extended period, the drug flow was severely curtailed or stopped for a while. Chief Burgher noticed. Charles couldn't have known how you were doing it but suspected it was you. When I brought the Schweizer to Del Rio and you got assigned collateral duties with the DOJ's Office of Internal Audit, it was probably enough for him to put two-and-two together that you were active in undercover counterdrug work. He couldn't have known who."

"I often wondered how Bashir got my name. Maybe it was from Charles. If it was, it makes sense why those Muslims tried to knock me off."

"It was probably Charles or one of his buddies."

"No doubt. Lights of Djibouti on the nose, Sir. Thirty-five

minutes."

"I also got an e-mail from Bullfrog."

Lynche hung his head, clicked the mic button, and asked, "What did he have?"

"Several things. He emails in bullets. You have to read between the lines. The first one was confusing. A bunch of mosques from Denver to Key West to Boston caught fire."

"Mosques? As in places of worship? Prayer centers?"

"I guess. I don't know why he thought it was important to let me know. Shit! Those were the locations where the SEALs were killed. Could he have found out they played a part in that?"

"Damned SEALs are like ninjas. I think they fancy calling themselves that."

"Don't fuck with them. They are ninjas, and they'll hurt you. Anyway, Bullfrog also said, in words to that effect, 'seems like Prince Bashir was lost at sea.' He fell overboard on his boat on the way to Monaco. It happened off the coast of Liberia. Have the article. It says, Al Jazeera reported Prince Azzam Mohammed Bakaar Bashir was lost at sea, 150 miles south of Monrovia, Liberia. Prince Bashir strolled out onto the fantail of his majestic yacht, the Sa'ad, when a fish flew over the side rail. The fish flopped around wildly, and Bashir caught it. He took it to the side of the boat and fell in. Guests were stunned. One second he was there, the next he was gone."

"Couldn't have happened to a nastier piece of shit." Lynche maintained his defeated posture and his hands on his helmet.

"I couldn't believe it when I read that. No way could that have happened. I wonder what really happened."

Hunter tried to suppress a spurious thought of a sexually satiated Bashir wandering out of his cabin in the night to see a fish jump over the side of the yacht. It wasn't a big fish, and, in three steps, he subdued the plain-looking fish, watching it gulp air instead of water. He was about to toss it over the side when he heard a low-pitched knocking coming from over the side, as if a log was banging against the ship's hull. As Bashir tossed the fish over the side, he looked at the horizon, then down and saw a light just under the surface. When he leaned closer to look, a frogman leaped straight up from the water, grabbed the prince's robe, and both of them disappeared underwater.

"Maybe SEAL Team Six caught another terrorist," Hunter said. "Who knows?"

"Whatever happened, good riddance."

"We also got notification the USG procured the rights to Weedbusters. Now the Department of State and the Drug Enforcement Agency, and everyone else can use it to eradicate cannabis, cocoa, and poppy. It may not be enough to retire on, but hey, that's huge, Sir."

"You're doing great, Mav. Your race-car and antique-airplane-restoration business is taking off. DOD has embraced quiet aircraft designs. What'll you do next?"

"What do you mean, what'll I do next? Isn't it *what will we do next?* Call ops and tell them we're ten minutes out."

"Roger. Connie wants me to retire. I'm surprised she hasn't pushed you to kick me out the door. We've got plenty of money and that huge sailboat, but we rarely use it. I've been thinking it's time to call it quits. If I go, what will you do?"

"Besides race my 'Vette? Fly the jet? Play some racquetball? I'm getting a bit thick in the waist."

"I'm serious."

"OK. Let me tell you a little story. I think we have enough time."

"Uh-oh. Is this a new story?"

"I was attending the Aviation Supply Officer's Course in Athens, Georgia, a few years before I retired. I played racquetball after class at the college or town. When I got back to officer's quarters, I found the walkways and walls of the building covered in cockroaches. I took my racquetball shoe out of my bag and started popping roaches, as many as I could until they heard the screams of their buddies being smashed and ran off.

"By the time I left Athens three or four months later, guess what? No roaches. That's what liberals and these Islamofascists are like. They hide during the day or from the light and come out in the dark to do all sorts of mischief and mayhem."

"I'm wondering where this is going."

"Sir, I'm awake to the seriousness and lethality of the left and the fascists in Africa and the Middle East. I'm fully aware of that and will never forget their ultimate goal is to overthrow our government and kill us. Everything the left does or embraces is bad, wrong, evil, or stupid. Wherever there are liberals and Islamofascists, something bad is happening or soon will be. It's in their DNA."

"All liberals are not bad."

"Real libs and radicals are. There needs to be a counterforce of good. Where we can make a difference isn't in the open but in the dark. To be a warrior for good means you go into the belly of the beast and fight them where they work, shining a light on them. You expose them and illuminate the others in the area. Then you pop them like roaches."

"To fight evil is to fight liberalism, socialism, communism, Nazism, and Islamo-fascism, like those roaches I killed. We have to keep at it until they're gone, and we need the right tools for the job. 007 is one of the best tools in the world. I want to continue using her to fight that special kind of evil. Landing checklist complete."

Lynche ignored the speech. "I'm all set. We're clear to land."

Hunter rushed to finish his thought before touchdown. The yellow light still shone brightly. "The only people capable of fighting that kind of evil, mischief, and mayhem are in the intelligence community. To play in that special sandbox, you need the right tickets and Special Access."

"I think I'm done." As the landing gear touched the runway, safe on deck, Lynche felt re-energized. A giant weight had been lifted from his shoulders. "This was my last flight."

"So maybe the answer is for you to retire and start being a job finder." Hunter taxied off the runway and headed to the inflatable hangar at the end of the tarmac.

"I don't think so. There comes a time when you have to say, 'I can't do this anymore.' One of these days, you won't be able to play racquetball anymore."

"Bite your friggin' liberal tongue!"

"My time has come. I'm through. It was a great ride, Sir."

Hunter didn't know what to say. Feeling emotional, he was glad Lynche couldn't see his eyes were welling.

After a minute passed, Lynche saved Hunter by asking, "So what else will you do?"

It took Hunter a moment to compose himself. "What do you mean?"

"Maverick, you basically deposed the President of the United States, and you didn't go to jail. Liberals will hunt you down and kill you if they ever found out what you did to their leader—so don't piss me off. No one knows you killed the two top terrorists in the world, and the Islamo-fascists will be after your ass in a microminute if they ever figure that you were responsible. Your nemesis from Border Patrol is dead, as is the DCI. Someone will start to wonder how shit like that happens when you're around. Then the real Prince of Darkness falls overboard under suspicious circumstances. Be glad you weren't anywhere near it when it happened."

"I swear I wasn't anywhere near him!" Hunter suppressed a smirk. He unsnapped the chinstrap from his helmet.

The yellow chip light remained on.

"What else is there, Mav? All the bad guys are dead, or you ran them out of office. What else will you do?"

"Greg, Marx spent his life living off other people's money and finding fault with just about everything and everybody. The Left has a penchant for selecting life's losers as their heroes. I'll continue to fight the Dr. Evils of the world wherever they are. I'll shine a light on them and pop 'em like bugs. There are plenty of roaches out there. I'm not even talking about the leaders of the Democratic Party. You mean something like that?"

"No."

As they taxied to the end of the ramp, Hunter saw there was too much light in the hangar and debated whether he should stop.

"Um, ah, what the hell's that?" he asked. "Grinch, we may have a problem. It looks like we've got a welcoming committee."

"What?"

"There's a small crowd with the twins. First glance, it looks like SOCOM thought it would be nice to welcome us home. Maybe you really got al-Zawahiri, Mr. Lynche. That you're a hero is good, but this is bad."

"This is bad?" Consternation filled Lynche's voice.

"Sir, some asshole blew our cover. There's your answer."

"What?"

"Some asshole blew our cover, and my partner just quit. Therefore, no cover, no partner, which means no airplane, no enemies to kill, no bad guys to find. No more Special Access Programs. Sounds to me like I'm now probably unemployed."

EPILOGUE

0430L July 6, 2011
The Spirit of Memphis C-17
41,000 Feet MSL over the Atlantic Ocean

Hunter, Lynche, and the two Bobs stretched out along troop seats with sound suppressors over their ears and sleep masks over their eyes. They were sound asleep in military, olive-drab-green sleeping bags.

A US Air Force air crewman in a NOMEX flight suit bespeckled with colorful patches on her shoulders and chest walked past the snoring men into the middle of the big jet's cargo area to the shipping container placed strategically in the middle of the aircraft. The petite African-American woman with hair pulled back into a tight bun checked the container's security by testing the tension of the heavy chains between the container's turnbuckles and the thick lashing rings mounted on the aircraft decking.

She kicked and stood on each chain with enough force to ensure the chains hadn't gained any slack, as the jet climbed to altitude. She climbed off the last chain in rotation and turned to look at the container, then back at the men sprawled across the seats. The unusual cargo and passengers that weren't to be manifested didn't pique her interest, but she gave them a snort.

"Nasty old spooks," she mumbled. "Don't have to play by any rules and get any damn thing they want."

Her cargo-security mission accomplished, the loadmaster turned and walked back to the cockpit.

Hunter lifted one side of his sleep mask as the woman walked by. As she moved out of visual range, he lifted a lazy eyelid toward the blue shipping container where the greatest little airplane no one ever heard about was nestled inside.

He rolled over on his side and fell back asleep.

631

* * *

Hunter woke with a start when Lynche kicked the troop seat. "Get up, Sunshine. We land in thirty minutes."

Duncan rolled over, peeled the sleep mask from his face, and scowled at Lynche, who was perfectly groomed and shaved. The Grinch's sound suppressors covered his ears, but the head strap hung down under his chin to avoid interfering with this coiffure. Hunter crawled out of his bag, looked around the C-17's cargo area, scowled at Lynche again, and checked his Rolex. They'd been airborne for fifteen hours and should be landing at Andrews Air Force Base soon.

Lynche sat beside Hunter, lifted the sound suppressor from his ear, and said, "That's not a pretty sight, Mr. Jones."

Greg Lynche removed his sound suppressors, and Hunter copied him before leaning close to his ear to say, "Be nice to me. You know I get gas on these flights, and you're in the frag zone."

Lynche leaned closer and said, "Hold your guns, Mav. Something's up."

Hunter looked at his friend in concern and confusion. For fifteen years, Lynche rarely uttered a cautionary line. It was usually Hunter's job to express random thoughts of concern or ask questions for clarification. The expression on Duncan's sleep-lined face changed.

"What do you mean, Mr. Smith?"

"I was in the cockpit when the aircrew was told they have to park in a different location and not to let us off the jet. We have a greeting party. I think we're going to jail."

"Maybe I'll go to jail for disseminating formerly classified documents, but not you. I'm the traitor. You're a hero, good Sir."

"We'll know in a few minutes."

The fifteen-year running joke continued. Hunter and Lynche operated extracurricular of dozens of legal systems. They broke laws with indifference. When a condition of success for a black program meant straying over the lines with every mission, the Special Access Program Wraith just quietly flew over local judiciaries. They smuggled their aircraft onto airports and conducted flight operations with no clearances, often penetrating another country's airspace without permission. They flew low to stay under radar systems to perform their mission, making nearly every time they flew a potential major international incident.

They operated a single-engine airplane over some of the most hostile territory imaginable, where the smallest incident meant the difference between having the aircraft or engine fail, which could result in the crew's being killed, captured, and tried as spies.

When someone broke the law for fifteen years, breaking a new one was considered "ops normal." The developing situation in front of the big jet concerned Lynche and intrigued Hunter.

Hunter's laissez-faire attitude sometimes infuriated Lynche, but this time, it was Lynche caught in the no-man's land of saying something, or sitting still and letting events unfold. Lynche nodded toward the front of the aircraft, as Bob and Bob departed the cockpit. Hunter saw real concern on his friend's face, as the crew closed the cockpit door once the old mechanics stepped off the ladder.

Hunter shook his head.

Hydraulic systems screamed and thumped, as landing gear went down, followed by flaps.

"Lowest price, technically acceptable!" Hunter shouted with a grin, pulling the sound suppressors over his ears again.

Lynche, appreciating the diversion, nodded with a grin. Their Gulfstream's hydraulic systems didn't squeal when activated. Corporate and commercial aviation could afford to pay for quiet hydraulic pumps and actuators. Noiselessness wasn't a priority for Uncle Sam's massive lowest-priced fleet.

After a landing that both men agreed was "very nice," the jet kept moving for an extended period, as the hydraulic systems screamed again when the flaps were raised. The auxiliary power plant's little jet turbine lit off, adding more high frequency to the cabin before they were jostled around, as the pilot heavily applied the brakes, adding more low frequency and high vibrations to the mix.

After taxiing for sixty seconds, the jet stopped, and the engines shut down, two at a time.

"Watch your head, as you depart the ride," the tall Bob said, as the four-man Wraith team huddled briefly to exchange handshakes and grab their rollerboards.

"Do you know this was our hundredth mission?" Lynche asked.

The aircrew opened the side door. Normally, they also opened the cargo door and leveled the ramp to expedite offloading, but they didn't.

Something's up, Hunter thought. "Seriously? I had no idea. I hadn't kept track. I thought it was the ninety-ninth?" He gave Lynche an impish grin.

The four men faced toward the front of the aircraft to depart when eight heavily armed Secret Service agents in black BDUs and clear earpieces poured through the door and hustled toward the four civilians. Hunter felt that the men's lack of drawn weapons was a good sign.

"Mister...?" one agent asked, looking at Greg.

"Aboard the plane," Lynche said quickly, "we're Smith and Jones, Jones and Jones, Smith and Smith."

Old intelligence agents knew the drill of properly addressing someone under cover to law enforcement and how to maintain their cover.

"Mr. Jones and Mr. Smith, do you have any weapons on your person?" the agent asked.

"I have a revolver and two knives in my rollerboard." Hunter offered his flight bag to the nearest agent.

Four agents stepped in and relived the civilians of their bags. "Assume the position, gentlemen."

Hunter spread his feet and placed his hands over his head in a coordinated, continuous motion. Lynche, Bob, and

Bob copied him.

"Anything on you that can hurt me?" the agents asked, as they frisked the men.

The US Air Force aircrew stepped out of the cockpit and watched as eight men in black frisked their Code Twos. It wasn't every day a troopie got to witness the equivalent of a general officer being frisked. After sixty seconds of being touched, prodded, groped, and otherwise molested, it was over.

"Thank you, gentlemen," the lead agent said. "Please come with me."

The four men followed the agent from the aircraft. Hunter thanked the bewildered aircrew for a great ride and nice landing, as he passed the cockpit. As the men stepped down from the jet, they were guided into the back seats of two black Suburbans.

Hunter saw the Follow Me truck leading the caravan of black vehicles. No one spoke until the line of trucks entered a hangar and stopped.

"Follow me," the agent in charge uttered with intrigue.

Hunter followed Lynche out the open door. He would've had to be blind not to recognize the six Marine Corps F/A-18s parked in the hangar in various stages of repair and readiness.

The men hurried through double doors and down a long, well-lit passageway before reaching another agent in black, who gave the lead agent a nod. He turned into a conference room. As the men gathered around chairs, a voice boomed behind them, "Gentlemen, the President of the United States."

All heads turned. Chills coursed through the bodies of the four flight-weary men, as the newly sworn-in President entered the conference room, followed by the Secretary of Defense, the Secret Service Director, and a man introduced as the Acting Director of Central Intelligence.

The three former military men knew what to do and formed a line abreast. Greg stood in the line-up between Hunter and the shorter Bob.

The President first stepped in front of the taller Bob and

shook his hand, exchanging a few words before the booming voice announced, "Attention to Orders! The President of the United States takes great pleasure in awarding the Intelligence Star to Robert J. Smith and William Robert Jones for outstanding achievements and services rendered, with the highest distinction, under conditions of grave risk."

After the short Bob received his medal, the President stepped in front of Greg and shook his head.

"Attention to Orders!" the voice booked again. "The President of the United States takes extremely great pleasure in awarding the Distinguished Intelligence Cross to Gregory Michael Lynche and Drew Duncan Hunter. Over a period of fifteen years, you performed one hundred of the most-challenging and sensitive national-security missions, as the pilot and copilot team under Special Access Program Wraith. Time and again, you demonstrated uncommon and extraordinary acts of heroism during the most-hazardous flying conditions possible, accepting existing dangers with exemplary courage. Your intrepidity and conspicuous fortitude were once again on display, as you wrestled with a severely damaged airplane over hostile territory and completed the mission, which culminated with the identifying, targeting, and destruction of key leaders of the terrorist group al- Qaeda."

The President said as if on cue, "America will never know your courage and heroism, Gentlemen. On behalf of every American, please accept our deepest appreciation and gratitude. This grateful nation will forever be in your debt. Thank you and congratulations."

The four men stood stunned, each holding a heavy wooden presentation case, as the former Speaker of the House and new President uttered a few closing comments. Before he left the room, the President leaned toward Hunter and said, "Come see me soon."

The Acting DCI sidled up in front of the four men and said, "Congratulations, Gentlemen. Now I need those back. They'll remain in the Director's safe until.... Well, one of these days, Wraith will be declassified, but I doubt it. You know the drill. Congratulations, Gentlemen, and well done. This didn't happen, and you can't talk about it."

"Easy come, easy go," Hunter said, as they surrendered their medals to the Acting DCI, who also left the room equally quickly.

The Secretary of Defense emerged from behind the row of men. "I think you two can go. Please close the door behind you." He pointed to the two Bobs. The SECDEF looked at Lynche and Hunter, shaking his head as if trying to clear an ugly thought from memory.

Lynche felt anxious. Something was wrong about the situation. It was ominous to have the SECDEF be the last one in an awards rotation. They hadn't done anything for DOD but use their gas.

"Nice work, Gentlemen. I had no idea. My predecessors knew something was going on all around the planet. They'd get a little intel here, a little there, but the DCI would never share the source. Now I know why. There always was a question about what happened to the remaining YO-3A that was on loan to the FBI. I understand it's in that container?"

"Yes, Sir," Hunter replied.

Lynche didn't glance at Hunter.

"And you have a G-four or five. You feel like you can come and go as you see fit from, let's say, Diego Garcia. Do I want to know what you were doing in Diego Garcia?"

"No, Sir. You do not."

"I think the President should've added 'highly inventive and audacious' to your citation. However, using a CIA-front company and the probable misuse of government aircraft, and who knows how much jet fuel you guys used to enrich yourselves, isn't consistent with the theme just articulated by the President when he just declared you two national heroes. Since he also signed an executive order, in essence a blanket pardon, for anything you two did in the execution of national security for the America, it would be difficult for me to send you two to jail."

"Here's the deal. I'm willing to strike those aircraft from the government's inventory and transfer ownership to you...."

"What do you want, Sir?" Hunter asked.

"The Acting DCI and I agree you have to start running a legitimate business. No more CIA-front company. And DOD wants to contract for some of your services...."

"Can do easy, Sir," Hunter blurted. He thought, "I'll still have to work, but this will be harder with every Tom, Dick, and Harry at the Pentagon knowing about the YO-3A."

"...and I want to see what you did with that airplane. Do we have a deal?"

"It's a deal."

Lynche and Hunter shook the SECDEF's hand.

As the Secretary of Defense left, Lynche turned to his friend. "I take it all back, Hunter. You're the luckiest SOB on the planet."

The men were about to leave the conference room when the Secret Service Director chased them back inside. Hunter made introductions. O'Sullivan offered the men his congratulations.

"I want you to know that Captain Bill McGee received the Navy Cross from the President," he said. "Someone at the CIA provided information that the intel was wrong regarding Osama bin Laden's whereabouts on Tora Bora, and McGee should not have been removed from command of SEAL Team Six. Bill's at peace and is with his teenage girls at a racquetball tournament. He said, if I saw you, to tell you they can kick your ass on the racquetball court."

"Thank you, Marty." Hunter pinched his lips, as the Secret Service Director turned and walked swiftly out of the room and down the hall.

Once all the government's senior executives were out of the conference room, Hunter and Lynche stepped into the hall to find their suitcases and a combat-ready Secret Service agent.

"I'm to take you wherever you want to go," the man in black said.

"Let's go. It's been quite a day."

Hunter and Lynche extended the handles of their rollerboards and followed the man in black down the long tiled hall. Lynche kept looking at Hunter, trying to say something, struggling to find the right words. Hunter noticed and stopped. So did Lynche. The man in black walked out the double doors, as the two friends faced each other.

"Have you any idea what just happened to us?" Lynche asked. "Greg, you're a hero," Hunter said nonchalantly and patted Greg on the shoulder. "I'm the luckiest guy on the planet. Not bad for Billy Ray Joe Bob Average."

Lynche's facial expression changed so fast, Hunter couldn't read them.

"No. That's not it. How about this…?"

Hunter could tell Lynche was on an emotional edge. Tears could form in his eyes.

Through a shaking jaw, Lynche fought to speak. "This has been the most-exiting fifteen years of my life. I'll miss you."

Hunter gritted his teeth and wrapped his arms around his mentor, partner, and friend as Lynche sobbed against him. When Lynche regained his composure, he pulled away.

"Distinguished Intelligence Cross," Lynche said. "They gave us a DIC! That's incredible."

"Hold it. Did you say we got dicked? I'm sure it was just a rumor. Did you see a DIC? I didn't see one."

Lynche burst out laughing. "You're friggin' incorrigible, Mav. OK, Asshole. That's it. I have a story to tell. Want to hear it?"

Hunter's brows shot up, almost touching his hairline. "You're finally going to tell me a story from your past? It has to be one hell of a story. You quit on me, and then you tell me a story. What is it, Mr. Lynche? I have to hear this." He crossed his arms and smiled broadly, waiting for the first of the bottled-up secret war stories his friend carried without sharing.

Greg looked down the hall to ensure they were alone and

then at the ground. He raised his head and said impassionedly, "I recruited you, all the way back to 1982 when you were sent to OCS and then to flight school."

"What?" Hunter almost shouted. "I had no dealings with you until you visited me at the Border Patrol in…1996!"

Lynche grinned like the Cheshire cat.

Hunter's brows furrowed, and his mind raced. Lynche never lied to him, but he couldn't believe what his friend just said.

"Mav, I ran the Special Activities Branch in the '80s. Your name crossed my desk. Somehow, you were some super-smartass world-class racquetball player who managed to get a commission in the Marines and get sent to flight school without a college degree. Have you any idea how unique that is? Of course not.

"I personally tracked intellectual and physical rock stars, and I tracked your progress for years under a Special Access Program called 17 Nails. One of these days, I might tell you about it.

"Do you remember filling out blue fingerprint cards for the FBI? Anyway, here and there, I…er, the Agency, helped with some of your assignments. I've known you for almost thirty years, and I've marveled at the last fifteen. You're an amazing man, Duncan Hunter.

"The secret is, I'm the luckiest man on the planet to know and work with you. Now please, no more with the Billy Ray Joe Bob Average bullshit." He walked toward the doors, leaving Hunter standing there with his jaw open.

The two men walked outside into a night of increasing fog. Hunter shook his head, his thoughts as foggy as the weather. He returned to the present when he saw men in black standing ready. A typical Secret Service black Suburban, antennas from every square inch on the roof, idled at the curb.

A man in black BDUs opened the rear door for Lynche.

"High misties," Hunter said, patting Lynche's back with his free hand. "Glad I'm not driving."

From the corner of his eye, Hunter saw a flash of red from a streetlamp. As Lynche got into the Suburban, Hunter waited for the flash and headlights to materialize into something more solid. He thought he recognized that particular shade of red even in the slightly swirling fog. More red came into view, as did chrome and the Tri-Star badge in the distinctive grille of a Mercedes SL.

Hunter turned to Lynche. "My ride's here. I'll talk with you later, good Sir. Hugs and kisses to Connie."

Lynche looked over his shoulder, then at Hunter. "Luckiest guy I know. Good night, Maverick."

By the time Hunter shut the Suburban's door and walked to the rear of the vehicle, a radiant Nazy Cunningham, in jeans and a polo, extricated herself from the coupe. The two ran into each other's arms, meeting in the fog spotlighted by the car's headlights.

The three men in the Suburban didn't move; their eyes focused on a screen between the front seats that gave the image of the man and woman embracing behind the vehicle. The Suburban's rear-view camera showed the couple in exceptional detail.

"Wow," the driver said. "I don't get greeted like that when I come home."

"That's one lucky dude," the man in the passenger seat said.

"You don't know how right you are," said Lynche. After a couple seconds, he added, "Gents, we probably ought to go."

The two lovers were so enraptured and entwined, they didn't hear the Suburban drive away and were ignorant they were alone.

Nearly breathless, Hunter slowly pulled his lips from Nazy's. "Well, hello, Ms. Cunningham. That's quite a greeting. Maybe we should get out of here."

With a nod, she walked to the passenger door on unsteady legs, holding Hunter's hand for balance. As he opened the door, she slid into the seat, watching him and trying to follow his every move.

They were soon leaving the big Air Force Base. He held her hand, and she stared at him with a grin that could only be described as devilish.

"Your place or mine?" he asked.

"The Gaylord is closer."

"The Gaylord it is. I was a little shocked to see you drive up."

"I would've been there earlier, but the President had business to attend to. Everyone had to wait until he was off the base."

An alarm rang in Hunter's mind, and he paused to close his eyes momentarily. "You've been a busy girl, Ms. Cunningham."

"I have. It's been a very busy week. I understand al-Zawahiri and a dozen other AQ were killed in Yemen."

"Your intelligence is very good. I wonder how you came by that information."

She smiled. "I have a new job in Operations and a portfolio of programs. I'm the Program Manager for several SAPs until they appoint a new DCI. I'm also the acting PM for an executive Special Access Program called Wraith. I learned that Wraith is a Scottish dialectical word for ghost or spirit. How apropos—and what a fascinating history. I was read in on it last week."

Hunter never shared the name of his program or what he and Greg did for the DCI, but now she knew all of it. The mood in the car grew somber.

"The former DCI didn't service that program very well," Nazy added. "You probably heard he passed away shortly after becoming the vice president."

Hunter spoke toward the windshield, worried about something he couldn't quite identify. "I heard something about that."

"It was fairly clear that the principals on Wraith had a remarkable string of successes going back almost fifteen years. They had a unique capability and performed some of the most-difficult missions for Langley, and no one but the Directors knew. The contract kept being extended, too.

"Then the former DCI moved to shut it down. I believe he wanted to kill the contract and replace it with unmanned aircraft. The case history showed Air Branch politicked to replace the manned Special Access Program with Air Branch unmanned assets."

"You blew our cover."

Nazy exhaled deeply and turned to look at him. The acoustics in the Mercedes were sufficiently good for her to be heard even when she whispered. "I did. CTC and SOCOM were wringing their hands over their inability to positively ID al-Zawahiri at his compound. After the acting DCI assigned me Wraith, I was to brief him after I was read on.

"I was surprised you were in Djibouti, very close to Yemen. The Acting DCI dragged me to the White House. I briefed the President, the Secretary of Defense, and the JCS Chairman. The President approved the change in the mission, then I had to fully debrief them on Wraith."

Tears streamed down her high cheekbones, falling onto her blouse. "Duncan, I made a mistake. I didn't think it through. I thought you could get him. I convinced myself after bin Laden you'd want to get al-Zawahiri. Once I realized what I'd done, I thought I sent you to die."

Duncan pulled into the driveway of the National Gaylord and was about to speak, but Nazy wasn't finished. She turned toward her window and squeezed his hand. "When I heard you had engine trouble, I almost had a nervous breakdown. I was so afraid I lost you, I wanted to die."

Hunter released her hand, put the transmission in Park, and reached for her chin, turning her head until she met his eyes. "Nazy Cunningham, you're going to be the death of me, but I can't live without you. Something has to give."

Nazy struggled to remove her engagement ring. Trembling and uncontrollably sobbing, she said, "I need to give this back to you. I...betrayed you."

Hunter exhaled as if punched in the solar plexus. When

he recovered, he spoke over the steering wheel and closed his eyes. "Other than that, how'd you like Dallas, Mrs. Kennedy? I've lost my job, my partner, and now my girl. This has been one hell of a day. And I didn't see any of it coming."

He turned his head to see Nazy confused and in despair. Even with mascara running down her cheeks, she was stunning.

Duncan shook his head and spoke over the steering wheel. "What am I going to do with you?" He fingered the large diamond ring back and forth several times as she sobbed. Finally, he reached for her trembling hand and slid the ring back on her finger.

Nazy held onto his shoulders as hard as she could. They struggled to kiss, wiping away tears with their shirtsleeves.

"I think we have to discuss the conditions of your future employment, Mr. Hunter." She moved into playful role-playing and trembled with excitement.

Hunter immediately played along. "Can I at least get a decent meal before you send me back out?" he asked.

"Negotiations might take several days."

"I'm fairly certain we can reach an agreement, Ms. Cunningham, though it may take a while. This place seems as good as any. What do you say?" He stroked the hand with the ring and looked into the eyes that captivated him from the first day he first saw her.

"You're lucky to get me. I've been a very busy woman."

He turned off the engine. He turned and looked deep into her dark green eyes. "Well, I *am* the luckiest guy I know. Time's wasting, Ms. Cunningham. I think you'll find me to be a hard negotiator."

"Then let's get at it."

GLOSSARY

A - Attack Aircraft

AB - Afterburner

AC - Attack Cargo

AFB - Air Force Base

AFCS - Automatic Flight Control System

AG - Attorney General

AGL - Above Ground Level

AH - Attack Helicopter

AIDS - Acquired Immunodeficiency Syndrome

AK - Avtomat Kalashnikova: Automatic Kalashnikov

AN/PRQ-7 - Personal Radio, Combat Survivor

ANVIS - Aviator's Night Vision Imaging System

AOR - Area of Responsibility

APU - Auxiliary Power Unit

AQ - al-Qaeda

AR - Automatic Rifle

ATC - Air Traffic Control

ATIS - Automatic Terminal Information Service, a continuous broadcast of recorded information at airports

BOQ - Bachelor Officer Quarters

C - Cargo Aircraft

CALA - Combat Aircraft Loading Area

C&M - Concealment and Maneuver

CAT - Crisis Action Team

CEO - Chief Executive Officer

CG - Commanding General

CH - Cargo Helicopter

CIA - Central Intelligence Agency

CMC - Commandant of the Marine Corps

CNO - Chief of Naval Operations

Code 2 - Distinguished visitor codes: President is Code 1, VP is Code 2

CONOP - Concept of Operations

COS - Chief of Station

CTC - Counterterrorism Center

D - Drone Aircraft

DC - Douglas Aircraft Corporation

DCI - Director of Central Intelligence
DEA - Drug Enforcement Administration

DEVGRU - United States Naval Special Warfare Development Group

DOD - Department of Defense

DOJ - Department of Justice

DOS - Department of State

DRMO - Defense Reutilization and Marketing Office

DSS - Defense Security Service

EA - Electronic Attack Aircraft

ECP - Enlisted Commissioning Program

EDA - Excess Defense Article

EP - Electronic Patrol Aircraft

ETA - Estimated Time of Arrival

F - Fighter Aircraft

F/A - Fighter/Attack Aircraft

FAA - Federal Aviation Administration

FARC - Fuerzas Armadas Revolucionarias de Colombia:

Revolutionary Armed Forces of Colombia

FBI - Federal Bureau of Investigation

FBO - Fixed Base Operator

FITREP - Fitness Report
FLIR - Forward Looking Infrared

G - gravity

GA - General Aviation

GAO - Government Accountability Office

GBU - Guided Bomb Unit

GED - General Education Development

GS - General Schedule

GT - General Technical

HAHO - High Altitude High Opening

HH - Hospital Helicopter

HUD - Heads Up Display

I&NS - Immigration and Naturalization Service

IC - Intelligence Community

ID - Identification

IED - Improvised Explosive Device

ISI - Inter-Services Intelligence: Pakistan's National Intelligence Service

ISR - Intelligence, Surveillance, and Reconnaissance

IT - Information Technology

JCS - Joint Chief of Staff

JDAM - Joint Direct Attack Munitions
JPAS - Joint Personnel Adjudication System

JROTC - Junior Reserve Officers' Training Corps

JSOC - Joint Special Operations Command

KIA - Killed in Action

LCD - Liquid Crystal Display

LD - Laser Designator

MBA - Master of Business Administration

MECEP - Marine Enlisted Commissioning and Education Program

MH - Multimission Helicopter

MOS - Military Occupational Specialty

MRTA - Tupac Amaru Revolutionary Movement

NASA - National Aeronautics and Space Administration

NAVAIR - Naval Air Systems Command

NCTC - National Counterterrorism Center

NCS - National Clandestine Service

NE - Near East Division

NECEP - Navy Enlisted Commissioning and Education Program

NGA - National Geospatial-Intelligence Agency

NHB - New Headquarters Building

NOFORN - Not Releasable to Foreign Nationals

NOMEX - A registered trademark for flame-resistant, meta-aramid material

NRO - National Reconnaissance Office

NSA - National Security Agency

NVG - Night Vision Goggles

NWC - Naval War College

OBL - Osama bin Laden

OBL - Operation Broken Lance

OCS - Officer Candidate School

OHB - Old Headquarters Building OICOfficer in Charge

ONI - Office of Naval Intelligence

OQR - Officer Qualification Record

PD - Police Department

PFT - Physical Fitness Test

PMO - Provost Marshal Office

POAC - Pentagon Officer's Athletic Club

POTUS - President of the United States

RAG - Replacement Air Group

R&D - Research and Development

RIO - Radar Intercept Officer
RPM - Revolutions Per Minute

SA - Schweizer Aircraft

SA - Special Access

SAM - Surface-to-Air Missile

SAP - Special Access Program

S&D - Search and Destroy

SEAL - Sea, Air, and Land SECDEFSecretary of Defense

SCI - Sensitive Compartmented Information

SCIF - Sensitive Compartmented Information Facility

SF - Standard Form

SIS - Senior Intelligence Service

SITREP - Situation Report

SNCO - Staff Non-Commissioned Officer

SOAR - Special Operations Aviation Regiment

SOCOM - Special Operations Command

SOF - Special Operations Forces

SOG - Special Operations Group

SSGT - Staff Sergeant

STE - Secure Terminal Equipment

STU - Secure Telephone

TS - Top Secret

TSA - Transportation Security Administration

UnitTHC - Tetrahydrocannabinol

UAV - Unmanned Aerial Vehicle

USAF - United States Air Force

USBP - United States Border Patrol

USG - United States Government

USMC - United States Marine Corps

USN - United States Navy

UV - Ultra Violet

VC - Viet Cong

VCR - Video Cassette Recorder

VHF - Very High Frequency

VTC - Video Teleconference

WMD - Weapons of Mass Destruction

WTC - World Trade Center

XO - Executive Officer

YO-3A - Prototype Observation: Third Model, First Series Utility Aircraft

CPSIA information can be obtained
at www.ICGtesting.com
Printed in the USA
FFHW02n1738101018
48760661-52855FF